Elizabeth Buchan lives in London with her husband and two children and worked in publishing for several years. During that time she wrote her first books for children, including *Beatrix Potter: The Story of the Creator of Peter Rabbit*. Her first novel for adults was *Daughters of the Storm*, followed by *Light of the Moon* then *Consider the Lily* — which won the 1994 Romantic Novel of the Year Award — *Perfect Love*, *Against Her Nature*, *Secrets of the Heart* and *Revenge of the Middle-Aged Woman*. Her most recent novel is *The Good Wife*. Elizabeth Buchan has sat on the committee of the Society of Authors and was a judge for the 1997 Whitbread Awards and Chairman of the Judges for the 1997 Betty Trask Award. Her short stories have been published in various magazines and broadcast on BBC Radio 4.

For further information go to www.elizabethbuchan.com

Against *her* Nature & Perfect Love

ELIZABETH BUCHAN

PAN BOOKS

Against Her Nature first published 1997 by Macmillan.
First published in paperback 1998 by Pan Books.
Perfect Love first published 1995 by Macmillan.
First published in paperback 1996 by Pan Books.

This omnibus edition published 2006 by Pan Books
an imprint of Pan Macmillan Ltd
Pan Macmillan, 20 New Wharf Road, London N1 9RR
Basingstoke and Oxford
Associated companies throughout the world
www.panmacmillan.com

ISBN -13: 978-0-330-44684-6
ISBN -10: 0-330-44684-3

3 5 7 9 10 8 6 4 2

A CIP catalogue record for this book is available from
the British Library.

Typeset by SetSystems Ltd, Saffron Walden, Essex
Printed and bound in Great Britain by
Mackays of Chatham plc, Chatham, Kent

Against her
Nature

For my mother-in-law, Hope Buchan (1917–1997), with love

Acknowledgements

Very many people are owed thanks. To David Forcey who showed me round Lloyd's, answered my questions with the utmost patience and read the manuscript. To Anthony Townsend and Natalie Rizzi of Rea Brothers who read the manuscript. Both gave freely of their time and allowed me to sit in on their work. To Andy MacNab who kindly gave me permission to make use of material from his book *Immediate Action* (Bantam Press). To Isabelle Anscombe, Carole Golder, Mike Morgan, Jennifer Pantling, Suzie Procter, Lance Poynter, Tim Stephenson and Ingrid Tress who offered their help and allowed me to bombard them with questions. My debt is unquantifiable. Any mistakes are entirely mine.

Two books in particular proved useful: *Ultimate Risk* by Adam Raphael (Bantam Press, 1994) and *For Whom the Bell Tolls: The Scandalous Inside Story of the Lloyd's Crisis* by Jonathan Mantle (Sinclair Stevenson, 1992). I took factual information and drew on ideas from both these works.

Finally, I would like to thank the Macmillan team for their faith and patience, in particular my editor Suzanne Baboneau, and Hazel Orme, Philippa McEwan and Morven Knowles. Also my agent, Caroline Sheldon who, as always, proved a rock and Peta Nightingale, who helped to nurture the book along. Friends too are beyond price and my love and thanks go to Anthony Mair and Julia Peyton Jones, for making France so easy, and to Marika Cobbold, for listening.

Once again my family took the brunt. I cannot thank them enough.

Chaos Theory: The branch of mathematics used to deal with chaotic systems, for example, an engineered structure, such as an oil platform which is subjected to irregular, unpredictable stress

From the *Hutchinson Encyclopaedia*

Prologue

Perhaps it was something to do with their height: tall women are treated differently from their small sisters. Being tall means that you must work hard to blend.

Perhaps it was their differences: one from a gentle, unthreatened upbringing in Hampshire, the other from the tough outreaches of a council flat in Streatham, and they recognized in each other the polarity essential to balance.

Perhaps it was the era, which promised that all things were possible. It was not so surprising that a girl nurtured in the city's anarchy should be drawn to one to whom it had always been suggested that the world was ordered for her comfort. They were not to know that a decade of excess was closing and, with the arrival of the modern imperialists and pirates blowing in from Europe and the unleashing of natural disasters, that a furious battle would be waged between the ghosts of the past and the spectres of the future. In the bitter clash would die the belief that we had wrapped up life, with antibiotics, insurance and social security.

Whatever, the two girls met at a reception given by Women in the City (WIC) a new and, of necessity, rather poorly subscribed association. For ten seconds or so, they scrutinized each other. Long seconds. Instantly, and to her immense surprise, a love, both deep and loyal, destined to outlive feelings for lovers, perhaps husbands, trembled on the edges of Becky Vitali's uninhabited and sceptical heart but drove a spear through Tess Frant's. And that was that.

'Let me draw sustenance from life,' wrote Tess in her childish five-year diary. 'I must not fail.'

1

Chapter One

It is written, somewhere, that if a butterfly flaps its wings – a delicate flash of orange, blue or white – over the grasses of an English meadow, the result can be an earthquake in China. Such are the connections between events that are, to begin with, considered random.

The first letter arrived on 25 June 1987, the day of the Frants' annual cocktail party. Like most letters, it looked innocuous: in a rectangular white envelope with a typed address.

> I am writing to inform you [it said] that the Quattro
> Marine Syndicate 317/634 will produce a substantial loss
> in respect of the 1985 Underwriting Account.
> You will see from the enclosed letter, which Mr Quattro
> has sent to his direct Names, that the overall loss is approxi-
> mately 200 per cent of allocated premium income . . .
> A schedule summarizing your underwriting position as
> of 31 December 1987 is enclosed from which you will note
> that your cash call will be approximately £6,400 . . .

Colonel Frant read it in the privacy of his study at the High House. Conscious that his heart-beat had raised a little, he frowned, laid the letter to one side and rejoined his family in the kitchen.

Of its contents he said nothing.

*

Summer had applied its colours over the shires and the day was filled with bright hot sun, and with the sound of skylarks swooping over the crops in the fields that lapped the village of Appleford. By six thirty the heat had distilled and rested heavily over the land. Clearly, the sun was going to take its time to set.

As this was England, the topic of the weather was on everyone's lips.

Mrs Frant moved or, rather, sailed through the drawing room and the coveys of guests. Recognizing a superior might, steam victorious over wind-power, as it were, they gave way and many followed in little dribs into the dry, manicured garden. From time to time, her snorting, slightly anarchic laugh, so at variance with her appearance, could be heard above the murmur of conversation.

'Margery, my dear,' she said, halting beside two women on the York stone patio, and kissing the powdered cheek that had been proffered. 'How lovely.'

'Lovely,' echoed Margery Wittingstall, middle-aged, divorced and depressed, but the sentiment did not seem to register with her hostess, who turned to the second woman.

'And Jilly. How lovely too.'

Jilly Cadogan smiled, safe in the knowledge that she was a beautiful woman who donated energy and attention to the maintenance of that beauty. 'With time and money, *any* woman can be good-looking,' she was heard frequently to say to her friends, and Jilly had plenty of both.

Jilly also proffered a cheek. 'How good of you to invite us.'

On a hot summer evening, Jilly would have preferred to have been sitting in her own garden, a careful – and fashionable – concoction of scent and colour, but she seldom allowed her preferences to override her social ambitions or duties. In Jilly's case, these were routed mainly through her husband, Louis, and it was for his sake that she had donned a black linen shift and lipstick, and stood making conversation with the abandoned Margery.

'That's just what that guru chappie said. "Think the unthinkable, question the unquestioned, say the unsayable . . ."'

Mrs Frant caught the tail end of a conversation, and a somewhat tired cliché she considered, between a young Turk in the City and the local Tory grandee who resided, with a lot of fake ancestral clutter, in the manor house to the north of Appleford. Both were endeavouring to impress the other.

She beckoned to her son, Jack, who abandoned the group that contained her daughter, Tess, and Tess's friend Rebecca, or Becky as she preferred to be called.

'Hand round the drinks, darling,' she ordered fondly, never ceasing to admire her tall, rangy, unusual son who, during the twenty-five years she had known him, had never given her any worry at all. Until now. 'Your father's being a bit slow.'

A toddler in an expensive and useless blue romper-suit, of the type favoured by well-off Parisians, clung to his mother's leg while a second, older one wove between the legs of the guests unfortunate enough to be in its vicinity. Mrs Frant's invitation had specifically excluded children, and it was with mild amusement that she saw that the mother, clamped, hobbled and flushed, was paying for her sanction-busting.

Satisfied, Mrs Frant moved on. A big woman, who had once been as slender as a dream, she was given in late middle age to wearing tweed skirts, floral blouses and pale stockings, none of which suited her. Today, however, in honour of her annual showcase party, which was designed to make the point – very subtly, of course – that families like the Frants were the real heart of the village, she was wearing an old-fashioned shirt-waister and flat sandals that revealed unpainted toenails. Yet, in contrast to the gaudy assembly of her guests, well-to-do and smart, there was something magnificent in Mrs Frant's refusal to submit to the tyranny of appearance: a spirit and independence that, if it had been recognized, might have been admired.

In fact, Mrs Frant was admirable in many ways, not least for her secret life. Like many people who are burdened domestically and tied to one bit of earth, a part of her had cut free, gone undercover, to explore the strange and awful regions of the spirit. Her epic journeys, she called them, secret voyages to match those of the Greek heroes, herself an Odysseus. In reality, Mrs Frant rarely ventured further than the south coast.

'Becky,' Tess Frant grabbed her friend, 'you must meet Louis Cadogan. He's rich and wicked and he's lived in Appleford for ages.' She turned to Louis. 'And this is Becky, who's also wicked but poor and wants to make lots of money.' Unfortunately, this was the sort of comment Tess made when she was nervous and struggling to be interesting and witty. Occasionally, she hit the mark. She finished the introduction in a rush. 'Becky and I met at a City do last year.'

Height, looks, energy: with his usual quickness, Louis summed up the girls. He judged Becky to be the same age as Tess. Twenty-two? Possibly twenty-three. Of course, he already knew Tess. Tall, fair, slightly plump and dressed to attract attention away from that condition, she combined innate, hopeless romanticism with innocence; Becky, tall, pencil thin and huge-eyed, hid, he saw with a clarity that startled him, an orphaned spirit under glossy hair and skin (and cheap clothes). Her face was dominated by those doe-like eyes above which were drawn, as if by a thick black pencil, a pair of eyebrows. Once seen, few would forget the curious combination of brow and eye. In that careless arrangement of features was cast her future.

And what would be the changes and transformations, wondered Louis, to dent those tender, unformed spirits and write on the untouched faces?

A significant proportion of the men she encountered were smaller than Becky. Louis Cadogan was not. He was big, but narrow, loose-limbed, well dressed and, she calculated, approximately twenty years older than she was. Instinctively she knew it was the moment to use her smile – a seductive smile that, along with her eyes and eyebrows, was the sole inheritance of any use bequeathed by the parents who had been so careless of her procreation and subsequent nurture.

'Let me guess,' said Louis, who even if he was dazzled recognized a wile. He studied the face in front of him. 'Fund management?'

'No,' said Becky. 'I've just started at Landes.'

Louis's interest quickened. Landes was one of the biggest managing agencies working at Lloyd's and, as one of Lloyd's noted underwriters (El Medici, said his friends and enemies), he knew it well. 'As?'

'A secretary. But I'm hoping to get a job as a reinsurance claims clerk.' She shrugged. 'Apprenticeship. It has to be got through.'

'And?'

'Well, I'll have to see,' said Becky. 'I don't intend to stay there long.'

Louis turned to Tess. 'How are things with you?'

After university (BA Hons, English and psychology), Tess had taken time off while she considered teaching as a career. After a year of reading through textbooks on semiotics and deconstructionism, and temping – a hideous combination – she had decided to flee the shores of literature. An active pursuit of money had been frowned on by the more intellectual under-graduates, the type with whom Tess had mixed. They had felt that Art and Culture were so much more important. At any rate, this was what they said, although Tess noted that the two who had been the most vociferous (and who had produced the plays with the most nudity and violence) had subsequently got themselves extremely well-paid jobs in advertising and the civil service. Tess was more honest and it was, after all, the eighties when, thank goodness, there was no nonsense about getting on and it was not unfashionable to be interested in making money. The upshot was that Colonel Frant made a telephone call to Louis and the job at Metrobank had materialized.

Lucky Tess. There was always some contact to fall back on. Some prop to hold her up. At least, that's what Becky had said once or twice when they'd talked over their past and their future (which did not appear to include marriage or children). It was not a bitter or envious remark, merely one that summed up the situation.

Lucky Tess.

While Tess talked to Louis, Becky was making a covert study of his English features, fashioned into good looks by generations of prudent marriage plus a fortunate deployment of genes. Those looks were lent extra interest by a pair of knowing, clever, slightly weary eyes and a mouth that suggested this was a man capable of feeling.

Then Louis made the mistake of turning his head towards Becky. Mutually startled, she by the honesty of his gaze, which told her that he wanted her, and he by the hunger in hers, they exchanged a look. This time, it was Louis who smiled at Becky.

'Hallo,' said Jack. Fed up with doing bottle duty and, wishing to chat up Becky, he pushed his way into the group.

Colonel Frant was dispensing drinks on the shaded part of the patio by the house. To the onlooker, he seemed entirely absorbed in his guests. In reality, he was mulling over his business affairs, to wit his run of profits (that is, until this morning), resulting from being a Name at Lloyd's.

Features set in a smile poised exactly between bonhomie and slight reserve, for he was a little shy at these affairs, he pressed a glass of iced champagne onto a latecomer who was in fact the chairman of the district council and a golfing companion. The glass was positively snatched from Colonel Frant's hand and the chairman, having exchanged only the briefest of greetings, hightailed it over to the group under the apple tree, which contained his mistress. Colonel Frant poured out another glass.

A man who, after leaving the Army at the age of forty-five,

had reinvented himself as a businessman and latterly as the chairman of a small fruit-importing company, he was both shrewd and cautious. But the eye contains a blind spot and it was possible that Colonel Frant did not see the whole picture with respect to his connection with Lloyd's.

Yet 1983 had seen profits of around six thousand, 1984 had jumped a little to over seven and, gloriously, in 1985 to more than nine. Nothing excessive but very nice, all the same. Colonel Frant's linen jacket was new, his shirt hailed from Jermyn Street and a gleaming set of golf clubs reposed in the hall of the High House.

'Over twenty-five thousand Names,' Nigel had said as he wooed. 'Capital base? No problem. Means requirement? Say two hundred and fifty thousand. The risk–reward ratio? Best ever. A hundred thousand underwrites three hundred and fifty and we'll split it up among some darling little syndicates.

'Covering yourself? Take out stop-loss. You know about that sort of thing. Must do.

'Good or what?'

'Tell me,' said Nigel Pavorde, members' agent, materializing at the side of Colonel Frant, 'who's the chap who's just moved into Threfall Grange?'

'Farleigh,' replied Colonel Frant. 'Made a killing with an estate agent chain in the West. His wife, though, has made him move back here.'

Nigel looked as though he had been fed a bone. 'Good or what, John? Introduce me.'

But Colonel Frant had caught his wife's gaze and picked up a champagne bottle. In its blanket of ice, the glass had sprung a delicate bloom and he wrapped it carefully in a napkin. 'Duty,' he said. 'Talk to you later.'

Nigel had a taste for outrageous waistcoats and possessed a great many. Some, the unkind, suggested that it was the only way he would ever appear interesting. Certainly, those who on first meeting him had been agreeably taken by his expansive figure and gestures found they were less so on the second encounter. Tonight, despite the heat, he was wearing a waistcoat striped in gold under a beige linen jacket, from the pocket of which he pulled a notebook.

'8 p.m. discomfort in lower stomach, 4 glasses champagne,' he wrote, on a page filled with similar notations.

He looked up to find Becky watching him. 'I like to keep a record,' he explained.

'Quite,' said Becky. 'So useful.'

'I'm Nigel Pavorde.'

Becky introduced herself, and set about finding out exactly what Nigel Pavorde did for a living.

They walked down the garden towards Eeyore's Paddock, where Tess had once kept a pony, beyond which was a meadow that Colonel Frant had bought years ago from a farmer who went bankrupt too early to be saved and subsided by the EU.

Becky had no interest in gardens but she could, and did, appreciate the sight of the meadow dotted with poppies and cornflowers, a lush, old-fashioned sight. Colonel and Mrs Frant were great conservationists and last year had been delighted to find that the tiny harvest mouse could be tempted to nest in a strategically placed tennis ball. To the south lay a flattish plain and the market town of Granton. To the west was the cricket pitch: a tended strip of emerald that managed to be both plutocratic and democratic at the same time. Jimmy Plover was hard at work mowing and the sound of his machine reverberated, vague and soothing, through bursts of the guests' conversation.

Appleford was a village in imminent danger of growing out of itself. Its centre was composed of old brick and timbered houses and of gardens awash with peonies, roses, sweet peas and verbascum. Two plaques for best-tended village were screwed into the wall above the local shop, which had recently metamorphosed into a mini-supermarket, and profits of the eighties bonanza were discernible to interested passers-by in the flashes of blue swimming pools and glimpses of conservatories to be had on the way to buy bread and milk.

At the north-east end of the village, and situated in a dip, which those who lived there swore was damp and those who did not swore was the opposite, was a housing estate, built in harsh, unforgiving red brick. Fortunately, for the aesthetically conscious, the estate did not intrude on Appleford's charm – although, now and then, some of its boys made it their business to smash windows and tear up fences fronting the listed houses.

'It's pretty here,' said Becky, who had no intention of moving into a period dwelling or of remaining in a council flat. Her full red skirt twined around her long legs and acted as a beacon to quite a few of the men present.

'Hallo again,' said Louis, bearing a bottle. 'Would either you or Nigel like a refill?'

'No, thank you,' said Becky, who was generally indifferent to food and drink.

With his free hand, Louis prised away her glass. 'You know, life is too precarious to pass up opportunities and you don't seem to me to be a natural puritan. You should never say no to champagne and you should drink the best, which this is. I advised John on the choice.'

A newcomer to the village, a widow anxious to be merry and to gain a niche, and who had made the mistake of moving away from the scene of her previous life, was circulating with a plate of rye-bread circles. 'Hallo,' she said to Louis and Nigel. 'This is my way of introducing myself.' The plate, held out to them with an obvious effort, shook slightly for Jennifer Gauntlet tended to tremble at the slightest hint of nerves.

Louis took a slippery circle and placed it in his mouth. 'How kind,' he said. 'Thank you. Now, do let me take the plate from you.'

'No, thank you,' said the Widow, who had gained control of the plate by holding it with both hands. 'It's my little duty to the kind hostess.'

11

'Louis,' said Jilly, gliding towards them, 'I think it's time we left.' She ignored both the plate held out to her and the Widow. 'Hallo, Nigel.'

'Meet Tess's friend, Becky.'

The two women assessed each other, neither drawing flattering conclusions. And, yet, they had several aspects in common.

'How very nice,' said Jilly, and turned to her husband. 'Louis, really, we should . . .'

'If,' said Louis, 'you would like to change your job, get Tess to give you my phone number.'

The Cadogans moved off, leaving Becky with Nigel, who shot his cuffs and said, 'Time for the old dins, I think.'

Tess slipped her hand into the crook of Becky's elbow and murmured, 'Thank God they're going.' But Becky's attention was fixed elsewhere.

Accompanied by a setting sun, the Frants' guests said their goodbyes and made their way home through Appleford's quiet, pretty streets, luxuriantly fringed with willow and beech, which had once witnessed Bad King John's hunting party and a progress of Good Queen Bess.

Suddenly, shockingly, the peace was shredded by three ambulances racing up the ridge, sirens blaring, towards the motorway.

Later that night, Tess lay awake in her bedroom. She thought – for she was rather interested in space and all that – of the world whirling on through the darkness and, in their eyries, of the men and women patrolling the furthest outreaches of the universe with their instruments.

Why, she thought, visualizing the winking screens and rows of mathematical calculations, if the watchers in the laboratories and observatories are slipping through time they must be encountering the future as well as the past; the conflict and cruelty to come, as chilling and devastating as that which has been.

As a child, her life had been one of sensation: ice cream dripping stickily down fingers; the whiff of new hay in Eeyore's Paddock; a scrape of leather against her thighs; stomach-aches like stones; bubbles of excitement held in her body like the first mouthful of Tizer; the strange, heart-stopping moments when she learnt something frightening, embarrassing, ominous, and wished she had not.

Now it was different. Lying there in the High House, Tess felt overwhelmed by the challenge of living, the sheer business of feeling, for her feelings ran deep and were often tempestuous and she despaired of mastering them. Above all, she longed to find God and was failing to do so, sometimes, even, berated Him for not being there. She also told herself it was bad luck to have been born into an age where there was no longer room for a Deity and where any mystery was given a scientific, rational explanation. Either that, or a documentary on television.

Longing for God was akin to feeling hunger. You could be plump, as Tess undoubtedly was, and still be a hungry person. As hungry as the thin, restless Becky. Starved. Famished. At least they had that in common. Sharing something with Becky mattered to Tess and it thrilled her to know that the need was returned.

Perhaps, if she relaxed her mind would be free to roam the highways and byways of knowledge and emotion and to make the connections that would fill her with power, energy and love.

Chapter Two

Round about the cheese course, Nigel had become a little drunk which, while not unpleasant, loosened his tongue. 'Bloody Americans!' He strove, as always, to impress his peers. 'I reckon all these court settlements will be disastrous.'

Nigel had been permanently allocated the role of buffoon (the waistcoats and notebook helped). However, it did not necessarily cancel the correctness of his observation. The willingness of American courts to settle in favour of plaintiffs – Shell was currently facing a bill for £200 million to clean up the toxic waters leaching into the water table in the Rocky Mountain Arsenal in Colorado – was affecting the insurance market.

The cheese, Cheddar and Wensleydale, was excellent, and its spicy, tangy taste was commented on knowledgeably and with affection, almost love.

'Bloody Americans,' repeated Nigel, to no one in particular, and ate his cheese. 'I wonder if this was made with pasteurized milk?'

The Bollys had met at Luc's restaurant in Leadenhall Market. A group of ten colleagues, they had been so dubbed because of their fondness for champagne by Chris Beame, who fancied himself a wit. They met to exchange gossip, because they liked one another and because it was both useful and agreeable to mull over the business. As an informal gathering, it counted two active underwriters, a managing agent, a members' agent, an investment expert and an accountant among the ten. With his beaked nose and hooded eyes, Matt Barker, an underwriter with a Midas touch and a member of Lloyd's council, gave it a welcome touch of gravitas, and Louis its glamour. Except that they all enjoyed healthy earnings, nothing of significance united them, neither taste nor lifestyle – apart from Louis's and Matt's mutual fondness for roses.

Yet once absorbed into the Lloyd's sphere something odd tended to take place. Much as patients given new hearts have been found to develop the tastes and craving of the dead donors, so recruits into the world of Lloyd's could be said to step inside the skins of the seniors.

Insiders, including the active underwriter, have by custom to demonstrate faith in their own judgement by investing their own money in their own syndicates. It was thought to be sufficient, and soothing, demonstration of good faith to the external Names. If the insiders were putting money where their mouths were, then the external Names – those like Colonel Frant, who knew nothing of the market only that they wished to make money for little effort – could rest easy.

Strangely, not one of the ten here at Luc's, neither the seniors nor the juniors eating their cheese and drinking their claret, had ever been tempted to place their personal business on the syndicates specializing in reinsurance, known as the LMX, which was reputedly flourishing. Or on those known to have long-tail liabilities. (For example, claims were coming in to some syndicates for cases of cancer caused by asbestosis as long ago as twenty years). Yet a percentage of Colonel Frant's underwriting liability had been placed in precisely these dubious areas by at least one of the men sitting round the table.

'The Far East . . .' Chris Beame had the sheen of excitement on his face. His syndicate was a relatively modest one, having around five hundred Names and an underwriting capacity of twenty million or so. Unlike some of the stuffier underwriters, he did not care – well, not *much* – if the Names on his syndicate did not include the royal and the titled. No, Chris argued that the aristocratic pot was empty and that it was better to concentrate on culling a new harvest of politicians, lawyers, accountants, businessmen, sports stars and – even – women. It was, he had been heard to say with only a trace of complacency, a remarkably progressive, democratic set-up.

'Self-regulation at Lloyd's,' Matt Barker had a trick of drawing his listener into a conspiracy, whose secrets promised to be intoxicating, 'will have to be seen to be better managed.'

Louis nodded and moved his glass around his knives. 'Tricky.'

Well back in the past, both men had been aware of, indeed had dabbled in, activities that were not criminal – no, nothing like that – but were open to criticism. Activities such as the creation of baby syndicates and, when taxes had been high, a little bond-washing.

Louis's position, which he shared with Matt, was simple: if the opportunity was there, take it. They knew how to operate the market, and operate it they would. There was, particularly with regard to the younger men, a lot of sabre-rattling and declarations of 'Let him who dares, dare.' Louis had reached the age when he simply did it.

As a result, Louis's personal wealth could now finance rose gardens from Arctic to Antarctic, and Matt, if he wished, could have bought up a couple of factories specializing in the production of his favourite bright-coloured ties.

Neither man was dishonest.

Sometimes Louis asked himself why the business fascinated him so much. Then he would recollect the childhood where each step had been proscribed, each thought tagged with potential damnation, each impulse questioned. A childhood in which the Virgin Mary's dreaming face and rose-bordered shimmering blue cloak suggested all manner of tenderness, but the cold, hard discipline exacted by her and her Son was anything but. A childhood where a sense of possibility had been whittled to nothing – and from which Louis had escaped.

In part, only in part.

After a satisfactory lunch the Bollys broke up and, in the gents' afterwards, Nigel examined his reflection in the mirror. Was he imagining things or was a touch of yellow painting his eyeball? He felt for the portion of his torso containing his liver and prodded it. Nothing.

It was tiring being a hypochondriac, tiring and burdensome, and it was an effort to stave off the terrors that threatened each corner he rounded.

'What a good party it was.' The Widow cornered Angela Frant in Appleford's mini-supermarket. 'Wasn't it? It was *so* nice of you to invite me.'

She looked for further affirmation to Jilly, who was buying *Tatler* at the counter on her way to her monthly appointment with her astrologer and then on up to London for a little lunch.

Jilly smiled but with not too much warmth, for the Widow had been marked down in her mental social register as a non-runner. She waited while Jennifer coaxed forth the coins in her plastic purse for a tin of soup, a small loaf, a half tin of baked beans, and then paid for her magazine.

She drove to Granton – once a solid market town, specializing in candles and cattle, now a vision of white paint and shop windows selling the *World of Interiors* magazine, artificial flowers and coloured bathroom fittings – more than ready for an expensive dose of reassurance.

Mercury is making a good aspect to Uranus, Jilly was told. Be prepared for changes. She must also take care not to overstretch herself. Jilly made an immediate resolution to cut down on her charity work.

Money, pronounced the astrologer, who did her homework, is there. Plenty of it. But beware the tricky aspects of Pluto in your House.

*

On the way home, Mrs Frant asked the Widow if she would mind signing up to help with the annual fête. 'Then,' she added, 'there are the cricket teas. I think Mrs Thrive would appreciate some help.' The gist of Mrs Frant's meaning was that Eleanor Thrive, who could not organize the contents of a lavender bag, was as usual making a hash of her rota. The implication was also that, being alone, the Widow would have plenty of time to give. But, Jennifer bravely concluded, it was infinitely more comforting and less bitter to be included on a dubious basis than not at all.

Mrs Frant walked slowly back to the High House, so-called because it had been built by a Regency remittance man on the top of the only rise in a flat swathe of rolling Hampshire land. The rise did not immediately strike the onlooker as very high but she liked to think of the house as occupying a rarefied stratum with purer air; it was a home that worked to make her better.

At present, she required the reassurance: Jack, her good and wonderful son, was becoming a source of worry.

If he had given her no trouble during his childhood, Jack had, nevertheless, been difficult to understand. Or, at least, his mother found his motives and ambitions, and the marked puritan streak, mystifying and, lately, a source of pain. Certainly, his progress since leaving Oxford with a degree in philosophy had not conformed – if taking a series of temporary jobs in reputable charities was not conforming. He had been lined up for a position at a merchant bank, and all would have been well. But he had had other ideas and held out stubbornly to work in Africa for a charity. It was Tess who had gone into the merchant bank.

'Jack is a missionary *manqué*,' Tess informed Becky as they waited at Waterloo for the train down to Appleford, the weekend following the party. 'He sort of burns with fervour to do good, or at least to flagellate himself.'

18

'Why?'

Tess raised her shoulders and stepped back to allow a flock of girls to scuttle down the platform. 'Some strange tic in his make-up. Maybe we have a saint in our past.'

Becky, who that week had been telephoned twice by Jack, had her own views. He had already declared his love for her (it took him five seconds, he had said) and when she protested that he did not know her, Jack asked why that mattered.

He was waiting for them at the station and drove them back to Appleford. Prowling and preoccupied, Mrs Frant fed them soup and roast chicken and watched her children – a maternal computer recording heart-beats, skin tone, mental fitness. Both the quality and intensity of her gaze, Becky felt, were disconcerting but, then, she possessed no knowledge, no memory of maternal love.

Like his sister, Jack was fair, but unlike her lush, moisturized-by-rain looks, his seemed bleached in anticipation of the sun.

'Tess was quite right,' he said, in a clever way, as he bore Becky off for a drink at the Plume of Feathers.

'About what?' Becky matched his pace and her red skirt swirled in a way that made Jack feel quite dizzy.

'You're a red colour. Vivid and scarlet. Like a poppy.'

Becky was amused. 'And Tess?'

Jack halted at the entrance to the pub. 'Let's sit in the garden. What colour do *you* think she is?'

'Powder blue. Soft and full of depth.' Becky tested a bench with her finger. 'This one's damp.'

'Come here, then.' As Jack sat down beside her, she felt his energy and fervour trap her in a magnetic field. They talked about his future and Becky's work and, every so often, Jack turned his gaze on the English countryside around them, bathed in the milky light of a high summer evening.

For Jack, the vista was bred into his blood and bone, as familiar as the skin on his palm, and it barely registered as he contemplated the idea of another landscape: lunar, unyielding, irradiated with intense light. One, moreover, where he would be needed.

'It's a wounded world,' he announced.

Becky stared at him. 'Really?' Endeavouring to understand what he meant, she said, 'The world has always been wounded, as you put it.'

Later Jack got up to fetch a second round and, a little hazy with wine, Becky watched his progress with an uncharacteristic mix of emotions. Desire, a worship of his beauty and strength, a yearning to be part of them.

'Where do you come from?' Jack put the refilled glasses on the table, spotted with mould.

'It's very peculiar.' Becky watched his expression. 'Everyone always wants to know where I've come *from*.'

'It's your surname.'

Becky's eyebrows rose. 'My father was Italian. Or so I'm told.'

'Your mother,' Aunt Jean informed her niece, 'sinned and she didn't stand a chance.'

'Why, Aunt Jean?'

'Because, because ...' Aunt Jean had been washing up during this conversation and up to her wrists in clumpy suds '... your silly mother listened to the first man who came along. Or rather, if she had stuck to listening and not laid on her back, it would have been a different story. And then she lumbers me with you.'

Aunt Jean had been lumbered with many things. Her heart complaint. Her religion. Her job cleaning offices in the evening. And, if I'm anything like my mother, Becky concluded, I know she was not taken in. She merely took what she wanted and made a mistake.

That's all.

'Your aunt Jean brought you up, then.' Jack's expression was tender as his blue eyes sought and engaged Becky's huge, deceptively soft ones. His compassion, not yet outweighed by middle-aged sternness or zeal, was a huge, slippery emotion that often gushed out of control. From suffering Africa to the damaged spider in the garden shed, his pity flowed indiscriminately. It flowed now, wrapping Becky in the downiest of coverings.

'My mother abandoned me when I was a couple of months old,' said Becky, whose reservoir of pity was, by comparison, limited. Especially, to be fair, in relation to herself . . . 'Which was hard for my aunt Jean who did not, does not, like children.'

'Poor baby . . .' Jack's gaze was now firmly anchored on new details: Becky's skin lustre, the sharp slash of her collar bone and, despite her height, her air of fragility.

A modern woman: clever, sensuous, knowing. Lover, siren, . . . achiever?

Jack found himself thinking foolish thoughts . . . that Becky had a flame burning inside her. A bright, leaping flame that would cast warmth over, that would be shared with, the right person.

'Sentimentality,' she was saying, 'is a weakness. I gather my mother is living up north somewhere. That's all I know.'

Jack took her home the long way, via the footpath that ran trenchant, across a cornfield. At its edge, he stopped abruptly, took her in his arms and kissed her. Unguarded and disarmed by the unfamiliar harmonies of earth and sky, Becky submitted, her busy mind for once still and quiet.

Heat rose from the baked perimeter of the field, the smells of chalky earth and ripening grain, and the chorus from the swifts high up accompanied the desire running through Jack and Becky.

I don't like her.

In her garden, Mrs Frant was marching her routes, which

she did every day. This one took her past the rose bed – too much orange, she decided – and along the herbaceous border. She stopped and bent over.

Where was the cosmos? Ah, there, almost hidden by the selfish, springy growth of a garnet penstemon. The cosmos was special – its deep blackish-purplish colour and chocolate scent promising all manner of revelations – and autumn without the cosmos (she liked the name, too) was not autumn.

Satisfied, Mrs Frant marched on.

Marching the routes stilled and soothed her. It imported structure and rhythm into her day, into her spirit, *on which she could rely*. And, provided she followed the exact path of the chosen route, things would be well.

'I don't like her, John,' she had told her husband. 'She means trouble.'

Angela Frant was a traditional matron, much concerned with parish matters, the WI and WRVS, but one with unexpected reserves. While Colonel Frant's daytime musings might focus on the pound's climb or fall against the dollar (the $1.55 during the dreadful 1976 providing a benchmark) or, latterly, *that* letter, Mrs Frant found time to ponder the implications of world famine, France's political configurations and the Russian nuclear disaster at Chernobyl. The broad sweep was Mrs Frant's territory, the minutiae her husband's. It was a standing joke between them that she never read the small print.

Yet when it came to her children, Mrs Frant was as parochial as it was possible to be; living proof that maternal love is an anvil on which the sharpest of swords are forged.

'Rebecca is not suitable for Jack.'

'Aren't you jumping the gun? Jack's enjoying himself, that's all. Becky is very taking.'

Mrs Frant had noted the 'Becky'. She walked on down the garden towards the paddock on her now thickened ankles. Rebecca, she concluded correctly, is on the make. With his job prospects, Jack would make a good catch and, clearly, there was a bit of money in the family. All the things she wants.

When she put this point of view to her husband, he surprised her.

'Don't be silly, darling.' Lately, Colonel Frant had only used 'darling' when he was irritated. 'Girls don't think like that, these days. Anyway, how do you know what she wants?'

'I know.'

The image of Becky buried itself in Mrs Frant's mind, and she carried it carefully and self-consciously, exhuming it from time to time for examination.

In fact, Jack was in a bind for he could think of little other than Becky. Quite apart from his African ambitions warring with the merchant bank, there was the thorny problem of Penelope (an earnest BA Hons in agriculture, and putative co-worker in Ethiopia), who was standing by at her home in Reading, waiting for the telephone call.

Instead of phoning and embarking on the Reading pilgrimage, which he had faithfully promised the faithful Penelope he would do, Jack tracked down Becky at Paradise Flats in Streatham.

Becky had just got back from work. She let him into the ground-floor flat in the block and ushered him into the main room, off which opened two bedrooms and a kitchen. The smell from yesterday's supper of tinned steak and kidney pie lingered in the air and a pile of clean washing roosted in one corner. In the flat upstairs, someone was trying to flush a lavatory.

Becky apologized for the state of the room. 'Aunt Jean's out cleaning and her work with the Holy Spirit during the day generally leaves her too tired to do her own housework. *Ergo*, God must be a man,' she explained for Jack's benefit, adding, 'the God Squad was over here last night. Tea, ginger biscuits and sing along with the Lord.'

But he was too full of other ideas to sympathize. 'I've been talking to my contact in HAT.'

'In what?'

'Help for Africa Today. It's partly funded by UNESCO, partly by a government aid agency. They need workers for a limited period in Ethiopia and it might be possible to get taken on. It would be perfect.'

A mental picture spread out before Becky. Of negotiating with officials and civil servants under a hot sun. Of walking between children with outstretched hands. Of being congratulated on her skills . . .

'Good God,' she said and, for an awful second or two, Jack thought she was laughing at him. 'What about the magnificent Penelope?'

'Penny? Well, I've confessed to her. She's . . . um sad, but she's going out to Africa whatever happens.'

I could, thought Becky, rummaging in the dark areas of her heart, allow Paradise Flats to rule my life. They could be the template for the way I am. For ever. I could allow myself never to move on.

Deep-seated melancholy induced by a deprived background was a state of mind she had often mulled over and rejected. Not for Becky was the depression induced by unsatisfactory vitamin levels, high-rise vertigo or the tyranny of no hope. Nevertheless, she darted a look of dislike at her aunt's flowered overall hanging behind the door.

'Poor Penelope,' she said. 'I do understand her feelings.'

A large smile spread over Jack's thin face, and his expression grew tender at this evidence of his loved one's generosity. 'I knew you would.'

He yearned so to cherish her, much as he would cherish his starving charges in the camp. Becky stretched out a hand and Jack seized it.

'I've got a job,' she said. 'And I don't want to leave it.'

Jack's face fell. The script he had written during the long sleepless nights portrayed him as resourceful and irresistible. He studied his shoes. They required polishing and, clearly, so did he. Before he knew what he was doing, he had slid to his knees in front of Becky's chair and recaptured her hand. The upkeep of the floor had defeated Aunt Jean and an upsurge of dust accompanied the movement. Outside, a summer storm was lashing south London into a frenzy, a thrilling shuddering backdrop that Romantics demanded for the significant encounter. (Think Beethoven. Think Goethe. Think Brontë.)

'Oh, Becky,' he murmured, thus exposed and yearning. 'What have you done to me?'

Becky's eyes were enormous as she ticked off the consequences of being weakened by love. There knelt her would-be lover: a big, golden, nervous example of its power, stripped by it to the bone. She bent over and touched his mouth with a finger, letting it slide, light and uncommitted, around the contours of his mouth, and relishing the slight harshness of his shaved skin.

Somehow, for the moment at any rate, Jack had dodged through the entrenchments dug into her stoutly defended heart. Why Becky Vitali, she thought, dazzled, you've been missing out.

She noticed a tiny tremor in his hands and smelt the sharp aphrodisiacal tang of male sweat. 'What do you want, Jack?'

Afterwards, Jack gathered Becky in his arms. 'Why don't we forget all this?' He meant jobs, family, London. 'We'll do worthwhile things, you and I.'

He sounded energized and directed. A tangle of hair and limbs, Becky stared past his shoulder at the ceiling. (NB A web of mould appeared to have taken root at the junction of the two big cracks. Reason? Neighbour's overflowing bath? Decaying joists? The council had promised a makeover.) She was limp and deliciously drowsy.

'Why not?' she murmured.

*

'*Drive* to Africa! Drive there?' Mrs Frant was horribly aware that she sounded like a parrot. She was wearing rubber gloves and had a duster in one hand.

Jabbing her finger down on a pink oblong, Becky looked up from a map of the Sahara that she and Jack had unrolled over the dining-room table at the High House. She had pulled back her hair and was wearing khaki shorts and a T-shirt.

Jack ignored his mother. 'Which route do you think, Bec?'

'Tamanrassat would be the main stop. Presumably they'd have supplies out there.'

Mrs Frant sank down on a chair opposite them and listened. Phrases such as 'dry season' and 'wind factor' were being bandied about. 'Listen to me,' she lunged at the table with the duster, 'this is not on, Jack. You have your job to think about. So do you, Rebecca. They won't make allowances while you jaunt off to Africa.' She rubbed savagely at the table top: it could have been Becky's face that she was endeavouring to obliterate.

Her son looked up, and Mrs Frant's heart squeezed with fear. 'Don't worry, Mum,' he said. 'This is the final fling before we settle down. One glorious expedition and then I'll come home and be as good as gold.'

Mrs Frant's dusting movement continued. Does she dust in her sleep, wondered Becky.

'Promise,' said Jack.

Chapter Three

Colonel Frant's career had been distinguished by a certain sort of courage, the kind that did not question too much and got on with it. He was not used to asking favours or advice and was surprisingly diffident – at least, with regard to himself. It was with reluctance that he sat down in his study to write a letter to the managing agent.

'I am sorry to be bothering you on such a subject,' he wrote, 'but I wonder if you could clarify my position a little more precisely? Am I likely to incur more cash calls?'

The letter that came back suggested that the Colonel was worrying unnecessarily, and that his exposure was such that any cash calls would, in the event, be paid for by profits in other areas.

Looking back, Louis was aware that his meeting with John Frant in the Bluebell Wood had been of significance. That it was accidental, and incidental, did not alter or diminish its importance.

Both men were walking the dog and, as they approached each other from opposite directions through the greenish light filtered by the trees, the dogs wheeling and circling, they had time to make choices.

'I wonder, old chap,' said Colonel Frant, 'if you would give me some advice? I'm a little concerned about my exposure. Do you think I should resign from Lloyd's?'

Louis clicked his fingers and Brazen came to heel, bringing with him the odour of hot dog and saliva. The rankness curled under the noses of the men.

'No. I don't think so.' Louis was as aware as any working Name of the dangers of under-capacity. That is, of Names such as Colonel Frant not possessing enough liquid capital to pay for the cash calls in bad years. 'You should be fine. But if you like I'll have a word with Nigel, who should look into it for you.' He spoke with the advantage of possessing knowledge that he did not impart. Colonel Frant listened with the disadvantage of ignorance, which he should have sought to alleviate. Neither questioned further.

They parted. One to walk home, reasonably reassured. The other to pursue his way through the wood, dry and brittle with drought, up onto the ridge where Caesar and his men once camped. From this vantage point Appleford appeared untouched, for the road and housing estate were hidden. Only the grey stone spire of the church and a cluster of houses could be seen, drowsy and complete.

Becky and Tess were comparatively new friends and, as is the case with older friendships, areas had not yet emerged that were unwise to examine. They discussed everything, obsessively and at length. It was extraordinary, Tess exclaimed, how every detail, every nuance that they aired of their feelings drew them closer together, and how well they understood each other.

Becky was less sure of the last point but willing, for the time being at any rate, to go along with it.

'You really don't mind about me and Jack?' she asked Tess, for the fourth time. She seemed uneasy.

It was Friday night and the two girls had been to a French film in Notting Hill Gate and had emerged blinking into the night.

Tess did not stop to reflect. 'Of *course* not. I love the idea. Why should I mind?'

The certainty returned to Becky's expression. 'As long as you don't object.'

Her best friend. Her loved brother. Tess admired the neatness and symmetry of the affair and, since it did not occur to her that things did not always happen for the best, she sat firmly on the occasional stab of jealousy. Becky had been hers first and, sometimes, it pained her a little to see Jack claim her.

Funnily enough, for she did not often waste energy on such sensitivities, Becky understood. 'But I love you too,' she said, and gave Tess a quick kiss before running to catch her bus home. After a few paces, she turned to look back. 'Mind you go to that party,' she called.

Tess had been invited to a party by a colleague and Becky had had to work hard to persuade her to go. Tess had declared that she was too fat and the women would be beautiful. Becky replied that Tess was in danger of living too much inside herself and it was making her lazy.

'It's too easy to turn inwards,' she scolded. 'And, given half a chance, that's what you'd do. You'll end up holding parties in your head and becoming a recluse.'

Tess was so pleased and flattered that Becky had bothered to think about her in such depth and with such a degree of insight that she found herself agreeing to go.

London was swathed in late summer dust, whirling pollens and pollution, and the following evening Tess sneezed several times as she walked down the Chelsea street. So fresh and inviting earlier in the year, gardens were now filled with ochre and yellow, their city soil exhausted by the demands made on it.

The party was being held in a house owned by the portfolio administrator at Metrobank. By nine o'clock it was in full swing and Tess had been hating it for the last half-hour.

'Hallo,' said a square-jawed, square-shouldered man, with a

lock of dark hair falling over his forehead. 'I'm George Mason and I've been watching you.' (Watching Tess's treacherous, glowing skin with its frequent blushes.)

'Hi.' Tess hated herself when she said hi. She searched in her handbag for her cigarettes.

'And this is Iain MacKenzie,' said George, pointing at the older man who stood beside him. 'Fellow officer and friend who hauls me out of trouble. Frequently. I give you fair warning that where I go Iain comes too. Providing Flora, the wife – his wife, I mean – lets him.'

'Will you shut up?' Iain smiled at Tess. 'One glass and he reverts.'

'How do you do?' said Tess.

Iain took her hand. His was warm and large. 'It's nice to meet you but I can see Flora signalling, so . . .'

George watched his friend's retreating back. 'Ruled by his wife,' he said.

A youth lurched past them, pupils boiled-looking and drugged.

'This is the sort of party,' Tess said, 'where if anyone looks deep into your eyes, it's to see their own reflection.'

George bent over and looked deep into hers. 'In yours I see a maiden who needs rescuing.'

It is not often in a life that its course is determined within a second, but when it does happen, it is worth recording. Tess always remembered the exact scent of the tobacco plants in the terracotta pot on the patio, the colours of the women's clothes, the strange, whitish quality of the sky.

'You look interesting,' he told her, still looking into . . . What *was* he looking into? Her soul? 'I know you're interesting.'

Cigarette in hand, and bothered by his actorish quality, she looked back at him, her lower lip caught, in her confusion, between her teeth. Her silky, youthful bloom caught George on the raw.

'George!' shrieked a voice. 'Darling, darling! Where've you been with not a squeak out of naughty you?' In a Lycra dress that barely covered her rump, a girl wrapped thin arms around George's neck and kissed him over and over again.

Women, Tess had once been lectured by a feminist, should make the running. Consider for how long the chains have been round our necks. *Break 'em.* She considered what the running might be in this sort of situation and concluded, not for the first time, that theory and practice were not related.

George and the girl appeared to be wriggling about satisfactorily and Tess was awed to see that she was not wearing any knickers. Behind the girl's back, George raised one finger and pointed it at Tess. 'Wait,' he mouthed.

Tess slid away from him and the entwined nymph and went to admire the small, smart London garden. On balance, she did not rate being young, a condition that left her frequently depressed and underlined her inexperience and sense of powerlessness.

It was not a fashionable view, but bugger that, she thought.

She lit another cigarette. Nicotine, wonderful nicotine, burned its way into her system and the smoke hit the back of her throat with its customary thud. Glorious, unselfish cigarettes, little pencils of comfort and courage. Tess smoked hers down to the stub then buried it in the flowerbed.

'Dinner.' George Mason had detached himself from Miss Lycra. He did not seem to think that she might say no.

Nor could she.

Over dinner in a restaurant poised equidistant between the very smart and the avoidable, George spoke on the subject in which he appeared to excel: himself. Charming and persuasive, he threw disconcerting flashes of modesty and humour into the sparkle, much as dun-coloured feathers among fancy plumage soothe the eye. Yet Tess was not entirely convinced for she gained the impression that this display was an effort for him, even distasteful. She suspected, too, that he did not like himself very much, just as she did not always like herself either, and her romantic instincts stirred.

'The Army sent me to university. Edinburgh. I was lucky and got an early captaincy.'

'How old are you?'

'Twenty-eight.'

'And then?'

George's attitude suggested that what he was going to say did not matter at all. 'Northern Ireland. I had a good tour and my platoon found a cache of explosives.' Tess had an impression that she was looking at a file marked 'Top Secret'. George paused, his unmilitary hair falling across his forehead, and decided to close the file, leaving her tantalized. 'Success is always useful.'

For the life of her, Tess could think of nothing interesting to say. Her tongue was tied, her waistband was tight and never, ever again would she eat dessert. How else could she ever be naked in front of this man? She dropped her head between her hands and pushed back her heavy fair hair. When her face emerged, the skin was stained a pure rose.

'I wonder,' she said at last, 'how we would be, how we would think, if we did not have the Northern Ireland problem. Like the Empire, it shapes us.'

'Ah,' said George, eyes narrowed. 'The psychology of politics.'

He was teasing her, perhaps even patronizing her. Tess's flush deepened but she ploughed on. 'We have a dark edge running along one of our perimeters.'

After an awful moment, when Tess could have died for the banality of her remark, George said, 'Yes, I suppose you're right . . .'

On leaving the restaurant, George asked, 'Where do you live?'

'In Pimlico. I have a flat there. Or, rather, it's my father's and he lets me rent it.'

'Ah,' said George. 'That's nice.'

'Hurry up, petal,' said Freddie Ahern. 'Bill's been asking for you.'

Tess opened her drawer – a horrible sight – and stuffed her handbag into it. Then she remembered her pen, opened the drawer again and extracted it with her reading glasses. 'What does he want?'

'There's a dowager, rich, rich, rich, who he wants netting in and thought you should sit in on the meeting. Then he'll want you to set up the new portfolio.'

'Right.' Tess's hair had worked loose from its velvet scrunchy and she adjusted it before grabbing her things. As she passed him, she tapped Freddie on the head with her pen. 'Don't you look so smug, Frederick. Your turn next.'

Considering that he was sitting down, Freddie did a remarkable imitation of a flounce.

When she came back to her desk, feeling quite pleased with her performance, the office was an organized frenzy. The previous day there had been one of the biggest rights issues of the decade and the price had gone through the roof. Today, at 9.01 a.m., something had gone wrong and it was falling.

'What the devil . . . ?' Tess's director, Bill – thirty-fiveish, wearing a blue striped shirt, red braces and a red tie – stared at the screen where the Strip revealed a large wobble. 'You'd better offload the smaller holdings and top-slice the larger.'

Women, Bill had mentioned to Tess in passing when she had been hired, are not just good on the eye. Had she got it?

Tess had got it.

'OK. OK . . .' Kit, the assistant director – thirtyish, wearing a

33

red-striped shirt and blue tie – swivelled round to face Tess. 'Beam up my holdings,' he said. 'Give me the numbers.'

She sprang into activity. Since the stock had only been acquired the day before, the print-out was no help and she used the screen. 'OK, Kit,' she said. 'Here we go.'

She heard him get on the phone to the sales trader, who would get on the phone to market-makers, and sat back.

Freddie winked at her. 'Go and get me some coffee,' he said naughtily.

She looked at him, formulating something witty and stinging with which to reply, and froze. 'Oh, my God, Freddie. I've done something terrible. I've given Kit the total holdings. Not just his.'

'Christ,' said Freddie, and turned pale for her. After a moment or two, he said, 'I'll send a large bouquet to the funeral.'

Tess got up. Everything about her was shaking. 'Make it large and lilies,' she said, and made her way across to Kit's desk.

'You *what?*' Kit stared at Tess. 'You . . .' Words failed him. 'You know how much money we could lose? Well, you get on the phone and explain and now. Make good.'

By the end of a morning's frantic work, the situation was mostly retrieved, but not entirely. Bill had hauled Tess over the coals in front of the whole office, back room and all. 'Here is an example,' he had said, voice pitched exactly to take in everyone, 'of someone who has not got the little mind back into gear after a weekend of excess. Yes?'

Yes and no. Tess had spent most of Sunday in a daze, going over and over her meeting with George who had deposited her back at the flat in the small hours with the promise: 'See you sometime.'

Her punishment could have been worse, far worse. After all, she had made a mistake. Initially Tess had felt that she would die, but now detected a little iron creep into her soul. That was how it was. You made a mistake. You got on with it.

George waited a week then rang to suggest they had dinner. She came home weak with laughter for he turned out to be an expert mimic. After that, they met frequently but the affair did not progress. At least, not as Tess wished it to. Fuelled by laughter and an instinct that there was more to him than he was permitting her to see, she fell headlong in love . . . arms whirling above her dazzled head, her heart pulsing with the electricity of passion, her mind filled with images of glory.

'I can't work it out,' she confided to Becky, over an evening drink in a crowded bar in Broadgate. 'I'm not sure what he's playing at. He's taken me out several times, dinner, walks, that sort of thing. But he's being a gentleman.'

Becky ran over several possibilities in her mind as to why George was failing to come up to scratch.

Non-gentlemen, Tess had been taught by the careful Mrs Frant, ravished females with lustiness and the lack of consideration of William the Conqueror's knights. Gentlemen took their time. Tess had queried whether, since the ends appeared to be the same, the means mattered. 'Without a doubt,' Mrs Frant had replied firmly.

'What do I do, Bec? Is it because I'm too fat?'

'For the last time, Tess, you're *not* fat.'

'I feel it, and that's the same thing.' Tess helped herself to more crisps. '*What do I do?*'

But Becky seemed far away, preoccupied with matters of her own.

'Come back,' said Tess. 'I need you.'

'Sorry.' Becky pushed her mineral water round in a circle.

'How's Jack?'

'Fine,' said Becky, but her tone suggested the opposite.

'Everything's all right?'

Eyes veiled, Becky smiled at her. 'Everything's fine. I'm just tired, that's all, and Aunt Jean is driving me potty. I can't wait to get out.'

'You will soon.' Tess was thinking of the African expedition.

'Yes, I suppose so,' said Becky.

Tess returned to her own agenda. 'Well, what do I do, Becky?'

'Ask him, for God's sake. It's easy.'

Women, break your chains.

On the tube back to Pimlico, Tess analysed the battle-cry. What did it mean exactly? When hormones, passion and biology fused, it was impossible *not* to feel imprisoned. She raged at her stupidity at being felled by love just when she was required to be free.

She wanted to concentrate on her work, but instead she was mugging up topics such as 'Arms and the Modern World', 'Does the Army Have a Role in the Post-Nuclear Theatre?', 'The Ethics of Killing', in a jumble of will-he-won't-he? and does-he-doesn't-he?.

Love, it seemed, stole your wits, your conversation, your sleep and your muscle tone. What a thief it was. Mrs Frant had done her duty in lecturing her daughter on rape and rapine, but she had neglected to inform her how physical love was, how uncomfortable its effects.

Tess looked down at her handbag, bulging on her knee, and asked herself: What if this distracting condition is long-term?

'Surf the market,' said a naughty, malicious Freddie in her ear. 'Easy go . . . that's how the boys do it.'

That night, after a pasta dinner in Chelsea, Tess, exhausted as she was, looked George in the eye and said, 'Would you like to go to bed with me?'

George's attention was brought back to the flushed, yearning, tenderly disposed Tess, for he had been thinking of something else not to be shared and not to be spoken about. And it was that remoteness that nagged and galvanized Tess.

He is, she thought, observing every detail, beautiful. He was made of fine material: brocade, velvet and silk from the Emperor's garden.

George would have been mad not to have accepted the

invitation, and if George was many things about which Tess had no idea, mad was not one of them.

Latterly, the instructions from God to Aunt Jean had taken a more specific turn and Aunt Jean had been told to Involve Herself More With the Homeless. The result was confusion. While the Mission flourished, the flat and her niece were neglected.

God had caught her, Aunt Jean once confessed to Becky, not on the road to Damascus but on the bus for Streatham High Road, which was as good a place as any. He had caught her at the bit where Etam and Dorothy Perkins battle it out for customers by the traffic lights. At that vital intersection, he had arrived, scooped her up and irradiated her life with purpose and love.

As far as it was in her nature to be so, Becky was glad for her aunt. Sometimes she questioned why the aforementioned Love, which apparently brimmed over in her aunt for others, never flowed towards her, for Aunt Jean only tolerated her niece.

'Why does it have to be God?' Becky was driven to ask one evening, after Aunt Jean had come home stinking of a drug addict's vomit. 'Why couldn't you have fallen in love with Mammon? Or a pools winner so we could have a new bathroom?'

Small and, despite the heart condition, pickled in tobacco, Aunt Jean favoured Becky with a look that certainly did not contain Love but, rather, combined the ruthlessness of the righteous with pity for one who was so bereft of spiritual resources as to ask the question in the first place.

She peeled off her bright pink cardigan, dropped it into the sink and ran cold water over it. Becky shuddered.

'Why not God?' replied her aunt, as if that wrapped up most of the great questions posed by humanity. 'Why not Him?'

'Because He's selfish and He hasn't got His head round

plumbing,' answered Becky. 'I must introduce you to Tess. The two of you would get on.'

Her aunt whirled round: an ageing messenger on earth. 'If you say anything more, then you'll have to go.'

'Don't make it too easy.' Becky's eyebrows snapped together. 'Just say the word.'

'Huh,' said Aunt Jean, and added, with a dignity that tore at Becky's heart, 'What about the free rent I grant you?'

Even her language is Biblical, thought Becky savagely, and that damn rent.

Swaying a little, the two women faced each other, the older struggling not to give in to temper and sinful thoughts about the younger.

If Aunt Jean had made one move to touch Becky, to offer affection, then Becky might have been different, might have made different decisions. But none came.

Becky leant back against the cheap wallpaper, felt the uneven texture between her splayed fingers and laughed at the sight of the two of them squared up like gladiators.

Aunt Jean finished washing out the pink cardigan and laid it flat on the *Streatham Advertiser*. A series of drops plopped steadily off the end of the sleeves. 'There's a tin of chilli on the shelf,' she said. 'Heat it up.'

Becky peered into the courtyard of the flats. An iron pulse beat in her, pushing life around her body. Out there, framed by the council's plate-glass window, another life gushed and swirled with dust, pollution and effluent. With an almost righteous anger, she tallied up the peeling paint, the grimy net curtains, the broken glass lapping the dustbins.

'I love you, Becky,' Jack had said, when he phoned earlier, and she had looked out of the window facing the road where a huge advertising hoarding was plastered with promises and glossy lies. She had stared at it hungrily.

'Aren't you going to say anything, Becky?' Jack was jumpy.

'Love you too.'

Running alongside the crackle of static from the nylon carpet, the persistent drip of the tap, the smell of damp that made her nose prick, the billboard dreams were seductive and siren-like.

Becky made a second phone call.

We are used to plagues, concluded Tess pacing the sitting room of the flat, the Black Death, Spanish influenza, Aids, and we understand them. As humans we like to pay for our sins and, the link between oestrogen and guilt being apparently solid, women are good at exploiting the highways and byways of guilt's octopoid properties.

Actually, money is less easy to quantify and love is hardest of all. A connection between love and work is, indeed, being spun together in our minds, a linkage that has not been traditionally feminine. But this is what happens in human history. The myths change.

Becky and I are thoroughly modern women, for we considered *eros* to be only a part of our lives – or that is what we *want* to believe. Our work is important, our men are important but neither is of greater importance than the other.

'I am so happy, so happy,' wrote Tess in her diary. 'And yet so unhappy.'

Chapter Four

Before she met Louis for coffee Becky had already made a reconnaissance of Mawby Brothers. Close to the Lloyd's building, its offices were built with a similar flamboyance and arrogance. Yet it worked. Light refracted through plate glass, illuminating a temple filled with exotic plants and a tree whose importation costs had had to be fudged by the architect.

Water ran from a feature in the centre of the atrium, voices issued from offices built off the central area and a large board, around which clustered a permanent group, flashed up figures in neon red and yellow. Clad in post-modernist steel and glass, Delphi had apparently abandoned the scented hills and enamelled skies of Greece, whirled through the centuries and alighted near Lime Street. Becky liked what she saw. It made her feel alive, important, and told her that she was now in the sight of the right horizon.

Louis had suggested that they meet before the interview at Mawby's which, at her request, he had set up for her. It was, she supposed, a favoured method of seduction.

They met in an up-market coffee bar of the kind invading the City – cappuccinos and fresh, good sandwiches. Becky refused the latter and only sipped the former. Louis smiled and made no effort to conceal that he was observing her closely. However coolly she had determined to handle this encounter, his effect on Becky was precisely as he would have wished.

'I suspect you don't eat much.'

His acuteness touched her, for it confirmed that he had considered *her* not just her body. 'I don't.'

'Tell me what you know.'

'The crucial requirement of insurance, any insurance, is the need to spread the risk. The market is divided into two. The primary insurer, who does the deal with the broker placing the insurance, and the reinsurers, who reduce the risk of the primary insurer. The brokers place the business.'

She was pleased at her prowess and, infected by her pleasure, Louis said, 'Obviously you were a child who mastered the tongue-twister. Peter Piper picked, et cetera.'

Becky laughed. 'How did you guess?'

He picked up his cup and she smelt an expensive aftershave, and heard the soft little sound of his costly shirt moving beneath the material of his Savile Row suit. In his turn, Louis allowed Becky to scrutinize him. As yet, she was too young to have learnt to conceal her thoughts and he was more than a little stirred by her ambition and energy. A pilgrim, he thought. At the beginning . . .

He reached across the table and placed a finger under her chin – a gesture that he had no right to make. Very gently, she removed it. 'You mustn't do that.'

'Why not?'

'Because I haven't given you permission.'

'True . . .'

Louis felt a little ashamed when he saw her visibly relax.

'Sorry,' she said, worried suddenly that she had blown her opportunity.

'It's all right.'

Lloyd's dealt in money's mythical properties, or so Louis had once written in his younger days in a university newsletter, an article which he now disowned. In it he had waxed lyrical and drawn on the classics, as post-graduates often do before they grow up or transfer their romanticism elsewhere.

He wrote of money's capacity for parthenogenesis, its chimera promises, its zephyr breezes, its slaughterous revenge. His business as the underwriter, he wrote, was to chase money, unleash it, run its projections through his fingers. In doing so, he was continuing in the tradition of Britain's mercantile and imperial past, spinning a web (how could he have employed such overworked metaphor?) of insurance and reinsurance, which links a staggering 40 per cent of the world's merchant ships, its aeroplanes, mines, cars and its political risks. A great, glittering procession winding through the centuries of trireme (he should have said tea clipper) and dirty salt stack, of giant tanker and spice ship billowing with white sails. Myrrh. Oil. Bananas. Gold. The soft, tingling smell of cinnamon and corian-der, nutmeg and dried curry plant.

'You must always layer your risks,' Louis instructed Becky, over the second cup of coffee, 'vertically and . . . horizontally.'

'Of course.' Eager to learn, she pulled out a piece of paper from her handbag and scribbled something down.

'Don't do that,' said Louis. 'Listen instead. Otherwise you look amateur.'

Carefully, Becky laid down the biro.

Louis continued, 'No one should ever expose themselves to intolerable losses. That is the first rule.'

She was breathing faster than normal, and felt a pull of desire deep in her body (for what, she was not clear) and an exhilarating charge, like electricity.

'Always pass a layer of risk onto others.'

Clearly she was a fast learner, for he could not read her expression any longer and she sat quite still.

'What percentage of risk should I take, Louis?'

He spread out his thin, well-tended hands. 'The received wisdom runs that the insurer should never retain more than ten per cent of a risk.'

'So,' said Becky, her eyes soft and shining, 'how many levels of risk are there?'

'Are we talking business?'

Becky looked at her watch and adjusted the strap of her fake Chanel handbag. 'I'm so sorry, I'd better go. They'll kill me if I'm late.'

As Jack had once been, Louis found himself transfixed by the courage with which she carried herself and wore her evidently cheap clothes – and by her slightness which, being Louis, he translated as defencelessness and fragility. Perhaps he was right. Certainly his heart, a much deeper and more complicated place than either his wife or his colleagues suspected, was softened by pity, but a pity sharpened by lust.

'They'll like you at Mawby's,' he said. 'They've set out to be progressive.'

Her eyebrows climbed upwards. 'Oh, God,' she said. 'Tokenism.'

'Don't knock it.' He went off to pay for the coffee.

He walked with her down the street to Mawby's entrance and stopped. A girl carrying a large flower arrangement edged past them through a revolving door. Becky clutched the strap of her shoulder bag, and the knuckles turned a revealing white. The girl placed the flower arrangement on a pedestal near the door and began cleaning each leaf with a rag.

'Louis. Something tells me that your help is more than philanthropy.'

The awkwardness with which she said it made him pause, a little repelled. 'It's too early to say. You've met my wife. I have two sons, more or less grown-up, the upkeep of an expensive house, two cars, a gardener and a Vietnamese maid called Thuk.'

'And?'

'A lot of money.'

'And?'

'I stay married. I'm a Catholic without a God.'

Becky's knuckles returned to a normal colour. 'How inconvenient. All of the trouble and none of the benefits.' She laughed.

43

'True.'

'I live in a flat, on a council estate in Streatham, which has one toilet, one basin, a priceless collection of glass on the stairs and I'm working on the maid.'

He bent over her. 'You can make money, you know, from the broking. Even more, perhaps, than from underwriting, for the capacity is unlimited providing you can deal with the business. I suspect you're a quick learner.'

It flashed through her mind that he loved her already and she looked down at her feet. 'Yes, I think I am.' Then she raised her eyes to his, and both she and Louis imagined that they understood very well what each wanted from the other. 'You'll have to watch and tell me.'

'I will.'

The revolving door performed another circuit and Becky shivered. Exasperated by her starveling quality, Louis produced from his pocket a paper bag containing a doughnut. 'Here,' he said. 'I bought this for you.'

She cradled the bag between her fingers, as the fat stain colonized the paper. 'Thank you.'

She watched him walk down the street. Lust, it seemed, came tempered with kindness, seduction with rough-and-ready practicality, selfishness with an odd humanity – for that Louis was selfish she did not doubt. Then, so was she.

When he was safely out of sight, she threw away the bag with its sweet, sugary offering.

Once upon a time, Mrs Frant had been young. Now, she was not. She was getting old. Therein lies a paradox and, for some, tragedy: possessing a size forty bust and swollen ankles does not mean that you *are* old. Unlike some of her contemporaries, Mrs Frant could remember, for instance, the wild surges of feeling when, urged on by her mother, she had netted Colonel Frant.

And quite a business that had been. She could also remember, to the exact timbre, the wilder, infinitely savage grief of giving birth to a still-born baby, her first, and in the aftermath the drawn-out agony of piecing herself back together.

Then, as now, she fell back on the bit of herself hidden beneath her twinsetted, permed carapace, its existence private and unsuspected.

In Mrs Frant's secret self, a door was set between this world and the next. Every so often, she would give it a nudge open with her foot, look through at the unimaginable beyond and shut it again. It was her insurance and provided a strange and neccessary kind of freedom.

The clock in the drawing room of the High House was ticking away and the curtains – chrysanthemums on an ox-blood background – were drawn right back to let in the evening sun, now shining directly onto Great-aunt Alice's prints, which had been hung a little too high.

In the armchair opposite, Jack was studying lists. Settled in hers, Mrs Frant was stitching hellebores on a tapestry. Rubies, pinks, peaches and primrose yellows. The dark and exquisite Lenten rose. A white Christmas rose – 'Christ's Herb'.

Hellebores also have a secret life, a murky, hidden, poisonous existence. That was one of the reasons why she liked them.

'Jack.' He looked up, fair hair caught in the light. 'Don't get too involved with Rebecca.'

There, it had been said. Mrs Frant had gone into battle with resolution, if not exactly cunning. Why not? A taste for petit-point and tweed skirts does not mean your cause is unworthy or your fighting strategy limited. In went her needle, and out.

Jack went through the motions of tidily folding the lists, but she knew he had become wary. 'We're going to Africa together,' he said. 'You know that. We've discussed it often enough.'

'I don't want you to go, but if you have to, Jack, go alone.'

He made a movement to get up from the chair and, once

again, she was struck by the ascetic quality of her son's features. He could be a saint, she thought, half thrilled, half chilled at the idea.

'Don't interfere, Mum.'

Mrs Frant sewed two more stitches and the black hellebore was almost finished. 'Please. Don't make the mistake.'

'I want to marry her.'

During her life, Mrs Frant had been hurt several times in a variety of ways. The terrible episode when Colonel Frant had fallen in love with the blonde divorcée ... and, of course, the baby. The tapestry fell onto her lap. She clasped her hands together and sat up very straight, for she had learned that good posture, plus her cherished inner reserves, helped her to cope. 'You will regret it, Jack. She's not of your type. No,' she saw his raised eyebrows, 'I don't mean socially. What I'm trying to say is that she's not made the same way as you, Jack. She's different.'

'You don't regret the things you do do, only those you don't.'

'Hold me, hold me, Becky darling,' he had whispered, utterly vanquished by the brilliant and captivating shooting star that he had captured.

'I will. I am, Jack.'

Carelessly, we underestimate the power of maternal love, which rests on its ability to exact self-sacrifice: to suffer, to feel deep in the bones, to tear flesh. How often does it work secretly, through the judiciary, through business empires and through politics? (There is a famous photograph of President Kennedy at a state banquet leaning towards his mother, the two figures bound together for ever.) How many decisions taken in the board room, on the shop floor, in the bank have at their root the spectral figure of an older woman?

Mrs Frant picked up her tapestry and set the last stitch for the evening. Ripe and silky, the hellebore under her hands swelled and bloomed with life. 'She will hurt you badly, Jack. You must listen to me.'

He got up, came over to his mother and slipped an arm around her shoulder. Mrs Frant was suddenly dizzy from happiness. 'Don't worry, Mum. Everything will be fine.'

The day after the interview at Mawby's, Louis sent a bunch of red roses to Paradise Flats. Aunt Jean took the delivery and dumped it in the basin. There they sat, slightly artificial and incongruous, until Becky retrieved them and placed them in the window so that Mary Biggs opposite would be set to speculating.

Louis underwrote mainly political risk. Too wide an area to be specific, he had informed Becky. Too secret to provide any details. It was an area to which many rules were attached. Becky liked the idea of secrets, for secrets suggested power and the notion that their keeper was close to the centre.

The next day she rang Louis at his box at Lloyd's. 'Thank you so much.' Then she added, 'That was a cliché, you know.' She remembered touching one of the blooms with the tip of her finger, and how soft and insubstantial it had felt.

With his free hand, Louis rearranged some documents on his desk while keeping an eye on his junior, who had a habit of eavesdropping on his conversations. 'Possibly. But does that make them unpleasant to receive?'

'Not at all. Isn't it the sort of thing that an old Etonian with a soul to match would do?'

'Being?'

'Very clever, informed and prey to emotional surges at the sight of old buildings.'

'Enjoy,' said Louis, smiling, 'and let me know the Mawby's outcome.' He put the phone down and his junior turned away, with the quick movement of the listening animal.

Becky sat at her desk and pictured Louis at the box while a queue of brokers formed to do business with him. The image pleased her, and she wondered how corrupt he was. A little? More than a little?

Becky did well to ask. Observation had taught her that money has a habit of rubbing away at goodness, rather as practitioners of politics and teaching find that their good intentions are eroded. Not that she objected.

Money. Those without it counted the pounds on their fingers. The careful middle classes totted totals on their pocket calculators of those joyously pregnant deposit accounts and portfolios, offspring of a swaggering market, bullish profits and confidence.

At heart, though, he would be malleable and soft . . .

Becky was partly correct, mostly not. Louis, like his colleagues, dealt in results. The percentages netted in swiftly, stacking one upon the other, a mirror image of the layers of insurance, a *mille-feuille* of profit.

And what would she do?

She began to type with bad grace but, as with anything she did, efficiently.

The rubbish by the bins at Paradise Flats now included a decaying fridge and, with the arrival of the autumn rains, the brushstrokes of moss up the grimy brickwork had taken on new, vivid colouring. It was a geography of deprivation and, as she picked her way down the corridor, Becky vowed it would not be hers.

She let herself into the flat and waited.

The minute Jack walked in, Becky told him that she had taken a job as a trainee broker at Mawby's, starting in two weeks' time.

He sat down hard in the tacky armchair and, visibly, energy drained out of him.

Becky looked at the roses on the table. 'I'm sorry, Jack.'

At last he asked, 'Is it someone else?'

'I've got a job, Jack. A good one.'

'Can't it wait?'

She went over to the chair, picked up one of his hands and

held it to her cheek. '*I* can't wait, Jack, and I should have known.'

He turned his head away from her. Already he was retreating and, suddenly, she regretted what she was doing. Jack was young, directed, innocent and uncorrupt.

'So you never cared.' He made it sound like a statement. 'Why on earth did you bother?'

Trust, his mother had pointed out to him, and Rebecca are foreigners.

'You have your work. I have mine. That's all.'

'Work! Don't make me laugh.'

She put her hand on her hip. 'Yes, work, and don't be patronizing.'

'Oh, God,' he said, and ran his hands dramatically through his hair.

He raked the room, searching for answers among the few possessions: a couple of mugs on the shelf, a print of a pink Redouté rose on the wall, an old-fashioned clothes-horse. Bare of photographs, with no icing of china and knick-knacks, no clues as to how the two lives were conducted between the walls, it was as different as it was possible to be from the High House.

He gripped her hand. 'Becky. Please think again. You won't get another chance to do this. To do something proper and worthwhile. Don't give it up.'

She stared down at him. Without knowing it, he had assumed the pose that she had seen in a photograph at the High House, one taken with his grandparents. She had examined it carefully, identifying the links between the generations: the shape of a chin, the set of a head. Available and obvious, the links were there to read and she had been struck by the poverty of hers. But, if she had no patterns in which to fit her life, she was free.

'You're wrong, Jack. I'm taking up. Not giving up.' She flushed suddenly, a bright, unlovely red. 'It was all a pipedream. Africa.'

'I thought we would get married.' A cold, shocked Jack

watched her pleat the hem of her T-shirt between her fingers. Her fingers stilled and a storm of agonized desire was unleashed in Jack, his coldness melted by the burning wish to make her understand. He pushed himself to his feet, grabbed Becky tight and buried his head in the white flesh that he so desired, and for which he hungered, much as he hungered to walk over cracked, heated plains. 'Marry me.'

She lifted clenched fists to her chest, as if, he thought bitterly, she was defending herself against him and what he represented. 'No, Jack, I don't think so.'

'*Please.*'

Gently, she pushed at him and moved away, flaunting her delicacy and grace in contrast to his hot, heavy disappointment. Again she touched the roses with a fingertip. Then she swivelled and leant back against the table.

'Come here.'

He did so reluctantly. Becky reached up and slid her hands down his back.

'You . . .'

Helpless, and shackled to the spot, Jack watched as Becky pulled her T-shirt over her head and undid her bra, which she allowed to drop to the floor. The change in temperature turned her skin to gooseflesh.

'Jack . . . ?'

To his angry, grieving eyes, she seemed the epitome of willingness, trembling with abandon.

'You're a liar,' he said. 'You were never going to come with me.'

She undid his shirt. Her curves brushed against his bare flesh and he shivered. 'Listen, foolish Jack,' she pressed close to him, 'it's unwise to get to the bottom of things. You never know what you might find.'

She was so warm, so silky, so very alive.

'See?' she said later. 'There was no need for all that fuss.'

* ·

Afterwards, Jack wept in her arms and she soothed him as she might have done a baby. After a while, he got up and dressed and left the flat without saying goodbye.

While they had been making love that Friday evening, 16 October 1987, the American stock market crashed.

On Monday the nineteenth, Becky was hard at work at Landes typing with half an ear to the huddle of men by the door, who were discussing the situation, when the phone buzzed. It was Tess.

'Is anything happening with you, Bec? It's all hell here. The Dow-Jones and Tokyo have gone bananas and now we're crashing.' Tess was urgent, breathy and excited. 'The computers are throwing everything into chaos. The programme trading can't cope and it's bucking the system and selling everything.'

'Financial melt-down is the word here.'

'Oh, God. I'll speak to you later.'

'Tess, I've left your brother. Will you forgive me?'

'Oh, *Becky*.' Tess hesitated. 'For goodness sake, this isn't the moment. Ring me tonight.'

Becky returned to her work.

It was easy to lose a fear of sex and of being exposed by its intimacies. Perhaps it was as easy to lose a fear of love and its capacity to change a person? Becky could not come to a conclusion for she had not loved, but if you lose a healthy fear of money, treat it with the familiarity of lukewarm spouses, then you can become careless.

Was that what had happened? she wondered.

By the end of the day, fifty billion pounds had been wiped off the value of publicly quoted companies, the Dow-Jones had fallen by 508 points and, in the dealing rooms, the slaughter had turned the computer screens (red for down, blue for up) into a bloody and unforgettable crimson.

Chapter Five

'Follow me,' ordered Charles Hayter, Becky's new boss, unnecessarily.

It was unnecessary because she was already following him through Mawby's showy atrium but Charles, who had an endless fund of good nature but was worried by it, had a habit of issuing commands as an antidote.

'I want you to be my shadow, my tail . . .' he had said, rather dramatically, when Becky had first presented herself in October. 'You must watch and listen.'

She had offered no comment. Today she had watched and listened through the nine-thirty forthcoming-business meeting, watched and listened as Charles briefed the backroom staff and listed his appointments with his secretary. She had also watched and listened during the past eight weeks as she helped to prepare policy documents and slips, dealt with American correspondence and – once – delivered a cover note to an underwriter. Currently she was preparing to watch and listen for three months in the claims department.

'You will need to sit the Lloyd's Test as fast as you can. It's only set once a year and without it you can't work at Lloyd's. And I expect you to be sitting the ACII exam within four years. Without *that* you won't get promoted.' Charles had rattled out the objectives as if he was at target practice.

At least they were clear.

'Where are we going?' she asked, having a pretty good idea.

'Lloyd's, the Room,' he said. 'Where else? Where you are to watch me.'

'Ah,' said Becky. 'Of course.' She suspected that his more than usually rapid speech this morning hid a mind occupied elsewhere. (She was right. Charles was worrying about Martha, his wife.)

The street was full of men: men in a hurry holding sheaves of paper, men grouped confidentially, tall men, short men, fat men and, circling, lean and hungry prowlers. The tarmac was slicked with winter rain and the cold was of the damp, depressing variety.

Oblivious, Charles strode on, a little loud-looking, certainly confident-looking, but not stupid. Already Becky had come to appreciate his sharp, hustling, sniffing-out brain and his good nature, but failed to see the integrity he brought to his work, which, in a world of the sharp and the cutting, made him successful.

Brokers are the marketing arm of the insurance business, he had confided over their first lunch. We bring in the business. Someone like you will do it easily. She had been pleased that he did not once refer to her sex.

But now, as he ushered her through the entrance to the Lloyd's building, Charles peered at Becky, doubting her reception, unsure how to handle her. She sent him a look that suggested admiration, submission and the non-confrontational, and tried to convey that she had donned the white robe of the neophyte. He seemed reassured.

'Hi, Charley boy.'

Someone slapped him on the shoulder and Charles responded by grabbing the greeter's tie and continuing a conversation that had been started elsewhere. Then he beckoned to Becky.

She had been in the Room several times and was acquainted with the hum of light and activity that, after the first impact on the eye and ear, muttered subversively. It was a noisy, gleaming, arched marketplace but it was the trading that interested Becky, not its architectural swagger or spectacle.

Marine. Non-marine. Aviation. Motor. Charles made a stab at being a guide. Becky remained silent, contemplative even, and allowed his rhetoric to rush past her, staccato and urgent.

The active underwriter accepts the risk, at an agreed premium, and reinsures it; the underwriting agent handles the affairs of the syndicate's members, accountancy and related matters.

'Yes, I know,' Becky gently reminded him.

'There are over twenty-five thousand external Names.' And he added, a stranger to irony, 'Seventeen per cent are foreigners. Twenty-two per cent are women.'

'Names,' he pronounced, with the emphasis that she was beginning to recognize as a feature of Charles, 'are warned that they are liable to their last waistcoat button.'

'I thought it was cufflinks.'

'Oh,' said Charles, annoyed. 'Yes. You're right. Cufflinks.'

'How simple,' she said later. They had ascended to the top of the building and were looking down through the well sliced out by the escalators. Below them the underwriters' boxes clustered in ants' cells. A vision, Louis had told Becky, that an Old Master might have borrowed for his version of Usury, even Hell.

Becky could not quite see it. 'How beautifully clear,' she remarked instead. The space, the subdued hum, its dedication to a single activity, its sense of purpose, spoke to her as powerfully, perhaps as God spoke to Aunt Jean.

Charles's expression was that of the baffled male.

They retraced their steps and he led her towards a box. 'You must always start to get your project underwritten by a leading underwriter,' he explained, 'otherwise you won't get the followers.'

'Bit like one's life,' flashed Becky, and then realized that whatever other advantages Charles possessed, a quick wit was not among them. 'Should you always try for a specialist in the area?'

'Yes.'

'As a matter of interest, do you have to have a formal training to be an underwriter?'

He took the trouble to consider the question carefully. 'Yes. But listening is important. Theory is only useful up to a point. Having said that, the number-crunchers are becoming more influential than they used to be. But nothing beats the feel, the hunch, the seat of the pants.'

They stopped in front of a box where a small queue had formed. While they waited, Charles tapped his papers and fiddled with his tie.

'He does nuclear business.' He conveyed the information in a hushed voice. 'And oil and energy.'

Becky looked again at Matt Barker, a man who dealt in the biggest risk of all. Did he really believe that a piece of paper could bottle up the nuclear whirlwind? Pick up the pieces when it had ripped, shrieking and murderous, across a Russian steppe or an American plain? Probably not, for Matt Barker looked shrewd and experienced. Perhaps, Becky thought, having taken into account humanity's frail defences, Matt Barker reckoned that a piece of paper was as good as anything. You made money on it.

Eventually they reached the head of the queue.

'Becky, meet Matt Barker. Matt, this is our newest and brightest trainee.'

Matt got to his feet and they shook hands. His junior, a clone of the older man, did not. He ran an indifferent pair of eyes over Becky and returned to his calculations.

The formalities over, Matt stretched out his right hand. His knuckles cracked audibly. 'What have you got?' he asked.

Charles changed into the appropriate gear and Becky listened – primary policy, rate on line, catastrophe layers – and learned. As they made to leave, Charles turned back with a final thought. 'We think we've got a big sweetie coming up, Matt. FEROC are building a new rig. Two billion or so. All the latest equipment and suchlike. I'll be back.'

'Sure,' said Matt Barker, inscrutable and conspiratorial. Crack, crack went his knuckles.

'A big sweetie,' Charles repeated.

'How much is he likely to take on a new rig?' Becky enquired, when she and Charles were drinking coffee and debriefing themselves in the canteen.

'A ten per cent line. Once that's done the rest will follow.' Charles ran a hand over his chin.

He had a nice, healthy-looking neck, Becky decided. She asked, 'Will all the business on the FEROC rig – should it come Mawby's way – be done in here?'

Earnest and, in his anxiety to teach, a touch patronizing, Charles leant forward. 'Probably not. It's too big. We'll go to Europe.'

'And will Matt Barker reinsure the ten per cent he underwrites?'

'Yup.'

'I'm not sure he was very impressed.' Becky pushed her half-drunk coffee to one side.

That bothered Charles. 'Really. Why?'

Becky shrugged. 'Instinct.'

'He's one of the most successful underwriters in the business.' Charles, a little uneasy, wiped the foam off his upper lip. 'He keeps very cool.'

The coffee finished, Charles suggested that Becky wandered around the building while he did some business. She smiled at his obvious wish to be shot of her and picked her way through the aisles to Matt Barker's box where she waited.

Matt looked up. 'Have we forgotten something?'

Becky towered above him and widened her eyes. 'I'm told you're one of the most successful underwriters in the business and your syndicate one of the most profitable. I wanted to know why.'

Several phones were ringing in the box and the junior was fielding them all. Matt ignored them and considered the girl in front of him. 'Since you ask, you must invest the syndicate's funds well for the bad times. That is the key. That, and finding out exactly the risk you're underwriting. Keep asking questions, down to the tiniest detail.'

It was so obvious and Becky was disappointed. Again Matt stretched out a hand and cracked his knuckles. 'Come to me if you ever want any help,' he said, and his junior glared.

Half-way down the escalator, Becky passed Louis going up. She looked across to the dark, weary gaze and he looked back at her. He knew all about her, he told her silently. He understood the baggage of ambition, insecurity and appetite of which she was made. He understood that an orphan is orphaned many times throughout a life. Not just once.

No more powerful an aphrodisiac was required than that silent, generous comprehension.

Abruptly, she turned away. Louis continued up, she continued down and, around them, the making of money went on.

Back in Appleford that summer, Jack had accused Becky of making him feel like Gulliver in Lilliput, pegged out and helpless on the sands. He had confessed such to her in the wood: a vivid, fragrant, vigorous backdrop. Sun had exploded across her vision and, aghast at his vulnerability, she had allowed Jack to draw her deeper into the undergrowth. He had begged her to tell him that she loved him.

She had done so, cupping her hand around the contour of

his chin, for Becky truly believed that the world functioned on lies. Otherwise, civilization was impossible.

To his mother's grief and his father's despair, Jack continued with plans for Africa, merely discarding the plan to drive across the Sahara and changing the destination to Ethiopia. There, in exchange for Becky, patient Penelope – who wished to work in the Fistula Hospital in Addis Ababa – would join him.

Loyally the Frants gathered at Heathrow to see him off.

In the car Colonel Frant fought his way up the approach road to the terminal and unloaded a very small amount of luggage. Jack had insisted on keeping everything to a minimum. He had gone through his bedroom at the High House, discarding, discarding, until the room was bare and cold. As if, his mother thought with a catch in her throat, it had never been inhabited. It frightened her, this cleansing of a past.

Even so, Mrs Frant could claim victory over Becky but it tasted bitter.

Face rigid with the effort of not displaying her feelings, she dug her hands into the pockets of her camel coat, felt the warmth of her body through the lining and wondered where she had gone wrong. To lose a baby was grief enough, to lose a son, for she did not doubt that she had lost Jack . . . well, could she survive?

What you do is get your head down and march. One day at a time. One day at a time.

Oh, Becky, thought Jack.

The departure lounge throbbed and bulged with people and their possessions. Eyes underlined with fatigue and midriffs slackened, businessmen drank coffee and read papers. Whole families, clearly relocating elsewhere, stood guard over piles of hand luggage.

Oh, Becky.

Yet even as the pain drove its now accustomed dart through his body, the image of Becky was growing a little faint, and Jack was moving on to contemplate heat, physical discomfort and the satisfactions of dispensing charity.

He swallowed. Was it worse to remember or to forget?

Mrs Frant touched his arm, more alive and sympathetic to his unhappiness than he had supposed. Tess hugged her brother, embarrassed by her connection with Becky. 'She's my friend,' she had told him. 'I can't give her up.'

Now she said, 'Take care. Don't get kidnapped.'

'Jealous, Tess?'

'No way.'

'Have you got enough money?' asked his father for the third time, at a loss for what else to say. It was noticeable that Colonel Frant had lost weight and his colour was not as healthy-looking as usual.

They were being very good, his parents, despite their feelings. (Goaded, Mrs Frant had cried out, 'Why Africa? Why not somewhere we understand?') A rush of affection for them suffused him and he put his arms around his mother.

'Jack!'

Jack released his mother, so abruptly that she staggered slightly. He swivelled, heart pounding like a battery gun.

'Jack?'

Mrs Frant stiffened and Tess went pale as Becky carved a passage towards them, clutching a carrier bag. Tess hoped, she did so hope, that there was not going to be a scene.

'The tube was terrible, and there was miles to walk. But I couldn't let you go without these.'

'What on earth are you doing here?' Jack's yearning returned in a floodtide. But he was angry too. Becky and he had had their farewell scene. Why go through it again?

Becky ignored the question and the other three Frants who were apparently struck dumb. 'Sun-tan cream. Thrillers for the long, dark nights. An outsize box of plasters. Glucose tablets. I thought you'd need them. At least, to begin with.'

'Oh, Becky,' said Tess, wishing that Becky had had the sense not to come, 'how sweet of you.'

I hate her. Mrs Frant's face was set in granite. (If motherhood is influential, it is not always soft.)

Massaging her fingers, which were numb from the handles of the heavy bag, Becky turned, at last, to greet the Frants. Her hair drawn back into a fashionable French plait, skin porcelain clear and glowing, Becky was clearly embarking on a transformation. At that moment, Jack wanted her more than anything else on earth.

But he could not have her. Or, at least, not in the way he wanted and he was still too young to make do with spoilt dreams.

'Good luck,' she said, impervious to the Frant parents' frigid aspect. 'See you in a year.'

Dropping the bag, Jack captured Becky's hands. An aircraft screamed in the sky outside. There was an eddy of passengers towards the departure lounge. The Tannoy issued instructions. The world was in a hurry and on the move and it was time for Jack to leave.

She reached up to kiss him on the cheek. 'Good luck, and I'm sorry.'

'But you came to say goodbye.'

'Of course.' Her smile both mocked him and told him not to take her too seriously.

Mrs Frant positioned herself by her son. Go away, she was implying. Leave us in peace to say goodbye.

Between them, they were consigning Jack to the African sun and to its tawny landscape, which would seize and mould him. There Jack would encounter the strangeness, terror and violence that ringed the edges of existence, cancelling the strangeness, terror and violence of the feelings he had experienced at home.

Becky turned to Tess. 'Tessy,' she said, placing a hand on Tess's arm, 'can you lend me a fiver to get back with? I'll reimburse you later.'

Becky's office at Mawby's barely justified the name: it was a corner, cut off from a general space crammed with VDUs, print-outs, research literature and bodies. Somehow, she had created a space that was recognizably hers and bore her tidy stamp.

The possibility of the FEROC deal was whipping up general excitement, and Becky had spent some time thinking over the details of such a project. At the nine-thirty meeting on the Monday after Jack's departure, she took a deep breath and, when the topic was reached on the agenda, asked the exact composition of the personnel on a rig.

Tom Pritchard, the older partner, stared across the table at her as if she had raised a question concerning unspeakable practices. Becky did not flinch.

'The usual,' Tom said. 'As it happens, FEROC has not supplied that level of detail yet but you're welcome to look back at previous records.'

'Thank you,' said Becky and, for the rest of the meeting, confined herself to taking notes.

She spent the next week amassing data on oil rigs: personnel (what type?), turnover of said, ratio of accidents to claims, risk to accident.

Charles was intrigued and found himself increasingly drawn to this part of the office. He wanted to know why she wanted to know. He eyed up the coils of computer print-out on Becky's desk. 'Are you going through everything?'

'Why not? It's the business.'

Becky leant back in her chair, tipping it gently, a habit she had quickly adopted. The contrast between the relaxed, almost dreamy suggestion of sensuality and her obvious cleverness made Charles's blood quicken a fraction. He liked what he saw: the feminine casing folded over a quick mind; the reddened lips and the sharp, foxy quality of the bones in her wrists.

Hurrying along the career and marriage paths, Charles had forgotten about the chase. About scented flesh. The fullness of satiation. Now, he found himself remembering.

'Do you really want to know?' She looked up at him and he felt extraordinarily alive.

'Of course.'

'I was at the airport the other day,' said Becky.

'So?'

'More people work in an airline than the crews. Cleaners. Waitresses. Messengers. I wondered if they were all insured against the 747 crashing down. And would it be the same on the oil rig? What about the cleaners?'

'So what do you propose to do about it?'

Becky's chair returned to its normal position and she gathered up her print-out. 'I'll tell you when I've found out.'

'Look.' Charles leant over the desk a little further than was necessary. He held up his hand, revealing shirtsleeves that had been hitched up with a pair of elastic bands. 'I think your energy and interest are wonderful.' It was true. He found the intensity of her focus almost erotic. 'I mean it. But don't imagine you'll get a new take on the business overnight. There are people here who've worked at it for decades, and there's not much they don't know.'

Becky handed back to Charles the end of his yellow tie, which was hanging over her cup of coffee. 'Sure.'

To his amazement, Charles found himself walking round the desk where he pulled Becky to her feet and . . . let her go.

'Don't be too cocky,' he said, and left the room.

If Jack was all golden, young and idealistic and she had sent him packing, an indulgence, and Louis was the opposite, then Charles . . . ?

What was Charles?
Charles was a conduit for useful information.

Lavish, wine-drenched and civilized, the 1987 Christmas meeting of the Bollys at the Savoy Grill was no different from previous Christmas meetings. But the mood had changed.

Louis and Matt found time to hold a lengthy and serious conversation about the 1983 underwriting year for which, unusually, two sets of results had been published. The first, announcing an underwriting profit of £28 million, had not taken into account the disastrous results of a syndicate accused not only of carelessness but of fraud. The second figure added these to the bottom line and announced an underwriting loss of £115 million.

They talked about damage limitation, press involvement, their own profits and – again – the long-tail problems coming in from North America.

'American lawyers,' reiterated Matt thoughtfully, 'are not on our side.'

Louis sensed they were talking about the finale to the old days. The mood was changing, forces governing circumstances were changing. An optimism, or was it complacency?, had become pessimism. He did not care to question what was happening to himself, or to the others. For Colonel Frant he did not spare a second thought. (But for Becky and their as yet unconsummated affair, he spared many.)

'We must take care,' he said to Matt. 'Guard our castles. And someone clever should be put on the damage-limitation programme.'

'To the defence of our castles,' said Matt, and passed the port to Louis.

Chapter Six

Tess spent the weekend before Christmas with her parents at the High House.

People came and went, bringing presents of potted plants and mince pies or presented themselves for a regulation sherry. Chit-chatting and *Merry* Christmasing. Several times the postman toiled up the gravel drive, raising beneath his feet a sodden spume of pebbles. The house smelt of a combination of citrus fruits and mud. Its windows, recently cleaned by Jimmy Plover, reflected a merger between the neon street lamps and the Christmas lights.

One Christmas. Two Christmas. Three Christmas. Four . . .

The old rhyme that she and Jack used to chant echoed in her mind, a childhood reprise from the time when it mattered very much how well the day went. Children do not like change or, at least, they like to be warned of it. Quite quickly, Tess had learnt that adults can turn nasty at Christmas, or change out of all recognition. But she felt the expectation laid on Christmas was unfair. How could it live up to its promise? Much as chocolate, cinnamon and brandy are so seductive to the nose on first encounter, so elusive or cloying a second or two later.

It would have been lovely if George could have come, at least for some of the time. Plucking up courage, she had invited him to spend Boxing Day at the High House but he had told her he was busy. His refusal had caused her to waste a whole day as she probed minutely for its significance.

She had wanted very much to see him in her home, being normal, talking to her parents. Thinking about it, which she did incessantly, there were points of likeness between her father and George, the same set of shoulder, a corresponding manner of speech.

'I wish Jack was here,' said her mother, when Tess discovered her in the kitchen staring into a saucepan of boiled chestnuts.

Tess slipped an arm around her shoulders. 'It's only one Christmas. He'll be back.'

'Will he?' Mrs Frant seemed unconvinced. 'I think your friend broke his heart and he'll stay out there.'

Mrs Frant's melodrama irritated Tess, partly because she, too, was angry with Becky but had lost courage when she should have had it out with her, partly because she suspected that her mother was right. That was the trouble with Becky: it was impossible to pin her down.

'Yes, of course Jack was upset. But we all have love affairs that come to nothing and it's a very good thing,' she lied, thinking, *I'll die if it doesn't work out with George.* 'Just give him time to get over it.'

Early on Sunday evening she returned to London with an idea of doing some tidying up, and surveyed the prospect. Piles of newspapers had taken up permanent squatters' rights on the furniture and there was a lot of unhoovered carpet. With a sigh, she picked up the phone.

Becky was fizzing with frustration. 'I don't think I can bear it any longer. Aunt Jean is completely doolally and, if I hear one more prayer or hymn, I'll kill her. The whole bloody world's gone fundamental.' She added darkly, 'Fundamentalism will be the scourge of the age.'

'Becky,' said Tess, 'I've been meaning to ask you to come and live here. Why don't you?'

There was a pause at the other end of the line and Tess, impetuous, generous Tess, plunged onwards. 'Don't worry about rent, Bec, if that's a problem. This is Dad's flat, a little investment he made after a good year. You don't have to pay anything. Just the bills.'

The reply came within a second. 'I'll move in tomorrow.'

And she did.

'But I don't like Becky,' said George, who had come round for supper during the week. He was folded into the small sofa, which was waiting for a cover, his highly polished Chelsea boots propped on the arm. 'Does she have to come here? It'll be a bottleneck.'

'Here' meant two bedrooms, one cramped sitting room and a cupboard that masqueraded as a kitchen. George had a point. Becky was out, entertaining clients, but although she had brought little with her, the flat had shrunk.

'Yes, she does have to be here.'

Tess had been swift to pick up George's real objection, which was about sex. She lit a cigarette and focused on the contrast between the white paper and the dark, angry red of the burn.

'George . . .' she attempted. Everyone she could think of enjoyed frank and fearless discussions about it – pundits, agony aunts, friends. Adverts reeked of it, television was stuffed with it. Et cetera. Sex and everyone else were on excellent terms with each other. But, when it came to airing the topic, it and she were nodding acquaintances, polite, awkward and wishing to get to know each other better.

'George . . . ?'

'Oh, come here,' he ordered, and proceeded to demonstrate his predilection for the noisy, cavemanish variety and to feast on Tess's honey-coloured, satiny body. Drowning in love and desire, Tess's doubts about George and the progress of their affair loosened their grip and sank.

Afterwards, she lay still, tender and quivering, and reflected on the confusion existing between her mind and her body. Once, she had pictured a future in which she would exercise her mind, so painfully toned at university, flexing and contracting its muscles. She had wished to build into it capacious rooms for storage. To become a mental athlete. Instead, she was reduced to intense contemplation of – obsession with, even – the flesh. Her own flesh: yielding, weeping, longing and desirous. And other people's flesh: so desirable, so cruel, so on display. She dwelt on the contrasts, and the discoveries, to be made: the exact shades and tints of George's arm, the blue vein searching through his groin, the silk down on his chest.

'Kiss me again,' she demanded of George, and he obeyed with a mouth from which passion was already retreating. Tess tasted him, savoured him and demanded more. She had what she wanted and yet ... And yet it was not enough. She craved further, more tangible and absolute proof that she possessed and was possessed.

It was impossible to have too much love.

When it was quite over, George sighed and said, 'We'll have to watch it from now on, if Becky's around.'

He got up and went in search of a drink. 'Don't you have anything more serious than sherry?' he asked, naked but impervious to the chill.

'Only wine.' Tess was lying on the floor where they had ended up. Too lazy to move, she pulled her clothes over her and shivered. 'Why don't you like Becky?'

'She's on the make.'

'What's wrong with that? So am I.'

'She's too obvious. Women shouldn't be so obvious. Not with money anyway.'

She knew enough about George by now to know that he did not necessarily admire money-making. No, he talked appreciatively of Darwin's voyages, Watson and Crick's discovery of DNA, the making of the Challenger spacecraft and of the astronomers who patrolled the night skies. He also admired, believe it or not, the peace-makers.

'Women,' George was warming to the theme, 'should be careful.'

She did not quite believe him, knowing that he liked to stir things.

He shot her a look. 'I mean it,' he said.

While he dressed, Tess digested the implications. In his jeans and boots, George looked the part of an off-duty Army officer. Was he what he showed the world? She supposed he was. Not for the first time, she questioned how it was possible to be so in love with someone with whom she so profoundly disagreed.

Fortunately, these pinpricks, so significant when two people have almost reached the end of a road, so insignificant in an infant love affair, did not spoil the evening. When Becky returned in the small hours, she discovered a dreamy Tess on the sofa, smoking. She had twisted up her heavy hair, anchored it with a pencil, and was studying the varnish on her toenails, which needed attention.

'Disgusting,' pronounced the immaculate Becky.

'You are addressing the spirit of enquiry.' Tess stubbed out her cigarette. 'Pure science. I wanted to see how long it took to grow the varnish out.'

Becky had a glass of water in her hand, and pointed at the ashtray. 'You should choose your addictions more carefully.'

'Yours, I take it,' said Tess, 'will leave you wiser and richer.'

Becky drank the water in one go. 'Smoking ruins your skin.'

'Don't you know we're a dependent culture?' said Tess flippantly. 'I'm a child of it.'

'Perhaps you are,' said Becky, bored. In the pursuit of the perfect skin, Becky drank a second glass of water and went to bed after using up all the hot water.

'My darling,' Mrs Frant came stamping in from a Christmas Day march around the garden and caught Tess idling over breakfast, 'don't leave it too long to find someone nice to marry. I'm worried about your future.'

Was George nice? And had Tess left it too long?

Until George, the future had not concerned Tess overmuch, for she felt it to be manageable. The politics of feminine inactivity – all that sitting about on sofas by Jane Austen heroines while they waited and prayed for their lives to be completed, and suffered and loved in silence – had changed. The blackboard had been scrubbed clean. The chains had been snapped. Until George. Whereupon Tess had been made uneasily aware that the chains had not disappeared. They had merely been buried out of sight.

Her conclusions had shocked her. Along with the eighties children, Tess was too accustomed to assuming that the world could be put right. After all, there were antibiotics and welfare benefits, and it was inconceivable that either would run out. If Tess had been less of her time, for instance, she might have noticed that, during the unusually peaceful, fragrant Christmas of 1987, her father had been very quiet.

'Talking of antibiotics . . .' Dressed in a dull navy blue suit and navy blue tights designed to depress the remotest suggestion of sex, Tess buttonholed Freddie when she got back to work.

'Were we?' Freddie had a hangover and post-Christmas seemed more post than usual.

'Yes, we were. Their future needs looking into, don't you think?'

'I don't think anything,' said Freddie. He looked up at the air-conditioning duct, which blew straight onto his desk. 'Except that I'm in line for Legionnaire's disease.'

'The body count's high, I'm told.'

Kit wandered over and began to chat, thumbs tucked into his braces which he snapped from time to time. 'Are we settled?' he asked, kindly, which was touching in one who was only five years or so older.

'More or less.'

'Would you two like to join the rest of us for a lunchtime

drink?' The invitation was the first such issued to the two graduate trainees and marked an advance. Freddie's eyes were twin pools of *faux* eagerness and innocence. 'Of course,' he said, for both of them. 'We thought you'd never ask.'

Freddie's braces were patterned in black and white, Kit's were bright red and Bill's were navy. What dressers-up men were. Tess smoothed the dull skirt over her navy blue knees and prepared to slog away at the print-out.

Lunch was raucous, and she made the mistake of drinking two glasses of wine.

'Right,' said Kit, on their return. 'Time to make contact with one or two clients. On your tods. No more sitting in on meetings and looking pretty. You've got to do some work.'

As luck would have it, the first client Tess rang to introduce herself was a professional Northerner.

'Why should I trust you, Miss Frant?'

His objection was reasonable and logical, and Tess told him so. This elicited a laugh, and Tess was encouraged. Unwise. From there on the conversation took a downhill plunge.

'Look, Miss Frint or Frant or whatever your name is. I don't want some fanny in a tight skirt muddling about with my money.'

'I agree about the muddling, Mr Fitch.'

'Get your boss to ring me, not some wet-behind-the-ears bit of fluff.'

'You beast,' said Tess, after she had put down the phone and regarded her blank client sheet on which she had neither defended nor proved herself, and set about considering how to circumnavigate eleven centuries of North–South antagonism and an eternity of male chauvinism.

It took a bit of doing, but she won her point and a couple of days later Tess found herself on the Intercity 125 travelling north to Leeds. She had rung Fitch and asked him to clear space in his diary. She took as consent the silence at the other end of the line.

Balding, stomach nudging open the fastenings of his shirt, a man opposite Tess talked non-stop into his mobile phone, which rang repeatedly.

'Darling,' he said finally, sneaking a look at the passengers close enough to be impressed, 'it won't be long.'

The jottings on Tess's notepad grew increasingly wild. At the last 'darling', she struggled to her feet and leant over the table.

'I wonder if "darling" would mind shutting up.'

Surprised at and impressed with herself, she moved down the carriage towards the blessed peace of rattling crisp bags and the automatic door.

In his cluttered, down-at-heel offices with steel window frames and a dying potted plant, Ted Fitch looked at Tess. 'I knew you'd have a tight skirt.'

Tess looked briefly out of the window, at a narrow, claustrophobic valley bisected by streams that had cut through the fern-patterned rock. Here, for five generations, Ted Fitch's family had struggled to make a living. She could almost swear, but not quite, that their dark presences were there too, and the air was charged with the memory of their sweat and tears. Suddenly she understood. She was not up against regionalism or sexism, or any of the isms that were flung around, merely a man who wished to make the most of his hard-earned money.

'If you're out of your depth, swim, Tess. You know how.'

As she searched for the right opening, she could recollect the exact nuance in her father's voice. She picked up her briefcase, extracted the projections she had made and handed them over. 'Shall we begin?'

'I don't want any risk, mind.'

'No, Mr Fitch, that's why I've built sterling debentures into the portfolio, which are index-linked, and suggested a good spread between the sectors with a bias towards blue-chip FTSE 100 stocks. But, Mr Fitch, I must warn you, there's always some risk.'

Five minutes later, Ted Fitch had thawed sufficiently to switch his attention from Tess and her skirt to the outrageous cost of administering a portfolio and, from there, it was only a step to castigating bankers and their outrageous salaries. That subject having been beaten to death, Mr Fitch was ready to listen.

'You tamed the old boy.' Bill was approving on Tess's next showing in the office. 'He's like a little lamb and quite a chunk is coming our way.'

'Good,' said Tess.

'You were *very* lucky,' said Bill.

'So it seems,' said Tess drily.

Tess had learnt that institutions borrowing large amounts of money must not over-expose their flanks to interest-rate movements. They had to strike a balance – the golden mean, on which the ancient Greeks had been so keen.

Balance . . . agreed Tess, mulling over her love affair. Yes, balance.

Money was complicated and capricious, a shining stream running through our minds. From the goat or bushel of wheat used for barter to the rudimentary coin was one step in its history. From the coin (first seen in 800 BC) to the modern-day gradations and categories of M1, M2 and M3 was quite another.

Falling in love was equally complicated and required a similar balancing act – between the upward-sloping yield curve and the plunge into chaos and debt. And the emotional dividend? What would that be?

'Don't expect too much, Tess.'

In the flat in Pimlico, Becky and Tess were eating an evening meal of pizza.

'Why not?'

'I don't know,' said Becky, and Tess had an uneasy feeling

that she knew more than she was prepared to say. 'I don't want to see you hurt.'

'Don't be silly,' said Tess. 'Everyone gets hurt.'

'Yes, but you don't have to be. Manage the risk.'

Tess thought for a second or two, but the subject was too fraught so she steered onto another path. 'Risk management,' she licked tomato off her fingers, 'is really housekeeping. Women are good at housekeeping. They like to keep tins in the larder.'

Becky had also moved on. 'Do you know what Louis Cadogan's nickname is?' She sounded unusually dreamy. 'El Medici.'

Jack would have recognized Becky's delicate shudder of anticipation. A movement of lips ready to sample the ripe blackcurrant of the vintage wine.

'And Jilly?' asked Tess, after a moment. 'How does she fit in?'

Becky sat back, and crossed her endless legs. 'Apparently, Jilly's stars have warned her there'll be changes but no shortage of money.'

'Did Louis tell you all this? Bec, have you . . . ?'

'Not yet. But I will. Probably.'

'*You* be careful, Bec.' Tess leant over and helped herself to the rest of Becky's pizza. 'He's married.'

'They all are, Tess.'

'Jack wasn't.'

'No, no, he wasn't.'

After supper Tess, on impulse, took a taxi to George's flat in Battersea, which he was sharing with Iain MacKenzie who lived there during the week and returned to Flora in the country at weekends. She had cleaned her teeth, hoping that the mint would cancel the tobacco but knowing the tobacco would beat the mint.

She decided to give up smoking.

George had presented her with a key and she let herself in.

Nothing. Silence. Yet she knew someone was there. Knocking gently on George's bedroom door, she pushed it open.

'It's only me,' she said.

How many times had the same phrase been uttered by the dupe in the film: the betrayed wife, the vicar stumbling over discarded knickers? By the foolish, the cuckolded, the trusting?

'It's only me.' Each word a stone: bruising and hurtful. And a naked George rolled lazily away from the girl last seen clad in Lycra at the Chelsea party.

A curious buzzing invaded Tess's head.

'Oh, Lord,' said the girl, 'she's going to faint.'

Rather than seeing him, Tess sensed George's naked figure come towards her, felt his legs and the warm jumble of his genitals press against her arm as he helped her upright. The pain hit her a physical blow, and she gave a little gasping sob.

Wrapping herself in the sheet, Miss Lycra said in a light, indifferent tone, 'Have some water.'

Tess observed the pattern in the rug on the floor assemble and reassemble, much as patterns form and dissolve under water, and concluded that life without the burden of innocence was much, much easier. Nothing need be expected in the way of good behaviour.

Now that that was settled she must flee from George and the slippery, slender body wrapped so carelessly in the sheet.

It came as a relief, really, truly, that it was no longer necessary to pretend that dark areas did not exist. They did. They did.

Never quite sure how she arrived back in Pimlico, Tess bore for a week red marks on her leg where her shaking hands had caused the tea, made by Becky, to slop. During that time, when she travelled from grief, to anger, through the arc of revenge and back to misery, the world had changed in an unexpected and peculiar manner. Her room looked different, she looked different and there were cracks in the ceiling.

She told herself that, way up in the stratosphere, astral winds were howling and screaming. Astral dust was being blown into feathers and the fierce light of many suns was cutting through infinity. Down below on earth, trapped by a ring of pollution, the Odden Feature in the Greenland Sea was behaving strangely. According to the papers, it looked as though, for the first time, it would fail to form its tongue of ice, which powered the currents around the world's seas. The delicate ecological balance of the world was being threatened. That was more important than her darkened life.

Oh, where was God? If He was what He was, surely he would help her.

In the silence and indifference that surrounded Tess, it was clear that He was not there.

Balance, Tess.

'Grow up.' After witnessing a second week of Tess's weeping, sleeplessness and furious smoking, Becky was moved to speak her mind. 'It's stupid to get so upset. It means so little.'

'Does it?' Tess stared at the television.

Becky threw a packet of aspirin at her. 'Take these and stop crying.'

Canned laughter filtered into the room. A couple on the screen held hands and Tess was gripped by a fear of being left alone. 'Don't go out, Becky,' she pleaded. 'Stay here.'

But Becky was mascaraed and ready for an evening of entertaining clients.

'Sorry, Tess,' she said, in her cruel, charming way, and stroked Tess's disordered hair. 'In your present state, I wouldn't be any use anyway. And the clients are big ones.'

'Bugger the clients.'

'Well, I don't think I'll do that exactly ...' Becky fetched a glass of water. 'Take the aspirins.' She looked down at Tess. 'Have you talked to George at all?'

'No.'

'Well, you'll never get him back that way, will you?'

Longing for animal comfort and warmth, Tess was left to

stare at the space in the wall where a fireplace should have been.

OK, Jack, what would you do?

From however many thousand miles away, he told her.

Not surprisingly, Jack's telepathic message was an exact reflection of Tess's own wishes and the following evening it resulted in Iain MacKenzie letting her into the flat. He was kind and concerned, and retreated tactfully to his bedroom.

Tess faced George and demanded to know where she stood in the line-up of females. 'Don't I mean anything to you?' she raged.

'Of course you do. And if you hadn't come butting in, then you wouldn't have known.'

'Why give me a key, then?'

George raised his eyes to the ceiling, and Tess saw that he had accepted her on a different basis from the one she had conjectured. Neither had understood the other.

'I thought we . . .'

'We are. But . . . Sophie and I are old friends. That's how it is.'

'I don't think I want that kind of arrangement.'

'Grow up, darling.'

Everyone was telling her to grow up. Clearly, negotiations over fidelity and loyalty, which she had considered absolutes, had only just begun.

'People only tell others to grow up when they're on shaky ground,' she countered.

George poured himself a drink. 'I don't think this conversation is getting us anywhere,' he said.

Tess had always thought of pain as akin to walking over a chessboard, moving from square to square, with respites in between. But pain was being wrapped in tarred roofing felt, a sticky, squeezing material whose adhesive properties burnt strips off her spirit.

'Half the world is starving,' Mrs Frant said, quite frequently when faced with a crisis.

Tess looked hard at the faithless, swaggering, unfathomable George, and committed the sin of wishing that she *was* starving for it would take her mind off her famished heart.

In the end, Iain MacKenzie drove Tess home. He stopped the car outside the Pimlico flat and took her hand gently in his own. 'You will get over it,' he said, searching obviously for the right words.

I want to understand [Tess wrote in her diary]. *I want to understand what has happened. Why I react as I do. Why betrayal matters so much. If I knew it was likely that he would go off with someone else, and I suppose I did, why wasn't I better prepared for it happening? But I should also question myself closely as to why I bother with George.*

Fiduciary law teaches that greater risk requires a greater reward. I have decided to concentrate on that. If I agree with it, surely I feel that George is worth the risk.

Today, despite all my resolutions, I've eaten a Mars bar and a bag of Maltesers. My attempts to give up smoking are also hopeless.

Chapter Seven

In the kitchen, Thuk moved daintily from oven to table, juggling the production of roast beef, glossy vegetables and a trifle swathed in whipped cream.

Jilly and Louis were entertaining weekend guests over on a business trip from the South of France. Jilly knew the form and, like everything else she did, the Sunday lunch was well organized.

Permanently bronzed and plumped with expensive creams, Sonia Lambert stuffed canapés into her mouth. 'Delicious. How do you manage it, Jilly?'

'I have the wonderful Thuk.' Jilly offered the plate to Richard Lambert. 'A treasure without price.'

'Thuk?' Richard seemed puzzled.

'The maid, darling,' his wife explained, flapping her hand on which reposed a large emerald ring. 'She's Thai or Vietnamese or something like that.'

'Ah.'

'Lovely ring, Sonia.' Jilly eyed the emerald, which was surrounded by fine diamonds.

'Oh, darling. I can't tell you. André, my jeweller in Bond Street, says all sorts of wonderful stuff is suddenly flooding the market. People are selling. Strange, isn't it? Anyway, as soon as he saw this he knew it was for me.'

'Will you be staying in the French house this year?' Richard Lambert asked Louis.

Louis glanced at his wife. 'I don't think so,' he said. 'Jilly doesn't like it much.'

True. Jilly found France unsympathetic and the elegant villa with its grey-blue shutters on the hill above Vence a headache too far. Or, perhaps, she felt she could not compete with the smart crowd down there. Whatever the reason, they never went and the villa remained, a poised, expectant folly. Jilly sipped her champagne and smiled, and sipped, and it took Sonia two or three seconds to realize that the smile on her hostess's face had a frozen quality.

'Anything wrong, Jilly?'

Under the expensive foundation, Jilly was a fiery red. 'My tooth,' she said piteously. 'I think I've swallowed it.'

'Darling . . .' Sonia swooped like the Assyrian. '*Let*'s see.'

'No.' Jilly clamped her mouth shut and avoided the sight of Louis's raised eyebrows. *He*, of all people, could not help her. 'It's fine. False alarm.'

Untrue. Jilly could feel the large – achingly large – space where the false façade of a tooth had been gummed onto the real one. Where the façade was going to finish up, Jilly was not going to consider.

'Are you sure?' Sonia was persistent. Jilly nodded, she hoped convincingly.

That bloody dentist. He swore the technique was infallible and that he'd been to America to learn about it. He had *promised* that resurfacing the teeth, at great expense, in a shade up from their natural colour would make Jilly look younger, but the camouflage ripped away, what remained was a filed-down yellow stump.

Oh, how she hated ageing. It was a bloody awful business. She sat through the lunch, barely opening her mouth.

Becky was passing the weekend in working for her exam and in reading a copy of a samizdat report, slipped to her by the co-operative Charles. 'Many members of Lloyd's in senior positions,' it ran, 'were not even vaguely aware of the legal obligation on agents to act at all times in the best interests of their clients . . .'

'Tess,' Becky looked over to where Tess was slumped over the Sunday newspapers, 'have you ever talked to your father about Lloyd's?'

Tess sighed. 'No, I haven't.'

'Well, you should. Do you know if his syndicates are OK?'

Tess adjusted her waistband.

'Are you listening? It might be important. I hear a lot of gossip these days.' Becky got up and papers subsided in a fan on the floor. She bent over Tess, assessed her state, saw it had not progressed and her expression hardened. 'How often do I have to tell you? *George isn't worth it.*'

'He is, he was, to me.'

'It's lucky I'm prepared to put up with you,' said Becky.

Tess grabbed her hand and held it for a second to her cheek. 'Sure.'

Becky snapped the paper fan together. 'Don't forget to talk to your father.'

But Tess did forget.

If Louis was the sure-footed hunter, Charles Cadogan was the prairie dog: attractive, busy, honest. According to office gossip, picked up and pieced together, he was kind in his dealings with women, perhaps something of a chat-up man but devoted to his wife.

Nevertheless, cornering her by her desk and up against the noise of the photocopying machine, Charles shuffled, without *really* meaning to, over a line between sense and recklessness and asked Becky out to dinner – to discuss corporate strategy, of course.

'Just to go over things.'

Carole, the secretary Becky shared with four others, looked up from her battle with the latest software and raised her eyebrows. Do you wish to be rescued? she signalled, a willing member of the helpful sisterhood.

If Charles was not really aware of what he was doing and its implications, Becky was. At first assessment, he was not a patch on Jack but that was too bad. She ignored Carole's lifebuoy and directed her smile at him.

'Look,' said stirred-up, muddled Charles that evening to Martha, his wife, about whom he worried incessantly – more from habit than necessity. After the third baby, Martha had suffered some kind of temporary breakdown and had refused to leave the house, but she was better now. 'I'm taking the trainee out to dinner to discuss strategy. Just so you know.'

Martha moved with regained confidence between the kitchen table and the worktop. She reached for the correct knife and began to peel and chop an onion, which she did in a way that suggested she was probing and analysing its texture.

A thin, seemingly fragile figure, with a slackened stomach from childbirth and curious orange-coloured hair (quite natural), she had been watched by Charles a hundred thousand times. He was proud of her dexterity, her cool application achieved through will-power. Martha had battled with her illness and won.

'Do you mind about the dinner?'

Martha wiped her cheeks with the back of her hand, so white-skinned it was almost transparent. 'Of course not.' She reached for the frying pan and switched on the hob. Then she opened the cupboard above it and located a tin of tomatoes. 'Should I mind?'

'No.'

'Well, then.'

She listened to his feelings, applying the secret, additional sense that she had developed through her marriage. Charles was agitated.

'How are the girls?'

'Anthea fell over and cut her knee, Pammy had a tantrum and Tiny was sick.'

'Oh, Lord,' said Charles, deeply thankful that he had not had to deal with any of it.

There was an eruption of flushed, clean-smelling girls into the kitchen, followed by a weary au pair, and a general wail went up for biscuits, stories, comfort ... Instantly, Martha stopped what she was doing and scooped up Tiny who fell, stone-like, with an expression of utter thankfulness onto her mother's chest. The smile that curved Martha's lips was tender and sure in the knowledge that she was wanted.

Charles drank his wine. The confining walls and domestic focus were as welcome to Martha as they were unwelcome to a woman like Becky. This was Martha's domain: fiercely guarded and given additional sweetness and contentment by three daughters.

I am the spirit of maternity. That is my business.

No ifs, no buts. The knocks and intensity of motherhood insulated Martha from the things she did not wish to hear.

'Have you thought any more ...' Charles settled a billowing napkin onto his lap in an expensive London-playing-at-being-in-France restaurant '... about personnel on the oil rig?'

Before Becky could reply Charles was diverted by the wine list, over which he fussed and dithered. Finally, he ordered a Macon Lugny and looked up at Becky, transparent and boyish in his pleasure at having done so. 'I've a mind to go into wine importing.'

'Really.' There are some people, and I suspect he is one of them, Becky reflected, who are clothed in adult trappings: marriage, children, cheque books and sharp little pension plans. And yet, like the pantomime horse, they do not convince the audience.

'Back to the oil rig,' said Charles eventually, over the coffee.

'Like I said, I wonder, when rigs are insured, if it takes account of all personnel and their life assurance policies?'

'Well ...'

'If every cook and cleaner has taken out a policy and the rig goes down or there's an accident, that must add hugely to the liability.'

'Plenty.' Charles was aware that he should give the idea attention, but Becky's large eyes were disconcerting.

Becky switched the subject. 'Tell me about your family.'

'Three daughters ...' Charles plunged into an account of scenes from domestic life. The impression that Becky gained was of an overweening femininity into which Charles, shell-shocked from producing so many girls, had been sucked. Bubblebath and leotards. Floral wallpaper, a huge assortment of nightdresses in the daily wash and pet hamsters that gyrated all night in perspex balls.

'Does Martha work?'

'Martha? No, she's a mother.'

There was a long pause while Becky absorbed the infor-mation. Did it add to Charles's interest or detract from it? 'Presumably motherhood doesn't affect the brain,' she said.

'Martha decided she was needed at home. I agreed with her ...' Charles faltered, realizing that Becky might be one of those terrifying, nose-ringed, man-eating feminists circling the increas-ingly infertile male.

'Of course,' said Becky, and Charles relaxed.

Martha! Home-loving Martha. Becky pictured her in detail: a big-boned, big-hipped matron in an A-line skirt with little pads of fat beginning to attach themselves to the jawline. Women like that always conveyed an impression of a straining zip. Their body language flaunted the tally of sacrifices made for their children: peaceful baths, ambition, looks and a serviced mind.

In a practised gesture, Becky curved her shoulder above the scoop of her silk camisole. Look at me, it signalled. I am lithe, fatless and free.

'Right,' said Charles, his judgement and good nature diluted with lust. 'I think you're ready to do a little broking on your own. Supervised by me in the background.'

'Of course.'

'That Nigerian project requires five per cent to complete. See if you can get it tomorrow. But keep checking back with me.'

The following day, Becky went straight to Louis and queued for three-quarters of an hour at his box. Every so often he looked up at her.

'How much?' he asked at last. 'And what?'

Becky told him, itemizing the facts smoothly but flushing a little with tension. Behind them screens blinked, pasting information subliminally onto retinas.

Louis checked Becky's papers. The project was not his normal area and Nigeria was always tricky. Facts had a habit of turning turtle there, of being magicked into mist by the witch doctors. Had the right man, the right tribe been approached? he asked. And was she aware that the question of good faith meant separate things to separate cultures?

'Is everything here that I need to know?' he repeated. Underwriters had to be sure that they had been told all the facts, and non-disclosure by the broker was the greatest sin.

Becky knew the form and did not hesitate. 'Sure.' She gave the word as much emphasis as possible.

'OK.'

She reached out to take back the slip. Louis gave it to her and his fingers brushed her sensitized palm. 'Tomorrow,' he said. 'Twelve thirty. Outside the main entrance.'

In the taxi with Louis, Becky shivered, whether from danger or anticipation she did not know. Silently, he took her hand and placed it on his thigh. The driver navigated his way eastwards through the city. Louis turned the hand over so that Becky's wrist was exposed. Then he bent and kissed the thin skin at the point where the pulse beat.

'I'm taking you to Harvey Nichols,' he said. 'After that . . .'

They lunched in the restaurant on ceps and turbot, Becky leaving most of hers.

Louis raised his eyebrows. 'Let me see if I can't give you something that really pleases you.' He led her down to the first floor and said, 'Go ahead, I've got plenty of money.'

Becky did not bother to say anything conventional. Surrounding her were expensive women, experts in the demands made by beauty. They chatted, they conferred, they swirled in front of one another in a rich, oestrogen-steeped parade of dresses, skirts and suits, their jewellery flashing a Morse code of the exclusive.

Silenced, Becky paced along the rails of softly draped cashmere and silk. Once she stopped, allowed her hand to trail over a black chiffon evening dress, tracing its encrustation of jet beads: an archaeologist discovering the outlines of a new fossil. These expensive clothes had been made for tiny women with bird bones and skinny hips, which screamed for pelvic space in childbirth. They were not intended for housewives, big women who toiled and moiled, but for those small enough to be placed in gilded designer houses.

In the changing room Becky stripped to her underclothes and examined the triptych of her in the long mirrors. In the confined space, there was no place to hide, no protection from herself. She was what she saw: bone, flesh and ambition. Here, despite her meticulous grooming, was the slightly grubby skin under the armpit. There was the stray hair in the plucked eyebrow and, there, the suggestion of slack in the muscles.

No wonder a woman demanded her Armani, her Catherine Walker, her Yves – her hard-won, hard-pressed badges of confidence. Becky picked up the trouser suit that Louis would pay for and walked out of the booth.

'You've led me a dance,' Louis told her later, in the hotel room, satiated and almost tender.

She sighed, impatient and dismissive of his call on her

emotions yet powerless to deny his attraction. 'You know,' she murmured, 'you could be my father.'

'Not *quite*.' He shifted to put his arm under her and pull her closer.

'You'll have to pay.'

'I already have,' said Louis, thinking of the huge bill Becky had run up.

She smiled at him across the pillows, then laughed. He felt her thin, greedy hands dig deep into his emotions. It spelt danger, possibly change, and he knew it.

The hotel, situated on the south bank, was cheap. The bed was uncomfortable and the small amount of fruit in the bowl on the table must have been picked from a plastic tree.

'Yes,' Becky said thoughtfully. 'You've paid for me. But I've kept my side of the transaction.'

Louis frowned, and she knew in future that she would have to be more subtle. She hesitated while she worked out how best to deal with the change of mood and then, with one of her soft laughs, leant over him and brushed his lips with her own. Louis drew her closer.

'You're a witch, Becky.'

It was not the moment to ask him for information or gossip that she would have liked. That would come later. She relaxed against him and raised her hands into the air, twisting them this way and that.

Her blood-red nail varnish flashed memories to Louis.

It was the colour of Father Jerome's red morocco prayer book, which had faded in the exact places where his finger and thumb used to rest.

'Shall I tell you something, Louis?' Becky's arms fell back to the bed. 'I've discovered a conspiracy to make things seem difficult. You can see why, of course.' She turned towards him and, light as thistledown, Louis traced the contours of her eyes. 'To make money seem difficult, I mean. They like to make its language inaccessible.'

'Yes,' said Louis, his finger now making a second journey, a wicked, seeking traveller.

'Women in particular aren't supposed to understand it.'

'Stuff, Becky.'

A little later, Becky laid her hand on his bare shoulder and said, 'I must warn you, Louis, that I intend to seduce Charles, my boss.'

In reply, Louis bent over and kissed her. Underneath his, Becky's mouth opened and yielded. 'Why bother?' he whispered. 'Is this not enough?'

She struggled to resist him and to ignore the curious sexual bargain that, between them, they had constructed. 'Because . . . because you won't be leaving your wife,' she said with a rush, vulnerable and curiously exposed. Touched and guilty, Louis again took her into his arms and rocked the slender body until they could begin all over again.

In the taxi back to work, they were silent. Then, in the street ahead, the sky appeared to transform itself in a flash of light, turn white and explode. A moment of suspended silence gripped the shuddering taxi and released it. As Becky watched, a glinting flight of glass arched its way up to the leaden sky, hesitated and speared lazily back to earth, sprinkling a diamond dust over the black bonnet. In the background there was a sudden noise of gushing water and of burglar alarms.

'Jesus,' said the taxi driver. 'It's a bomb at the end of the street.'

He and Louis were out of the taxi and sprinting towards two blood-shrouded figures lying in the road. Beyond them were the smoking remains of a car and an office block with most of its windows blown out except, curiously, the ones on the ground floor, which remained shinily intact.

Several seconds behind the two men, Becky had hung back. 'Don't!' she tried to call after him. 'There might be a second bomb.'

Now, the silence was replaced by screeching brakes, shouts, pounding feet, orders, and the terrible cries of the injured. Becky ran after the men.

The taxi driver was endeavouring to calm a group of hysterical tourists. Louis had dropped to his knees in the road by one of the victims and Becky did likewise by the second. A young, red-haired man, who looked up and through her. He moved his head from side to side. Just like the wooden tortoise I used to have with the waggling head, she thought, appalled at the randomness of the recollection.

The man began to emit hideous choking noises, and Becky fumbled in her handbag, among hoarded bits of string and sachets of shampoo which she had filched from the hotel, for something to mop up the blood. In the end, fearing she might vomit, she pressed her hand against her mouth, pulled her scarf from her neck and wadded it over the biggest wound. The man's right hand was horribly mutilated, but his left seemed untouched, a dirt-engrained hand with nicotine stains.

It was not so much an innate sense of humanity that made her take it in her own, rather the sense that it was expected of her and she must perform. The man's flesh was cold with shock and heavy in her equally cold palm and she continued to hold it, not knowing what else to do. When she looked up for a second or two, it was to see one of the tourists, a man, calmly taking photographs.

So Becky sat in the blood-spattered road holding a stranger's hand until help arrived, feeling curiously detached and remote from the scene. Neither was she surprised. Sometimes the truce made between violence and non-violence held. Sometimes it did not and the results spilled over into the streets. Life in Paradise Flats, Streatham, had taught Becky that lesson. You made love in a ditzy hotel. A bomb went off in the London streets. That was how it was.

After a long, long time, but in fact only a few seconds, Becky began to stroke the man's hand. If he registered a human touch, she was not aware of it.

'It won't be long,' she told him, but it was apparent that he was too dazed to understand.

The paramedics took over and Becky and Louis left the scene separately. In her taxi, Becky examined her blood-stained skirt and cried with shock and the driver refused to accept a fare.

That evening as she watched the news, she learnt that, in all probability, the men she and Louis had attempted to comfort had been the terrorists themselves, their smallish bomb intended for a bank in the City. Instead, they had blown themselves up and killed a tour guide shepherding visitors to the Tower of London.

'If you had known they were terrorists,' asked a shaken Tess, supplying Becky with cups of tea, 'would you have comforted them?'

Becky concentrated on holding her cup of tea. 'I don't know.'

Tess bit her lip and said, 'You were so brave, and it could have been you.'

'Rubbish,' said Becky, who would never confess her lack of feeling even to Tess, and began to shiver uncontrollably. 'I didn't think. If I had, I would have run away.'

Tess put her arms round her friend and drew her close. 'So brave,' she repeated lovingly.

Which were, more or less, the same words that Jilly addressed to Louis at breakfast the following morning, adding, 'Still, Jupiter is on your ascendant, it was unlikely you would have come to harm.'

'Thank you,' said Louis.

The planets having been assigned their place, Jilly stretched out for the marmalade with a hand that was showing the tiniest symptoms of age.

'Don't be late this evening,' she said. 'The Coopers are coming.'

'Oh, God,' said Louis, and threw down his napkin. 'Why?'

Jilly was puzzled. 'You know why. Bridge.'

Louis got to his feet and placed his hands on the table. He leant towards his wife. 'No. Not tonight. Cancel them.'

Jilly searched her husband's face for a clue to his behaviour and concluded that he was more upset by the bombing incident than he had let on. 'Bridge will settle you,' she said soothingly. 'You'll see.'

'No,' said Louis, and left the room.

In the pretty green and white breakfast area with a watery March sunshine filtering through freshly curtained windows, Jilly sat and assessed the physical condition of her hands with a thoroughness that she never applied to her soul. Clever Sonia Lambert had told her about hand lifts and she really must enquire further.

She was due to have coffee with the Widow – Jennifer had earned the outing with a skilled application of flattery. And since Jilly categorized her meetings with the latter as charity, both parties were happy. In her customary organized way, Jilly began to make a list of Things To Do.

The aqueous light turned the room and its glossy arrangements into an aquarium, through which Jilly – not normally given to flights of fancy – imagined herself swimming, sure in the flip of her strong, lazy tail. Whatever else she may have been, Jilly appreciated her buttered bread and never whined. She understood the terms of her existence. If Benisson fabrics, trips to Henley and Wimbledon and an account at Harrods could be said to constitute life, then life had been good to her.

Chapter Eight

'Thank you for your communication,' went the letter of 21 March 1988 to John Frant. 'We have noted its contents. We regret to inform you that it is not possible for you to resign as a Name while the year 1985 remains open.

'Meanwhile, you might find it helpful to have the enclosed summary of your financial position.'

The letter suggested that a third cash call, to the tune of £10,000, would be coming his way.

During their marriage, the Frants had learned, if not to understand, at least to read each other. While it was true that Mrs Frant was more adept and fluent, it was also true that the Colonel was no mean pupil.

He knew that his wife knew that he was worried, to the degree that he was almost sick with it, and that in the mutual collusion that made their life possible, she was turning over his worry in the part of her that she held back from him. That spring he watched, with a heavy heart, her progress around the garden, clipping the clematis, targeting infant tendrils of bind-weed for extinction, inspecting the compost or marching along the beds and round to the paddock. Fighting cold and damp, she was out there. Most days.

Business life was full of reverses. Importing apples and bananas was a positive drama of bad weather, deficient cold storage and unpredictable transport and he had waged war against them. And yet, Colonel Frant was not sure that he could fight this last battle. He had neither the men, the weapons nor knowledge of the terrain.

Lead weighed down his spirits, and he sensed that his body was struggling to maintain its customary patterns.

The wind, whistling down the valley, held the sharp, cold notes of March and, as she moved down the border, checking the position of the plants against the diagram in her notebook, Mrs Frant was glad of her thermal vest and thick herringbone stockings. She noted the temperature, lower than last year, and wrote a summary of the weather in the section at the back of the notebook. Later, she would enter it up in the leather book in the kitchen.

Weather was important and she had always been fascinated by it. Jack had written to her of the heat in Ethiopia, and the freezing nights, of rock cracked by the extremes of temperature, and dry, scrubby vegetation. Faithfully, she pictured what he described.

He also described death, as it made free with the starving and the depleted, and she pondered over his version – death, the cruel thief. For Mrs Frant, death was the tease with whom she flirted when the life outside her secret life seemed especially worthy of contempt or unreal. Like her daughter, she had also searched for God. Unlike Tess, she had found him, but he was a smaller, less compassionate, more wayward figure than she had hoped. It pained her to admit it, but try as she might, Mrs Frant could not admire the Deity.

She got down on her sponge garden kneeler, pulled off her glove and cupped her favourite hellebore in her hand: dark and fascinatingly freckled, contained, strong and faithful like the best of friends. Hellebores enjoy a remarkable longevity, some living for fifty years or so, and there is something comforting about growing old with a plant.

Such beauty, she thought, such joyous beauty.

The Widow, who happened to be passing the High House, was treated to the sight of Mrs Frant on her hands and knees under the lilac trees. Quite, quite strange, she confided to Jilly Cadogan over biscuits and coffee, Angela was talking aloud but no one was there.

'What do we do?' asked Mrs Frant of her husband, over a lunch of cold meat and salad.

Her husband shuffled the unappetizing slices of lamb around his plate. He loved his wife but, by Jove, she was no cook. 'I've had a word with Nigel who says there's nothing to worry about.'

'How can one believe the reassurances of someone who is no more than a dating agency?'

She had a point but Colonel Frant wanted to believe Nigel, and that made a difference. 'You can't make an omelette without breaking eggs. And we've had a straight run for several years. I'm sure the syndicates have proper reserves, invested in the best way, and we won't get any more calls.'

'Yes,' agreed Mrs Frant, for there was no point in doing anything else.

Naturally, both spoke from a position of ignorance.

The phone went on Tess's desk at Metrobank and, one eye on the screen, she picked it up.

'You win,' said George. 'I was a naughty boy. Spend the weekend with me.'

'No,' said Tess, and the screen in front of her blurred.

'Yes, you will.'

'Stop behaving like an ape. Anyway I'm going down to my parents.'

He spotted the opening in her flank. 'I'll drive you.'

After a long crawl out of London on the Friday evening, they nosed onto the A3 and began to pick up speed.

Tess sat with clenched hands: she was finding conversation a little difficult. She had discovered before that it was easier to say things on the phone and the silence in the stuffy, dark car seemed pregnant with disappointment that neither had come up to scratch for the other.

Guildford flashed by, a paradise of business parks and heavy traffic, the angel on top of the city's cathedral gamely illuminated by its spotlight. Tess's nails made little red crescents on her skin.

George cleared his throat. 'I want to get sorted.'

He usually ducked out of making personal statements and the directness took Tess by surprise.

'What sort of sorted?'

He swung off the road and onto the Hogs Back. 'Have you ever thought about Northern Ireland?'

'You know I have.'

'I'm going back to Belfast. Soon.' George flipped back his hair with his free hand. 'Difficult. The whole place is crazy and everyone is busy convincing the other side that their prejudices are correct.'

She sneaked a look at George. He was difficult to see in the dark, but his outline suggested a frightening remoteness and Tess was too much in love to realize that this quality only added to his attraction but did not, necessarily, add substance.

'I think you'd better marry me,' he said, pressing the accelerator.

It was as if, she reflected at three a.m. the following morning, she was an appointment in his diary that had to be ratified. *Sorted.* If she married George, they would be sorted. Into what? Paper bags? Piles of china?

But she wanted to marry him, oh, how she did. She wanted for herself George's handsomeness, his air of mystery and his challenge.

Yet she had imagined events differently. The private, female part of her had craved, expected even, the sweetness and excitement of being pursued and captured. She had imagined gazing down on George's glossy, bent head and allowing a little time to elapse before she consented.

In the event, she said yes before one second had ticked away and, for the rest of the drive, they conducted an adult conversation about Army quarters, children, her work, his work. Nothing about fidelity, which she very much wished to get straight. Nothing about craving or needing each other. Tess had wanted, too, to be told that she was loved.

I'll make it work, the romantic Tess avowed, lying in linen sheets in her white cotton nightdress. Accommodation is part of love; the bending and flexing. Corn in a rainstorm. The object: to survive.

In the spare bedroom across the landing, George was also staring into the darkness. Tess was lovely. She was good. Maybe, just maybe, she would bring order into a rackety existence.

George also considered the comfortable home in Appleford, the flat in London and Tess's expectations. The equation appeared to satisfy him for he fell asleep, suddenly and deeply.

Like Tess, Mrs Frant remained awake, praying for the future happiness of her daughter. George Mason was exactly the clean, salaried, well-mannered type of man that she would wish for her. Unfortunately Mrs Frant was not sure that she liked him.

She leant over and shook Colonel Frant awake. 'What are we going to do about the wedding, John? We always promised that we'd give her the best we could manage.'

For the first time, a spurt of anger fuelled Mrs Frant's feelings towards the husband who, after all, had got them into a financial mess and her maternal anvil was emitting sparks.

'Of course we'll give her the wedding,' he said, from the isolation of his side of the bed. 'If it's the last thing I do.'

Outside in the garden, Mrs Frant's hellebores shook their heads in the night wind: secret, beautiful and poisonous.

*

George deposited Tess back at the flat on Sunday evening and a radiant Tess burst through the front door with her news.

On hearing it, Becky sat down hard on the sofa. 'You'll want me out of the flat.'

Her reaction took Tess aback. 'Yes. I mean no. Sometime.'

Becky did not smile. 'That'll be the end of us, Tess.'

She was right. Tess had a vision of Becky not being in her life. Not being in the bathroom, on the phone, in the everyday housekeeping calculations. 'Don't be silly.'

'Well, congratulations.' Becky sounded as flat as Tess had ever heard.

It was with a curious sense of disappointment, even anger, that Tess went to bed. She wished that she dared to ring George just to say goodnight but, feeling she did not know him quite well enough yet, had not done so.

She was stuffing papers into her briefcase early the next morning when Becky emerged from her room into the hall. 'I want to apologize.'

Tess said nothing.

'I should be happy for you. I should have said so.'

'That's all right.'

'I don't like the idea of change, that's all. You'll disappear behind a front door, children, all that sort of thing.' Tess listened, scarcely breathing. 'We'll lose touch. In the *real* sense, I mean.'

'Don't,' said Tess. '*Don't.*'

The Good Fairy ... Tess swung through the doors of Metrobank ... never points out in the stories that getting married involves death. Granted, only little ones of friendship and habit, but deaths all the same.

'Where've you been?' Bill was irritable. 'You're late.' Tess glanced at her watch: eight fifteen. 'Fitch has been on the phone. Wants you to go up there again.'

'Oh, Lord.'

Tess retreated to her desk.

'Dollar's up,' said Kit. 'And the word is Brewsters Bank will be fined for not declaring its overdraft.'

'*Naughty!*' Tess was beginning to feel better.

The room was filling up. Freddie lounged over his desk drinking cappuccino, looking raddled and blown. Computer screens winked and the printer emitted sighing noises.

'Why are you late?' Clearly, Bill was in a ferreting mood.

'Well,' said the flushed Tess, pushing back her hair, 'I'm getting married.'

Bill regarded her. 'I didn't think women got married any more. I mean, women like you.' He called over to Freddie. 'This mad woman's getting married.'

Sharp and louche, Freddie looked up. 'What the hell for?' He seemed genuinely puzzled.

Tess beamed at him. '*You* don't have to worry, Freddie. Not your neck of the woods.'

'Touché.' Freddie struggled to his feet. 'Listen, you lot. Tess is getting married.'

'Fuck me . . .'

'Champagne's on you!'

'Will you warm *my* slippers?'

'*Don't.*'

'You'll turn into your mother.'

'Watch it,' called a voice from the back. 'A big wave's building on the FTSE futures.'

There was a dash back to the screens, Tess among it.

All morning she watched: tracking and cross-tracking numbers that slipped, dodged and ran. Behind their configurations lay a story: nervousness, fashion, good management and the struggle to maintain a positive relationship between the return on an investment and its costs.

I'm more at home here, Tess reflected, threading her way through the figures, with this work and this language, than with anything else. I understand better what to do when a yield curve inverts than how to handle the man I'm going to marry.

'You talk of self-regulation at Lloyd's,' said Becky, 'but surely, at best, it's an idea with elastic tendencies. No one, not even the saints, self-regulates themselves.'

She was sitting at Louis's box, having persuaded him to take another 5 per cent on a second Nigerian project. They were discussing a reinsurance scandal that was emerging from a syndicate that had run into trouble – fortunately, still only a mutter in the press.

'You realize that Nigeria and this project are not my area,' Louis had commented, after examining Becky's slip, but scribbled his signature all the same.

He opened a drawer, took out a packet of paracetamol and swallowed a couple.

'You take a lot of those,' Becky pointed out.

'I get headaches.'

Risk identification demands a clear head and Louis's was aching. Whether social or financial, it requires skill to isolate, finance, reduce and manage risk. Greed fuels risk. The trick, in the language of the insurance game, Louis and Becky's game, was to avoid the trap of unplanned risk assumption. (Definition in *Dictionary of Insurance*: that which results from ignorance and inertia. Colonel Frant might have done well to ask whether ignorance and inertia had been the cause of his financial predicament or whether his risk had been well managed on his syndicates.)

A steady file of underwriters and brokers in suits walked up and down the aisles. Up and down. Round and back, in a pattern that can be observed in insect colonies.

Louis looked at Becky. 'It's all very well to criticize but the economy depends on the invisible earnings, the business here, otherwise the level of exports is affected. You must understand that the insurance market ensures that we remain the money market of the west so we can't rock the boat too hard,' he said. 'By and large, we manage. Someone like you just fixes on the things that go wrong.'

'Funny,' said Becky gently, 'so do the press.' She smiled at her lover. 'You mustn't be so sensitive, I'm not accusing you,' she said. 'I'm greedy too.'

As always, she exuded the suggestion, irresistible and marked, of intense life. She was, he thought, all slenderness and tender flesh tints. In a shortish skirt and tiny-waisted jacket ('Dress to kill,' Charles had advised), he knew that she knew she was a focus in the male-dominated Room.

A battle was being conducted in Louis between his customary assurance and a new disequilibrium. As the expert in risk analysis, Louis understood perfectly that, if permitted, Becky was a bully. He also understood that he was attracted by this.

Stacked behind him was intelligence data on Syria and Iraq, which had been beamed, via CNN satellite, onto his desk. A client was requesting cover for a trade delegation to this area and Louis was conducting an assessment of the probabilities.

Becky got gracefully to her feet. 'Louis . . . which syndicates is Tess's father on? Do you know?'

Louis reeled off the names.

There was a moment of profound silence. 'Oh, God,' said Becky. 'Isn't he the run-off man who's in big trouble?'

Louis shuffled his papers and, again, resisted picking up this problem. He asked quietly, 'How's the seduction of Charles progressing?'

'Fine,' said Becky. 'He's nice.'

'Why lumber yourself with him? There are others.'

'True. But the point is . . .' Becky turned away her face. 'The point is, I haven't met them so the question is irrelevant.' Papers folded to her chest, she looked up at Louis.

Father Jerome's thumb had not only pressed an imprint, whorled and grained, on the red morocco of his prayer book. It pressed also on Louis.

Becky slotted her papers into her briefcase.

'Hallo . . .' A curious Nigel Pavorde broke into the conversation. 'I was passing and since we're all lunching . . .'

'Hallo, Nigel.' Becky twitched at her jacket cuffs. 'I was just going.'

'Good business?'

'This and that in Nigeria,' said Louis.

'Oh.' Nigel's expression adjusted up a notch. 'Not your line, really, Louis.'

Becky waved her fingers as a goodbye and moved off. Nigel observed the retreating back. The muted rings of telephones gave the impression that the building was covered by a large blanket. Black was the dominant colour, overflowing in the boxes, moving along the aisles, sprayed in dots up and down the escalator. Among that subfusc, Becky's long legs, sheathed in opaque black tights, and the hair, caught back in the French plait she favoured, were startlingly noticeable.

'Ambitious, isn't she?' commented Nigel.

'Very.'

'Good thing she's not ugly.'

They walked out of the building together.

Two hundred thousand asbestosis-related deaths are predicted by the Yale School of Organization and Management over the next twenty-five years. Cost $50 billion.

Where did I read that? Louis searched his memory. Where? In the stack of documents on his desk?

'I wonder,' said Nigel, blinking in the daylight, 'if things aren't on the turn. There's a lot of talk about Names kicking up stink.'

American actuaries are predicting that the cost of cleaning up polluted America will be in the order of $1000 billion.

'There is,' Louis replied. 'But we sit tight. We make provision.'

'For ourselves?'

'As much as anyone.'

The silence of men, such as an underwriter and a members' agent, contemplating financial crisis, even melt-down, is akin to the silence of women contemplating childbirth. The impending event is too big for mere words.

Becky finally told Charles about the bomb over dinner, the third to which he had lured her in a fortnight. He surprised her by turning pale and shaking.

'Oh, Becky, Becky, I could kill the bastards.'

A little surprised but touched by his concern, she endeavoured to shrug it off.

'It was pure chance,' she said, deceptively cool, for her sleep had not been entirely untroubled since the incident. 'That's life and we shouldn't bother about it too much. I won't allow myself to bother about it. It's someone else's war.'

Throughout the meal, Charles worried at the subject until it had been beaten thoroughly. 'I can't believe how near to death you came. How I might have lost you.'

'Look,' said Becky, who had noted the personal pronoun. Her smile was calculated to remove the sting from her words. 'We can overdo this. Let's forget it.'

After coffee, Charles insisted on escorting her back to Pimlico and on coming inside with her. 'I want to tell you something,' he said, looking mysterious and important.

'What?' But she had a good idea as she led him through the vestibule and into the lift. The doors closed and Charles put his hands either side of Becky, trapping her. 'I love you, Becky. I can't eat. I can't work. I can't think of anything else.'

She had been expecting a request to enter her bed not a

declaration of love and it rocked her equilibrium. Perhaps this transaction would be conducted on a different basis from the one she had originally envisaged.

Charles was gazing at her with moist, loving eyes, and it was clear that he had meant every word. Becky closed hers for a second. So had Jack and Louis ... Well? Who knew? Charles was more insistent than Jack, more experienced, and that told in his favour.

The lift jerked upwards and Becky and Charles's stomachs were left behind, adding to Charles's sense of euphoria. He waited for Becky's reply.

She did not give one verbally but, once inside the flat, she took him by the hand and led him into her bedroom.

Chapter Nine

'*To wed*: To wager or stake (now obsolescent). To bind.' *The Dictionary of Historical Slang* also defines it as 'emptying the necessary house'.

Tess hoped that 'to bind' and 'to empty' were not linked.

Weddings are exercises in irony. They are occasions that demand and are granted the broad brushstroke: the exchange of big promises, the public passage from one state to another, the marshalling of individuals into unity before the centre breaks and the congregation disperses.

That's the theory, Tess thought, in some exasperation, having discovered that a wedding is an accumulation of small details. Or, at least, the wedding that Tess was having.

Flowers. What colour in the hall? In the guests' lavatory? Where should the umbrellas be sited? Iain and Flora MacKenzie required a taxi at five fifteen. Jenny Parsons's mother was coeliac – could the caterer oblige? Who would give the caterers their lunch?

Sometimes Tess looked up from the lists, the piles of presents, the smoothed-out stack of tissue paper, and talked to St Jude the patron saint of lost causes.

'I hope you don't mind,' she said, 'but I don't want you taking an interest in the wedding. *It is not a lost cause.* I may look at the end of my tether, but I'm perfectly well aware that in order to arrive I must journey hard through the politics of tetchy relations, my mother's wishes – a hard one that – and George's lack of co-operation. In good time, I will also deal with a superabundance of pickle spoons, decanters and three toast racks, and George's hostility to the pile of knick-knackery that sits in the corner.'

St Jude remained silent.

I don't really know George . . . Tess found her nights restless. I don't know him at all. There's no point of reference with someone whose parents are dead and whose only brother works on the other side of the world.

What if George had the Aids virus? A secret life? Perhaps a child somewhere?

During this period, Tess returned to the poets she had abandoned after university and searched out the ones that, once, had meant something or given pleasure. She yearned to read about the tap of chestnut blossoms on the bedroom window, of a sun rising in fierce splendour over misty fields, or descriptions of satin and silk whispering against skin and of the blood rising hotly through the body.

Each morning, Mrs Frant telephoned her daughter at the bank and dictated the tasks for the day. Thank-you letters. Queries. Dress fittings. And Tess obeyed.

A week before the wedding Colonel Frant caught her reading one of the poets after Sunday lunch.

'Oh dear,' he said. 'It's got to that stage, has it? Who is it?'

'Francis Thompson.'

'Don't know him. Should I?'

'He was a Catholic poet.'

Colonel Frant's feet were planted so solidly in the Anglican tradition and his grasp on its doctrinal tenets was so unwavering that it would never occur to him that Tess might look for comfort elsewhere. He laid a hand on her hair.

'I hope you'll enjoy your big day. Your mother and I have done our best.'

'Oh, Dad.'

'By the way,' he nodded at the book, 'be careful. I was young once and I remember well the temptation of extremes.'

He succeeded in astonishing his subdued and rather troubled daughter, who had presumed that her father's ruminations did not extend much past the theory and practice of well-placed capital and that his youth had been long forgotten.

Her presumption was misplaced. Yet, entrenched in the habits of years, neither was prepared to explore further.

'We are not,' Tess wrote in her diary, 'in the habit of talking to each other.'

Jack was flying over a couple of days before the wedding, adding mysteriously at the end of the letter that he had his own news to tell them. (Oh dear, said Mrs Frant, placing a hand over her eyes. Oh dear.) Becky was to be bridesmaid. She and Mrs Frant had almost, but not quite, come to blows over the subject of the dress, Mrs Frant favouring a floral pink, Becky white with a coloured sash. Becky suspected that Mrs Frant only favoured the pink because she could see that it did not suit Becky.

Perhaps Becky was right. Mrs Frant was not a woman who neglected her vendettas or forgot her wounds – and an image of Becky forced into a dress she did not like would offer a tiny recompense for the exile of her son.

The colleagues at Metrobank clubbed together and bought a very large silver photo frame onto which Freddie had stuck a packet of condoms in Day-glo colours. He was in agonies over which waistcoat to wear: too elaborate a one, he felt, would be at war with the marquee's décor.

In the peaceful green paddock, the marquee went up. A stretched white canvas temple, lined with pale blue and white stripes, dotted with clusters of white roses, lilies and scented stocks. Stippled with graceful summer flowers and rippling with grasses, the meadow beyond gave an impression of lapping gently at the edges of the busy activity. A sea running with wild beauty, at peace with its own nature.

*

On 6 July, the day before the wedding, there was a scream of escaping gas in the North Sea, followed by two explosions ten minutes apart. The sea boiled, the metal platform buckled and twisted and men leapt, human torches, into blazing salt water. The oil rig, Piper Alpha, self-destructed.

The newspapers were full of images: stark representations of unimaginable pain and anguish. Gagging from nerves, Tess stared at them in the kitchen of the High House on her wedding morning and tried to eat a bowl of muesli. At first, they made no impact, and she thought, instead, of sheer white tights, of silk and pearls.

'Give me those,' said her mother. 'It's bad luck to look at things like that.' She dumped the papers on the window-seat and stood over Tess. 'Eat up, darling. You'll need your strength.'

Tess looked round the familiar room, at the clutter of the well-to-do: china, flowers, shopping lists and notices of charity events. Nothing was ostentatious, nothing there that did not have a purpose – her careful mother saw to that. Obediently, she bent her head over the cereal bowl.

In front of the mirror, she felt differently. She felt, suddenly, that the world she knew had been too small and she was too inexperienced to have any understanding at all. Violence was reflected in the silver mirror – Becky's bomb pulling apart healthy flesh, a bullet carving a tunnel through bone, men twisted by an oil-lit fire – and the gleaming whiteness of the dress hanging on the wardrobe appeared to turn crimson.

These were the things with which George was involved and about which they never talked. But she had not asked.

Needing to hear him, she left the bedroom and, in search of a phone, went into her parents' room. Her mother's outfit, blue shantung, lay on the bed, her father's morning coat arranged neatly beside it. The windows had been flung wide open and high summer streamed through. There was the smell of sensible talcum powder and a light drift on the carpet where her mother had shaken the tin too vigorously.

While she waited to speak to George, she crossed and uncrossed her legs, already sheathed in white gossamer.

'George.'

'Tess. Everything all right?'

'I just wanted to say hallo.'

'Well, hallo.'

'Are you happy?'

'Of course.'

She felt a slight chill stroke her skin under her new underclothes. 'I love you, George.'

'Ditto,' he said, in his impersonal way.

After Becky, also in white silk but with an apricot sash (she had won), and Mrs Frant had departed, Tess made her way cautiously downstairs. At the door of her father's study, she halted and looked in.

Colonel Frant was reading a letter which he put down on the desk when he saw Tess, but not before she had caught sight of the name of his managing agency and tabulations of figures.

'All right?' she asked, alarmed.

Colonel Frant was struggling to cope with his losses, his daughter and his money and, in contemplating their significance, he felt lessened.

'All right, Daddy?'

He gave himself a few seconds, then stepped forward and took Tess in his arms. 'Absolutely dandy,' he said. 'Don't I have a beautiful daughter?'

Oh, God, she thought, alerted by the letter and the strain on his face, Becky did try to warn me.

But she swirled round on the spot to show off the dress, her veil floating out around her. 'Thank you for all this.'

Thus Tess went to her wedding, dressed in a virgin's white and shrouded in a veil, carrying lilies, her heart thudding, not to the music of the organ or to high emotion, but in response to jumbled images of death and pieces of paper with Lloyd's written on them.

As she stood by the church door with her father, she waited to be seized by an enormous sensation of feeling, by God, but felt, instead, a detachment as if the veil had spun a membrane between her and the rest of the world. Then she felt a touch on her elbow. It was Iain MacKenzie and his wife, Flora, late and out of breath.

'Good luck,' he said, and entered the church. Flora sent her a little smile with a mouth that puckered at the corners.

George's regiment formed a colourful guard-of-honour outside Appleford's ancient church. George seized Tess's hand and pulled her through. And then, only then, did she quicken with excitement, and go gladly with him.

Waiting in the receiving line with the bride and groom, Colonel and Mrs Frant exchanged a long look and the Colonel gave a tiny smile.

'My goodness,' said Nigel, in an aside to the Widow as they waited in the line, 'there's been some money spent here.'

He spoke in a speculative and, the Widow felt, rather unpleasant tone.

'Well, of course. She's their only daughter.' The Widow shuffled out of Nigel's proximity. He was eyeing the champagne. A glass or not? Champagne was hell on the veins in the legs. Better to wait for the Puligny-Montrachet he had spotted on the menu for lunch.

The Widow edged towards Jilly. 'Save me,' hissed Jilly to Margery Whittingstall. 'I can't take another dose of Jennifer just yet.' However much Jilly might pander to the Widow in private, she was not prepared to take her on at public functions.

'Cost you a lunch,' said Margery, and surged forward.

Jilly turned away and bumped into Jack who, if she was truthful, looked yellow rather than brown.

'Hally, Jilly. You look wonderful, as always.'

There was, she decided, ignoring the puritan set of his nose and chin, a fascinating suggestion of the exotic and erotic about him. 'So do you, Jack.' She pecked him on the cheek. 'Tess looks nice, very nice. Of course, you won't have had time to get to know George yet.'

It was a second or two before Jack replied and, following the line of his gaze, Jilly realized that it rested on Becky. All flushed skin and gleaming hair, Becky was dancing Ring a' Ring a' Roses with two toddlers, white skirts swirling and whirling and her sash tossing lazily behind her.

Aha, thought Jilly.

'Do you know that I got married?' said Jack. 'Last month. At the camp. I thought I might as well.'

'Oh, how lovely, Jack. Congratulations. Um. Is your wife here?'

'Penelope? No, she felt she was needed in Addis as there's a crisis brewing. I'm going back at the end of the week.'

After lunch, things became noisy.

'Ra, ra . . .' A chorus went up from the regimental contingent, who were doing an impromptu hokey-cokey in the middle of the marquee. Standing at the centre, Freddie whirled his cravat above his head and was drinking glasses of champagne as fast as he could from a tray held unsteadily by the best man.

Nigel watched them. 'This must have cost a packet,' he repeated to no one in particular, and shook his head.

By midnight, the flowers in the long-deserted marquee had drooped and the specially laid floor was encrusted with food. Remains of the cake were crumbled onto plates and flakes of salmon oozed between stacked ones. Still clad in the shantung suit, now spotted with champagne stains, but in her bedroom slippers because her feet had swollen, Mrs Frant surveyed the scene. A smell of cigarettes, damp lawn, old drink, food and a residue of expensive perfume hung over the debris.

All was quiet.

Inside the house, Colonel Frant sat in his study.

Beyond the marquee, the paddock and the meadow, with its corncockles and poppies, slept under a black summer sky. Mrs Frant switched off the electricity supply into the marquee and stood, quite still, for a long time in the dark. Then, in an odd gesture, she raised her hands palm up to the black sky, and walked back to the house.

On the second day of their honeymoon in Crete, which he had organized, George disappeared into a nightclub and failed to return until four o'clock in the morning. He found Tess sitting up in the bed, hands clasped over her knees, watching the first harsh fingers of sun reach across the horizon. In the hill above the village, several donkeys were braying.

'Why aren't you asleep?'

She favoured him with a look that he had not seen before. 'Why do you think?'

He gave a snort of laughter. 'I'm sorry I kept you awake.'

She wanted to show how angry she was but did not dare for she was not yet sufficiently sure of her husband to allow herself to be angry with him. Instead, she looked out of the window at a balding landscape with its patches of scrub and rocky outcrops. George sat down on her bed, hair flopping, stinking of drink.

'Why don't you tell me I'm a beast? Go on.'

Uneasy, she fingered the bedspread made of cheap cotton. Once or twice before she had noticed that George seemed to like – need – confrontation.

'Go on. Say it.'

Sick with misery and disappointment, she was silent.

'*Go on, Tess.*'

Abruptly, she pulled the sheets around her. 'Go to sleep, George.' She lay, burning with the anger she had not expressed, and listened to him moving around the room, his bare feet making a soft sucking noise on the stone.

Having breakfasted alone on yoghurt and coffee, Tess picked her way to the beach across scrub and lumps of concrete abandoned from the building programme further up the hill and settled herself on the only unoccupied and clean bit of sand she could find.

The heat was colossal and the beach was full. Hot stones stuck into her bottom, the sand was a burning cradle, there was no shade and the sea looked like warm soup.

So there she sat, alone and unhappy, under a blue sky and yellow sun, on a beach fringed by aromatic marjoram and thyme, bullied by the heat into releasing their aromas.

She lit a cigarette and inhaled deeply.

Suddenly, it was whipped out of her hand. 'No, you don't,' said George, grinning like a boy. 'No more smoking but plenty of swimming.'

He half lifted, half dragged Tess down to a sea the colour of pulpy black grapes. She gasped as her feet were burnt as they ran, and gasped again when the water hit her body and George pushed her under. When she came up for air, hair streaming down her back, he caught her round her waist and kissed her salty mouth.

'I love you really, Tessy. Darling Tessy.'

She kissed him back. They were to be a normal honeymoon couple after all and, weak with relief, she clung to him.

'You know, I'm not so stupid,' said Becky, on the phone to Charles.

'Did I ever suggest you were?'

'Matt Barker told me that the pay-out costs on Piper Alpha are going to be bigger than originally calculated. Why do you think that is?'

'You're going to tell me, I know.'

Becky gave one of her soft laughs. 'Apparently, the insurers hadn't taken into account all the life assurances of the catering and cleaning staff.'

She was clever, his Becky, so good on detail (in bed too), and that cleverness was the most erotic of aphrodisiacs. Pricking and stirring him until he was driven mad with desire.

Sometimes, Charles reasoned, if you put your head down and don't look up, a problem goes away. He knew this to be true from his experience at work. Skilled prevarication was an art and, from time to time, he had proved he was a master at it.

But he had reached a juncture where he felt desperate. Desperate to have Becky, and equally desperate not to hurt his family. He owed Martha much; he owed his daughters an unclouded, straightforward future. Security. Structure. Good parenting.

So, he had got his head down during that spring and summer, but what he felt for Becky would not go away. It was, it seemed, indelible. Charles's awakened passion accompanied him to the office and wound hot, sticky tendrils around each thought. It returned with him each night to the meticulously maintained house in Clapham. Sometimes Charles (who was not an imaginative man) imagined that it took a physical form and he was walking in through the door with it clinging to his back.

He was aware that the last thing on earth he should do was to hurt his troubled Martha. He also suspected that that was precisely what he was going to do.

'Leave him alone,' Louis had warned Becky.

She had thrown back at him, 'Don't be a dog in the manger.'

'And you,' he said, 'mustn't be a bitch.'

'Well,' said Becky, 'that wraps up the canine imagery.'

'Why do you want him?'

'He's kind. He's well off.'

'And what about the children?'

Becky did not hesitate. 'Children survive.'

One evening after supper Martha tackled Charles. 'What's going on? I think something is.'

She waited for his reply, every sense strung taut, listening to his mood while she twisted a lock of orange-coloured hair around her white fingers. Charles took a surprised breath. He had never imagined discussing the subject over pork chops and boiled potatoes. 'I've fallen in love with someone else.'

Martha's hand made a journey back to her lap. 'So?'

Charles, who had been prepared to act deeply sorrowful and guilt-ridden, sat up. 'What do you mean "*so*"?'

'So, my poor Charles, you've fallen in love with someone else. It happens. It happens quite a lot.'

Dynasty, the cat, wandered by and Charles concentrated on the tortoise-shell fur. 'I'm so sorry, Martha.'

Martha's mouth was twisted with distress. 'It doesn't surprise me. I'm not the most glamorous creature in the world. But I'm prepared to help you.'

He could not bear the flash of bitter hurt that she revealed in the remark she had made about herself. Could not bear it.

'I don't think you understand,' he said, and suddenly his decision was made. 'I want to leave you.'

'Yes, I know,' she said, listening frantically to what he was feeling. 'You think that at the moment, but you can't. Because of the children.'

'Can't I?' He ran impatient fingers through his hair. Just like a boy.

'No. Be patient and the feeling will pass.'

A net had been thrown over Charles, and instead of striking out into open sea he was thrashing in the circle made by the fishermen's boats. But he fully intended to swim out.

Martha's questioning had released the torrent of feeling damned up in her husband, and he made the additional mistake of imagining that no further hurt would be inflicted by talking. He got to his feet and paced the kitchen.

'I've never felt like this, Martha. Never before. Never so strong. It's quite extraordinary.'

He fiddled with postcards stuck on the noticeboard, snapped the lid of the breadbin shut, and seized an unopened bottle of wine and proceeded to uncork it.

'I didn't see,' cried Martha. '*I didn't see.* The wife never sees.'

There was a clatter of plate pushed against glass and the harsh grind of a chair pushed back. Hands on stomach, Martha was bent double as if she had been punched. Charles let go of the wine and a glass fell to the floor where it bounced on the cork tiles with a dull sound. He leapt towards his wife and crouched down beside her. Gasping and breathless, she pushed him away.

Wincing, Charles squatted on his heels. 'You mustn't worry, Martha. I'll make sure you and the girls have enough money.'

The view of the run-off insurer is this: having covered the first layer of possible loss with a time and distance policy up to a certain figure, any claims arising would, statistically speaking, occur only over a long period. This long period allows for profits to be made from investing the insurance premium, which should make enough money to cover any subsequent loss. Providing, of course, that the premiums charged by the one underwriting the risk had been adequately pitched for the risk being carried.

In some respects, this practice provides an excellent blueprint for the conduct of our personal lives.

That night Charles lay awake in the double bed, shifting with the greatest care away from Martha, who was also sleepless. It had not occurred to him that the first loss in a dissolving marriage was the freedom to move around in a double bed. Frozen into their respective sides, the Hayters resembled effigies under the duvet, mourning the death of a partnership.

Whereas Louis, clad in pyjamas from Simpsons, lay in his

bed and considered the architecture of disaster. Asbestosis, pollution, earthquake and, yes, marital breakdown.

The rules are written in stone, Father Jerome had taught him. Big immovable blocks against which you may battle all you wish and end up only with bleeding fingers.

Had he, the sharp and successful underwriter, investigated the risk sufficiently? With a combination of lust and gentleness, Louis lay and thought of Becky.

And Becky? What did she think?

Certainly she was not contemplating rain dripping off freshly washed trees, or the smell of earth invigorated by summer. She did not, like Mrs Frant, dream of the hellebore, or, like Tess, fall asleep with a heart soft and palpitating with love. Reining in the more slippery of her longings, Becky totted up the advantages of her position and set her face, metaphorically, towards the dawn.

Chapter Ten

Some acts are embedded in the memory for ever, so shameful and so sharp that the skin that grows over them has to be doubly thick. After a while, a second skin is formed. Then a third. But it cannot hide the true nature of what it conceals.

These days, lots of people leave their wives and get divorced.

At the moment of walking down the stairs with his luggage, after two unspeakable days of argument and bitterness, Charles was assaulted by violent doubt. What on earth was he doing? Was this the action of a civilized man? He dropped the suitcase at the top of the stairs and looked down at Martha in the hall below.

'You should have tried harder to stop me,' he said.

'*I* should have stopped *you*!' Martha made the gesture, now almost habitual, of pressing her hands into her stomach, as if to press it out of existence.

Charles picked up his suitcase. 'What am I saying? I didn't mean that.'

Martha had cried so hard that the skin on her face had sprouted reddened patches. 'You have a nerve,' she said. Anthea, who was clinging to her knee, whimpered, and Martha placed her hand on the child's head. 'And I imagined, Charles, that you would never do anything to hurt the children.'

Charles felt his mouth grow dry. 'It's better this way.'

'Better! Have you learnt *nothing*? Except clichés? What possible reason do you have for this to be better?' Martha raised her arm, and her patterned jumper fell back along it to her thin

116

elbow. She seemed all skin and bone, a rattling witch, he thought, and was instantly ashamed.

Upstairs on the top landing, the Swedish au pair leant over the banisters and watched.

'You're wrong to do this, Charles. Wrong. Wrong. Wrong.' Martha spoke in a low tone.

Once again, Charles paused.

'Remember what we wanted, Charles. It wasn't that ambitious. The house. The children.'

'Daddy? Where are you going?' Anthea watched her father finally descend. At the bottom, he hesitated and his wife caught her breath. Then he moved towards the front door.

'Daddee?'

He continued out into the Clapham street and away from his home. At the end of the road were two men, drugged and ravaged. One propped himself against the wall, shaking. The second, defiantly filthy, was talking to him quietly. As Charles passed, the comforter lit a cigarette and guided it into his friend's mouth.

He walked on towards the car parked a street away, ricocheting between his infatuation and a deepening astonishment at his newly discovered capacity for ruthlessness. The man who quibbled over stealing a paper-clip from the office was to ask himself over and over again: How did I do it?

After camping in various friends' flats for a couple of weeks, and in order to celebrate, Charles bore Becky off for a ten-day holiday in Thailand.

Charles did not enjoy himself in the way he had anticipated. More than once he had been forced to acknowledge that, for a new lover, Becky paid him little attention. The air had been seductive with scent: jasmine, cardamom and hot human life. The hotel was a triumph of discreet service, the food magical. But Charles had spent a lot of time sitting beside a brilliant turquoise pool watching Becky chat up a merchant banker, whom he suspected of being deeply into recreational cocaine, and the blonde he had introduced as his wife.

It niggled him that Becky was blind . . . no, he should not use that word . . . *oblivious* to his aching wish to be alone with her and to his desperate guilt.

Had it been during that first dinner? Or the talks over the coffee? The times when, a Ruth to his Boaz, Becky followed him into the Room and he would glance over his shoulder and know that she was there.

During those lonely moments under the tropical sun, he had found himself searching to locate the point where he had really decided to make changes. He found no illumination, no intersection on the graph between the intent and the action, just an all-consuming hunger and need for Becky.

On the plane back home, Charles played a game. At the airport, he would kiss Becky goodbye and leave her. Waiting in the concourse would be Martha and the girls, flushed and sticky and smelling of babyness. 'So glad you've had a nice break,' his wife would say. 'Now let's go home.'

'I'll see you have enough money,' he had promised, in an agony of guilt that later turned to rage that Martha was not taking the business quietly, which would have allowed him to feel better. Scenting plunder, Martha's lawyers already looked set fair to making sure that he kept his word.

He turned to Becky, who was reading a book on oil politics. She had recently sat and passed the Lloyd's test and was going hell for leather for the ACII. 'Do you love me?'

She looked over the edge of the book and thought of Louis who had been so unreasonably angry when she announced her decision to live with Charles. 'Of course,' she said, her eyebrows drawn together, and went back to the text.

'Really?'

She did not look up but patted his thigh. 'Really, really.'

I'm like a dog, he reflected savagely, who has been flung a bone.

To her credit, Becky (who was far too smart to do so) made no comment whatsoever about Charles's financial arrangements. She had set, she informed Tess, her own agenda. For her part, Tess was not at all sure about this latest development in Becky's life.

'Why Charles?'

'You sound like Louis. Why not Charles? He wants me. He's nice and he's got stacks. And . . .'

'And what?'

'Nothing,' said Becky. 'Nothing at all.'

'Listen,' said Tess, with the authority of the new bride, 'if Charles leaves one wife, he'll leave a second.'

'Perhaps it won't matter by then,' said Becky enigmatically.

Once Charles had declared his intention of living with Becky, she had set about flat-hunting and within days she had pounced on a riverside development in Battersea. The three-bedroom flat was over-priced, although not quite as over-priced as it might have been a year ago. Property, the estate agent informed them, was iffy, a bit volatile. The complex included a gym, a swimming pool, a fresh-fruit juice bar, and its flashy atrium was the size of a small aircraft hangar. Facing north, the flat was not exactly sunny but it had a vista of the river which, on the best days, could be described as dazzling.

At first, Charles declared they could not afford it. Becky, whose business vocabulary was continually being added to – words such as upbeat and combative – spent some time extolling the attractions of the flat as an investment. When he pointed out the estate agent's misgivings, Becky kissed him and brushed her mouth against the exact spot below his ear, a tactic that always sent him wild.

The next day she got on the telephone, and by the evening she had negotiated herself another job and better pay at the rival Coates Brokers (who had woken up from the sleep of centuries to the value of the token female, especially one with Becky's potential profile), handed in her notice at Mawby's and committed herself and Charles to a hefty mortgage.

As he signed the relevant papers, Charles knew he had been outmanoeuvred.

Becky set about filling the flat with Ralph Lauren linen, glass coffee tables, huge sofas and a chandelier from Murano in Venice. There was also talk of a housewarming party.

They moved in two days after returning from Thailand, Becky bidding goodbye to the Pimlico flat that Tess had insisted she share with her and George, and Charles to his depressing *pieds-à-terre*.

'Becky . . .' Charles eased his sunburnt shoulders into a shirt on the morning of their first weekend in the flat. 'We have to cool it a little. Expense-wise. Do a bit of down-trading.'

Becky picked up his hairbrush and handed it to him. He looked at it. 'What's this for?'

'They were over on my bit of the dressing table. You must keep your things in your bit.'

'Good God.'

Becky's loosened hair swung from side to side. 'You don't mind, do you, darling? I do like my things to be just so.'

Charles threw the hairbrush onto the bed where it made a soft indent. 'I suppose I don't.'

She flicked him a look from under lashes that, to his dazzled eyes, had grown even longer during the night. 'How about the party?'

'We can't afford it.'

In a trice, Becky was beside him, twining her arms around his neck and Charles was inhaling her scent, jasmine mixed with tuberose.

'Think credit,' she said. 'Think of the freedom that credit gives. Freedom to give a party.'

'Stop it,' said a helpless, uneasy Charles, never sure whether Becky was joking or not.

'Have now. Pay later.' Becky undid the shirt that Charles had just put on.

He had *nothing* to complain about, Charles concluded, drowning in physical sensations that had long since faded with Martha. Rediscovering the itch of the flesh was magic: the exhaustion after a night's passion, the taste of feminine skin on the tongue, the surprising fullness of a slight breast under his hand and the terrible desire to lose himself in another.

Becky liked the walk from Coates to Lloyd's. It allowed time for reflection. Anyway, she liked the City. The big buildings, and the wind that whipped around them.

Today, however, the sky was plum-coloured with incipient rain and the air tasted nitrous. It seemed colder than it really was. Darkness was gathering in corners, but in buildings glaring with light dealers and pundits strove to hold steady a queasy market.

How would Tess describe it, Becky wondered, and decided that Tess, romantic Tess, would see the market free-fall in relative – and poetic – terms. She would say that when a star falls in a burning arc through space, and asteroids whirl around the solar system, formulae are shaped and put on paper to provide an explanation. We *need* explanations, she always insisted. It doesn't matter that we don't know if they're correct or not. Ah, thought Becky in her turn, but the confidence that seals together a network of shares, bonds and investment has to be explicable. Otherwise, a huff and a puff, and away it goes. Just like that.

Inside the Room there was a cluster of men round the rostrum and the talk was all, still, of the disaster on Piper Alpha.

'Yup. The investors were Texaco, International Thomson,

Union Texas Petroleum, Occidental Petroleum . . .' one broker was saying into his mobile phone. He paused. 'Spread throughout the world, of course, but mostly reinsured here.' He stamped his foot lightly on the word 'reinsured'. 'No. Not good.'

A huff and a puff, thought Becky, then made her way to Matt Barker's box and waited for fifteen minutes in the queue before handing him a prepared slip.

'Talk me through the clause four here,' said Matt, after a second's perusal. 'And twenty-one.'

Becky gritted her teeth for she was fluent in neither, a mistake she would not make again. 'Ask me about clause ten.' She smiled at Matt. 'I'm an expert on that one.'

'Go away,' said Matt, letting her off lightly, which made his junior, who was used to watching scenes of carnage between Matt and brokers, gasp. 'By the way, why did you leave Mawby's?'

Becky took another risk. 'That would cost you a coffee.'

The previous night, Charles had knelt in front of Becky, who sat on the impractical, primrose-coloured sofa. 'Becky, I miss my daughters.' He had bitten his lip. 'I miss them very much. You must help me.'

'I can't,' she had said. 'I wish I could.'

'As soon as we're married we'll have a baby.'

'Sweetie, I have a job to think about.'

'Think about it, won't you? Please, Becky.'

'Done.' Matt cracked a knuckle, and Becky laughed with delight. 'Coffee it is. Then we'll do business.' After she had left, Matt turned to his junior. 'That girl's got character, which I prefer to the prat who number-crunches.'

The junior did not comment.

The Frants regarded each other silently over the breakfast table, neither wishing to broach the subject. In the end, it was Mrs Frant who took the initiative.

'There's the Regency side table, John, and the Lalique vase.

We could sell those.' She paused to gather strength. 'And the silver.'

Colonel Frant's toast had gone cold. 'Yes.'

'We could do bed and breakfast. Lots do.'

'Yes.'

Mrs Frant's irritation again rose to the surface. 'Well, we must do *something*, John.' His quietude bothered her. 'Unless you're not telling me everything.'

Colonel Frant did not feel well and had not for some time. The worry was one thing, the effort at concealment was another, for he had confided in his wife neither the whole extent of his debt nor what he was planning to do.

'What went wrong, John?'

His shoulders lifted briefly then sagged. 'I've found out a bit more about it all. It seems that Nigel was linked in with an agency that was not so keen on the old kind of syndicate. Like the marine ones, for example. The managing agency he was pally with specialized in reinsurance. They thought it was copper-bottomed. Anyway, they probably paid him a lot in introduction fees.'

'Is it too late?'

There was a silence.

'Look, I'm going up to London to meet someone who might be able to help.'

Mrs Frant looked out of the kitchen window to the paddock. 'It seems a long autumn,' she said. 'And I expect it will be a long winter. Christmas will not be the same this year.'

Colonel Frant looked over towards the dog basket. 'I think . . . I think we should have Sage put down.'

His wife's coffee cup crashed back onto the saucer. '*No*, John. Not that.' She dropped her head into her hands. 'Surely not that. Give him away. Don't kill him.'

'I couldn't bear anyone else to have him,' said her husband. 'I just couldn't bear it.'

*

When Louis woke, which he did in a blink, he always sneezed, and Jilly groaned.

'I can't understand why you do that.' Smelling of sleep and yesterday's bath essence, she rolled over.

'I know why you sneeze,' Becky had teased him. 'You sneeze because you don't want to wake up. Your subconscious doesn't want to take second place.'

'So?' he had replied.

'So,' asked Becky, 'what is it, Louis, that your subconscious can't bear to let go?'

It was quiet in the bedroom, silent with carefully assembled luxury: deep-pile carpet, interlined curtains, *en suite* bathroom. Louis lay still.

He thought of grey stone walls, dotted with invasive ferns. The suck-suck of the river winding through the 'swold village where he had grown up. Of his boyish self ured in the church – aching knees and incomprehension. He thought, too, of the frame imposed on his mind by a faith that prided itself on its grip. Stubborn and adhesive, it had stayed with Louis. An old companion. An unwanted companion, at times a clamorous companion, but as much part of him as his blood.

He looked at the clock on the bedside table and braced himself. Jilly slid her legs out of bed and inspected them carefully. He heard her give a tsk before reaching for her dressing gown.

'Up, Louis,' she said.

Over breakfast she became business-like and asked if he had any plans for the weekend.

'Are either of the boys coming?'

'No. Are you going to mass?'

'Probably.'

Jilly opened a letter. 'Why do you keep going?'

'Why do you go to church?'

'To be part of the village, of course.' The subject dealt with, Jilly now cleared her mind of inessentials. 'Would you object if I bought some furniture for the conservatory?'

'Not at all.'

Louis finished his breakfast and went to catch the train. Because he was running late, he was forced to park the number two car (Jilly used the Jaguar) at the furthest end of the car park.

The breeze blew specks of wood ash from a fire on the embankment into Louis's eyes, which made them water and he did not recognize John Frant until he had virtually bumped into him. Sometimes, in a rare moment of empathy, it is possible to penetrate through the surface of skin and bone to a truth undercutting the exterior. Underneath John Frant's neat, dapper exterior – check shirt, Army greatcoat – Louis sensed inner sickness and fear.

'How are Angela and Tess?' he asked.

'Fine. Thank you. And Jilly?'

'Fine also.'

The moment when Louis could have acted, said something, offered help, came and went. Nothing too substantial, for that was not possible, but a gesture of support *was*, even morally imperative. Yet what was Louis to say? John Frant had been placed on syndicates that were now in deep trouble, of which two remained open for 1985. Piper Alpha was going to make matters worse.

One of the defining factors of a morality is its absoluteness, to which one should cling in the teeth of the wildest gales, the hottest holocaust.

The moment came and went, and both men retreated into their newspapers.

Later, installed in his box, Louis knew he was guilty and was diminished by the knowledge.

Oh God of the grey stone church walls, I am guilty of silence.

The Mafia have the tradition of *omerta*. We are all silent about the inevitability of death otherwise it overwhelms us. But John Frant had been owed, at the very least, a sentence. A word.

I am guilty of not helping.

*

Fortunately, the word was with Aunt Jean, who opened her mouth and sang louder than normal in the Chapel of the Pentecost in Streatham. She found her singing satisfactory (and presumably God did, too), even if it was a little hard on the big black lady sitting next to her who shifted further down the bench. Despite her air of fragility, Aunt Jean was capable of a great noise: something to do with air resonating, perhaps, in an entirely fat-free body.

A woman, or so she liked to think, in whom pride and desire had been whittled to a minimum, thus making her powerful indeed, Aunt Jean was strong in her faith. This was fortunate for her heart, whose daily heavings for oxygen and blood caused it to knock against the thin shell of her ribcage, was failing.

'You want to be free for God,' Aunt Jean whispered to it as it banged about in her chest. 'Be patient. You'll be there soon.'

Her neighbour decided to issue a challenge, opened her mouth, let forth and the chapel was filled with ebullient sound. After all, even if inflation was running at 6.4 per cent, Christmas was coming.

Back home in Paradise Flats, Aunt Jean filled a kettle and sat down with a thump in the armchair. Flashing shapes and whirling lights danced across her vision. The kettle was boiling, but she was distinctly disinclined to get up. Pity that Becky wasn't there any longer.

Becky. Aunt Jean placed a weary, shaky hand on the arm of the chair. For as much as I have sown, so will I reap. I did not love her. I never loved her.

When she was next aware, it was to experience the sensation of a straitjacket. Both arms were pulled tight and needles had been drilled into them. There was an unfamiliar hiss of machinery. On turning her head, a fold of green curtain with an unfamiliar pattern presented itself. Someone spoke.

'She's conscious.'

'Of course I am,' she said crossly, and discovered that her throat had turned into builder's sandpaper.

'Aunt Jean?'

Becky swam across the horizon, a blow-dried, lip-glossed Becky who looked as though she should be somewhere else.

Somewhere else – a major client meeting intended to bring in major business, the first she had attended for Coates – was precisely where Becky should have been. 'Your aunt,' the exhausted-sounding registrar had reported on the phone, 'has only a slim chance. She was discovered late last night by a neighbour who did not know where to find you.'

'But,' said Becky, 'I have a meeting.'

'Don't we all?' replied the registrar. 'Don't we all?'

Becky had dressed, thinking perhaps she could juggle locations. Pop into a deathbed scene then pop into a meeting. Charles seemed appalled when she outlined her strategy.

'It doesn't matter about the damn meeting.'

Becky frowned. 'It does to me.' The past was never safe, and she had ducked and woven, hoping to find a place of safety and of affection. And never had. 'Aunt Jean never loved me,' she said.

'That doesn't matter,' said a shocked Charles.

Whatever, her aunt lingered long enough to scupper any chances of Becky attending the meeting, or the one the following day where the deal was negotiated. Instead of drinking champagne, she forced down cups of hospital coffee.

Towards the end, Aunt Jean opened her eyes and smiled happily. 'I'm very near,' she said, meaning to God.

Not unnaturally, Becky misunderstood. 'No, you're not,' she said sharply. 'The hospital's at the other end of London and I'm thinking of moving you.'

'Don't bother.' Aunt Jean closed her eyes. Her thin, transparent hand crept with infinite effort over the bedclothes towards her niece. Becky watched it knowing that Aunt Jean was asking her forgiveness.

A hot, choking feeling gathered in her chest. To pick up that hand or not? To make peace, to acknowledge forgiveness.

With an uncharacteristically rapid and graceless movement, Becky got up from her chair and left the room.

Aunt Jean's eyes remained closed, the mask lying over her features gradually congealing. Half an hour later, she whispered, as if surprised, 'It's come,' and died, leaving the hiss of machinery to fill the denuded room.

Chapter Eleven

'Becky wanted a quiet funeral but, apparently, her aunt left instructions for a rousing, happy-clappy send-off. Her friends at the chapel are organizing it. Becky's terrified at what they might come up with.'

'Really?' George was lounging, naked, in bed and not listening. He was concentrating on a memory that bothered him a lot and had changed his thinking. It was of Rainey O'Shaughan, her grief and the shooting in Belfast that had turned her modest dwelling into a slaughterhouse, and her husband and two sons into butcher's meat.

When George and his men had raced to the scene, Rainey had let herself out into the back garden and there, on her knees by the small patch in which she cultivated flowers in Republican colours, she said, 'At least my men died in front of me who loved them. Not in front of strangers.' She added, 'They won't be on the run any more. They were homesick in the south, you know. My boys.'

Tess stepped into the skirt of a black suit and struggled with the waistband. Then she brushed out her tangled fair hair.

The bedroom in the Pimlico flat was not a scene of order. Added to Tess's natural chaos there was an additional layer of wedding presents not yet stowed, some still in the packaging in which they had arrived. It was the kind of jumble of a person who had most things. Or, perhaps, the kind of jumble to remind someone that they were newly married.

She added a black velvet hairband to the ensemble. 'How do I look?'

'Very Army wife.'

'Very promising banker, you mean.'

There was a tiny, but significant, chilling of the air. The lowering of temperature between two people who are not understanding one another very well.

Oh, God, thought Tess. Not again.

George flung back the bedclothes and got up. Tess sat down at the stool in front of the tiny mirror allotted for her dressing table and made up her face with quick slashes and dabs. She had to say something to break the silence that had descended.

'Have you heard from Iain and Flora? Are they well?'

'They're fine. They've asked us to go and stay for a weekend.'

'How lovely,' said Tess, aghast at how uninterested she sounded. 'Do let's.' She picked up her handbag and threw her brush and lipstick into it. 'I've got to go and support Becky.'

Will we ever beat it? George asked himself, as he got dressed. Or will it take the end of the world to scrub the martyr complex out of the Republican heart?

Of Tess he did not think at all.

Among the congregation, composed of friends from the Mission, bingo cronies and neighbours, was Aunt Jean's solicitor. He was a bright-eyed, bobbing young man with a taste for thick-soled rubber shoes and evidently smitten with Becky. As Tess slid into a pew, Becky pointed him out and hissed, 'He's just told me that Aunt Jean left virtually nothing except two hundred pounds to my mother.'

'Your mother! I thought she was dead.'

'She *is*. To me.'

'Jesus loves me,' sang the congregation, at the urging of the minister, and swayed and swooped to the music in their pews.

The women sported an amazing array of hats. *Loves me . . . loves me . . .*

Standing beside Becky, Charles stuck his head forward in the manner of the embarrassed English male. Becky allowed her eyes to wander around the large, bare room with fake green marble set into the floor and plastic flowers.

'Jesus loves me,' she sang and it was then that the implications of a remark made by Charles in the car struck her. What Charles, stupidly, had let slip was: Mawby's had not yet signed with FEROC because it was insisting on more detailed figures.

Becky reckoned that, if she was clever, she could work on a few figures in the loo with her pocket calculator and make the call to Coates during the funeral tea. Then she thought better of that. Once released, information is hard to control and she wanted to manage this deal.

The funeral and the tea afterwards were as Becky had feared. There was much hugging, sistering and brothering and curiously dignified sorrow directed as much to the smart outsider that Becky had become as to the dead woman.

You fools, she wanted to tell them. I was never an insider. That was the trouble.

Afterwards, Becky insisted on taking Charles out to an expensive restaurant, as a reward for being so good and understanding and, after he had drunk a bottle of white burgundy, she grilled him gently about the FEROC deal.

Divine Nights, alias Art and Hal, the party planners, had short dyed white-blond hair and leather aprons. They also possessed visions of grandeur and excitement whose scope was not necessarily limited by space or finance unless they were dealt with firmly. But they knew what was what. They definitely did. Buck's Fizz was out. So was *nouvelle cuisine*.

'The things you learn,' said Becky.

'Can't beat a gooey roulade,' said Art, on the night of Becky and Charles's party, bearing one in each hand towards the draped table in the drawing room.

'Quail's eggs.' Hal was right behind Art, holding a plate of beautifully speckled ones in their shells arranged around a pile of peeled ones and a saucer of brown and white salt. 'And lots of *Boy's Own* puddings.'

His tone held a hint of acid for the boys had wished to art-direct the party as either a Japanese forest or a Winter Wonderland. Charles had put his foot down and they had had to be satisfied with eau de framboise champagne and spraying the room with scent and artificial cigar 'for that rich and opulent feeling, darling'.

'Where did you pick them up?' asked Tess, sprucing up her hair in front of Becky's bedroom mirror.

In the bathroom – French tiles, his and hers basins – Becky was applying make-up.

'Oh, the grapevine, you know. Amelia next door recommended them.' She drew a wisp of violet under her lids. 'It's a good thing Aunt Jean didn't pop off two weeks later than she did otherwise it would have interfered with the party.' Becky now lowered her lids and applied mascara.

'Do you miss her?'

'Not really. I don't have anyone to worry about now.'

Tess regarded her neatened hair in the mirror. 'There is Charles,' she said drily.

'He doesn't count. Not in that way, I mean.'

Tess shifted on the stool, perturbed and not a little unhappy. 'Something smells wonderful.'

'Joy.' Becky sprayed a mist of it around her, and felt the pinpricks of moisture descend onto her skin.

'I could do with some joy, Becky.' Tess wanted Becky to stop preening, to sit down beside her, to take her hands and say: Tell me. Let me help.

Of course George loves you.

Becky recognized the plea. 'Darling,' she said. 'Not now.'

They entered the sitting room whose curtains had been swept back to reflect the river, and which had tiny white fairy lights scattered throughout and over a huge orange tree in a pot. Becky turned to Tess. 'I rely on you,' she said. 'You know the worst of me.'

Jangled and unsure, in love with love and with George, yet sick at heart with its roller-coaster rides and also prone to the feminine propensity to self-sacrifice, Tess replied, 'Of course. Rely on me.'

Composing a guest list has points in common with acquiring a new lover. Pored over, admired, contemplated at night, relegated to the wastepaperbasket the following morning, it can be milked for drama. Baffled by its theatre, Charles had enquired of Becky if their party was meant to be an endurance test. By that time, Becky had netted two lords, whose aristocratic blood had been thoroughly diluted, an MP, involved in a cash scandal and, thus, delighted to be invited anywhere, and an actress, recently sacked from a West End role for reasons not specified.

Yet ... Charles admitted to himself ... Becky had a gift for this sort of thing, and it did not matter that he felt a stranger in his own sitting room and that the guests were quite different from those he would have invited to the house in Clapham.

Dressed in Armani, the bill for which ticked on Charles's credit card, Becky moved gracefully from one group to another, dispensing Divine Nights' canapés and caviar.

'I shall think of you, sitting on the balcony on summer evenings,' Louis murmured into Becky's ear.

She smiled up at him. 'Do I detect a wistful note?'

Charles was dispensing drinks, a little eagerly perhaps. 'Yes,' he replied, to an enquiry, 'Becky and I will be getting married when the divorce comes through.'

'I'm on my third,' stated his interlocutor. 'Imagine.'

'You look tired, Nigel.' Becky paused on her way back from the kitchen. 'You need to get out and play a bit.'

Nigel's hand found its way to his midriff, which he prodded. 'A touch of gallstone trouble,' he said.

'How's it doing?' Hal, marooned in the kitchen, asked a cruising Art.

'Riff-raff,' replied Art, with dignity. 'Only riff-raff.'

When Lily let herself into the flat through the front door, which had been propped open, the party was well into its stride. Short, not above five foot four, and fat, balanced on a pair of white leather high heels, she was wearing an expensive dress whose colours could only be termed recklessly bold, and a raft of thick gold bracelets which jangled on her arm. She was out of breath from the exertion of negotiating the lift.

She stood in the doorway surveying the scene, a flamboyantly coloured insect, and since it was not what she had quite expected, her shoulders sagged for a second or two.

She pushed her way into the sitting room. Nigel was closest to the door.

'Do you know what?' he was saying. 'Some regulatory prat has decreed that members' agents should go on courses to bone up on the law of agency—' Noticing the apparition, he broke off. 'You must be lost,' he said.

She bristled at the implication. 'Rebecca,' she said, in a tone that was an enlivening combination of South London larded with Manchester, 'I'm looking for Rebecca Vitali.'

'Are you sure?' asked Nigel.

'Just point her out, will you, sonny?'

'There . . .' Nigel's finger traced Becky's progress.

Lily stared hard, features creased into little sausages of fat.

'Oh,' she said, and seemed disappointed. 'Not bad. But looks a bit of a tricksy mare.'

Nigel was not sure that he had heard correctly. 'Would you like me to call you a taxi or something?' he asked. Lily favoured him with a look and he amended his words. 'Or, rather, would you like a drink?'

'First bit of good sense I've heard from you.'

Nigel grabbed a glass from an extremely blond, extremely slender young man with a tray and looked, for a moment, into his eyes. Then he refocused on Lily. 'Could I ask who you are?'

Lily accepted the drink. 'Who are *you*?' She was not to know that Nigel often considered that question and the answers gave him some unease. Lily addressed the slender tray-bearer. 'I've left a suitcase with the porter downstairs. Could you get it? On second thoughts, you don't look strong enough.' She turned to Nigel. 'Perhaps you could.'

The tray-bearer tittered.

Lily took a swig of champagne and, holding the glass to her bosom, barrelled her way through the pin-striped suits and minimally dressed women towards Becky.

'Rebecca,' she said, in her loud and unmistakably alien voice. 'Is that Rebecca?'

Glass in one hand, a plate of caviar on pumpernickel in the other, Becky was radiant with the success of her evening and innocent of what was about to unfold. She swivelled towards Lily. She was, she had told herself many times, a free spirit now, unimpeded by superstition, religion or ties and she watched, puzzled, as Lily teetered towards her.

'Rebecca?'

'Yes.'

'I'm Lily.'

'Yes ...' Becky's down inflection held, just, a note of apprehension.

'I'm your mother.'

The reply was instantaneous. 'I don't have a mother.'

The insect was seen to wince. 'True, but that which is lost shall be found.'

Becky swivelled. 'Oh,' she said. 'Oh.' The syllable cracked and splintered with her shock. As Louis stepped forward to help, Charles remained frozen to the grey Wilton, and Becky whispered, 'That's just the sort of thing Aunt Jean would say.'

'How extraordinary, how bizarre ...' The girl to whom Louis had been talking was a professional mistress, and her over-made-up eyes were bright with malice.

Louis said nothing but turned, once, to look at Becky and did not look at her again.

Outside the flat, the river continued to wash its dirty water over the mud-flats, the last aircraft of the night stacked around Heathrow and the tramps were being let into the doss-houses in Vauxhall.

Still bustling, Art lit a Manova-scented candle, which he always reserved for the end of an evening. A light, flowered scent stole through the gathering.

'Darling,' whispered a riveted Nigel in Becky's ear, slipping his hand under her elbow, 'do you want me to get rid of her?'

At the other end of the room, Tess tried to move through the crush but George put out an arm and restrained her. 'Leave it alone,' he said. 'It's not your business.'

'But it is,' she hissed at him. 'Becky *is* my business.'

'No,' said her husband. 'I'm your business.'

Shuddering inwardly for, like Tess, he hated scenes, Charles knew it was incumbent upon him to direct proceedings. He held out his hand, his good-natured features wreathed in a polite and welcoming smile. 'How do you do?'

Louis beckoned to Art and exchanged the professional mistress's empty glass for a full one. Then he proceeded to tell a story that made her shriek with laughter. At a stroke, the scene reanimated and attention was switched away from the two women.

Without a doubt, Lily's entrance had made Becky's party in a manner Becky had not calculated.

Fifteen or so minutes later, Louis shepherded a group towards the door. 'Thank you so much,' he said to Charles, but did not hold out his hand. Neither did Charles hold out his.

When Louis kissed Becky, their faces brushed together for a second longer than was necessary. She looked at him and, once again, he told her silently that he understood.

Then he was gone.

'So delightful,' said a departing guest. 'How exciting.'

'Yes, wasn't it fun?'

The room was being drained of noise and warmth, the overflow washing down the stairs and into the street.

Tess retreated into the kitchen and put on the kettle. George poked his head in. 'Come on. We're going home.'

'Not quite yet. I must help.'

George watched her bustle around with the tea-pot. 'Right,' he said. 'I'll take a taxi.' And he tossed her the car keys.

Tess whirled round. 'Please wait.' But George had gone.

When the last guest had departed, Tess brought in a tray of tea to find Becky sitting at one end of the smart sofa with hands folded in her lap and Lily at the other, hers likewise, looking as if she was in training to be royal.

'Do you plan to go to sea in this thing?' Lily was asking, and her bracelets clinked as she moved.

Becky ignored her. She was exploring the sensations that accompanied profound surprise. First nothing much. Then a feeling that her skin had been lifted from the flesh underneath by an electric shock.

I don't want a mother.

Outrageously dressed, slashed with lipstick, with small fat feet, Lily was an incarnation of a future that Becky had not dreamt of.

Lily ignored Tess's tea and nursed yet another glass of

champagne. 'I'm not sure,' she said, 'that you're quite what I had in mind. But the lawyers had contacted me so I thought I ought to have a look.'

With a visible effort that made Tess ache for her, Becky pulled herself together. 'What have you been doing all these years?'

A sliver of tongue appeared between Lily's scarlet lips. 'I've made money and don't be asking me how.' She shot a look at Becky. 'That'll interest you, won't it?'

'Yes, it does actually.' Becky noted this strange woman's liver-spotted hands and papery skin, an older version of hers.

'What a noisy, dirty, hard world it is.' Lily looked pointedly around the luxurious room. 'Motherhood's a responsibility, you know.'

Quick as a flash, her daughter suppressed, as she always had, memories of anguish and loss that writhed through her past. She said, 'How would you know?'

'Here,' said Tess. 'Drink this.'

Becky sipped it gratefully and looked up at Charles. 'It would seem,' she reflected, 'that you won't be getting out of a second mother-in-law, after all.'

Charles was consumed by the need for a whisky, made for the drinks tray and poured himself a large one. On cue, Hal and Art emerged from the kitchen and began to rip down the fairy lights. Little eddies of plaster dust drifted to the floor, which they brushed away frantically. When they had finished they stowed the lights in a bag that had 'Lunch is for Wimps' stamped on it.

'We're off,' they chorused.

'Cheerio,' added Art.

'Do you bear me a grudge?' Lily was inspecting the plate on the kitchen table at breakfast the following morning. She shot Becky a naughty look. 'What are these?'

Becky returned the look fairly and squarely. 'You've seen a croissant before.'

'True.' Lily helped herself to a large one. 'We're quite civilized up north.' She took a bite. '*Do* you?'

'Bear you a grudge? Not really.' Which was not the sentiment she had expressed to Charles in the privacy of the bedroom.

You did not want me. You left me.

In daylight, it was possible to see that Lily's eyes and brows had once been as remarkable as Becky's but the eyebrows had surrendered to harsh black eye pencil. 'And Jean,' she was asking. 'What did you make of her?'

'She did her best.' At this point, Charles dragged himself into the kitchen in his dressing gown and Becky shoved a cup of tea towards him. 'But she didn't like me much.'

Lily assessed the fashionable, if not entirely functional, kitchen: the French oven, the *batterie de cuisine*, the twin sink. 'You haven't done too badly out of it. And it doesn't do to be liked. It softens you up.'

'What do you want from me?'

Lily's bracelets almost played a tune as she helped herself to another croissant.

'Well?' said Becky.

'I'm getting old,' said Lily unnecessarily. 'I thought I might see if I could live with you. The clever solicitor who traced me gave me your address.'

For once, Becky's hair was loose and flowing around her face and she ran her fingers through it thoughtfully. The effect was of extreme, untried youth. 'Why?'

'I was curious.'

'You must have been curious before this.'

'I need looking after.'

'You didn't,' Becky found herself saying, 'look after me.'

Painted in frosted pink, Lily's nails tapped against her plate as her fingers scuttled between pieces of croissant. 'Is it conducted like that?' She sounded surprised. 'If you do this, I do that.'

'In general, yes.'

Courtesy of the eye pencil, Lily's raised eyebrows seemed much fiercer than her daughter's. 'You don't know anything, my girl. And you probably did better without me.'

'It killed Aunt Jean.'

'Jean spent her life searching for martyrdom,' said her surviving sister. 'I gave it to her.'

'Yes.' Becky felt a rare tug of loyalty to her aunt. 'You certainly did that.'

At this point, Charles woke up. 'How do we know you're not a fraud? I think we'll need some proof. Some assurance that you are who you say you are.'

'I haven't any,' said Lily. 'You have to take me on trust.'

'Trust!'

Then Becky succeeded in truly astounding him. 'Oh, I wouldn't worry, Charles. I don't think there's any doubt at all that this is my mother.'

Lily looked from one to the other and saw the differences between them. 'I could tell she was difficult from the moment I saw her,' she informed Charles. 'Too tricksy by half but smart.'

Becky stirred as if from a dream. 'Takes one to know one.'

'Why aren't you more surprised?' Charles asked Becky later. 'That's what surprises *me*. This woman bursts in on us out of the blue.'

'She's been waiting to happen,' said Becky. 'I just knew it.'

Chapter Twelve

Tess came home from the party to an empty flat, which did not surprise her. She removed the little Lycra dress, which was really too tight but showed off her long legs, and stowed it on a padded coat-hanger. After that, she brushed and cleansed and, gradually, her face lost its glittery public look and emerged from the flannel dimmed into weariness and disappointment.

'Prince Charming has turned into a frog,' she wrote in the diary, 'the Princess into an overweight nag, the hearth is piled with ashes and Cinderella's contract looks a bit dodgy. I did not realize that conflict is the basis of marriage, not harmony.'

She lay in bed, waiting for sleep, and planned the diet that she was *definitely* beginning in the morning.

Tess phoned Becky early the next day. 'Do you need any help and how's your mother?'

While she waited for Becky's reply, she cradled the telephone with one shoulder and practised her nose exercises in the mirror. Unlike other extremities, your nose, she had been told, continues to grow throughout life, a reliable indicator of age. If length of nose tallied the years – Tess squinted at hers – then she was a hundred.

In the bedroom, George was sleeping the sleep of the drunken and guilty.

'Lily's fine,' said Becky, 'and I've got a firm to come in and do the cleaning.'

'Where does she live?'

'Outside Manchester. She was married once but left him a couple of months later.'

Tess recollected the terrible but expensive dress and gold jewellery. 'She looks reasonably well off.'

'Don't ask me where she got that.'

'Tell.'

'She informed us that she's been quite a party-giver too, in her time.' Becky sounded genuinely admiring. 'I reckon she's been a madam, and must have survived the pimps and the fuzz. Anyway, she also tells me she's made quite a lot of money.'

Tess's professional instincts rose to the challenge. 'I hope she's not letting it sit around. Tell her if she wants any advice . . .'

'I will,' said Becky, 'especially if I benefit.'

During the unpredicted and strange encounter between Becky and her mother, Tess imagined that Becky had died a thousand deaths, as she would have done, and she quivered with loyal anger. One minute, Becky was living her life, discreet and, but for Charles, solo. The next she was being presented with a woman in a dreadful frock.

'It was cruel to turn up just like that.'

'Oh, I don't know,' said Becky, carelessly. 'No time is a good time.'

Tess concluded that Becky was tougher than she had given her credit for. Either that or she was pleased. 'How's Charles taking it?'

'Charles?' Becky seemed genuinely startled at the question. 'He's all right.'

'Be kind to him, Bec. He's vulnerable, you know.'

'Tess, you've got to stop saving the world. Charles is a big boy now.'

'And Louis?'

'I haven't a clue.'

Tess heard Becky's intake of breath and probed further. 'How do *you* feel?'

'I feel fine,' said Becky, and followed it with a silence that alerted Tess to the probability that this, despite Becky's insouciance, was a delicate area. 'Oh, Tess,' Becky sounded choked, 'I was doing fine without her.'

Tess took a deep breath while she searched for something to say. Courtesy of Freud, she decided to interpret events in terms of the psychological rather than the obvious. 'You might have been searching for her, Becky.' She added knowledgeably, 'Many do.'

'Well, I wasn't.'

Tess tried another tack. 'Didn't you say she's going back up north?'

'I don't think she likes me,' said Becky.

'So? She didn't like you when you were born. You can cope.'

When Tess put down the phone, George had surfaced. There was a silence as they faced each other and Tess made nervous remarks to the effect that Becky's father must have been very tall.

George scratched his head and Tess softened at the spectacle of his handsomeness and assurance, trophies that, as a wife, she wore with pride. 'Or,' he said, 'some marauding Viking got in on the ancestry.'

That was good: he was talking to Tess normally and reasonably. Sometimes their conversations were like walking on bits of glass. Then, inadequate and fearful, Tess darted hither and thither to avoid the slice into her flesh. Desperate love was all very well for Shakespeare and other writers, but in real life it paralysed. Imperceptibly, she was fumbling towards the idea that, perhaps, love and marriage were not a good combination either. Or, at least, the two put together constituted the highest risk.

In the tiny galley kitchen, she ran hot water for the washing up. Question: Is quivering passion the best or worst basis for negotiation?

'Any chance of some breakfast?' George had put up his feet on the sofa and was reading the paper.

'Sure.'

Fool, Tess told herself, needing to realign the balance of power. She examined the prone figure of her husband. One day, I'll earn more than you, she thought. And she entertained a delightful playlet of George marooned behind a pile of washing up while she floated out of the door clutching a Vuitton briefcase. She was changing. These days there was less of an urge to search for meanings. To find God. Or to find the energy and grace she had once been so anxious to locate. From those deductions, the syllogism looked a little bleak for, it appeared, neither love nor modern life had either room or time for God.

London water is hard and unyielding and Tess had allowed her hands to get into a bad state. 'It is never too late to take steps,' *Vogue* instructed. Tess searched among the muddle of dusters and polish for rubber gloves, failed to locate them and gave up. As she fried bacon and eggs for George, she tried to concentrate an analysing the Zen of investment but every nerve was straining to see what George was doing.

Had he looked at her as she prepared his breakfast? A couple of times? Once? Not at all?

'Here.' She placed a tray in front of her lounging husband and looked at him with a combination of passion and need which, if she but knew it, always made George irritable.

She dried up the knives and put them away in the drawer and then retrieved them for she had put them in the wrong way round.

'Tess ...' George cut into his wife's ruminations. He had draped himself over the doorpost, loose-limbed but curiously watchful. 'Listen, Tessy, I'm being sent on a course, training and things, and then it's Northern Ireland again. You won't be coming.'

The skin on her fingers had gone prune-like and she picked at a cuticle. 'Oh, no pay, pack and follow?'

''Fraid not. This is a sort of special assignment.'

'Can you say what?'

'Not really.'

'Oh. Oh, well, then.'

'You wouldn't have wanted to leave your job, Tess. Be honest.'

'How dangerous will it be?'

George straightened up and Rainey O'Shaughan's wild weeping sounded in his ears. He was being seconded to the 14th Intelligence Unit, which was run by the Army, as opposed to the secret services, devoted to intelligence gathering and surveillance. Long-term surveillance. 'Well, Tessy. It is Northern Ireland. And the players are clever. Worse, fanatics.'

He was as serious as Tess had ever seen him and, suddenly, the intimacy that she so craved was there between them, and she ached with a rush of love. Then George spoilt it.

'You have my permission to take old boyfriends out to dinner.'

She pushed past him with more violence than she had intended, sat down in the sitting room and lit up. The absence in her infant marriage of an element, mysterious, glowing and perhaps as dangerous as the radium that Marie Curie had searched for over the years through the piles of pitchblende, was the one that Tess also sought. It hurt and offended her that he should make such a suggestion.

Marriage did not make for wholeness, that was for sure.

George opened the post and glanced at a letter. 'Good Lord,' he said, 'did you know about this?'

Tess stubbed out the cigarette and read the letter, which was from her father. 'That's a bore, him wanting us to sell the flat.'

'When?'

'In the spring.'

'Why do you think he wants to do that?' George looked a little uneasy. 'Well, I suppose there's Army quarters. But . . .' He did not add that, in marrying Tess, he had hoped never to inhabit them.

'I'll talk to Dad. He'll sort something out.'

As the words left her lips, it occurred to Tess that *they* should sort something out. Together. George should be offering.

He bent over Tess, ignored the generosity and tenderness in her expression and saw only her misery and bewilderment. Tipping up her chin with a finger, he said, 'You mustn't get so het up. You're a big girl now.'

Sensibly, they gazed into each other's eyes and the chemistry of desire was activated. George made the first move. 'Four months is not a long time,' he murmured, as he kissed her. 'Now will you shut up?'

Since what followed possesses a remarkable facility for blotting out the short term, all was well and George made up for his differences with a fine, sweaty show of lust.

The following day, he rang Tess at the office and announced that the two of them, plus the MacKenzies, were going to Berlin for a quickie pre-Christmas weekend, where they were borrowing an Army quarter.

'Nice?' He seemed to want her approval, and Tess felt small and mean that the prospect of two days in a military camp in Berlin, rather than a hotel in the West Indies, did not excite her.

'Nice,' she echoed. 'But why?'

'It's a cheap weekend and I thought you and I could have some time sightseeing or something together.'

'Are you going to say anything to me at all?' George asked on the plane over. He was on his second mini-bottle of wine.

'Sorry.'

The plane cut through the air corridor, and circled over the divided city, doubly divided now that it was evening by glowing electric light shining wastefully on the capitalist side, by dark on the Communist.

Tess considered the geographical division below. Single, you carried your own burdens of disappointment and your expectations were mercifully private. Being married, it seemed, had the effect of taking a tin opener to the lid kept on them. That was the point of it. Wasn't it?

'How long have you known Iain?'

'Ages.'

Their friendship was puzzling, inexplicable, really. George so swaggering, Iain so contained and watchful. 'He's a good sort,' she said carefully.

George tapped the window of the aircraft to indicate Berlin below. 'I love Iain,' he said. 'He's my anchor. My lifebelt.'

'Oh,' said Tess, and swallowed painfully.

Iain met them at Tiegal and whisked them off in a borrowed Mercedes. 'I know the city well,' he said. 'We were posted here four or five years ago. Flora's making some supper. She's looking forward to seeing you.'

If Flora was pleased to see them she managed to hide it, and Tess got the impression that she would have preferred the weekend alone with her husband. Inclined to mousiness, emphasized by a brown skirt and cream blouse, she led them round the house, exclaiming, in her soft, reedless voice, at the efficiency with which it had been built.

'See?' she said, leading them to the basement. 'A dedicated washing and drying room. Only the Germans would be so clever and so organized.'

Tess gazed at this palace of housewifery and felt, unaccountably, depressed.

In the morning, the men disappeared for a couple of hours. Tess looked at Flora and her heart sank. Her vision of feasting on a froth of white and gold rococo palaces retreated. Flora suggested coffee and then a nice walk in the woods.

'It's quite tricky out here,' she said, giving Tess her coffee and pouring hot water for herself. 'The wives get restless and homesick, especially if hubby is away. There're drug problems, beatings-up, and when I was here a quartet of wives set themselves up as tarts and earned quite a lot of money.'

'Did the husbands know?'

'No, thank goodness. They'd have killed the women.'

Tess had an idea that she was being rehearsed and briefed.

'Mess nights . . .' Flora was saying, with the air of someone who had been born to shoulder burdens. 'Playgroups, lunches for the wives . . . You've got all this coming.'

'Have I?' Tess was startled. 'I suppose I have. But, of course, I have my job.'

'But you'll give that up?'

'No, I don't think so.'

If disapproval could be measured in colour, Flora's expression would have been black. 'So the Army can't count on you.'

'Not in that way.'

'Goodness me,' said Flora, in a soft voice. 'How things are changing. Of course in the past . . .'

What past? A great deal of past. Consider the network, the huge web spun by women's work stretching across continents. Soothing, caring, child-rearing, underpinning welfare states with voluntary work, being unselfish and receptive and loving. Entirely unpaid.

Flora recollected herself. 'You're in investment.' The subject brought a faint colour to her cheeks. 'Terribly grand.' She leant forward. 'Do you have any tips? The Army pay, you know . . . and there's talk of cuts, which we're *terribly* worried about. Everything is so unpredictable and depressing, don't you think? I was even thinking of buying one of those Amstrad thingies and having a go at a children's book.'

Tess did a good job of looking interested.

Flora's breathy little punctuations continued. 'I was terribly against buying shares in British Gas and those sort of utilities. I didn't agree with selling off the family silver.' She sipped her hot water. 'On the other hand, it's silly to ignore an opportunity.'

'Quite,' said Tess.

On a diet of disapproval Flora's pallor improved steadily during the day, and she confided privately to Iain that she rather thought Tess would have to learn a thing or two. Iain annoyed her greatly by replying that, these days, women were entitled to their own lives. This had the effect, Flora concluded, of downgrading her own sacrifice of a career as a successful hospital administrator. In a very soft voice indeed, Flora asked him just where he thought he would be if she had pursued her life rather than his.

If she had reservations about Tess, Flora would have hated Becky. Sometimes Tess disapproved of Becky, but only in relation to Louis. A newish bride struggling with the intricacies and silences of living together, Tess felt that Becky's liaison was not supporting the institution.

'How do you know I'm not propping it up?' was Becky's invariable response.

During the Berlin weekend Tess thought about Becky in little flashes, much as the stone in the stream is sometimes visible, sometimes not.

Becky would not have cared for Berlin. Too decayed. Too much ancient history and suffering. When the party set out for some serious sightseeing, Flora confided to Tess that when she had been here, among the empty spaces and pocked buildings, she had found herself longing for the ordinariness and reassurance of a congested M4, of marigolds and polythene-covered Cheddar.

Tess longed to ask George what Iain had seen in Flora but thought better of it. If women had a loyalty to each other, so did men. George remained silent on the subject of his best friend's wife, which she was beginning to see held its own significance.

On the Saturday night, they went to the opera in the eastern sector. Passports held up to the window of the coach, the security camera winking, they drove through the checkpoint through a cityscape of cold winds and concrete tower blocks to the old opera house.

Fresh, fit-looking and smiling, Iain had touched Tess's elbow and pointed out the more exquisite features. Suddenly, Tess scented danger. Or, rather, disturbance.

The opera was *Cosí fan tutte*. Mozart had also scented danger and skirted around it with delicacy and tease, to which the cast responded with passion.

'I was warned once by a mad English professor that disguises are more dangerous for those who put them on,' Tess remarked to Iain, in the interval. 'They end up seeing things they didn't bargain for. You wait, it's the men who are going to suffer in the end for testing the women.'

'What rubbish you talk sometimes, Tessy.' George smiled at Flora.

In soft blue, with large gold earrings, Flora looked at the floor and murmured, 'Well.'

'And the women?' asked Iain.

'They're tougher. They get away with it. Their toughness surprises the men.'

To Tess's amazement, Flora nodded in agreement with more vigour than Tess had imagined she possessed.

On the way to the western sector, Tess watched the lights of the restless, stricken city.

What chance did one small marriage have of working when it was framed by such fractures, such dangerous movements in the world? Such betrayals. And such slippages of faith and flesh.

Other than in sleep, Tess and George had not spent one moment alone.

'Right . . .' George called from the bedroom, closing his suitcase. 'That's it.'

Tess was on the phone. It was early February and post-Christmas malaise hung over the flat. She had not got round to removing sprigs of holly from the pictures or to folding up Christmas wrapping paper and only that morning her lack of housekeeping had been a source of marital sniping.

'Lodgers, Daddy? Are you quite sure?' She listened to her father. 'How will Mum cope with the extra work?' There was another pause. 'Of course we'll get out of the flat. It's about time George and I stood on our own feet.'

At the other end of the phone, her father signed off gratefully and said her mother wanted a word.

'Mum,' she said, 'I know things are bad but have you really got to do this – what's it called? – yes, this Wolsey Lodge business?'

Angela Frant had spent some time trying to decide whether her heart was breaking from anger, grief or routed pride. 'Well,' she said in her practical tones, 'we could sign up with Amway. We have to eat and it doesn't make sense to sell the house. Or, at least, I don't want to sell the house.'

'I see.' Tess was ashamed. 'Bed and breakfast it is.'

George had dragged his suitcase into the hall and was checking through his pockets. Tess finished her conversation. 'Listen, Mum, I promise to come down and help you.'

She traced a pattern on the plastic casing of the phone with a finger and did not look up. 'If the flat is sold while you're away, I'll find somewhere to rent.' She sighed heavily. 'Mum and Dad are in big trouble.' Tess could tell that George was not pleased. 'You might at least say you're sorry or something,' she burst out.

'I've told you how sorry I am.' George stuffed his wallet into his jacket pocket. 'I can't keep on saying it. We had a flat, now we don't. It's a bore and a pity, but there we are.'

He smiled as he spoke and Tess, looking up swiftly, caught the smile, and her suspicion that George was not focused on her was swept away by a familiar surge of excitement.

'When shall I phone you?'

'I'll phone you,' he said. 'When I've got a moment. So don't worry if you don't hear immediately.'

So much had gone into George and so *little* was coming back, however hard Tess tried, however hard she hoped. With a shocked gasp, she ran at him, grabbed him by the shoulders and shook him hard.

It was the first time in her life that she had ever done such a thing, the first time control was impossible. 'I *can't* think why you bothered to marry me. You're so . . . so . . . bloody detached. I seem to be nothing but an encumbrance. Or a free lunch or a free flat.'

'Hardly the last any more.' Calmly, George prised off her hands. Tess resisted and he brought to bear his considerable strength. With a moan she gave up. 'Now you stop this,' he said. 'You've got to grow up.'

She dropped her hands and averted her wet face. 'I thought you'd make me whole,' she said miserably, realizing, finally, that George would not understand.

He shoved his hands into his pockets. 'I think you think you married your father, someone who'd baby you and look after you,' he said. 'But you haven't, you know. And the sooner we agree on that, the better.'

She stared at George, at the fit, handsome body that she loved and desired so passionately. 'Oh, go away,' she whispered. 'Go away and play at soldiers, if that keeps you happy.'

'That,' said George, and again he smiled, 'is the silliest thing I've ever heard you say.'

He picked up the suitcase, let himself out of the door and banged it behind him.

I was wrong, wrote Tess. Marriage is a power struggle. A bitter, bloody power struggle between what we expect and what we get.

Chapter Thirteen

Becky's fact-finding trip to a rig on the North Sea was put off because of wild and angry weather from late February until milder mid-April. This made it possible for her to combine the expedition with the trip to America to attend a conference on oil pollution.

Anxious to demonstrate its lead in technology and safety, the oil-rig trip had been organized by FEROC, and its guest list was a painstakingly composed mixture of brokers, financial analysts, underwriters and a couple of hand-picked journalists who could be relied on to file the right report. Becky was the only woman.

'Why you?' asked Charles suspiciously, when she told him her plans. 'It should be us at Mawby's.'

'My legs, darling. What else?' If Charles had been in an observant mood, he might have spotted a suspicious light in Becky's eye. 'Why not me? FEROC has put a big budget towards training and public relations. It needs friends and it's making sure it has some. Anyway Dick, the corporate-relations chap, has become a friend, we must have him to dinner, and he promised me a peek at the real thing.'

It may have been spring, but in the North Sea, off Aberdeen, subtleties of seasonal change were irrelevant. Swooping in from the air, the rig metamorphosed from a toy castle on a grey sheet into a vast, airy cathedral, and Becky experienced a fleeting moment of fear. Piper Alpha was only recent history.

As they struggled out of the helicopter onto the landing pad, the wind lashed savagely at the members of the group and flayed a layer of salt onto their skins. A month here, thought Becky, and I would be as dried and brittle as salt fish.

They filed into the reception area. The door closed behind them and, miraculously, the weather was shut out.

'You'll be wishing you were back in a cosy office.' One of the party, a rugger-playing type called Jim, turned to Becky.

'Will I?' said Becky sweetly.

They were inhaling an odour peculiar to extra insulated and heated buildings. Becky wrinkled her nose and the smells and enforced intimacy of living in close confinement were borne in on her. Tact in bucketfuls would be necessary to survive. Or, maybe, one learned to put up with the worst. Or went mad.

She looked out of the window. The rig was a monument to endeavour. To profit. It was poised on the edge of the world, and she did not underestimate its rapacious nature.

Harnessed, hatted and carefully marshalled, the group were shown around. They watched the oil flare, listened to the ceaseless rattle of machinery in the wind, and felt the prickle of nerves in response to their exposure. At times, as they clambered down steps, they appeared only just to be hovering above the sea's bluster. As they clambered up, they grew remote from its roar, gathered up instead by the astringent wind.

After the first futile attempts, no one took notes.

At lunch, they were served with soup, fish (of course) and a good fruit tart. Unusually, Becky was hungry and ate all the courses, a serene-looking female among the men.

'How about a drink this evening?' The rugger player was trying his luck.

'I think not,' said Becky politely. He flushed and turned away.

Back in an over-furnished hotel room in Aberdeen, Becky ignored the message from Charles: please ring. Instead, she sat down to write up her report on the new, state-of-the-art laptop she had wheeled out of Coates.

Only then did she permit herself to pick up the telephone and to ring Louis. 'What are you doing?' she asked.

'Can't tell you.'

Becky examined her reflection in the mirror. 'Louis. I wish you were here.'

'I've got to go home. Jilly's expecting me.'

'Yes, of course.' She lay back on the bed. Her skin felt tight and wind-lashed. At some point, age would get to work. Mottling and dulling skin. Thinning bones, sculpting flesh into folds. What then?

'Becky,' said Louis, 'I love you.'

Becky was so astonished that she put down the phone.

She rang Tess's home number and left a message on the answerphone. 'Tessy. Can you have Charles over or something? He needs cheering up and he's useless on his own.'

Finally she rang Charles, who sounded a little drunk. 'Bec,' he said eagerly, 'had you forgotten you were supposed to be ringing me?'

'I'm ringing now,' she pointed out.

'How did it go?'

She gave Charles an edited account. 'Good,' he said, sounding like the decisive Charles to whom Becky best responded. 'We're working night and day to get the figures sorted for the FEROC deal.'

'Charles,' said Becky, then thought better of it. She looked down at her expensively shod feet (Aunt Jean had never in her life bought a pair costing more than twenty pounds) and reflected on the flat by the river, filled with objects that she had desired and bought. She thought, too, of her old life and her new one and of money, the commodity that made perfect sense.

'So nothing's been signed up?' she asked.

'No. The boss has been away. He's back tomorrow.'

'Listen,' said Becky, 'Tess will be ringing and asking you over for a meal.'

She realized Charles had drunk more than a few glasses of

wine when he confessed that Martha had also rung and wanted him to go over to Clapham because Anthea had been bedwetting.

'Fine,' said Becky. 'But take a Resolve first. You'll find it in the bathroom.'

'Hang on.' Charles abandoned the phone and returned. 'Got one,' he said, a boy discovering treasure after the adventure. 'Thanks, Bec. You are good to me. Love you.'

The telephone receiver was warm and slightly damp. As she dialled Coates's number, Becky tapped a martial rhythm on her knee with her free hand. She got through to her boss at once.

'Mawby's still reckon they're in on the FEROC act,' she said quickly.

'Don't worry, it's more or less wrapped up. We'll announce it in the next day or two.'

'That's good.'

Her boss seemed puzzled. 'Doesn't your chap work at Mawby's?'

'Yes,' Becky replied. 'Does it matter?'

'Not to us ... unless there's a conflict of interest, as we discussed originally.' His tone was unsure, even sounding a little repelled. 'But maybe to you.'

'No,' said Becky. 'Not at all.'

Before dinner, she went out for some air. The hotel was situated on the outskirts of Aberdeen, and behind the city's formal Georgian composition, which had been so rudely thrust into the twentieth century by the discovery of the oilfields, was the Scottish countryside.

She stretched up her face to the flat cold expanse of sky and breathed in deeply.

If she was truthful, the burden of Charles was beginning to press on Becky. The little boy, the troubled lover, the guilty man. To a degree, she had been the architect of the last. She had taken him on because he had money, he was willing, he was good at his job and, yes, he was nice.

How quickly reasons turn dull and lose their urgency.

The sky was empty, a grey and unyielding expanse. Courtesy of God, Aunt Jean had been sure of what she was doing. Like aunt, like niece. Becky was sure too. She knew where she had come from, and precisely because she was clear on that, she knew where she was going. And what lay at the end.

Clutching the collar of her expensive coat around her neck, and in her expensive shoes, she trod back towards the hotel, which smelt of pot-pourri and gussied-up food. If doubt and disappointment ever speared through the cunningly contrived armour in which Becky had clad herself, she did not acknowledge it.

It was after eleven o'clock when Becky left the hotel dining room. Fatigued and a little bored, for the men at play were tedious, she stopped in the foyer to examine one of the glass cases containing jewellery and china.

The intense, and idiosyncratic, manner in which she looked at the objects, the waterfall of hair caught up in a pair of combs, the long, long legs impressed the interested onlooker on the nearby sofa with a curious combination of familiarity and rediscovery.

'Becky . . .'

She whirled, for once unguarded and wordless. At last she said, with a little gasp, 'Louis.'

'As you see.'

'Good heavens. You took a risk.'

'Who better?'

He picked up his briefcase and together they moved towards the lift. Outside her room, Becky slotted the plastic card into the lock, let them in and leant against the door. 'How did you do it?'

'Easy. Got the last flight.'

'Tell me.'

Her insistence on the details amused Louis and he spun out the story of last-minute dashes, taxis and booking details. Then she asked about his work and he replied that he was dealing with business in Northern Ireland.

'George is there.' Becky wore her teasing, witchy smile.

Louis had had enough. He pulled her towards the bed, flung her down and unzipped the tight skirt. 'Will you shut up?'

She did nothing to help him, but after a minute she was naked.

Half-way through, Becky said, 'I've betrayed Charles.' She did not need to add 'again'.

'How?'

Becky told him about the FEROC deal. Above her, Louis smiled and she smiled back.

They rang for room service and ordered champagne. Louis got up and took a couple of aspirin. When he came back to bed Becky lay as close to him as she could manage and filled him in with the details.

'All's fair in business. I believe that.'

Louis recollected the cool grey stone church and, conducted inside it, his halting confessions and the absolutions. Shamefully, both his desire and the degree of his complicity increased. 'All is fair,' he said, 'but not necessarily right. Let's be straight about that.'

With a quick movement, Becky buried her face in his shoulder and ran her hand up his body. 'Who are you to talk?'

'I can't.'

She was alerted by a heaviness in his voice. 'It's all we've got,' she said, meaning work. 'Otherwise there's nothing. You're greedy and I'm greedy.'

He rolled towards Becky and gathered her up in his arms. 'You're wrong, Becky. And you're wrong because you've been wronged.' He began to kiss her eyes, then her cheeks, then her neck. 'You mustn't make the mistake of imagining I understand or I don't know.'

'Know what precisely?' She seemed puzzled.

Louis checked himself for he saw no point in continuing the conversation and raking up Becky's origins. Instead he kissed her again. 'It doesn't matter,' he said. 'Enough. It's all too short to worry about.'

It crossed Becky's mind that Louis was the only person who ever made her feel safe. At least for a minute or two.

'Talking of which ...' Louis continued, 'who knows about us?'

'Only Tess,' replied Becky. 'She knows most things about me.'

Both were silent, for a dim but unmistakable intimation of their mortality had crept through them, a cold contrast to the sensations of their warm, naked bodies. It drew them even closer. For as they had shared their bodies, they also shared the knowledge that both had a dark and restless spirit.

If he loved her ... then. If she loved him ... then. Breathing him in, his flesh against her face, Becky found herself crying helplessly.

Out of the blue, Louis said, '"I will not leave you orphans."'

'What's that?' she asked, and wiped away the tears on her cheeks.

'A promise I heard as a child. So you must be quiet now.'

'Sometimes,' she said, through fresh tears, 'you talk rubbish.'

Louis held her against his heart until she stopped and murmured over and over again that he loved her.

The following day, Louis flew back to London, without having noticed that he had been in Scotland.

'Surely ...' Tess gave Charles a hefty gin and tonic then poured a strong one for herself, 'you don't regret being with Becky. Do you?'

Charles had come over to the Pimlico flat for supper, a depressed-looking, half-packed-up flat in which Tess was uneasily anchored, not knowing whether she was to be here or there. It was proving difficult to sell and the property market was showing signs of a serious slump.

'I *can't* understand it,' her father kept repeating, each time with a degree more desperation.

Charles sucked eagerly at his drink. 'I don't regret it at all. But Becky is a bracing person. Martha was . . . is not. It takes time to adjust.' He added in a low voice, 'One makes one's bed.'

This did not sound the song of a happy man.

It takes one to know one.

Surveying him over the rim of her glass, she concluded that he *did* have a depressed air and that troubled her. She had grown fond of Charles in a safe, platonic way, perceiving that he had two sides, often at war with each other. Anyway, her own unhappiness made her sensitive to his.

The lightest of fingers stroked across her tender heart.

'Becky's the best person I know,' she said. 'You won't go wrong with her.'

'I know.' Charles thought it over. 'Of course, she's quite brilliant.' He gave a self-deprecating laugh. 'Too good for me, really.'

'Charles . . .' Tess stood over him with the gin bottle. 'Stop it. Another one?'

He held out his glass and, for the first time, she noticed the bright blue eyes. So English, and hiding confusion and doubt. 'I sometimes wonder . . .'

'Let's have supper.'

Over fresh spaghetti and tomato sauce, they got through two bottles of burgundy. They touched briefly on holidays, where and how expensive, a film they had both seen on which they disagreed. After that, the conversation, which was a little sticky, faltered. Only those who know each other well can indulge in the luxury of silence. Eventually, after another pause, Tess made an inspired guess and mentioned an investment she was evaluating. Immediately Charles brightened up and responded with an anecdote about insuring bicycles in Holland, which made Tess laugh.

Over the cheese, they talked money, assessing its waywardness, its black magic and the cloud that had folded over the eighties economy.

During this conversation, Tess was aware of big, boiling emotions below the surface.

After the ice cream, she brought up the subject of her parents and the mood changed. Taking the wine, they moved to the sofa.

'I don't know what to do about them,' she confided, and her eyes grew wet. She rubbed them impatiently. 'The last demand was for fifty thousand pounds. I feel Dad was misled or, at least, not properly advised. In fact, I know he wasn't.'

Whatever failings he had, Charles was excellent on tears. Feeling strong but, of course, detached, he slipped an arm around Tess's shoulders.

'What does George think?'

'I haven't *really* talked about it with him.'

So sympathetic and, somehow, so buoying up, Charles's arm tightened and Tess found herself in one of those situations where what she thought was happening probably was not. Yet indubitably it was.

At that precise moment, her reasoning was not brilliant but good manners suggested that it was bad manners to imply to someone that they were seducing you when they were merely offering comfort. Equally, it was very bad manners to allow your best friend's lover to seduce you as part of the comforting process.

'Poor Tess. Your poor parents ...' Charles poured more wine for them both. 'And ...'

'Yes?'

'Poor Martha.'

Pity is an excellent aphrodisiac with a facility for demolishing barriers. Pity shared can achieve all manner of results.

Why, thought Tess, I have been too conformist all my life. Too restricted in my behaviour. Ungenerous, too, with my body. I should share it.

I've stepped over the line once, thought Charles, and it's impossible to go back. So what does it matter? I need help. Reassurance, not reinsurance. Some way of assessing what I'm worth. Otherwise, I'm lost.

Help me, Tess.

Tender-hearted Tess, so anxious to give, responded and when Charles leant over and kissed her, she did not move away. Then he buried his face in her hair, letting it drape between his fingers. Five minutes later, Charles was kissing her and pushing her into the pillows.

In Belfast, George was asleep, worn out and over-full from a late supper of fried bacon and sausages, which had been left to stew on a hotplate. He had eaten it doggedly and resolutely because his body required fuel. The night had been difficult, but he would sort out the implications after he had slept.

It had been tiring, bloody tiring, and he hated the clothes. A pair of grimy jeans, with a 9mm Browning tucked into them, and a donkey jacket that had seen better days.

While Tess was otherwise engaged, George had been staking out a bomb factory on a housing estate to the north of the city.

Eyes slow. Keep walking. Look the part. On the target. Squeeze pressal button on radio to tell Alpha on the net where he was.

Who was that talking to the tall man in the anorak? George dropped his eyes and lit a cigarette. That was Kelly 'all-British-are-fascist-pigs' senior. And if Kelly senior was around, the likelihood was that Kelly junior was too.

It was time to move. From the staked-out house came the

sound of grinding. A bomb was being made in a large coffee grinder. Alpha whispered in his ear to get out.

George made his way along the street up to the Shamrock pub and eased his way through the crowd to the bar. He ordered a whiskey.

The Kellys came in after him. He could feel them. He could hear them. Last time George had seen them close up was after they had been brought in for questioning. He hadn't liked them then and he didn't like them now.

Around him, the talk went on and on. He caught at snippets. So much hatred lurking in hearts. And it didn't matter how capital was poured by the government into shopping malls and supermarkets, it didn't buy out hatred.

Who knew? This pub was probably crammed with more undercover agents than *bona fide* rebels.

Someone was singing, rather beautifully, and the man next to George joined in. George lifted his glass and drank and, as he did so, his eyes collided with those of Kelly senior.

Understanding flickered over the older man's face, and a strange out-of-place compassion. Why, thought George, you're as trapped as I will be.

He was burnt.

Tess woke with a start and a headache. I went to bed with this man because, in the end, I did not want to seem bad-mannered, she thought.

'Look,' said Charles, from beneath the sheets, 'I'm very sorry about this.'

She searched to recapture the sense of liberation and wild mood of the previous evening. 'So am I. So am I. But I understand.'

Blue-eyed and tousle-haired, he reared up from the pillows and questioned her eagerly, 'Do you really?'

'I think so.'

'Thank God.' He shot a look sideways at Tess's peachy skin and the mass of hair. 'I didn't mean it to happen,' he said thickly, and reached over to touch her.

Tess clutched the sheets around every bit of her bare body and shut it off from him. 'Would you mind closing your eyes, Charles? I want to get dressed.'

Obediently, he did as he had been bidden and Tess put on her clothes, shivering and a little queasy. Then she sat down on the edge of the bed.

'Charles. You must go.'

'But what are we going to do?' His eyes were round.

'Do? Nothing. George comes back for the weekend tomorrow and Becky will be back in a week's time. We do nothing. No, that's not quite right. We forget.'

'We forget,' said Charles, and sat up. Tess softened for he was, without question, handsome. 'This is our secret. We'll never talk about it again.'

'No,' said Tess, 'no. That's agreed.' And with that undertaking, she was changed, utterly and for ever.

Chapter Fourteen

Lunch at the Lloyd's Club was a mixed affair. The beef was voted not quite up to scratch but the mood veered between the sombre, because warrants for the arrest of two underwriters had been issued by the Serious Fraud Squad, and guarded optimism, because the American court had ruled against Shell and in favour of insurers over the question of the pollution of the Rocky Mountain Arsenal (from which the company derived profits of between $12 million and $20 million a year, using open-air evaporation basins for its toxic wastes).

The Bollys made up for the beef with some excellent claret. It was not quite enough to square the future favourably but it helped to make the atmosphere a little more congenial. The pollution crisis was not, Matt and Louis agreed, going to go away.

'Met someone the other day,' Nigel announced.

'Really?' Matt's knuckles cracked.

'Told me about this new expert emerging in the States, the insurance archaeologist. They trawl the archives digging out old policies with loosely worded general-liability clauses.' Nigel had no need to add that many of the clauses would be thrown back at Lloyd's.

'Hate the buggers,' said Chris Beame.

'We've survived worse,' said Nigel, searching in his pocket for an antacid pill. 'The chatter in court of moral responsibility,' he was referring to the Shell case, 'doesn't end in us having to pay.' He paused. He chewed another pill. 'It isn't our fault.'

'No,' said Chris Beame.

'Nigel,' interjected Louis, 'I think you'll find there are approximately four hundred thousand hazardous waste sites in the United States, all requiring to be cleaned up.'

After that, the lunch seemed to lose its point and the Bollys dispersed.

Colonel Frant was of the school who believed that personal calls should not be taken in the office so Tess was surprised when he rang her at Metrobank.

'This is just to let you know, darling, that since we haven't sold the flat I've had to make other plans and I want you to come home at the weekend and discuss them, if you would.'

'Of course,' said Tess, who had one eye on the screen and a rather important stock that was not behaving as she wished. 'How's Mum?'

'Worried sick about Jack. But we think he's better.'

Jack was in hospital in Addis Ababa with a dysentery bug; according to Penelope, he was taking his time to get better.

'How was George?'

'Oh, Dad, it was only two days and then he was off again. Not long enough, really. We just lazed around and went out to dinner. You know, that sort of thing. Dad, I must go. I'll see you on Saturday.'

On arriving back for the weekend, George had said, 'Let's not think of our differences, Tess. Let's think of our similarities.' And Tess had rejoiced, for it was the first such sentiment George had voiced. It made her feel, in a curious way, that she was seeing him properly at last, and she felt anticipation and optimism stir strongly inside her.

Then she remembered what she had done, and her feelings became muddled with pain and anxiety, and she grieved for her own shortcomings. What's the point? she thought. What *is* the point?

George had been loving to Tess but quiet. He spent much of the time either sleeping or watching television, but before he left he pulled her close and said, 'We'll make it, Tess. You'll see.'

The letter was waiting for Becky when she arrived back from her ten-day trip to the States.

I hope you've recovered from the shock [wrote Lily]. I should, I suppose, say sorry. But I don't feel sorry. I always say that you should never be sorry for things you do, only what you don't do. I wanted to see you and now I have. You seem to have done all right and I respect you for that. Perhaps it runs in the blood.

As you will have gathered, I'm not one for mothering. For all her God-ing, Jean was a much better bet. If you feel hard-done-by and resentful, think about that.

I don't expect we'll meet very often. I refuse to be robbed by British Rail and my feet swell on the coach. But if you want to telephone me at any time, I'm here.

Becky read it in the hall, surrounded by her luggage, and found herself smiling.

Charles was also waiting for Becky, on the primrose sofa, anticipating the sound of the taxi and the opening door. Becky's palm tree, which he considered hideous, threw spiky shadows on the wall. A huge drinks tray sat under a lit Provençal landscape that she had also insisted on buying.

These were visible appurtenances of a particular life. Bought at cost, maintained at cost. The showy familiars of an economy whose murmurings and eruptions, egged on by the boys in striped coats, the brokers, the insurers, the punters, the plodders and, of course, the vultures, were Charles's daily fare. Not that he thought of his affluence in those terms, if he considered it at all.

The habit of introspection had come only recently to Charles and it tended to concentrate on one subject: a slow, awkwardly conducted investigation into emotions that threatened to become too painful. 'I love her, I *love* her,' he repeated often to himself, aware that tiny seepages of distrust and disappointment were draining his reserves.

He sat quietly, legs crossed in a manner reminiscent of the days when he had been in control. When the front door opened he did not get up but waited until the sound of a heavy suitcase being manipulated into the hall ceased.

'Charles? Are you there?'

He remained silent and Becky put her head round the door, a tired-looking, travel-smudged Becky.

'You *are* here. Why didn't you answer?'

'Hallo, Becky.'

Puzzled, she advanced into the room, and threw a new Chanel bag onto the chair. 'Not even a kiss?'

'Since when,' Charles heard himself saying, 'have you minded whether I kissed you or not?'

'Oh dear, it's that bad.' She bent over him, trapping him with her arms and he caught the waft of her perfume, the jasminy one that she loved and he loved because she loved it . . . 'Are you going to tell me?'

He fended her off, knowing that his strength and resolution were less clear cut than he wished. There were no buttons he could press. No figures from which he could form a conclusion. He had imagined that by leaving his wife, loved with the depth of a long association, for a new passion that snared him in wild and haunting dreams, he would be empowered, as other men had appeared to be. Too late, Charles had discovered that he was not a dreamer, would never be a dreamer. He had tumbled at the wrong time to a secret: he did not match the models he had chosen. In that discrepancy, however small, can be hidden a tragedy – in this case, the tragedy of Charles's betrayal.

'Mawby's,' he said heavily, 'were informed yesterday that FEROC would be giving the business to Coates.'

Becky straightened up. 'Ah.'

'Did you do it deliberately, Becky?'

If possible, Becky's eyes seemed larger than normal but that, Charles decided, was the effect of blurred mascara. 'Do what?'

'Tell them we hadn't signed. There was a delay on our side. Whatever. Apparently your big guns were sent in and wrapped it up in twenty-four hours.' He sighed. 'Funny how they got hold of the figures so quickly.'

'Don't ask me.' Becky folded her arms and looked down at Charles.

'You must have done it, Becky. There's no other explanation. You set out to do me down.'

She sighed. 'Don't be so stupid, Charles. Lots of people had the information, all of them with their own agendas. Of course I didn't set out to do you down. You mustn't be so self-centred.'

Charles gave a snort.

Becky's expression was reassuringly untroubled. 'It's possible that I said something and, if so, I'm sorry. But there's business to be done. Good business. That's how it works.'

'You *did* say something.'

She shrugged. 'If I did, not deliberately.'

'What were you thinking of?'

'Money, business, profit,' said Becky. 'What else?' She seemed bewildered by his question.

'Becky, let me ask you something. Have you one shred of loyalty in that body of yours?'

'Charles. Do you *have* to talk in clichés?'

Where had he heard that before?

'All right. If you didn't care enough to be careful about me you should have cared about your own reputation.'

There was a tiny silence. Becky sighed. 'Don't give me that

nonsense about honour. If you can't accept how the business works, that leaks happen, whether knowingly or not, you shouldn't be in it. There's no great drama. Coates moved quicker than Mawby's, that's all.'

Stung, he raised his voice. 'Don't tell me about the business. I was in it before you were out of nappies.'

'Well, then,' she said, quietly and reasonably.

Charles lifted his hands and let them drop. The prairie dog, so delightful and brisk when busy and purposeful, so miserable when not. 'I'm now out of a job.'

Becky sat down on her handbag and put her hand up to her head. 'I think I'm jet-lagged.'

'Did you hear what I said?' Charles sprang to his feet and flung himself over to the window. 'I've bloody lost my job. They had me out of there before I could say P.45 because they reckoned we'd enjoyed some pillow talk. Do you know what that means to me? Do you know how I'm being laughed at? Do you know how long I took to build my reputation?'

Yet another silence punctuated the conversation.

'Come here, Charles.' He remained where he was. 'Please.' Treading heavily over the deep-pile carpet, he did as she asked. She took his hand and stroked it gently. 'Don't look like that, darling. Are the lawyers handling this?' He nodded. 'Listen to me,' she said. 'I've been thinking it's about time you upgraded. You need to be more innovative and use your expertise. Mawby's were holding you back. I know. I saw when I was there. They reckoned they had you tamed. But you're better than that.'

'Oh,' said Charles nastily. 'I haven't come up to scratch, then, in your expectations? Backed the wrong horse, have you, darling?'

Then he remembered Tess and what had happened.

But what had happened there was not the same. It hadn't meant anything.

Becky sat very still, every line proclaiming patience. 'Charles, you're a big boy now. The FEROC deal was common knowledge. Mawby's was dragging its feet. It could have happened at any time.'

Frantic to have things back on course, he searched her face. She was so tired that the skin had turned a chalk colour, but her expression seemed genuine. Honest – loving, even. In the old days, when moral relativism was a term for a party game, life had been uncomplicated and Charles was swamped by a rush of longing to have it back.

'If you have a mind for it, Becky, you can make black look white,' he said dully, and she knew she had won.

Her fatigue was so intense that she felt sick. She rummaged in her handbag and tossed a package to Charles. The wrapping paper said Cartier.

Charles held up a pair of enamel cufflinks. 'Not quite thirty pieces of silver,' he said, 'but they'll do.'

The enamel was blue and vivid. Becky was right. He needed a new job. He had been undervalued and, with things as they were, he could do with earning a bit more loot.

Tess was coming to terms with her new self and she hoped that no one had rumbled the process, certainly not Becky.

Her outer layer worked and played and adapted to the shapes of her life. But at her centre, reverberating with energy and anger, was her secret, and she was astonished that she, Tess Frant, well-mannered and well-intentioned, had done what she had done.

She was astonished that, out of the airy ambitions she had set herself to achieve in her life, she had finished with this lead-like disappointment and deceit.

'Been overdoing it, duckie?' Freddie passed her on the stairs. 'Do we look a tad used? Old liver curling at the edges?'

Tess managed a smile and the nausea that had plagued her for the last few days returned. 'I think I've got a bug.'

'Money bug, dearest. It gets us all in the end. The antidote is champagne. Gets a boy into proportion.'

He vanished into the foyer.

She sat at her desk and flicked through the pages on her screen. What a sticky and neurotic market it was. Naturally the clients were in a fair way to being the same. She began to take notes and then made some phone calls. Bill came over and told her off for not taking enough trouble with a potential client. 'The dear little clients don't want someone whose eye has wandered from the ball,' he informed her. 'Lots of love and undivided attention. OK?'

Tess took herself off to the ladies' and hung over the basin while her stomach settled. Then she applied a bright red lipstick and brushed pink onto her cheeks. She looked into the mirror.

'How do you do?' she said. And in that encounter Tess was formally introduced to her new self.

The six thirty train drew into Appleford station dead on time on Friday evening and disgorged a load of white-faced, sweet-eating commuters.

At the ticket barrier, Tess bumped into Louis. 'Hallo,' she said, never quite sure, these days, how to treat him.

'Hallo, Tess.'

'How's the family?'

'Jilly's fine,' answered Louis. 'Andrew has a job at Warburg's, and David's still working at Sotheby's and very happy.' He stepped aside to let her through the ticket barrier. 'I'm glad I've met you, Tess. I presume you've been talking to your father about his plans but I should warn you there's a great deal of feeling running against him in the village.'

She stopped abruptly, forcing Louis to follow suit. Bodies brushed against them and she swayed.

Louis drew her aside. 'Did you know that he's gone into partnership with an organization and applied for planning permission for a showground stretching over your paddock and field?'

'Eeyore's Paddock,' said Tess involuntarily. 'A showground? My father?'

'Eeyore's?'

She shook her head. 'It's a nickname. As a child, I thought Eeyore lived there.' She stared at Louis, so assured and expensive-looking, and hated him. 'Thank you,' she said. 'For all your help.'

It gave her pleasure that Louis flushed.

Formerly, Friday nights at the High House used to be rather sedate, rounded off by the *Nine o'Clock News*. Today, Tess was greeted by strange cars in the gravel drive and her mother in an apron, face dusted with flour. She was making bread for the guests' breakfasts, she explained.

'It's cheaper.' Mrs Frant forestalled her daughter's protest. 'Look, darling, you'll have to make your own supper tonight and please stay in the kitchen.'

Tess was conscious that something was missing in the kitchen. She looked over to the niche under the cupboards normally occupied by Sage, along with her smelly tumble of rug and rubber toys. It was empty.

'Mum,' her voice rose, 'where's Sage?'

Her mother did not look at Tess. 'Darling, I think your father wanted to talk to you about Sage.'

I'll think about Sage later, thought Tess, riven by the foreboding that, these days, was a frequent companion.

She took her bag upstairs, pausing to look into the drawing room in which sat four strangers, neatly dressed and drinking sherry. With a shock, she saw that the Lalique vase, which had stood for ever on the table between the windows, had been removed.

'From the north,' said Mrs Frant, slamming the oven shut with one foot while balancing a tray filled with chicken wrapped in filo pastry. 'They want to do the south.'

She looked tired. Tess got up to help but the smell of the food made her feel so sick that she sat down again with a thump.

'Easter's coming,' said Mrs Frant, 'and we're full for the next two weeks.'

Tess ate a supper of scrambled eggs and a sliced tomato and went up to bed.

Over breakfast in the kitchen – 'Don't go into the dining room, darling' – she tackled her father. Her mother was hanging up sheets in the back garden.

'What's this showground, Dad?'

Her father appeared guilty, defiant and determined all in the same second, none of which she recognized in him. 'I've never made use of them before, but the Eeyore's P. and the meadow are a source of potential income, which I need.'

'So? I'm in the business. Tell me.'

'Well ...' Of the generation where women in a family did not handle financial affairs, Colonel Frant was not expansive. 'It's bad,' he said reluctantly. 'Bad.'

'And?'

'There's an organization called the Countrymen who specialize in setting up big events in the countryside. They hunt out sites, contact the owners and draw up programmes. Um ... Clay-pigeon shoots, athletic events, motocross, that sort of thing and um ... part of the organization deals with rock festivals. These rock things being held at the moment are illegal and they want somewhere permanent, which is all above board. The Countrymen handle all the legal work and the planning permission. In return, I lease them the fields and receive a royalty on ticket revenue.'

'*Rock* festivals,' said Tess. 'Am I hearing you right, Daddy?'

'They would have two, possibly three, a year. A maximum of a hundred thousand or so is estimated as an attendance figure.'

Tess abandoned her breakfast and went over to the kitchen window. Bright with new growth and tussocky, hiding secret caches of insect life, the meadow rolled like an enchanted sea; riding on it were ghostly ships carrying her childhood and Eeyore and Pooh and the rest of her companions into the past.

'I'm surprised you haven't been lynched, Daddy,' she said, deadly quiet. 'A hundred thousand people in Appleford.'

He made a little sound, half-way between a cough and a sneeze.

'Have you thought what this will do? You, the conservationist who gets upset if a litter bin is put outside the shop? The cars, the buildings. It will need loos and that sort of thing. Then the land will go down in value. The clever and well-off will move out. Those who can't will remain and suffer.'

'There is money to be made.' Her father bowed his head.

Tess retreated from the window and picked up a piece of paper lying on the sideboard.

SAVE OUR VILLAGE

Dear Appleford Resident, I am writing to you because you may be aware of the proposed plan for a showground to the east of the village at the High House, plans which have already been considered by the District Council.

They include provision for five toilet blocks, three service buildings, and several structures for formal shooting in the field. These will be visible from the highway, the main street and some public footpaths. In addition, there will be marquees and other temporary structures present on the site for up to 161 days in the year . . .

'Where did you get this?'

With a shade of his old self, he replied, 'It came through the letterbox.'

She shoved it into the open file lying beside it, which she banged shut with a clenched fist. Then, without looking at her father, she went to find her mother.

Mrs Frant was folding sheets. 'What do you think, Mum?'

The latter dumped a pile into Tess's arms. 'Hold those.'

'Mum. This is serious. You've got to stop it.'

'Tess, your father and I are in trouble. I don't like it any more than you do.'

'But the village . . .'

Mrs Frant piled more sheets into her daughter's arms. Good linen sheets, well worn and well cared for but hell to iron. These days she stayed up late at nights to get them done. Tess smelt their sweet-hot smell from the airing cupboard and saw the care with which they had been folded, order from disorder, and was silent.

'Help me make the beds, will you?'

Obediently, she followed her mother into the spare room. Curtained in faded glazed cotton, with sprigged wallpaper, it had always been a warm, successful room, but never over-indulgent, a place into which she and Jack had ventured at their peril.

It had lost some of its charm. Yet another picture, the one of Edinburgh from Arthur's Seat, had vanished from the wall leaving a mark. A litter of cotton-wool balls and tissues on the dressing table proclaimed recent occupation. A pair of tights was stuffed into the wastepaper basket and there was an unfamiliar smell. Lavender? Face powder? Tess was not sure.

Her mother stripped the beds deftly and, together, they remade them. Stretching. Patting. Smoothing. Out of such actions a life was made, a woman's life in particular, and Tess was out of practice.

'In the end,' said Mrs Frant, arranging a pillow, 'survival is the most important thing. Other considerations have to go.' She spoke with some bitterness.

'Surely not. Not the things that *really* matter?'

Mrs Frant looked at her fair and lovely daughter. 'I hope you never have to find out.'

'Why didn't Dad ask me for some help? There's probably some sort of package we could have put together.' But Tess knew that the odds were low on such things being possible. She tugged a bedspread straight. 'How will you live with the hostility?'

Her mother took time to rearrange the pots on the dressing table and to pull straight a lace mat. 'Very easily,' she lied. 'As you will appreciate, it's a question of living . . . or not.'

Mrs Frant's loyalty was a fine and perfect thing to behold.

Dimly, Tess heard a scrunching in the gravel outside and voices growing louder as they approached the house. At the front door, they ceased.

Guests, she thought.

The bell pealed through the house. She heard her father's tread through the hall, a questioning murmur after he had opened the door, the answering counterpoint of his deeper voice. The door closing.

After a minute, Colonel Frant came into the spare bedroom. He trod heavily and with care. 'Tess, darling, you're wanted downstairs.'

'Me?'

One step. Two steps . . . The childish game tugged at her memory as she came down the stairs, each foot planted carefully below the other. Then, across the hall and into the drawing room that was no longer their own.

Two men waited by the window. One she did not recognize. The other, face creased with distress, was Iain MacKenzie.

'Tess . . .' He walked forward and took her by the arms. 'I'm sorry. I'm sorry.'

She was bewildered. 'Why?'

His grasp intensified and she winced. She looked up into his kind eyes and grave face, and the nausea rose from her stomach into her throat. 'No,' she said, uncertainly. 'No.'

'George was killed in the early hours of this morning,' said Iain. 'An ambush.'

'Ambush.' Tess was puzzled. 'George would never let himself be caught in an ambush.'

'It happens to the best,' said Iain, and pulled her towards him so that she could lay her head thankfully on his shoulder.

Chapter Fifteen

Somehow, within twenty-four hours, the Widow found her way up to the High House, slipping through the front door, a small, nervous but ruthless rodent.

'I'm so sorry, I'm so sorry, I know what you're going through.'

Trapped in the kitchen – the drawing room was full of guests, which added a farcical quality to the events – Tess observed Jennifer Gauntlet through unfamiliar sensations of nausea and sleeplessness. It crossed her mind to ask how the Widow had heard the news, but the question became muddled with another thought that slipped in and then out of her mind.

Jennifer patted Tess's arm with her trembling hand. 'You think me intrusive . . .' She nipped out the words through her small yellowish teeth (no American facings for the Widow). 'But I know. We widows must stick together.'

Yes, thought Tess. Fat, thin, old, young. A net of black-clad, sharp-chinned women cast over the world.

Mrs Frant swooped. 'Jennifer, how sweet of you to come but I think my daughter's in shock and really can't see anybody.'

Tess remembered her mother's face seen over Iain's shoulder. Underneath the coral lipstick Mrs Frant favoured, her mouth had appeared bleached of colour, and it had seemed to Tess that two colours, red and white, were stacked, like sheets of tissue, one on top of the other.

Iain had gone now, taking the other man (who was he?) with him. Apparently, Mrs Frant said, Iain had made huge efforts to be the one to break the news (why?) and the Regiment had done their best to make it possible. The Army was good on death.

The High House was echoing with noise and a bustle that was continually shushed for her benefit. Its life was being suppressed so that hers might be given breathing space. As if Tess minded. The drive was parked with unfamiliar cars and every lavatory in the place was in constant use. Her mother served coffee ceaselessly to strangers, and the vicar had rung to say that he was in the intensive care unit at the hospital but he would come as soon as possible.

'As soon as he's dispatched whoever it is,' said Tess.

'Now, darling.' Mrs Frant was remarkably calm. 'Now, darling.'

Tess fled into the garden and found herself pacing one of her mother's routes. First to the rose bed, down to the wild patch under the tree and back to the mixed border.

'I like my routes,' she could hear her mother say. '*I need them.*'

The early spring flowers had come and gone. Patient and watchful but their time over for this year, the hellebore blossoms were running with sticky sap as their death throes began. But, in the border, great leafy coronets were unfolding: the lupins, peonies and poppies that Mrs Frant also favoured, planted so precisely.

Actually, thought Tess, I don't think I like the way Mum does the garden. I would do it differently.

Beyond Tess was a green and tender countryside, old and dragooned into obedience. Peaceful and uninvaded, marred only by the pylons scything through it.

Actually George is dead.

Later, after the guests had been served lunch and a pitiful attempt had been made by Tess and her parents to swallow what had been left over from the beef casserole and apricot mousse, Tess asked, 'Dad, *where* is Sage?'

Having no option but to tell her, Colonel Frant said, 'Darling, I had her put down.'

Tess digested this latest piece of news. 'What you mean is you've murdered her. Just like George has been murdered,' she said, in a light conversational tone. Then, and only then, she began to weep.

She looked *very* odd, poor thing, reported the Widow, popping into the Cadogans' on her way home. *Very* pale. Wearing an expensive Escada suit, Jilly tsked, a gesture that she judged could be interpreted as neither too heartless nor too sympathetic.

Jilly got on the phone to Louis. 'Tess Frant's husband was murdered yesterday in Belfast. Jennifer told me. God knows how she knew.'

Louis took a moment or two before he said, 'Yes. I was aware there'd been trouble.'

'Why didn't you tell me?'

'Jilly,' said Louis, 'I didn't know the exact details, nor whom it involved, and, besides, the family had a right to know first.'

'The question is,' speculated his wife, 'can we bring ourselves to write? Given we're now sworn enemies.'

'Of course we'll write.'

'No of course about it . . .' Jilly brushed aside Louis's implied criticism. You could always rely on him for a conventional answer. 'You feel as strongly as I do. John Frant is doing terrible harm to Appleford. Worse than death.'

Jilly had never been a woman to reflect on, or even appreciate, ironies. In that, Louis conceded, as he terminated the conversation with an 'I won't be late', lay her strength.

He rang Becky and was informed that she was in a meeting. 'Get her out of it,' he ordered the flustered secretary.

After a minute or two, Becky came on the line. 'Louis? You mustn't do that.'

'Listen,' he said. 'Tess is in trouble. George has been killed. It's on the news now.'

'Oh, my God . . .'

'Can you go?'

Becky cast around while she tried to get a grip on the situation, to stabilize her position in the picture. 'I don't think the old bat will have me in the house. Anyway, I'm in the middle of this huge meeting. The final details . . . FEROC.' Becky ground to a halt, all manner of images crowding through her mind, so strong and so vivid that she screwed up her eyes.

'Becky . . .'

'All right,' she said. 'I'll go tonight.'

'Good girl.'

Becky gripped the telephone. 'Louis. How did he die?'

'He was spotted in a pub car park getting into his car. They kidnapped him and took him into the country.'

'And . . . ?' Becky's knuckles were white.

'I can't bear to tell you any more.'

'I don't understand tribalism,' Becky cried. 'I just don't understand what makes people do it.'

He was not quite sure what she meant, but let it pass.

After work Becky drove down to Appleford. Due to road-works, the A3 was blocked and, at the best of times, she was a bad driver who attacked a route with gritted teeth and damp hands.

'Why did you have to go and die?' she addressed George, and narrowly missed a collision at the junction of the A3 and the Hogs Back. 'Think what you've done. You've turned into a statistic, to be worked into future probabilities, and introduced violence and interruption into the conveniently sanitized.'

That's twice now that I've been engaged with spilt blood, she thought, gripping the wheel extra hard, for her life seemed full and very sweet. Is that an average? Is that the total actuarial risk that Mr and Mrs Bloggs should expect as their years dwindle in Acacia Avenue? Two encounters with spilt blood?

The drive at the High House was choked, and Becky was forced to park in the street. She got out of the car and stood for a moment, gathering strength.

Mrs Frant answered the doorbell. 'Oh,' she said, on seeing the tall, smart figure on the doorstep. 'What do you want?'

Becky was hoping to be invited inside but Mrs Frant did not move. 'Mrs Frant, I'm sorry to arrive so unexpectedly but can I see Tess, please?'

Mrs Frant considered. A daughter lay upstairs, widowed and sick with grief. A son sweltered under an African sun, his health and looks and, more important, his prospects draining away. How and why she made a connection between the two situations and the girl on the doorstep, Mrs Frant was not capable of explaining. But of the limits of maternal authority and her right to exercise jurisdiction, she was absolutely sure.

'I don't think so,' she said coldly. 'Tess isn't well enough to see anyone.'

The two women assessed each other.

Becky's black eyebrows climbed up her forehead, a fighter acknowledging a fellow fighter. 'She'll see me, Mrs Frant, I know she will.'

It was unlike Becky to misread the script but she happened to choose the words most calculated to inflame Mrs Frant, who did not consider that anyone except herself knew what her daughter wished. Yet however much she wanted to hustle Becky down the drive, Mrs Frant's cast-iron training in good behaviour propelled her to step aside and allow Becky into the hallway.

A pile of post lay on the table and two bouquets, still in their Cellophane, had been stacked – and forgotten – beside the letters.

'Wait here.'

Becky watched as Mrs Frant, not bothering to quicken her pace, trod upstairs. As she did so, Becky's mobile phone shrilled. Mrs Frant froze and, her back still to Becky, said, before continuing magisterially up the stairs, 'I would rather you did not use that thing in the house.'

The idea that Tess might need Becky did not enter her head; otherwise she might have stopped to reconsider her objective, which was to drive Becky out of the house. As it was, she went into her daughter's bedroom and asked only if she wished for a cup of tea.

She returned downstairs and waited for Becky to finish her telephone conversation, her face composed into distaste.

'Couldn't you finish? As a favour?' Becky was saying. 'The master rig line slip? That's under control. Look ... I'll talk to you later. I'm a little tied up.'

The unfamiliar vocabulary only underlined Mrs Frant's determination to exorcize Becky. 'She's sleeping, I'm afraid.' The lie tripped neatly off her tongue. 'The doctor gave her a pill and she probably won't wake until tomorrow. I would offer you a bed but we're full.' Her tone grew regal. 'I'm so sorry, but I'm sure you can't help. No one can.'

Before she could calculate a riposte, Becky found herself out of the door and trudging back down the drive. Half-way to the gate, she stopped, returned to the house and stood under Tess's window.

Upstairs, Tess was curled up like a child on her bed in an effort to ballast herself against the sensation, impossible to describe, that had taken possession of her body. Somewhere, in the distortions that were wrecking her sense of time and place, she wondered why Becky had not come.

A week later, after the funeral, Tess returned by herself to the flat in Pimlico.

She stood by the sitting-room window, looking out at the window-box she had placed on the sill.

'If that damn thing falls off,' George had said, 'we'll be done for insurance.'

He had not reckoned – or, at least, she did not think he had – on bits of himself being scattered over a country lane in Northern Ireland. Then, again, perhaps he had. During the past few days, Tess had relearnt the lesson that, in the urgency of living, she had forgotten. No assumption should be cast in iron.

The variegated ivy in the box straggled over the edges and drooped. Tess decided to look at something else. What? What could she possibly look at?

She knew what she did not want to look at. George's side of the bed. Or the jumper thrown over the chair where he had left it that last weekend. Where next? She certainly did not want to look inside the wardrobe where his suits hung on their hangers. Or on the shelves where his socks slumped in a badly constructed pyramid.

No, none of these things justified her scrutiny – for they induced a pain so serious that, if she relaxed her guard for one second, it made her gasp.

George's things.

She wandered back and forth from the sitting room to the bedroom, from the bedroom to the kitchen. A silence had folded over the flat. Dust had been added to the accumulation from Tess's desultory housekeeping and a smell peculiar to unlived-in buildings had crept in too – infiltrating under the door, through the window, up the lobby stairs.

The experience of grief is to encounter yourself, she had concluded. In funny ways, too. I didn't know I possessed nerve ends in unexpected areas of my body and heavy, oh, so heavy, bones. Grieving is to sink into a deep, inner selfishness. I want to say: Thank God it's not me that's dead, but I daren't. Instead, I listen to my own speech scrambled by fatigue into nonsense and I watch my performance on the centre stage.

How I shock myself.

The previous day Jack had phoned on an appalling line. 'Tess, oh, Tessy, what can I say?'

'Tell me about Africa,' she had replied. 'Just talk to me about something normal.'

'Nothing is normal in Africa,' Jack shouted through the static. 'Famine, plague, drought, fundamentalism, fatalism.'

'What do you mean?'

But the line was so bad that Tess had given up.

She tried to think about codes, structures, strictures. So far, she had failed to make sense of any of them, except to conclude that she had failed. She had failed to husband her resources sufficiently to see her through . . . *this*.

George had not been interested in the subject of death. Now that she considered, Tess realized there had been many subjects in which George had not been interested, or that he did not wish to discuss. She sank down on the sofa and lit a cigarette. It tasted disgusting and she stubbed it out.

'George,' Tess addressed the empty room, 'we had only just begun.'

Out of a weary spirit and the emptiness, she must remake herself.

When Becky let herself into the flat with the key that she had kept, she found Tess sitting so still and quiet that, for a second or two, her heart went into freefall. Then she scolded her for giving her such a fright and asked the question that others were asking over and over again.

Have you eaten? Have you slept? Have you looked at the will? Have you signed papers? Which, what, where?

'Have you eaten anything, Tessy?'

Tess looked up. 'Not you, too.'

Becky sat down beside her and took her hands. 'All right, then,' she said, chafing them gently. 'I'll lay off.'

Tess's mouth was set in the wryest of lines. 'My baggage of grief is private,' she said. 'I don't want it opened up for public display.'

'No,' agreed Becky, continuing to stroke Tess's trembling fingers. 'But what's that to do with eating?'

'You do see, though?'

'I do see.'

'What's the time, Becky?'

'Drinks time.'

'I don't think I can face alcohol.'

'Funny, nor can I.'

For a long time they sat in silence while the sun slid to the west and disappeared. Eventually Becky sighed. 'I've done something stupid.'

This succeeded in producing a reaction from Tess, who turned her wet face to Becky. 'You never do anything stupid.'

Becky looked unusually thoughtful. 'This time I have. I've just come from the doctor. I've gone and got myself pregnant.'

Tess absorbed this news. 'Is it Louis's?' Then it struck her that the question should have been formulated in the opposite way. *Is it Charles's?*

That's what's wrong, she thought. Everything is the wrong way round.

Becky's face was contorted with passion and feeling that sat oddly on its beguiling features.

'It's Charles's, of course. There is some honour among thieves. Not much, but enough. It was after I got back from America. After a disagreement about the FEROC contract. I came home with a stomach upset and the pill didn't work.'

Tess's second question was not much better. 'Will you keep it?'

Becky punched the dusty sofa cushions. 'Charles caught me heaving the other morning. And that's that, really.' She looked appalled at the prospect, trapped, angry. 'Tessy . . .' She lowered her voice. 'I look to you to set me right, hold my hand and all that. I don't know . . . I don't know how to behave well.'

Fatigue was again scrambling Tess's speech and lack of interest – grief was insatiable. 'When?'

'Mid January. Ish.'

Charles had been a warm body, warmer than George who was – had been – chilly-skinned. Charles had been needy, hurt and passionate. 'I love her,' he had told Tess, again and again while he made free with Tess's body. 'I love her.'

There are worse violations than seeking comfort.

Tess looked at Becky and, with a whimper, dropped her head into her hands and wept.

'Tessy . . .' Becky dropped on her knees beside her. 'I'm sorry. I shouldn't have told you. I thought it might introduce a lighter note, a bit of black comedy into the awfulness. You know my views on children.'

But Tess only wept the harder.

Becky wanted to take Tess back to the flat on the river but Tess refused, saying that she needed to be on her own.

She was the bereaved, the widow, two stages on from the child and the bride. Becky was not, and from that fundamental division of experience would flow their different courses.

'Well . . .' Freddie was in good fettle. He watched Tess slide back into the seat at her desk. 'Are we managing?' He peered at her. 'I'm afraid we're not looking as glam as the Scottish widows in the adverts. Here. I got you a cappuccino.'

He pushed the cup towards Tess but the sight of it made her nausea return. She put up a hand to hide a retch and Freddie's eyes narrowed.

'You got through?'

Tess's recollection of the funeral was of George's cousins crowding into church, of piles of sandwiches and flowers, piles of letters and not much else. 'It was like one of those television plays, all camera-tracking and no script,' she said. 'Yes, I got through.'

'Bill's been fidgety without you. Fitch has been on the line several times and there's a big cheese that Kit wants you to chat up. Apparently your legs have something to do with it. Lunch in the boardroom, best suit and muzzles. And there's a couple of divorcées with fat settlements.'

'Oh.' Tess opened and shut her drawer without purpose.

Freddie tossed his head. 'Are we working through the numb and angry stage? No? Are we merely patrolling the perimeter of grief? Tut, tut. My shrinky friends, such bully boys, tell me that you must positively throw yourself into the centre. Go for grief's core, darling. Otherwise, it won't be a meaningful experience.'

Tess felt unwilling laughter claim her. 'Freddie, you're always spot on. All sorts of people have been telling me what to feel. Anger, bewilderment. I don't feel any of those things. Just sad and bitterly, bitterly sad. That's all.'

'You be as numb as you like, darling. I can take it.'

'Sweet Freddie.'

'No, not sweet,' said Freddie. 'Not sweet at all.'

What had George been doing?

'He was killed,' wrote the commanding officer to Tess, 'while doing his duty. He was a good officer, popular and efficient, and he will be missed by his Regiment.'

No details. No catalogue of events. Neither of the scene, nor of what was said by whom. Merely the phrase 'killed while doing his duty'.

What had George seen in the course of doing his duty?

Loitering in the shadows, he had observed a section of the city in detail, a shadow-play of dense blocks and moving shapes, none of which or whom had offered him refuge.

He was angry. Earlier in the day one of the men, Ginger from Newcastle, had been blown up while removing a Republican tricolour from the top of a telegraph pole. The men had picked the bits up from the road and the hedge, and the locals had leaked out of their houses and clapped and cheered.

News of violent death always spread like marsh gas, flickering as fast as light and leaping out of control. George had heard about it sooner than Louis, for all his technology and watchfulness. George had known and liked Ginger.

Money had been poured into this country, a bloody and

obstinate place. Money that was intended to mend and build. But it did neither of those things.

From the pub opposite, George heard the strains of the same Republican song filtering out into the night. Briefly, he fingered his new moustache. Lives here were hard. But these stone people were also expert in enriching themselves with the gaudiness of martyrdom, and with the comforts of being a rebel.

Ah, yes, thought George, minutes before he was bundled into the car that prowled out of the shadows at the top of the street. There must be comfort to be had for the Republican in behaving precisely as your enemy, the British pig, expected.

In the situation in which he found himself, neither the pressal button nor the Browning were any help.

Half an hour later, he knew there was no hope. The car had been driving too far and too fast. The men were too nervous. He could smell it. He could also smell country through the gap in the window: a rain-washed, innocent mix of smoke and silage. Then one of the men leant over George and sweat and cigarette smoke drove away the other smells.

This was the end of his life. Blood trickled down from a cut above his eye and he darted out his tongue to taste it for he did not imagine that many sensations were left to him. Would he manage what was coming without talking? The question pressed down on his bladder and squeezed his heart.

George doubted it. But he had to try.

The car swooped and bucked to a halt, and George was thrown out of it onto mud-slicked tarmac.

'You pig,' said a thick, Irish voice.

And that was all.

As he died, George thought, I've managed well enough.

My business, wrote Tess, is not to think.

I'm angry with you, God, for not being here. You could have saved him.

That was all.

Yet in the respite granted between the bouts of wild and frantic grief crept a quite different sensation, one of relief.

Tess was aware that she had been given space. However she chose to reinvent herself, it would be in her own time and at her own pace.

Chapter Sixteen

On Midsummer's Day, the first lorries drove into Appleford and successfully clogged the road outside the village stores. A man in jeans with a pony-tail hopped out of the largest and went into the shop to ask where he would find the High House.

The Widow, who was buying the cheapest baked beans and margarine, craned her head to see what was going on. Within minutes of paying for her purchase she was back in her cottage and on the phone.

Edging down the narrow road, the lorries ground past the verges, harvesting bits as they did so, and manoeuvred round the back of the High House and into Eeyore's Paddock. In turn, they were followed by a flotilla of cars out of which emerged several bare-chested young men in shorts.

During the morning, the bones of two marquees had been constructed, rising high above the summer grass.

'Vandals,' cried the Widow, from her vantage point over the fence where she and a group of equally irate supporters were standing. 'You should not be here.'

One of the pony-tails heard the cry and looked up. He was young, muscled and glistening with sweat. 'Get a life, lady.'

But the Widow had a life, and it was raging inside her depleted body, giving it extraordinary strength. With a shout that might not have disgraced a football fan, she broke free from the group and propelled herself into the field. Running so hard that her modest dress flapped up over her thighs, she panted around the paddock, feet lifted like those of an old-fashioned sprinter, and waved a branch broken off by the lorries.

'Go away. You will destroy us,' she shrieked, blind to the picture that she made.

The foreman had a hasty word with one of his lads and stepped up to the back door of the High House. Almost immediately he returned with Colonel Frant, who managed to grab Jennifer Gauntlet by the arm and end her strange progress.

'Jennifer. Please.'

The Widow turned her hot gaze on the Colonel. 'How dare you?' she panted with contempt. 'How dare you destroy the village?'

Colonel Frant removed his hand. Years of chairing committees had taught him a few things about human nature and he did not ask why she alone was shouldering the village's defence given that she had only lived in it for a short time. Yet, indisputably, she was, and he was diminished by her gasping breath and wild gestures.

'You must not allow it, Colonel.' The Widow struggled for control. 'Once it starts, it's unstoppable.'

He knew that she spoke the truth. But debt performs conjuring tricks, and it had done so on the Colonel, turning an absolute belief into a relative one, overshadowing regret and guilt with something far stronger.

Peter had to pay Paul.

Sending out waves of lavender soap, the Widow swung round to confront the half-assembled marquees, which now resembled jagged teeth, eating up grass, space, light and peace. 'I curse you,' she said, a witch from the black haunts – and for a second Colonel Frant admired her. 'And I curse them.'

Colonel Frant opened his mouth and lied. 'My dear Jennifer. It's only this once. And, if I may say so, you know nothing of the matter.'

The Widow may have been on a state pension, plus a meagre contribution from her late husband's employer. She may have been nosy and neglected, and have lived in a house with a fake portico (commented on by purists), but she knew untruth when she heard it. Furthermore, sacrificing without a pang her social ambitions for Appleford, she was going to make her feelings clear. 'You know it isn't,' she said. 'You know you won't stop there. You have been greedy and wicked. And I am afraid I will not be able to bring myself to speak to you in future.'

The Colonel did not reply. The foreman and his lads had downed tools and were watching the drama without much interest. In the course of their work, they had seen and heard this sort of exchange before.

Silently, Colonel Frant led Jennifer Gauntlet towards the gate where her supporters, which included two mums from the council estate and the chairman of the local conservation society in a bright green dress with strawberries on it, waited and exchanged urgently delivered opinions on the scene unfolding in front of them. Jennifer was ushered out of the field.

'You have not won,' she said defiantly. 'Whatever happens, Colonel, you have lost.' The little group closed around her and moved off without anything further being said.

Above them, the blue sky was irradiated with summer sun.

John Frant returned to the High House where the sound of hammering filled every room. Having reached a state of mind where nothing but his terror and anxiety held any validity, he did not waste a second in reflecting as to whether, as the Widow had put it, he had won or not.

During the afternoon, Mrs Frant made a check on her provisions and, noting that she required coffee and sugar, set out for the shop. It was hot and the shop interior was stuffy. In its efforts to maintain a correct temperature, the deep freeze emitted a fractious note.

Tilda, Molly Preston's daughter, was serving behind the till. She smiled at Mrs Frant. 'I'm thrilled with my free tickets, Mrs Frant. It's very generous.'

'Free tickets?'

'Tickets to the tribal gathering at your place, this weekend. It's our perk if we live here. The company gives them out. I don't know what all the fuss is about and why people are so against it. It'll be fun.'

Molly Preston was rearranging bottles of Fanta and Coca-Cola and overheard the conversation. She frowned at her daughter.

Jilly Cadogan came in to pick up *Tatler* and *House and Garden*. Mrs Frant was counting her change and looked up. 'Hallo, Jilly. How are you?'

If men make war with weapons, women do so with a gesture. Jilly sent Angela Frant a look that declared hostilities and turned her back.

'Oh,' exclaimed Molly Preston, helplessly. 'Oh dear.'

'Thank you, Molly,' said Mrs Frant, and handed over the correct money.

Trapped between her natural instincts and taste – that is, an aversion to a rock concert in her own back garden – and her loyalties, which decreed that she should support her husband in sorting out his financial nightmare, Angela Frant was to be pitied. On the way home, the string bag containing a jar of coffee and a bag of sugar banging against her legs, she struggled with her pride and to staunch her wounds. The wounds of a woman who had spent her life endeavouring to live in the correct manner, only to discover that the formula did not run true. In return for her good behaviour, she had expected, indeed been taught, that a home, husband, children and, of course, a degree of material comfort would be hers.

But to rail against her false indoctrination was not in Mrs Frant's nature. She had married John for better or worse, and stick it out she would. She must.

That she considered his financial decisions imprudent, greedy even, would not pass her lips.

No one watching the tall, competent-looking figure continue on her way down the village street would have guessed that underneath the floral blouse raged many battles to keep the ship on course. Or that a door in Mrs Frant's mind was being pushed ever more open.

Remaking – reinventing – was more painful than Tess had anticipated. Her father had done it, in his transition from Army officer to businessman. Becky had done it. To a degree, Charles had done it. Even Jack had done it. Her mother was doing it. Recasting, recomposing. It was, Tess told herself, the spirit of the age. Its self-consciousness.

And what was she doing? Struggling to be a widow. Struggling to be the investment expert. Struggling to make sense of what was happening to her parents. Struggling with money – or, to be more precise, with debt whose reach appeared to run through everything she surveyed.

But, yes, Tess was also beginning to understand that she did not know herself and, until recently, she had been ignorant and fearful of her capabilities.

She fought on.

'My goodness,' commented Nigel Pavorde, on meeting Becky in the Room. 'You don't look very well.'

'Nor do you.' A white, somewhat frail-looking Becky raked huge eyes over Nigel's compact figure. 'You look dissipated.'

'Yes, well. One or two parties.'

'And Ascot. And Henley. And the little weekends in Normandy.'

'It's a nice life.'

Becky was amused. 'Yes, it is, isn't it?' She beckoned him closer. 'How're the gallstones?' she whispered.

'Bad.' He was grave.

Becky spotted Louis talking to Matt Barker by the huddle

that had gathered at the Rostrum. She allowed her eyes to rest on him briefly. 'And how's business, Nigel?'

His expression was not happy and he seemed overly nervous. Bad publicity had driven away potential Names and the commissions gained on the introductions to the Lime Street agencies were no longer so easy to obtain. If you are dependent on a river source, it is a matter of panic when it dries up. Nigel was not made of the stuff that enabled him to pack up the tent in a hurry and move on.

'Bad business, Piper Alpha,' he said. 'And the hurricane.'

By chance, Nigel used the same words of the disaster as Charles had. Becky was forced to conclude that these men had been taken by surprise that, in the end, insurance was in place to deal with emergency. In the glut of easy business, they had lost sight of the end. They, she, all of them had grown used to dealing with the form, not the substance.

'Keep off the cream, Nigel,' she advised, and moved on.

In fact, Charles had been strangely affected by Piper Alpha. He confessed to Becky of dreams filled with images of that awful death, and of other terrors. Wild winds, dying animals, stunted children whose blood flowed white not red.

Becky's response was to tell him to cut down on the wine and to lay off whisky altogether.

'It's part and parcel, my duck,' said Lily, during one of the phone calls that were beginning to be a regular event, 'of the all-talk-no-bottom brigade with a conscience.'

Becky had laughed. 'He's a nice man,' she replied, at her lightest and most charming. 'He cares about things.'

'You should know,' said her mother.

'Whatever,' said Becky. 'He's very trying at the moment. Still, when he starts his new job at Viscount's he'll calm down.'

'Didn't take long, then?' Lily was properly admiring. 'Lots of readies on offer, I take it?'

'Lots. They wanted Mawby's secrets.'

'Will they get them?'

'With *Charles*? Never. But they don't know that yet.'

Rebuffed by Becky's indifference, Charles found himself – on the pretext of sorting out child-care schedules – treading inside the front door of his ex-home and discussing his nightmares with his estranged wife.

'Those poor men.' Martha gazed angrily at Charles. 'I hope the families are being looked after.'

'Normally,' Charles looked down at his tea and wished it was whisky, 'one doesn't care too much about these things. We just move on.' He replaced the cup on the saucer. 'Martha, do you have any . . . ?'

'It's too early.' Martha anticipated his request.

He sighed. The kitchen was much the same: shabby, overloaded with toys and children's equipment, albeit stacked with precision. Tell-tale money-off coupons were stuck to the fridge door with magnets.

'Martha?' She leapt with alacrity to her feet. 'Have I given you enough money?'

She stopped dead in her tracks and ran her fingers through her orange hair: fatigued and wearing a T-shirt splattered with the tomato sauce she had been making, she was as far removed from Becky as it was possible to be.

'Money,' she said quietly, 'is not the problem.'

Sighing, Charles noticed, was becoming a habit with him. 'Tell me about the children.'

Martha explored her T-shirt, reconnoitring the tiny encrusted patches of red. 'What can I say? Once upon a time you were here, then you weren't. You can't expect them to be settled.'

'Don't say that.'

Martha had planned no scenes, had promised herself guile and patience. But now she quivered with anger. 'What do you expect, Charles? What *did* you *expect*?'

He remained hunched over the tea-cup. Martha had turned

into an avenging angel, the essence of the mother defending her children, of the authority he had discarded. 'Becky and I . . .' he said.

'Yes, Charles?'

'Becky and I are having a baby.'

Silence.

'Get out,' said Martha. 'Get out. Go.'

Feeling as if his anchor-line to safety and coherence had been cut, Charles did as she asked. On the front doorstep, he turned back to look at the house where he had spent ten years of his life, and encountered only strangeness and hostility.

Two days later, he received a letter from Martha.

I don't want to see you again but we must think of the children. You must have a divorce for the sake of the child and you must see our children as often as possible.

I will behave as best as I can manage. Whatever else you do Charles, whatever we do to each other, they must suffer as little as possible.

For most of her early and middle pregnancy Becky felt ill, exhausted and worn to the bone. Dark eyes and brows set in startling contrast in a bone-pale face, she seemed low and lustreless. Fortunately, her tall, narrow body only swelled a fraction, which meant that she could conceal the lump from colleagues until she judged it an appropriate time to reveal it.

She said nothing to Louis.

When her colleagues were informed, they were properly admiring to her face of her ability to carry on. They thought the pregnancy's lack of evidence simply *amazing*. Indeed, the general conspiracy to ignore it conspired to make the impending birth something of a miracle.

But, behind Becky's back, the same colleagues had marked her down, finished. She would, they agreed, be gone before the birth.

Becky hated, oh, how she hated, the whole business. The discomfort, the slowing down, the sensation that something inside her flounced and fluttered with the abandon of the truly at home.

April, May, June, July, August. Still she said nothing to Louis.

'Now you know why I packed my bags and fled,' said Lily, yet again on the phone. 'Packed my bags and went. It's a bloody awful business.'

Becky always had difficulty with the word father. 'Did *he* know about me?'

Up north, comfily installed in her favourite chair and surrounded by cushions adorned with lilac tassels, Lily wrinkled her forehead.

'He didn't stick around long enough.' There was just a trace of something in her voice that might have been called regret. 'But he was gorgeous and sort of hungry, if you see what I mean. I enjoyed being on my back with him.'

'You make it sound easy.'

Lily's lips were the product of smoking, criss-crossed with fine lines. 'But it wasn't, chuck. Not at all. In those days we were supposed to be good girls.'

Becky made a valiant effort to attach shame to sex, and failed.

'I thought,' Louis remarked, when he met Becky for lunch in one of the city's duller, but discreet, restaurants and she reported her conversation with Lily, 'that you wanted nothing to do with your mother. And there's you holding regular conversations.'

It was true. The garish insect had turned into something much more comfortable. A friend? A mother, possibly?

Louis had just returned from three weeks in Tuscany and looked brown and oiled. Becky drank some expensive mineral water, poured from a blue-frosted bottle. 'There's a lot of things I thought would go one way and have gone the other.'

'Why don't you go and visit her?'

'That old bird,' said Becky sweetly, 'abandoned me when I was a month old. Is there not justice, not to say self-preservation, in keeping my distance in her old age? She might dump me for a second time.'

But he was not listening. She leant forward, quivering with the love she habitually ignored. 'What's wrong, my Louis?'

But he was distracted and she was forced to ask the question for a second time. 'What's wrong?'

He smiled at her, and she was conscious of relief that she was not the cause of his evident distraction. 'Disasters all round,' he said. 'I think . . .' His hand circled above the breadsticks in a parody of a blessing. 'I think things . . . the LMX spiral may be out of control.'

'No,' she said. 'You're taking fright at the press reports. You just have to sit it out.'

'Not this time, Becky. I don't think.'

'You mean,' she was extra tart, 'that shunting excess-of-loss policies around the market each time for ten per cent commission has made some of you a lot of money and you don't want anybody else to get to know about it.'

He smiled and she sensed she had lost him. 'Something like that.'

'Listen.' In a bid to get his attention back, Becky circled his wrist with her fingers in a hungry movement, noting how the hairs had turned gold with the sun. 'You're not on any of the LMX syndicates?' He shook his head. 'Then what are you worrying about?'

'Lloyd's will get it in the neck. It will be seen as working for the benefit of insiders while the external Names are squeezed.'

'So what? So does the Bank of England. Or Parliament. Just sit tight.' Her fingers clamped down on his. 'Do you have anything to cover up?'

'Not really. And if things go wrong I have back-up.'

Becky refrained from asking what the back-up might be but her eyes narrowed a little. She removed her hand and sat back. 'Is Jilly very expensive?'

Becky rarely referred to his wife. Louis knew he was on dangerous ground and that he was, perhaps, missing a clue to what Becky was driving at. 'Yes, she is. You know that.'

At his answer it was Becky's turn to retreat. After a moment, Louis said, 'You're right. Sit tight.'

'After all, isn't that what generals do?'

After Louis had paid the bill, they went out into the street. Traffic dammed the road and a cache of litter rustled in the gutter as a wind whipped round the high-rise buildings.

I love this place, thought Becky.

At the traffic lights, Becky touched Louis's arm, a gesture not normally permitted in public.

'Louis, I'm pregnant.'

That evening, when he came home from work, Charles discovered Becky weeping in the bathroom.

'Darling . . .' He tried to gather her up in his arms. 'What on earth . . .'

'Don't touch me, please. Go away.'

This was unlike Becky and he grew alarmed. 'It's not the baby?'

She swivelled round to face him, her face reflecting into infinity in the three-sided mirror. 'No, Charles. It's not the baby.'

But it was the baby. The baby that was Charles's and not Louis's. 'I can't bear it,' he had said despairingly, jabbing the button repeatedly at the pedestrian crossing. 'Why isn't it mine?' The woman beside him, clutching a plastic mac, had looked at him with unconcealed curiosity.

'I can't have your baby,' Becky had flashed. 'Anyway, I don't *want* anyone's baby. It's a mistake.'

Louis had run his eyes up and down her body, and Becky had been overwhelmed by panic for she knew instinctively that he was saying goodbye.

They crossed the road and he turned to face her.

'But you took me,' she cried. 'It was you who led me, seduced me, taught me and I followed. Willingly. You can't abandon me now.' Without knowing it, she echoed Tess's words to George. 'It's unfinished. Our business together.'

A deep tan often has the effect of making faces appear good-natured and untroubled. Louis seemed unperturbed as he said, 'There's a child to consider,' but his voice had darkened.

'Why these antiquated notions all of a sudden?' Becky demanded. You don't care normally. You're a buccaneer not a vicar.'

'Even I,' said Louis bitterly, 'have limits.'

'What about your children? Did they come into it when you had me?'

'They had gone.'

'You want to get rid of me.'

He was very gentle. 'Do you really believe that?'

She looked up at the features she knew almost as well as her own. 'This is nothing to do with the good of a child,' she said, gathering together her shrewdness and courage. 'This is to do with your jealousy.'

He knew her inside out. Her passions. Her ambitions. Her careful control. Her wounds. And if Louis loved Becky against his will, he loved her too well to lie. 'Maybe,' he said, 'but it doesn't change my mind. And it does not invalidate your baby's need for a secure home.'

'I'll get rid of it.'

She spoke in a furious whisper, and the woman with the plastic mac who had stayed to watch this street theatre was thrilled by the tender gesture that Louis made in cupping one hand around Becky's face and stroking her hair with the other.

'No, you won't,' he said. 'You know you won't. You like to

think you're capable of anything, but it would be killing yourself.'

She shook free of him. 'All right.' She gave in. 'That's it, then.'

'Goodbye, Becky.'

'If you think, Louis,' she said, with the first real despair he had ever seen on her face, 'that this guarantees my baby's future security, then you are far, far more stupid than I had ever imagined.'

'Take care, Becky, won't you?'

We like to think that we are shaped by our surroundings, our families, our climate, our jobs, our lovers. Yet there is a point where the process is arrested and the remainder of the business of fashioning a life remains with us and only us. In the end we shape our own lives, assume responsibility for our thoughts, are endowed with a power to choose.

Becky understood the point very well.

'Listen,' Charles coaxed a still sobbing Becky, 'you'll hurt the baby, if you don't stop. Please stop.'

She allowed him to draw her out of the bathroom into the sitting room where he sat her down. 'How can I help?' he asked.

Becky looked past him through the window. 'You can't.'

'Yes, I can. You see, I've done it before.'

'Go away. Please.'

Charles made for the kitchen and paused by the drawing-room door. 'I'm looking forward to a son.'

How strange, ran her thoughts between the dying sobs, how strange. In the end, it was not death separating her from Louis, as it had intervened between Tess and George, but the prospect of a new life.

Charles bustled out of the kitchen, carrying a tray with neatly arranged cups and saucers on it which he put down on the table. He spread a napkin over Becky's knees and placed in front of her a plate of exquisitely cut bread and butter.

'Eat up,' he said.

With a startled look, Becky obeyed. Watching her force down the food, Charles was reminded of the time he had looked after Martha. The memory gave him pleasure.

Chapter Seventeen

Temporarily, the Bollys had lost heart. A couple of its members were abroad, one was ill and the rest were submerged by work. The autumn lunch was put off until the late autumn.

Matt and Louis met for a drink in a wine bar which was already occupied by Boulderwood, one of the more flamboyant and hugely successful brokers in excess-of-loss policies. Louis drank his wine and watched Boulderwood, who had a party of younger men, with cleverness and ambition written all over them, clustered around him.

'I gather he's just bought a third Ferrari.' One of Matt's more likeable qualities, and for which Louis admired him, was his lack of personal cupidity, and he spoke without envy.

Louis smiled. 'So?'

Matt returned the smile. 'So?'

For a moment both reflected on the differing styles of being rich. At the bar Boulderwood oozed and dripped with the stuff. Matt and Louis had money built, like the calcium deposits, into their bones. But it was not to be denied that they were brothers under the skin, just that Louis and Matt went about their business more subtly.

They talked in low voices about the scandal that now looked inevitable. Their conversation made references to various terms – 'excess-of-loss', 'under-reserved', 'asbestosis', 'computer leasing' – and, with a note of incredulity, to the name of a syndicate that had agreed to reinsure the run-off of a second syndicate with a large exposure to asbestosis and pollution. The two men agreed that, in normal times, these problems were containable. Placed in the context of a market that had been sent reeling by a series of disasters, beginning with Piper Alpha, and add to it a nosy press and a band of ruined Names who, if reports were correct, were fighting back, the picture was less reassuring. But they also talked of unease in Korea, the rise of China, and terrorism, the areas of turbulence in which Louis, the expert in political risk, was interested.

'If I was dealing with all that,' said Matt at last (who, it must be remembered, underwrote nuclear matters), 'I would have ended up very pessimistic indeed.'

'Nonsense,' said Louis. 'It's the same as betting on the horses.'

Yet the immediate outlook, they agreed, was somewhat rocky, a prospect that, strangely enough, Louis rather relished. Not that he would mention it to Matt. Why he should feel so, he was not sure. Bloody-mindedness? An idea that it was impossible to wrap up matters securely? Approval that nature hit back? Father Jerome had held strong views on retribution and perhaps . . . perhaps, he had been right.

He recollected Nigel's declaration: 'We haven't done anything wrong.'

The inverse logic, however, was not to conclude that anything had been done correctly. Louis put this point to Matt.

Matt and Louis were men from the same mould. As was usual with any problems, they resorted to figures. Yet, having mulled them over, these did not offer much comfort to Matt, sharper on the immediate. But Louis, whose mind was strategic, was more robust.

'Don't lose your nerve,' he said.

'No indeed.' Matt seemed more conspiratorial than ever.

More champagne was being consumed at the bar and when Matt and Louis left Boulderwood was in full flight.

*

During the spring and summer a small battle had been waged among the by-laws and regulations concerning the English countryside. The District Council had refused permission to hold the first rock gathering at the High House. The magistrates' court had decreed an unequivocal no but the Crown Courts had wavered.

'Par for the course,' a representative of the Countrymen debriefed Colonel Frant. 'It's just a question of sitting it out. We tend to win in the end. We have the funds, the time, the expertise. Locals don't. Look at the bypasses.'

A petition signed by two thousand people was handed in. Advertisements for the gathering were heard on Radio One. The anti-rock gathering brigade in Appleford held its breath, and many bitter opinions were aired about the Frants. The pro party felt a blow was being struck for liberty: the liberty to enjoy themselves in their own chosen fashion.

The party of the indifferents was too small to make its voice felt. What happens, asked one of its members, if the gathering is cancelled and all these people turn up anyway?

Colonel Frant's necessary journeys through Appleford, once such pleasant excursions, were painful reminders of his fall. As he performed his errands, it was borne in on him that a life that had been conducted so moderately – and moderately successfully – was in its latter part proving quite the reverse.

At the beginning of September, the magistrates' court ruled that it was permissible for the rock gathering to take place.

'How many back-handers did that take?' demanded Jilly Cadogan of Louis.

As promised, the Countrymen paid any bills that were owing, and the District Council retired, smarting, to consider the second application for a permanent showground at the High House.

'I can't understand it,' was the most frequently heard refrain in conservationist quarters – from whose ranks Colonel Frant had been banished for ever. 'How could he?'

A financially secure position was, as always, a comfortable place from which to criticize.

On 21 September fifty thousand people converged on Appleford.

Their vehicles, which included a couple of clapped-out London buses, clogged the roads and rendered the lanes impassable. Their occupants were noisy, mostly good-humoured and young. Some were drunk, some drugged, some neither. Within hours, the village had been turned into a vast car park.

From mid-morning to midnight, the music beat, a pulsing accompaniment to the fleshly delights being pursued in the marquee and the fields beyond. At Riley's Farm, the music affected the pigs, who ran in wild circles and refused their feed. A skim of litter settled on the roads and in the gutters, and blew over Appleford.

Meanwhile, at the east end of the village, the Appleford Beekeepers Association set up their annual stall. Molly Preston stacked the pots and set out her till with a ten-pound float in it.

She stood for a long time but, in the end, her varicose veins played her up and she sat down. After a four-hour vigil, the tally of honey-buyers amounted to three.

In the afternoon, the *pétanque* club, for which the village was noted, began a much-debated match with a rival team. After an hour, the match was abandoned for the noise was too great for concentration.

In the church rooms, the jumble sale to raise money for the playgroup was a fiasco: it was invaded by strangers, who picked over and plundered the knick-knacks and old clothes and left without paying.

Throughout the long day, protesters and supporters went about their business and, eventually, to their unquiet beds.

During the night the Widow was woken by a pounding on her door. A little dizzy with apprehension, she padded downstairs and opened the door on the chain. In the porch light, a figure with large staring eyes stood swaying. 'They're coming,' he announced. 'Hide me.'

'Go away.'

'HIDE ME.'

The Widow slammed the door and fumbled her way towards a telephone. Later, peering out from her bedroom window through the curtains, she watched the man being led towards a car by a policeman.

I fought the fight, she congratulated herself, and returned to her abandoned, and now cold, bed.

I'll never get used to living alone, she thought, and climbed into it.

The telephone rang in the Pimlico flat at two-thirty on 22 September. Woken by its first ring, Tess waited until her head had cleared before she picked it up.

It was her mother. She spoke fluently and clearly and issued instructions. 'Your father has collapsed and has been taken to Blackwater Hospital.'

'Oh, Mum.'

'Ask for intensive care. It's serious.'

It was only after she had put the phone down that Tess realized that the car was in the garage being repaired after her unfortunate collision with the lime tree outside the flat. After a second or two of panic, she acted on impulse and picked up the phone. Why she chose to do so, what inner prompting directed her action, Tess never knew.

Within half an hour Iain MacKenzie was outside her front door.

'I can't thank you enough,' she said, as she got into the passenger seat.

'I'm sure you'd do the same for me,' he said.

'I hope Flora didn't mind too much.'

On the subject of Flora's feelings, Iain remained silent. He concentrated on driving, and soon the smell of the river filled the car as they passed over the water, grey and shot through with neon light.

'Why don't you try to sleep?' Iain's voice sounded in the darkness. 'You never know what's going to happen during the next few days.'

Tess leant back and closed her eyes. 'I wonder,' she said, and stopped. Iain waited. 'I wonder if my father chose to be ill. Things have been so difficult.'

They reached the Kingston bypass, and Iain put his foot down. After a minute or two, he asked, 'How is your situation? Do you need any more help with pensions or with any of the red tape?'

Iain was the sort of person who used expressions like 'red tape'. There was a long pause, then Tess sighed. 'Everyone's fallen over themselves to be helpful. Only . . .'

He turned his head to look at her. 'Only . . . ?'

She put up a hand to her mouth and was surprised to feel it shaking, so she replaced it in her lap. 'Only,' she gave each word due weight, 'I appear to be pregnant – quite pregnant, actually – but I've managed not to tell anyone yet. I didn't want anyone to know. *I* didn't want to know.'

The situation struck Iain as odd. 'No one knows?'

'No.'

'Is it not rather wonderful?' he asked quietly.

'*No!*'

He was taken aback by the passionate quality of her rejection.

'I can't cope with a baby.'

The car sped on, rapier headlights stabbing through the darkness.

Eventually, Tess said, 'I hope you're not too shocked by my reaction.'

He reflected. 'I've learnt not to be shocked unless I know the story and I don't know yours.'

Tess shifted in the seat and the discomfort eased in her groin. In archaeology a distinction is drawn between methods used to establish absolute dating (the sequential placing of events in a fixed time-scale) and relative dating (the ordering of events by cross-referencing one to the other). Driving into the dawn towards her stricken parents, Tess placed a marker on the precise moment when she acknowledged and cross-referenced her pregnancy and, with it, her doubt, her guilt and the question as to whose baby it was.

'I don't want it,' she said. 'But I can't possibly get rid of it. I know I should be pleased, but women aren't necessarily pleased any longer to have babies.'

Iain glanced at his watch. Three fifty-five. 'Flora and I couldn't have any.'

He did not mean to administer a corrective, but he was tired and the subject was one that remained raw. In the dark, Tess flushed bright scarlet. 'I'm sorry,' she said, and added, 'Thank you for doing so much for me.'

Iain negotiated the slip-road off the motorway and cut the speed. 'George was my friend. And I hope you're also a friend.'

'Stupid, isn't it? Being pregnant and widowed.'

Tess's voice quivered, and Iain detected a touch of hysteria. He stamped on the brake, brought the car to a standstill, reached over and took Tess's hands in his own.

'Difficult, certainly. But not, I think, stupid.'

Weak, and fearful of what lay ahead, she said, 'I don't know. I don't know.'

After he had escorted her to the reception desk at the hospital, Iain said goodbye and drove back to London.

He was greeted by Flora sitting up in bed with a knitted bedjacket around her shoulders, drinking tea from a Thermos.

'I can think of better starts to a day.' She drank from the cup with one of her slurping noises. 'Is the Colonel all right?'

'I didn't ask, Flora.'

'We'd better watch that girl.' Flora unscrewed the flask and poured herself a refill. 'I reckon she'll use us, given half a chance.'

Iain towered above her. 'Do you think,' he asked coldly, 'I might have a cup?'

'Of course,' Flora was at her mildest and most gentle.

It was during her elevenses, when she was checking through the supermarket bill, that Flora recollected Iain's face as he had got into bed. For some reason, the memory made her uneasy.

At eight o'clock the next morning Tess and Mrs Frant drove back to a silent, shaken Appleford.

'The ambulance couldn't get into the village because of the traffic,' Mrs Frant told her daughter. 'There was . . .' she bit her lip '. . . a delay.'

'Yes,' said Tess.

As they drove by, Ron Davis was standing in the recreation ground surveying the litter, which was stuffed into hedges, up trees and dumped in heaps. A layer of broken glass flowed, glittering treacherously, over the grass where the dogs and children walked.

But in the Three Horns pub, Dave was bagging up his takings with a smile. Upstairs, his wife was bed-bound with three aspirins. Normally well attended, Betty's jump and pump keep-fit club had only one participant, Jeanne Rudge – she had adopted the French version of her name after working as a waitress in the Dordogne. The rest could not face it.

Ron Davis told Jimmy Plover that he doubted if the mess would ever be cleared up. As he was imparting this view, there was a shout from the other end of the recreation ground and Dan Preston waved frantically. Ron and Jimmy broke into a run.

'There's a body in the grass,' Dan informed them. 'Alive but out for the count on something.'

Looking neither to the right nor to the left, Mrs Frant drove on.

'We have to be thankful that Daddy died peacefully,' said Tess, as the car eased into the drive of the High House.

'Do we?' Mrs Frant felt as if the words were being dragged out of her.

By mutual consent, the two women hovered on the doorstep, reluctant to go in. It was as if they both sensed that, once they crossed the white stone into the hall, what had happened would acquire the status of truth.

Then Tess pushed open the door and stepped into a hard, painful future.

During the afternoon the marquees were struck and stowed. The foreman rang the front-door bell of the silent house, whose curtains had remained drawn, and stood, square and uninterested, on the doorstep.

'We're very sorry to hear of the death of the Colonel,' he said to Tess, who answered the door.

She murmured, 'Thank you.'

'You won't be wanting us next week, then. Not till the funeral's over.'

'No, we won't be wanting you again. I don't think.'

But the foreman had a timetable, which he produced. 'The hard-core is due for next week, for the permanent toilets and access to the car park.'

'You're joking. I had no idea.'

'Then there are the litter-bin facilities and the refreshment point.'

She stared at him. 'What do you mean?'

The foreman stared back and his expression suggested that he was not going to get involved but she ought to find out what was going on. 'Well,' Tess swallowed, 'my mother and I won't be pursuing the project.'

'I see,' said the foreman, and took his leave.

Metrobank were not pleased. The personnel officer, pompous, middle-aged and something of a bully, telephoned Tess to inform her that, of course, she must take compassionate leave. Again. But, he underlined the words, the bank could only see their way to giving her four days. Tess must, of course, take time off to help her mother with the funeral, he continued, but . . .

Four days after the funeral, Tess returned to the office and Bill put the situation into perspective. He sat Tess down by his desk and plied her with coffee she could no longer stomach. 'It's most unfortunate, Tess, but we can't keep covering for you. Clients are not interested in your personal affairs.'

'No.' Tess was perfectly ready to concede the point. She had opted to work in a world that rejected making time to grieve. Familiar with its laws, she accepted them.

Weary and apprehensive, she looked up at Bill. He cleared his throat and panic squeezed her stomach. It would be so easy for everything to fall apart. She summoned the reserves of her energy. 'What's been going on?'

'Good girl.'

She indicated the piles of papers and prospectuses on his desk. 'Looks like the nine layers of Troy. Why don't you give me some?' she said wryly, in a way that was becoming habitual. 'I can bone up on them between wrestling with probate and maddened villagers.'

Bill leafed through the top layer and pushed three thick documents towards her. 'I'd be glad of your views on these.' He got up from his chair and walked around the desk. A hand, impersonal and dutiful, dropped onto Tess's shoulder. 'I'm sorry,' he said, as the phone began to ring, 'I really am.'

At least, Tess reflected, I have a place. She smiled at Bill as he muttered into the phone, careful not to appear too grateful, and got to her feet, noting as she did so that a brochure for a business in the Caymans, which he had retained, had an air ticket secured to it with a paper-clip.

Freddie was away. GONE TO CRUISE THE CASBAH IN MOROCCO, said a large notice on his desk.

The others went out of their way to welcome Tess back, and then, as quickly, returned to their desks. They did not refer again to her father's death. Yet, for a second or two, they had stepped out of the circle drawn around their desks to make a verbal gesture and she was touched.

Back home in Appleford, the phone and the doorbell would be ringing. There was a structure for dealing with a death in the village and an unwritten rule that, however despised the deceased, it would be observed. It was a way of ensuring that one's own death was honoured.

Molly Preston had come round with one of her shepherd's pies. Jimmy Plover house-sat during the funeral as burglars were known to strike at such times. Ron Davis supervised the car parking. Eleanor Thrive organized the team of sandwich- and cake-makers. Jilly Cadogan made an ostentatious point of arranging the flowers in the church.

The Widow had insisted that she stayed for a couple of nights with Mrs Frant, just in case.

'Come and live with us,' Becky had urged Tess. 'Please. For a bit.'

But Tess, who had a shrewd idea of the limits of Becky's philanthropy, said no. Anyway, she preferred her isolation: the safety of the dust and silence of the unsold Pimlico flat where she could think.

George. Her father. The unborn baby.

Tess surveyed the office: the screens guarding their neon information and the figures of her colleagues.

'Since the heart of the capitalist system is profit, it is not surprising that the profits are a vital component of corporate valuation.' (From *How the City Works*, a manual to which Tess had referred frequently in the early days.)

That was a fact, and a simple one. But the edges of the fact were blurring, slipping, gathering doubt and ambiguity. What was profit? Clearly, it was not just a matter of deducting costs from revenue. There were also questions of depreciation to consider, of earnings per share, and much, much more. According to the Bible, it profited a man nothing if he had lost his soul, yet Juvenal, the Roman satirist, felt that all profit was sweet, whatever its source.

It could be argued that her father had lost his soul in search of profit, and it had profited him nothing.

Tess returned to a theme she had discussed with Becky. We are not entirely fashioned by our nurture. We choose to make ourselves.

'Of *course* we do. Of course,' Becky had insisted. But then she would, wouldn't she? 'You can,' she added. 'You must step outside the frame.'

Knowing this, and accepting it, but beset with doubt and fear, Tess was posed the question as to how she was to steer her pregnant barque around the sharks and barracudas cruising the City's water.

How was she going to wrestle and kill the monster that was feeding off her family? How was she going to interweave the moral, physical and spiritual, and profit from the deal that had been handed to her?

How?

She did not know.

'When I told Becky I was pregnant,' she wrote in her diary, 'she did not seem that interested. Sometimes I wonder why I love her. But I do.'

Chapter Eighteen

'I'm afraid that the news is not good,' said the smart, successful and ruinously expensive Rufus Metcalf to Tess, during a consultation after Colonel Frant's funeral.

Rufus had been recommended by Louis as a red-hot lawyer who would help her to grapple with her father's estate, which invoked the undying enmity of Colonel Frant's country solicitor with whom he had originally placed his affairs.

Tess could not afford a Rufus but, if she had lost a few illusions during her widowhood, she had acquired prudence. Prudence suggested that successful people tended to have successful people on their side and she had two priorities: to keep her job and to keep her mother afloat. Wily, foxy fighters were better on your own side.

On the fate of Appleford, she had less time to expend in speculation and subsided into a weary fatalism. Viz., what was happening to the village had been bound to happen anyway.

Of the baby she thought little. Except for the times when she wondered, twitchy and fearful, why she had not got rid of it while it had been possible.

Very often at great turning-points, men acquire new wives and women cut their hair. Tess had taken to putting hers up, piling it in a coil, shiny with pregnancy hormones, on top of her head. It suited her. Now, she leant forward over Rufus's desk.

'The bad news?'

'According to Mr Flee, your father's original solicitor, your father had not taken out estate insurance. And I'm afraid he had failed to renew his stop-loss insurance too. Probably he felt that he had no more funds to do so.'

'Meaning?' The question was superfluous.

'There is no insurance against the Lloyd's claims on your father's estate. At the moment there is a large cash call outstanding, with which your father was attempting to deal at the time of his death. Indeed, he is owed money from the Countrymen organization. But I must warn you that the likelihood is there is more owing.'

Organized and unmoved, he waited for her reaction. 'Oh, Dad,' she murmured.

Refus had seen this play before. A members' agent trawling through dinner parties, prowling Henley, the private views and cocktail parties, the Rotary Club dinners. A word slipped into a ready ear. The introduction to the Rota Committee. The acceptance. (And, of course, the payback to the member's agent.)

His own parentage of sufficient vagueness, he understood perfectly the allure of Lloyd's for the man and the woman in the terraced house or the modest colonel in the shires, who had made a little money. For, as much as its promised yield, Lloyd's seductiveness lay in its establishment dazzle and its exclusivity.

'How does that leave my mother and me?' Tess's hair slipped from its anchorage and she tucked it back into place without a hope of hearing anything positive.

Rufus glanced at the papers in front of him, which was unnecessary for he knew what they contained. 'There are additional problems. Your father signed a five-year lease for his fields with the Countrymen, which makes it difficult to sell your house for its proper value. Normally, it would be very valuable and I think the best advice is for your mother to stay there, for she will then have a roof over her head. You will, at least, have some income from the Countrymen.'

'Do we know about the planning permission for the showground?'

Rufus shrugged. 'Tricky but the Countrymen are experienced in this kind of operation. They know the loopholes in the Criminal Justice Act. They argue that they wish to be legal and above board and, indeed, that is exactly what they are. They also have access to the best legal advice. These events have to be held somewhere and they maintain they are the most responsible set-up to arrange them.'

Tess stood up. 'Dad must have been desperate to do this. But I didn't realize quite how desperate. Imagine that weight of worry crushing you. All the time.'

'He was certainly badly advised over Lloyd's and, it would seem, placed on some dubious syndicates. But your father could not have predicted the disasters. Nor is he the only one.'

'No, I suppose not.' Fearing the size of the bill, Tess terminated the interview.

'It is anticipated,' ran the opening lines of the Chairman's speech to the meeting of the Appleford Society, the first to be held after the rock gathering, 'that if the plans for the permanent showground go ahead, which seems likely, there will be an anticipated annual tally of traffic movement of approximately two hundred and fifty thousand vehicles. This will have considerable impact on village roads and streets and on the nearby B5032.'

It was Saturday morning and Tess was sitting with her mother in the High House reading the minutes of the meeting. On the table between them lay Colonel Frant's ties, which they had been trying to sort out. But, somehow, the pile for throwing away had become muddled with the one for keeping.

'I can't throw this away.' Mrs Frant had held up a tattered regimental tie. 'I can't.'

In the end the women had given up and sat staring at the melded heaps.

'Apparently,' Mrs Frant now stared at the calendar on the wall, 'there was uproar at the meeting. I got some hate telephone calls afterwards.'

'Oh, Mum.' These days, Tess found she was often inarticulate, words having been chased away by events and emotions that were too big.

Mrs Frant gave her odd laugh. 'Nigel Pavorde . . . *Nigel Pavorde* cuts me dead, if you please.'

Tess read on. 'Seventy-five per cent of weekends between March and October could have one or both days affected by the planned activities, including three weekend music festivals a year.' She dropped the paper. 'They're probably exaggerating in order to have a better bargaining position.'

Her mother's hands twisted together. 'It doesn't make much difference, does it?' There was a desperate, anguished silence. 'I don't think your father understood quite what he had done. I don't think he would have countenanced living with this . . .' she, too, searched for words '. . . this nonsense and noise. He intended only to have the rock gathering, make some money, pay the Lloyd's bill and then return to normal.' Another painful silence. 'I blame myself. He never talked to me about this sort of thing because I'm so bad at detail.'

Tess poked at the morning's post and extracted the letter from the Countrymen, which had arrived in it. It was polite but inexorable. Anticipating a favourable decision on Planning Application No. 12/341, the foreman and his lads would commence 'the erection of nine toilet blocks, three service buildings and some structures for formal shooting'.

The letterbox rattled but neither woman moved. Later Tess, passing through the hall, picked up a white envelope on the doormat whose contents were soft and heavy. As she did so, her nostrils wrinkled and her stomach heaved. Suppressing a desire to open the door and pitch the envelope outside, she went instead to fetch newspaper, Sellotape and a plastic bag.

I will be calm, she told herself, as she deposited the parcel in the dustbin. I will be calm for . . . and added, with a sense of extreme detachment . . . for the baby.

That evening Mrs Frant took her longer route around the garden but avoided the spoilt paddock and the meadow. From a deckchair on the terrace, Tess watched her, a less vigorous figure than of old marching the pathways of a life that had vanished in a garden blazing with orange and red. She resolved to make no mention of the envelope and its contents.

Her mother returned. 'I like to look at border when I'm particularly agitated,' said Mrs Frant, and pointed to the strip of lawn running beside it. 'You can see how worn it's become.'

Tess handed her a cup of tea and Mrs Frant settled herself in the deckchair. 'At least,' she drank thankfully, 'you've got George's baby.'

It was eight forty-five on Monday morning and Tess's phone rang on her desk at Metrobank.

'Dear,' said Mrs Mantle, 'how did the funeral go?'

Mrs Mantle was one of Tess's more idiosyncratic and favoured clients.

'As well as could be expected. Thank you.' Tess could hear Mrs Mantle's budgerigars shrieking in the background – Mrs Mantle had a passion for pedigree birds. This suggested that she was in the kitchen, probably surrounded by bills from the morning post which was why she had got on the phone.

'Now,' said Mrs Mantle. 'The tally, dear.'

Tess had already extracted the printout and was flipping through it. 'Fifty-three thousand, Mrs Mantle.'

'That's nice, dear. Now, I need a little something to help me out. I've been such a naughty girl.'

'How much?'

'Three and a half, dear.'

Good God, is that what one paid for a pedigree budgerigar? Tess assessed the figures on the Strip – Bid, Ask, Mid-Close, Vol, Sector. 'I was thinking of top-slicing your holding in Quaxocos. Will that do?'

'Fine, dear. Just send the cheque.'

Tess had bent over to shove the printout back into her desk drawer when the size of her stomach struck her. Then she knew she could not hide it for much longer. She looked up to see Freddie's raised eyebrows.

'Confess, darling.'

She sighed.

'It's so obvious, Tess. Everyone knows. They just don't say.'

'I . . .'

Freddie waggled a finger and spoke into his phone. 'Give us a price for size, then.'

Tess's phone rang again. It was a solicitor with whom she had struck up a friendship – always wise in her business.

'I've got a plum for you, Tess,' he said. 'Half gaga, I'm afraid, and living in squalor until his nephew returned from Canada and found a whole raft of stock hidden under the carpet. He's worth about three hundred grand and the nephew wants to set up a structure to put him in a decent home. Doesn't have to be too long-term. He's eighty-five and apparently, in his day, quite a famous cricketer.'

'Fine, Andrew. Send me the details. And, Andrew, thank you.'

'Location meeting.' Freddie chucked a file over to Tess. 'More, more of the same. The company view . . . who cares? Far East. Blah, blah. Bloody old Willis will drone on as the expert and, therefore, no one's allowed to contradict him.'

Freddie knew that Tess knew that he did not mean a word of it. 'Tess, darling. You've got to face up to it. Take it from one who's had to do the same.'

'OK, OK.'

They walked down the corridor, Freddie chattering *sotto*

voce. 'Now when's it due? George came back for the last weekend in April. You stopped being sick secretly in the loos July-ish. January, then. Ish.'

'How do you get to know everything, Freddie?' Tess was grateful for his bothering. A second elapsed. Then another. 'What am I going to do? They'll sack me.'

'So. Get another job. *Penses-toi à ton* brownie-point mountain, as they say. Our very own tragedy queen. Just think. Widow bravely bears dead hero's baby, he who gave his life for peace in Ireland. So touching. And Metrobank sacks her. *Not good copy.* I've a good mind to ring up the *Mail* and graciously grant them an exclusive.'

'I want my job, Freddie. I don't want a baby. I like my job and I'm just getting good at it.'

'Tough, my darling. You should have thought of that.'

She raised a pair of angry eyes to his. 'Biology is a bugger.'

'Now on *that*,' said Freddie, 'I am the expert.'

Tess stopped outside the ladies. 'You go ahead.'

When she arrived at the meeting room, they had begun without her. As she came in, the men stopped talking and Tess was terribly conscious suddenly of the tell-tale click-clack of her high-heeled shoes.

After the meeting Tess asked to see Bill and confessed to her pregnancy. Bill was not amused. 'Good God,' he expostulated. 'What next?'

He did not mean to be unkind or callous, but his priorities were different. Quite, quite different. As Director of UK Equities and Special Situations, he had a margin to achieve to justify the existence of his department. In what she hoped was a considered manner, Tess outlined her plans for maternity leave and childcare.

'I can give you eight weeks max,' said Bill. 'Then, Tess, you've really had your whack of compassion.'

When she returned to her desk, Tess consulted the *Estimate Directory* and studied the form for several companies she had marked. Employees of Metrobank could only deal on the market for themselves after their clients had been serviced. But Tess required capital. What was the point of being passively feminine and non-opportunistic with regard to herself if she was the opposite when it came to clients? What was to stop her making some money? Surely the risk entered into on behalf of another was the risk you also assumed for yourself.

Dear Iain [Tess wrote],

I hope you and Flora are well. Forgive me for bothering you yet again, but I wondered if I could ask you to check if there is any possibility of more money from the Army? My father left quite a few debts and I am exploring all avenues in an attempt to meet them.

'If you write back . . .' After she had read the letter, Flora spoke across the breakfast table in a very soft voice indeed, 'I shall think the less of you, Iain. She's just using you and taking advantage of your good nature.' Iain replied that afternoon, writing from the office.

Dear Tess,

I am sorry to hear of your difficulties. I have today made some enquiries about possible *ex gratia* payments but whether or not we can squeeze you into the correct category I don't know. I will get back to you.

Yours, Iain.

P.S. I am hoping to be made redundant in the first round of the Army cuts which are being threatened, and going to live up north.

His letter coincided with the one containing Rufus Metcalf's staggering bill. Fortunately, the estate agent phoned to say that, at last, there was a cash buyer for the Pimlico flat, provided that Mrs Mason vacated the premises within the month.

Before she closed the door for the last time, Tess stood in the tiny hallway and said goodbye to her dead husband.

The flat felt stale and unresponsive and, however hard she tried to call up something of George, an essence, a wisp of memory of the man who had once lounged in and out of its rooms, she failed. Only the taste of grief remained on her tongue.

She closed the door, deposited the key and drove over to Becky who was accompanying her down to Appleford.

'How are you feeling, Bec?'

'Ghastly. How are you feeling, Tess?'

'Ghastly.'

'Why are we in this jam?'

'Biology,' they mouthed at each other.

'The funny thing is,' said Tess, 'the bigger this baby grows, the less I think about it.'

'Liar,' said Becky.

Tess negotiated the car down the Kingston bypass. 'It seems that Dad increased his underwriting limit to three hundred thousand in 'eighty-five and four hundred thousand for 'eighty-six. The managing agent suggested it.'

Becky glanced at her. 'There could be some profits from the good syndicates, you know, if he was on any. You must sit tight and trade through.'

'I don't think he *was* put on any. Anyway, I've made a bit of money on the market. It's pitiably little, but it helps. The only trouble is, the rail fares from Appleford are going to slaughter me. Still, Mum will help look after the baby.'

As they drove into the High House, Becky had an uninterrupted view of the lavatories, basted in grey concrete and hooded in green corrugated iron. 'Oh, my Lord,' she exclaimed. 'They look awful.'

'I know,' said Tess miserably.

Becky pinched Tess's arm between two fingers. 'Listen, I promise not to fight with your mother.'

Tess smiled at Becky and felt better, for this declaration of a cessation of hostilities was a mark of profound affection.

Without doubt, Mrs Frant's trials and tribulations had weakened her support for the absolutes of good manners and of restraint. There is not much else to recommend them, but worry and fatigue can and frequently do provide a licence to be rude and Mrs Frant availed herself of it. The battle inside her was being waged, but it was not at all sure that her training would remain in place. Indeed, it would be true to say that, at the end of her life, Mrs Frant was not half as well-mannered as in her heyday when it would not have mattered. Nor was she as controlled. On occasion, and this frightened her daughter, she showed an open contempt for the world that had let her down.

Mrs Frant greeted Becky with barely concealed dislike and immediately switched the conversation to Jack, who was back in hospital with his stomach complaint.

'It was bad enough that he couldn't get back for the funeral,' said Mrs Frant, with longing. 'I was so hoping to see him. Still, Penelope,' she emphasized the name and stared at Becky to underline the point, 'is a very nice girl and keeps me fully in touch. It's so lovely how they are just like that.' She crossed her two forefingers. 'Like that.'

'I'm so glad,' said the leashed-in Becky.

'Really? I didn't imagine you would care one way or the other.' Mrs Frant was icy.

Lunch was eaten in a strained atmosphere and afterwards the two pregnant girls lumbered outside for fresh air.

It was busy in the main street and two large delivery vans were parked outside the stores, which had been outlined in scaffolding. A notice explained that, due to demand, the shop space was expanding and a tea-room was also opening.

Becky worked it out. 'This means that the planning permission for the showground has got the OK. You bet. Someone's leaked it. Or he's got a crony on the council.'

Tess knew that Becky was almost sure to be right.

In silence, they turned off and walked up the lane towards the fields. Gradually their figures lost their substance and became silhouettes: dark, distorted, fecund outlines against the grey goose-down winter sky. At the top, they paused and looked down on Appleford, whose lights were being strung, one by one, onto an electric necklace hung round the village. A Jaguar was being driven along East Lane and turned in at a house with the scrunch of tyre against gravel.

'That's probably Jilly Cadogan,' said Tess.

'I first met Louis here, do you remember?'

Tess touched Becky's arm. 'Yes, I do.'

Becky did not respond to the gesture. 'Charles badly wants a son.'

Tess had never been so conscious of her isolation. 'Does he?' she said, and moved ahead. Then she stopped. 'Do you ever think about Martha?' she asked.

Becky's answer came on the rebound. 'I can't afford to.'

Burdened and heavy, the silhouettes walked on and, like the sudden release of a blind, night descended over Appleford.

Chapter Nineteen

Becky's attempts to ignore her pregnancy were, Tess informed her, truly magnificent. She neither read a book on the subject nor attended a class, and demanded an elective Caesarean of her immensely expensive gynaecologist. 'If you don't give me one,' she informed his startled eminence, 'I won't pay the bill.'

'I don't want to huff and puff with the beard and sandals brigade,' she snapped at Charles, who had suggested, gently, that she should consult the National Childbirth Trust.

If only ... he caught himself thinking, forgetting that it was precisely Becky's unusual and unpredictable qualities that had attracted him to her in the first place ... if only she could be more like Martha. Gracious and feminine about the whole business. More accepting.

If only ... thought Becky in turn, if only I could see Louis. Then I think I could bear all this.

She knew she had taken the wrong path. Because she was honest and it wasted energy not to be clear, Becky acknowledged that the fault was hers and called on her still plentiful reserves of energy to get through. Being trapped was, after all, the fate of many. Becky's was an optimistic and opportunistic spirit not easily quenched and nor would she allow it to be so. The nature of nature was change, she lectured herself, and if she was pulled down by pregnancy's peculiar alchemy, which had changed a slim, fast-moving woman into a huge, curved, rooted bolus, then she must endure it and wait.

'Who was it who declared that pregnancy was God's joke on

women?' she asked Tess, after the latter had forced her to accompany her on a shopping expedition to Mothercare. They had taken a taxi back to the riverside flat.

Tess was sprawled on the primrose sofa. 'God knows,' she said wearily.

Becky shot her a look. 'How are you feeling?'

'Fat and boring. Apparently . . .' there was a tiny hesitation which Becky did not notice '. . . I'm big for my dates. How are you feeling?'

'In a state of suspended animation.'

'Why are we in this jam?'

'Biology.' By now they had perfected the timing of their chorus.

'Not long to go.'

'Not long to go. Christmas and then . . .'

Beached and exhausted, the women sighed in unison. Becky roused herself. 'What's the latest at the bank?'

Tess showed signs of coming to life. 'Quite good, actually. I've pulled in two more clients with lots of dough. An author who's just made a killing with a novel and yet another farmer. Farmers are rolling in it. How's Coates?'

'Quiet. But I'm doing a lot of chatting up. The rumour shop is operating at full tilt at Lloyd's. Lots of external Names talking to the press and big talk of a huge year-end deficit.'

They fell silent for the shop talk had lost some of its savour, but neither would ever admit it. Tess poked with her foot at one of the many shopping bags dropped onto the floor. It fell over, disgorging a pile of white terry Baby-gros. 'I can't quite believe what's happening to me.'

Another silence.

'Becky.'

'Um.'

'Are you sure you want a Caesarean? Isn't it a bit drastic unless you have to have one?'

'Quite sure. You should do the same.'

'You forget.' Tess was at her driest. 'I'm on the National Health.'

'So you are.'

'Becky, why are you having this baby?'

Becky turned a pair of tired eyes on her friend. 'I can't think. Charles, I suppose. I wasn't quick enough off the mark to hide it. Or do anything. I can honestly say it's the very last thing I wanted. Anyway, I owe him *something*.'

Tess balanced a Baby-gro on the end of her foot. 'In the end, there is reproduction.' She sounded grave. 'And we made the mistake of thinking we were cleverer. Unless, of course, you really wanted this baby.'

'Shut up, Tess.'

Tess retrieved the Baby-gro and stowed it away. Secret lives were so much more interesting than the surface life, the one by which others judged you, and could be compared in its relative truths and falsehoods to others and was plainly in view. But the true Tess, the real Tess, now operated under cover. That much, she had learnt.

She looked across to Becky, the friend whom she had betrayed. Becky operated secretly too, in the darkness, and the essential Becky was also hidden.

Soon after that Tess said goodbye for she craved, as she so often did now, the solitude of her flat.

There had been many jokes to endure at Coates about pregnant oil-and-energy experts. Ships in port. Lubricated working parts. Etc., etc. Becky put up with them good-naturedly, for their crudeness, sometimes vulgarity, indicated something important: that she was accepted. It was a relief, too, to be treated normally rather than as the china doll into which Charles apparently considered that she had turned.

'We've never had one of you before,' observed her boss, indicating Becky's bump. They were sitting in his office, decorated with hideous lumps of Christmas tinsel and the large, ostentatious cards with printed greetings that only firms can afford to send, discussing her maternity leave. 'The question is, can one insure the stable once the horse has bolted?'

'Very funny,' said Becky, who had established that kind of relationship with him.

He cleared his throat, a sign that he was on uneven ground. 'Are you sure about coming back?'

Half Lebanese, half English, he was a kindly man with three children of his own. 'It's a huge commitment and you're not taking much time off. You women can overdo things. It's not easy.'

Becky made to cross her legs and thought better of it. 'I've never been surer of anything in my life. Six weeks is my entitlement. I'll take it and I'll be back. David will handle my work and keep me up to date on anything urgent and I've invested in the latest technology I can lay my hands on so I can do some work at home.'

Her boss seemed thoughtful. 'You must think of the baby.'

Because she knew him to be just, Becky was prepared to overlook her boss's interference. 'But also of myself,' she said. 'And the firm.'

He then said something unexpected. 'Take care, Becky.'

On New Year's Day 1990, and without any warning at all, Lily arrived at the riverside flat clutching, among other things, an enormous shimmering blue patent-leather bag.

'Oh, no,' exclaimed Becky on opening the door, but stood aside to let her in. 'Is this a long or a short stay?'

'As long as it takes.' Lily dropped bags and baggage onto the floor, bracelets tinkling like the evening angelus. 'I've come to be a grandmother.'

'Good God.' Becky leant on the door for support. 'I have to hand it to you, Lily. Omit the mother bit and go straight to grandmother. Do you collect two hundred pounds when you pass GO?'

Lily looked all at sea: she had no idea what Becky was talking about. 'Ha, ha,' she said, tip-tipping in her white high heels into the sitting room. Her voice issued back into the hall where Becky was still rooted. 'Don't you Londoners go in for Christmas decorations? Or is it not smart?'

'You're a Londoner. You should know.'

'Not any more.'

'Did it ever occur to you,' Becky appeared in the doorway, one hand pressed into the small of her back, 'that I didn't invite you for a reason?'

Lily swivelled on her swollen feet. 'You didn't invite me, my girl, because you're not in the habit of having a mother.'

The humour that buoyed Becky through tricky encounters threatened to vanish, and she gritted her teeth.

After the long journey, Lily was in chatty form. 'Where's Charles?'

'Seeing his children.'

'Jean's God-botherers have been on to me. They wanted a contribution to the church hall. In memory of Jean. I imagine they need the money to fund the bribe to the council.'

Becky relived the sharp, intrusive memories and smells she carried as permanent luggage. The nose-pricking scent of mould, fetid urine and rotting food; kicking orange polystyrene hamburger boxes into the air (no autumn leaves in Paradise Flats); listening to the interchange of voices that never ceased. Angry. Hungry. Hungry for something . . . what? Alone.

'Did you give any?'

Lily looked evasive. 'I sent them a bob or two,' she said carefully. 'On condition they never bothered me again.'

Becky rubbed her back. 'Lily, I don't think I can cope with you so you can't stay long. I've got a maternity nurse coming as soon as the baby's born and that's scheduled in ten days' time.'

'*Scheduled*, is it?' Lily plonked herself down on the sofa. 'I had Jean,' she said. 'Cheaper than a nurse.'

Becky stood over her mother. 'You're unscrupulous and wicked.'

Lily darted a look at her daughter. 'Pots calling kettles black?'

'You can't stay for long.'

'That's a pity.' Thoroughly at home, Lily sat back among the cushions. 'I was planning to settle some money on the baby.'

Sometime during the night, Lily was aware of movement in the flat. Struggling with sleep and the embrace of one gin too many, she struggled out of bed.

The sight that greeted her in the hall was clearly not one that Becky would have built into her schedule. Her daughter was clinging to a door frame, weighed down by a suitcase and various bags, and Charles was fussing over her.

'Save us,' was Lily's dopey comment.

At the sound, Becky raised her head and sent Lily a look of pure hatred and fury. Trapped, my duck, thought Lily with a touch of malice. It gets you in the end. 'What happened to the famous schedule, then?' she asked, and beat a strategic retreat back into the nice dark womb of her bedroom.

'I don't ... like ... this,' Becky uttered, between whitened lips, as Charles drove at high speed into the hospital car park. 'I want to go home.'

'Well, you can't.' Charles jerked on the handbrake unnecessarily hard and leant awkwardly across Becky's bulge to unsnap the safety belt. 'It won't be too bad.'

'Only a man would say that.' But she clung to his hand for a second or two. Deeply moved by this unusual display of need, he stroked her hair. It was so unfair that the one time she was in trouble – and he had prayed for such an occasion – he could not help her at all.

As it turned out, Charles required all his wits. The baby was early and Becky's consultant was on a skiing holiday. Furthermore, at night only two theatres were operational and they were currently occupied with the remnants of a car crash that required putting back together.

On being told that she would have to go it alone, for the anaesthetists were also in theatre, Becky spat venom and sobbed. Then, as he dabbed at her face with a damp flannel, Charles saw her pull herself together and from then on conduct herself with . . . well, he felt it was courage.

The doubts that had plagued him lately melted away in admiration and he wielded the flannel with the fervour of the worshipper at the shrine. Whatever Becky decided to do, she did it well.

Eventually, Sister Liquorice, a large and beautiful Nigerian women, who giggled when she introduced herself as the midwife, commanded Becky to push.

'If you mean push off,' Becky's teeth had drawn blood on her lower lip and she was bathed in sweat, 'I am. To the Bahamas.'

'Push, lady. Push. Push your baby into the world.'

Sister Liquorice nudged Charles aside and took up her position at the business end of proceedings.

At the moment Becky gave birth, surrounded by Charles, nurses and the registrar – 'This is a flaming cocktail party,' she ground out, during one respite – the mobile phone in her overnight bag emitted a shriek for attention.

'Get it, will you?' gasped Becky.

'Don't be so stupid.' Charles dived towards it and snapped it off.

'Probably Australia.' Becky's face screwed up in anguish as Sister Liquorice told her to kneel. 'You should have answered it.'

At eight o'clock the following morning, Charles reeled out into the winter morning, the father of a daughter. The baby had taken a great deal of time and trouble to arrive but she was healthy and lusty, and Charles had wept – as he had wept three times previously – when she was placed in his arms.

My daughter, he thought, gazing on the little face that had not had time to unfold. My daughter. Slightly jaundiced, a little battered. My *fourth* daughter.

He must guard her, as he should guard her sisters, against the prowlers and the predators, sane and insane, who waited in the shadows. That was his absolute duty.

Later that afternoon, he returned to the hospital with Lily, whose bold slashes of red and green on a yellow background hit Becky between the eyes.

'Well.' She usurped the only chair in the room and her bracelets gave off their usual cacophony. 'Keeping the florists busy already, I see.'

Becky smiled with a touch of complacency for the bouquets had not stopped coming all morning.

'Where is she, then?'

Becky pointed somewhat wearily at the crib and Lily heaved herself to her feet. 'She's got her grandfather's eyes,' she pronounced.

'How do you know, you old fraud? They're shut.'

'So they are.' Lily sat down again. 'I could do with a cup of tea.'

The well-trained Charles went to find one.

After a second or two, Becky said, 'I'm not surprised you abandoned me.'

Lily's expression was a mixture of defiance and, yes, regret. 'In my day, there was less choice.'

'Do you want me to weep, Lily?'

From beneath the layers of fat, Lily's shrewd gaze raked her daughter. 'You look as though you've already been at it,' she remarked. 'Are you feeding her yourself?'

'No.'

Lily opened her large shimmery bag and produced a hand-

kerchief. 'Nasty thing, feeding,' she remarked. 'I wouldn't do
it.'

'Well, you didn't.'

Lily snapped the handbag shut.

'I must speak to Tess,' said Becky later, fretful and a little
feverish. 'I want Tess.'

But the phone at Metrobank rang and rang and no one
answered.

Earlier in the day, Tess had been talking on the phone to
Louis, whom she had rung for advice. But first she told him
Becky's news and then, somehow, because it was a subject they
wished to discuss but felt inhibited in doing so, they found
themselves discussing the implications of the plunge in the
property market and the number of articles in the press about
the City fat-cats.

'Of course, journos seize on telephone-number salaries and
make lots of noise about takeovers. That's their game and good
luck to them. But, at bottom, the business is safe and secular.'

Tess was puzzled. 'What do you mean, secular?'

'Long-term. Steady. As a society we're growing older and
require pensions. That's why the funds dominate and they build
in a self-adjusting mechanism.'

Tess was tempted to interject that it was a pity Lloyd's did
not share this advantage.

'What is worrying,' she cast around for alternative topics, 'is
the erosion of our manufacturing base.'

As they talked, Tess experienced the strangest sensation,
almost as if her body had moved onto another plane.

Oh, baby, she addressed it directly for the first time; no one
has thought about you.

'Do I gather,' said Louis, eventually, 'that you feel your
father has been treated badly by Lloyd's?'

'I do.'

'But your father was aware of the risk he was taking.'

'No,' said Tess, 'I don't think he was.'

Before she put down the phone Louis asked, 'Becky is all right, isn't she?'

An hour or so later, Tess realized that she was in labour but continued to work, taking an obscure pleasure in denying it up to the last moment. When the contractions were fifteen minutes apart, she beckoned Freddie over.

He sized up the situation. 'Oh, my God, ball and string. Hot water.'

'Shut up, you idiot.'

'You can't have a baby in a merchant bank. It isn't done.'

'Unless you help me, I'll be setting a fashion.'

He was suddenly concerned. 'Isn't it early?'

'A bit,' she said reluctantly, and with sudden terror.

Within minutes Freddie had arranged the taxi and taken her to St Thomas's, where he kissed her heartily and said goodbye.

Alone and minus luggage, Tess was wheeled up to the labour ward.

It's not so terrible being alone, she decided, as she laboured through the afternoon and into the evening with strangers attending her. The body is too busy, too convulsed to worry much about other things. Like dying, birth is solitary.

She was surprised to discover, therefore, when David was placed in her arms that she had been wrong. Giving birth had ensured that she would never be alone again.

Two days and two fitful nights later, Becky pulled herself painfully upright in bed and reached for her earphones to listen in to the financial news. Poppy, as she was called, had spent the night in the nursery but Becky had been woken twice in the night by a kerfuffle in the corridor. Her stitches hurt: tightly knotted into her tender skin and she was filled with indignation that sacrifices of whole, sweet flesh should be so demanded of the female.

'No one tells you that you'll be mutilated as well as disfigured,' she had informed Charles. 'No one tells the truth.'

Serviceable but not comfortable, the hospital pillows bunched around Becky's hot body. No amount of money was capable of replacing as new the bits of her body that had been cut and sewn. No amount of money could restore to their rightful place in Becky's psyche the bits that had been destroyed when Lily had tossed a few things into a bag and left.

But it helped.

She rang the bell, asked for her bed to be remade with fresh sheets and took a bath. She stepped on the scales: not bad, not good. The mirror reflected a face plumped out by pregnancy and a soft flab of torso and, to her extra-critical gaze, seemingly enlarged shoulders. Only the eyes, with their marker eyebrows, remained to remind her of the past.

Afterwards, she was left in peace to eat the breakfast she did not want.

She toyed with the fruit juice and, as she did so, bewilderment and a fear she could not place clustered over her like homing pigeons that had not flown far.

She gasped with shock and, in the compromised light of a winter morning, wept. She sensed that the life she had fashioned was in danger of slipping away, much as the good times were slipping away with a decade that had been spectacularly careless.

As she wept, tears running over her sore mouth, Becky retraced a wasteland of the solitary spirit, taught to her from the first glimmer of consciousness.

Already she observed her daughter through a glass, darkly and with detachment. Yes, evident were tiny feet and hands tipped with shell. Yes, a body rearing in primitive reflex, a tender stomach and tiny spine. There was, too, a suggestion of intelligence behind the mostly shut blue eyes.

It was expected of her that she, the mother, would respond to her baby in the approved manner. Then everyone could relax. Yet, for Becky, the building of bridges to another human being was something she regarded as impossible, even to a child.

'Bloody hell,' she said aloud, and her weeping stopped.

The nurses had remained impassive when Becky had informed them that she would not be breast-feeding, and gave her lessons in bottles and formula. Poppy struggled to take nourishment but it was a wearing business: although the baby fed and survived, the formula did not soothe and please her. She cried a lot. The nurses clucked over her and, more than once, bore her away for observation, leaving Becky quivering with relief and resentment.

Breathing space.

Yet Becky had to face the truth: there was no space left any more, and her sense of loss was profound.

She was flicking through *Tatler* when the door opened. 'Pouting lips and thighs that dazzle in Lycra, paint a chilly town a blazing scarlet in your own way . . .' She did not look up.

'May I come in?' asked Louis.

Pouting lips . . . thighs . . . blazing scarlet. Dazzled, but by electricity sending bolts through her body, Becky looked up. He reached for one of her hands, and sat down on the bed and, in the private, well-remembered gesture, ran his thumb gently over her dry fingers. 'Are you well?'

Again tears threatened and Becky choked them back. 'What do you think? I know now it's the second worst thing in the world to have a baby.'

'What's the first?'

'To repeat the experience.'

He laughed. 'And the baby?'

'She's fine.' Becky gestured towards the empty crib. 'Or so they tell me. They're doing something with her at the moment.'

Despite herself, despite everything, she grasped his fingers in hers. 'Louis . . . don't. Please don't ever leave me again.'

The door opened and the thin, tired wail of an unhappy

baby could be heard. Young and too plump, a junior nurse handed Poppy to Becky.

'Why is she crying?'

'She won't take enough of her feed. We thought perhaps you should have a go.'

'Oh.'

The nurse had no time to spare. She plonked the bottle on the side table and left the room.

'Why don't you feed her yourself?' Louis watched the struggles with the bottle.

'I don't want to.' Becky turned her now sparkling eyes on Louis. 'I have to get back to work.'

He observed the little face. 'It would be better for her.'

'Don't,' pleaded Becky. 'Not you too. Charles hasn't stopped on the subject.' She stroked Poppy's cheek in an experimental manner. 'It's for me to decide.'

Louis reflected. 'You needn't feed her for long. Just enough for her to know.'

'Babies don't know.'

'How do *you* know?'

'Louis, you're as guilty as the rest of them. When a woman has a baby everyone considers that her autonomy has vanished and she's public property. I've given birth, not lost part of my brain, and I've decided not to breast-feed.'

She spoke over a hunched shoulder but avoided Louis's gaze and he knew that it was not the whole truth.

'Point taken,' he said, reached over and pushed down the straps of her satin nightdress, to reveal swollen white flesh.

'This is the mother,' he said, running his hand down her body. 'You shouldn't ignore her.'

'I've had an injection to stop the milk.' Becky made no move to stop him. 'And don't go all Catholic on me.'

'Does that invalidate anything I might have to say?'

'You haven't listened to me.'

241

'Just concentrate, Becky.'

Scenting her mother, the baby turned her head towards the unused breast. Louis's presence had a hypnotic quality and Becky's skin goosefleshed. As she had banded the intricate patterns and cool beauty of her DNA on her daughter, his clean, hard elegance was burned into her make-up. So, too, was the knowledge that he understood the exact pathways of her greedy nature. There was no point in denial.

Then Louis said something very strange: 'You must build the bridge, Becky.'

Louis won and Poppy drank, then gorged on her mother's milk and he had watched, as tender and satisfied as he had ever been.

Was it possible that, after all, the grey stones, the incense and the calloused knees, the incomprehension of a small boy had had a point?

It was probably the drugs she had been given. Probably. But for an intense, vivid moment, Becky experienced the condition of complete femininity, acknowledged it, and moved on.

'I suppose you'll disappear now, won't you, and not come back?' she said to Louis.

'I don't know. If I have the strength.'

Perhaps, ran Tess's diary, which had been shoved carelessly among the bouquets that had been delivered to the High House and written in a deceptive state of euphoria, perhaps, I will be happy again. My son is perfect.

Chapter Twenty

If the world is arranged into noisy, aggressive tribes who wish to have nothing to do with each other, then it must also be acknowledged that its parts are interlocked. Unless we understand that, we understand nothing of the modern world . . .

It was six months later and Becky was making notes on her laptop for a lecture on insurance broking that she had been ordered to give by Coates to a girls' sixth form. She had noticed before that it was a job frequently allocated to the token female.

Tess was coming up to spend the day and Charles was preparing lunch in the kitchen.

. . . For example, if the American Congress had not passed the Comprehensive Response, Compensation and Liability Act in 1980, which required the clean-up of polluted sites retrospectively 'and irrespective of cost, a selection of Lloyd's Names, who live on the other side of the world, would not be facing enormous cash calls. This may seem strange or unfair to you and, in one sense, it is. But it is the reality of the world in 1990.

Like it or not, tribe is connected to tribe by a network of financial commitments, and disaster in one area links it with another.

Becky paused and stared at the screen. Since Piper Alpha, there have been enough disasters, she thought grimly, Hurricane Hugo, the Enchova oil-platform fire to name only two, to turn the world into one happy family . . .

Back in hospital that January and greeted by the sight of a milky, drowsy baby, Charles asked Becky, with a leap of his heart, what had made her change her mind.

Perhaps, he thought, it is possible we will pull together.

Becky was cross and suffering from the post-partum low that comes after experiencing strong emotion and did not bother to answer him properly. Charles satisfied himself instead by stroking his newest daughter's head with a gentle finger and tried not to worry about the question that bothered him not a little: how on earth was he going to afford to launch four daughters into the world?

Martha left it until June before ringing him at the flat to ask if the baby was doing well. Otherwise, apart from messages via the nanny when they exchanged the children, they had not communicated.

'How nice of you,' said Charles. 'Life was hell at the start, with a frightful old bat of a maternity nurse plus Becky's mother, but we got rid of them smartish and now it's a question of struggling with the nannies.'

'Oh dear,' said Martha at her end, hands trembling.

'Martha, we *are* friends, aren't we?'

'Are we?' Martha wanted to shriek that what she felt for her soon-to-be-ex-husband had nothing to do with friendship, but everything to do with outrage and violent longing to have the old happy days back.

'How are the children?'

'Oh, you've remembered them?'

Charles grimaced at the familiar note in Martha's voice. It spelt lecture with a capital L. With his free hand, he manoeuvred a file out of his briefcase and flipped it open. 'Is it really going to cost three hundred a term for Tiny's nursery?'

Martha sighed. 'I know it's a lot, Charles, but it's so convenient for Anthea's school and fits in with the run. More important, it's the best place for her.'

As usual, Martha had her arguments marshalled.

'That reminds me.' Charles recollected a previous conversation. 'Do you think Anthea should have some remedial help? Should I talk to the school?'

'Well ... she's picking up a bit. Did you get her to read to you when you took her out on Sunday?'

Ranging over this and that, the trivia, but not trivial, aspects of a shared life and shared children, their conversation continued for another twenty minutes or so.

'I must go.' Charles disengaged himself reluctantly from this warm and cradling exchange. 'Becky's friend Tess is up for the day and I've got to finish the lunch. But it's so nice to think we can talk. It's good to be civilized about these things.'

By now, Martha had run her hand through her hair so often that it stood on end, and she had resorted to picking at the bobbly bits that always appeared on her leggings however she washed them.

'*Civilized!*' she exclaimed. 'My God, you do say the most stupid things sometimes, Charles.'

Charles was left to reflect uneasily that his grasp on the situation was less clear than he had supposed, which Martha, had she been consulted, would have pointed out in the first place.

As part of the paring-down procedure, Mrs Frant had sold her car. This left her reliant on Tess's, a somewhat tricky situation as their needs clashed. They had clashed today and, thus it was that with enormous difficulty – nappies, buggy, bottles, cuddly toys – Tess had brought David up to London on the train to have lunch with Becky, Charles and Poppy. The purpose was to celebrate the babies' first six months. The new decade babies – the 'deccies'.

'I never thought I would feel old,' Becky had said to Charles, in a rare confiding moment. 'It's a curious feeling. I'm so used to thinking of myself as a beginner.'

'I think I've always felt old,' replied Charles.

The outing threatened to exhaust Tess before she reached Becky: she had got up early to help her mother prepare the guests' breakfasts and dinner. The journey to London, which she had imagined would be fun, only served to underline her double life. During the week, she was free and successful, at weekends the reverse.

'I'm not a natural at motherhood,' Tess confided to her son, worried that she found it so difficult.

She looked down at him, wriggling in her lap. *You sleep when you want, cry when you want and you don't care about anything except your own needs. But I love you.*

'Tessy,' said Becky, as soon as Tess had disgorged herself and David into the hall of the flat, 'I must warn you that you can no longer smoke in this flat. Banned.'

'Oh? Yes, well, I suppose you're right.'

Later, Tess stood on the balcony and smoked defiantly and held a conversation through the door. 'Another letter came last week. The loss for 'eighty-seven was £217,985.'

Becky's voice sounded thin and disembodied through the glass door. 'I don't know how to help, Tessy.'

She exhaled. 'Just be there.'

Both women were aware that the difference between the onlooker on the bank and the swimmer in trouble is the one between death and life.

'Have some coffee.' Becky held up a cup and Tess tossed her cigarette into the street below and came to sit on the sofa. It was, she was glad to see with a prickle of malice, less pristine than of yore. David was grizzling in his portable chair and she picked him up, which meant that she had to perform one of those contortions, noticeable in new mothers, to ensure that the cup did not pass over his head.

Becky watched her, and her heart pinched with unfamiliar empathy. 'How's your mother?'

'She's incredible and she drives me dotty. Grandmother likes to think that she knows best. And yet, Bec, there she is getting up at dawn like one of those tough colonial ladies in Somerset Maugham, refusing to give up . . . We're giving guests dinner now, you know. They're not quite as up-market as they used to be because of the showground. Less *fungi* and balsamic vinegar, more prawn cocktail.'

'Some income, though?'

'Yes. Without it . . .' Tess tugged at the waistband of her full cotton skirt. It was still too tight and she had attempted a poor disguise with a T-shirt. 'Why are you so thin?' If anything, Becky post-Poppy was slimmer and smarter.

'You've been stuffing chocolate,' she accused Tess, accurately as it happened, knowing how the jibe would make her smart.

'You need energy to diet. The pundits never tell you that.'

Becky softened. 'You're gorgeous all the same, Tessy.'

They could hear Poppy wailing in her bedroom. Unfussed, Becky called out, 'Charles, get her, will you?' She looked at Tess, who wore a wooden expression. 'Is anything the matter, Tess?'

'No, nothing.'

Charles appeared with Poppy draped over his shoulder and placed her on Becky's lap. Poppy lay back and scrutinized her mother with the infant's urge to rediscover. Becky looked down and smiled. And, with a dazzling imitation of her mother, Poppy smiled back. Becky picked up a wooden toy, of the type favoured by parents and usually ignored by their children, and dangled it in front of her.

Tess took a deep breath and plucked up courage to look at Charles, an action, simple as it was, that was becoming more difficult as more time elapsed. As with many sins, it seemed worse the more it was brooded upon. 'How are your other daughters?'

He groaned. 'Expensive.'

After tea, Tess said that she must go and Charles got to his feet. 'I'll fetch the car from round the corner.'

In the car Charles looked straight ahead at the road and said, 'I understand your feelings, Tess, and we just have to get over this uncomfortable period as best we can. It will get easier, I'm sure.' He was handling Tess, whom he did not love, better than he ever handled Becky, whom he loved desperately, and managed to defuse the situation rather gracefully. 'I understand about the guilt and all that. And I've made up my mind to forget the incident completely.'

Craving release and the peace of post-confession, she almost said something about the troubled source of her guilt, but held back.

Not knowing.

But, if she did not forgive herself, Tess forgave Charles there and then. He handed her onto the train and efficiently stowed the mountain of equipment.

Charles's eyes rested on David for longer than necessary. *A son?* he thought, painfully and with longing.

'David's a lovely boy and the spitting image of George,' he said finally, and raised his eyes to Tess.

They looked at each other. He suspects, she thought, and was deeply moved by his effort to give her peace. How generous he was. In the split second between his remark and her reply, a layer of earth was brushed over a truth. Perhaps for excavation later. Perhaps not.

'Thank you,' she said.

Left alone with Poppy, Becky poured a final cup of coffee and put her feet up. Poppy sat silently in her bouncy chair on the floor.

On the rare occasions when she examined her life, Becky was aware that she flew close to the sun.

Aunt Jean imagery?

Yet, so far, her progress, an acquisitive, worldly pilgrim's progress, had been achieved with a mixture of luck, shrewdness and life-saving selfishness, the last being the most crucial. She was partnered, well funded, and, if the baby was a tie, she could throw money at the problem.

Lily was not so sure. 'Don't imagine you've got it sussed, my girl,' she informed Becky, before she left to go north after Poppy's birth. 'Money's no insurance. You can't buy order. You may fancy yourself rotten as the rich bitch but, at bottom, Becky Vitali, you're just the same as the rest of us.'

'Do you have to be so depressing? Or so smug?'

'Things have a way of not working out. Look at Jean. She set out to be a model housewife and mother – that's why I left you with her. And look what happened.'

What *did* happen to my pink-cardiganed, zealoty aunt? She had been forced by domesticity into being a saint, Becky concluded with a faint cadence of guilt, because that was the only way she could survive. For the first time ever, a lump ached in her throat as she recollected the years of Jean's impatient sacrifice – a reaction she put down to post-baby hormone displacement.

Wise Lily. She knew a thing or two about love, money and the whole damn thing. 'It pulls in two ways, you dozy mare,' she pronounced mysteriously.

'Meaning what?'

'Look at you,' her mother pointed out. 'Living with Charles and mentally shacked up with someone else with a poncey name.'

Becky wished that she had never confided to Lily the secret of Louis.

True, Louis loved her but he was married to Jilly and bound to Jilly by the strictures of a Church in which he no longer believed.

'It's called . . . I don't know what it's called but it's a situation that I can't alter. The trick is to get round it.'

'Will you ever call me Mum?'

'No, I don't think so.'

'It's lucky,' said Lily, 'that you weren't born when I was. You wouldn't have lasted a minute. It's easy now. One yelp from a so-called minority, the one-legged, single-parent lesbian, and the Queen sends you a telegram. It's all birth control and free market and whatever. And very wicked.' Lily looked as though she did not mind too much about the last. 'Suits you, though. All spend and top coat.'

'You're forgetting Aids and negative equity.' Becky could not help laughing. 'You're an old bat, Lily.'

'Mark my words.'

Fine, thought Becky, who minded Lily's mild criticisms more than she cared to admit. If the wicked grow and put on leaf like the green bay tree, so be it. Sodom and Gomorrah were much more interesting places than Eden.

However, every equation and every bargain has its tricky and often stubborn area.

'Becky,' said Charles, after he returned from depositing Tess on the train, 'I want us to get married as soon as possible. But I want to know that you mean to stick by it. And that you're married to me.'

'Ah,' Becky's answer darted towards him with the speed and accuracy of a snake's tongue, 'but would you be married to me or to Martha?'

It was, they both acknowledged, a fair question. Becky had made the discovery that, if you appropriate a person from someone else, the shadow of the latter remains. In their life together, Becky and Charles traced a Martha shape every day.

'Have you been seeing her?' Becky asked.

'No. But we've talked on the phone. I hope you don't mind.' Charles rather wanted Becky to mind very much.

'Oh, no,' said Becky, wishing that she could oblige. 'I do see that it's necessary.'

Buoyed up by his handling of Tess, Charles asserted himself.

'We must get married as soon as possible.' He allowed Becky a few seconds to digest this then added, 'And you can look after Poppy until bedtime because I have work to do.'

Becky regarded him blankly and he wondered if she was going to lose her temper. He should have known better because she rarely allowed herself to do so. Instead she threw back her head, exposing the delicious area at the base of her throat that drove Charles mad with desire, and laughed.

'You win,' she said, hefted Poppy onto her shoulder and headed out of the room to change the baby's nappy, adding over her shoulder, 'for the time being.'

He walked over to the balcony, where a drift of ash betrayed Tess's previous presence, and shoved his hands into his pockets. Sometimes Charles was driven to think that the only act that had given his life significance was to leave Martha.

He dated events mentally from before and after: before M., he had been an emotional innocent; after leaving M., he had turned into a bad father, an abandoner of wives, the seducer of friends and, lately, into the broker who had allowed his lover to sell him, professionally, down the river.

What astonished Charles to the depth of his soul was that he had never intended that any of this should happen. Yet it was done. Life crept up on you and leap-frogged over good resolutions. Because he took no comfort in solidarity, it made no difference to Charles that many others experienced the same.

At Coates business was booming. Its staff younger than Mawby's – the fruit of the human resources officer's forward thinking – Coates was attracting big international contracts.

Becky's team were rootless and excellent at their jobs. Coinciding perfectly with Becky's, their aims were to enjoy the business and their personal enrichment. Why not? They were required to survive and the world was shuddering with risk. After a while, opportunism becomes a state of mind and, if they cared to judge by the behaviour of financial, industrial and political leaders, the words 'fraud' and 'greedy' could be said to possess chameleon properties. Anyway, whichever way the business went at Lloyd's, the brokers earned their commission.

Becky put her finger neatly on the mood. 'The City likes short-term business. Quick profits. Quick cash. We lost our ability to think long-term with the Empire.'

'You mean men did,' said Tess. 'Women have housekeeping imprinted into their bones. Fruit-bottlers.'

'But they don't think big enough,' Becky replied. 'And they're lacking in the confidence department.'

Heigh-ho.

But they worked hard, these short-termists. They worked morning, noon and at night on corporate entertaining. Once, perhaps twice, a week Becky would phone Dominique, the French nanny – Poppy being destined to learn French with her formula – to tell her that she would not be back until late.

Unfortunately, Charles was often late, too, and they agreed to add a third to Dominique's wages, which was fine for the latter but left Poppy seriously depleted of parental attention.

One day in August, driven to it no doubt by the idea that the whole of her country was on holiday, Dominique decided to depart and did so that evening, with less than a day's notice.

Two days later, a grim Becky announced that Charles would have to look after Poppy for she had an all-day meeting and left him holding the baby. In desperation, he did the only thing possible and picked up the phone to Martha.

The situation remained dire. The nanny, who arrived on the Friday, was discovered with her head out of the window smoking and was dispatched back to the agency. Her replacement the following Tuesday announced that she had a rare blood virus and she was not sure if it was infectious or not. She, too, was dispatched smartly.

'This will not do,' said Charles, on the Wednesday night as, stupefied with tiredness from coxing and boxing Poppy, they undressed. 'We haven't seen her properly for days.'

He had just been in to check on the baby and had been transfixed by the skin drained to white wax by sleep, the closed half-moon crescents of her eyelids, and by his love for her.

'She'll survive.'

'I've been thinking. Martha ... might ... *possibly* help out.'

Becky slipped her lace knickers down her legs and reached for her nightdress. 'Did I hear correctly?'

'Yes.'

'Martha!'

Charles had not confessed that he had already used Martha. 'Martha could do it and we're in a big jam.'

'How do you know she could?'

Charles sighed and told the truth. 'She helped me out last week.'

The Martha-shaped space in Charles and Becky's relationship was, at that moment, more than usually noticeable. But Becky was a working mother and no one who is not quite understands the cocktail of desperation and ruthlessness that sweeps over a woman faced with the prospect of an all-day seminar with FEROC and no childcare.

For the next month, while the right nanny was recruited, Charles took to dropping by at Martha's once or twice a week when Becky was working late. Sometimes, he helped to bath Poppy with the other children before bearing her away to the riverside flat.

Mentioned casually by Becky, the arrangement took Tess's breath away. Yet, of all people, Tess should have been used to the idea that the surface of our everyday hides strange, subterranean accommodations and unexpected passing places.

The summer meeting of the Bollys was held at a restaurant near Fenchurch Street.

The weather hung over the City, a heavy, back-end-of-season mood that drained energy, and a perpetual wind whistled between high-rise blocks and buffeted plate-glass windows.

As chef was on extended holiday, the lunch was not good and the wine was too heavy. The talk was of syndicates racking up huge losses, the predicted Lloyd's deficit and a strange coincidence of disasters and the approaching millennium.

'It's a matter of adjustment,' Louis suggested. 'Of a new psychology.' His colleagues seemed only partly interested. 'Of accepting that events do not, necessarily, go all one way.'

'We know that,' said Dick Turner impatiently. 'But we over-expanded. And the press are on our backs.'

Louis raised his eyebrows. He turned to Nigel, who was writing. 'How are you?'

Nigel closed his notebook with a little snap. 'Having a bit of trouble,' he said. 'It's very odd but the skin between my toes has split and it's hell. It makes walking difficult. You've no idea.'

'No, I haven't,' said Louis.

'I'd never paid any attention to my toes before.'

'No, indeed.'

Louis stared at the waistcoated Nigel. Unlike the Munich Re, for example, which held massive reserves, Lloyd's had less to call on. The stock-market crash of 1987 had wiped millions off the value of investments, which formed part of the reserves, yet the level of underwriting had remained the same.

'Imbalance,' he said.

'What?' Nigel looked puzzled.

'Dietary imbalance,' explained Louis. 'Your toes.'

Waiting for Becky that evening, Louis was filled with a sense of loss. For a safe past. For his own mistakes. For the certainties that he should have re-examined and had neglected to do so. For the fact that he should have helped John Frant.

'What do you think?' he asked Becky. 'Apparently the resignation rate of Names is running at twenty per cent . . .'

Sleek in her favourite olive linen and in the knowledge that it was seven-thirty in the evening and she was not going home to deal with a tired baby, Becky wrinkled her nose. 'Keep your nerve.'

'And?' He waited for the answer that he knew was coming.

'Trade through.'

'Clever girl.'

'Story of my life.'

He piloted her into a taxi and they glided through the London streets. 'Remember the bomb?' he said.

She shivered. 'I never forget it.'

He moved close to her. 'Say it again.'

She closed her brilliant eyes. 'You'll have to make me.'

He touched her breast and she moved imperceptibly. Then he ran a gentle finger just behind her ear. She smiled, and Louis bent over to kiss her. Just before he did so, he allowed his lips to hover over hers. 'Trade through . . . darling.'

As he kissed her, his sense of loss grew unbearable, swelled to terrible proportions, and then, as Becky looked up and murmured that she loved him, vanished.

They dined at San Lorenzo, touching each other at intervals very discreetly but not, it transpired, discreetly enough. They emerged into Beauchamp Place followed by a journalist on a tabloid newspaper, who had also been dining in the restaurant. By random chance, the journalist was sniffing at the Lloyd's story and recognized El Medici. It did not take him two seconds to ascertain that Becky was not his wife.

Louis took the last train back to Appleford and arrived home well after midnight. He was surprised to find Jilly still awake.

She was wakeful because she was thinking. Lapped in pure cotton sheets and flounced nightdress, she had been reflecting on the knowledge that, once again, a third party had joined her marriage.

She did not mind. As her astrologer to whom she confided most things had pointed out, she had her own agenda. Anyway, Mars was in the ascendant and he was the god of war.

As with war, which she would now wage, acceptance was a skill, requiring the discipline of the *réligieuse* and, early on, Jilly had set about perfecting this art. Until now.

She looked up, and the pink shade from the bedside lamp threw a flattering light over her beautifully serviced face and skin. Not for the first time Louis was struck by how little he knew of the exact calculations and directional voices of his wife.

Abruptly she told him that some bills were outstanding and he apologized. He finished undressing and got into bed.

'Any news from the boys?'

'No.'

'Any interesting post?'

'No.'

Louis rolled over towards Jilly. 'Are you all right?'

'I'm getting old, Louis.'

He was amused. 'Is that all?'

'How like a man. Forty-eight is old.'

Louis sighed and rolled away. Jilly's periodic wrestling with the spectre of ageing required patience and, tonight, he had none.

I have journeyed from the land of lost content.

'I don't want wrinkles. I don't want to be a bore.'

Louis closed his eyes. 'Go to sleep.'

Jilly switched off the light. 'I think we should move. Thanks to the Frants, Appleford has changed and we should get out before the value of the house drops further. Anyway, with the boys gone, it's too big for us.'

'Talking of waste, I'd like a visit to France.'

'Oh.'

He knew very well that she disliked the beautiful shuttered villa in Provence, run at great expense and seldom visited. 'I don't want to move,' he said. 'Not yet.'

'But the village. It's going downhill.'
'Go to sleep, Jilly.'

Half an hour later, Louis got out of bed and went into the bathroom where he searched for his headache pills. Gasping slightly from the pain, for it was worse standing up, he shuffled back to bed and waited for the thudding to grow quiet and leave him in peace.

Chapter Twenty-one

By chance, Becky passed Louis on the escalator at Lloyd's as she had once before, before the adventure had begun. On that occasion, she had been coming down and Louis had been going up.

They exchanged a look, brief but complete.

A reporter from a tabloid newspaper rang Becky in her office.

'Am I speaking to Becky Vitali?'

'Yes.'

A brisk, young-sounding woman, she was doing a piece on Lloyd's and how it worked, and was interested to know how the pieces fitted together. She was also interested in women in the insurance business. Could she interview Becky?

Becky indicated she could give her five minutes on the phone.

After a quick gallop through the business, the reporter suddenly asked, 'Is there a degree of co-operation between the broker and underwriter where the relationship is in danger of passing the boundaries of what, business-wise, I mean, is acceptable?'

'No.'

'Not at all?'

'Of course, if you're particularly friendly with an underwriter it might be the case that an insurance broker uses them without properly assessing the rest of the market and without keeping the interests of his client uppermost.'

'Quite,' said the journalist.

'But I've never heard of it happening,' added Becky coolly.

'Does your employer, Coates, use one or two, possibly three underwriters to the exclusion of others?'

'It depends on the business.' With that Becky terminated the conversation.

The same reporter rang Jilly Cadogan.

Afterwards, Jilly rang Louis and said, 'I've had a reporter on the phone.'

'What?' His shock was uncharacteristic.

'Asking about you and . . . this woman. An insurance broker. Apparently you've been in cahoots for some time. She wanted to know if I had any comments on this professional relationship.'

The silence that followed was frightening.

It was worse than anyone had imagined. It always is.

Louis read the paper on the train to London. Jilly read it over the breakfast table in the green-and-white breakfast area. Becky read it on the bus. Charles was the last to read it as he had been giving the nanny and Poppy a lift to the baby clinic and did not have time for newspapers until he reached work, and then wished he had not found time for them at all.

The piece was matter-of-fact and avoided direct allegations. Under the headline 'What Does Go On By the Lutine Bell?', it referred to the ongoing researches of the recent Finance, Trade and Industry Committees and pointed out that while many external Names were suffering ruin, working Names, by and large, had escaped. Names such as the dashing Louis Cadogan, nicknamed El Medici, a noted figure and hugely wealthy underwriter whose Midas touch made him a legend. He was, the report went, just the sort of figure that up-and-coming insurance brokers did well to cultivate. Brokers like the beautiful, ambitious Becky Vitali and, indeed, they had been spotted dining together only the other night in one of London's most fashionable restaurants.

Jilly stared at the white tablecloth and let her coffee grow cold. This, she thought, was not part of the bargain. Charles felt sick. Louis phoned Rufus Barker, and Becky ...? Becky shrugged and an old recklessness that had lain quiet in her for a long time was ignited. Battle lines were being drawn.

'All right,' said Jilly, when Louis returned that evening. She was sitting in the swagged, toile-de-Jouy drawing room. The french windows were open onto a serene autumn garden filled with roses and coryopteris. 'What have you been up to?' She was very angry. Naturally.

Louis sighed, and the memory taunted him of a distant, sunlit time when they had been innocent and young. 'I don't know what to say.'

'Well, that's a first.'

Jilly twisted on the sofa to reach for her gin and tonic. 'I suppose I have to congratulate you on being exposed as a liar and a cheat.'

He leant against the mantelpiece. 'I'm sorry.'

'You'd better tell me.' The gin was ice cold as she liked it. 'All of it. I gather the rise of this woman has been pretty spectacular.'

Louis looked straight at Jilly and told the truth, and with the confession arrived a sensation of release and relief and of walking out of the shadow.

'You understand I don't mind about the woman,' she said, for Jilly always played fair. 'I know your first loyalty is to me and the boys.'

That was true. The houses in Appleford and France, the bank account and the portfolio of shares. The solid wedge of capital, although she was never quite sure where Louis put all his assets, was the deal. Their bargain, struck when Jilly, deeply in love with a man with a failing veterinary practice in Essex, chose to marry Louis instead, was the stronger for being unarticulated.

'But,' she added, a tight, joyless look descending over the immaculate visage, 'it was unforgivable and careless of you to get into the press. How do you think I feel, knowing that everyone we know is discussing us over breakfast or sniggering into their gin?'

'I agree,' said Louis, impressed as always by the immutability of his wife. Jilly's instinct was for form rather than content, and in some ways it was admirable. You knew where you were. 'I'm sorry, Jilly.'

'Have you been up to tricks at Lloyd's?'

Louis considered the question, which was less simple than it appeared. 'Put it this way. There were opportunities and I have taken them. And I've been lucky and in the know. Those who have lost out have been none of those things, which is, perhaps, not fair. Their losses are not their fault, but they are a consequence of a decision. They need not have taken the risk in the first place. Anyway, quite a few insiders have lost money too. The press never prints that.'

Jilly was growing bored. She held out her glass for yet another refill and Louis obliged. 'If the John Frants of this world elect to take on unlimited liability and not enquire as to what it means and where their risk is being placed, then there is a case for saying they're foolish. If they don't cover themselves they're foolish.' He paused. 'Wherever you go, whenever you go, there are always insiders. Sometimes journalists can make very stupid assumptions.'

Jilly's mind, however, was ranging over a variety of options. She never encouraged Louis to talk about his work, and never listened when he did. Except, of course, for its proceeds, Lloyd's did not interest her. She searched for an opening to make the best of her advantage.

'I've known about all your women, Louis, over the years.'

'I imagined that you did and I hope I never overstepped the mark.'

'Until now.'

He ignored her interjection. 'In return, I never enquired into your activities.'

'No,' said Jilly, thoughtfully. 'You didn't.' They both knew – or, at least, Louis thought he knew – that Jilly's activities had been more to do with spending his money than in taking lovers and he had been careful to pay her the compliment of never referring to what might be construed as a wounding lack of candidates.

The gin required more ice and she got up to replenish it. 'Is she *much* younger than me?'

Tall and elegant as ever (Jilly often thought that Louis would have that tailored English look on his deathbed), he walked over to the french windows and stood looking out. 'She has courage.' And humour and a carefully controlled recklessness that made his heart turn over in his breast. 'And she's tall.'

'Oh. Not like me.' Jilly crossed her thin, bird-boned ankles.

'No, not like you.'

Behind his back, and to her surprise, Jilly winced with pain.

That night, Charles did not return home and Poppy had whimpered a long time for her father before she went to sleep.

The next morning the other tabloids had jumped on the wagon. Louis and Becky figured in two diary pieces and in a scurrilous little article tracing Becky's career from Streatham to Lime Street in which she managed the no mean feat of being portrayed as both a bimbo and a ruthlessly ambitious career woman. The piece also conveyed the suggestion that insiders such as she and Louis made a fortune out of fleecing poor witless Names, who had been reduced to begging on the streets.

'Congratulations.'

She looked up from rereading the worst bits to see an unshaven Charles in the kitchen doorway.

Becky knew then that an episode was at an end. The battle had been fought, and it was time to sew the jewellery into the hem of her skirt and depart with the retreating army. A voice in her head sang a song. Whether it was of liberty or lament she was not sure, but she lifted her hands, palms up, in a gesture of penance for she owed something to Charles. 'I'm sorry, Charles. Truly.'

'When I think . . . Becky . . .'

'When I think,' she supplied the rest of the text, 'what I gave up for you. Is that what you're going to say? Am I right? If it was so precious what you gave up, darling Charles, why did you do it? You didn't have to leave Martha.'

'But I did.'

Becky regarded him out of her impossible eyes and Charles was very much afraid that he saw contempt in their depths. 'This is not a moment to debate free will, but you did have the power to choose.'

'It seems I chose wrong,' said Charles, grinding his foot into a newspaper that had slid to the floor. 'And I will pay for it.'

'You've certainly done that.' Becky thought of the huge sums that departed Charles's bank account each month for Martha's.

In the grip of the strongest emotion he had ever experienced, Charles struggled to speak. 'You tempted me, Becky. And you've betrayed me and made me look a fool.'

She studied him with incredulity. 'Charles, darling,' she said at last, 'you must grow up.'

'Yes.' Charles picked up one of the other newspapers and gazed at the front page without seeing it. 'At thirty-six, that's something I'll have to do.'

The telephone rang and Becky got up to answer it. It was Tess.

'If you need a home, you can come and live at the High House,' she said, and Becky found herself fighting back tears.

Very quickly, Becky discovered that public morality, in contrast to what went on in private, came decorated with teeth. Scenting copy, the press proceeded to cast her, unequivocally, in the role of the scarlet woman, the articles by other women being the most vitriolic. Louis's dash and cash, however, appealed to readers who, apparently, cherished in their collective memory the icons of Sir Walter Ralegh and Sir Francis Drake. In the press, at least, Louis was forgiven for philandering. Press and readers alike enjoyed that aspect but there was more to milk.

'Was it expertise or lust that caused El Medici to underwrite a bad risk in Nigeria,' asked the journalist, 'which contributed to the spectacular losses? Judging by his superlative track record, it had to be the latter. The question must then be posed, "Given livelihoods are dependent on it, is lust the correct fuel to run Lloyd's?"'

On reading this article, Louis experienced a degree and intensity of anger that he could not remember ever having felt before – a common reaction when an uncomfortable truth is being aired.

'Bad or what?' expostulated Nigel, when he read it – free, for once, from the envy of the big boys that had accompanied his working life.

Yet penance was necessary. The scene in which Louis, on the advice of Rufus, stood on the front step of his home with Jilly at his side and read a statement, checked by Rufus, to the assembled rat pack would remain a scar on Louis's memory. Their marriage was solid, he told them, very much the establishment figure in his pin-striped suit. His wife, immaculate in Escada, was supporting him.

More painful was the scene with Becky.

'Even now,' said Becky, when they met secretly after work in a pub in darkest Fulham, 'you're not going to leave her?'

'I can't,' said Louis. 'You know that.'

'So we go on as before?'

'Yes.'

'I just don't understand,' said Becky, her courage and stamina for once on the ebb, 'how a posse of men in frocks and a theology that went out with the ark can exert such a strange hold over you.'

'You have to take my word for it,' said Louis. 'It's too difficult to describe. Unless you know.'

Feeling bitterly excluded, she looked away. 'How can you be such an ogre at work and something quite different in your private life? An earthshaker in the office, a mouse at home. How can you reconcile such different visions?'

'I can't explain it,' said Louis. 'I wish I could. But it's me and bred into me. I have to abide by it.'

'But you have the morals of a polecat. And I'm an expert so I know.'

'Becky.'

'Is it my background, Louis? Streatham and all that?'

'If I told you, Becky, that your transformation is one of the best I've ever seen, then you must take it as a compliment.'

The implications were not what she wished to hear. 'Thank you for putting me in my place. You've just ratified an outdated class system. But,' her venom was watery, 'that makes sense to you.'

'No,' he contradicted, more sorry than he could say. 'That's gone. It's what you make of yourself.'

'Tell me about Louis.'

'Becky . . .'

'If you know the right people, of course.'

He leant forward and took both her hands in his. 'If I also tell you that I love you more than anything or anyone ever in my life, would you believe me?'

Becky's face was running with tears. 'You've done this to me once too often, Louis,' she said, 'and I believed you. As I've believed no one else.'

'The first thing we have to learn, Becky, is that nothing is straightforward. I can't let go of what I believe to be right.'

'You don't, really, and it's outdated nonsense.' She wiped away her tears with the back of her hand, an inelegant gesture that conveyed to Louis the depth of her grief. She waited for a moment longer, granting him the benefit of the doubt. Hoping. 'Louis, I've made up my mind. This time, I'm going for good.'

The drums sound and the Army departs, sweeping up with it its baggage and women.

He released her hands, sat back and, with that gesture, Louis let Becky go.

Charles had to be dealt with.

'I can't understand why you behaved as you did,' he said. 'You owed loyalty to me. We were happy, weren't we? Or did I calculate it all wrong?'

They were in the bedroom of the flat and Poppy could be heard wailing in the background.

'Nobody,' said Becky, beginning to pack, 'is owed loyalty. You earn it.'

'And didn't I?' Her quiet, dispassionate tone had made Charles livid.

All trace of the ease and unquestioning good humour that had once distinguished him were erased from his expression – and Becky, with an uncharacteristic genuflection to the part she had played in it, accepted that it was her fault. She favoured him with a long look. 'Up to a point.'

Jane, the latest in the line of nannies, appeared at the door holding in her arms a pacified Poppy dressed in a red sleepsuit. 'I'm going now,' she said nervously, eyeing the heaps of Becky's clothes on the bed and chairs. 'She's all bathed and fed.'

'Oh, you're going out?' said Becky, startled.

'Yes, it's my evening off and Mr Hayter said I could.' Jane held out the baby to Becky who, after a second or two, took her. Hair all mussed and fluffy from the bath, lips as red as the flower she was named after, Poppy snuggled into her mother's shoulder and her thumb found its way into her mouth. Despite herself, Becky allowed her hand to curve around the infant skull and cup it.

Charles's gaze sought and found a picture on the wall, which he had insisted on buying. A chic little oil of an autumnal landscape, its creator had given full rein to a series of clichés. There were apples laden on trees, hips in the hedge and a glorious spectrum of orange and gold in the painted trees. Then his gaze transferred to the white sanctuary of the bedroom he had shared with Becky, where only a hint of colour was permitted.

Ripeness had eluded him, and he was ashamed.

Poppy was in bed by the time Becky had packed, her underwear and suits folded as she preferred. On top of the open suitcases lay a couple of fat jewellery rolls. In a move that was to haunt him for years, Charles snatched them up.

'You can't have those.'

'No?'

He knew of old the raised eyebrows and half smile that Becky adopted when he behaved badly, and flinched. It was an expression he hated and, at that moment, Charles was aware that he had touched rock bottom.

'Naked I came and naked I went. Is that it?'

'I gave you every single piece.'

Becky put her head to one side and stepped back. 'Fine. Take them. I don't mind.'

On reflection, *that* was the cruellest thing she had ever said for Charles had chosen the watch from Kutchinsky, the pearls from Mikimoto, the Tiffany ring, and the earrings from Van Petersen – those sparkling milestones that Becky had flaunted – with passionate love and passionate care.

With a sound that could have been a sob, or a muffled groan, Charles turned on his heels and, still clutching the jewellery, left the room.

Before she fastened the suitcases, Becky assembled her

papers, her Filofax with its contact addresses, the joint building-society account book and, finally, she helped herself to the blue enamel cufflinks she had given Charles.

She fastened the suitcases and zipped up the small bag. Then she unzipped it, extracted the box containing the cufflinks and laid it on the pillow on his side of the bed.

They would do more damage there than anywhere else.

The suitcases were heavy and she slid them experimentally onto the floor. In the event, they proved too much for her to carry and she called to Charles for help. There was no answer and thus it was that Becky found herself pushing two large suitcases with difficulty down the passage to the front door while Charles sat and watched her from the white drawing room.

'Welcome to the club,' said Lily, when Becky rang from the hotel in which she had taken a room. Becky could hear her bracelets at the other end of the line. 'Chip off the old block.'

'Looks like it,' said Becky. 'But it's for the best. Charles is a much better father than I am a mother. Still . . .'

'Do you want to come up here?' Lily interrupted. 'You can, you know.'

'No,' said Becky, but she was pleased. 'Thank you.'

'You'll see her. You have your rights. The lawyer will make sure of that.'

Becky hesitated and then plunged in. 'What was it like, Lily? The missing-the-baby part, I mean. Did it bother you a lot? *Did* you miss me?'

'You get over it,' said Lily, who preferred not to explore memory. 'I wouldn't worry about that.'

'You're an old liar, Lily,' said her daughter, shrewdly.

'Yup. That's me, chuck.'

Loneliness, Becky repeated fiercely, after she had put down the phone, was the condition of being human. *Never* forget it. As a nostrum it had served her well over the years when she was learning to grasp at the tempting fruit on the tree. (Charles's painting must have affected her more than she had realized.) But a tree drives roots into the earth somewhere, lets loose a scented whirl of blossom into the storm, ripens its seeds and, when it dies, leaves something behind.

Becky stared at the notice on the wall, which stated that patrons were requested to leave the room as they found it.

She had left her baby behind.

Coates Brothers did not like scandal of any sort. Young-based and go-ahead they might be, but the firm, nevertheless, relied on a reputation for probity.

'You made a mistake in getting found out,' said her boss. 'And I'm afraid I've had one or two comments from some of our clients. None of whom bear too much examination themselves. But the markets, you know, they're not what they were. The Lloyd's fall-out being only part of the problem. There's nothing to stop the big multi-nationals bypassing London and going elsewhere. The Munich Re, the Swiss Allianz. You know . . .'

'I see,' said Becky. 'So it's garden leave, is it? Till things die down? How long?'

'No,' said her boss. 'It's not garden leave. It's the sack.'

Becky looked down at her lap and back up again. 'Have none of you erred and strayed?'

'None of us got into the newspapers.'

Becky got to her feet. 'That's life and the going was good while it lasted. You win some and you lose some.'

Her boss heaved an inward sigh of relief. You never knew, these days, with women. Sometimes, in situations like this, they got uppity and took you to court. Becky favoured him with her most dazzling smile, and left him reflecting that it was unfair that she should be so penalized. Then, after an hour or so, he forgot about her.

She spent the next two days on the phone in an attempt to

get another job, and realized rapidly that discretion was going to be the better part of valour. Publicity-wise, she was red hot and to touch her was to risk being burnt.

Time wasted, she told herself, was time gone. A spent echo, that left her a little older, a little more brittle. That it was unfair that she was losing the job she loved, and furthermore, did with brilliance, was not to be thought of, for Time, she told herself, was greedy and she would *not* waste it.

Thus, seething with stratagems, some grand some not, Becky made her plans and worked out the debt and credit of her pecuniary loss.

Her family, such as it was, she did not consider at all.

On the Friday after Becky had left Charles, Tess and she travelled down together to Appleford on the evening train, Becky burdened with her suitcases and Tess spilling papers out of her increasingly battered briefcase. At the station, Tess got into the car and drove it gingerly into the village.

'I hate driving,' she said. 'I hate it. We must pick up David first from the baby-sitter we use when Mum's busy. I must warn you, the High House is not like it used to be.'

'You know what they say about beggars.'

Tess was offended. 'I hope you don't feel quite like that.'

Becky touched Tess on the arm. 'O doubting one,' she said, 'I meant only that we're all beggars these days.'

'Don't let my mother hear you say that.'

The village had changed, even in the comparatively short time since Tess and Becky had waddled pregnantly up to the rise. Building was going on in two fields, and a third had been turned into a permanent car park. A pastiche period house had filled the gap between two rows of houses. The butcher had packed up – couldn't compete with Sainsbury's, Tess explained. The road down to the mini-supermarket had been widened, and an antique shop now proclaimed itself opposite the new tea-room. The air of the village was busy, preoccupied and unafraid of profit.

However, several of the larger houses were up for sale and there was talk that one would be made into a conference centre.

'Reilly's pigs went completely off their heads,' Molly Preston had informed Tess, not entirely innocent of wishing to make a point. 'The noise, you know. He's had to sell up.'

Tess had taken the point.

Mrs Frant was out playing bridge, and Becky sensed a strategic feint. The house had decayed – well, no, she thought, not so much decayed as given up. It was no longer a well-kept, well-ordered home. It was a place for a through-put of people, hedged on each side by parked cars and buildings.

After a drink, Tess scooped David into a pushchair and they went out to inspect the showground.

'I think I told you that Dad only signed a lease for five years. The Countrymen were covering their back in case there was new legislation or the appeals were thrown out. They're anxious to be seen to be law-abiding because in the eighties they ran into trouble when they tried to organize rock-festivals all over the country.'

Eeyore's Paddock, scene of the Widow's protest dance, was ruined, only an escaped comma of soft virgin grass here and there to remind them of what it had once been. Becky shaded her eyes and looked up and out over the route where she and Jack had once walked.

A long time ago.

'What happens this weekend?'

'I have an awful feeling it's an historic battle. At dawn a whole load of fanatics in Civil War dress will be turning up to re-enact Naseby or something. Actually, they're not too bad. Apart from the shouting and the gunpowder, the noise is moderate. Watch out for the camp followers, though.'

Becky dropped her hand. 'Louis doesn't know I'm here, Tess. I'll have to be very careful.'

'Is this really it? No more Louis?'

'That's it.'

'What do you feel?'

'I feel like one of those leaf skeletons, if you must know.' Tess gave a little exclamation of grief for her – she understood so well what Becky was feeling. Becky added, 'But leaf skeletons travel and they survive.'

'Well, you're only here for a week or two. Just until you sort something out. And Mum could do with some help.'

Now I know I've sinned, thought Becky.

Chapter Twenty-two

'Have a tissue.' Wilbur poked a box across his surgery desk, which was littered with drugs manuals and oddly shaped rubber tubes. The room smelt of the insides of old pill bottles.

Tess cried harder.

'It's perfectly natural to feel up and down for some time after having a baby.'

'As long as nine months?' Tess sobbed harder. 'I can't look at anything with suffering in it. Or read it. I cry over the *Evening Standard* in the tube, and I cry if I see a beggar in the street. I cry if I see an advert for Dr Barnardo's. Or children starving on the *News at Ten*. I can't go on. I can't work like that. Apart from anything else, it's exhausting.'

A recent arrival to the village, Dr Wilbur had acquired the reputation, discussed in low tones, of an earnest but thoroughly up-to-date psyche picker. (He had been known to ask his more elderly patients about the contents of their dreams.)

He leant forward. 'You're still grieving, you know, Mrs Mason. But, I wonder, is anything else troubling you that you would like to tell me about?'

'No.' Tess felt as if the denial had been snatched from her lips by a superior force. *That* option was no option. It was finished and final. Or was it? Tess was honest enough to know that, in a curious way, she had come to like her secret, for it gave her power, to tell or not to tell, with which she played.

In other words, she had become a subversive.

'No, nothing else is bothering me,' she replied. 'I mean, yes, there is one thing. When am I going to get thin? That's what's really bothering me, Dr Wilbur, and I've got to the stage when I'd eat a raw egg if I thought the stomach upset would get me to lose weight.'

Faced with this peculiar female logic, Dr Wilbur retreated into textbook-ology. 'In the majority of cases, the mother's figure snaps back to normal within eight weeks or so. But it *can* take a little longer.'

'If you really believe that's how women's bodies behave,' said Tess, 'then you're a tile short of a roof, Dr Wilbur.' She smiled to show that she bore him no ill will.

'I'll give you a tonic,' said the somewhat flushed Dr Wilbur. 'It might soften you up.'

Tess emerged from the surgery. I can't go on crying, she told herself. I have to stop it.

She wondered if she might be going mad.

These days, there were not many private places left at the High House except for Colonel Frant's study. Here Mrs Frant struggled with the correspondence and kept her photographs of Jack and Penelope. The latest, framed in cheap wood, was taken after Jack had left hospital in the summer. If do-gooding could be stamped on an expression like a flag, Penelope had hoisted hers aloft. Jack, thin and pale, was less certain and more tortured.

Often, on her way to and from her bedroom, Becky caught sight of bits of the photograph – Jack's chin, his leg, Penelope's bright and definite smile. Finally, she had ventured into the room to look at it properly and, after studying it, concluded that Jack had not stood a chance of escaping his wife.

On Sunday evenings, mother and daughter sat in the study and made up the accounts. They tended to speak softly for they felt that another presence shared the room. Banished from the rest of his house, Tess's father seemed almost palpable among his books and papers.

'You'll ring Nigel Pavorde in the morning?'

Nowadays, Mrs Frant's voice held a permanently anxious note. Tess looked up from puzzling over the figures in the account books and noticed that her mother's embroidery basket, with an unfinished tapestry folded into it, had been shoved into the corner and clearly had not been touched for weeks.

'Mum, darling. I've done so several times. The answer is always the same. They won't release the deposit because of the open years. That is, as I explained before, they can't close the accounts until they know every claim is in.'

Her mother sighed heavily. Looking at her, Tess grew frightened. It seemed to her that her mother's bones were eroding internally and that her height and solidity were melting. She was no longer invested with the maternal authority that had kept Tess rooted in childhood. A vital essence of Mrs Frant was being leached – as water, whittling out scoops and hollows, harvests soft limestone.

You can't go too, she thought. Not yet.

George and their marriage, and what had taken place and what she had learnt of him and herself, had never seemed so remote.

'I can't *bear* not knowing.' Her mother's face puckered with feeling. 'And I don't see why, at my stage of life, I have to put up with it. I dream of those men ... laughing at my predicament, asking for more. Of letters ...'

'Mummy.' Tess was appalled. 'Perhaps you ought to see the doctor.'

An expression, which could only be described as cunning, flitted across Mrs Frant's face. 'Perhaps I should.' She brushed back some hair from her forehead and looked away.

'Oh, Mum,' Tess said, and drew her close.

Undermined by her daughter's sympathy, Mrs Frant allowed her fear to gush over. 'Your father *never* meant to do this to us. Did he? He was not a bad person. Only trying to do his best.'

Death usually brings revisionism of one sort or another.

Grieving and requiring reassurance that her husband had indeed been the man she had thought him, Mrs Frant's voice ran up and down the register of bewilderment and anguish.

Downstairs David cried and Tess released her mother, for she knew that it was unlikely that Becky would go to his aid. Looking round for help, she retrieved the unfinished tapestry from the basket, banged it gently to remove the dust and unfolded it on her mother's lap.

'One more hellebore to go, Mum.'

Alone, Mrs Frant picked up the canvas and jabbed a needle into a hole. She pulled the purple thread through with a savage motion.

'Morning.' The Director of Marketing and Investment Trusts addressed the eight-thirty Location meeting. 'I want to focus on two long-term issues. One, the prospect of a Labour government. Two, what are your views on biotechnology and should we be doing more with it?'

'Doing more with it' translated roughly into 'making money from it'.

'Labour won't get in.' Kit sounded definite. Freddie shook his head in disagreement.

'No, they won't.' Tess was with Kit. 'However strongly the electorate feels about the muck-up in health and education they'll resist more taxation.' She was conscious that a steel band had taken up residence around her forehead. Five o'clock. At *five o'clock* she had been up with a fractious baby.

'OK,' said Fergus. 'Let's assume they do get in. We're struggling with recession and it has hit the City and our manufacturing base. At the same time, the government has been forced into more market-oriented policies ... privatization, contracting-out and deregulation. Labour wouldn't be able to halt the process, however much they would like to, because the pressure on government finances would be just too great.'

Unobtrusively, Tess pressed her head into her hands and wondered whether, if she located the precise spot, she could kill the nerve that was torturing her.

'Tess,' interjected Fergus, 'are you with us?' He emphasized the word 'with'. 'Would you like to add anything else?'

Just then, Tess had no views whatsoever. Paracetamol, she thought desperately, *where did I put them?*

'Just to reiterate, I don't think high taxation will be acceptable during a recession.'

'I think that's been agreed,' said Fergus.

Kit studied his agenda and Freddie stared raptly at the floor. Bill drank his coffee with little slurps. No one looked at Tess and, suddenly, she understood that a new agenda had been set. It explained every tiny lapse in her concentration or effectiveness in terms of her biology: working mother.

She was damned if that was going to happen and set about retrieving the situation. 'Can we move on to biotechnology and the related area of nano-technology, which is still terribly new and experimental but which we should bear in mind?' The men waited. 'Like Japan and micro-technology, biotechnology is worth looking at. Companies run on low overheads, they have highly motivated staff, they operate as the discovery arm for the pharmaceutical industry where they are highly cost-effective. Granted, they cannot be seen as blue chip but the pay-off is their nimbleness . . .'

Tess was now fluent in this language. Yet running under the surface was a seam of other words from another language. Nappies. Weight percentiles. Formula. Teething. Safety gates. Mummy.

Mummy.

Freddie took over. He pushed a paper covered in tabulations across the table towards Fergus. 'We've done some research . . .'

Freddie was being nice. It had been less of the 'we' and more of the 'I'.

The meeting continued. As it broke up, Fergus said, 'By the way, I want you all in the boardroom at six thirty. There's a presentation scheduled for a new venture in insurance partnership. No ducking out.'

Tess's head beat out its protest in waves of pain. A tom-tom banging a message of despair. Six thirty. Six thirty.

At home, David will be needing me.

Mrs Frant was not disposed to make Becky feel welcome at the High House, and did not do so. Becky's presence diluted the pure air that Mrs Frant so prized.

Why should she welcome this cuckoo? she asked herself. She disliked and distrusted Becky and, despite the years, the hostility had not abated. The physicality of dislike now struck Mrs Frant, for it was akin to stretching after sleep or eating when hungry and gave a piquant pleasure. Since many pleasures were now denied her, Mrs Frant had no intention of exercising restraint.

At times, and secretly, Mrs Frant thought of herself as already dead – a shade, winging though layers of time that had been folded back on themselves, searching for John. (Mrs Frant had been reading the latest theories in the science section of the *Sunday Times* and rather fancied herself as a post-modernist ghost outwitting relativities.)

In her stronger moments, panic and fear temporarily capped, she decided that hatred was useful: it was one way of confirming that she *was* still attached to the world. And, as the woman born and bred to manners but who was losing the habit, she was also amazed to discover that she was comfortable with hatred.

'This telephoning business.' She accosted Becky in the hall as the latter was finishing a long session on the telephone. 'You have to pay for it, you know.'

'Of course.'

'I've decided to put in ... well ... a payphone.' Mrs Frant

had difficulty articulating the word 'payphone' and, for a second, Becky felt pity for her.

She took the bull by the horns. 'Mrs Frant,' – 'Angela' was, of course, out of the question – 'I know Tess had to persuade you to let me stay here but I am grateful.'

Like many women, Mrs Frant operated elliptically. But, faced with the girl she had demonized, she felt an upsurge of power. Glancing through to the drawing room in which sat two interested guests (why could these people not get on with their lives?) she shovelled Becky into the kitchen.

Stock bones boiled on the cooker and the now shabby kitchen was impregnated with a moist, gelatine-flavoured atmosphere. A crate of milk sat on the table with three cartons of cut-price margarine. A catering tin of cheap instant coffee and two kettles took up one sideboard. The window over the sink, which looked out onto Eeyore's Paddock, now provided an excellent frame for the row of concrete lavatories.

Mrs Frant took up a battle position by the table. 'I didn't – I don't – want you at the High House but Tess does. Because you're in trouble and because she wishes it, I'll do my best to put up with you. But I insist that you pay your way.'

'Of course,' Becky repeated.

The riposte was sharp. 'There's no "of course" about it. We both know that.'

Becky's polite smile did not falter. Indeed, it held a hint of mutual understanding. 'Do you dislike me because of Jack?'

Jack?

Strange. These days, these terrible days, Mrs Frant barely missed him. But, in its way, that was worse than missing.

'Yes. And no. Jack would probably have gone and half killed himself running around with refugees without you dumping him.'

'Because . . . because I left my own baby?'

Leaving a baby was too ghastly a subject to tackle. Mrs Frant turned to poke ineffectually at the boiling bones with a wooden spoon. 'I hated you long before that,' she said. 'And I hate all this business,' she said angrily. 'Cooking. Stock and margarine. Thinking about every penny. Widowhood. I wasn't brought up to expect that things can go wrong, you know. I don't have the resources to cope.' The spoon banged against the edge of the saucepan: the clack and clamour of an unquiet woman. 'I admire Jack, though. And I admire Tess.'

Once embarked, Becky was not going to give up. 'Why *do* you dislike me?'

Wooden spoon held like a sword, Mrs Frant swivelled to face Becky. 'I dislike you, Rebecca,' she pronounced her verdict, 'because you have insufficient heart.'

With a clumsy movement, Becky turned away and her hair flew around her cheeks. As surely as if a bullet had drilled a hole in Becky's beautiful breast, Mrs Frant had inflicted a wound.

After lunch, a humbled Becky offered to look after David and take him for a walk. While she was gone, Tess rang up.

'I've spoken to Nigel, who's been negotiating with the managing agents. It's just possible they can release the deposit but nobody can be sure. If they do, it will cost us.'

'How much?' Mrs Frant laid a hand on the region of her heart.

'About ten thousand.'

'Robbers.'

'They have to keep back a reserve, just in case.'

'At this rate, I won't have any money to live on.'

'Listen, Mum, I'm doing my best and playing the market a bit. It's difficult and the market is bumpy but I should make enough to pay some bills. Till things are sorted out.'

Mrs Frant removed her hand from her chest. 'Did that idiot have anything else to say?'

'No. But I thought I'd talk to Louis Cadogan again.'

When Tess managed to track him down, Louis listened with courtesy and attentively, and she became conscious of the difference in their age and experience.

'It's an impossible situation,' she said. 'Daddy's estate has been wiped out by the cash calls. My mother needs capital to live on. She can't sell the house. Or she could but for practically nothing and, anyway, the money would be whipped away. And Lloyd's won't release the deposit because of the lapsed estate insurance.'

Louis listened and then said, finally, 'It was a pity that your father didn't renew.' Tess bristled. 'It's a great pity that Nigel and the rest didn't do a bit of housekeeping which, after all, they're paid to do.' She felt treacherous tears gathering and fought to get the words out first. 'Daddy was ill and frightened and there was no one prepared to help or advise, or to take responsibility.'

'Tess.' Louis sounded weary and he was. '"Help" and "responsibility" are not applicable words for insurance, which is a matter of rules and regulations. I must point out that, in your father's case, these have been followed to the letter.'

Tess's fury routed her tears. 'And in *your* case?'

He was silent.

'I do hope,' Tess was dry and bitter, 'that if you are ever in a situation which requires help that no one suggests that responsibility and help are abstracts that do not apply to you.'

'Dear Tess,' went the letter the secretary tossed into her in-tray at Metrobank, 'I hope you are well and the problems have sorted themselves out.' Tess, who had been crying again in the ladies' and frantically endeavouring to hide the traces, blew her nose.

A voice cried in the wilderness.

She was going mad.

'As I think I mentioned to you, I was hoping to come out of

the Army and it looks as though that is going to happen. We are very pleased and hope to move north to Scotland ... After so many years in the Army, I hope I can adapt. We are looking forward to it very much ...' Clearly Iain was neither a stylist, nor a poet.

In fact, the drama had unfolded a little differently from the harmonious arrangement his letter suggested ...

When she watched him come through the front door on a Friday evening, Flora MacKenzie had known, and she beat at her ungenerous bosom with a (practised) little fluttering gesture, a sure indicator that she was angry.

'You've put in for redundancy?'

Iain chucked his briefcase onto the floor where it landed with a thud. 'A free man, Flo. Mind you, it took some persuading.' Leaving her frozen, he stuck his hands in his pockets and went in search of the drinks tray.

Flora pursued hotly, 'Are you telling me that you had to beg them to let you opt for redundancy?'

'Affirmative.'

She sat down hard on a chair, whose stretch covers were plain and severely practical. 'Iain, have you *any* idea of what's happening out there? Or are you like one of those things that live buried in the sea bed?'

'We'll find out.'

She closed her eyes and her hand continued its tattoo against the green Marks and Spencer lambswool. 'I thought you were joking about Scotland,' she almost screamed.

'I would love to meet up with you again before it all happens,' Iain terminated his letter to Tess, 'because, I imagine, we will lose touch when we move. I was going through some of my things the other day and came across some photos of George in the early days. You might like to see them.'

The telephone rang. It was the bright and bushy-tailed reporter from the tabloid newspaper. She was searching for

Becky to do a follow-up piece and had heard that Tess might be able to help. Could she tell her where she might contact Becky?

'No, I bloody could not.' Tess put down the phone and regarded it for a moment. 'Bugger,' she said aloud.

Freddie looked up. 'That's better, sweetie. *Much* more life. Like the old Tess. Professional widder-wimmin can be a tad dreary.'

'Shut up, you heathen.' The blood was back in Tess's cheek.

Again the phone rang. It was the agency broker. 'Tess, that order you placed for the Epigram shares. We've had a spot of trouble with the registering. Can you enlighten?'

Tess shuffled through the print-out. 'Half the stock is held in Guernsey and half here. OK?'

Two seconds later, the phone rang again. 'Tess,' said Bill, 'I've got a little project for you in darkest Humberside. A local landowner who's made some money selling off land for a supermarket. It means an overnight stay.'

She felt her hands clench. 'Is that necessary?'

'Afraid so. I want this one netted in. Best bib and tucker.'

Oh, God, oh, God.

No, don't call on Him. He isn't there. Clearly.

What does my son look like these days? How many teeth has he? When did he first smile? When did he crawl?

Do I care?

Is the face of well-to-do England changing? [ran one of the think pieces, entitled 'The Wages of Greed', in a quality Sunday paper, as the winter of 1990 laid its chilly finger on the land.]University professors are quietly removing their children from fee-paying schools, the cricket greens are deteriorating in picture-postcard villages. There is a rash of FOR SALE signs in the stockbroker heartlands.

Why?

Quite a lot of it is to do with the crisis at Lloyd's. Some

call it 'The Lime Street Factor'. Others who find themselves struggling with impossible cash calls call it 'legalized' theft by Lloyd's insiders, who regarded the external Names as so many sheep to be fleeced.

But if the villages of Middle England are having the stuffing knocked out of them and the sheep are being sheared to the bone, it must be pointed out that the Lime Street Factor extends a bony finger around the world. In Canada and Australia, too, there are those reeling from cash calls and very vocal about it.

Clearly, with the recent revelations and a new militant mobilization of burnt Names, the reputation of Lloyd's has taken a nose dive that will affect future business as other insurance markets around the world leap into the breach . . .

It was decided that the Bollys' Christmas lunch should be austere: they would forgo one course and give its cost to charity. There was much discussion as to whether the smoked salmon or the flambéed crêpes in brandy should constitute the sacrifice.

Nigel Pavorde read the article during the cheese course. 'Bad or what?' His notebook lay in his pocket. 'Stomach uneasy. Bowel movement 7.30.' Unsure of what his response should be, he looked to the others for the lead. What should he think? His business was to tie a small knot on a parcel.

He was not sure but he thought, maybe, his guts were on the move again.

'What do you think, Matt?' Chris Beame was flushed with wine.

Matt seemed troubled and more than usually conspiratorial but he was safe in the knowledge that it was not he who would suffer. 'The publicity will do damage, but we must remember that the core business is sound.'

'We are guilty,' said Louis, who had grown thinner and more lined, which rather suited him, 'of sins of omission.'

It struck him again that, whatever he did, wherever he was, it would be impossible to fillet the Catholic theology out of his blood and bone.

'What are you talking about?' Nigel was thoroughly bewildered.

In revenge, Louis gave a lecture. 'Decline and fall is quite usual. Predictable, even. You know that, Chris, from history.'

'Is it?' said Nigel.

'But so is resurgence. We must reinvent ourselves. There are ways . . . Offer limited liability. Shares in the business, etcetera.'

The port was circulated, and Matt lit up a cigar. 'We'd better get on with it.'

'You're sitting on the port,' said Chris Beame.

Chapter Twenty-three

'We ought to invite Angela onto the committee.' Eleanor Thrive operated on the assumption that her charitable impulses made up for her hopeless inefficiency, with the result that no one took her seriously, of which she remained in blissful ignorance.

The members of Appleford's Christmas co-ordinating committee were drinking coffee in the Cadogans' dining room. The table was spread with a rug, which was covered in bits of paper.

'No,' said Jilly Cadogan. 'I think not.'

Today the Widow's trembling was obvious, and the more obvious it became the more it was ignored. From politeness – and from terror. 'Won't it hurt her?' she said, recollecting the slights that had come her way.

'Angela is no longer one of us,' said Jilly. 'I feel sorry for her.'

'Yes,' said the Widow, greatly daring and with the reckless-ness of the worm who had turned. 'Of course, you would understand. The publicity and gossip and all that . . .'

Jilly flushed a deep, angry scarlet and set her mouth in a thin line.

'Well,' Margery Whittingstall decided to pitch her tent in Jilly's camp, 'I think that after all that's been done to Appleford there's no way we should invite her to help with the Christmas flowers. Or the party either.'

'Oh,' said Eleanor Thrive faintly, and gave one of her silly laughs. 'We *are* sending her to Coventry, then.'

*

Becky was not versed in the classics but she understood the role of fortune in history. One had only to think of Queen Victoria's luck in marrying a man who was interested in drains and Christmas trees. But Becky also knew that fortune must be wooed and – another vital requirement – it was best to be in its path when it came along. In other words, she was not going to give up. Somewhere in the busy, greedy structures that supported Lloyd's, there would be a job that fortune was keeping open.

Stubbornly she worked through her contacts. Was there anything in the brokers'? The underwriting agencies? The syndicates?

'Oh, yeah, oh, yeah,' jeered one of her more macho ex-colleagues. 'Think again.'

'Your name's too hot, baby,' said another, a cocaine-snorting high flyer, currently occupying a senior position in one of the top brokers. 'Just a bit awkward right now.'

Others, more sober, were tactful. Their message, interpreted collectively, ran thus: the situation was difficult and a lot of mud was being slung about. It was whispered that the 1989 year of account looked as though it would be disastrous and heads might roll. External Names were rattling sabres and the press was prowling.

Sorry.

The headhunters who had heard tell of Becky were sorry too. Jobs, they said, were not quite as plentiful as they had been. There were no longer stories to relate of whole teams being poached, hardly any of apocryphal golden hallos or goodbyes or sweeteners to rack up in the tally of City folklore. They told Becky other tales. Something had happened to confidence. The mood had changed. The ecology of the bedrock had altered, and the easy provender had vanished. When a tide recedes, they implied, the creatures who have been too slow, too old, too disadvantaged are beached. In 1990 – and we should have seen it – the death toll had climbed, leaving victims bloated with a decade's glut gasping on the sand.

If rebellion seethed in Becky, she hid it. Patience was an art and she was greatly practised in it. Energy was finite and she would not waste more than a second or two in analysing the anomaly that it was she who had lost her job, not Louis.

'You know I've never been into isms,' she told Tess, 'and I refuse to interpret what has happened to me from a feminist perspective. It's what happens, that's all.'

'We're different,' she said, on another occasion when they had been discussing the subject of the modern woman. 'We don't sit and look out of windows any more. We've let ourselves out by the front door and we do things. We cannot be expected to be treated differently from the others out there.'

Tess, struggling with guilt and weeping, wanted to cry out; You've forgotten the wretched biology we always talked about, but realized that that did not really apply to Becky.

This, I believe, is true, Becky told herself. I am the new woman taking on an old world. Let's see what happens.

'No use crying for the moon,' said Lily who, on hearing the news, had winched herself into a new frock and white high heels, grabbed her shimmery patent-leather bag and got herself down to London on the coach. Once there, she had demanded that Becky join her for a night out in a wine bar in Victoria.

'I'm not. That's the way it works.' For once Becky had allowed herself a glass of wine. Louis liked wine. Good wine. 'Never waste your palate on indifferent stuff,' he had said (the one with the money), and he had looked at Becky. 'Only the best. The finest.'

Dozy mare.

'That's it, chuck.' Lily was on her second gin and French. 'Tell you what, Bec, let's drink to that.'

'From Paradise Flats to a penthouse in Battersea to where? From no money to plenty to none . . . Well, I was paid off.'

Lily looked shrewd. 'Keep it safe.'

Becky leant back on the leatherette bench. 'You'll have to

be careful, Lily. You're beginning to take your duties seriously as a parent.'

'Ho hum, as Jean would say.'

Both women laughed.

Lily got drunk. Becky did not: she supported her mother back to the hotel in Kensington and put her gently to bed.

'Mum,' she said, looking down at the recumbent figure. The word was foreign on her tongue.

Poppy took a minute or two to recognize her mother. When she had run through the images in her mental filing cabinet and made the connection, her smile illuminated her face.

Becky took her in her arms and felt the small body fit against hers. A smell of baby invaded her nostrils and she buried her lips in the light, curling wisps of hair. She knew then, irrevocably, that it was impossible to travel through life without some luggage, even if it was only a memory.

Charles was not speaking to Becky. As soon as she arrived, he left the flat, leaving her with Poppy and the long-suffering Jane.

'I'm sorry,' said Becky, to the girl. 'This is all very difficult for you.'

'Not at all,' said Jane, sturdy and sensible-looking. 'All my families have been split up.'

'How many have you worked for?'

'Five,' said Jane. 'Do you want me to make Poppy's lunch before I go out?'

While she was in the flat, Becky took the opportunity to read through Charles's papers, pushing aside the personal stuff to concentrate on work documents.

Nothing big appeared to be going on, just a few whispers of a deal in Brunei. But, then, everybody has whispers in Brunei, it was part of mythology. Plus, they were erratic about paying. A trip was planned to America and another to an Alaskan oilfield.

Charles's work diary for the coming week had three lunch engagements with a couple of well-known underwriters with whom he used to do business at Mawby's. Becky smiled. Charles was working the floor.

In a rare, unbent moment when out walking David, caught between the polite *froideur* of the present and the last hostility, Mrs Frant had shown Becky the mark left by a horse-chestnut leaf on the twig. 'See,' Mrs Frant had said, 'look at the tiny nails in the horseshoe-shaped scar. You can see exactly which bit belongs to the other.'

When she said goodbye to Poppy, Becky remembered that image.

Back at the High House, she and Mrs Frant preserved a more or less civilized front, Mrs Frant because she loved her daughter and Becky because she loved her friend and because it suited her position to behave well. If the High House physically dominated the rise at the end of the village, it also contained two women intent on occupying the moral high ground.

That Christmas, the air seemed polluted and there were no log fires and soaring Christmas trees. No spice, no crackers and, to be truthful, no hope.

During the days after Tess had left, David kept the two women endlessly occupied. So did the guests. Becky worked hard. Her cuticles grew rough from washing-up and her hair less smooth and curbed. Sometimes she imagined that her clothes smelt of baby, and she was forcibly reintroduced to plastic toys and other joys, such as plastic bibs in which bits of food lay festering, which she had imagined that she had left behind – in that other life. She was also reacquainted with the snobberies, many and various, dispensed by those spending money to those providing the services. Being Becky, she laughed at this manifestation of human behaviour in a way that Mrs Frant, sliced to her aching heart by her predicament, never would or could.

Estranged from Appleford (Mrs Frant had taken note of the

Christmas rejection), she resigned from rotas, councils and committees. Considering what she had given over the years, the silence was unforgivable. But there had been too much bad feeling, and too many wounds inflicted over the business of the showground for Mrs Frant to be a welcome presence, even among her friends. Especially among her friends, for friendship depends on a commonality of interest. But if she mourned the finish of an old life, if she missed its fabric, if the isolation was not good for her, she said nothing. Fed by grief and something worse, impotence – for it is imperative to our sanity that we can control our affairs – her hatred, rich, black and festering, grew.

What, then, did Mrs Frant have left?

Courage? A determination to see things as they were? Perhaps. Yet it was odd that Mrs Frant, that most maternal of women who might have been expected to fall into the doting-grandparent category, appeared curiously unmoved by her grandson, so smooth of cheek and so deliciously silky-haired. But, thought Becky, who had no energy to waste on regret for her own position and certainly none for Mrs Frant's, she had always been odd.

Only two factors could possibly be said to unite the women: their dislike of each other and their fear of the post – Becky's because it yielded nothing, Mrs Frant's because she lived in daily dread. Sometimes, when the postman's tread sounded on the gravel outside, Mrs Frant shook with anticipation. Sometimes, she fled into her depleted garden and marched and remarched her routes until she could face whatever lay on the table in the hall.

'I am sorry,' Becky ventured one morning, when Mrs Frant finished reading a letter. The older woman had turned chalk white. 'I wish I could help.'

'You have *no* idea,' said Mrs Frant, 'no idea – of what it is like to live in limbo. I expect,' she turned her drained features towards the kitchen window and the ruined paddock beyond, 'it amuses you to see your victims close up.'

'Victims?'

'The ones that suffer for the mistakes made by others. The sheep that you fleeced.'

'Some of them are suffering with you,' said Becky, battling with her patience. 'There are ruined insiders as well as outsiders at Lloyd's, you know. Less fuss is made about them in the press.'

'Good,' said Mrs Frant. 'If I'm down to my last penny, it is fitting that they should be too.'

Mrs Frant's world view, united with the draconian cast of her outrage and her rigid sense of fitness, was remarkably similar to Aunt Jean's. Maybe, thought Becky, it has something to do with being an older generation. For a second or two, she envied Mrs Frant the beliefs built on such a bedrock, for flexibility was tiring and held a quotient of risk.

'At least,' murmured Mrs Frant, casting aside the latest letter from her lawyer, 'I have my life insurance.'

She shot a speculative, secretive look at Becky but the latter, busy assessing the odds for the future, did not notice.

She remembered, early on in their marriage, remarking to John that it was comforting to think that one could grow old with a plant. She had meant the hellebore, whose hidden aspects she so admired. A gardening reference book had yielded up the knowledge that the word hellebore stemmed from the Greek verb 'to kill' and that the *Hellebore niger*, 'the black hellebore', was so-called for its black root. (This discovery had coincided with Mrs Frant's second, and more important, discovery that the guarding of private areas in a marriage were vital to its success.)

In the twilit tundra in which her life was now conducted, Mrs Frant concentrated on the idea of the black, fibrous taproot anchoring the hellebore. As an image, it lent her strength.

The Black Root was the code name she now gave to her preparations.

*

Did Becky think about him? Did her shallow, disloyal soul crave his forgiveness? Did she regret his absence from her life? Did she regret her daughter?

Unvarnished truth is plain and heavy. Sometimes, it is bitter. Unvarnished truth teaches us that some people are forgettable – who as soon as the door is shut or the coffin lid fastened on them are as if they had never been.

Left in the clinical white flat (which would have to go on the market), Charles sensed that he had left no impression on Becky, and a terrible desolation swept over him. Outside the windows, the Thames failed to sparkle, and each morning Charles regarded the dull sludge movement of the water and reflected on the ills in his life that had now accrued emotional compound interest.

In her area of the flat, Jane attended to Poppy, moving through the days with practised routine skills. But in the evenings when he managed to get home Charles took Poppy from Jane and put her to bed himself.

Frequently, he felt ill. Nothing he could lay his finger on. A vague sore throat. An ache in a joint. As the winter drew down, he felt even iller and drained of resources.

Martha was ironing and listening to *Woman's Hour* when the doorbell went. Switching off the iron and the radio in one practised movement, she hefted Tiny onto her hip and, sighing a little, opened the door.

'Charles . . .'

He was a sorry sight. Pale, unshaven, crumpled, swaying just a little.

She smelt the stale drink on him and got the picture. 'Heavens,' said Martha, her kinder impulses blunted by the lengthy attrition of grief and anger. 'You again.'

He tried to say something but failed.

'What on earth . . . ?'

Once upon a time, a long time ago, before the story had taken an unexpected twist, had spiralled like the LMX, Martha would have leapt forward and drawn him in, absorbed him into the circle that contained her love and nurture. Instead, an unfamiliar, defensive woman was staring at Charles as he occupied the doorstep like a vagrant. With an awful heightening of additional guilt, he realized that part of the punishment for his actions was the destruction of the old Martha and the emergence of this stranger.

'Martha . . .'

She stood still, reading the signs, absorbing the terror in his blue eyes and suddenly, with an inner prompt, understood that her patience had been rewarded. Nevertheless, she made no move.

'I'd gathered she'd left you.'

'It wasn't quite like that.'

'Well, whatever—'

'Please, Martha. Let me come in.'

'Why should I?'

'Please.'

Tiny wriggled with pleasure in Martha's arms, banging down on her mother's hip. Looking away, for a hidden smile was playing around her mouth, Martha stood aside and Charles walked back into his home. In the hall, he slumped against the wall and asked for a glass of water. Martha put out a hand and touched his forehead.

'You're ill, Charles. I hope you haven't got a bug which you'll give to the children. If you have, you'd better go. I can't cope with anything more right now.'

'No, I don't think it's a bug. Where are Anthea and Pammy?'

Martha sighed. 'At school, Charles.'

With an effort, Charles pulled himself upright. In the dim hall, Martha appeared to have grown so thin that she was in danger of vanishing. Disappearing into the essence of abandoned wife. Then he noticed, with an observance of detail that, until now, had not been a habit with him that her hair had also grown sparse and dry.

'Oh, Martha. How do I say I'm sorry for everything that's happened?'

'In the normal way,' she replied, and kicked the door shut. 'But it would be better if you didn't say anything.' She seemed unmoved by his outburst and the obvious release that flooded through Charles, and bent down to put Tiny on the floor. 'There, sweetie pie. You're too heavy for Mummy.'

Immediately Tiny metamorphosed into a limpet on Charles's right leg. He made as if to touch his daughter but his dizziness made him stagger.

Martha unpicked Tiny from her father. 'You'd better come and lie down.'

While he lay and shivered, Martha made him a cup of tea and brought him a couple of aspirins. Charles groaned and pressed his head back into the pillows of the bed that had once been so familiar and drifted in and out of a doze.

Could a clock be made to turn back? And which one? For some reason he was lying on Martha's side of the bed, and he swivelled his eyes to the left. The patterns on the wallpaper responded by fusing into a grotesque and nightmarish tracery, so he closed his eyes and watched sparks float behind his lids. Then he fell asleep.

In the kitchen, Martha traced with her fingertips the dates on her calendar, which was pinned onto the noticeboard, but in the end she had spent too many weeks as the abandoned wife to tally them and she gave up.

When Charles woke, Martha was sitting on the edge of the bed with a second cup of tea. 'You must go,' she said. 'It's getting late.'

Charles tried to raise his head and muttered in a thick-sounding voice, 'May I stay?'

'No,' she replied, and got up. 'Drink your tea before you go.'

He struggled upright and did as he was told. Martha busied herself in stowing the ironing in the chest of drawers. Vests and knickers that required replacing. Once upon a time, there was a busy, innocent and virginal girl. Along came a prince and promised to lay the riches of his love at her feet and the girl had believed him . . .

'Martha?' Charles interrupted the story and she lost the ending. She hesitated, a hand on the drawer, then closed it. Charles pushed back the duvet and manoeuvred himself to his feet. Then he walked three steps across the bedroom and fell against the chest of drawers where she stood, whether from penitence or as a result of flu he never knew.

'Take me back,' he whispered. 'Please.'

Martha's thin knuckles tightened and her bones sprouted beneath the white skin. Take him back? Every nerve end throbbed with outrage at Charles's presumption – and yet, and yet, this was a moment of triumph.

But forgiveness?

In a well-remembered gesture, she reached out and placed her hand on Charles's cheek, testing the texture of the hot skin under her fingers. Then slowly, and with infinite care, she moved her hand down his body, encircling his wrist, running the length of his hot fingers with her cool, possessive ones.

He submitted, and while Martha read him as she would read a book, he felt the past soak away.

'Go back to bed, Charles.'

She manhandled him to his feet and together they collapsed in a heap on the pillows. With a groan that wrung pity from her deepest soul, Charles rolled over and buried his face – awkwardly and rather painfully – in Martha's breast.

And there they lay, bound together, by their shared years, circumstance, habit, their children, and by Martha's frail, unbeautiful arms.

After a minute or two, Martha stirred. 'We must get Poppy.'

*

If Charles was in the process of obliterating the past, Iain and Flora were facing a future that, apparently, did not include each other.

Flora was very, very sorry but she could not relocate north. She cried as she said the words, which was unusual in itself, and Iain was moved to try to take her in his arms but she shrugged him off.

'You can't let me down now,' he said. 'We agreed.'

She twisted a handkerchief around her capable fingers and he noticed that the velvet on her hairband had frayed slightly. 'I've changed my mind. I can't live up there. It isn't me. I don't want to live among strangers. I belong down here. So do you.' Her voice was low and soft. 'You don't have the right to tear me away from my roots.' She considered her husband. 'The male menopause does odd things, you know.'

Furious and speechless, Iain had slammed out of the house and driven for miles through the night. When he returned, Flora was asleep and he woke her. 'Do you still mean what you said? About not coming?'

Half awake and neat, even in sleep, she seemed much younger and more the girl with whom he had fallen in love and sworn to cherish.

'Yes,' she said.

'You married me for better or worse.'

'Not for the unspeakable, not for exile,' she flashed, and, for the only time he could recollect, her voice sounded loud and harsh.

'That's that, then,' he said, expecting to be contradicted.

By now, Iain should have known that life specializes in surprise.

The look Flora gave him was one that had chilled him in the past, and it chilled him now. She sat up in bed and she looked her age. It was then that she told Iain she was not sure if she wished to remain married to him anyway, and this mad scheme of his had forced the issue. The years of Army life had taken their toll, she had lost heart packing up house after house and he had never appreciated her sacrifice and her discomfort. Of course, if they had had children, it would have been different.

Iain sat on the edge of the bed and dropped his head into his hands. 'If you really feel like that,' he said, 'then there's no future. I'll give you a divorce.'

Seconds fled, never to be compensated for.

'Iain . . . listen . . . maybe . . . perhaps . . .' For once, Flora seemed lost for words.

But he cut off any possible reversal. He stood up and, with a rush of relief, acknowledged something that he had suppressed for years: he thoroughly disliked his wife. 'We've said enough, I think. I'll make up the bed in the spare bedroom.'

Within seconds of climbing into it, he fell into a deep and refreshing sleep.

Chapter Twenty-four

Louis should have known that it was rare for Jilly to give up. 'You know,' she said, while they waited for Thuk to put the last touches to the Sunday roast, 'there are lots of houses for sale in Appleford. The Barfords are going. They say they can't stand the place any longer. It's quite spoilt. We really should think of moving out.' She paused. 'You owe it to me, Louis.'

Jilly was exacting the price for the publicity, which did not surprise her husband. 'The Barfords have lost money,' he said. 'That's why they're selling up.'

'Oh.' Jilly's expensive forehead wrinkled a fraction. 'They didn't say anything.'

'Would you? By the way, have you seen Angela Frant lately?'

'No,' said Jilly, flatly.

The phone rang and, for some reason, Jilly went to answer it in the hall. Louis could hear traces of a conversation conducted in a low voice. It did not interest him in the least.

The temperature had crept slowly downwards and he had not noticed. By and large, the autumn had not impinged on his attention and neither had the winter. He had not been aware of the gold and red taking over from the dying green of the trees, the brittleness creeping over Jilly's garden and the transformation of his roses from lax bushes into stark sculptures.

What Louis had noticed was the change in himself; what he could only conclude was a seepage of optimism and energy.

It came as a shock to realize that he was grieving. For all manner of things. Not necessarily his youth, which he perceived as nothing special and he strove always to see through the commonplace. Besides, he had not enjoyed being young. No, Louis was mourning something more significant: the years to whose passage he had not paid enough attention.

He grieved, too, for Becky, with a curious grief that was almost physical. Sometimes it sat, large and hot, in his chest, very often in the old place in his head, or, like dry rot stealthily colonizing the hidden infrastructure of a building, spread through his spirits.

Louis had arrived, and he knew the place well, at the intersection of an affair when the absent lover still makes free with the mind and absorbs the desires.

(Louis was not aware, and Becky took good care that he was not aware, that he had only to walk to the other end of Appleford and ascend the rise to see her.)

The question he asked himself was: What now? A decade had run its course, and a shift was taking place in his life, and he had little doubt that the easy times had vanished. He had talked of reinvention, that rabbit-out-of-the-hat trick, which he, as yet, had still to work on himself.

It was an open secret that the total losses at Lloyd's for 1988 were likely to be enormous.

'Will we be affected?' were Jilly's first words when Louis mentioned it.

'To a degree. But it's containable. I've ring-fenced and there are funds.' He had not specified what or where. 'I'm afraid others will suffer. The wretched Nigel has taken a hit or two.'

Jilly had considered the issue. 'I wouldn't want to miss skiing.'

'No,' said Louis, 'of course not.'

The telephone conversation in the hall was now punctuated with long silences and, then, a burst of rapid sentences. At last Jilly hung up and came back into the drawing room. She had, Louis noticed, a heightened colour.

'You don't look very well, Louis,' she commented. 'Aren't

you? Which reminds me. Since you're sleeping so badly why don't you move into the spare room?'

'As you like.' Louis seemed indifferent and Jilly got up to instruct Thuk to make up the bed and they went in to lunch.

If she was truthful, Jilly enjoyed having the bedroom to herself after all these years. No little mutterings, no snores, no heaving body beside her. Just silence and the comforting (i.e. flattering) pink glow of her bedside lamp.

In the spare room, it was a different story. Jilly was correct: Louis was not sleeping. Tired and fractious, his mind continued to run through strategies and to wrestle with problems. An underwriter with syndicate losses running into millions had shot himself and his death, a violent and particular circumstance, fixed in Louis's mind in a way that alarmed him.

His headache, which hovered all day, grew worse and he got up to do something about it. Gratefully, and greedily, he swallowed the pills.

Later the headache turned crushing, then malevolent, and he began to moan with pain.

A voice said distinctly in his ear: You must save your skin. And he heard himself answering, I can't. It's too big. Too final.

He fell asleep once more, a twitching, anxious sleep. Then, as the demons prowling in his subconscious rose from their depths, the weakened blood vessel, situated near the surface of his skull, burst.

Some time later, he was conscious of a conversation being conducted over his body. There was a high, anxious-sounding voice. Jilly? Then the slower, deeper tones he recognized as his eldest son's. Then the speakers went away. Or was it Louis who went away?

Later, there was another conversation, a slower exchange between two people when he caught the words 'not too serious' and 'lucky'.

Am I, indeed? Louis tried to summon a response but was too tired. He endeavoured to move but found it impossible, indeed painful, for he appeared to be anchored by ties to a hospital bed. An immense weight held him down, heavier than anything he had ever lifted. Ever imagined. He set about locating a mental image to find the one that fitted him. Ah. That was it. Fixed to the bed with tubes. A Gulliver of the intensive care ward, for he had worked out that that was where he was.

But how odd that his mind should feel so liberated. Extraordinary how it seized the day with a wild, joyous abandon to perform all kinds of tricks. At one point, he chose to glide above his body and look down. At another, he sank through endless dark air towards . . . he was not sure. The huge debt? The final reckoning?

Perhaps I'm about to meet God, he thought, and a warning darkened his exhilaration, the tocsin sounded, and he was back in the grey stone church.

'Louis?'

No, he was not meeting God but Jilly. Pale and preoccupied, she bent over him as he forced open his eyelids.

'Thank goodness,' she said and, finding a spare space between the tubes, touched his shoulder. Even that hurt, and Louis winced, for it would appear that each nerve ending in his body had forced its way to the surface of his skin.

He made a supreme effort to look normal and was rewarded for Jilly's face cleared.

'You did keep the insurance updated, didn't you?' she asked, her fingers burning into his skin. 'You did, didn't you, Louis?'

Returning was a more difficult process than might be supposed. First of all, it was frightening. Every breath was a conscious one. Every thud of his heart a herald of possible trouble. Every dawn the last. Every step hedged with qualifications. Every word spoken qualified by a question mark.

He had suffered a minor stroke, which had affected his left side. In future, he would not have to bother to reinvent himself: that had been done for him. No butter. No wine. No stress. No this, that or the other if he was to recover: the consultant painted a picture that filled Louis with boredom and despair. As it happened, the consultant warned with a downward inflection, the situation was retrievable but it must be looked on as an alarm bell to which he must listen.

Alone, sweating, clammy and without a prop, Louis contemplated a future that had changed.

After two days, he was moved into a private room, away from intensive care and the activity centred on the prone forms, whose silence exuded an intense, threatening quality. His sons came, unable to look him fully in the eye, and went away again. Jilly came and went. Outside in the corridor, the nurses and other mysterious figures of authority and knowledge passed to and fro in a practised hurry. Ladies bearing books and magazines put their heads round the door. Meals arrived, to be contemplated and then removed. Louis was being sucked into a panoply of medicine and illness, falling into routines, needing them even while the world outside became pale and remote.

He slept often and dreamt strange, vivid dreams, one dream in particular.

The door opened.

'Good God,' said Becky in his dream. 'You look awful.'

So did she, in dark glasses and headscarf patterned with horses. 'Disguise,' she announced, throwing them off onto a chair. 'I said I was your sister.'

Worry had drained the colour from her face and he knew that she had suffered. She sat down on the bed, light, insubstantial, leant towards him and smiled her smile, full of humour and wickedness. Louis's overburdened heart and circulatory system throbbed with love. 'Let me ask you something. Are your insurances rock solid?'

Louis felt the dark lift from his spirit. Risking the pain, he laughed and the weight of tubes and the prognosis became feather light. His hand inched over the starched counterpane towards Becky's. Their fingers touched and held. Louis felt tears run down his cheeks.

Her face touched his and Louis knew that she was crying, too. 'Oh, Louis. You fool. You might have left me.'

A smell of medication, illness and his fear filled the room. On his tongue, Becky's tears tasted salty and normal while his were thin and ungenerous.

In his dream, Louis moaned.

Still holding his hand in hers, she leant back, the thick arresting eyebrows raised above the fabulous eyes. Ironic and utterly compelling, doubly so now that he was ill.

'You're not a good proposition, Louis. Any longer. But . . .'

The 'but' hung over him. There was, he wanted to tell her, no safety in human relationships. No love, really, except of the self and sometimes not even that. No security. No insurance. Except for the 'but'. . . and on that hung everything.

'Kiss me, Louis,' she ordered.

On that small, dreamt word – 'but' – Louis began to heal.

'Two down,' said Matt, poking his conspiratorial face above another terrible tie into the bunch of hothouse flowers on the dressing table. 'You and Nigel, who's having his piles seen to. By special dispensation, lunch has been set back a month or so, so you can make it.'

Matt had made the journey at some inconvenience to Appleford where Louis was now convalescing, and Louis was touched. 'Fine,' he said. 'Tell me what's happening.'

'General mayhem.' Matt's face lost its geniality. 'A body called the Outhwaite Action Group is suing.' He did not seem concerned. 'Nothing squeals as long and hard as a man or a woman who thinks they've been defrauded. But if they win, a nasty legal precedent will have been established that members' agencies can be held liable for the failures of a managing agent. We shall see.'

'The Name bites back.'

'Quite a few suicides, one way or another. Pareham got a letter the other day from one of his lot enclosing a death threat.'

Louis shifted in the bed and turned his aching mind to business, from which he had been detached. 'If the bad publicity continues we'll lose capacity. You can see their point of view.'

'Yup.' Matt sat down and looked hard at his friend. 'You all right? Really all right?'

Before Louis could answer, Jilly came in bearing a coffee tray. 'So good of you, Matt. Louis has been a bit down and needs cheering.' Louis recognized the tone that she had used to address the children when they were young and uncontrollable.

'Thank you, darling.' He restrained the urge to bare his teeth at his wife. He watched Matt drink his coffee, and lusted after its strong dark fragrance. 'In the future we'll have to think corporate. Woo in their funds somehow.'

'You're supposed to be ill . . .' Matt put down his cup.

The two men continued their conversation until exhaustion hit Louis, a hammer appearing out of nowhere, and Matt said goodbye. Louis watched him go, and listened to the car draw out of the drive.

A business on the brink of a crisis was already finding ways to adapt and mutate. That was the way it happened, he concluded, as Matt's engine faded into the distance. The idea of those schemes fabricated to turn disadvantage around, as ever, intrigued him.

Take the days one at a time. Slowly. Carefully. Eating, washing, walking, talking required thinking about, and energy had to be hoarded.

The left side was scheduled for re-education. And what would he teach it?

On the bad days, when he experienced the double assault of hurting body and depressed spirit, Louis's bedroom was a place of torture, which was inflicted with an indifference that he, used to control, found shocking. A fever of impatience and despair seized him, sending his thoughts swooping and dipping into the dark. His illness, his unreliable vein, were, he supposed, the encounter with the very devil who had been promised by the priests of his youth. *Lucifer was there. He was there. Like God, he never went away.* Louis had imagined that he had discarded such fatalism. But no. The devil, it seemed, had merely bided his time.

Jilly made some attempt to understand, but her ability to enter Louis's hushed arena was limited. After the initial shock had faded, it was clear that her impatience was held in check. Just. However, she exhorted Louis frequently to get out of bed and do his exercises. Illness frightened her, and she wished it banished from her house for it carried with it a spectre of her own decay.

He thought back on the marriage they had shared. In the early days, he had loved Jilly and she had loved her penniless Essex vet. After a while, Louis had stopped loving Jilly. And Jilly? Louis did not know what Jilly felt, and in his lack of curiosity lay indictment.

That was the way it had worked.

Jilly kept herself busy. The phone rang often and Louis could hear conversations accompanied by gusting laughter, or low-voiced, urgent exchanges. She went out: massages, facials, hair, some committee work, she explained, groomed and perfumed in contrast to the unkempt quality imposed by illness and of which Louis was conscious. But the house was always immaculate, the sheets fresh, the fridge full, the garden a delight and the flowers perfect. Jilly kept her side of the bargain.

'Becky,' Louis addressed the dream Becky, 'I am frightened of my own body.'

'Nonsense. You're merely renegotiating its limits.'

He laughed, as he always did when he talked to her, and felt its healing quality trickle through him.

'All the same, you'd better tell me.'

He sighed with pleasure. Becky listened to the list of physical changes: the long journey between bedroom and the adjoining bathroom, the effort required to take a bath, the hard thump of his heart inside his chest, the nagging headache that descended in the afternoons, his hunger at being deprived of butter, cream and coffee. And wine. Of course, wine.

'Tough,' said Becky, who did not care either way if she had these things or not.

At last he said, 'Tell me about you.' But that part of the dream went blank for Louis did not know where Becky was or what she was doing. All she could say was: 'I'll manage. I always do.'

Yes, she would, he thought, his heart overwhelmed by a tenderness that constantly took him by surprise.

Before Christmas, he was surprised by a visit from Tess who brought from Mrs Frant's garden a carefully culled bunch of witch hazel, which had come into bloom. Its light, sweet scent floated through the drawing room to where Louis had now progressed. Jilly had given up making coffee and Tess was presented with a glass of sherry while Louis received yet another carafe of water.

'You're privileged.' Tess pointed to the witch hazel. 'My mother doesn't yield up her precious plants easily.'

She was lying: Mrs Frant had not wished to yield up anything, but Tess had insisted.

She looked round the room, which was decorated with Jilly's customary flair. Louis imagined that Tess found it a little too dressy for her taste as he himself now did – these days, he found himself longing to strip clean, white and bare all the rooms in the house. 'Louis, I must apologize for being so rude to you. It's on my conscience.'

'Don't even think about it.'

'But I must,' she said, pressing the point, not entirely disingenuously. Nowadays Tess did not mind what Louis thought.

'How is your mother?'

'Hanging on. Just.' One of the advantages of being hit by tragedy, and there were not many, was that if you did not feel like it there was no need to put a brave face on things. 'She has been put in an intolerable situation.'

'I'm truly sorry.'

Tess saw that he was. 'I wish I could help her but it's beyond help. I need a miracle. Trouble is, God doesn't provide them these days.' She looked straight at Louis, her thick hair tumbling down from its loose knot. 'It's strange, isn't it? All his life my father was so careful with money. But when it came to Lloyd's, and Nigel's blandishments, he developed a blind spot.' She stared at her fingers clasped round the glass. 'He simply developed a blind spot.'

'It was a business proposition, Tess. And it went wrong.'

'A blind spot,' she repeated wearily.

There was no adequate answer and Louis did not presume to make any. After a few seconds, he asked, 'Did she send you?'

Tess knew perfectly well to whom the 'she' referred. 'No, she didn't.'

'But she knows I've been ill?'

'Oh, yes.'

'Is she well and where is she?'

'She's fine but looking for a job and I'm not answering the second part of your question.'

'I'll see what I can do about the job bit but, given the circumstances, it will be awkward.'

Rarely had Louis been so conscious of failure: the failure of his wretched body, of commitment and courage. He looked at the girl sitting opposite him in the affluent room: drawn and a little too plump. She, too, was struggling.

Worse than his failures, perhaps, his beliefs were threatening to prove inadequate. In maintaining loyalty to the structures taught him by his faith, imperfectly held, imperfectly enacted,

...an was perhaps consistent with someone who had ...culated the odds. Risk-taking did not end when you ...reets of Belfast. If I don't, then . . . well . . . Iain had ...n an articulate man and, at times of powerful emotion, ...me in second place.

...great lump,' as Flora would say, unaware of the ardour ...t in her husband's sometimes too silent breast. If she had ...t been, the future would have been different.

The train from Oban sped southwards, through the High...and defiles clenched by winter: dark, snowy and swathed in silence.

At Edinburgh, which was swarming with people after the Christmas break, Iain changed onto the Intercity for London and sat in second-class listening to the muffled beat of Walkmans and the conversations of mobile *phonistes*. He looked out of the window. Already the contours and signposts of the North were changing, reknitting into lighter colours and Midlands' plains. Even the air looked different.

The young man opposite was again wielding his phone. 'Tell Bev to make sure the respray job's done . . .'

The showmanship amused Iain. Along with the extra bills and never being out of reach, the owner acquired an auxiliary set of behavioural rules.

When things change, they change quickly. Obviously, he and Flora had agreed that the marriage was over but the speed with which it disintegrated had appalled Iain. One minute Flora was there, the next she had moved out, got herself a job as chief administrator in a private hospital and, her hair newly high-lighted with blonde streaks, dispensed authority and clutched ...pboards as content as he had ever seen her.

Iain had packed his bags and left the South for a decaying ...se situated on the Sound of Mull from whose windows he ...d observe his fish farm, bought from a couple who had had ...h.

...w, he was coming south, leaving behind a bare refriger-

Louis had seen the only way possible to manage. He had not reckoned on the contrariness of feeling and impulse that made his decisions seem meaningless.

The trick was: hang on whatever.

Trade through, Louis.

He pulled himself together. 'How are you, Tess? And, of course, the baby.'

'He's fine.'

He was conscious of a slight detachment on her behalf. 'Sleeping through the night?'

Her '*No*, unfortunately' gave Louis the answer. Tess added drily, 'Metrobank's hours were not constructed with the working mother in mind. In fact, I think there's a plan to make it as difficult as possible. But I've rumbled them and it's a fight to the death.'

'I hope not,' said Louis, and because it had been forced to his attention, 'you must look after your health.' Tess made a gesture with her hands that suggested she did not have any choice in the matter and Louis added, 'I've never really told you how sorry I am about George. It was cruel.'

The new bold Tess told him the truth. 'I'll survive without him.'

'More sherry?' Jilly appeared in the doorway.

God tapped on Louis's shoulder quite a few times during the stuffy, wakeful nights that he endured as he got better. What have you done with your life? he asked.

I accrued money, Louis answered. On political risk. Some-one has to.

Indeed, said God. And was it enjoyable?

Very.

And is it difficult to let it go?

Very. Neither do I wish to.

And your duties and responsibilities? What about those?

Don't ask me, said Louis, involuntarily. Those, I fear, are on the debit side.

Quite, said God. And there is always a reckoning. Would you not say?

Chapter

Not all old habits become otiose and some are useful, necessary. Unlike the habits of a failed marriage, which the instant of dissolution are redundant. A case in point – Iain's vocabulary would, perhaps, never shed its Army embellishments – was the habit of thinking out even the smallest of manoeuvres in strategic terms. As an ex-Army officer, and one trained to be congenitally opposed to waste, Iain had made a thorough reconnaissance of his feelings, identified his objectives and targeted his mission. Now he must wait until he had healed a little, and the shock of Flora's departure – and his relief – had subsided. Until he was able to admit freely that he was relieved. This was not automatic. He did not care for the idea that his marriage had been so lacking in adhesion and rootedness that it had been as easy to end as pulling a weed from the earth after spring rain.

Yet, for all the thoroughness of his emotional investigations, Iain was unable to see the blind spot (how could he?), or even admit to myopia, when it came to the subject of Tess, a condi that had shaped the downward course of his marriag which the sharper-eyed Flora had spotted. On sitting ination on the subject of ourselves, it is impossibl marks. Iain scored higher than most but, nur that was beginning to astonish and delight h enough.

Christmas and New Year came and move. Why should I not? he as

ator, an unmade bed and an infestation of sea lice on his salmon.

Why were his fish infested?

The profit for this, his first year in the business, would be nil.

Sea lice.

Mobile phones.

Flora with blonde highlights.

At King's Cross, he indulged in a taxi. The capital folded around him: choked with cars and now alien, whose surface anarchy concealed a profounder one. At Covent Garden, he got out, paid the taxi and walked into the restaurant where he sat and waited until Tess arrived, rushed and breathless, a mass of papers stuffed into her briefcase. She was dressed in an unflattering dark suit, chosen to suggest just how serious she was about her work.

Iain seemed both taller and thinner than Tess remembered him, browner, too, and rather too conventionally dressed. Halfway through the main course, he put down his knife and fork.

'Don't you like it?' Tess was eating her (theoretically slimming) sole enthusiastically.

'Food can get in the way,' said Iain, 'and I don't want it to just now.'

Tess felt her body miss a beat. A second of change, of reassessment, or realignment into a new position. 'Well, I shan't waste a mouthful.'

They talked fish farms, Scottish politics and Scottish money, much as once, long ago, she had talked Irish politics with George, until she put down her knife and fork and said, 'Iain, I never really understood what George was up to in Ireland. Are you allowed to tell me?'

He considered. 'Put it like this—'

She interrupted, 'Put it straight, Iain. That's all.'

'Over there, the Army operates its own unit for intelligence-gathering. George was part of it. He would have been trained in

313

surveillance and countersurveillance. He would have been out on the streets or whatever, doing just that.'

'He never said.'

'It wasn't, isn't, something to talk about. For obvious reasons. The players know all the tricks of the sneaky-beakies. Sometimes it's stalemate. Sometimes we're cleverer than they are. Sometimes the players are cleverer than us. When George died it was the latter.'

With a weary gesture, Tess pushed back her hair. 'You're all the same. It would have been a lot easier for me if I'd known.'

'Of course.'

'I suppose I should have thought harder, asked more questions.'

'There was no need.'

She looked across the table at him, sharp and defensive, but there was no trace of patronage in Iain's expression. Neither was he going to continue the conversation.

'Coffee, Tess?'

Tess ate all the petit fours and eyed the adjacent table's quota with longing. Iain laughed, which she considered suited his face, and ordered a second plate. 'Don't they feed you at Metrobank?'

'I'm on a diet, so most of the time I'm famished. Anyway, with things at home as they are, every penny counts.' Tess rummaged in her bag and produced a packet of cigarettes. 'I know I shouldn't but it's a way of subduing the body. Otherwise I think of nothing but food. It's unfair,' she held up the lit cigarette and a youthful resilience illuminated her face, 'but I was born in bondage to my appetites. So there's no escape. Sometimes I can't wait to be old when it won't matter any more if you can't see me for chins.'

Tess might have added that she was famished for colour, music, passion and some kind of form, the things that she craved, while she grieved for her father and her husband, struggled to put things in order for her mother and to love and cherish her son. Struggled to make work work.

'Tell me about David.'

She took a breath. 'David? He's . . .'

Midway through describing him, Tess wondered if Iain sensed her ambivalence. 'I love him, oh, I love him to bits,' she assured the listener, 'with feelings I didn't know were possible until I had him. But it's difficult. I don't think motherhood is a natural condition.'

Psychiatrists are familiar with the syndrome of burying a fact in the subconscious, of willing it into the never-had-been. But Tess's secret was proving protean and quicksilver, as tenacious in its hold as the bindweed that was beginning to creep through the garden of the High House. Was David George's or Charles's? Perhaps that, as much as anything, shaped her view of her son.

Forced back onto old hunting grounds, and to the diary, Tess nagged at the old question. How can you reconcile the longing for faith without belief? Would faith make it possible to keep and carry her secret and her anxiety? To hold the ambiguity steady between her cupped hands. Faith would confer a measure of absolution because it held out the promise of forgiveness. Faith would give her strength to get through.

'Are we,' she wrote, 'victims of our age? Willing but rudderless, longing for the infinite but educated into scepticism. Children of science and privatization.'

The concept of the lost generation rather pleased her.

Suddenly, Iain leant forward and took one of her hands. Taken by surprise, Tess blushed a deep red.

'Tess, I've loved you for a long time, longer than I realized, and I want you to come and live with me in Scotland.'

No one ever sheds risk . . .

'You know nothing about me.'

'I've astonished you.'

'Yes, you have.' She added, unaware (unforgivable, she

315

reflected later) of the hurt it would inflict, 'You're not like George, after all.'

Iain closed his eyes for a second. 'I want to rescue you.'

'Good Lord,' said Tess, who had never suspected that he was a romantic. She stared at him with wide eyes and retrieved the situation. 'No, you're not a bit like George and I was stupid not to see it.'

She heard Becky's voice in her ears.

Take it, take it, you fool. March with the Army.

The next morning at the High House, Tess got up at five thirty and crept into Becky's room where she lay, a restless mixture of limbs and quick breathing. Tess snapped on the bedside light and bent over her. 'Bec.'

In the light, Tess's face was clearly sleepless, and lines had arrived around her eyes. Fine lines that traced their own history. Becky's face was better preserved: its smooth skin suggested the survivor, a high-octane energy that maintained its taut, lubricated look. It was the face of less reflection and sharper-focused ambition.

Becky stirred, flung out an arm and said something incomprehensible. Then she opened her eyes and shut them again. 'You're only waking me up because you want me to deal with David. Am I right, or am I right?'

'Right.'

Becky sat up. 'Or is it Mr Right we should be talking about?'

'I need to think and I can't do it here. I'm going for a walk.'

Becky shivered in the cold bedroom. 'Only for you . . .'

Tess sat down on the bed. 'I don't know what I would have done without you.'

Instead of saying, 'Nonsense,' or the equivalent, Becky just said: 'No.'

'But what would you have done without me?'

'Sleep.'

When Tess left, Becky lay and thought. She hated being awake at this hour for she was at her most vulnerable. She turned over and pulled the thinning sheets over her shoulder – the good ones were used for the guests – and tried to doze.

She heard Aunt Jean singing one of her hymns, a thumping, jolly number, and at odds with the careworn face and body. 'I expect,' she muttered to her dead aunt, 'that Up There they're begging you to shut up.'

Becky ran a hand over her thin haunch. She wanted her job back. She craved the adrenaline rush, the whiffs of fear and exhilaration, the precise calculations, the beat of business in the Room, its faint suggestion of old socks and men's changing rooms. Insurance was a world to itself, and its idiom was the background mutter in her brain – reinsurance, settlements, renewals – words arranged like inviting canapés at a party.

Strange how she never thought of Charles. Or, much, of Poppy. The horse-chestnut-leaf scar was fading. She was free again, free to operate and to move where she wished. To make money. The jewellery was, indeed, sewn figuratively into Becky's hem and who knew what was coming next?

But she thought of Louis.

She pictured his broken head. The blood pumped by the stricken heart.

Louis.

Tess took the car and drove out of Appleford up towards the trigonometrical point and parked in the field below. It was dark, and cold, and her breath plumed out around her. Dawn was trying hard to make itself apparent, but the weight of the winter night was almost too heavy to lift. In the distance, Appleford was shrouded in ghostlike livery and, as she watched, a few lights stole on in upper storeys.

As a child, Tess had run through fields such as this one, arms wheeling, breath heaving. Innocent and free of knowledge.

Now she was walking with maturity on her shoulders, and all that came with it.

Up, and further up. The walk of a woman chased by devils and goblins, accompanied by the crack of ice and frosty silence.

What have you done, Tess?

She had learnt to strive, to compete, to do business. To outwit the sharp, predatory life in a medium where it flourished and fed. The dip of an index and its climb upwards, and she could move. The quiver of a rumour and she was there. The suggestion in a tone of voice, and she could repackage it in financial terms. Yes, there was no doubt that she had not done badly. Unlike her mother, Tess was fluent in the language of a non-domestic arena. Both she and Becky had abandoned the view from the kitchen window and chosen to go out through the front door.

Yet it was not enough. No, it was not *enough*.

She stubbed her foot and stumbled. Toe stinging, she looked down and dimly made out the stone's white surface threaded through with a seam of crystal.

It was the metaphor that she sought. Around the stone flowed the rushing impulses of the spirit. Restless, hungry rivers of feeling and yearning, pushing over the hard lump of work and motherhood. And in the stone, the crystal that she longed to extract.

She moved on, the grass crisp round her chilled feet. She was no longer a girl but a woman, who woke, dressed, made breakfast, changed her son's nappies, commuted, worked and occasionally remained awake to watch *News at Ten*.

A fish farm in Scotland. A second marriage to be built on the residue of the old, as Troy was rebuilt each time on its previous destruction. A marriage to be conducted in the shadow of the mountains and ruddy glens, in the wind and the rain of the north. And this for Tess, who had been bred in the good-mannered landscape of the south?

A breeze got up and smacked the tree branches against

others. Its ice stung Tess's cheek and sent the blood diving away from the surface of her skin.

She raised a hand and brushed her wet eyes where the skin felt pulled and taut with fatigue. Slowly she turned and made her way, feet crunching slightly on the long grass, back to the car. Behind her, a silence closed over her path and returned the landscape to the winter.

Ambiguity, the not knowing, was the condition of living.

When she let herself back into the High House David was shrieking. For once, there were no weekend guests, and Mrs Frant, who had been ordered by Tess to rest as much as possible, was still in her room. Dressed in leggings and a jumper, Becky was dashing around the kitchen endeavouring to mix hot-oat cereal. Tess peeled off her outdoor things and dropped them in a heap on the floor.

'Pick 'em up,' said Becky.

'Later.' Tess sat down and began spooning cereal into David's mouth. 'You should be doing this yourself, my boy,' she informed her son, who ignored her.

Becky subsided thankfully with a cup of coffee. 'Better now, are we?' Her tone was more sympathetic than the words. 'Walked it off?'

'Sort of.'

Becky shrugged. 'There's a chance of a job,' she announced.

'*Becky*. Where?'

'Abroad. Swiss Securité. Dennis Badge rang, but it's very iffy so I won't say anything.'

'Oh, Bec.'

After breakfast, Tess sat with David on the sofa in the now unfamiliar drawing room and read him a story. It felt cold, for they did not light the fire unless there were guests. In the old days, at her father's insistence, a fire had roared throughout the winter.

David laughed and wriggled, stabbing his finger on the pages emphatically and with huge enjoyment. After Tess had put him down for his morning nap, she took a cup of coffee up to her mother.

Mrs Frant was sitting on her bed in her underwear, staring out of the window, caught midway through dressing by the more urgent desire to look at her garden. Beside her was a large envelope that Tess knew contained her will. Its flap was open. In reminding yourself of your mortality, did the idea become more acceptable or less? On balance, Tess concluded, it was worse. She kissed her mother and gave her the coffee and Mrs Frant announced, in something of her old manner, that she would be down for lunch.

'Mum,' Tess sat down on the bed and put her arm round her mother, 'if you had a chance would you like to leave Appleford and start afresh somewhere else?'

Mrs Frant did not ask why Tess had introduced the subject. She did not look at her and the silence was charged with the old, heavy imperatives that Mrs Frant's love and passionate will had laid on her daughter over the years. Then the older woman shook off Tess's arm, sat down at her dressing table and picked up the silver-backed brush that Colonel Frant had given her as a wedding present. 'Don't be silly, Tess. We can't leave this house.' She banged the brush on her head so hard that Tess heard a crack.

'*Mum!* Do be careful.'

There, thought Mrs Frant with satisfaction. Now my head hurts and I can think about that. For a second, Tess struggled to understand what was going on. 'If it would make you feel better.'

'I'm not going to Africa.'

'Did I say that?'

'No.' Mrs Frant made an effort, visibly reassembling the pieces of the calm, capable maternal figure that she had been.

A force that, once, had almost smothered her children. No longer, Tess vowed, in a split second of revelation between her mother banging down her hairbrush and the moment of impact. But it hurt her to watch.

'Sorry, darling.' Mrs Frant turned to face Tess. 'I'm not quite myself these days. Sometimes I don't feel quite real, sometimes all too real.'

'Mum, I wish I could help.'

Mrs Frant stroked her daughter's thick fair hair. 'You're doing your best.'

They got through the weekend.

On Monday morning, Tess left the house as usual. Becky fielded David and waited for Mrs Frant to come downstairs. She failed to do so and, after a suitable interval, Becky laid a breakfast tray and took it upstairs. She knocked on the bedroom door and pushed it open.

'Tess asked me to bring you up breakfast.'

It was dark and absolutely still in the bedroom. Becky took in the flowered curtains, the old-fashioned furniture and a large photo of the Colonel on the dressing table, now slicked with a film of dust. There was a smell of toothpaste and of damp towel, and the wastepaper basket needed emptying.

Mrs Frant raised herself on one elbow and inspected the tray. Then she heaved herself upright, pulled the sheets straight and smoothed back her hair. The persona she presented to Becky clicked back into place.

'Are you all right, Mrs Frant?'

'How much longer are you going to stay here, Rebecca?'

With the cruelty of which at times she was capable, Becky observed the heavy furrows engraved into the face below her. Absent hormones and age had long ago banished the feminine. Becky took note. Age obliterated gender.

'I won't be here much longer. But I hope I've repaid you by helping out.' Becky produced her smile.

White and shivery as she was, Mrs Frant was proof against

Becky. Even so, as she pulled a knitted woollen bedjacket around her shoulders, her hands were trembling. Becky placed the tray over Mrs Frant's knees and a hand shot out and trapped her wrist.

'You've always taken advantage of Tess's good nature and generosity.'

Becky calmly removed the hand. 'Why don't you stay in bed today, Mrs Frant? You need the rest. I can cope downstairs.'

The two women looked at each other. I've had enough, said Mrs Frant silently. I want to go. Because you are indifferent and heartless, you will help me. Not understanding, Becky stared back. You awful old woman, she thought.

Mrs Frant gave a nod, so slight that afterwards Becky thought she had imagined it.

Something made her say, 'You wouldn't do anything foolish would you, Mrs Frant?' The stuffiness in the room was overpowering and Becky quivered to escape.

'Oh, no, I always think of my children,' said Mrs Frant, feeling the beat of her love for them. Inside her head the door was flung wide open but no onlooker could possibly have known. 'And you must allow me to judge what is foolish or not. My husband is dead, leaving me to cope. My son . . . well. I miss my home, for the High House is no longer mine.' Mrs Frant's hands locked together. 'I miss my life and I can't have it back. Simple enough to understand but not to accept.'

You're mad and awful, thought Becky, and I won't have you putting a hex on me. But Becky also knew that she must protect Tess, whom she did love. For her sake she said, 'Would you like a bath, Mrs Frant? Shall I run one?'

'Don't be mis-led,' said Mrs Frant. 'The obvious is not necessarily the best solution.' A spark of animation suddenly smouldered in the drawn face.

The chaos theory. A butterfly flaps its wing, and an earthquake shakes China. Where did this drama begin? With a letter? No, further back with Colonel Frant's desire to make his capital work twice. No, with the mining of asbestos, with the seeping of oil over sweet land, with the whirling of hurricanes, the rip of escaped gas, with the desire of the first human to step out of Eden.

'A bath, Mrs Frant? I really think you should have one.'

Mrs Frant's hands wandered over the tray and lighted on a piece of toast. 'Will you stop bothering, please,' she said. 'I resent it and it isn't necessary.'

Becky stepped back. 'That's more like it,' she said, with satisfaction. 'I'd better go and see to David. But,' she turned at the door, 'I will be watching and, if necessary, I will summon the entire might of the social services to ensure that Tess isn't overburdened.'

Left to herself, Mrs Frant was quite calm and cool. Death, she thought, gazing through the door to the other side, and a very good thing too. Until now, she had not understood that an integral ingredient of a good death was the taking control of it, as her life, her middle-class, unambitious life, had not been, in the end, controlled.

There was joy to be had in sloughing off the armour, in tearing through the layers of what had been taught as appropriate behaviour, in the sacrifice – the pelican tearing out her own bloody, painful breast to feed the young.

Let it finish.

Cut the Black Root.

Chapter Twenty-six

'Louis.' Jilly Cadogan addressed her husband in the draped, immaculate drawing room. It was just before dinner and Thuk could be heard banging saucepans in the kitchen. 'Louis.'

'Yes.'

Louis was aware that, behind the cover of her excellent care, Jilly had been watching him during the weeks of his illness and slow, oh, so slow, recovery. The soft-hard scrutiny of the big cat.

'I don't know how to put this . . . In fact, I don't know how to begin.' Jilly's smooth segue into the next sentence suggested exactly the opposite. 'I think your time is up, Louis. I mean our time. We've come to the end.'

There were no guests for dinner but Jilly was in full fig: dressed in cashmere and silk, made up, scented and bejewelled. Louis's thoughts ricocheted wildly and came to rest on one: how like Jilly to go into battle, for he had no doubt that this was battle, daubed so skilfully in her war paint.

'Oh?' He had been considering the impact of an out-of-sorts body on the mind. He was sweaty from the effort of walking from room to room, depressed that it should be so difficult. Depressed that re-education meant precisely that.

Jilly went over to the drinks tray on the table – under the portrait of Louis's grandfather in the red hunting coat – and poured herself a sherry, her manicured hands tipped with varnish moving gracefully among the bottles and glasses. Louis had no such recourse. Alcohol was still off limits: one more thing, one more subtraction (those luscious wines, fruity and flinty, he had drunk in the past).

Glass in hand, Jilly swivelled. 'I want a divorce, Louis.' Oddly enough, her announcement added nothing to the inner darkness that now filled Louis. His first thought was: I'm in no state to move. His second was: Why now? His tired response was instinctive: No.

Jilly sat down opposite Louis and crossed her legs. Then she got up to corral into safety a glass poised too close to the edge of the drinks table and sat down again. She pulled gently at the pearls at her neck and straightened her shoulders. From one foot dangled an expensive high-heeled shoe, and that carelessly appended shoe did more than anything else to rouse Louis.

'You choose your moments, Jilly.'

She favoured him with a look which, after the first, kinder years of their marriage, Louis had come to know and understand.

'You know what I mean,' she said, and Louis knew that his days as a cheque-book husband were over. 'I've enjoyed being married to you, particularly in . . .' Jilly's expensive and precarious top teeth bit her carmined bottom lip '. . . the early days. I've stuck by you, yes?'

'Was that *such* a hardship? It didn't appear to be, if I remember correctly.'

Jilly, however, had a case written in her head and there is nothing so immutable as the middle-aged woman who, having hovered on the stepping stone by the shore, decides to move to the next one. 'I've done what was expected. The children have grown up, yes?'

'Yes.'

'So . . .' Jilly's slenderized shoulders lifted under the cashmere and silk. 'It's at an end.' She did not add, You are at an end, sick, finished. He added it silently for her. But, because illness had thrown him back on the senses and had killed logic and deduction, Louis was not prepared for what came next.

'I want to marry someone else.' Jilly's shoe fell off onto the carpet with a soft sound.

Shaken by extreme surprise, Louis could only manage, 'Who?'

Jilly told him and Louis said, 'Why don't you put your shoe back on?'

'Oh, really, Louis.' Jilly shook her head angrily, and contained in that exchange were the reasons why, in the end, they had failed to love one another.

The man in question, Gerald, was one of Louis's colleagues: rich and successful and in the process of divorcing. If life held out the ever-present threat of dissolution – explained in terms of the guilt, sin and retribution – one element had remained predictable and, curiously, consolatory. Jilly had always been both honest and consistent in her approach to the management of her desires. Now she was taking out further reinsurance. In that moment frozen between unwelcome news breaking and the nerves activating, Louis admired her.

'How long has this been going on?'

Jilly put her head on one side and considered her answer. 'As long as you have been involved with that woman.'

Louis was surprised for, adept in deception, he had flattered himself that he could read the signs.

'I didn't think ...' Louis struggled to his feet before he finished the sentence '... you would be quite this cold-blooded.'

'Ah,' she bit out, 'but I didn't imagine I would be put through so many hoops.' She shuddered at the memory of the newspaper articles and the gossip that had hummed and circulated – and the Widow's revenge. 'Anything but that.'

Suddenly, Louis understood Jilly's humiliation and saw how her life in Appleford had been placed by the publicity on another footing, how her hard-won equilibrium and status had been shaken, roughly and without mercy. 'I owe you an apology.'

'Thank you.'

'Will you pass me my stick?'

He caught a glimpse of tears as she got up to do so and, his own weakness making him extra sensitive, did not take advantage of that exposed flank. He leant heavily on the stick and felt the handle bite into his flesh.

'What do you want to do, Jilly? Tell me and we'll work it out peaceably.'

Her eyes widened in surprise for, lacking empathy with his weakness, she had been expecting Louis, the buccaneer, to fight. Her tears disappeared. 'You're pleased, really, aren't you? You've been planning to go off with that woman.'

He sighed. 'How little you know me, Jilly, even after all these years.'

'How little you know me, Louis.'

He summoned energy. 'But I accept that is partly my fault. You must know that I won't divorce you, and I had intended for us to stick it out together.'

'Don't worry.' Jilly got up and placed her glass on the table. Her heels moved over the edge of the carpet onto the parquet and gave a hollow little tap. 'I reckoned you would come up with the Catholic nonsense, so I'm divorcing you. And you can't stop me.'

Tap. Tap.

'Soon, actually. Gerald would like us to get married as quickly as we can. He's doing up a villa in the South of France and wants me to help.'

'France!'

'Yes. I think we'll live there for a couple of months a year.' Complacent and triumphant, Jilly again tugged at her pearls, buoyed by the red blood of conquest, proof that her femininity retained its power. 'Don't you have anything to say, Louis?'

In a flash, he perceived that Jilly, like the maiden who craved her token flaunted at the joust, craved him and Gerald to wage combat. He was almost prepared to oblige her but, stick in hand, left arm and foot unre-educated, he would make a poor champion.

'What is there to say? Except shall we have supper?'

Jilly remained where she stood by the drinks tray. She looked at her feet. She looked at her hands, with their sparkling rings, spread out in front of her. 'You always were detached.'

'That's not true.'

'You wouldn't know what truth was if it sat in your lap.'

His blood thundering in his ears, Louis concentrated on lifting his left foot in front of the right. Good. It worked. Then the right was placed in front of the left and Louis shuffled, a limping cavalry, towards the dining room, yearning for peace, for resolution and for an easy path through what lay ahead.

None of those comforts would be granted – indeed, are ever granted. Louis was feeling . . . what? It had been best described as 'the weight of life', a phrase, so Becky had once told him, that Tess had read in a book on Eskimos. They used it to describe the important emotions.

'Of course,' Jilly said, over Thuk's leek and potato soup, 'I was going to wait until you were better. It looks rather bad but Gerald wants . . .' She left the rest unsaid.

Louis remained silent.

Eventually Jilly put down her soup spoon. 'What about the money?'

'What about it?'

'I warn you I shall be employing a good lawyer. Gerald's, actually.'

Louis felt sweat break out over his skin. 'Why bother, Jilly? They cost money and cause trouble.'

Jilly dismissed the idea with a contemptuous little *moue*. 'Even if you don't, I need someone to advise me. Which is, perhaps, the point.' She flicked her gaze over the Meissen in the cabinet, the silver on the sideboard, and her eyes darkened. 'Suggesting that I don't need advice is a cheap trick, Louis, which might prove expensive. And, by the way, I won't under any circumstances take the dog.' He saw that she was pleased with the way in which she had ranged her defences, and it saddened him to think that they had reached that stage.

'Lawyers are divisive because it's their business.' He, too, pushed aside his food. 'I repeat, Jilly, I am not divorcing you. I won't for the reasons you know perfectly well and I did not, do not, seek it.'

'You certainly did nothing to ensure it didn't happen.'

'What we had worked,' said Louis.

Later, sleepless between the sheets, he concluded that he had neglected to look. I had stopped observing. I had failed to read the signs.

I did not change. Why? For change is the condition of a successful life.

Mea culpa.

Inside Louis the darkness deepened. Oh, Becky, he thought. How like Jilly you are. The difference being that Louis loved Becky down to her last disgraceful fibre.

It rapidly became clear why Jilly had insisted on lawyers, for she intended to go for the jugular. She wanted to be bought out of the house, and she wanted a lump sum.

The amount she named was staggering. 'You can't have that much,' Louis informed her, via the solicitor although they were still living in the same house.

'Yes I will,' she said, via hers.

'I will give you half of that.'

'Three-quarters.'

'Done.'

'You see?' she snapped at him as they passed in the hallway, several thousand pounds the poorer in extracted legal fees. 'We did need a lawyer.'

The news of their impending divorce trickled through the village. In itself, a divorce was not sufficiently startling or remarkable to take precedence over other village matters. The proposed bypass to accommodate the extra traffic generated by the showground and, in some quarters, the evolving spectre of a future Labour government were inciting far stronger passions than a mere marital breakdown. A stream of people was moving out of the village, a corresponding stream moving in, and in the flux small matters were lost.

Nevertheless, the Cadogans' break-up, a source of distress to a few friends, gave good theatre to some watchers. And, as it is with these issues, sympathies that had lain with Jilly, the wronged wife, did an abrupt turn. She, it was said, was a woman who was planning to abandon her sick husband.

Her swan song in Appleford was a soup and champagne rally for the Conservatives, which, Louis said, rousing himself from apathy, summed up the straddle that the party was being forced to make to win supporters. In preparation, Jilly packed her clothes in neat, tissued layers and went round the house fixing labels on furniture and objects. Red for her. Blue for Louis. She wanted to be quite sure that there was no mix-up by the furniture removers, and the house began to resemble a French nationalist fête.

'Don't you trust me?' Louis asked, watching the precise way in which she divided the spoils.

Jilly's answer was swift and unhesitating. 'No.'

On the day of her departure, Louis woke early, convinced that someone was moving around downstairs. There goes Jilly's furniture, he thought with a spark of malice, for burglars had been operating in the area.

He pulled himself together. His leg and arm were more co-operative now so he hauled himself out of bed and searched for a likely weapon. There was none. Then, as noiselessly as his disobedient body would permit, he crept downstairs and stood in the open door to the drawing room. Scissors in hand, Jilly was on her knees by the Regency card table over which they had argued and which Louis had insisted on keeping.

'For Christ's sake, Jilly, what are you doing?'

She started, guiltily, and he caught a glimpse of her set, determined face – and a transparent plastic bag containing five or six blue labels that she had removed from his furniture and replaced with her own. Red stained her face to match the labels.

In that moment, Louis knew he had now experienced the best and the worst, as he was capable of the best and the worst. Why should he have expected differently? For he was as greedy and duplicitous as his wife.

Sweat dampened his striped pyjamas. Viewed by his inner eye, which had been so blind, the structure and beliefs of Louis's life appeared to dismantle and reassemble in wholly unfamiliar configuration. Jilly's action provided both his salvation and a glimpse of the abyss, as dangerous and terrifying as any encountered on the course of his illness.

'You devil,' he said quietly.

Jilly leapt to her feet. 'And if I am,' she said, 'what can you do about it?'

The blood beat and roared in his ears. A tide swept through Louis's unresisting body, bearing him along strange pathways. With a groan he stepped forward, swayed, lifted his face to the light, tried to say something and slid to the floor.

At the other end of Appleford, Becky heard the ambulance siren in the distance and turned over in bed.

Then she heard Tess get up and go into the bathroom, followed by the sound of taps running. David stirred in his cot. Small movements, intimate and reassuring. Not that Becky required reassurance. She had taken stock and it was time to move on: unencumbered and free. For this she was grateful. Becky's gaze could be as fierce and focused as she wished. She was not required to look either side, or to stretch out a hand to hold up a child, or to think of anyone else. (By spring, scars on chestnut twigs have healed.) Lily may have been no mother, but when she reappeared in her old age, she had had the good manners and good sense not to bother Becky. In the end, they understood each other well.

If she thought of Louis, she only permitted herself a second or two of recollection, a mental cameo of him sleeping at the other end of the village. Having taken too much of her, he was now finished and gone.

The front door opened and shut. The gravel scrunched as Tess wheeled her new bicycle down the drive. Then there was a brief moment of peace.

The mewing, snuffling sound from David's room grew louder. Becky swung her legs over the bed and scrutinized them. Still glossy and lightly muscled. Still long, no shrinkage there.

Good.

She glanced at the mirror. Suddenly, she stuck out her tongue at her image and grinned. She would require all the assets that had tumbled randomly out of the gene pool into her face, and she must – she must – move on.

Clothes neatly to hand on the chair, Becky got dressed, intent on her plans.

Guests were due that evening and, as usual, Mrs Frant had made the preparations, but she was not seated in her customary place in the kitchen. Becky peered briefly into the empty drawing room, and got on with feeding David. Apart from the baby's noises and the clink of Becky's tea-cup and plate, the house was silent.

After breakfast, Becky wheeled David to the child-minder and left him, weaving unsteadily but happily among the other toddlers. When she returned to the High House, the silence still held sway. There was a mark on the wooden floor, a crack had sprouted on the wall and there was a stain on the plaster under the stairs. This was a house brought to its knees by a poverty of energy.

The door to Mrs Frant's bedroom was shut. Sensing trouble, Becky paused in front of it then knocked.

No answer.

She knocked again and pushed open the door. Inside, the silence was clamorous and the room smelt of cheap talcum powder, dust and an unquantifiable something. Age? Despair? Neglect? Mrs Frant lay on her bed, motionless.

Drawing closer, Becky looked down. Stockings neatly pulled up over her strong legs, tweed skirt brushed down over her knees, lambswool cardigan shielding a floral blouse, Mrs Frant was fully clothed and decently assembled except for her mouth, which was wide open. At long intervals her breath soughed in and out of it.

Lying there, she seemed inexpressibly lonely, an embodiment of muted grief and of the many things that had been left unsaid.

On the bedside table was a letter in one of the cheap envelopes that Mrs Frant so hated using. To Becky's surprise, it was addressed to her.

You won't have resisted reading this. I know you too well, Rebecca. But no one else is as selfish and uncaring as you are, so I know I can rely on you to do nothing.

Do not revive me. I have had enough of life. This is my wish. You will see me out, Rebecca, you will see me out. Get rid of this before anyone gets there.

If you care for Tess, you will do this. It is for her and Jack's sake.

An unpleasant sound escaped the dying woman, and Becky flinched.

The obvious thing was to return the letter to the envelope,

to leave the room and to walk out of the house. To wash her hands of this act.

The obvious thing was to pick up the telephone, call the emergency services and wrench Mrs Frant back into the life she had arranged to leave.

More publicity, more branding in the tabloids, another awkward reputation sullying her job prospects ... 'Broker in death pact ...' Talk, gossip, speculation, Tess's wrath and bewilderment. The probable results of Mrs Frant's act inched their way through Becky's brain which, for once, was refusing to work.

She looked again at the letter. The cheap envelope nagged at Becky, for it symbolized the fall of Mrs Frant, a hard, bitter and, apparently, endless fall.

Mrs Frant stirred, her eyes fluttered, opened and stared at Becky for a second, admitting Becky to her Gethsemane, and then closed. During that second of exchange, Becky was forced, once again, by Mrs Frant to look into the shallows of an insufficient heart.

Sew the jewellery into the hem, and march with the Army.

An empty pill bottle on the table and a drained glass. That would be Mrs Frant's last courageous march.

Outside, in her empty garden, the sun was dim and unsure of itself, but the light peculiar to spring, papery and the perfect foil for yellow spring flowers, was shining over the land busy with growth and over the new roads, the new houses, the new shops.

Frozen to the spot, Becky's mind drifted.

The master rig line slip. Rate on line. Excess-of-loss. Excess-of-loss.

In front of her lay a suffering, dying woman. As surely as she stood there in the stuffy room, Becky was being punished for her deficiencies and her knack of survival. A punishment set all those years before, when Mrs Frant had first cast her eye over Becky and decided that she would not do for her son.

Mrs Frant's breathing was noisier now, but less predictable. And each strained inhalation and exhalation tore at the watcher. Becky was repulsed, terrified and, yet, curiously exhilarated by the power Mrs Frant had granted her.

She undid her watch and placed it on the bedside table beside the empty pill bottle and the letter. Then she sat down on the side of the bed, as she had not done for her aunt Jean, sought and found Mrs Frant's hand, the strong, capable hand with its surprisingly artistic fingers, and held it. With a tenderness that was new to her, she stroked the aged skin, sprinkled liberally with its flowers of death, the age spots. The flesh was cool and slightly damp. Becky visualized the chill, like a sheet of ice, spreading up from the fingers, through the palm, moving steadily through the arm towards the heart, its target.

Struggling with terror and threatening nausea, Becky forced herself to keep stroking the hand. No one deserved to go out of life unattended, without anyone to pretend to care.

Oh, Aunt Jean. At least, you knew your God was waiting.

And Becky, loving Tess better than she had imagined, owed it to her to usher Tess's mother – if not lovingly, then as politely as Mrs Frant had endeavoured to live – out of the final exit. For a brief moment, that fractional pulse of the butterfly's wing, and with a compassion that she was not aware flowed within her, Becky did just that.

After half an hour, Becky got up, smoothed the dent she had made on the bed, picked up the watch and the letter and went downstairs towards the phone.

Her explanations were even, measured and convincing. After Mrs Frant had been loaded into the ambulance, Becky gave an account to the policeman that timed her arrival back at the house five minutes later than it had been and her entry into Mrs Frant's bedroom twenty-five minutes after that.

Sergeant Franks and Dr Wilbur both admitted that it was

deeply regrettable, and the latter signed the certificate and let slip that, of course, he had been prescribing tranquillizers and sleeping pills. It was possible that Mrs Frant had been confused as to the dosage but . . . he did not think so.

'Ah, well,' said Sergeant Franks, who had witnessed similar scenes, even in Appleford, 'ah, well.'

Of Tess, Becky did not like to think. But as she waited in the High House to greet her, unaware that silence and their secrets were to be the element that bound each of them to the other for ever, Becky vowed that her silence would last the rest of her life.

Tess was remarkably calm. She insisted on remaining at work, taking no days off.

'They'll sack me if I do so let's not discuss it. You can cope.' When questioned by Becky about the funeral, she said, 'Just use Dad's. Same hymns. Same service. Same grave. It's all there. Same sandwiches.'

The only time she broke down was after the funeral when Jack, who had flown back, and she were sitting in the dusty drawing room. The mourners had gone and Jack, whiplash thin and tanned, was drinking whisky. Tess and Becky had hit the wine.

'Do you know the worst thing?' said Tess.

'No.' Even Jack's voice now seemed sun-baked.

'It's funny,' said his sister. 'Awfully, awfully funny . . .'

'Tess,' said Becky, and put her arm around her. Easy.'

'Mum did this for us, you know.' She swivelled to look at her brother. 'But you wouldn't, of course, because you're never here. Too busy bloody helping the world. Mum killed herself because she thought that the life insurance would give us capital to pay off Lloyd's.'

'Oh, my God,' said Becky.

Tess raised her red-rimmed eyes and clenched her fists.

'Mum could never read the small print, could she? She just didn't have it in her. Between her and Daddy—'

'You mustn't think,' said Becky. 'Don't say any more.'

'Mum killed herself for no reason. The insurance companies won't pay up for suicides.'

Chapter Twenty-seven

Fortunately, David took to the journey on the train. Very fortunately, for it was punctuated by delays and, finally, at Doncaster, engine failure. Along with the other passengers, Tess and her son waited on the platform for an hour until an alternative engine could be located.

The wait was tedious and Tess had grown tired of pointing out features of the station to the restless child by the time they climbed back into the carriage. David settled to sleep and Tess watched as the land began to throw up lumps of folded rock and hill and outcrops of stone grey slate – a fitting backdrop to the harsher world through which she now passed, having left behind a sunlit childhood.

Becky had accompanied Tess to the hospital to identify Mrs Frant's body and she had slipped her hand under Tess's elbow. Strangely enough, after the first outpourings of shock and horror, Tess was not as angry and guilty as most relatives are of a suicide. The thing was too big and, in deciding to remove herself from its path, Mrs Frant had acted logically. Her peaceful dead face had given away nothing to her daughter.

'But I didn't think that anything else could happen,' cried Tess.

Becky's hand was comforting and Tess felt the faint suggestion of relief, of having been released.

Yet having certainties so decisively dismantled sapped strength, as did grief and bereavement. Tess had experienced both, and quite early. Now there was only one thing of which

338

she was certain: suffering did not ennoble. Whether or not she would retrieve her energy she had no idea.

Jack's certainties were of a different order. He had returned to Africa, to the patient Penelope and his African children. 'I'm doing what I wish,' he told his sister. 'You cannot ask for more.'

Freddie had said she was a damn fool.

In the train David slept on; her ruffled, radiant son who, save for the push-pull of his strong appetites, was unmarked. Looking down at him, Tess smiled. Then, as sleep was a subject of abiding concern, she thought, I'll have hell getting him to bed tonight.

At Glasgow, they left the train and went to spend a night in a hotel. Iain had offered to drive down and collect them but Tess, feeling that this was a journey that she and David should make alone, declined the offer.

But the next morning Iain was not at Oban station, and Tess's heart gave an unreasonable thump of disappointment. Holding hands, she and David stood at the station entrance, shivering in the sharp, clean air. Essence of fish and brine filtered through the other smells and, in the sky above, gulls tore past in noisy formations.

Eventually, Tess spotted Iain walking up the station approach. He lifted his hand and waved, and she was rooted to the spot by an overwhelming fear.

'I'm so sorry,' he said, panting slightly. 'The fan-belt on the van snapped and I had to leave it at the garage.'

He seemed paler than before. Nerves.

They drank tea and ate sandwiches in an adjacent café. By now, David was over-tired and over-excited but he was a convenient focus for attention while the ice was being broken.

Once or twice, Iain directed a look at Tess, considering and speculative, and she became aware of a hunger to *get things sorted*.

Oh, George.

Finally, they bundled into the van – it, too, smelt of fish –

took the ferry across the strait to the Morven peninsula and drove along a silent, twisting but gloriously open road, fringed by the Highland glens and mountainous outcrops.

The solitude settled over Tess, much as a piece of clothing settles over the body.

'You'll never do it, sweetie-pie,' Freddie had said. 'You can't leave the real world for some toy fish farm.'

Can't I?

'*Think*, darling. Think red veins in the cheeks. Horny hands from toiling. The broad beam from stuffing yourself with plum duff and doorstep sandwiches. The utter, utter loneliness of never wearing a decent rag.'

The utter loneliness of a brain on permanent hold.

Will I be running away?

She had consulted Becky, and Becky had replied, 'It depends what you're leaving and what you're going to.'

Quite right.

I certainly haven't found God in the marketplace. So I might as well go and look for Him elsewhere.

'But the marketplace,' said an acerbic Becky, 'is precisely where you should be searching.'

'Even so,' said Tess, realizing at that point with a wrench of her gut that, if she left, she would be saying goodbye to Becky too, 'I should go and look at what Iain is offering.'

'I hope you're not expecting too much,' said Iain at last, signalling left. The van snaked up a single track road, breasted a rise and then dropped down towards the edge of the Firth where, sailing mistily through the water, was the coast of Mull. Iain pulled up in front of the manse, a house with many windows. He got out, walked round to the passenger side of the van and held out his hand to Tess.

'Welcome.'

The silence struck Tess: a rounded, uninvaded, complete silence.

Inside the house, courtesy of the generous windows, it was

surprisingly light and sunny. On the Sound of Mull side, there was no garden to speak of, only turf, a rough wooden bridge over a spring and the water beyond. Behind the house, the moorland stretched into the distance. The view was breathtaking, for the house had been positioned to take advantage of the point where there was a gap in the mountain range. The composition of water, house and highland suggested to Tess's southern-acclimatized vision both marvels and space, and also terror of the unknown.

Iain led Tess through the house and up to the spare bedroom. Dust – the dust that she and her mother had fought unsuccessfully at the High House – was evident here, too, dredged over window-sills and furniture. A curtain ring had sprung loose from the rail over the big window on the landing. In the kitchen, a clock ticked on the wall, ten minutes slow, and a half-empty tin of baked beans occupied the fridge.

In the evening, after Tess had put David to bed – he was a little apprehensive in the strange, beautifully proportioned room with a large single bed – they sat down to a bottle of wine.

'Is this crazy?' Tess folded her hands around her glass, a gesture that was calmer than she felt.

Iain stared into his. 'I don't think so. I've loved you for a long time.'

'I'm sorry about Flora.'

He sighed. 'So am I.'

'Why did you decide to come here?'

He shrugged. 'Family and things. Anyway, I didn't think it would be easy. But whether that's a fault or an advantage, I don't know.' He grinned. 'Do I sound like a masochist?'

'The winters?'

'Are pretty dreadful, or can be,' he finished. 'I'm not going to pretend that anything is better than it is.'

'You're very kind, Iain.'

She shifted round in the seat to look out across the darkening water. 'I should like to tell you . . .' She paused. She wanted to warn Iain that if he took her on, he would be taking on someone whose first marriage had been difficult and whose search for a faith had yielded nothing so far, but she thought better of it. Perhaps these topics would never get aired and perhaps it would not, in the end, matter. 'I'd like to tell you many things, but I think I have to take it slowly.'

Iain gestured to the still, shrouded landscape. 'It'll be peaceful.'

She got up, went over to the window and listened to the sound of the water on the beach. 'Yes. And very beautiful.'

Iain was silent.

'Funnily enough,' Tess breathed on the glass and wrote a + and a − in the misted patch, 'I don't think I'll miss the bank, all that tension, drama and excitement.'

'You won't find those here.' Iain came to join her by the window. 'You do realize that, Tess?'

She was conscious that she had hurt him and turned to face him. 'But that's the point, Iain.'

'I don't propose to hijack you. Only to live with you.'

Contrite, she turned towards him. 'How indifferent I must seem, after your kindness. I'm sorry. I think grief makes you selfish. Forgive me.'

'Over there,' he said, pointing to a house whose lights made patterns in the gloom, 'are the Knights. He was a merchant banker who made a fortune, and she's an artist. I must introduce you. Further up the valley in the big house are Wendy and Martin. *They* used to live in Birmingham – he was a personnel manager, I think. He's now a prawn fisherman.'

'Is he surviving?'

Iain gave a short laugh. 'Only just.'

She remained by the window. 'Tell me about the fish, Iain.' She held out her glass for a refill. 'I tried to read up on the topic before I came, but I didn't get very far.'

The next morning, they drove back to Lochaline to do some shopping, Iain having had no idea of Tess and David's requirements, where she searched in the shop for David's currently favoured cereal and yoghurt. At the check-out, she looked at the women with carrier bags and thick coats. A tough breed, she supposed, but not necessarily. Perhaps their battle with wind, weather, land and water was as profound and prolonged as, should she stay, hers would be.

In the afternoon, Iain took them out in the boat to inspect the fish farm. There was not much to see, he explained, only the platform, the electric light and a dim view of threshing forms.

She balanced David in the crook of her arm. 'Do you use a lot of chemicals?'

''Fraid so. Disease is a big problem.' Iain leant over and cupped some water in his hand. 'Sea lice are the biggest. With salmon, at any rate. But I've heard tell of a light someone's developing that attracts the lice off the fish which, if they can get it off the ground, would be better.'

Ecologically acceptable? Non-polluting? What was the fish farm's value in the market?

'And the downside to fish farming?'

Iain laughed and touched Tess's hand briefly. 'We speak another language here. This isn't the stock market.'

'Sorry.' She flushed and then, recollecting her wits, adjusted the balance. 'But it is, was, my language, Iain.'

He gave her a long look. 'All right. Well, a fish farm doesn't hold the answer to over-fishing and chemical pollution. We are forced to use chemicals. The fish catch diseases, which are passed on to the other fish. The sea bed becomes polluted with the chemicals and also fish faeces. So, you see, it isn't simple. But it's the best I can do.'

Far out to the west – seawards – the weather gathered in ominous-looking clouds.

'Do you miss things from your other life?' Tess fought with a piece of hair whipping across her face.

He searched for the words. 'I've been amazed at how quickly

you forget what you imagined was engraved into you. I grew up with the Army, breathed it, worked it. And yet, the moment I stepped out from under it, I forgot. It left me.'

Tess could not quite agree, for his language and bearing proclaimed his former profession, but she said nothing.

Again – David blissfully asleep on a cocktail of fresh air and unaccustomed exercise – they shared a bottle of good wine for supper at the kitchen table.

'The year begins,' Iain said, and she listened attentively, for in the recital of a timetable she could learn about him, 'when the sheep and pregnant ewes are brought down from the hills.'

Sleepy and lazy, Tess pictured the ewes, back legs bandy with their burden, picking their way down the paths, accompanied by the dogs. An expectant progress towards the lambing sheds, the bitter night and the exhausted aftermath of birth.

The hinds are still being culled then, too, Iain told her, before the real winter descends. In February the Highland Cattle Society holds its bull sale. In March they burn the heather to improve the grazing.

As he talked, the pattern of the year was picked out, as ancient and recognizable as the pictures in a Book of Hours. April saw lambs back in the fields and, since the grass was young and sweet, it was the best month for heifers to have their calves. In May, the hunt for vermin on the moors begins and the ferrets are let loose on the hill fox. June is shearing time and the moment to make repairs to the land and house.

'Don't tell me,' said Tess, 'August is grouse-shooting, followed by pheasant and stag season. Slaughter.'

'Not if you weigh it up fairly. It involves skill, too.'

'Yes.' Tess pushed back her hair impatiently.

She turned, as was becoming a habit, to look out over the water.

'A fair fight, Tess.'

She shrugged, but smiled at him all the same.

On their last day, Iain was up early. Tess found him in the

kitchen making sandwiches. 'I thought we'd go and take a look at the deer.'

'Can you spare the time?'

'Johnny McAndrew has agreed to stand in for me today. He sometimes does.'

They drove up the glen and took a road winding up the hillside. Down below them, the water was grey and white and the fish farm grew small and insignificant. Near the summit, Iain parked the van and picked up David in his arms. 'Come on.'

With Tess bringing up the rear, they scrambled up the heather and over the rock, David sometimes held by one or other, sometimes held between them.

'He's doing well,' said Iain. 'A trouper.'

'Yes,' said Tess, the shade of George crossing her mind. Then she remembered Charles and was silent.

If I come and live here, she thought, no one will ever have the chance to guess about David.

Before reaching the top, they sat down to rest. A wind whipped around their faces and the air was as clean as starched sheets, scented with heather and the rain that had fallen during the night. Iain got out his binoculars and swept the hill behind.

'This will probably be impossible with David,' he said, 'but never mind. We need extreme stealth. If you disturb the sheep or grouse it'll alert the deer and it'll be hours before they settle.'

Tess gathered her son into her arms and hugged him. 'We're going to be very quiet, Mousy, otherwise we'll frighten the deer.'

Iain wriggled further up and peered over the ridge. He stiffened, then wriggled noiselessly down.

'They're up there,' he whispered. 'Go and take a look. I'll hold David.'

Tess took the binoculars and inched, rump up, towards the vantage point. It took her some time to get the deer into her view but, eventually, she was rewarded by the sight of a couple of hinds grazing on the opposite slope. Large, warm-looking, liquid-eyed animals enjoying a leisured graze. Undoubtedly an ancient sight, full of pleasures and interest, but it did not stir Tess in the way figures on a print-out did. After all, it was only deer on a hillside.

Her lack of response depressed her.

She turned to signal to Iain and David. As she did so, she dislodged a flurry of small stones. Immediately, the hinds' heads shot up, their laziness vanished in a second. Together, they scented the wind and vanished.

'Sorry,'' said Tess, slithering down. 'That was stupid.'

His arm firmly around a contented-looking David, Iain said, 'It takes years of practice.'

They exchanged a look. 'Yes,' said Tess. 'Yes, I see that.'

Tess looked around the drawing room at the High House. 'I never thought I'd leave this house without a backward thought.'

'Oh, good,' said Becky, 'you're growing up.'

'*Thank* you.'

'While we're at it,' said Becky, 'growing up, I mean, don't you think you should give up the fags?'

'Nope,' said Tess. 'I must have one vice.'

Becky wrinkled her nose. 'As you like. Do you want to go for a walk?'

'My hair will go frizzy in the drizzle.'

'You'll go Afro in Scotland.'

And so, for the last time, the two walked through a changed and transmogrified Appleford, and along the old Roman way. The lane followed an ancient route and skirted an equally ancient field, now laid out as a golf course and car park. For a moment, they watched its flag beat against the club house, and the stream of cars rolling in through the gates, then continued upwards.

'Have you met the tenants?' Becky loped easily up the rise.

'No. But Rufus says they're fine.'

'Don't you think it would be better to sell it?'

Tess held out her hand for Becky to pull her along. 'No. It would never achieve its real value. Anyway, it's an insurance for the future.'

'Ah,' said Becky.

'I want to thank you, Bec. You helped me a lot.'

'Sure,' she replied, aware as Tess was aware that their friendship would alter, subtly but irrevocably. From now on, their lives would no longer match one another's, and their tastes and needs would differ. With no more daily exchange, no chance of intimacy, there would be no necessity for each other and the immediate pulse connecting them would weaken.

Ah, well, thought Becky, it's best to travel alone. She turned her head towards Tess and said, 'You never did tell me what made you decide.'

'I'm forty-five, you know,' Iain had said, after they had washed up and drunk their coffee on Tess's last night.

'What are you trying to say?'

'Only that.'

'I bring problems. A son and debt. Or, at least, resolving it might be a long-term problem.' Abruptly, she turned away. 'You never know where that can lead you. My mother killed herself as a result of debt. And that was the very last thing I would ever have imagined.'

If Mrs Frant had been listening to her daughter, and it was probable she was, she might well have given one of her snorting, anarchic laughs.

'I want to help.'

She glanced up at him. 'You always have done, Iain. You are the perfect gentle knight.'

He was amused. 'Thank you.'

She touched his cheek. 'Do you think I can tough it out here? I don't like the north very much.'

('God, Tess,' said Becky, and raised her eyes to the sky. 'You do sail close to the wind, sometimes.')

'I don't want to hurt you, Iain, I don't want to let you down.'

He stared at the woman he had loved for so long. 'I don't know the outcome,' he said, 'but the battleplan looks good.'

'Once a soldier,' said Becky, 'always a soldier. But you could do worse.'

Tess got undressed in the spare room, tossing her skirt and jumper at the chair, which she missed. They fell in a soft lump to the floor. For a second or two, she stood and stretched her naked body, feeling the cold air tease her skin into a thousand bumps.

She knew how hard it was to live with someone else and her marriage to George had not supplied her with a map for the road she had chosen.

The water ran, soft and reddy brown, into the basin; she splashed her face and neck then the rest of her. She towelled herself dry, observing a faint pink creep up her arms and legs as she did so. She had placed a foot on the chair and bent over to dry it when the knock sounded on the door.

Tess straightened up. I can, of course, she thought, tell him to go away. A second passed. Two seconds. She was struck by his courage, for Iain had no idea what he was taking on, what secrets she bore and would protect him against. Nor did she know his.

She glanced down at her bare limbs. 'Come in,' she said at last, and turned towards him as he stood, tense and unsure of her reply, in the doorway.

At dawn, she heard David cry out and Tess drew away from Iain's tenderly proffered, but overly protective, arm and slid out of bed. It was freezing cold and it took a few seconds to locate her jumper on the floor. By the time she reached David he was wailing heartily.

Half an hour later, when she had given him a drink, which he had demanded, and cuddled him back to sleep, every muscle was stiff with cold, and the skin between her fingers felt cracked with it. She thought she would never be warm again.

That would be the life here.

And yet. And yet. On an impulse, she bent and stroked her son's hair.

She had proved she could flourish in easier territory, but it was time to take on the tough. Out of it she would fashion a life. Out of her lessons in subversion, she would fashion a transparency and a structure.

If she moved her head, Tess could see, or rather sense, through the gap in the ill-fitting curtain the mountain, and trace its huge, uneven outline. She pictured herself toiling up it, carrying her griefs like a stone. The desire to reach the top pushing her onwards, the hard-won breath, the slight, very slight disappointment once the summit is reached. Leaving the stone on the top.

After she laid David back in the bed and tucked him in, she bent over him, breathing in his innocent child's smell. Then she went over to the window and drew back the curtain, just a little. On the horizon to the east, the black was invaded by violet, rose and opal, and land and water met in a clash and fusion of light and shape.

God was in his heaven?

She would never know. *That* was the basis of existence: ambiguous, ambivalent, fluid.

Tess slipped to her knees and rested her chin on her arms on the sill. The cold crept relentlessly through her body and her teeth began to chatter. But, as she watched, the light redefined.

Ah, yes, she thought. Yes.

'Yes?' said Becky, handing Tess a tissue.

'Yes,' said Tess.

Chapter Twenty-eight

In the end, the job in Switzerland came to nothing. Perhaps, the potential employers had not liked what they had heard.

No matter.

Becky's money was running out and (Tess was very apologetic) she was required to quit the High House within the month before the new tenants – he had made a fortune in designing software packages – moved in.

Becky craved London. She craved the terrible red city brick, and its softer greyish-yellow companion. In her bones, she knew the strip of acid soil in front gardens, the back yards, window-boxes slipping off cracked sills, the wild and beautiful patterns of dry rot, the spreading damp and litter deposits. She knew London's smells – rich, unpleasant, historic and peopled – its reach and its depravities. The city gave her a purpose.

As nimble as ever, her mind sorted out the possibilities and weighed them against the probabilities. Hair in a French plait, linen suit pressed, she took the train up to London and made her way to Mawby's who, after sacking Charles, had decided he was too valuable and had re-employed him at a vastly better salary. Becky demanded to see him.

When she was led through the open-plan area, she sensed a ripple of recognition, unease, even, and felt regret. But for a few miscalculations, Becky might be sitting in the senior office directing operations.

Was it a case of becoming institutionalized by a career? There were other avenues Becky could have sought out that would not have meant approaching her ex-lover and the father of her child.

Had Becky flung off the chains of Streatham only to become a prisoner of the workplace? She knew from experience that the most successful and brilliant of business strategists can possess the most impoverished of imaginations, visualizing no further than life in office. She need not have worried. By birth and circumstances she was a realist, by temperament one who seeks out the glitter of gold in order to spend it. She knew that the good, clever, foxy broker makes money. Masses of it. Given this potential, it was unlikely that Becky would busy herself with running a tea-shop or, equally, become dull. And dullness was the worst crime of all.

'Blood is a funny thing,' Lily had said. 'You're just like me. Big ambitions.'

Becky was not quite sure about that, but she let it pass.

Carole, the secretary, recognized her and rushed forward. 'Hallo,' she said. 'How are you?'

'Fine.' Becky glanced at the banks of computer terminals attended to – mostly – by young men in shirtsleeves and braces, talking their private language. 'The techies are still in control.'

As one of life's non-techies, Carole did not understand. In the office light, she looked a little sallow and disappointed. She led Becky towards Charles's office.

'Come in,' said Charles, cradling a phone with his head, and continued his conversation.

Becky sat down. He was dressed in his uniform of striped shirt and loud braces and looked no different from the moment she had first seen him.

'How are you?' she asked, when he put down the phone.

Suspicion clouded his face and he glanced uneasily between her and the computer terminal. Then he reached out a hand and turned it off.

'No need to worry.' Becky was amused.

'Is this a social call?'

'Not exactly,' said Becky, 'but I wanted to know how you and the admirable Martha are.' There was a silence. 'And Poppy.'

Intense wariness crept over Charles's face. 'She's fine. We're all fine. In fact, thriving. She's looking forward to seeing you next weekend.'

Becky crossed her legs and sat back in the chair. 'I rather thought it was time Poppy came and lived with me. When I'm settled, of course.'

Charles's flinch was genuine and his reaction spontaneous. 'No. She can't. We agreed, Becky. Poppy lives with us and her sisters and she's happy and settled. Martha loves her.'

Becky raised her eyebrows. 'Surely her place is with her mother.'

'She hardly knows what you look like.'

'Really?' Becky's tone was neutral which, from of old, he knew was a warning.

'I mean, she thinks of you as a sort of aunt.'

Charles shifted in the chair and walked his fingers up and down the dialling buttons of the telephone. Walking up and down the memories. Suddenly he understood. 'What do you want, Becky?'

'All right,' she said, and turned the full force of her eyes on him. 'I'll tell you. Poppy in return for a job.'

'I see.' He swivelled in the chair so that Becky was presented with his profile. 'That's not so easy.'

'Sorry, Charles.' The trace of a smile hovered on Becky's lips. 'But a girl has to live.'

He ran through the options and likely scenarios. 'They wouldn't give you Poppy.'

'Want to bet? In court, mothers tend to be flavour of the month. You *can't* bet on it, Charles, and you might end up burnt.'

'I have been burnt,' burst from Charles, with the force of pent-up pain and regret. 'Badly.'

'Come on. We had a good time, good fun, at one point. Now

it's over. And don't pretend that your heart wasn't with Martha a good deal of the time because it was.'

Every line and curve of Becky stirred memories of mysterious elements of sex, and of cruelty, to which Charles had responded so powerfully but with which it had been impossible to live.

Oh, silky-fleshed, scented, *hard* Becky, who had so teased and blinded him. He looked down at the pad on his desk and then at the pile of papers in his in-tray. 'You wouldn't dare take Poppy away.'

'Look,' said Becky, who, of course, could not appreciate the exact irony of what she was saying, 'you're not exactly a paragon and the issue is not clear cut. A mother is a mother, you know.'

Quick as a flash, he fought back, 'How would you know?'

She shrugged and smiled and said, in her disarming way, 'It's true I took time to learn, but I didn't have much of a start. There you go.'

Carole bobbed her head round the door. 'Coffee, Mr Hayter?'

Charles was never sure, never quite sure, if Tess had kept her word about *that* episode. It was in his memory, an excess liability, and he wished it was not. And, because he did not reflect on it unless driven to, he had no notion that it had been that unthinking coupling, as much as Becky, which had driven the good nature from his heart and outlook.

'If you get me a job, a good job, I'll undertake never to try to take Poppy off you. Simple.'

'You are *extraordinary.*' Like most cowards, Charles was only rude when he thought he had the upper hand. 'I don't believe you're real.'

'Needs must.'

'But can I trust you?'

Becky picked up her handbag and got to her feet.

'OK,' he said quickly, 'it's a deal.'

Becky surprised Charles by blowing him a kiss. 'You'd better not let admirable Martha know.'

'Blimey!' Becky was provoked into the exclamation when the phone rang at the High House and Jilly Cadogan invited her to lunch in London.

'You'll have to pay,' she said.

'That's the idea,' said Jilly.

The restaurant was expensive and fashionable, and Jilly, in short navy blue skirt and jacket with a silk body underneath, swept into it on a cloud of Giorgio, wearing the faint smile designed to accentuate her teeth.

At the sight, Becky gritted hers and redoubled her determination. 'How did you know I was at the High House?'

'You were spotted some time ago.'

'Is Louis better?'

'I'm divorcing him, you know.'

'No, I didn't.'

'You haven't been listening to Appleford's gossip, then.'

Out of Jilly's soft, pampered mouth issued hard truths. 'He's not the man he was, you know.' She took a tiny mouthful of poached salmon and washed it down with mineral water. 'Poor Louis. I've probably cleaned him out. I stood my ground and got, more or less, what I wanted.'

Becky was curious. 'What do you want from me?'

'I'm giving Louis to you. And I just wanted to be sure that you'd be nice to him.'

'Is he aware of your touching concern?'

'No.' Jilly took another miniscule mouthful of steamed spinach. 'Where is he?'

'In hospital having a rest. He had a bit of a setback and they wanted to keep an eye on him. They're giving him a rigorous dose of physiotherapy. All knee-bends and parallel bars, poor thing.' She shrugged. 'The insurance pays, you know, so why not? The problem will be when he comes out of hospital next week.'

Becky had given up the pretence of eating. There the two women sat, surrounded by crystal, silver, the swags and loops of expensive décor, the French wallpaper and Irish linen napkins, and by the half-eaten remnants of exquisite food that would be thrown out.

'That's your problem,' said Becky.

'Men are so self-indulgent,' said Jilly, avoiding Becky's eye. She fumbled in her Chanel handbag, produced a silver box, opened it and popped a pill into her mouth. 'They think we are, but the truth is quite the opposite.' She pursed her glossed lips and smiled. 'You're welcome to him.' She thought for a moment and added, 'And you get the dog.'

Becky smiled back. 'But I don't want Louis any more.'

'If the techies get to rule the world what will happen to the non-techies?' Becky was on the phone to Tess in Scotland. 'Those who can't cope with computers. There's plenty of them.'

'Frankenstein lives again,' said Tess, who was watching a couple of fishing boats from the drawing-room window of the Manse. 'No, I'm wrong. Frankenstein was capable of love. Computers aren't.' She waved at Iain coming up from the beach with David. '*Why* have we got onto this subject?'

'Oh, I don't know,' said Becky. 'We ought to keep an eye on the future. By the way, I've been offered a job by Osbrooks. Director. So I'm in business.'

'*Osbrooks!* Goodness.'

'I've had the house cleaned and I'll hand over the keys on Saturday.'

'You've got somewhere to stay, Bec?'

'Well, sort of,' she said. 'Don't worry about it. Tess.'

'Yes.'

'You know you've opted out. Lost the battle for wimmin?'

'If you like.'

There was a silence.

At her end, Tess stirred. 'Bec. Will you do something for me?'

'Of course.'

'Will you go and look at the graves from time to time? Just to keep them tidy. I wouldn't like to think that they were left. Please.'

As ever, Becky packed quickly and neatly in a quiet, abandoned house, discarding anything she considered superfluous.

Tick-tock.

She was disposing of papers when the doorbell rang, a sharp, questing sound. Holding a sheaf in one hand, she opened the door.

The man on the doorstep was in ambulance uniform and behind him in the drive was the ambulance. As Becky stared, the driver got out of the cab, went round to the back and opened the doors. 'Wrong house,' she said, and tried to close the door.

'Nah,' said the chap, a big, brawny fellow you could trust to haul you out of a car smash. 'He said here.'

'He?'

The man consulted his clipboard. 'Mr Cadogan.'

The colour fled from Becky's face. 'No. You've made a mistake.'

'I don't think so. It's been arranged.'

Becky pushed past him towards the ambulance and jumped up the steps between the open doors. 'No,' she said. 'I'm not looking after you.'

Louis looked up from the wheelchair in which he was confined. 'Yes, you are.'

'You never even asked.'

Thin, pale, but still elegant, he spread his hands in an old gesture. 'You don't ask for a last chance, you take it.'

Becky swivelled. 'Take him away,' she said furiously. 'He doesn't belong here.'

The driver did not much care either way. 'If you would make up your mind, sir.'

Louis lifted up his re-educated left hand and held it out to her. 'It's not as bad as it looks, Becky. Truly.'

She looked out through the ambulance's doors, which provided a frame for the ruined paddock. 'I've just got everything organized. I don't want you. I don't want *anybody*.'

A burden. A slobbery, needy, disintegrating, energy-consuming burden.

Wasn't that just like a man? At the bottom of the pond lies a mud-slick of sentimentality and a conviction that, in the end, people will act for the best.

'What makes you think that after all we've been through I'm going to drop everything to nanny you?'

'It's precisely because we've been through, as you put it, everything.'

Passion and sorrow. Did these bind a man and woman? She supposed they did.

'How can I be sure?'

Louis took his time to answer. 'There is no insurance,' he said. 'Ever.'

'Well, tough,' said Becky, and she had never looked so beautiful. Tall and lustrous-eyed. 'I've done enough lately to fill the book of saints. So, Louis, I'm sorry, I think not.'

A sound made Becky turn her head. Louis had put up his good hand to his face, and she knew without being told that behind it he was hiding tears. Another sound escaped from him and, this time, he turned away his head.

The ambulancemen were embarrassed and became angry. 'Can't we get on?' asked one aggressively.

'I'm sorry,' said Becky, letting herself down into the drive, filled with a sudden wild grief and a light-headed sensation. 'I can't afford you any more, Louis.'

What was it that Jilly had said? Becky fought the anguish that was threatening to swamp her and the memories. That she had cleaned Louis out. He hardly had a bean left (even allowing for a bean, in Jilly's terms, being relative).

But Louis was also a fighter, and a veteran one.

His eyes sought and found Becky's. 'There's the bank account in Switzerland,' he said. 'I thought we'd go over and arrange things. Possibly live there.'

'*What* did you say?'

'Money in Switzerland,' said Louis. 'It was in transit when Jilly's lawyers were asking questions. So you see . . .'

Slowly, Becky positioned her foot back on the ambulance step and hauled herself up. Then she stood over Louis, her wretched heart beating like a hunted animal, and placed a hand on his shoulder.

Louis waited.

Then she bent over and kissed him.

The Bollys welcomed Louis back. No. It would be more precise to say that it was as if he had never been away. The meal, in the Lloyd's Club, was up to scratch. A frost had come down over the country but, in London, its clean, astringent dazzle was routed by the orange neon and press of traffic.

All in all, the mango mousse was voted a success.

Less satisfying was the comparison made in the press that day between Lloyd's and the Munich Re. The article was written in a pessimistic vein. Who could judge whether, after all the recent disasters and Names' revolts, if Lloyd's could pay out sufficient compensation? Would it not be better, as an insurer, to go somewhere else where the equity was not tied up in hundreds of what, after all, were only modest houses in the Shires and Home Counties?

Nigel's waistcoats had grown more outrageous. In the notebook lying in his breast pocket, the timetable of his digestion had been duly noted. 'Wind, 10.32. Bowel movement, 10.35.' The wine had made him sleepy and he was not paying attention.

Matt, greyer and more gaunt but just as sharp, was discussing with Louis the welcome development of corporate underwriting. A little sunburnt from sitting in the mountain café (while Becky skied the morning away) surrounded by the rich who had descended on Gstaad ('Euro-trash,' said Becky, 'I love 'em'), Louis was jotting down notes.

'You know, Matt,' he said, 'I think we might have trouble in store with the problem of organo-phosphates. I think we should look into them.'

As he left the restaurant, his mobile phone (which Becky had insisted he carried) shrilled.

'OK, darling,' she said. 'I want you to be a very good boy and just put your stamp on . . .'

That night, in the flat in Knightsbridge, Louis twitched in his sleep and groaned. Then he woke up properly. 'Hold me, Becky.'

Painfully, for she was very tired, she inched her way across the large double bed and held him until he was quiet.

And thus it was, in her way and, yes, with love, Becky paid her dues, for little by little, understanding had crept into her insufficient heart.

In its chrysalis, the butterfly dreaming of a past life when it soared, light and powder blue, into the sunlight, twitched its embryonic wings and was quiet.

I wonder what I have done?, ran the entry in Tess's diary. *What have I done?*

Meanwhile, the frost stole over the two graves in Appleford's churchyard and transformed the shared headstone into a tablet of ice.

Perfect
Love

In memory of my beloved father, Peter Oakleigh-Walker
(1917–1993)

Acknowledgements

Many thanks are due to many people including my agent, Caroline Sheldon, and my editor, Suzanne Baboneau, for their back-up and expertise, to Peta Nightingale whose input was vital, and to Hazel Orme, on whom I rely absolutely. Last but certainly not least, to my mother, sisters, children and husband.

There is a huge body of work devoted to the life of Joan of Arc and I would like to mention two in particular: Edward Lucie Smith's *Joan of Arc* (Allen Lane, 1976) and Marina Warner's brilliant *Joan of Arc: The Image of Female Heroism* (Weidenfeld & Nicolson, 1981). I took factual information and drew on ideas from both of these works.

'Love seems the swiftest but it is the slowest of all growths. No man or woman really knows what perfect love is until they have been married for a quarter of a century.'

Mark Twain

Prologue

Let me tell you a story about an adultery, a heroine, a child's anger, voices, Joan of Arc and, since it was 1992, recession.

None of these things is new. In fact, since human beings and economics do not change much in the essentials they constitute an old story. Yet there is always something a little different each time it is told: a different twist, a different happiness, a different sadness – and suffering is an individual business.

Outside, a winter wind blew down from the ridge but, to all appearances, the frost of recession had only touched the fringes of the village of Dainton – the parish being a Nazareth to Winchester's Jerusalem – for the money expended on the Christmas of 1991's flowers had been generous. Euphorbia, lilies, and imported narcissi do not come cheaply. Making a rough computation of the cost, Prue Valour was puzzled. Perhaps a newcomer, buying their way into the village, had donated them. Perhaps the church flowers had been put above other claims on the Christmas purse (the insulated mats for the homeless, for example) but Prue thought it unlikely.

Kate Eliot, Prue's friend and confidante, and a woman fond of a challenge, providing there was every chance she could master it, had taken the trouble to decorate the

1

Christmas tree with real candles – not, of course, to be lit because of the insurance veto. This was a shame because the candles looked beautiful elsewhere in the church. Nevertheless, swaying on the tree, forced through the green like white asparagus, they cocked a snook at regulations, their colour suggesting the purity and hope so lacking elsewhere.

Content, certainly better-looking and more serene at forty-one than she had ever been at twenty-one, and just about organized (turkey stuffed, extra fruit salad made, emergency presents wrapped and stacked in the cupboard) Prue joined in the singing of the last carol. If God had withdrawn from England in disgust, there was still a chance he might drop in, briefly, to Dainton's parish church and cast an eye over his faithful: struggling, well-meaning, frayed and nibbled at the edges by existence, imperfect and, in Prue's case, a little cushioned, a little unwilling to listen to new voices . . .

Unlike Joan of Arc who had listened to them all too well. You see, as Prue had discovered during her researches into the life of the saint, apparently Joan had been in her father's garden in Domrémy when she first heard the voices towards noon on a summer's day. After that, they visited her at various times, often when bells were ringing – the bell for vespers, compline, or the lovely clear tone of the evening angelus.

The bells were important, you must understand that. They introduced order into lives that had none. They told the time, they spread news, issued warnings and because France lay split open – so many segments of a fallen peach over which fought French, Burgundians and English – many warnings were needed.

The bells suggested routine and peace and, when despair set in at the obvious lack of either, they hinted at God's purpose. Of God's goodness.

Whatever time it was, it does not matter. For into the broken silence, the backwash of displaced air that shuddered over the fields and village torn and ravaged by war, came the voices of St Michael and St Catherine and changed Joan's life for ever.

Oh, yes, thought Prue into whose consciousness was creeping the knowledge that her own life had remained much the same during the past twenty years, it was right that the voices spoke when they did – and for Joan to listen to their message.

Spring

Chapter One

'It's in the stories,' Jane had once insisted on a Friday car journey home from school. 'Everyone hates the wicked stepmother, and the wicked stepmother schemes to get rid of the beautiful stepdaughter. Think of Snow White.'

'*I* don't go "Mirror, mirror on the wall",' Prue protested, only half amused.

'You don't have to, Mum.'

'Thank you,' said Prue with dignity. Beauty had never been her problem – and now that she was fortysomething and understood that more elements lay below the surface than on it, she realized that beauty *was* a problem for its subject. Not that she considered the problem to apply in any way to herself for, in Prue's view but not necessarily in the opinion of those who came to love her, she did not possess beauty. Whereas Violet did, in bucketfuls.

Happily, Violet was safely in New York with her new husband and baby and well out of Prue's way. Or she had been until that morning in January 1992.

'*When* did you say they're coming?' asked Prue, pouring milk into her saucer for the cat. Bella placed an elegant, bangled paw on Prue's knee, leapt into her lap and was surprised when Prue clutched her hard against her midriff.

'I wish you wouldn't do that. It's so unhygienic,' replied Max, her husband, watching the milk spray the tablecloth. It was not the first time he had protested. Nor would it be the last. 'February. Because of the recession the bank is cutting staffing levels on its overseas operations. Anyway, apparently they want Jamie back home to head up the London bit of the European arm.' He pushed the airmail letter over to Prue.

Prue picked it up with reluctance and Max, aware of what was going through her mind, said, 'It's only till they can buy a house in London. Jamie can commute and Violet will be looking for a job.'

'Lucky Jamie.' Prue gave the letter a brief glance and then ignored it. Meanwhile, Max creased *The Times* into a raging sea.

'You don't object too much, do you, Prue?'

She leant over the table, nipped the paper out of his grasp and folded it into order. 'I object to you doing *that.*'

'Do you mind?'

She considered his question, the familiar sleepy look in place that meant she was thinking hard. Was sharing a kitchen with her stepdaughter a good thing because it would shake Prue's moral fibre into a bracing workout, or a bad thing because the inevitable clash would cancel any Brownie points thus gained?

I hate you, Prue . . .

'It's Violet's home and you're her father.' Fairness, she reflected bitterly, was the curse of the middle class, the fatal weakness. 'They can look after themselves.'

Bella's purr broke the uneasy silence which fell between them. Oh, Max, thought Prue, you look so pleased at the prospect of your daughter coming home. How can I possibly deny you?

Max looked at his watch and got to his feet, wincing at the twinge that occasionally attacked his right hip. 'Time to go.' He retrieved *The Times*, which he had no intention of yielding up. Prue swallowed half a cup of coffee so strong it made her tongue go dry, but that was how she liked it. One day she intended to renounce caffeine, being reminded daily by the inside of her cafetière what her stomach lining must resemble – but not yet. She squinted at Max. He looked irritable and impatient, two things which until recently had been alien to his nature, brought on, she suspected, by panic. For Max was sixty and he did not like the idea of retirement.

Tick, tock.

These days he maintained, a little too frequently, that he was still in his prime. Still capable of good things. Oh, yes, his listeners agreed, but then they were not likely to disagree. To be fair, Max's large, fit-looking body gave the impression of strength and a well-oiled mind, both of which were true.

Prue did not relish the idea of his retirement either, but there was nothing to be done. Sometimes, she caught Max looking at her as if to say: It's unfair that you're twenty years younger. Other times, she sensed that he almost disliked her for it. I can't help it, she wanted to cry out. I would take on your years if I could. It did not occur to her that it was not her business to shoulder Max's advance into old age, it was his. But, then, it is almost impossible for the lives of people who are bound together by deep feeling and habit, not to seep into each other's.

Meanwhile, it *was* Prue's business to help negotiate this tricky period. She pushed a reluctant cat on to the floor.

'You've got the big meeting today, haven't you? I won't expect you home until late.' She paused to insert the first plank in the bolstering-Max programme. 'I don't know what the firm would do without you.'

Max tapped his right hand on the table and the little white scar on his index finger – Helen's wound – attracted Prue's gaze as it had done a hundred thousand times during their marriage. 'I've made noises that I would like to take over the working party into setting up the European structure.' Max's large and profitable law firm in the City was in the process of setting up a working relationship with likeminded firms in France, Germany and Spain, the idea being that clients would get the best advice on all fronts. 'I would like to get it,' said Max, whose fluency in French, German and Spanish certainly put him in the running, 'so spare a thought.'

'I will, darling. I will.' She fingered her coffee-cup. 'They would be foolish to ignore you, I think.'

'Thanks,' he said, a touch drily. He adjusted the silk handkerchief in his lapel pocket, his only sartorial indulgence, and flashed her one of his disconcerting smiles, which told her that he was not going to let his feelings get the better of him. 'Good try, darling. Butter the old boy up. I might just bring a decent bottle back for supper on the strength of it.'

Palm up, he stretched out a hand across the table and curled his fingers in invitation. Prue tapped the edge of the table with hers and her mouth twitched.

'Darling Prue . . .' said Max. 'Don't be mean. Give me a kiss.'

She laughed, leant forward and traced a circle on the exposed palm. He caught her hand and kissed it.

'My lovely Prue,' he said.

'I love you really,' she said.

'That's fortunate,' said her husband. 'You've got me for life.'

Prue removed her hand, looked down at her lap and endeavoured to brush the cat hairs from her skirt.

The car nosed into Winchester station only just in time. Max wrenched open the passenger door to show his annoyance at Prue for insisting on changing her skirt at the last minute. It had made them late and the road from Stockbridge had been full of feeble drivers unwilling to go above 40 m.p.h.

'Nobody looks at your bottom half if you're behind the counter,' Max had pointed out, not unreasonably, which made Prue feel quite exasperated – unfairly she knew. All the same, there was a diminution of the goodwill of breakfast.

She swerved to avoid a squashed hedgehog, which had made the mistake of imagining the station was a safe place. There was no need to add insult to grievous injury and, besides, the idea of going over the bloody little body was too much at this time of the morning.

'I'm sorry I made you late,' she said.

'So I should think.' Max dropped his large, squarish hand on to her thigh for a second and she covered it with hers.

Although Prue's life was oriented around her husband's, the minute he was out of her sight she forgot him. She often puzzled over the conundrum. Was it a normal stage in a twenty-year-old marriage? She supposed it was. After all, she did not notice her wedding ring from one week to the next, despite its tendency to make her finger swell. It was there, much as her nose was (which she disliked), or her legs (marginally better) or the rather startling mole, positioned above her right eyebrow.

Once upon a time, as all good stories go, there would not have been a day *not* dedicated to the idea of Max. Every breath she took, every meal she ate, every stamp she licked (Prue had been a secretary when they met) had revolved around a Max-shaped space. And why not? He was older, wiser and infinitely sadder, and, thus, irresistible to a nineteen-year-old, a *young* nineteen-year-old whose favourite childhood game had been to re-enact Florence Nightin-

11

gale's lamp-lit passage through suffering men at Scutari. Perhaps a too-young nineteen-year-old?

What she got with Max was love that showed no sign of running out, fishing rods, a pair of guns to which he was devoted, gentleness in all their dealings, a village life and a degree of comfort.

Prue drove through the city and realized that too much reflection on what constituted normal was not a good idea. Stones were upturned and worms exposed.

With a lot of extra exhaust and gear changes, she manoeuvred the car into her secret parking place behind the market square. The morning was still sharp and exuded depression, and wherever Prue looked as she made her way to the bookshop she was accosted by 'For Sale' signs.

Whatever else she had expected, she had learnt quickly that bookshops are not peaceful places. Certainly not Forsight's. It was busy, which was good, but it was also haphazardly organized, which was bad. Any ideas Prue had entertained for browsing, paid, through Fict., Class. and Fict., Pop., or even Hist., Med., vanished by the end of the first week. Since then, she had tried for two years to impose order, but order – and Prue was a mother – is a slippery animal and slithers away at the slightest opportunity.

Books were delivered daily, others were piled up waiting to be returned, publicity material buckled in corners and gangways, and Gerald, the owner, had a knack of sabotaging Prue's ideas for display with his own. Still, most days the shop was full, and not only with browsers who had no intention of buying. The family holiday might be jettisoned along with the new car, you might be a witness to the repossession of your house, be forced to sell the BT shares, weep at the destruction of your life, but buying a book remained an achievable goal, particularly if the bookshop offered free warmth and the comforting evidence that others felt the same.

Disorder is relatively easy to accommodate, particularly if you were Prue. She was used to smoothing paths through problems yet, if challenged, she would stick on one thing. To her surprise she was not prepared to yield up her job. You cannot make compromises with oxygen and, devoted as she was to the hearth and the Hoover, Prue's three mornings a week at Forsight's (cash and no questions) were like three draughts of pure air.

'What do you think?' Gerald held up a paperback with an explicit cover.

She directed her sleepy look at it. 'It will sell.'

'Winchester doesn't like sex. Hadn't you noticed? But stack it on the table, will you, Prue, after you've served the customer by the till who wants a book on hats.'

Sometimes, Gerald sounded remarkably like Max. Prue threw her scarf into her basket, twitched at her blouse and refrained from asking if he had had a bad night.

By half past one, three people had placed orders for a book on coping with bankruptcy.

'You should stock some,' Prue informed Gerald, much struck by this neglected window in the market, as she put on her coat.

'Can they *pay* for it, dear?'

Next door to Forsight's was a bakery, the kind that sells 'Olde Worlde Bread' and pipes a smell of cooking yeast into the retail area. Prue bought a sausage roll and an almond croissant to which she allotted four out of ten and ate them as she walked to the public library. It gave her satisfaction – still – to flout one of her mother's rules: never eat in the street. In fact, the transgression gave her so much pleasure that she was tempted to conclude that the more draconian and senseless the rule, the more excellent it was.

It is the small things, rule-breaking, sleep positions, a way of brushing the hair, that provide a continuum through the years. The eternalness of habit, and Prue, now accustomed to the library and its best positions, made for 'her' niche and was forced to restrain a frown when she saw it was occupied. She retreated to a position by the door, arranged her books and began to write.

'It was in my thirteenth year when God sent a voice to guide me . . .'

Thus Jeanne la Pucelle, *fille de Dieu*, as those mysterious voices addressed her, describes the moment when her life, the hard-working, simple life of a daughter of a well-to-do peasant, was stopped in its tracks. 'Say what you will', Prue wrote in her notes, then came to a halt. Say that Joan was born with the compulsive exhibitionism of many of our public figures, which drove her to invent something, any-thing, which would stamp her life in bas-relief on the often dark and frightening medieval chronicle of life and death. That she was schizophrenic, that she was a transvestite driven to extremes by the limits of the age in which she lived. Say anything you like, but as Joan stood in the garden, carpeted with lilies-of-the-valley and wild strawberries, a heroic poetry, a meaning, a clash of arms and a terrible beauty flowed into her life.

Prue had never regarded herself as a woman given to a hot rush of feeling, or a candidate for the steel grip of the *idée fixe*, and her ambition to write a biography of this woman and saint, Joan of Arc, took her, and anyone to whom she confided it, by surprise.

Do it, Max urged, when Prue faltered out the idea to him. Do it. Do it.

Do it, echoed the obstinate part of Prue which she kept hidden, folded into the dark areas of her mind (of which she was secretly afraid). She obeyed, and that was why she was to be found in the public library on every spare afternoon.

Prue's biography was intended to be the unacademic, ordinary woman's view of the medieval equivalent. Where the idea had arrived from was mysterious, but arrive it had as a sunburst over a bleak landscape. Even now, Prue maintained a level of extreme surprise at her daring, for nothing in her life had trained her for a project like this. That obstinacy, a quivering response to the colour, the boldness, the surrender, the excess of St Joan, and perhaps an unconscious need to change an element in her own life, fuelled Prue's researches. Not that she would explain it as such.

The results so far were headings, 'Life', 'Death', 'Battles', in a red-and-black notebook imported from China, and notes made on A4 paper which she kept meaning to transcribe under the headings, once she had got through the stack of reading she had set herself. This was composed of biography, to guide her as to what she should be doing, history, for its background information on labyrinthine politics, gold-encrusted artefacts, and the collection of John the Bolds, the Fearlesses, the Bads, and degenerate Valois that had littered medieval France.

The library smelt of polish and, less fortunately, of sweat, which was not surprising for the central heating had been turned up to furnace level, and the faces at the tables were varnished with an unnatural sheen, Prue's included. She sensed the stain that crept up her neck when she was hot and bothered, spreading like red ink above her blouse. Somebody should tell the council. *She* should tell the council.

Shopping. St Joan. Ironing. Jane. Bank managers. Max. Councils. This was a life indeed.

She looked at her watch. It was time to pick up Jane from

the excellent but staggeringly expensive school where she was a weekly boarder. She stacked her books together and got up.

Outside, the cold wind blew, cooling Prue's flush and she put up a hand to her neck in a gesture that was becoming habitual. Still smooth, she thought, a little guilty that she minded.

In front of her flowed the life of the city – an arterial stream of traffic, punctuated by the ganglia of shops, precincts and the market. Looming over this commercial activity was the cathedral, whose massive symbolic and physical presence used to exert an osmotic force on the life of the city. *Mutandus mutandi* ... (Prue was learning some Latin.) Today, having been trampled in the rush towards science and commercialism, its supremacy was composed mostly of memory and the reverence the British accorded to the past. But Prue took delight in the building, and often made a detour as she did today to wander in its precincts or look inside. The January light failed to penetrate the dim interior, lit here and there by the bright, isolated stars of candles. The aisle was shrouded in a green-tinged dimness, and echoed to the half-whispers of tourists and church officials going about their business.

Her basket weighing on her arm, Prue hovered in the transept, thinking about people and their separate circles of isolation, sometimes overlapping others, sometimes moving forward without contact. It was perfectly possible to live a life thoroughly boxed in by Christian habits but lacking the essential core of belief. She knew because she was making a good job of it herself, and occasionally she told God off for not being there. Life would be easier with him.

A group of Japanese tourists fluttered and fussed in the aisle, and some nuns were praying in the pews. Presumably

God loved this stone tribute to him. She trusted that he did, for it had been built on sweat, lives and ambition. Of course, the same could be said for motorways and supermarkets.

Prue left the smell of wax and ripe flowers and returned to the daylight.

'Wicked, Mum, you're on time.'

Jane was preceded by a collection of bags slung into the back seat, then a great deal of green uniform and green tights, and plaited fair hair.

'How's the week been?'

'Fine.' Jane always made the question sound irrelevant.

'The French test?'

'Oh, Mum. Don't ask me those questions the minute you see me.'

It was windy and rather bleak on the hill where the school was situated. To the east the motorway, always crowded, cut away to London, and to the west a new section was being hacked out of the chalk downland, much to the bitterness of local protesters. That view was not pretty.

Jane sighed.

'What, my sweetie?'

'Nothing. Just glad you're here.'

Prue drove out of the school yard. 'Violet and her family are coming to stay for a bit.'

Jane sat up. 'Oh, Mum,' she repeated, this time with a dying inflection indicating her disapproval. 'That's a real pain. Where will they all sleep?'

'In the spare room, of course. Luckily it's big enough for the baby as well. If not, they can put him in the guest bathroom.'

Jane bit her lip.

'Aren't you curious to see your new cousin?'

17

'Not really,' said Jane, who preferred computers to ballet and software to clothes. 'Babies are boring.'

Prue smiled. 'You weren't. You were marvellous.' She observed her daughter from the corner of her eye. The approach always worked, mainly because she meant every word. 'I used to wonder what I'd done to deserve such a good baby. Sometimes, I imagined a big foot in the sky waiting to squash me because I was too lucky.'

'Truly?'

'Truly.'

Actually, there *had* been the equivalent of the foot in the sky and that had been Violet. But Prue would not permit herself to say so to Jane.

Jane went quiet for several minutes. They drove on between hedges lightly tipped with new life – nature always got on with things much earlier than you imagined – over mud islands from last night's rain and past telegraph wires on which rooks and moisture were equally strung. The landscape was suspended, but also secretly in flux, waiting for the moment it tipped over into spring proper. Every so often, a cascade of water hit the windscreen and, as they descended the hill to Stockbridge, the road became slippery.

What had I done to deserve such a good baby – and such an awful stepdaughter?

The car skidded slightly and a vision of Jane lying crushed and bleeding by a roadside, calling for her mother, flashed by Prue, so vivid it almost made her choke. It was the old nightmare, come back to visit, the old anxiety. It meant many things.

Prue tried to explain her fears for Jane to Max, and how they were connected to the idea of perfection. They'll vanish quickly enough when she's a teenager with a safety-pin through her nose, he said.

Jane broke the silence. 'It's a pity you don't like Violet. You don't, do you, Mum?'

'Why do you ask?'

'My intuition,' said her eleven-year-old daughter. 'Don't worry, it's quite normal in the circumstances.'

It was then that Jane explained the Snow White theory.

What did it matter? All over Britain the lights were going out. A fog was stealing over northern towns and masking the classy shopping developments in the south. Desperately worried men and women prepared for the weekend, and talked to each other about banks calling in loans, high interest rates, the behaviour of building societies, about the dole and sleeping rough, of businesses collapsing and redundancy.

Then, again, perhaps they kept silent. Perhaps you do not talk about things that are too pressing. Perhaps silence is easier. Perhaps it is human nature to ignore the thing that looms largest and most awful in your life.

Prue climbed into bed that night and said nothing to Max about Violet.

Chapter Two

'Can you meet us at Heathrow?' Violet never bothered to ingratiate herself with her stepmother – that point had long ago been passed if it had ever existed – but since the last thing she wished was to struggle to Dainton by public transport or incur the expense of hiring a car, she managed, 'If you would, Prue.'

Prue made an effort and said she would, adding, 'It will be lovely to see you and to meet Jamie and the baby.'

'Five a.m., terminal four.'

'*Five a.m.!*'

'Afraid so.'

'Violet, that's hideously early.'

'Well, if you feel you can't, Prue, could you organize hiring a car for us?' Violet calculated two things. One, the request might shame Prue into agreement. Two, if it did not then the likelihood was that her father would pay. It was a measure of her current state of mind that she forgot that Jamie's bank was paying most expenses. Or perhaps she wished to put Prue to considerable trouble.

Same old tricks, thought Prue, powerless before Violet's determination. 'Don't worry, I think we can make it.'

'See you, then.'

In Dainton, Prue was accounted something of a saint – older husband with two tragedies, or at least incidents, in his past, and a stepdaughter who thought rather too well of herself and made it her business not to cooperate. Violet was well aware of Prue's putative sainthood and had lived with it for those difficult, uneasy years before she had left home; it had sharpened her quick, but essentially unsubtle, mind. Our characters are shaped by those we hate, as much as by those we profess to love. Thus Violet was very much Prue's creation, a fact that would have astonished both women.

'I hope we're not *too* much trouble.' Violet pondered the *coup de grâce*, which proved too tempting not to use. 'After all,' she modulated her voice sweetly, 'you don't have that much else to do.'

The conversation left Prue to stare at the calendar on the wall, unsettled and disturbed. Only Violet managed to prick the skin, so soft and gracious, in which Prue clothed herself without having to try. Only Violet could make her feel so angry and unwilling. Picking up a pen, she scrawled: 'Heathrow, 5 a.m.', in such a way that the whole of the day's space for 7 February 1992 was obscured.

Violet's recollection of her childhood was a fractured, uneasy jumble of dreams and memory. On one hand, she took comfort from a cosy, firelit nursery, a cross between Enid Blyton and Charles Dickens where she knew she was safe (*OED* 'safe': uninjured, entire, healthy). But, perhaps, this was wishful thinking. On the other hand, and the sensation was indisputable, her memories or dreams, whichever, precipitated Violet into a terrain across which she fled, running from a terror she found impossible to describe.

Oh, that white dust churning in her face and choking her mouth and nostrils as she panted across her inner landscape. The torn nails she used to batten on to blank rock faces blocking her way. The sweat that ran like lava down her body. The terror that clawed at her back.

Those who lose their mothers young can be subjected to mirages like Violet's warm nursery, and the terror swimming in the darkness outside. Violet's dream figurations could have been less obvious, but that did not diminish either their import or their impact. They were cruel fantasies, both for the fear they stirred and, worse, for the false suggestion of safety enshrined in a leaping nursery fire, the rag-rug, the rocking-chair and the cupboard in which lived Ned the Teddy and Muffin the Mule. Oddest of all, Violet bore no recollection of her mother and she had been almost six when Helen had gone away for the last time – all of six when she died.

Jamie understood. 'By dying your mother let you down,' he said, 'and you're angry with her and you've blocked her out.'

Violet regretted her impulse to confide in Jamie – but the marriage was still young. 'I wonder', she commented acidly, 'what the world would have been like before Freud reinvented it. Fresh and innocent, perhaps?'

'I don't mind my concern being rejected or abused,' said Jamie. 'My sense of humour remains intact.'

His reproof did not go unnoticed. 'Sorry,' said Violet who was still delighted by the acquisition of a new, handsome husband and, furthermore, loved him.

They were in the bedroom of the New York apartment packing the last bits of luggage. Jamie inserted a pastel wedge of Brooks Brothers shirts into his suitcase and closed it. Violet watched. Because she could not fathom them, she distrusted Jamie's occasional silences.

'I *am* sorry, Jamie.'

He placed the suitcase alongside the others by the door. 'I'll think about accepting the apology.' He had his back to her and she was unable to see his smile.

Uncertain how to take the last remark, she sat down on

the bed. 'I never know where I am with you, Jamie.' When baffled, Violet had a habit of clicking a nail against another. The sound filled the pause. Then she continued, 'I don't want to be left out, if you see what I mean . . . Because I am your wife and I want to share everything.'

'It's simple.' Jamie came over and pushed her back on to the pillows. 'I love you and I can take your nastiness.'

Violet should have replied, 'I love you, too, and thank you for being nice.' Instead she said, 'Mind my breasts. They're sore.'

'I won't.' Jamie edged closer. 'Beautiful, clever wives must put up with interest in their breasts.'

This was familiar ground. Violet gave a laugh and ran her hand down Jamie's back. 'Friends?' she asked softly, meaning lovers.

His arm reached over her body. 'Friends.'

After a moment, she wriggled free. 'I must pack.'

Jamie rolled over and folded his hands behind his head. 'Are you going to have a minor panic or a major one?'

'Neither – and do you have to joke *all* the time?' Violet pulled open the top drawer of the chest and surveyed the contents. Muddle, she hated muddle, and muddle stared back at her. 'Jamie?'

'Yes.'

'You don't think having a baby addles your brain permanently, do you?' She bit her lip as the words left it. A bundle of crawling, post-partum neuroses was not the best aphrodisiac.

'It's not your brain I'm interested in.'

She raised her eyebrows. 'Ignoring the base metal of yours, do you think I'll ever be normal again?' She sifted her fingers through a Liz Claiborne scarf and a Ralph Lauren belt and let them drop. 'My memory is haywire, so's my ability to organize. I've always been so good at remembering.' She wanted to say, 'I've always shone at whatever I've turned my hand to', which would have been true.

She poked furiously at the scarves and belts and slammed the drawer shut, trapping a belt. There was another silence. 'Jamie. I seem to have lost my will to do things,' she said helplessly.

It was so uncharacteristic of Violet. In a flash, Jamie was on his feet and cradling her in his arms. 'Listen,' he said, 'having a baby, running a department and the home takes a toll. Your body is telling you to slow down, that's all, just until you recoup your energies.'

'You think?'

Jamie stared over Violet's dark, glossy head to the New York landscape framed by the apartment window. 'I know so.'

Violet stiffened. Before meeting her, Jamie had lived with Lara and her daughter, Jenny, for ten years. That meant he had ten years' extra experience and nothing would ever alter this advantage. Violet's competitive instinct was nettled. It was not so much that she had missed out on ten years at Jamie's side, rather that she had launched herself into a relay race where she was forever condemned to the outside track. Whatever Violet did, however fast she ran, Jamie was pounding away on the inside track.

It irked her, for at twenty-seven Violet was still too young to have broken through the shield which protects the young from the knowledge that, very often, a reversal takes place in later years.

She leant against Jamie's cashmere-clad shoulder. Then she pulled back and stared into his face. I want to read you, she thought to herself. I want to gather up what is *you*. But I can't.

Under her scrutiny, Jamie's eyebrows lifted a fraction and Violet was swept by desolation for she was failing to grasp something important, and she did not know what. She reached up and pulled his head down and gave him one of her soft, dry kisses on the lips which he always found incredibly erotic. 'Thanks, Jamie.'

A howl from the second bedroom made her jump. The howl increased and Violet folded her arms across her stomach and tightened her mouth. (If she had known how the gesture changed her face for the worse, she would not have done it.) 'I can't, Jamie. He was only fed a couple of hours ago. I just can't.'

Jamie pushed his wife gently away. 'You stay there and I'll bring him in.'

As it was fashionably situated – they had agreed on fashion over comfort – the apartment was tiny and, thus, Jamie was back thirty seconds later. He held a squalling Edward out to Violet. Reluctantly, she accepted him. The baby was red and furious, and the rash sprayed over his face appeared embossed into his skin.

'Oh, baby,' said Violet, angry at his thoughtlessness. 'How could you?'

'I'll get you a cup of tea,' said Jamie.

Edward smelt and it was a toss-up between enduring the crying or the smell. The second option was easier. Violet forced herself to hold the baby and, hating herself for hating him, dragged up the front of her designer jersey and allowed him to latch on. Silence broke over the room, the kind when the breath hisses out in release.

Jamie came back with a tray and gave her a mug. With her free hand, Violet engineered it to her lips but, worried about dropping hot tea on the baby, only managed an unsatisfactory sip. Even having a cup of tea was an effort, these days. The biscuits remained on the saucer. Officially, she ignored them but unofficially their sweet and infinitely desirable image burnt a hole in her stomach.

Edward made satisfied sounds. Bully for him, she thought. She was sucked dry, an arid, slackened arrangement of tubes and organs, no longer pumping sweet juices but bile. The baby's mouth at her breast tugged and worried her flesh with the arrogance of complete possession. Violet looked down at the incubus that had recast her life, and tried not to hate him for his being hideous with spots, because he had made her hideous and her clothes did not fit, and because she was stretched to screaming point by sleeplessness and the scars from her stitches still hurt.

Nobody had warned Violet.

What shall I do? she thought with real panic. A baby and leaving New York. Can't we turn the clock back, Jamie? she asked him silently. Why are you making us go back home?

It had been four hugely exciting years. Of all the great, glorious metropolitan cities to choose from in the world, New York was Violet's. She had made herself there, and the pulse-beat of urban life thudding day and night thudded in time to hers.

New York suited her brand of good looks, her sharp, smart shrewdness, and applauded the terrier quality that made Violet excel in the rights department of a publishing conglomerate.

'I know, I know,' Jamie had said four months ago when he told Violet that the American arm of the bank was being scaled down because of the recession. He knelt in front of the white sofa where she had been sitting. 'But I'm going back to a good job.'

Violet had not moved. 'What about *my* job?' she had asked him. 'Can't you get another one over here?' In reply, Jamie had gently splayed his fingers over her pregnant stomach. 'There are other things,' he said.

'Evidently not for you,' she spat at him. 'Your job comes first.'

Edward continued to feed at her breast as though his life depended on it which, of course, it did. She placed a thumb on his chin and, with a sound of released vacuum, Edward was forced to relinquish the nipple. Face averted, Violet held him up against her shoulder and waited. After he had belched into her ear, she transferred him to the other breast.

A future of eternal broken nights, feeds, milk dripping down her shoulder and an enlarged stomach – almost worse than anything – was visited on Violet. It seemed so awful, and she felt so desperate that she bent her head over the baby and cried. Afterwards, she took Edward into his room to change his nappy.

She had taken infinite pains with the room – more pains, Jamie had commented wickedly, than she had with the baby. It had *had* to be blue and white, ordered, stacked with white towels, clean-smelling and resolutely non-adult. As with most things, Violet achieved her aim and by the time the nursery was finished it was a strong candidate for *Interiors* magazine.

That was before Edward was born and cotton-wool balls had migrated like starlings across the floor and the snowy towels had acquired indelible marks.

Violet pushed back a lock of hair which fell stylishly on to her cheek – the haircut by Kelvin requiring a bank loan. The cut was terrific with the power-suit but irritating at home. Skewering Edward to the changing mat with one hand, she felt in her pocket for a kirby-grip and jammed it into her hair. Edward whinged.

'Shut up,' she told him. 'Just shut up.'

The Filippino maid who came in once a day had left everything as per Violet's instructions, except for the Beatrix Potter cot bumper which, for some reason, she always tied on upside down. A protest? Perhaps Peter Rabbit made more sense that way. Violet untied and retied it correctly.

The baby settled into the cot without too much fuss. Violet checked his position, stuffed a nappy under his back, rewound the tape of *Womb Concerto* and clicked it on.

Unspeakable noises filled the room and she backed out.

How long? An hour? An hour and a half? Two hours? How long before it all started again?

Goodbye, New York. Goodbye, joggers, muggers, impeccably dressed women walking to work in trainers, designer salads, designer sex, designer divorce. Goodbye, Canal Street, SoHo and the best pasta bar in the world on 5th.

Goodbye, where I made myself.

Violet craned out of the plane window to suck in the last traces of land. Below, the gigantic spawn of the city heaved with life and death. Once again, New York girded itself for another night.

Goodbye, sweet, sweet New York.

Jamie smiled at his wife across the BA flying cradle into which Edward had been lowered. I understand, said the smile. No you don't, thought Violet, because you have got your own way. Then she repented and returned the smile before settling back in her seat. Night flights were hell.

They flew on into the dawn, and it was so cold in the stratosphere that the rising sun failed to melt the ice crystals on the aircraft's wings. The light turned from bruise purple to mauve, to lilac and then rose pink. After that, came opal and turquoise and tender pink-grey. Violet caught her breath, for up here the world was beautiful and unstained.

'We'll look for a house with a reasonable garden,' murmured Jamie, who was not sleeping either. 'Near a common or something.'

'Not too far out.' Violet's instinct for the city did not desert her. A new thought imposed itself. 'And near a good school.'

'Near a good school,' confirmed Jamie.

'With an extra room downstairs so we don't have baby things cluttering up our room.'

'Anything you wish, Violet.'

Jamie was happy. After eighteen months of marriage, Violet knew him well enough to gauge a mood. She sneaked a look at him as he peered into the cradle and talked to a wakeful Edward. There were such huge areas in Jamie's life of which Violet knew nothing, and Lara was one of them. Not that Violet wished to explore the past – she was not a *Titanic* survivor who went back to look at the iceberg. No, it was better to sail on.

At that point, Edward decided to be thoroughly traumatized by the unfamilar surroundings, the strange cot and the popping in his ears. An hour later, Violet thrust a still-crying baby into Jamie's arms.

'*You* take him,' she whispered, spitting vitriol, and scrambled out of the seat.

She reached the lavatory and slammed shut the folding door. Inside, she examined her reflection in the mirror: The Woman Who Could Not Keep Her Baby Quiet, the object of every eye on board. She dabbed with a tissue at a stain on her blouse. That was mistake number two, dressing up to fly home with a manic baby. For a second, the humour of the situation struck Violet, which was not usual, and she flashed a grin at herself. Then it disappeared, and did not return.

When she got back to the seat, she found Jamie holding a peacefully sleeping Edward in his arms. The baby's features were slack with sleep and his skin had acquired its usual translucence.

'Nothing to it,' said Jamie, and it was all Violet could do not to whack her handbag down on the complacent head of her husband.

Her father never changed much. Huge, grey-haired, a little shambling, given to corduroy trousers and green sweaters and to taking off and putting on his bifocal spectacles, Max was a reserved man except when it came to his daughters. When he saw Violet, he stepped forward and swept her into one of his bear-hugs, which came close to inflicting injury.

'Darling,' he said, with the brand of awkward tenderness that always made Violet's throat tighten, 'I had to come.'

It was a minute or two before Violet worked out what Max was talking about, until her jet-lagged mind took in that it was Friday. Max had taken a day off work because, he told Prue, he could not miss the homecoming, and added as an afterthought that she might need help with the driving.

Although neither of them had made it to the wedding – so quickly decided on, so romantic – Max had been over to the States to meet Jamie and pronounced that he was a good choice. But he had not met Edward and as soon as he released Violet he turned to examine his grandson, who was almost obscured by his wrappings. Virtually ignoring the other two, father and daughter bent over the pushchair, which also did duty as a pram.

'He's a fine little chap,' said Max. 'Handsome, too.'

'No, he's not,' said Violet. 'But I'm glad you like him.'

'Hallo,' said Jamie, standing by the heap of hand luggage. 'You can only be Prue.'

Prue transferred her attention from the family vignette to Jamie. For a second her eyebrows were pulled together in a frown, as if she was trying to sort out a problem, then her eyes widened a fraction. Violet's husband reminded her of someone. Who?

He turned to see to the luggage, and then she realized that Jamie was a younger version of Max. He was very tall and brown-haired, with a similarly shaped face and large but elegant hands. He wore better clothes than Max, and an expensive aftershave, which would never darken the bathroom shelves at Hallet's Gate. But, like Max, there were humour and curiosity in Violet's husband's face and the suggestion of deep feelings that the photographs had ignored. The photographs had, she concluded in that second's assessment, conveyed only two dimensions and missed the third.

'Hallo, Jamie.' Prue held out her hand.

The Basingstoke stretch of the M3 was even uglier than she remembered, Violet announced in the car after survey-ing, admittedly, some of the worst excesses that had mush-roomed during the last four years. *If* that was possible. Violet tended to have A Subject tucked up her sleeve which she aired at parties and dinners. It was a useful defence. Having reasoned that motorway architecture was a conversation in which she could adopt the politically correct stance, she embarked on a trial run on the way back to Dainton. Max joined in and while they batted the topic back and forth, Violet searched assiduously, and unobtrusively, for signs of age in her stepmother.

It had taken her years to realize it but Prue's were the sort of looks that responded to scrutiny. At first sight, the verdict on her was good-looking, attractive, pleasing. On second and third sight, a curve of her eyebrow, the set of her eyelids, the well-shaped breasts, suggestive mouth, thin wrists prodded the onlooker into thinking: There is more.

Search as she might, Violet could not isolate much. An extra pound on the hips and stomach, perhaps. A line under the eye, which Violet hoped she had not seen before, but nothing else. Otherwise Prue's dark brown hair, swept behind her ears, and clear skin were as she remembered. Nor did the breasts show any sign of sag. Somehow, Violet reflected bitterly, her stepmother always managed not to look her age.

Violet had reached the stage where she no longer endeavoured to censor her reflections; from early in their acquaintance, Prue had been fair game. Occasionally she wondered if Prue knew how much she disliked her, and, if so, did it hurt? Prue never gave anything much away – that was what made her so infuriating, and such a difficult enemy. To the angry, grieving child, her soft implacableness had been . . . terrible.

Motorway architecture having had its airing, Violet moved on to discuss the job that was possibly on offer in the publishing house she most favoured. Underneath the Armani trouser suit, the child that she had been wept at yet another change and beat out her grief.

'Can I help?' Prue stood in the doorway of the spare bedroom at Hallet's Gate. 'You must be dead tired.'

The men had gone off for a walk to work off the bottle of wine that both, unwisely, had tackled over lunch. Edward was asleep and Violet was unpacking.

'I can't believe it was yesterday I put this lot in.'

Prue knew that Violet had not wished to leave New York and felt some sympathy. She picked up a pin-striped skirt and shook it out. 'Liz Claiborne,' she read on the label. 'How chic.'

'Yes, isn't it?' Violet handed Prue a tartan-padded coat-hanger from a stack. 'Hang it up for me.' She paused. 'Please.'

Prue shoved the wire coat-hangers she had saved from the dry-cleaners to one end of the cupboard and did as she was asked. The wire hangers rattled in their exile as she arranged dresses, suits and skirts on their padded rivals, and inserted them in special wardrobe bags. 'I never do this,' she said.

Violet threw her a look, and Prue declined to interpret it. 'Do you have any rough clothes?' she asked. 'You'll need them here.'

'Jesus H. Christ, Prue, I've only lived here for twenty years.' Longer than you, Prue, she wanted to add, although that wasn't true any longer. But I was in the house long, long before you. All those years ago, when Helen, beautiful, drunken Helen, had abandoned her little daughter and sent shock waves through the village equivalent to the death of Grace Archer. Prue had not arrived until three years later, an interloper from London. 'I know the mud-flats as well as my face. And yes, I have plenty of sweaters and leggings.' Violet pronounced 'sweaters' with an American twang.

Violet flung her hairbrush on to the dressing-table, and Prue winced for the glass top. 'I think I'll get some sleep now.'

Prue did her bit. She fetched and carried hot-water bottles, a cup of tea, an extra rug and Violet, who did look grey with exhaustion, settled down gratefully.

She got half an hour's rest before Edward let everyone in the house know that he, too, had taken up residence. Furthermore, he demonstrated it throughout the small hours of Saturday and Sunday night, but spent the days in exhausted slumber. Thus, it was a frayed group that convened for Monday morning breakfast.

'I thought you said, Mum, that you can sleep through other babies' cries,' said Jane, who had been kept back from school for a dental appointment. She spooned up cornflakes in a dazed fashion. 'I would like to remind you I have a Latin test this afternoon.'

Violet was washing Edward's bottle at the sink. She swirled round. 'Think yourself lucky it isn't every night – which I have to put up with.'

Jane's spoon descended to the bowl and she observed her half-sister without affection. 'I was giving fair warning as to why I will do badly in the test,' she said. 'That's all.'

Prue broke an egg into the frying-pan for Max's breakfast. Anyone who caught the 7.33 day in day out deserved padding, even if it was pure cholesterol.

'Would you mind if I use a ring?' Violet brushed up against Prue.

Prue endeavoured to make herself as small as possible. 'Of course not.'

Violet produced a bag of organic, cold-pressed porridge oats, labelled 'DelMonico's New York, Your Organically Sound Delicatessen' and measured a cupful into a saucepan. 'Part of the strategy to keep Jamie healthy,' she said. 'All those business lunches.'

Prue assessed the porridge, which certainly had 'organic' written all over it, and transferred her attention to achieving, within the limited space available, the perfect fried egg, sunny side up.

'Good morning,' said Jamie arriving in the kitchen smelling of soap and Vetiver. 'That bacon and eggs looks good. Can I have some?'

Violet placed the organically OK, ecologically sound breakfast in front of her husband. 'No, Jamie,' she said. 'I've done this for you.'

Chapter Three

Expensive, lacy, wispy, the spectacle of Violet's knickers accosted Prue from the pile of clean laundry in the basket. Prue entertained a vision of the slender torso and entirely cellulite-free thighs to which they belonged, and sighed. Once Violet had been a skinny, burning-eyed little girl, all bones and angles, who proceeded, in the course of only one year, to surprise onlookers by developing beauty.

I hate you, Prue.

Beside the fantasies in the basket lay Prue's own knickers, safe and sensible Marks and Spencer. Prone to cystitis, Prue liked her kidneys to be covered. She bent down and picked up one of Violet's daring black numbers. Comfort versus style. The terrible old sofa versus the love seat. Knickers were a clever way of deploying and maintaining an ingrained male fantasy, and Violet would know just how it was done. If pressed, most women would admit that keeping their kidneys covered was a great deal more comfortable than wearing minuscule bits of lace but, like Violet, endured the chill and unsightly lines. As it happened, Prue was misjudging her stepdaughter – something to which well-intentioned Prue was prone. Violet wore her underwear entirely to please herself.

Prue did not doubt that Jamie loved his wife and, because she herself was loved and therefore understood its language, read the signs, but she wondered if he was smug at the trophy he had captured to put on his mantelpiece. It did not occur to her that the idea might apply the other way round. She let the knickers drop back into the basket.

'Day-dreaming, Prue?'

Jamie entered the kitchen with the evening paper under his arm. It was seven o'clock on a Wednesday evening and he had changed into corduroys. Prue's answering smile was particularly sleepy.

'Thinking about laundry, actually.' She kicked the basket under the table because the notion of Jamie making the same knicker comparison and arriving at the same conclusion did not please her somehow.

'Can I help with the supper?'

The request stopped her mid-track. 'Is that a *serious* question?'

'Surely.'

She indicated the potato peeler and Jamie dumped the newspaper, ran cold water into the sink and set to. Taking pleasure as always in the routine, Prue chopped an onion and fried it and watched while the slices softened and turned translucent.

'Did you ever see that play when they fried an onion on the stage? The audience was in agony from hunger.'

'No, I didn't.' Jamie replenished the water in the sink, adding, 'I don't go to the theatre much.'

Prue added mince to the frying pan and the slightly rank smell of meat joined the other smells in the kitchen.

'We must be a lot of extra work,' said Jamie.

'Yes and no. Max always has a cooked meal in the evening.'

'Where is he?'

Max had phoned to say he would be late, she told him. Although he would never breathe a word of criticism against Violet, Max, Prue suspected, was finding the full house as trying as she was. Extra noise. Night activity. Stuff everywhere. A borrowed pram blocking the hall. Baby clothes overflowing in the laundry basket. A half-emptied suitcase on the landing. Every room had an occupant and the house had shrunk.

Where are the spaces in my tranquil, drowsy house? she cried silently.

'Still,' Jamie persisted, 'it's extra work for you and we're grateful.'

Prue nudged back a lock of hair with her wrist. Provisioning and providing were her business, but it was nice to have it acknowledged. 'Any luck with a house?'

'Well, yes.' Jamie launched into a description of one they had seen in Wandsworth and for which they had offered, explaining that it was expensive but he could get a cheap mortgage.

'Ah,' said Prue.

There had been a report in Max's *Economist* which demonstrated that the richest 1 per cent of the population owned 18 per cent of the marketable wealth – a member of which category was helping her to make shepherd's pie in her kitchen. This was in contrast to the poorest 50 per cent who owned only 6 per cent of the marketable wealth.

Of course Jamie Beckett would be able to secure a cheap mortgage, he was that sort of person. The sort who knew people and who had a network thrumming discreetly to his wishes.

The knowledge did not enrage Prue for, she reasoned, it did not mean that Jamie was not lacking in either morality or feeling and, although she worried about the disadvantaged and was happy to make cakes and sell raffle tickets for the homeless, the Bosnians, etc., etc., she had never burned with passionate involvement in their fate. How, then, could she cast a stone?

'How are you doing with the potatoes?'

Jamie pushed a full saucepan towards her. 'Anything else?'

'Could you lay the table? But are you sure?'

'It's my duty day,' he said. 'Or rather night. I share the nights with Violet.'

Gosh, thought Prue, silenced.

Jamie's night duty did not run smoothly. Violet had decided to get Edward completely off the breast within a week and he hated the bottle he was offered at one-thirty a.m., and the bottle he was offered at two-thirty. He cried and cried, emitting the angry, despairing wails of an air-raid siren. The members of the household not involved in the drama cowered beneath their bedclothes, including the baby's mother who informed his father that Edward had *got* to learn.

At three o'clock, Jamie took Edward downstairs and, in desperation, walked him through the hall, around the dining room, up and down the drawing room and round and round the kitchen table. In the dark, he whispered to his son to shut up and, in the dark, he remembered his own childhood nightmares and terrors.

'Please be quiet,' he begged Edward.

The baby's down-dusted skull pulsed angrily under Jamie's chin, and the little body was rigid. Back Jamie paced through the hall, and a shape emerged on the stairs.

'Is he ill?' asked Prue in a normal voice. Under the circumstances, it seemed pointless to whisper.

'I don't know,' said Jamie. 'He won't take the bottle and I'm not sure if it's obstinacy or stomach-ache.' Jamie was beginning to feel exhausted and, not unreasonably, panicked.

Prue led the way into the kitchen and turned out the light. 'Shall I have a try?'

Jamie handed over the baby thankfully. Prue took him

and, in an automatic gesture, drew him into her breast. Conscious then of his gaze, she said without looking up, 'I wanted more after Jane but it didn't happen.'

She was wearing a blue dressing-gown, minus its belt, revealing a soft, white-cotton nightdress underneath. She looked warm and rather sensual, with the blurry languor of mussed hair and drowsiness, and he was suddenly conscious that he was looking at a private side of her. Perhaps fatigue acted as a filter on Jamie, for the colours that made up Prue, blue, brown hair, and the white skin, veined and intimate at the junction of her neck and collar-bone, dry and slightly stretched on her hands, painted themselves on to his vision.

'Where's the bottle?' she asked, after a slight pause, aware of his scrutiny.

Jamie handed it over. She settled Edward in her arms and tested the milk. 'It's cold,' she said. 'I bet he doesn't like that.'

'We never heat it up at night.'

Prue raised her eyebrows and then lowered them again. It was not her business. She got up and switched on the kettle, talking to the baby as she did so. Jamie could not make out what she was saying, but her voice was steadying. Evidently the baby agreed for he quietened and when Prue offered him the warmed milk he nuzzled at the teat. After a hiccup or two, he began to feed.

'This might take a while, Jamie, because he's been so upset. Do you want to go back to bed?'

Yes, he did very much. And no, he did not. 'I'll wait with you.'

The cuffs of Prue's nightdress had slipped up her arms and Jamie found himself fascinated by the movement of her surprisingly delicate wrist-bones under the skin and the long fingers that were working magic on the baby. The kitchen was quiet and very cold. Neither of them said anything, but every so often Prue shifted the baby and Jamie was reminded of paintings of the Madonna and Child – the calm and potent icon from which we demand comfort.

'Like the Virgin,' he said aloud.

'St Joan called herself the Virgin.'

'What?'

'An interest of mine.'

'Tell me.'

Prue told him. During her life Joan had been given several names, even more after her death which, Prue said, again adjusting the angle of the bottle, was an indication of how puzzling and incomprehensible Joan had been to her contemporaries. Joan herself preferred the term *la pucelle* which means virgin, but a virgin who anticipates a change in her state.

'Oh,' said Jamie.

It was a condition, continued Prue, that suggested flux, a condition that she had at first found difficult to understand. 'But now ...' she looked up at Jamie '... I think I do.' It pinpointed the maiden, both innocent and nubile, spread-eagled on the cusp.

There was a pause.

'Ambiguous, but not,' Jamie supplied.

'But how acute,' said Prue. 'How psychologically sound for a so-called unlettered peasant. And it fascinates me how she knew.'

The chill deepened. Prue addressed the now peacefully sucking baby. 'I suppose I'd better wind you.' She draped Edward across her shoulder. 'Did you have trouble at night in New York?'

'Sometimes. But it's far worse when you're responsible for someone else's household stuffing its fingers into its ears.' Jamie began fiddling with an orange from the fruit bowl and looked up at Prue with a smile rendered devastating by its rueful irony. 'I'm learning.'

She smiled back. 'If you mean that parenthood is a state of extended exhaustion . . .'

'I do. I do.'

'Actually, it's extended terror as well.'

'Meaning?'

'You're constantly frightened for your children.'

Jamie was silent.

'Do you think . . .' Prue sounded tentative. 'Do you think Violet should be going back to work quite so early?'

He frowned and tossed the orange from one hand to the other. 'That's up to Violet.'

She thought for a moment, digesting the rebuke.

The light was not good in the kitchen but good enough for Jamie to witness the flush flooding Prue's cheeks. The desire to leap up and comfort her cut into him with the speed, thoroughness and surprise of a knife, and he dropped the orange. 'I didn't mean to be rude, Prue.'

'But justified,' she said, got up and handed Jamie his son. 'I think he'll be fine now.'

She left him holding a damp, but silenced, baby.

As a result of that last episode, Emmy Horton came into their lives for Violet insisted that she just *had* to have help. Period.

All right, Prue conceded wearily and wrote out the postcard for the village shop.

KIND, CARING, TEMPORARY MOTHER'S HELP
WANTED TO LOOK AFTER FOUR-MONTH BABY AND
DO LIGHT CLEANING. GOOD CONDITIONS AND
PAY. REFS. APPLY MRS. VALOUR, HALLET'S GATE.

The notice attracted a good deal of interest, not least because it was placed beside the one announcing the sale of bankrupt Jack Woodham's personal effects on 26 February. Jack had been the head of the local fern-growers' association and his greenhouse collection – now in jeopardy because he could not heat it – was being fought over.

'Has Mrs Valour had a baby, then?' asked Anna Vigas, reading the postcard.

'No,' said Emmy Horton.

Anna's attention span was never great and she lost interest in the subject. She scuffed a bit of mud with the toe of her Doc Marten's and, in a prize-winning imitation of Annalise in *Neighbours*, flipped her blonde hair over her shoulder. 'Are you coming tonight, then?'

Emmy was searching her bag, a huge, floppy leather affair with a fringe, for a biro. 'Hang on.'

'You're not going to apply, Em? A baby *and* cleaning?'

'Unemployment plus extra cash equals nice idea,' said Emmy. 'I like babies and I want something to do.'

'You could do lots of things,' said Anna unfairly, for her own horizons were not vast.

'But I don't, do I?'

It was a bitter day but neither girl was wearing much. Thin T-shirts, leggings and jackets from the discount store. Both of them were skinny and, clearly, cold but neither appeared to mind. Emmy sniffed the air.

'It's going to get colder,' she said. 'I think I'll go and try my luck now with Mrs Valour.'

Flip went Anna's hair.

'The baby is still very young,' said Prue later, in the kitchen of Hallet's Gate, worrying about the thin T-shirt and goose-fleshed arms, 'but it's reasonably simple to look after him.

My stepdaughter wishes to have some help because she needs a bit of a rest and she has to go up to London quite a bit.' Prue outlined the situation.

Emmy shifted on the kitchen chair and her eye lit on a framed photograph on the dresser of a beautiful girl with black hair and rather remarkable eyes. She looked smart, in control and well off. I see, thought Emmy, who was no fool. Madam needs her beauty sleep.

Prue apologized for Violet not being there and asked when Emmy could start. Emmy replied she could then, that moment.

Aren't you going to ask me about my experience? she projected silently, feeling almost embarrassed for Prue. As if on cue, Prue produced a red-and-black notebook and scanned the last page where headings such as 'martyrdom' and 'treachery, Burgundians,' were interlarded with 'check hourly rate', 'no smokers' and 'notice period' which Violet, who reckoned she knew about management, had dictated to Prue.

'Do you have experience with babies?'

'No.'

Prue stared at Emmy and then smiled. 'Nor did I when I had my daughter.'

Her smile was infectious. OK, thought Emmy, not bad. She was aware that she did not look her best. She and Anna had been out drinking the previous evening and it had been an effort to get up. She felt the outline of dark circles under her eyes, the lank feel of her awful hair at its worst, and she was thirsty.

'First aid?' Prue was searching her notes. 'Do you know what to do when a baby chokes?'

'Turn it upside down?'

It did not rank with one of the great answers, but it would do.

'Could I get you a cup of coffee?'

Emmy hesitated. 'Could I have tea, please?'

She watched Prue organize the cups, familiar with the type. Mrs Valour was the sort of person who bent over backwards not to offend but, in so doing, sometimes did. I wonder if she knows she's beautiful? Emmy considered herself ugly and measured her sex from this relative position, and Prue's well-tended hair, English skin and unforced, untampered feel struck her. Is her husband as nice as he looks? Both Valours were well known in Dainton, but Max's large, hunched figure, his courtesy and his willingness to sit on committees and councils made him especially popular.

The warmth in the kitchen was making Emmy's cheeks glow. Evidently she had caught Prue just as she had returned from a shop. Ordeal-by-trolley at the local Sainsbury's and, judging by the amount, ordeal-by-chequebook as well. She bent down to retrieve a rogue tin from the floor.

'Thank you,' said Prue. 'Do you mind if I unpack while we talk? Some of the stuff needs to go into the freezer.'

'I'll help.' Emmy got to her feet.

'That's kind of you.' Prue shoved a polystyrene tray containing twenty-four chicken thighs towards Emmy before she could change her mind. 'Special Price', it said on the red sticker. 'Family bargain.' 'Could you bag those up in fours, please, in the freezer bags?'

Emmy touched the sticker. 'Favouritism. Do you ever get a bargain if you're an old bat on your own?'

Prue handed the roll of plastic bags across the table, and the light caught a couple of strands of hair at her temples, which were lighter than the rest, 'No, I don't think you do.'

Emmy took a gulp of tea with an unfamiliar taste, ate Prue's biscuits and began work. A stack of polystyrene, plastic and clingfilm mounted on the table. Prue stuffed it into the rubbish bin.

'I know, I know,' she grimaced guiltily, 'it's not good. I keep meaning to protest about the amount of packaging.'

'Gives someone a job, though,' said Emmy.

It crossed Prue's mind that she and Emmy might not get on, and it crossed Emmy's that this was a very different world from the one she knew.

She stood bottles of sherry and wine on the table, piled butter and low-fat spread into a heap, and marshalled tins of *petit pois*, flageolet beans and green lentils for the larder. There were bags of different pastas and pasta sauces, but no gravy browning or salad cream.

'"Farfalle",' Emmy read out from a packet. 'I don't know why they bother. It's all the same at night.'

'There's a theory that sauces bind better to the pasta the more surface there is.'

Prue gathered up the bags and Emmy repressed her reply.

The larder impressed her, however. It was one of those cold, shelved, walk-in rooms, ventilated by mesh and dubbed game-larders by pretentious estate agents. Tins – lentils, artichoke hearts, plum tomatoes – were ranged one side, jars of chutney, expensive jams, bottled fruits and emerald-coloured olive oil on the other. There was a ham, the remains of a truckle cheese and a half-empty jar of Quality Street. Someone had a sweet tooth.

Emmy closed her eyes for a moment.

'You must help yourself to anything you want,' said Prue in a rush, anxious to make up for her slightly superior attitude over the pasta. 'I'm out at work three mornings a week and Mrs Beckett will see to her own meals.'

By that, Prue meant that Violet had categorically refused to do any cooking for the mother's help. 'And, anyway,

Prue, I have just gone on a *vicious* diet in order to get into trim for London.' Do you not have to be in trim for Hampshire? Prue wanted to ask her.

'Do you have a microwave, Mrs Valour?'

Prue handed Emmy the final tin to be stowed and took so long to answer the question that Emmy was not quite sure if her question had been offensive.

'No, we don't.'

Prue had been thinking about Jamie's rebuke over Violet.

Anna was suspicious. The idea of the cash was OK, but babies spelt work. 'They want something for nothing,' she repeated, endlessly in Emmy's opinion.

'Shut up,' she told Anna, finally.

Anna adjusted a migrating shoulder-pad under her jumper and scrutinized her friend. Emmy wore her miserable-and-alone look, which she did from time to time. 'Sorry, Em.'

Emmy grinned suddenly. 'I'll watch out,' she said. 'If they overwork me, I can always clean the baby's bum with Jif.'

Scanning the gardens and fields that lapped the village boundaries for the things that interested her – earth thrown up by a mole, a stream swollen and flowing with energy, the bright green of grass sated with winter rain – Emmy walked home. Almost too dazzling for the gloomy day, a burst of winter jasmine was draped over the wall of Horton's farm. Further up the road, rooks were nest-renovating in the beeches that edged the copse up the rise. Good. That indicated spring. Not spring because the calendar said so, but spring because things were happening in the earth.

Emmy considered the subject of spring. She knew quite a lot about wildlife and bits of this and that picked up from GCSE biology and the snippets of medical detail with which her mother, a clerk at the hospital in Winchester, occasionally regaled her. Knowledge that surprised her sometimes, for Emmy, though sharp and shrewd, did not consider herself in any way bright and school had been an experience to get over and done with as soon as possible.

The wind shifted, and she responded by hunching her shoulders. Where in the damp, frozen woods were the fritillary butterfly caterpillars overwintering? Hidden in the violet leaves? She hoped so because it sounded so nice, and they must be there because last summer had seen fritillaries. Emmy had spotted a rare pair of Monarchs, too, blown 3500 miles across the Atlantic by the winds.

Imagine being blown all that way.

She bent to pick up the discarded husk of a beech nut which cracked between her fingers. Gently, she prised it open and was rewarded by a glimpse of secret, intimate green at the centre. Its unexpectedness, and the contrast – death and life, sweet and bitter – pleased her greatly.

These days, Father was on a reduced shift, Mother was on night duty, because it brought in more, and her two elder brothers had joined the army and she never saw them. In the empty space that remained was Emmy, a solitary girl, in an empty house on the edge of Dainton. Either that or it was full of people trying to sleep at awkward hours.

A green Range-Rover followed by a Volvo drove down the road and sent up a spray of water. Emmy stepped back smartly.

'Sods,' she said half-heartedly.

The Volvo had a FOR SALE notice pasted on to its back window. GOOD PRICE FOR QUICK CASH SALE.

Emmy's lack of obvious prettiness was not helped by the pinched look characteristic of someone who did not eat quite enough, in contrast with the glossy hair and skin of someone who did. Like Mrs Valour, for example.

47

In one respect, unremarkable bone structure and lank hair made life simpler: the race was so unequal there was no need to enter it. Observing Anna's unrelenting attention to her body – haircuts, face packs, depilations – Emmy appreciated her freedom and was grateful for the anonymity granted by ugliness. People looked straight through Emmy to the blonde, full-lipped Anna, who then had to cope with the attention.

'I don't know,' said her mother, often enough. 'You won't even *try* to look nice.'

She reiterated the complaint on Emmy's return to the house and stepped up the pressure when she heard Emmy had got herself a job. She suggested that Emmy got herself a perm, at least, and emptied the contents of her straw basket on to the table. Having located her wallet, one of those fat-bellied affairs into which you can stuff a life, and extracted a twenty-pound note, she held it out to her daughter. 'Here, have it on me.'

'You really think it'll help?' asked Emmy.

Mrs Horton's own face was framed by a construct of ice-blonde curls. 'Of course,' she said impatiently, and picked at a flaking cuticle. 'You see, Emmy,' she confided, and clicked her frosted nails on the Formica table, 'you're so much on your own and I don't do enough for you.'

'And a perm will alter that?' Emmy flashed back.

Mrs Horton was tired from having raised three children, harassed by the family's reduced income and the demands of running a home and a job. ('Thank the Lord,' she often said, 'I won't have to empty a Hoover bag in my coffin.') She did not feel equal to pulling Emmy's life into shape. A perm was the best she could offer. Emmy knew that, and knew her mum tried, and was grateful. 'Stand by for the mob, then,' she said, 'and for the suicides under my window.'

The perm, as she could have predicted, was not a success. In the seconds before her scalp disappeared under the baking foil and chemicals, Emmy allowed herself to fantasize: from under them a woman of power and beauty would emerge. Then she pulled herself together and studied her reflection in the mirror while Neil worked her over. Surrounded by lights and bottles of shampoo and conditioners promising Nirvana, it was not a kind mirror. Its object was to strip its prey to the bone, and it did. There sat Emmy, a plucked chicken with nodular wrists, peaky features and collar-bones that made lines under her T-shirt. She lit a cigarette.

'Shouldn't do that,' advised Neil, 'it destroys your Vit C level. Have a cup of herb tea instead. Else,' he shouted across the saloon floor, 'bring us a cup of Blackcurrant Bracer.'

Neil was a great deal prettier than Emmy and she could see from his clear eyes and fresh skin that his Vit C level was kept topped up. A wholesome, tutti-frutti, blow-dried walking advert for citric acid.

Else placed a mug in front of Emmy and a sweetish smell rose from a curl of steam.

Two hours later, Emmy alighted from the bus at the Dainton stop. Patches of frost glimmered in the light thrown from the houses edging the road, and the landscape was how she liked it best: stark, with gaunt, skeletal plants. She liked the smooth bark, bleached branches and cleanness of stripped winter trees. It was growing even colder and her hair fizzed and burned around her face. She pushed it back and contemplated doing a Sinead O'Connor and shaving her head.

At eighteen she had not got far with her life, but exactly what she was to do with it was as yet a mystery. Three moderate passes at GCSE, as Mrs Horton also pointed out, were not a passport to a briefcase and a company car. Silence lay over the other subjects with which Emmy had wrestled and lost. Since leaving school, she had made do with odd jobs here and there, but they never lasted more than a month or two, and never engaged her interest.

She halted by the big oak at the bottom of the lane which was flanked by hawthorn scrub. Earlier that morning, a fieldfare had been sitting there, fluffing out its grey and russet plumage. Emmy had enjoyed that.

Her shoes cracked on the frozen puddles and the sound was magnified in the cold air. In the field ahead, the livery horses were clumped together. A big bay had a New Zealand rug strapped around his girth, thicker than Emmy's jacket. Round here, livery horses got treated like hotel guests – linen sheets and hot-and-cold running.

Emmy rounded the corner and Hallet's Gate came into view. She recognized the Valours' voices in the drive as she drew nearer and saw them standing, talking.

'Don't get cold,' he said, and there was a degree of tenderness in his tone that made Emmy halt temporarily in her tracks. Sometimes the unfairness with which love was dished out, some people getting so much, made her jealous. Emmy had no idea that its presence could create more trouble than its absence. She hovered for a few seconds more, a dark, rather anguished shadow with a perm that imperfectly disguised a spirit that longed to expand but did not know how.

Then, Mr Valour put his arm around Mrs Valour and she leant briefly against him before they moved towards the front door from which light was streaming.

Suddenly, Emmy knew. She did want something from life. She wanted her own home. Not a big one, just a couple of rooms, with a kitchen, and a bathroom with a decent bath. A back garden. She wanted white walls, fringed lampshades, coir matting and plants. She wanted order and quiet, not the deadly quiet of Number 5, but her own peace. The yearning solidified in the pit of her stomach, surprising Emmy by its physicality.

As Emmy let herself into her own home, which smelt chilly and unoccupied, the boiler leapt into life. She switched on the light, which sent down harsh rays through its frosted glass shade on to the patterned carpet.

In the kitchen, Mrs Horton had left a message on the back of an envelope. 'Get your own supper. Dad and me out.'

Emmy sighed.

Chapter Four

Emmy proved a godsend and, for someone with no experience of babies, a natural. Edward took to her and so, after the initial week, did Prue. Quick to pick up the basics, she was not too talkative, apparently reliable and, above all, willing. Prue relaxed, and Violet exploited all these advantages.

'I'll be away a lot more in the future,' she explained to Emmy, and sipped mint tea while Emmy struggled to change a nappy. 'I need to be in London to supervise the new house. After all, I've done my whack with breast-feeding, whatever Sheila Kitzinger says.'

Emmy did not hold any opinions on breast-feeding, neither did she know who Sheila Kitzinger was, but what did strike her was that Violet was on the defensive. Guilt at offloading the baby? No, Mrs Beckett did not look the guilty type. Intuitively, Emmy felt it was more complicated. People looked and sounded like Violet when they were not sure how to behave: she had seen it with her mates at school, and particularly with the bullies. Violet, Emmy eventually put her finger on it, to her satisfaction, was only pretending to be a mother.

Emmy liked the baby, without feeling any passionate attachment to him, but when he was presented with a bottle instead of the warm breast and occasionally cried, his desolation rendered Emmy sweaty and uneasy. She was not, therefore, surprised that Violet made herself scarce.

'She's a madam,' she told Anna.

Anna inspected the expensive pushchair. 'With loot.'

'With loot.'

'Are you going to stick it, Em?'

'Of course. The more spoilt Madam is, the more's in it for me.'

'You've lost your deck.'

Emmy considered Prue's kitchen and larder, the scent bottles on Violet's dressing-table, the stack of sweaters and shirts with classy labels, and shot a look at Anna. At the back of her mind, she harboured an idea that if she stuck out the job some of the luxury and exclusiveness would rub off on her – like glitter flaking from a Christmas card. Whether that was sensible or not, and what she would get out of it in the end, Emmy was unsure. Neither Violet nor Prue wore T-shirts and there was not a leather jacket to be cast off between either woman. Packets of pasta? An insider's knowledge of Sainsbury's layout? Instant recall of Radio 4's timetable, Monday to Friday?

It was not the *savoir-faire* that would get Emmy by in the disco or the factory, or the supermarket packing division – if it came to the latter, the thought of which made Emmy screw up her face.

'Bear up, Em,' said Anna, flicking her hair. 'We'll go drinking tonight.'

From the first – and always – Violet had inhabited an uneasy terrain in Max and Prue's life together. 'I can't cope with her, I *can't* cope,' Prue had been driven to shouting at Max from her mess of hormones and leaking body just after Jane was born. She hates me. She hates the baby.

Max's large, heavy hand on her shoulder and his silence, which she interpreted as condemnatory, hurt badly, and drove Prue to say something she regretted: 'She's like a bad fairy in our marriage.'

Instantly, Max had removed his hand and left the room. Later, Prue discovered him in the study polishing (forever polishing) the two guns from the gun-safe. Max always used his uncle's Purdey for shooting but the other, which had belonged to William, his father, received equal attention. She had endeavoured an apology and ended up weeping hysterically in the armchair. Max dealt with Prue's tears and moved into action. He had put her to bed, summoned her mother, who was still going strong at that point, and Mrs Blake from the village was recruited to take charge of Violet until the worst was over. All wonderfully practical solutions that he effected without drama, fuss or recrimination, and Prue was grateful.

'We all need breathing space,' he said when she tried to thank him. 'Otherwise we crowd the spirit too much.'

And Prue was left in peace with her new baby, and her mind was allowed to drift in and out of dreams, to go over and over the birth until it was settled in her memory, to struggle with the sense that she should be giving thanks to a God, but that she could not find him. At least, she had been given the silence in which to try.

Max had never commented on Prue's outburst. Yet she felt that its memory, and its import, remained, submerged but there.

'Violet looks exhausted,' said Max, sitting down and peeling off a sock. It had been a full week and everyone had opted for early bed. Violet had arrived back in Dainton after a two-day trip to London full of talk of the new house and the job she had been offered.

'I'm worried it's going to be too much for her.' Max took off the second sock. He held up a hand to forestall Prue. 'I know, I know, it's what women want.'

The echo from the conversation in which she had been the one to query Violet's decision pricked and bothered Prue. Instead of confessing that she had been thinking along the same lines, she said, 'You sound like something out of the ark.'

'Maybe. But I watch these working mothers struggling to keep the show going and I wonder. Delphine Watson, for instance. I told you about her before. She used to be pretty but these days looks dreadful. I took her out to lunch to find out why. Apparently her two-year-old hasn't slept through the night yet and her husband's no help.'

'Being at home makes no difference if you have no sleep.' Prue got into bed beside Max and leant over and dropped a kiss on his hair. 'It was nice of you to bother.'

'That girl has a good job, and I require to know why she looks like something out of *Marat/Sade*. How can she do her job properly in her state?'

Prue withdrew to her side of the bed.

'What I'm saying is this. I don't want Violet ending up half dead with fatigue and heading for a nervous break-down.' Max punched his pillow and settled down.

He interpreted Prue's silence correctly and flung a sop. 'Actually, the working mother is nothing new, only the dames who ran the manors and demesnes in history had family back-up. Nowadays, you use girls like Emmy.'

'Emmy is very reliable.'

'Maybe.' Max swivelled on the pillow to look at Prue. Underneath the blankets his hand felt for his wife's. 'But she has no brains.'

'You don't know that.'

'Anyone who wears only a T-shirt in February is brainless.'

'Very funny.'

Prue turned off the bedside light and composed her body into the position she preferred for sleep. After they had first

55

married, Max had forbidden Prue to work. Well, not forbidden exactly, he had just kept up a powerful lobby. 'Look,' he said, 'I've lost one wife, and Violet and I need you at home.'

She remembered he had stood over her as she sat on the sofa, his large features creased and urgent. Then he took hold of Prue's hand and held it against his cheek. 'Please, Prue. I want a family and a home.'

There had been no glittering career for Prue to fight for – the role of secretary then research assistant did not warrant a lot of drum banging, and insisting on her right to work promised to be a Pyrrhic victory.

'*I want a home,*' insisted Max. '*You have a job here at home surely?*'

Practicalities were a consideration, too. The prospect of daily outwitting British Rail made Prue wilt – the cattle truck of the rush-hours, the furtive Mars Bars at the end of a long day and falling asleep over the *Evening Standard* did not seem to be positive affirmations of life. Who would look after the children, the many she envisaged sitting around the kitchen table? An Adam and an Edmund. An Eleanor and a Freya.

Prue turned over, aware that her distaste for the commuting life would cut no ice with those who had no option but to do it. Her hand sought and found the corner of the pillowcase and she rubbed it between her fingers. She liked the feel of the texture on her skin, and to run an edge under her fingernail.

Max was asleep. This was Prue's time, and her mind flowed up and over the rocks and hills of her life, trying to make sense of problems or the restlessness that occasionally tormented her. Sometimes, in the moment suspended between waking and sleeping, she sloughed off the sense of herself and floated free. Just for a few moments. Then she would feel extraordinarily peaceful and receptive but, paradoxically, charged with energy. *I have been lucky.*

Yes, so far, Prue had been lucky: in her marriage, in her circumstances, in her daughter.

Men are good icon-makers, and Max had shaped Prue into a familiar and infinitely comforting one, and she had not objected. A French peasant girl wearing a man's armour and a man's haircut had also been turned into an icon through the medium of the masculine eye and pen. (Although women's tongues must have had quite a bit to do in shaping Joan's story and sending news of it far and wide.) As far as Prue knew, there was only one documented instance of a woman describing Joan, which affirmed only that from what she could observe Joan was a virgin. Stranger still, as often in the business of forging icons, men like to ascribe weird purities to the female version. Extreme, tortured virginity. Suffering. Untouchableness. Immaculate conception.

A virgin then, the *pucelle.* A woman on the brink of change.

Before she fell asleep, Prue relived the moment in the kitchen with Jamie and Edward: the sensation of the baby against her breast, and Jamie's tired, tenderly composed face. He was a stranger, and different, one whose possibilities were foreign. Of one thing only she was sure: the sum of Jamie was hidden below the surface. Her mind drifted on ... Jamie holding his baby and telling her to mind her own business. His touch on her arm, as violent in the sensation it provoked in her as the swords of Joan's men running through English flesh.

After Prue had fallen asleep, Max turned and looked at the dark shape, tipped by a luminous lick of white linen. He stared at his wife for some time. Then, very carefully, he turned back to his side of the bed.

Jamie leant over to kiss Violet goodnight. Burrowed into the bedclothes, she was already half asleep and the waterfall of hair on the pillow was motionless. He turned off the light.

Blue was the Virgin's colour, the Madonna's colour, and it suited Prue as it did not suit the unMadonna-like Violet who favoured reds and greens. He stared at the ceiling while his eyes adjusted to night vision. Blue was a colour into which to sink, rested and calmed by its serenity.

Prue was secret, or rather private, and Jamie suddenly perceived that walls and thorn hedges offered temptation as, let it be said, they did in matters of work. How high could you, would you, climb? Did you dare to cut and slash your way through to the princess wrapped in blue who lay sleeping within?

To reassure himself, Jamie slid a hand across the sheets and placed it on Violet's slender haunch. It was cool and firm to the touch.

Goodnight, wife.

'My mum's always worked,' Emmy informed Prue over the sterilizer, which took up too much space on the sideboard and made the kitchen stink of Milton.

'Who looked after you when you came home from school?'

Emmy looked at Prue as if she was sizing up a visitor from Mars. 'No one. Mum left a meal out for me to warm up. Sometimes my brothers were home. Sometimes my nan came over. The neighbours were there if I wanted something.'

'Yes,' said Prue. 'Of course.'

Emmy flicked through her file of mental images. One of its documents was the picture of a warm house, a bright fire and a mother in the kitchen, baking. It was a picture to which she only referred after careful consideration, or after one too many at the pub, because it hurt her to think about it.

'How do you find dealing with a baby?' Prue sat down at the table to count out the housekeeping money.

'I was dead frightened.'

Prue looked amused. 'And now?'

'I like it. He's a nice baby and it's sort of planning, really. Working out a routine. Understanding his language. I should be quite good at it.'

'Oh?' Prue slid a heap of coins back into the tin, which had 'Fortnum and Mason. English Breakfast Tea' written on it.

'Yes,' said Emmy. 'I'm good at crosswords.'

Prue was not and the conversation lapsed. Anyway, she was not quite sure of the logic of Emmy's argument.

She was quite clear on one point, however: her longing to have the house back to herself. A baby provoked such big upheavals and such big emotions – panic, inadequacy, crippling tenderness. When it was yours myopia was added to the list, for it was hard to see anything beyond its milk-blistered mouth and your own exhaustion. With Jane, Prue had looked up from time to time to the world outside and found it alarmingly narrowed but, battle-happy and at that time more or less on an even keel with Violet, thanks to Mrs Drake, had longed for a bigger family. When a second one did not arrive, distance set in and, after a few years, so did relief at no longer being on the front line.

Unlike Joan, who had placed herself fairly and squarely on the front line.

Joan had possessed an advantage. God. From the beginning, Joan had been in touch with him. She had been an exceptionally pious child, even in an age of piety, if you believe the depositions of Jean Waterin and Mengette Yoyart as they appear in the *Procès de condamnation et de réhabilitation de Jeanne d'Arc*. In his deposition, her godfather Jean Morel also states that often when Jeanne [*sic*] was supposed to be watching the cattle, she played truant to worship at the shrine of Our Lady of Bermont. God must have made life easier even in war-ravaged France, particularly if he sent instructions down via St Michael and St Catherine, and less frequently St Margaret.

Instead of battling on to the 7.33 to Waterloo, or with the school run, Joan had abandoned her patched red frieze dress, the traditional costume for women in the area, borrowed a tunic and hose and taken herself off to a bigwig in Vaucouleurs, Robert de Baudricourt, and badgered him into listening to her crazy idea of rescuing and crowning their moribund Valois dauphin. This being the age that allowed, encouraged, a dialogue with God and miracles, she succeeded, and set off for Chinon with six companions wearing a new set of clothes and a horse bought by the good people of Vaucouleurs. Note: The saddle was of a design that supported the small of the back and the thighs. Otherwise, how else would a peasant girl unused to riding have mastered such a mount?

The wool stuff of her newly acquired leggings would have rubbed unfamiliarly between thighs that had known only a skirt. She would have been aware of the different freedoms permitted by a shirt and doublet, the constriction of leather boots, the smell of harnesses and male sweat. Noise, too, would have afflicted Joan, accustomed as she was to the rural peace of the village. She complained later that her voices sometimes had trouble coming through because of it. Prue empathized with this as she read of Joan searching for a little peace among the clamour of conflict and communal medieval life. Today, she would have stood no chance at all against aircraft, breakfast television and the new, improved A303.

'Did you get the organic oats?' Violet enquired, as Prue was packing away yet another gigantic Saturday shop. It was the first week in March, and everyone was waiting for spring.

'Sorry, I forgot.'

'Camomile tea?'

'Oh, Lord.'

Violet pushed the sterilizer under the window and stacked tins of infant soya milk powder in the place where Prue usually kept the bread crock. Prue bided her time until Violet was occupied with the kettle, pushed the milk tins to one side and replaced the bread crock. She felt thoroughly childish.

Violet looked up. 'Were they in the way?'

'No,' said Prue coolly. 'But I keep the bread there.' Violet's expression prompted her to add, 'Oh, for goodness' sake, it doesn't matter where the bread goes.'

'Quite,' said Violet, 'that's what I thought.'

Emmy, Violet and Prue sat and drank coffee at the kitchen table. Once upon a time, Violet would have been drinking orange juice and demanding a story, a diversion she used to demand constantly.

If Prue had loved her – and she tried, she *did* try – Violet would have been fascinating. She had been a funny little girl, a great collector, comics, *Girl* annuals, cheap jewellery, shells, abnormally tidy and over-fond of fluffy toys. Each toy had a house in her bedroom, a shelf, a corner, an area of the bed and a second establishment downstairs, and it went

61

ill with Prue if they were moved. Every so often, Violet gathered up her menagerie of bears, cats, dogs and dolls, shut herself in the bathroom and washed them. The hair-dryer then whined continuously. Eventually, damp, groomed and fluffy, the objects of Violet's passionate care returned to their homes. The tidiness had created an extra barrier between stepmother and stepdaughter.

'By the way,' said Violet holding out her cup for refill, 'I've got the official letter today. Group Rights Director.'

The magnitude of this achievement was lost on Emmy, but Prue said, with unfeigned delight, 'Congratulations.'

'It's the one I really wanted.' Violet's red-tipped nails tightened on her cup. 'It's the most exciting publishing group in the business.'

'Will the house be ready in time?'

'Sorry, Prue, I forgot to tell you. Jamie told me last night. We exchange contracts on Monday and complete in two weeks. Jamie's making them work double quick.'

Dear God, only two weeks.

'Lovely,' said Prue. 'We should celebrate.'

At her end of the table, Emmy shivered. 'I'm freezing,' she said.

Prue met Violet's gaze and, for once, there was complete accord between the two women.

'You're not wearing enough,' said Violet.

That was the weekend when Prue first became concerned about Jane who had arrived back from school subdued and pale. Prue had overdone her concern, insisting on a double dose of tonic and supper in bed. This had pitchforked mother and daughter into a battle. Jane wished to stay up to watch *Home and Away*, *Neighbours* and *Eldorado* and Prue had said no. Jane had insisted on three good reasons as to why the ban was in force, and Prue had made the mistake of saying she did not want Jane's head stuffed with that rubbish. 'You don't want me to be left out,' Jane wailed as she went upstairs, 'everybody watches them. Anyway,' she added, 'we see them at school.'

This left Prue to reflect bitterly on the relationship between school fees and soaps. She came to the conclusion that the subject was so enraging that it was best not to dwell on it.

She was tackling the ironing after lunch on Saturday when Jane surprised her by sneaking up behind her and sliding her arms around her waist.

'Hallo, poppet,' Prue said.

Jane pressed her cheek into her mother's back. 'I've done my prep, Mum.'

This was Jane's apology. Touched by its elliptical approach, which was so typical of Jane, Prue inserted the tip of the iron under a shirt collar and the material wrinkled into creases. 'Bugger,' she said under her breath.

'I did an extra bit as well because it was easy.'

'Well done.'

Jane's arms tightened around Prue. 'Victoria's mum and dad are getting divorced, you know.'

Prue did not know. She plonked the iron down on its stand and swivelled round to face her daughter. 'That's awful. Poor Victoria.'

'She's quite happy. She says she can play them off against one another. Me and Sally have a bet that Victoria will have a pony by Christmas.'

This report did not accord with Prue's image of Victoria who was a shy, rather withdrawn child, and she ached to think of the bravado that had gone into her statement.

'And what would *you* aim for, Janey ... if you were playing Dad and me off against one another?'

Jane's eyes gleamed. 'You know what I want, Mum. A 389 computer. MSDOS, four megabytes of RAM. Windows ...'

Prue searched her daughter's face, so little and so unfinished, and smoothed back some hair from the unmarked forehead. It was a source of amazement that she had produced a creature of science and mathematics, of computers and suchlike when she herself cared for and knew nothing of these subjects. 'I should have known,' she said tenderly.

'Can we light a fire, Mum, and watch telly together?'

When Max came in from his walk, mother and daughter were settled in front of the drawing-room fire enjoying themselves. They made a good picture and he watched them fondly for a moment.

'Hallo, darling.' Max leant over the sofa and gave Jane a kiss.

Jane reached up a hand and Max tugged at her fingers. He pointed at the newspaper lying on the table in front of the sofa. 'Did you read that the pound's in a mess?'

Prue sat up. 'They won't put up interest rates, I hope.'

'It's possible,' said Max.

It was only then Prue registered that another figure stood behind her husband.

Quite by accident, Prue's and Jamie's eyes met, explored, and exchanged a message which neither quite understood.

Chapter Five

At last the Becketts had moved into their house in Austen Road. Prue had longed for their departure but, in the contrary manner of the human psyche, found the space left behind in Hallet's Gate empty and unsettling.

'It's odd,' she told Max as they wheeled the borrowed pram back to its owner, 'how ungrateful you are for getting the things you want.'

Max's expression was inscrutable. Then, looking straight ahead, he said, 'I'm grateful for getting what I wanted, even if it is obsessed by a saint.'

For a second Prue was blank, then she realized he was joking. She prodded him in the ribs. 'Unlike wine, Max, your wit does not improve with age.'

He laughed, and they walked on together and, because they were enjoying the walk, took the long way home.

But the peace was not to remain unbroken.

A couple of weeks later the telephone rang.

'Can you help, Prue, do you think?' Violet managed to make her request sound remarkably similar to a command, explaining that it was imperative that she attend the spring sales conference as a run-in to the new job. Apparently, the nanny hired for the week had phoned to say that, after all, she did not fancy the job.

Not fancy it? Violet was not often floored. Not *fancy* it?

was all she could manage at her end of the phone, the grail of the sales conference whisking out of sight. You *can't* do that to me, I have a job to do. Tough, said the defaulting nanny who, in contrast to MPs and civil servants who hold the balance of power in the country, holds the balance of power in a significant number of homes.

In Dainton, Prue toyed with the idea of saying no.

Violet, knowing she was at bay, changed her tactics. 'I'm desperate, Prue.'

It was true. She was desperate to get out and away and shake off her appendage. In her more anguished moments when she fell back on cliché, Violet thought of herself as a bird unable to take flight, caged and encumbered – which, of course, she was.

Prue checked out the *Prunus autumnalis*. Planted strategically so that washers-up at the sink – her – could benefit from its winter blossom, it was now past its best, but tanking up nicely underneath were the narcissi and chionodoxa she had planted at the last minute. London was another world. Not hers and, she suspected, dangerous.

'It's only from Tuesday to Thursday afternoon,' said Violet, who did, indeed, sound desperate.

Prue relented. 'I suppose I could do some work on Joan when Edward's sleeping.'

Violet refrained from replying that she thought it most unlikely. 'Of course,' she said in the tone she had found useful in New York when lying, business lies being part of business. 'I would be so grateful.' Gratitude was not an emotion she usually felt for Prue, but Violet was a strategist.

There was no one at Waterloo to meet Prue, not that she expected it, and the taxi queue was enormous. Nudging her case along with her foot, she took stock of the city, a station being as good a place as any to begin. As a child, Waterloo, to which she had journeyed frequently on school trains, had seemed immutable and unchanging, like the areas in her atlas stained pink which, her teacher insisted, represented decency and order.

Now the station was under wraps. Bits were falling off it and a skin of litter, leaves and dust overlaid the pavements. A couple of homeless men had set up base by the entrance. One of them had a puppy stuffed into the front of his coat, which was tied with string. The other breathed in greedy slugs from a paper bag and turned a drugged, drowning face towards passers-by who did their best to ignore him. Prue supposed he was in his twenties.

According to the taxi driver, Albert Bridge was out of commission, and life was a bloody nightmare. Prue sat in the taxi, swamped by a sea of cars. She sniffed at the benzine and exhaust, overcome by the miasma of houses and humans competing for existence in a confined area.

Colours in the city are cast in a different foundry. Leaves are heavy with yellows and ochres dripping acid tints into the greens. Dun-coloured cement pointing in brickworks is slicked by a powdering of carbon. Curved grey roof-tiles gleam in the rain; a flat counterpoint of greys sit alongside the harsh, unbeautiful red of London brick.

Prue pressed her gloved hand against the taxi window and rebellion at being there streamed through her fingertips and on to the glass. Was her protest at Violet? Or was she protesting about the fin breaking through the surface of the now calm, unstormy waters of her marriage?

A cyclist paddled alongside the taxi and flipped the wing mirror.

'Idiot,' said the driver, mildly, out of the window.

The Becketts' house was situated in a road wider than the others, in the area between Wandsworth and Clapham

Common. Prue was deposited outside a late-Victorian house with good proportions and a brown front door.

Violet had been hovering and opened the door before Prue had rung. 'Hideous colour, isn't it?' she said, referring to the front door.

Prue followed her into an open, light-filled hall, littered with painting equipment. Almost at once, she sneezed. From upstairs came a clatter of boots on bare floorboards and a volley of interesting language. Violet apologized.

'I thought you said nothing needed to be done to the house.'

'Well, you know how it is,' said Violet. 'In the end, Jamie needed a dressing room and the nanny must have her own bathroom. Some of the rooms needed decorating, and the kitchen wasn't quite as I wanted it, so it's being redesigned. Don't worry, they're working on the nanny bit at the moment and won't bother you.'

It is possible to know how you feel about a house when you step over the threshold, and Prue was interested in this one's incompleteness. By the time you enter them for the first time, most houses have settled.

'There's a good feel to the house,' said Prue.

'That's lucky.' Violet led the way into the kitchen. 'I'm not moving again for a long, long time.'

The kitchen was large, sunny and the floor had just been relaid with planks of sanded wood and varnished to mirror brightness. Prue negotiated a pile of builder's overalls and huge tins of varnish and sat down.

Violet loomed over her, a creature, Prue fancied, out of a Fuseli engraving, brooding darkly, wings straining for flight.

'Edward's in the next room, asleep. I've made up his bottles for the day and they're in the fridge. He should sleep for an hour or so. Give him a drink when he wakes.

After his lunch he likes a walk, then pray for six o'clock when you can put him to bed.'

'Bath?'

'If you like.' Violet seemed indifferent. 'Have some coffee.'

She disappeared and returned ten minutes later, groomed and made-up, wearing an olive wool suit, her eyes sparkling with a different light.

'Do you think you can cope, Prue?' Violet was straining to be gone.

Prue transferred her gaze from the garden (20 ft × 50 ft) which currently resembled a municipal tip. 'Good luck.'

Suddenly, momentarily unsure, Violet hugged her briefcase. 'I'll need it. I've got to make a good impression. Show them that the baby makes no difference at all.'

'I think that's impossible,' said Prue gently. 'You can't have a baby and pretend that nothing's happened.'

'I can,' said Violet, and the old, assured expression was back in place. 'By the way,' she added from the doorway, 'you'll have to buy something for supper. Northcote Road. The *A–Z* is in the hall. Alfalfa sprouts are in the fridge.'

Edward did not bother to wait for an hour and was yelling for his bottle within twenty minutes of his mother's departure. Prue gave it to him – there was no point in not and she had been blooded in the Baby-Knows-Best school. The afternoon walk was advanced by three-quarters of an hour but Prue enjoyed snooping. Anyway, the prospect of a supper composed entirely of alfalfa drove her shopwards.

Colonized by late-Victorian housing developers, the area had mouldered during the fifties and sixties but, clearly, was now enjoying a renaissance. Many of the houses had been painted in pastel colours, a backwash from the British love affair with the Mediterranean, and wreathed in fashionable plants, clematis and old roses definitely favoured over utilitarian mahonia and laurel. The effect reminded Prue of medieval gardens she had seen in Books of Hours, indisputably pretty but lacking robustness.

Pelmets were in fashion. Tart's-knickers blinds had been ousted in favour of swags, poles and ornate curtain rods. Velux windows sat fish-eyed in roofs so that neighbour, it seemed, was looking into neighbour.

Edward stirred in the pushchair and opened his eyes, which were now bright blue, blinked and, soothed by the motion of the chair, dozed.

'You little blighter,' Prue told him.

By the time she reached the butcher, she had decided that her taste in curtains was boring, and she should do something about it. On an impulse, she bought a copy of *Interiors*, which featured pages devoted to old Swedish furniture, swathed in muslin and photographed in light as white and sunny as a dream. They were delicious and beautiful, and utterly removed from her life.

Prue took the magazine back and exchanged it for *Good Housekeeping* and a part-work on computers for Jane.

The shop local to Austen Road turned out to sell French cheeses, Italian salami and extremely expensive vegetables. Next door was a florist whose window display was composed of lilies and mimosa, and the off-licence further down the street had Australian wines stacked in bins.

How like Violet. How clever she was at situating herself. No run-of-the-mill corner shop for her. No wedges of cheese wrapped in industrial strength cling-film, or one-size pop socks. All the same, Violet was right. These commodities exuded attraction. Vignottes and Chaumes cheese sitting on a bed of, admittedly, fake straw, pesto, Häagen-Dazs and Bach Flower Remedies exuded the allure of fantasy made real.

Back at the house, which seemed cold and dark, Prue sat

in the kitchen and fed Edward, conscious of the uncurtained window making a rectangle in the wall. Because he was tired, Edward fussed. Suddenly, two days seemed a long time.

She phoned Kate, at home in Dainton, and did not feel at all guilty at talking for half an hour at the Becketts' expense.

'You are kind,' said Jamie when Prue served him sausages with baked potatoes. 'We batten on you, I'm afraid. Do you mind if I start? I'm so hungry.'

They sat opposite one another at the table, with a candle stuck into a bottle. Prue was wearing a jersey in her favourite blue which allowed Jamie to see the outline of her breasts.

How soft were they? Softer and more yielding than Violet's?

Jamie made himself concentrate on his plate.

'Ketchup?' she asked.

They passed mustard, chased sausages around their plates and drank wine out of tumblers, because nothing was unpacked, and shared the kind of intimacy that is usually shared by people who know each other well.

Jamie talked about his work in the bank, and used his knife and fork to emphasize points. He talked about the Australian economy, the promise in Europe – 'still a bit iffy' – and the bogey of ERM. Prue described the protest against the motorway extension at Twyford, which was gathering momentum, and explained that she was concerned it might turn violent.

'I'm not sure how to act,' she confessed. 'I disapprove of violence but I feel driven to wield a stave.' She drank her wine. 'I know I'm talking liberal middle class . . . but it's the best I can do.'

The thinness of her aspirations struck Prue with depressing force, and if she expected to be reassured about the purity of her intentions, she was not. The motorway reference had reminded Jamie of a file he should have checked before leaving work and his attention wandered. Frightened that she was boring him, Prue came to a halt and then sneezed a couple of times.

'It's the dust, sorry.'

'Like Lara.' Jamie poured out more wine.

'Lara?'

'I lived with Lara before I met Violet. She always sneezed.'

Prue was unprepared for this knowledge, which hit her hard as bolts of jealousy generally do. 'I didn't know about Lara. What happened?'

'She met someone else, upped with her daughter and left.'

'I'm sorry.'

He looked down at his empty plate. 'I was too. But I went to America soon afterwards and met Violet, so I gained in the end.'

After a second or two, he looked up, his expression suggesting that he appreciated the sympathy. In fact, he had just noticed that the electric light gave Prue's hair fascinating highlights.

'Do you keep in touch with them?'

'I write to Jenny now and again.' Jamie sounded sad. 'I watched her growing up, you see.'

Prue drank several mouthfuls of wine. 'Do we regret mistakes as much as we regret the things we don't do?'

An ancient but renascent message was sent over the table. A second elapsed. Then another.

Jamie took his time to reply, rolling the possibilities around his mind, well aware that if you took even one tiny step across a boundary line it is impossible to return.

'You don't look as though you make mistakes, Prue. You're too careful a person.'

Was she? Prue asked the curtainless bedroom, and went to look at the London-scape spread beneath the window. Roofs touched by tungsten-light. Black tree shapes. Patches of gloom where the back garden met others. Who knew what was sliding through them? Foxes? Cats? Burglars?

At home, she thought with a catch in the throat, the earth would be wet from the rain and sodden mulch would be masking the spring growth. In the moonlight, her *Prunus* acquired the witchy grace of a Rackham painting, and silence spread under the night sky, with only the occasional fox bark to break it.

Prue let the sheet which covered the window drop. She had discovered that Jamie was thirty-nine. She had not imagined he was virtually her own age.

Nanny agencies kept Prue busy on the phone for a good part of the day, time she had wished to spend on Joan but which was filled instead with taking details of Alisons, Sarahs and Annes for Violet to consider. Were they NNEBs? Could they drive? None of them seemed ideal.

She rang Max and told him that it was the job to be in, car, flatlet, good pay, and you could demand the world. One had asked to bring her own baby, the other was into riding and wished to stable her horse at the nearest livery. Even the last failed to raise Max's interest. 'Tell me the news,' she begged.

'Met the new occupant of the Dower House, a Lady Truscott.'

'And . . .?'

'Silly woman. Huge pearls, nicotine-stained fingers and when I asked her what her husband had been she said, "A gentleman."'

Prue laughed with real enjoyment. 'Wonderful,' she said.

'When are you coming home?'

His need for her was palpable down the phone and Prue, once again, was conscious of the seethe and prick of rebellion.

'Friday morning,' she said. 'How's the cat?'

Max was not to be deflected. 'I hate meals from the freezer.'

'Darling. Half our meals are from the freezer.' She visualized him, hunched over the phone, performing his ritual dance with his glasses. 'Have a fry-up or something.'

'It's lonely without you.'

'Max, it's only two nights. What has got into you?'

His voice cleared. 'Nothing.'

'The baby's crying, I'll have to go.'

'Bugger the baby,' said Max, but Prue knew it was a good-natured cut-off.

Unable to settle to research, she spent the time while Edward slept rifling through Violet's glossy collection of cookery books. Her finger stopped on a recipe: to cold-press a tongue first scrub it, soak for half a day in cold water and cook. The tongue is ready when the skin along the surface has blistered, and the T-shaped bone at its root comes away easily. After this destruction, it is arranged in a suitable dish, port-flavoured jelly is poured over it and it is pressed down by a heavy weight until it is ready. It is completely unrecognizable when it is served.

Could the procedure be said to be a metaphor for certain types of wives?

Prue's finger released the page, and she moved on.

On Thursday morning, Edward woke late and refused his milk, screwing up his mouth and pushing aside the bottle. Tramlines dribbled down his cheeks and on to Prue's sleeve. She put the bottle down to examine him more closely – and a fist squeezed in her chest. There was a blue shade to the baby's mouth, and a red flush on cheeks normally like pale shells. He did not look well and when Prue took the minute hand in her own and gently felt the matchstick fingers, her flesh made contact with burning heat. Without thinking twice, she phoned the doctor.

After an interminable wait in a hot, noisy, overflowing surgery, a young and indifferent-seeming doctor took a look at Edward. Just a passing temperature, she informed Prue. Babies do that. It always seems worse than it is. Give him plenty of fluid and don't bundle him up in too much clothing.

Her coolness only intensified Prue's anxiety, otherwise she might have laughed at the cheek of the dewy-behind-the-ears patronage. Instead, she drove back to Austen Road and spent an uneasy morning hovering over the cot. From time to time, Edward wailed and his body twitched in between fractured dozing. Each time Prue forced Dioralyte down him, he vomited.

At half past three, Prue was once again on the phone to the doctor. The receptionist, who could detect genuine panic from 'panic', promised to talk to the doctor when she had a moment.

An hour passed. Prue sponged the little body with warm water and, in her fright, she imagined that flesh had already slipped from the bird-like bones, and the frog stomach was hollowing – like the poppyhead which ejects its seeds and dies.

Not to worry, that wretched doctor had said. Babies do this. Yes, they do. Babies do this and have died. Think, think of the millions of babies' bodies which have piled up during the centuries.

Edward seemed to appreciate his blanket bath, for he sighed after she had finished, tucked his hand up by his neck and fell asleep.

Prue got herself some tea.

Edward's piercing wails interrupted her and she rushed into the nursery. The baby was bright red and had been violently sick. Prue phoned Jamie.

'I think he needs to get to hospital.'

Jamie did not hesitate. 'Get a taxi to St Thomas's. I'll meet you there.'

He was waiting by the time Prue arrived, white and anxious-looking. 'I've cleared it with the receptionist,' he said, taking the baby from her. 'We go straight in.'

Prue discovered she was trembling.

Jamie held Edward while the doctor examined him. He looked up once to thank Prue, otherwise he concentrated on his son. Prue held her shaking hands tight, and went outside to wait.

Casualty was awash with people, sitting on benches in the corridor in various states of dejection. Each time a nurse or a doctor went by, they looked up. Along with their bodies, perhaps they were hoping that their spirits would be patched up as well.

Prue closed her eyes and opened them when Jamie emerged, walked over to her and took her hand in his. 'Don't fret. They think it's only a twenty-four-hour bug.'

He was followed by the doctor, and a nurse hovering at his heels carrying Edward.

'Mr Beckett, you can take him home now. We've given him a thorough examination and paracetamol to bring down his temperature. He is a little dehydrated so you must try to get some liquid into him. If you're worried, bring him back.'

They made the journey home in the taxi in virtual silence. Prue leant back against the seat and closed her eyes, luxuriating in relief. Her eyes opened a crack and she found herself observing Jamie, narrowed to a squarish shape which smelt of expensive aftershave and a whiff of cigar. Emptied of everything, she absorbed the contrast of his brown hair against his navy coat, the skin tones and the way in which his big, elegant hands emerged from his cuffs.

'Why are you looking at me, Prue?'

Prue's treacherous hands trembled in her lap. 'Am I?'

Light-headed and consequently reckless in the aftermath of adrenalin, Jamie leant over, pulled Prue towards him and kissed her.

'Oh, Prue, oh, Prue,' he muttered into the white skin of her neck, relief for his son translating itself into physical need.

She felt her own body burn with desire and knew that if she gave it only the slightest leeway, pandered to it in the minutest form, it would make her forget that she was someone else's wife, and that Jamie was her stepdaughter's husband.

Back at the house, Prue fed Edward boiled water and Dioralyte, and Jamie hunted for a bottle of sherry.

'It's only five o'clock but . . .' Prue drained her glass.

Jamie said he would ring Violet because she would want to come home. A conversation took place on the drawing-room phone with a great many pauses. Prue concentrated on Edward who was taking his time, the sherry warming her gullet, sweet and wonderfully welcome.

Jamie returned and poured himself a glass. 'Violet isn't coming back till tomorrow. It would be difficult to leave as there's a big dinner tonight, especially if Edward is over the worst.'

Prue found it impossible to gauge his expression. Instead she held out her glass for a refill.

'I can't,' Prue said gently when Jamie appeared in her bedroom in the small hours as she lay thinking about him.

He looked down at the coils of hair and rounded shoulder illuminated by the light from the corridor, and his gaze travelled down the shape under the bedclothes.

'No,' he agreed, but in his imagination he was imprisoning the full, tempting breasts under the white cotton and the unknown territory of her body with his own. He bent over, and brushed her cheek with a finger.

'Goodnight, Jamie.'

'Goodnight.'

Chrysalis-like, the sheets enclosed her body. She felt their weave against her skin, smelt the detergent and wool in the blanket. In the dark, the sheet across the window became a mask, hiding the slippery feelings and heated imaginations that raged behind it.

Prue had imagined that her desire centred solely on Max. It was a shock to discover that this was not true.

Violet arrived home on Friday morning. She stepped out of the taxi wearing a defiant expression and hugging her leather briefcase. Prue knew that look. It meant: I am not going to show that I feel guilty.

Brushing past Prue, Violet ran upstairs into the nursery. A couple of minutes later, she emerged holding Edward. 'He looks fine,' she called down. 'You gave me such a fright. I couldn't concentrate.'

You couldn't concentrate. Reminding herself of the scenes with Jamie, Prue fought with herself to give Violet the benefit of the doubt. After those, how could she climb on to the rock of moral superiority? It was hard work turning into a mother, a process that did not come automatically. Violet, as she had, needed the time to learn.

Was Prue overreacting? Lusting after your stepdaughter's husband, though bad enough, is not quite the same sin as neglecting a baby.

Talking to Edward in a breathy way, Violet came downstairs and went into the kitchen and put him in his chair. 'It wasn't very kind of you, baby, to get ill. I almost think you did it on purpose.'

She was aware that Prue would judge her, and knew she should have come home. But she had been frightened to leave, and equally frightened to return. She put Edward into his chair and surveyed the kitchen. 'Goodness, how untidy.' She began stacking the china on the draining board.

'Sorry,' said Prue, 'it's been a bit hectic.'

'Of course,' said Violet.

Prue made an effort to remove the constellation of saucepans that had migrated to the stove, and then thought: Dammit. 'Was the conference successful?'

Violet put out a foot and prodded Edward's chair. The baby juddered like an apple at apple bobbing. 'You know,' she said vaguely, 'lots of talks, too much to drink and far, far too much food. I'm sure I've put on masses.'

She was busy opening and shutting drawers, rearranging contents and stacking plates, with the result that Prue felt deeply inadequate.

'Did you impress the bosses?'

A smile spread across Violet's beautiful face. 'Yes, I think so. They were very nice about me. And there is some good business coming up.'

79

Prue produced the bit of paper with the doctor's name written on it, and the dosage for the Dioralyte. 'You should have this.'

Violet glanced carelessly at Edward who, mercifully, had stopped bobbing. 'I hope I won't need it.'

With obvious reluctance, she peeled off her olive jacket and draped it over a chair. 'Thank you, Prue, for all that you have done.' She spoke like a child at the end of the party. 'Do you want me to call a taxi?'

If a seed is planted it grows. No, that is not correct. A seed grows when the conditions are right. When there is water, when there is light. When there is a chance that the root, a rudimentary bud at first, can push out from the confining cotyledon and drive deep into the warmth and secrecy of the earth.

That is what Jamie had done. Planted a seed. And Prue did not want it to grow.

Chapter Six

Emmy did not require much time to think over Violet's phone call, inviting her to accept the post of nanny to Edward.

'*Pro tem*,' Violet added hastily (none of the Alisons and Sarahs having measured up to her standards), leaving herself leeway to say goodbye to Emmy if she found someone better. 'You might not like London. Or us.' She gave a laugh which suggested that the latter would be unlikely.

At Number 5 Hallet's Lane, Emmy stared into the mirror positioned above the Phone 'N' Sit table and grimaced. She moved her foot, sending a wave of static across the nylon carpet. 'I'll come,' she said.

Violet rattled out some details about pay, conditions and use of a car. Emmy kept on repeating yes, it all sounded fine but could she ask if Violet would deal with the PAYE?

'PAYE?' Violet's tone sharpened. 'I don't think that will be necessary.'

Emmy realized she had made a mistake. On the other hand, her rights were important – they were all she had. 'And National Insurance,' she added.

'Oh.' Violet became thoughtful. '*That* makes it a lot more expensive.'

Emmy thought it wiser not to comment.

Violet recouped. 'If you decide to stay on permanently, Emmy, then, of course, we will be putting you on PAYE.'

She was cursing silently, having relied on the grapevine that alleged that nannies preferred to be paid in cash.

'Thank you, Mrs Beckett.'

'Er ... Emmy, that being so, if you *do* stay on, I might reduce your pay a touch because of tax and insurance, which makes it a little expensive for us at the moment. I'm sure you understand, with the recession and everything.'

Lying b—, thought Emmy, and made conciliatory noises. How come Madam was so mean? She had plenty of money. Enough, as Anna pointed out with irritating frequency, to have a boob, hip and face job when the time came.

Question: Did having money make you meaner or were you mean in the first place? Never having had any, Emmy could not hazard an answer. As she moved through Number 5, dusting her mum's horse brasses from Devon, the blue Maltese glass and bulbous china cherub from Portugal, the problem occupied her.

No enlightenment, however, emanated from the silent lounge and hall. In the kitchen, early spring sunlight filtered on to foil rectangles which sat thawing under a tea-towel for tonight's microwave banquet. A solitary tea-leaf decorated the shining sink. Emmy removed it between her finger and thumb and the kitchen was perfect once again, scrubbed sterile and as ordered as a sergeant-major's kitbag. Suddenly, she felt desperate to get away, from the silence and the unyielding concordance of crimplene and nylon.

As the days lengthen with the approach of spring, it sometimes happens that the cold increases, and the last week in March had been icy. A hard chill hugged the bottom of the valley and, in defence, birds had gathered close to the houses. They were hungry and probably frozen. Emmy hauled a pair of secateurs out of her jacket pocket and headed for the holly tree at the end of the garden, which formed part of the hedge bordering the road. For some reason, the birds never touched it. Emmy cut off the largest branch she could without doing damage and backed on to the lawn where she stuck the branch into the grass. Then she retreated.

After a minute, the first berry-eating birds arrived hot-foot and tucked in. Hand on hip, Emmy watched. Eat up, she advised them silently. It's on the house.

Emmy headed up the road towards the airstrip which sloped up from the depression in which Dainton was sited. Up in the open, the frost which had closed in a week or so ago had rampaged unchecked and had burnt sections of hedgerow which gaped like lost teeth. A partridge ran across the field on Emmy's right and she came to a halt. Partridges would be paired off by now and if she was lucky she might spot some.

Most people had paired off by now.

Wasn't it better, though, to hold your life in your hands, cupped and shaped as you wished?

Emmy swung to her right and plunged into the tiny strip of wood that led up to Danebury Rings. Her feet sank into the softened earth and gathered mud as she passed. As she reached the foot of the steep rise, the first primroses greeted her.

She tucked her frozen, ungloved hands into her jacket, pulled it tight across her thin stomach and felt better.

The builders were creating a bathroom out of a cupboard and Mickey was regaling his team with a story to make a sex therapist blush when Emmy pushed open the spare bed-room door at Number 6 Austen Road with her foot. A flush stormed into her cheeks and, not at all sure what to do, she stood awkwardly with the heavy tray.

'Hang on, love.' The tall, glossy-skinned one with a pony-tail took pity. He detached himself from the Black and Decker and removed the tea-tray from Emmy. 'Don't listen to Mickey, he's a throwback.'

Was her face scarlet or bright scarlet? 'Thanks,' she said. 'I've heard it all before.'

'Have you, now?'

She liked pony-tails on men: they stirred a residual memory of childhood fairy tales, complete with illustrations of men in boots with flowing hair, where the maiden is saved, or is merely the helpless female swept away by a superior masculine force. Whatever. Emmy reckoned that being passive had its advantages.

Pony-tail winked at her. Why, he's beautiful, she thought. The counterpoint that never failed her echoed: And I am not.

Later Emmy – having sorted the kitchen, emptied the tumble-dryer, washed the floor and changed Edward – was watching the birds feeding on the fat she had hung from a branch of the sycamore tree. After a minute or two she became conscious that she was being watched and whipped round.

It was Pony-tail bringing the tray back. 'Thanks.' His physical presence filled the room – all hair, skin and bones covered with lean flesh. Beside him, Emmy was transformed into a delicate and tiny nymph, the maiden trapped on the rock waiting for rescue.

'Do you want seconds?'

He nodded and Emmy moved towards the kettle.

'What's your name?'

She told him and he replied that his was Angus and she suppressed a giggle for Angus always went with kilts.

'Are you interested in birds?' He pointed at the tableau outside.

'Love them,' she said, handing him back the tray.

Angus appeared to consider her reply. 'No accounting,' he said finally but his expression was kind. Emmy flinched, for she imagined it was the sort of kindness reserved for cripples and defectives.

'No accounting,' she agreed.

London was a shock to the system that kept Emmy reeling for the first weeks. How did people breathe in this air? How did they sleep with the noise, traffic, alarms, late-night talks in the streets, crashing milk bottles – and the constant light?

For much of that time, Number 6 Austen Road was in uproar. In places, the house resembled a building site, the baby was teething and fretful and Violet was too snappy and nervous to help her son.

Some things never change, and Emmy found herself at the beck and call of an employer whose rage for order was as bad as her mother's – a difficult situation since the builders made it their business to import an impressive percentage of London clay into the house.

'I'm growing shoulder pads on my knees,' Emmy confided to Anna on a long – and illicit because it was after nine a.m. and before twelve o'clock – phone call.

'Very sexy,' said Anna.

'How does she suppose I'm going to look after the baby if I spend my time on my hands and knees scrubbing?'

'Don't do it, Em.' Emmy could hear Anna inhaling cigarette smoke. She longed for a fag herself but Violet had laid down battle-lines and informed Emmy that if she ever caught her smoking that would be *it*.

London notwithstanding, Emmy did not want it to be *it*.

'What's her clothes like?' Anna performed another noisy exhalation in Emmy's ear.

'Must have cost a packet. Mind you . . .' Emmy paused. 'They don't look comfortable.'

'Yeah,' said Anna. 'Don't expect they stay on her very long.'

'Don't think she's that type.'

'Where do you shop?'

'Sainsbury's.'

'And . . .?'

'What?'

'The bill, stupid.'

'About two hundred quid. She's very fussy. The cleaning stuff is all ecological. Trouble is, it doesn't clean very well.'

Anna pressed for more details and Emmy obliged. Thus did the tom-tom beat out all sorts of private facts. If the employers of nannies and mother's helps ever considered the extent to which the detail of their lives, down to their chosen brands of soap powder, were in the public domain, they might have had second thoughts about working. Was it worth it? A salary in return for an itemized list of your habits, your knickers, the colour of your toothbrush and what precise terms you flung at your spouse when he came home drunk from a 'quick one after work'.

'Met anyone, Em?'

Emmy reflected on the lonely evenings spent upstairs with the black and white television ('Just till we can afford a colour one, Emmy'), tucked up with Bovril and a smelly gas fire because the heating did not *quite* reach that far up the house. 'No,' she said.

Apart from registering that she was pleasant and capable, Jamie did not pay much attention to Emmy. He was thankful that the problem of childcare had been dealt with and, once satisfied that his son was in good hands, switched off. But Emmy watched Jamie and compared him with the men with whom she was familiar.

For a start, Jamie took a lot of stick from Madam. On the other hand, he was capable of dealing with it and telling her to get lost. From time to time, he helped out with Edward and got up in the night and changed nappies. He even did his bit at breaking eggs into a bowl and whisking them up. Accustomed to bad-tempered men, Emmy found his good humour puzzling, then suspicious, then seductive. Nevertheless, just in case she was tempted to elevate Jamie to sainthood, he succumbed at intervals to patches of irritation. They tended to occur when Jamie and Violet both arrived back late from work, played out and hungry. Edward, of course, was always at his worst.

'You deal with him,' Jamie ordered Violet one Friday evening. 'I'm going to have a bath.'

'I'm too tired,' said Violet flatly. 'Anyway, why does it have to be me?'

'Because you're his bloody mother, that's why. Although no one would guess it.' Jamie ripped off his tie.

'That's outrageous and unfair,' said Violet.

'Is it?' said Jamie in a dangerously quiet voice.

Edward's screams interrupted further discussion and Emmy, who was hanging about in the corridor feeling useless and a gooseberry, retreated to her room. Later, percolating through the *Coronation Street* theme, she heard sounds of impassioned argument over who should do what, which intensified until she heard Violet clattering down the uncarpeted stairs.

She wished she was not living on top of the Becketts and she wished she did not have to be a fly on the wall.

At seven o'clock on Monday morning, Emmy tramped blearily downstairs to join Jamie and Violet in the kitchen.

'She has a long enough day as it is, Violet,' she caught Jamie saying as she arrived in the hall. 'You can't ask her to do any more.'

'Try me. She sits here and eats us out of house and home.' (Emmy started at that one. Whatever else she may have been, her appetite was modest.) 'She is warm, housed, uses our phone, makes free with the car, it won't hurt her.'

Emmy grasped the banister. It was bad enough breaking into someone else's intimacy – and at breakfast time at that – worse if you were the subject of discussion. It made her feel raw and jumpy. Emmy had no intimacy to safeguard and no pacts to make over the toast. But although she did not mind her solitude, indeed sought it, she did mind being discussed as if she was a fitting for the bathroom or kitchen.

Violet was scraping vegetable spread on to her wholewheat toast as Emmy entered. Jamie looked up.

'Hallo, Emmy. We were just talking about you.'

Still at war with her perm, Emmy had scraped her hair on to the top of her head and anchored it with an elastic band. Bits of it fell down her neck, which Emmy was aware resembled a plucked chicken's. It was, however, a remarkably slender neck.

Violet rubbed at hers as she spoke. 'Emmy, would you be prepared to put the baby to bed? I *know* I said I would do it, part of the bonding process and all that. But, frankly, Edward leaves me very unbonded and I feel exhausted. If you could do the evenings, then I can cope with the mornings.' Violet's manicured nails were like scarlet petals on white silk.

Emmy shot Jamie a look. Whatever he was thinking, he was keeping quiet. He returned her look and, suddenly, Emmy felt her mouth twitch. Jamie did not appear to have the situation under control. Despite this, Jamie's mouth also curved at the corners and she felt that she and Jamie understood one another.

'If it'll help, OK.' Emmy sat down, remembered that the

Becketts drank coffee and she liked tea, and got up again. Jamie took refuge behind the *Financial Times* and Violet quivered almost visibly with impatience to be gone – out and away. She cast a look at her husband.

'Men have it easy,' she said, clicking her nails on her coffee-cup, and her bitterness was both shocking and ageing.

'For God's sake,' said Jamie, and retired into the paper.

Emmy ate a piece of toast and drank lapsang souchong, which she did not like, preferring plain old teabag.

It was odd, she confided to Anna later, being a sodding Peeping Tom. She wasn't quite sure what she felt about the Becketts. 'I mean,' she said, 'they get quite lovey-dovey and all that,' but she wondered if they got on as well as it first looked. When ordered to explain, Emmy said she didn't know what she meant.

She returned from taking Edward on his afternoon constitutional, as long as the cold would permit, and was unloading baby and shopping in the hall when Angus peered over the banister.

'Thought you'd done a runner,' he said. Emmy gave an uncertain laugh, conscious that the tip of her nose was raw. Worse, it might have a drip.

'I've got something for you.'

Emmy heaved the enormous bundle that Edward made in his outdoor things into her arms and followed Angus into the kitchen. He pointed through the window and Emmy's gaze followed obediently until it rested on the sycamore. Her eyes widened. Nailed on to a lower branch was a small wooden platform. She turned to Angus and he nodded. Clasping Edward under one arm, Emmy fumbled to open the back door and flew down the lawn.

If rudimentary, the bird table had been made with care and sited out of reach of the cats.

'I thought the birds should eat in comfort.' Angus stood behind her as Emmy inspected his work.

Emmy felt a smile begin at the corners of her mouth, pulling them gently but inexorably wider and wider, until she was smiling all over her face. In her head, the sound of a nightingale in full throttle trilled clear and joyous.

'Thanks,' she said, shifting the baby. 'That was dead nice of you.'

In the days that followed, however, Emmy began to wish that Angus had not singled her out. Not that the bird table did not give her pleasure. It did – a lot. She spent a great deal of time gazing out of the window at the tits and yellowhammers and shouting at the starlings to get lost and to pick on someone their own size.

No, it was because Angus had opened a floodgate to a different type of self-consciousness, whose newness acted as an abrasion on soft skin, rendering her uneasy, expectant and vulnerable all at the same time. Why had he made the bird table? It can't have been friendship. It could have been impulse. Or . . . surely to God he didn't fancy her?

How could he?

This was one problem on which Emmy did not consult Anna and remained silent.

One morning, having disposed of the breakfast things and made a stab at the ironing, Emmy sneaked upstairs, washed her hair and larded on conditioner and spent an uncharacteristic amount of time drying it.

The results were not much different. Emmy fingered a lock and assessed the image in the mirror. At least, it *felt* soft – she had been afraid that the perm would leave her with a permanent Brillo pad on her head. Then she searched for a sweater which had some pretensions to style.

Her efforts were wasted for Angus did not turn up with the team that morning. Emmy spent the day in an uncomfortable state when every nerve was on red alert. Was he going to come? If not, why not? Perhaps he had moved on to another job?

She made tea for the team as often as she dared without overdoing it and padded upstairs with the trays in the hope of discovering some information. It was not forthcoming.

As she gave Edward his evening bottle, Emmy debated fiercely with herself. Was she *so* deprived, *so* insecure that a small gesture (which he would have forgotten by now) started her thinking she was a cross between Meryl Streep and Madonna? OK, nice gestures were thin on the ground, but that was no reason to prance around wiggling her bottom.

Where was her famed liking for independence? Solitude? For the rewards of organizing her life just as she pleased?

Emmy's highly developed instinct for self-preservation told her that blokes spelt trouble.

Edward choked and she ripped the bottle out of his mouth and held him up while she dealt with the paroxysm. After he had regurgitated enough to float the London docks, Edward resumed a normal expression. His eyes travelled up to Emmy's face. He studied it, blinking now and then and breathing noisily in through his mouth. Who are you? he appeared to be asking and Emmy found herself grinning. Edward blinked again, awarded Emmy a ravishing smile and pulled himself into a sitting position, using Emmy as an anchor.

'My God,' said Emmy. 'You little devil. You've never done that before. Wait till I tell your mum.'

On the face of it, Mum did not seem interested. 'At least he's developing normally,' she said. 'We need a reward for all the hard work.'

Having just got in from work, Violet was burdened by a long camel coat and a bulging briefcase. She fiddled with her gloves (Italian, black leather), squatted down, stuck her face towards her son's and parted her lips. Edward did not care for this – perhaps his mother had startled him – and wailed.

'Oh, no,' said Violet in a resigned fashion. 'We're in for it.'

On Sundays Emmy was free. Technically, Saturdays were too, but Violet had pleaded with her to help out, just for the first few weeks while she settled into the job, and promised that if Emmy stayed on permanently the contract proper would be drawn up.

'It's either that, or I'll have to get Prue up to help,' she said when Emmy showed distinct signs of non-cooperation.

'Mrs Valour?' Emmy said stupidly.

'Yes, my stepmother. I said that, didn't I? I really don't want her around unless I have to.'

'Oh?'

'She's ... she's not very good with children. As well I know. I use her only when I have too.' Violet sounded strained.

As far as Emmy was aware, Mrs Valour appeared to be a warm, comforting and more than adequate mother. She raised her eyebrows and started to fold a stack of Babygros. Better not to enquire closely about how many pots were calling kettles black.

That Sunday, she got up late and, armed with the A–Z, let herself out of the house. In her bag were two weeks' worth of wages which she had not had an opportunity to broach. The A–Z informed her that Clapham and Wandsworth Commons were close and because she was hungry for a sight of some green she decided to explore.

Emmy spent a reasonable half-hour circuiting Wandsworth Common, watching parents masterminding toddlers and children on tricycles and skateboards. Dog-owners were exercising every kind of breed and the keep-fit brigade was out in force.

Emmy was curious. Londoners seemed to be so much more aware of themselves. In Dainton, the village people lived, worked, pottered and walked without thinking about their image. She avoided the puddles dug by bicycle tyres and the quagmire that spread from the toddlers' play area and, hungry for breakfast, made for the terrace of shops. Once there her heart sank for it was very smart with a wine bar, and a restaurant that looked expensive. Not a McDonald's in sight. Emmy's skin goosefleshed with fright. She could not go into any of those places. Not with those glossy joggers, mothers and dog owners.

The only place remotely approachable was the newsagent and Emmy went in to buy the *Mail on Sunday*. When she emerged, she had persuaded herself not to be intimidated and made her way to the brasserie and ordered coffee and a sandwich. The coffee arrived all fluffed up and sprinkled with chocolate and the sandwich was made from French bread.

Emmy stared at these with a new and acute insight into how an alien might feel when he arrived on earth. She took a bite and the sandwich filling spilled over and dropped yellow egg dollops on to her jeans.

She walked back past big Victorian houses and past a pub whose windows glittered. A group of people stood outside by the railings, bikers in leather with serious leather boots and lots of fastenings. One of them had his back to the road and Emmy's stomach contorted for she imagined she recognized the big back and the pony-tail.

Head down, she hurried on past. Whoever it was did not look round.

Chapter Seven

Freud suggested that we forget things, lose things or omit to finish them because we really wish to do so. If this is true, the Lost Property Office in Baker Street is a very interesting place indeed, and those mountains of homeless umbrellas, briefcases, handbags and artificial limbs, plus the items left off shopping lists and the unwritten thank-you letters constitute an excellent but unwritten history of humanity.

Prue had left a jumper behind in Austen Road.

'Typical,' said Max folding his arms across his chest when she told him. Since he felt fondly tender about Prue's occasional lapses, and enjoyed the manifestation of what he considered a mild dottiness, and Prue was aware of this, she had not, in the past, minded Max's mildly patronizing attitude. Indeed, she had not considered it as such.

Apparently, the relativities of the position were changing and, in this instance, she did mind. Yes, there was an unfinished tapestry in her work basket, *circa* 1984. Yes, she did mean to go back to the art classes, *one* day. And, yes, Joan of Arc *was* waiting to be written. But, she protested hotly, ramming her weekend case back into the cupboard, anyone who runs a house, produces a meal each night, has a job (granted part-time) and does more than her bit with flower rotas, village fêtes, and masterminds the 'Teddies for Tragedy' sew-in could reasonably expect to be considered organized.

'I think you're most unfair,' she finished.

Max blinked at his wife's unaccustomed tartness, looked blank for a second or two, and then a wariness crept into his face which Helen would have recognized. Prue did not.

'Sorry, darling. That was a bit tactless.' Max unfolded his arms and held out his hand and the white slash of Helen's wound caught her eye. 'I expect coming back after the dazzle of London is a let-down.'

'Dazzle of London? Max, I spent the whole time changing nappies and coping with a sick baby. Don't be witless.'

Max went quiet. He turned on his heel and left the room. Prue heard him later, moving around the study. She heard, too, the soft clink of cold metals and smelt Rangoon oil, so she knew what he was doing.

Jamie left it a week. The telephone rang at Hallet's Gate and he suggested that Prue and he meet for lunch when he could hand over the jumper.

Prue struggled to say, 'Please put it in the post,' and failed. 'I'm coming up to do some research next Wednesday.'

'We owe you a big thank-you, Prue, especially for your suggestion about hiring Emmy as the nanny. How about the Ivy?'

Prue would have needed to have possessed the detachment of a St Augustine, sated to the point of asceticism, to say no.

'Yes,' she heard herself say, resolving to sort out a few points with him. '*Yes*, please.'

When she arrived at the Ivy her jumper was waiting, exquisitely packed in tissue, in a smart carrier bag. In it, Violet had also put several give-away samples of face creams from one of the most exclusive and expensive make-up houses as a thank-you present. 'I thought you should try these', she had written. 'Thank you again.'

Prue replaced them carefully at the bottom of the bag. 'How thoughtful,' she said.

Flushed from a struggle with the *A–Z* and the briskish walk from the London Library, she sat down at the table, spread her napkin over her knees and realized she had made a mistake. If a course of action is likely to change the image of ourselves and our lives that we carry tucked into our minds, then it is as well to read the government health warning. Within seconds, Prue knew that this lunch – knives, forks, some meat, a salad, a bit of bread – would be a profoundly disrupting experience, and the needle carefully balanced between the poles of contentment and tormenting yearnings would be set quivering.

Why did she do it? Why did she sit there, innocent of her understated beauty and its effect, dressed in a grey crêpe wool suit and white blouse, and eat the lunch?

Who knows? Perhaps it was something to do with the search for St Joan. For a second, Prue was back scrutinizing Decari's mezzotint of Joan's burning. Already, the toes were disintegrating, the bony, slender fingers (this was a highly idealized representation) cramping in agony, and Joan herself was translucent and insubstantial, like a photographic negative.

She directed her attention at Jamie and, once again, his likeness to the younger Max nagged at her. 'I gather this is the place to be.'

'It is,' he replied. 'And I intend to be smug about the ease with which I procured a table.'

Prue decided she was impressed by the close proximity of two actors and a television mogul. 'Wait till the WI and Kate hear about this.'

Jamie gave her a look usually reserved for clients who wished to play the coy game. 'Prue, do I look taken in by the hick-comes-to-town bit?'

Prue's eyes were hidden suddenly by her eyelids. Behind them coalesced a picture of Joan riding away from Vaucouleurs, an ignorant, unlettered peasant girl with ideas above her station, struggling to master a warhorse and the unfamiliarity of her longed-for breeches.

'You should be,' she said coolly. 'I am from the country. And the WI has a healthy interest in most things.' She sipped her wine. 'You're being rude about them.'

Jamie sent his knife spinning in a circle and watched the flash of silver. 'Yes, I was,' he said.

She enquired after Violet and the new job, and then how Jamie's new job was going. 'What *qualities* do you need for it?' Prue was anxious to understand what an asset manager did. She cut a piece of *carpaccio* and ate it slowly.

Jamie was amused, then intrigued, by her interest. 'Energy. The nerve to know when to act when the consensus is right, and that's difficult. You have to play devil's advocate, and keep your ear finely tuned to what's going on.' In contrast to Prue's slow progress, Jamie's Caesar salad disappeared rapidly. The energy that he cited flowed over the table and sucked her in, pulling her, unresisting, along. Jamie was over twenty years younger than Max and it made a difference. Jamie was expanding: his knowledge, his job, his life. Max less so. As he had once remarked when they had talked about his retirement in 1997, he had finished climbing the mountains and was now on the plateau. At the time, Prue had not understood.

It is a matter of luck when you meet someone. Prue smiled across the littered table at Jamie who smiled back. It was luck whether or not that person had reached the same point as you, and bad luck if you were too far ahead.

Jamie made a joke. Prue laughed. Then she became quiet, and so did Jamie. Holding her gaze, Jamie offered her a second piece of bread from the basket which she accepted.

'Sleepy Prue,' he said.

Her eyes widened at his tenderness, and the bread turned to stone between her fingers. Dressed in that deceptive grey, Prue Valour gazed, with an abundance of . . . what was it? . . . illicit interest and delight, at her stepdaughter's husband and, for once, felt remarkable.

She knew suddenly that she needed to have everything quite open and honest between her and this man. It was important that the dark things, the past and its accretions, its mistakes, should be laid on the table between them. 'I don't know what Violet has told you, but she was cruel to me sometimes,' she said with a rush, breaching a dam she had resolved would never be breached, but impelled by an honesty that determined he should see her worst side. Now. Before it went any further. 'And I wish I could say that I don't blame her, but I did mind. Still do. That is not to suggest that Violet did not suffer. I know she did, and badly.'

It was not a pretty piece of self-justification, but Jamie had a Lara in his past, and understood what prompted Prue's confession. Vulnerability always stirred him, and Prue looked so woundable, and so embattled by a complicated family situation, not unlike a child herself. 'You tend to see things the way you're told them,' he said, 'and I had no reason not to accept Violet's version.' He wiped his mouth with his napkin and threw it down on the table. 'Violet never said *that* much, you know.'

'I'm sorry about the disloyalty,' she said quickly. 'It's unforgivable. Yours, I mean, in listening to me. It's not your fault, and you didn't start the conversation.'

He lifted and let drop the crushed linen. 'If we accept truths about those we love, does it make us disloyal?'

'"I hate you, Prue. He didn't want you. He wanted Mummy but she's dead."' Prue repeated the words that had reverberated in her mind for so long, and which she had kept hidden from Max because she knew she should not pay attention to them. But she had.

Equally, her loyalty at this lunch, or lack of it, was past retrieving, and the intimacy of the confession had ... well ... she drank more wine very quickly, an erotic compulsion to it.

Daddy doesn't really like you. He loves me and he wants Mummy only she's dead. Granny says she thinks Daddy married you because you were convenient.

'I was cruel, too, Jamie. First from ignorance then, perhaps, because she hurt me so often. It made me understand that being innocent doesn't prevent you being wicked.'

Jamie listened in silence. Then he refilled her glass.

'Sorry,' she said. 'That's enough of that. I won't mention it again.'

No fool, Jamie understood when it was time to back off. Besides, it was a long time ago, before he was on the scene. He steered the subject away from Violet and, because his work was never far from his thoughts, asked her if she thought the City had changed.

A little surprised, and disarmed, Prue considered. People tended to solicit Max if they wanted an opinion, and Prue if they wanted help with the school-run or harvest-supper. It was habit, and Prue forgave male chauvinists and related species, like maiden aunts, for she herself was as habit-bound as they were. Still, she had felt some resentment in the early days and then grew used to it, as women did the layer of fat on the hips.

'What do I think?' Prue prodded into action a brain that

felt as murky as Loch Ness. 'I think recent events show that politics doesn't influence the City any more. Money markets influence politics.'

'Politicians are past their sell-by date?'

'Sort of.'

'Is that a good thing? At least, we elect politicians.'

Prue's attention was caught by a blonde in a short black suit settling herself at an adjacent table. Pulled back by a tortoiseshell clip, her streaked hair framed a face cherished by artifice into plate-glass flawlessness. She was as unlike Prue as it was possible to be.

She returned to unemployment and the City's underbelly. '"The centre isn't holding,"' she remarked.

'That's a quotation, isn't it? I can't remember where from.'

'Nor can I.'

Joan might have said the same thing, except she was not given to philosophy and mysticism. France was in a mess, Domrémy was in a mess, its church partially destroyed. How did she feel about her tranquil, fertile Meuse valley as she watched dawn slide over the dew-laden meadows and tear apart the mist draped over the famous *bois chenu*? What did she think after the Anglo-Burgundian band had swooped down on the cattle and plundered the church? That the centre was not holding?

Jamie talked on about the Russian aid programme, a junk-bond king's deal with the courts to reduce his sentence, and the rise of the new right in Germany which had grabbed 13 per cent of the vote. Prue listened to the world being dealt with across the lunch table – economics, high finance, bomb explosions, the politics of greed, aid and consensus. Such a big place, the world, in which small acts repeated themselves until they became huge – greed, power-seeking and polluting habits.

Jamie was in his stride. Prue listened and interjected now and again, and it seemed to her that a transparent bell-jar lowered itself over the table, trapping them inside its shiny, revealing dome. Prue knew she should beat at the sides to be let out, even smash through them, but did nothing.

Afterwards, they walked down St Martin's Lane and Jamie asked Prue why she was so interested in Joan.

'Because she practised the art of the impossible, I suppose,' she said.

When she looked back through the window of the taxi into which Jamie had handed her, he was standing quite still, looking at the pavement. Nothing had been said about the shaming incident in the other taxi, or what had taken place afterwards.

The interlude is over, it is closed. Prue sat back. Cradled and protected as she had chosen to be, she now understood that passion could arrive out of the blue, like a bunch of flowers from Interflora with a tag on it saying: Your turn.

Jane's rats were giving problems. When had they ever not? thought Prue, disloyally reflecting on their brief, but incident-strewn, careers. Not only did they act as a magnet to Bella the cat – and the danger of a rat holocaust was ever present – but they had acquired a taste for liberty. Thanks to Jane, in whose scale of priorities animal comfort ranked highest, the rats took morning and evening constitutionals around her bedroom, driving Prue to shampoo the carpet at regular intervals and to reassure herself constantly that domestic rat droppings could not possibly be harmful.

Worse: a rat's life runs out fast and, for the past fortnight, Toffee had been ailing. When Prue picked up Jane that Friday, Jane insisted they took him to the vet.

'He's ill. I *know* he's ill.' Jane pressed her nose against the wire cage where Toffee's tail stuck out cold and limp from a pile of shredded newspaper.

Prue bent down and studied Toffee. Her heart sank. 'OK. Let's take him to the vet.'

Jane's expression was a compound of distress, fear – and complete reliance on her mother. 'Do you think he'll be all right?'

Do you lie to reduce a child's terror? Should you erase that look, which strikes straight to an adult's heart, for the sake of few minutes' grace? If Jane suffered, Prue suffered, and she was never sure if she lied to ease Jane's pain or her own.

In the event, the journey to the vet proved to be Toffee's last. By the time they had manhandled the cage into the surgery, he was dead. Prue would long remember Jane's cry of anguish, and the sight of her daughter sitting on a plastic chair surrounded by a clutter of *Country Lifes* and give-away magazines clutching a dead rat to her chest.

'I'm trained in bereavement management, Mrs Valour,' whispered the vet, gently disengaging Toffee, 'I'll deal with her.' In his experience, humans grieved more bitterly for their animals than for other humans – it was amazing how many widows became merry. He produced a cardboard box from a pile under the counter for Toffee's coffin and laid him gently in it.

'Come and choose the label to put on it,' he invited Jane, closing it up. 'You must write his name and his dates.'

'If you want any help, Mrs Valour, in the grief management – it takes a little time you know – come and see me,' he said as he examined Buttons, the survivor, whom he pronounced fit and well. Just a little top-up of vitamins to make sure, he said, producing an enormous syringe and an equally enormous bill.

'What will Buttons do without Toffee?' Tears washed in a sea down Jane's cheeks. 'He'll be so lonely.'

Prue's own throat jammed up at this point, and she cursed the day the rats had entered the house. 'Perhaps he won't notice too much, darling. It's not like a human being.'

Jane interrupted her crying to stare at her mother, and Prue felt as if she had been chastised with a whip.

'How do you know, Mum?'

She drew her daughter close. 'I don't, darling, but I think there is a good chance he doesn't feel like us.'

Jane clung to Prue. 'It's so awful that everything has to die. Why do they?' and added, 'Toffee wasn't doing anything. Just living in his cage.'

Prue stroked the wet face. 'People have been asking those questions since time began and I don't know the answers.' She thought for a second or two. 'You might think this odd, but death improves life, Janey.'

Perhaps, she reflected, piloting a still weeping daughter into the car, a rat mortality in the home is a useful aid in the teaching of metaphysics to one's offspring.

Jane got up on Saturday having slept badly. Pale and heavy-eyed, she spent the morning hanging over Buttons in his cage. At lunchtime, Prue went upstairs to investigate.

The bedroom resembled a bomb-site, but Prue bit her lip and merely drew back the curtains. She bent down to pick up a pair of rollerboots apparently left in the middle of the room with express intent to kill.

'Lunch,' she said. 'Didn't you hear me calling?'

Jane looked up from the cage and Prue's irritation vanished. Her daughter's eyes were underlined with what a previous au pair had termed 'suitcases'. From long habit, projections of the direst kind – anaemia, leukaemia – surged into Prue's mind.

'Are you feeling all right?'

'Fine.'

Jane was lying. Prue sat down on the bed and studied her. 'Everything OK at school?' This time the hesitation was obvious and enlightenment (with relief) dawned on Prue. She patted the space beside her. 'Tell me what's going on.'

Jane tensed, and Prue divined that a battle was being waged between keeping up the pretence and the comfort of casting her troubles on to her mother.

'Everyone hates me.' Jane made the confession sound shameful. 'They all tease me.'

'Ah.'

'Nobody wants to be my partner. I was left by myself at CDT lesson and Miss Cook had to do it with me. I thought I'd die.' Jane slumped against Prue's shoulder. 'If I died at least I'd see Toffee.' Jane tried hard to stop her lip trembling, and she said, 'I don't care really, Mum.'

Any suggestion of attack on their daughter drew elemental feelings from both Max and Prue, chief among them desire for vengeance, mixed with hurt for the child. It did not matter how often Prue lectured herself, and Max, on being too emotional, or that Jane needed to learn some lessons for her survival or that they, the parents, could not, should not protect her. Not trusting herself to speak, she took Jane's hand in her own and rubbed her thumb up and down the palm.

'Alicia hates me, and she makes everybody else say I'm stupid and ugly. Even Lydia.'

Technically, Lydia was Jane's best friend, with whom she had swapped wrist snappers and, in a major demonstration of best friendship, Julip Horses. Prue concentrated on achieving a perspective while suppressing the wish to shake Alicia until her teeth rattled.

'What shall I do, Mum?'

The virus of hate in the fourth form was as disfiguring and contagious as smallpox, and here it was disfiguring her eleven-year-old daughter's face as surely as the evil blotches. Prue cradled Jane's head between her hands, feeling the bony plates of the skull as if it was her own, and kissed it.

'Listen to me. It won't last. Nothing ever remains the same. I know, it happened to me.'

Jane went rigid and still against her mother. 'Did it, Mum? Did it really? You're not just saying that?'

'I begged Granny and Gramps to take me away from my school. They didn't, and I discovered that being unpopular is like a switchback. Sometimes you are, sometimes you aren't. I bet you next term Alicia hates someone else.'

'A whole term, Mum.'

'Listen. If you show you mind, Alicia will make it worse. She wants you to look miserable, so don't. And tell her to shut up if she attacks you. Bullies don't like to be told to shut up.'

Jane appeared to be absorbing the advice. Prue breathed in the smell of her daughter – a combination of Prue's best jasmine soap and cheap shampoo – acutely conscious of the growing body against hers. Love flowed out of her in a hot, aching tide and lapped the suitcase-eyed little face, unformed hands and too-thin shoulders.

Please (God?), please, see to it that I carry on protecting her until she's big enough to cope.

'Just one thing, Janey. If they start on someone else, don't forget what you've felt. Don't forget what it feels like to be miserable.'

'No, Mum.'

Even if they resemble a cross between Little Nell and Barbie, children are not natural Christians. Abnegation was for adults and even then it was comparable to a white Christmas: you should not bank on it. Prue was not going to bank on it.

Jane grabbed Prue's proffered handkerchief. 'Thanks, Mum,' she said in a small voice. 'I don't know what I'd do without you.'

Never, ever will I take risks with Jane, resolved Prue. She is my absolute responsibility.

Never, ever.

Jamie telephoned.

Prue gripped the receiver until her knuckles turned white.

'Next time you're up, perhaps we can have lunch again?'

She shut her eyes and thought of Jane. 'I don't think it's a good idea,' she addressed her corpse-like knuckle, and thought, If I bang you hard against the table perhaps it'll kill the devil that has got into me. She was taking the call in Max's study, facing the photographs on his desk. One was of a family group – she and Max with Jane between them. Max was looking towards Prue, fondly and she now perceived, a little possessively. Her knees felt weak, and her heart was pounding. She inhaled deeply and continued. 'I think you know why.'

The pause at the other end of the line became ominous with unsaid words. She pictured it as a summer sky grown plum with incipient storm.

'You don't have to worry, Prue.'

With breathtaking fickleness, Prue's emotions did a *volte-face*. She had been wrong, after all – the kiss in the taxi had been one of pure relief from tension, only that. The nocturnal visit a politeness in a circle that took making love as one did meeting for a drink, or for a meal. Not wishing to insult her after the taxi episode, Jamie had made it a point of honour to invade the bedroom – from which he undoubtedly retired in relief. That was it. Jamie had not wished to hurt her feelings. All that had been required of Prue to extricate herself from a solecism was to hide them. Instead she had blundered. In the blessed privacy of the study, she balled her fingers into a fist and knocked it against her stomach hard.

'I'm sorry. I made a mistake.'

'No, you didn't.'

She found herself smiling like an idiot with relief. You've gone mad, Prue Valour. Mad and dangerous.

'But you're right, Prue. Lunch is probably a bad idea.'

The study seemed very cold and dusty and the silence that followed the replacing of the receiver an ungrateful one. Prue studied one of the photographs. She had been thinner in those days and it had suited her. She studied her younger image critically, comparing it to the photo of Helen that also sat on the desk.

'I don't like you at all', she told the beautiful countenance for the umpteenth time, 'and, dead, you have been nothing but a menace.' Helen's glistening eyes and scarlet lips did not move. Neither did a tremor disarrange the shining hair.

Prue picked up Helen's photograph and placed it at the back of the desk so that it was partially obscured by one of Max at a company dinner.

At his end of the phone, Jamie sat in his office twirling the biro stamped with the bank's logo around and around between his finger and thumb.

'Daydreaming?' asked Dyson, one of his fellow asset managers, putting his head round the door. 'Of the millions you're going to make?'

'I was thinking about clichés.'

'Good God.' Dyson parked himself on the chair in front of Jamie's desk. 'Have you got the answer to the great cliché of the economy?'

Jamie was suffering from a sense of shock at his own behaviour. 'Just because a cliché is a cliché it doesn't mean you should underestimate it.'

'Good God,' repeated Dyson, unimpressed.

Chapter Eight

The alarm shrieked into the darkness and tore Violet from sleep. For a few seconds she lay motionless, flattened and exhausted, before the adrenalin shuddered through her limbs.

The Scandinavians devote a whole vocabulary to snow. Mothers have evolved one entirely for sleep. Oh, that leaden, deliciously unenabling warmth. That languor licking softly over a body quivering with need. Come, come fast. Stay.

Sleep.

Get up. Dress. Make breakfast. Feed Edward. Brush teeth. Go to work ... Come back. Make supper. Brush teeth. Go to bed ... Struggle up to Edward.

A cry sounded from the baby's room and uncapped the borehole that fed Violet's rage. Anger streamed through her and she jerked the sheet up over her shoulders. How much more could a baby demand of its mother? And how old would he have to be before he slept properly? She had been up twice during the night to service the ravening monster that apparently inhabited her son's body and refused to respond to her nurturing. There was no *reason* for Edward to cry; and her anger was fed by the unreason. He received every possible attention. He was fed. He was clean. He was talked to. He was cuddled. But no amount of feeding, changing or rocking propitiated the ever-open mouth whose *raison d'être*, it seemed, was to scream.

Under the bedclothes, Violet strove to remember what it was like, not so long ago, for God's sake, when she had no baby, and failed.

Jamie was making groggy-sounding noises and she turned over towards him. 'See to Edward, Jamie, please. I'm finished. There's juice in the fridge.'

'Must I?'

'Yes,' said Violet sharply.

Jamie struggled out of bed and padded out of the room. Violet sank into the goose-down pillow. She craved peace, stillness, the utter bliss of not being wanted – and the certainties back by which she had lived her life before Edward.

She listened to Jamie talking to the baby, and to Edward responding with little grunts and giggles. Father and son went off downstairs. Violet let out her breath, rolled out of bed and stripped off her nightdress. Low-cut and lace-edged, it was part of the pre-baby existence, inadequate for night sorties, and she reminded herself wearily to buy some sensible ones. The idea of her, Violet, in a sensible night-dress intensified her rage. Gritting her teeth, she forced herself into the bathroom and to the mirror to start the armour-plating process with which she began the day.

The nakedness of her face never failed to set Violet's fingers metaphorically itching, for here was the best, and most docile, material of all to shape, refurbish, alter and mould into the image she wished.

Cleanse, tone, nourish. Violet rarely deviated from the regime self-imposed after reading articles on skin care at an impressionable age in the sixth form. The articles had been high on scientific data, and a slightly sceptical but deter-mined Violet had taken note and looked to the products they recommended much as the fully paid-up atheist might secretly cleave to the idea of the saviour – you have nothing to lose by assuming the benefit of the doubt.

If you wanted to believe, then liposomes offered one possible route to eternal youth. Violet was canny, choosing the most exclusive and thereby enhancing its mystique.

She glanced at the clock and picked up a moisturizer which had come in an icily elegant package and apparently incorporated these desirable liposomes in spoonfuls. A gremlin dancing at the back of her mind informed her that she had been conned: advertisers lie, it said, it's their business. From long practice, Violet ignored it.

She applied the cream over her face and neck. Then she brushed her hair vigorously, this way and that, and studied the effect, checked her eyebrows, combed out her eyelashes and nipped at her cuticles with a special pair of pliers.

Jamie padded back into the bedroom and deposited Edward on the bed. Reluctantly, Violet yielded the bathroom to her husband. The baby's gaze locked on to his mother and a smile revealed four white teeth.

'He seems all right this morning.' Jamie retrieved a towel from the floor. 'Thirsty, though.'

Violet proffered a finger to her son. She did not pick him up, however, because she was now in her office clothes and there was dribble on his face and a patch of something dubious on his Babygro. Edward seized her finger and transferred it to his mouth where he bit.

'Ouch. Little beast.' Violet removed her finger and Edward whimpered with disappointment. In the bathroom, Jamie frowned at his shaving-soap-wreathed reflection.

'Careful,' he said through the door. 'I've just got him into a good mood.'

Violet interpreted the remark as criticism and yet another wave of fury crashed over her.

'I'll sort out the breakfast,' she said bad-temperedly, and meant: Lay off me, Jamie.

'Do you have to be so cross, Violet?'

She wanted to run at him and bang her head hard against his chest until the breath was driven from his infuriating, superior, smug body.

'Oh, do shut up,' she said.

A flare of meanness and dislike leapt between husband and wife. Sensing the atmosphere, the baby began to cry but Violet made no move to pick him up.

Jamie looked at Violet and turned his back.

At weekends, Violet anticipated the sharp relief of walking out of the front door on Monday mornings, much as the patient anticipates relief from the doctor. The click of the lock, two paces down the red-tiled path, out of the gate, into the street – and there it was. Freedom. Air.

All weekend she toyed with the vision. A whole day, a whole week without my baby.

'Morning, Vi,' said Lavinia, her secretary, as Violet came in at nine fifteen sharp on Monday morning, 25 May, the day after a Palestinian assassinated a young Jew and the day before a tribunal opened in Nantes enquiring into the alleged child murders of Gilles de Rais, executed in 1440 for the crime. Gilles, of course, fought alongside Joan of Arc.

Not that Violet would pay attention to matters so removed from her world, but her good mood was punctured. 'Good morning,' she replied, took off her jacket and hung it carefully over one of her padded tartan hangers. 'Any messages?'

Lavinia scrutinized her pad covered in hieroglyphics. 'Don't think so.'

Violet squeezed behind her desk. 'Lavinia, would you mind not calling me Vi.' Lavinia looked blank and then turned pink. 'It's not my name.' Violet's tone was kindly – and deadly. 'It's a bit like me calling you Lav or Lavvy.'

'Sorry,' said Lavinia.

Violet requested a cup of camomile tea and began preparing for the marketing meeting, which promised to be difficult if not stormy. She arranged facts in her mind, honed what she knew to be a tricky argument over overseas discounts and read a report on a 'big' book that had come in for auction which, in the attempts to secure it, was reducing everyone to mania.

Gradually her irritation lessened and a warm, happy feeling began to grow inside Violet.

Unfortunately, the meeting *was* stormy and the wash hit Violet. Having neglected to produce some figures (which on reflection she should have anticipated), it was then pointed out that she had permitted a contract to go through that specified overseas royalties on the old basis of the published price, instead of the new practice of price received.

The criticism was listened to in silence. Nevertheless, it was a fair bet that behind the studiously blank faces – including Sebastian Westland's – ranged around the table, busy minds were constructing defences to cover their backs, or engaging in *Schadenfreude*. Recession induces iron in the soul; redundancy is a direct result of recession – and the publishing industry was prone to the latter. Violet's fairy godmother should have told her that it did not do to be unprepared.

The room grew stuffy and a scent of animals on the prowl hung suggestively over alert bodies and faces, blanched like mushrooms by city light.

Violet fixed a slightly widened gaze (it usually worked)

on the publishing director, an attractive man but given to bouts of temper.

Even if you'd had one baby, two babies, three babies, and were hollow-eyed and boneless from lack of sleep, it made no difference. You couldn't fall back on the excuse of exhaustion. That was no quarter. She had to be up there with the rest of them: just as tough, fighting and hungry as they were.

'It would have been helpful to have had those figures,' the publishing director reiterated and his tone was biting. 'Can we have them next week? If not, someone else can do it for you, Violet.'

Never. Violet would have flung herself to the wolves first.

'Leave it to me,' she said, and arranged her mouth in what she hoped was a convincing smile.

There was a pause after this interchange before the next topic was introduced. Violet scribbled something, anything, on her notepad. They're all looking at me, she thought, forgetting that most people concentrate on themselves (a school in which Violet was a premium scholar). They think I can't cope. Or else they're pleased I got it in the neck.

'Violet?' probed the publishing director. 'What's your view?'

The obstinacy and pride that lurked in Violet came to her aid and she raised her head and told them.

When she got back into her office, Lavinia had decorated Violet's phone with a yellow Post-it sticker. 'Emmy phoned: what do you want for dinner?' For one moment, Violet thought she might scream aloud. For heaven's sake, couldn't Emmy work that one out? She seized the phone.

'Is there something in the freezer, Emmy?'

'Stewing steak, I think.'

'Could you make a stew?' Violet did not approve of them

but she was beginning to see the benefits of their elastic properties.

'I don't know how.'

'Didn't your mother teach you anything?'

'No. We bought them ready-made.'

Violet could hear Capital Radio playing in the background. 'If you bought some mince round the corner, what about a shepherd's pie?'

'Sorry. I'm not sure how to do that either. Could you tell me down the phone?'

For God's sake!

'Right.' Violet spoke very carefully. 'Get down to Marks and Spencer's and buy one of their fish pies or something. Do you have any housekeeping money left?'

'I used it up when I bought Edward's juice.'

In a very even, careful tone, Violet told Emmy where to find an additional supply. Meanwhile a buzz cutting through their conversation every thirty seconds informed her that calls were backing up. Lavinia was also waving at her from her desk and mouthing, 'New York.'

Violet's sense of well-being had well and truly dissipated. Irritation (I pay this bloody girl, why can't she use her wits?), fury (why is everything left to women?), and a niggle that she had not made up the morning's spat with Jamie threatened to swell into neap-tide proportions.

'Look, Emmy. Just do what you think fit. Get anything just as long as there's something to eat tonight. Got it?'

Violet flung down the receiver and then, to Lavinia's extreme surprise, dropped her head into her hands. Pressure from the ball of her thumb made sparks float across her vision – great, flaring, yellow sparks that danced with a freedom that Violet no longer possessed.

*

115

Jamie thought about a report he had read on the Israel–Palestine situation as he struggled through St Mary Axe, which was still being cleared of millions of pounds' worth of damage from the IRA bomb in April.

He tried to put himself into the terrorist's mental shoes. How could anyone be so driven by hate or doctrine – the one usually involved the other – that he or she was prepared to set foot over a line dividing those that did not act violently and those that did? It took only one step, but once taken the irreducible logic of the foot over the line made it impossible not to go forward. Jamie did not enquire of himself whether kissing his stepmother-in-law in a taxi constituted stepping over the line.

'Jamie. Do you think your life has changed much having Edward?' Violet asked later, over the Authentic Fisherman's Pie and (not often seen on Violet's table) tinned peas.

'Of course.'

Violet took a tiny forkful of mashed potato while her desire grew to wallop down greedy mouthfuls until her stomach ran with juices and food. She put the fork down on the plate. '*You* are not rung up at work and asked what's for supper.'

'True.' It was a fair point and Jamie always tried to be fair. In times past, it had made Violet love him. Tonight it appeared to madden her.

'I think you should share running the house. I have an important job, too.'

She knew perfectly well that her sharpness stemmed partly from the drubbing she had received at the meeting, but she was not going to tell Jamie that.

It was quite clear that Jamie considered her suggestion a bloody awful one. Violet sharpened the whirling blades and went into battle. 'Don't interrupt my important job with questions about baked beans and nappies, is that it?'

'In a word, yes.'

'I see,' she said. 'Come home and expect to find supper on the table but ask me not how it gets there.'

Jamie had the grace to look sheepish but he also knew that, with Violet, attack was the best form of defence. 'Don't be so nasty. I promise to help when I can.'

His half-apology lanced the atmosphere which had threatened to grow poisoned, but did nothing to solve the problem – which was probably insoluble anyway.

Nevertheless, Violet returned to the subject of their changed life during the nine o'clock news. The Duchess of York had, apparently, jetted off somewhere exotic and pictures of her arrival flashed on the screen.

'We can't do that any more,' said Violet. 'I thought we would be able to, but we can't.'

'Why ever not?' Jamie picked up a strand of his wife's hair and smoothed it between his fingers.

Violet considered the logistics of going on holiday. Push-chair. Sterilizing equipment. Nappies. Baby food. Travelling cot. Bottom ointments ... An anchor chain had wrapped itself around her neck and was tightening.

'Think of transporting all the stuff we need.'

'It's been done before. Successfully, too.' Jamie stroked her cheek. 'Cheer up.'

'How do you know?' she flashed at him before she could stop herself and added, 'Of course. Jenny and Lara. You've done it all before with them.'

She wished then that she had remained silent: Lara and Jenny were the big, burning areas which she knew, *she knew*, were wise to avoid. Jamie's hand dropped away from the back of the sofa and he turned on her with a mixture of pain and anger that conveyed more clearly than words that Lara's defection had inflicted a massive hurt.

'Shut up, Violet. Leave the subject alone.'

It was so unusual for Jamie to show anger, or to reproach her, that Violet was silenced.

On the television screen, figures focused and faded, and the images danced.

'Sorry,' said Violet. 'Kiss me.'

He bent over her, considering the beautiful but stormy face, and she breathed in his smell which she found so attractive. 'Sorry,' she repeated.

Jamie kissed her gently and without passion, then got up and left the room. The anchor chain jerked tighter around Violet's creamed and liposomed neck.

'We'll do the assessment first, Mrs Beckett.'

The supervisor assigned to Violet in the gleaming gym to which she had rendered up a staggering fee for membership was dressed in pedal-pusher leggings and a T-shirt which said: 'Workouts are healthier than sex.'

Violet did not feel qualified to comment and allowed herself to be ushered into a cubby-hole, grandiosely labelled 'Assessment Room'. It contained a treatment couch, a machine which disgorged coloured wires, an exercise bike, a computer and various charts in different typefaces and colours, which specified respiration rates, calorie values and fitness categories.

The supervisor shut the door, thereby trapping air so laden with sweat that the effect was of an old-fashioned wet woollen blanket. Violet swallowed.

'I'll measure your body fat first, Mrs Beckett, on the machine here and the computer will work out your needs and then we'll construct your personal fitness programme.'

She spoke with the driven energy of the fanatic and Violet began to relax.

'Thank you,' she said. 'I need attention because I've had a baby and I've not had the time or energy to get myself back on form but I need to look my best for my job.'

The girl nodded sympathetically. 'It's hell on the thighs and hips,' she said.

Violet did not ask her if she meant the job or the baby.

'My name is Carole,' said Carole, scrawling it across a virgin chart which she had clipped on to her board. 'Let's go . . .' She produced a tape measure. 'Bust.'

Violet gazed at the bobbing head busying itself around her hips and thighs and, for the first time in months, felt curiously liberated and soothed.

'Thirty-six and three-quarters hips.' Carole flicked the tape measure. 'Waist twenty-seven.'

'Thighs?' Violet hardly dared to ask.

Carole told her and threw in the circumference of her upper arms for good measure. The two women shook their heads at each other.

'Not good,' said Violet between clenched teeth.

'Well, we'll soon see to it.' Carole spoke as the zealot faced with the task for which she had been searching. 'Let's measure the composition of your body. Please lie down.' She indicated the narrow treatment couch. 'I'm going to attach these electrodes to your feet and wrists. Don't let your thighs touch each other.'

Violet gazed at the ceiling and recollected that the last time she had been strapped to machinery her legs were raised and something dreadful was happening to her exposed body. She closed her eyes.

Carole applied the pads, read the machine and fed data into the computer which, after a couple of seconds, flicked up a breakdown of the constituent parts of Violet's body.

'Not too bad,' said Carole. 'Actually quite good. You need

to lose three pounds of fat. That's pure fat, remember, so you'll have to lose about seven pounds altogether to do that.'

Three pounds of fat! Violet stared at the screen. On top of everything else – fatigue, work, food, baby, house, husband – how was she going to peel away those glistening yellow collops?

'Blow, please.' Carole held out a lung-capacity monitor. Trusting it was germ-free, Violet blew into it as directed. The result was not startling, but not bad either.

Carole wriggled herself up on to the couch and swung her purple lycraed legs in a relaxed fashion while she wrote busily on the chart.

'Now, getting thin is your primary objective. I shall put you on the thigh abductor. Then the abdominal stretch and the treadmill.' She wrote on. 'Your next assessment will be in six weeks and we'll keep a close eye on progress. But first, the StairMaster. I promise you, it will make your buttocks beg for mercy.'

'Good,' said Violet.

Thereafter, as the days grew longer and warmer, Violet went to the gym whenever she could, plunging out of the spring sunshine into the dark, electrically lit intimacies of an exclusive female mystery. She invested in a plunge leotard, leggings and designer trainers, and with her dark hair and magnolia skin, she resembled an exotic hummingbird.

At first, she was wary of exposing her body in front of so many potentially critical gazes, but soon discovered that she had been judging others by her own standards. Granted, the gym was a temple to narcissism, lined from floor to ceiling with mirrors designed to catch every muscle twitch, and, granted, it was filled by women driven to desperation by a culture that demanded they should be thin. But the neophytes at the temple were too absorbed in the drama of thigh abduction and abdominal stretching to take much notice of others. It was their own panting, bulging, sweat-rimed bodies that absorbed these women's time and concentration, and there were no extra grammes of energy to expend on others.

Violet was effortlessly absorbed into the ranks, snatching every minute to come and worship, to tread out the litany of hope on the StairMaster and watch Jane Fonda on the video screen, whose changes of outfits were as numerous as stars. (Even Violet wondered if a black lace body cinched in at the waist by a designer belt was quite suitable.)

By the middle of June, Violet had lost an inch all round and Carole, who regarded it as a personal triumph, was delighted.

'Your thighs are looking *really* good. We'll beef up the programme.'

Oh, yes, thought Violet, bending her will to master her protesting, hungry body. More, please.

Jamie did not approve. 'You spend all weekend at that place,' he said as Violet handed Edward to him on Sunday morning. 'Don't you think you're overdoing it?'

'No.'

They were in the hall in Austen Road and Violet was packing her holdall. Jamie hefted Edward from one arm to the other. He was in playful mood and bumped around on his father's shoulder and reared back in what to him was a wildly funny game.

'Don't go again, Violet. After all, we only have the weekends to be together.'

Violet stuffed a pink towel into the holdall. 'It's only an hour or so. I'm not disappearing for the weekend.'

Just in time, Jamie prevented Edward from dive-bombing to the floor. An inner, and honest, voice insisted that it was not only the prospect of being deprived of his wife that was driving him to protest, but the knowledge that even an hour with a demanding child is a long time – especially when you want to read the Sunday papers.

'Why don't we go for a walk instead and then have a drink somewhere?'

Violet's face set into obstinate lines. Jamie was acquainted with the look but had never quite appreciated how etched in stone it was. She bent over and her hair fell in a waterfall over her shoulders. She looked smooth, sweet-smelling and very desirable and Jamie ached to have her back as they once were.

'Don't nag,' she said. 'I'll be back to cook lunch if that's what you're on about.'

(Which she would not eat.)

Jamie hunched his shoulders, a habit when he was offended, and put Edward down on the floor where he made for the doormat and the curls of mud lying on it. 'It wasn't what I was getting at,' he said untruthfully. 'Don't worry, I shall demand my pound of flesh and go for a jog when you get back.'

He was left looking at the freshly painted front door which closed with a snap, aware that Violet would be hurrying out of the gate and into the street as if her life depended on it.

Perhaps it did. But Violet left behind a vacuum and into vacuums creep replacements. Or sometimes they arrive with a roar. Jamie bent down to retrieve Edward and an image of Prue flashed across his mind. What was she to him? A pair of grey eyes above a grey crêpe jacket and a pair of delicate wrists. She had raised one towards him when she had told him to leave the bedroom that night. Yet she

had been willing, flattering to him, interested, her stillness infinitely seductive. *Her* foreignness begging to be
explored.

I must have been mad, he thought.

Scented, yielding, mysterious. His image of Prue. Always
softness, and the idea of fire burning quietly inside her.

He bent down to pick up his son and, at that angle, the
blood beat and roared in his ears. Jamie held Edward's
compact, wriggling body and stroked the now curly head
and, once again and against his better judgement, fell in
love with his wife's stepmother.

You pay for everything, reflected Violet as she sped in the
car over Westminster Bridge. Someone up there is
appointed full-time to work out the sums. If you take here,
the result is debit there. Accountancy, really. That Violet
resented being in debt to Jamie and wanted her old life
back did not make the balance more palatable.

'Who's the hottest kid on the block, Violet?'

Violet concentrated on keeping her eyes open. She was
lunching in a fashionable restaurant in Covent Garden, the
kind she loved, with a visiting American rights director with
whom she had been friendly in New York.

Nicole was a highly successful, blonde-streaked, long-
nailed career woman without children. Her colleague,
however, with whom they were also lunching (who was
Nicole's lover), was married. His name was Colin and the
trip to London provided an admirable opportunity for a
real get-together with Nicole.

The bout of drowsiness routed, Violet studied Colin over
the undressed radicchio and artichoke hearts for a trace of

guilt that might indicate he had mixed feelings about what he was doing. She found none.

'Come on.' Nicole was impatient. 'You look half asleep.'

Violet bit back the urge to say, Oh, God, I'm going to die if I don't get a night's sleep, but knew it would expose her flank. Instead, she said, 'There's a rumour that Dinsen and Fraser are going to be taken over.'

Her companions digested this admittedly not very exciting gossip.

'Honey,' said Nicole. 'I've got a hundred times more dirt than that.'

She drank tiny sips of her wine as she told Violet who was sleeping with whom, which famous novelist's book had virtually been rewritten by the editor (who had then been sacked), and the cock-up on Helen Hines's publicity campaign which had cost Nicole's firm close on a hundred grand.

A little scene re-enacted itself behind Violet's dark eyes. Of her stumbling up at night, of cold creeping up her legs, of a wide-open baby's mouth and of the horrifying but quite clear urge to smack him. Hard.

'What did you think of the Hines novel?' asked Colin.

'Very good,' she answered, automatically. 'I liked the way she handled the love story.'

'But, Violet, it's an anti-love story. It's a hate story. Love is a piece of cultural crap according to Hines.' Colin looked smug in his Armani shirt and well-cut suit. Pleased to have caught her out, she thought.

The world, it seemed, was full of vindictive, uncooperative men.

'Yes, that's what I meant,' she said.

Nicole laughed and poured out more wine. Her bracelets clinked against the bottle and Violet forced herself not to wince.

'Do you have children?' she asked Colin.

For a few seconds, she imagined that colour stained the tips of his ears, then concluded she had been mistaken.

'A three-month baby and a two-year-old.'

A baby and a two-year-old and you are sitting here in the pink of health and energy ... with your lover. She was surprised by the strength of her outrage.

'Your wife holds the baby, then?'

'Sure, she enjoys all that,' said Colin. 'We agreed that was her role.'

Violet drank her wine and said nothing.

Across the table, Nicole raised one shoulder in a little shrug which said: What did you expect, darling?

Chapter Nine

'Jamie,' went the message, written on the bank's distinctive yellow memo paper, 'I think you have been ignoring me and I find your attitude difficult. I would appreciate a good morning when you come in. It would make a great difference to our working relations.'

Jamie read it twice to make sure he was not hallucinating. Dyson was a good chap, friendly, cooperative, clever, and not given (overtly) to indulging in scenes.

Written communications such as this one between colleagues were not uncommon. Jamie was also well aware that flare-ups of irritation, hurt and worry were not the sole property of either sex and, in the pressurized world of high finance, flare-ups raged like bush fires in unexpected places.

The points where humans make contact with each other require insulation grease of the thick electrician's kind, a viscous, stabilizing blanket which protects against the pinpricks and uncertainties of this world. Stroking it on was part of the business of life, Jamie knew that well. He grabbed a cup of coffee from the machine, made his way to Dyson's office along the corridor and said, 'Good morning,' pointedly. Flushing, Dyson looked up from a spread-sheet.

'Look, I'm sorry if I've offended you, I certainly didn't mean to.'

Cup in one hand, Jamie lounged against the door jamb. 'I don't know what I've done but whatever it was, I'm sorry.'

The casual pose irritated Dyson and he said stiffly and with an effort, 'Perhaps I've overreacted, but I felt I had to say something after that meeting.'

Jamie searched his memory until he remembered that he had confronted Dyson over the issue of privately funded motorways. That in itself was not a problem; locked antlers frequently resulted in spilt blood. It was rather that both the chairman and the chief executive had been present at that particular meeting – and Dyson had lost the argument.

'Sure.' Jamie heaved himself upright a little, shocked at how little he cared about Dyson's pique. That and the knowledge that the London job he had so keenly antici-pated was, for the moment, of less importance than he had imagined – a state of mind that was new to him. 'Why don't we meet for a drink after work and sort it out?'

Back at his desk he chucked Dyson's memo into the bin and stood looking down at it.

The world's great sins – murder, torture, rape, the taking of a good name – claimed the headlines' attention. Yet was it not true to say that laziness and evasion did as much damage in a quieter way, and were practised on an even larger scale?

Oh, yes, continued his inner dialogue, given that human beings were endemically lazy and evasive, it was astonishing that goodness infected the world at all. Jamie's emotions were too confused at this point for him to add adultery to the list, if indeed he ever would. Naturally, he did not exempt himself from any of the above sins but, as most of us do, tended to ascribe to his reflections deeper powers of perception than, perhaps, he possessed.

His conclusions, however, did not make him feel better and he turned his attention to his in-tray, which contained a letter marked 'Personal' in familiar writing. It was from Jenny who, young as she was, had quickly grown old in the

ways of jealousy and taken to sending letters to Jamie at his
work address in order to avoid Violet.

Dear Jamie [she wrote],

I'm off to the Brazilian rain-forest to work for a
couple of years. If you would like to contribute some
dosh to a good cause, I need a pair of boots.

Love Jenny.

Jamie smiled and pulled out his cheque-book. Jenny was
very dear to him and he did not like the idea that Lara's
new man saw more of her than he did. 'Good luck, Jen,' he
wrote. 'Make sure you have the right jabs.'

Jamie had not meant to loop his life into an extra twist
and, a conventional person at heart, had intended it to run
along a straight line. It had not been sensible, therefore, to
hitch up with the fascinating but unstable Lara. But she had
been ripe and golden – and on the search for a new man.
He had been romantic, passionate, and in a hurry. That was
that.

Subsequent events squashed the idea that Jamie had once
held that good things remain intrinsically so, and taught
him the opposite. Good things could, and did, turn into
bad things.

Jamie looked out of the window. The dusk outside
possessed the white, peeled quality of late spring that he
loved. It made him think of Prue walking down the lane at
Dainton, and an unfamiliar tension gathered in his throat.

How he wanted her, as he had once wanted his wife. His
hand moved towards the telephone and stopped.

When you grow older you can lose the habit of love (and
probably acquire the habit of bad temper), and if love

arrives in a burst of feeling it is, without doubt, that much tougher to cope with.

Jamie folded up Jenny's letter. As the years lay down hard accretions round the body and soul, it is harder to fight through habits of selfishness to find those initial impulses towards niceness that, once, he had been so ready to deal out. Indeed, he wondered if there was anything left of that in him at all.

Eve Watts knocked and came into the office. She was the corporate PR officer. Tall, slim and given to linen suits with short jackets that showed off her waistline, she had long red hair which she wore in a French plait. She wanted to talk to him about the company's results and how they should pitch them to the public. Eve was clever and fluent, and knew how to sit in a chair without fidgeting, and after they had sorted out the strategy she stayed on to gossip. Eve made it her business to know down to the last sneeze what was going on. They discussed office antics and the row brewing between the Conservative Party and Lloyd's.

'Could be quite a fight ahead.' Eve's linen skirt hitched up to reveal a very nice thigh. 'Stand by for heads on Tower Bridge.'

Jamie recollected a conversation with Prue. She had been describing Joan of Arc's famous relief of Orléans in 1429, and how Joan had woken one morning to sounds of the citizens of Orléans attacking an English garrison outside the walls at St Loup. Joan had leapt to her feet and dashed into battle. Apparently, she had wept at the sight of spilt French blood before planting her standard on the edge of the ditch and storming the *bastille* built around an abandoned church. All manner of English blood had then been shed, but it was not recorded if Joan wept for it.

He studied the thigh laid out for inspection and Eve,

sensing his dispassion, twitched her skirt down. 'Do you have any views on Lloyd's?' he asked her.

She did, of course, and confidently planted her standard on the edge of what Jamie suspected was an abyss. He pulled himself together and responded, aware that Eve was a little puzzled by his lack of enthusiasm and his failure to respond to the direct signals she was sending him.

After a while, she got to her feet. The red plait danced back over her shoulder and the linen skirt was pulled straight.

'See you, then.' She paused. 'Perhaps we could have lunch?'

Jamie's 'Let's' sounded unconvincing.

She got the message and shrugged elegantly. 'We younger women differentiate love from sex, you know. Rather as men have always done. Yes?'

'Aren't you generalizing somewhat?'

Eve moved towards the door. 'In a recent survey it was shown that over fifty per cent of married women are unfaithful at some time or another.' She raised her fingers and waggled them at Jamie. 'Just a thought to be going on with.'

It occurred to him later that the word 'evil' was 'live' spelt backwards. Once again, he stared out of the hermetically sealed window. What did 'love' spell backwards? What did 'love for someone else's wife' spell backwards? What did 'fool' spell backwards?

Should he phone Prue?

In Dainton, Prue knelt on the kitchen floor, like a bloody penitent, she thought, and scrubbed at the tiles decorated with the stew she had just dropped all over them.

I won't phone him.

The pain of being married and forty-one, of saying goodbye to expectations that youth enjoys without thinking about them, knowing you are passing over a bridge and you will not return, was sharp. People Prue knew were beginning to die. Her parents had gone, and one or two friends, in particular Mary, who had died protesting that she still had so much to do. Their ghosts sometimes haunted her. Elements of Prue were also dying. Relinquishing the right to nourish intense feeling – or, worse, the ability to provoke it because cellulite, slackening skin and gravity interpose themselves between your desires and their object – was harder than she had ever supposed.

As she listened to the wind blowing rain and cool wet air through the garden, Prue grieved for her youth and listened to the voices from the past. Once, she had imagined that she could touch the furthest planet if she had wished.

So Prue scrubbed, her hands stinging from the hot water and detergent.

Max and Jane, she thought. Max and Jane.

The phone rang.

Jamie's mother came from Scotland, he told Prue, the last in a long line of a well-bred family that had gradually lost its faith in itself and, more important, its capital. Beautiful in her way, she had Celtic black hair and white skin and not a spare ounce of flesh. She always dressed in tailored tweed suits, linen blouses, and wore diamond earrings and a double-stranded rope of pearls, the remains of the MacIndrews' assets. She did possess one thing, however, in abundance: a strong sense of family. One of her chief amusements was to cart Jamie and Amelia, his elder sister, around the relations.

'You should *know* who the family are, darlings,' she would

say when her children protested. 'You must know where you belong.'

We should know each other, darlings, because we are responsible for each other.

Imagine, he told Prue. Picture the scene. And Prue, who wanted to suck in every detail, listened with a hunger bordering on the ravenous. Imagine.

One of his abiding memories was of being made to recite Kipling's 'If', dressed in too-big grey flannel shorts and a tie, in front of a panel of great-aunts who lived in a vast and gloomy flat in Edinburgh. They had been a grey, fluttering group, smelling of camphor and Indian tea. After he had finished, several pairs of hands, worn down to the bone by age and making-do, patted him and offered cups of tea and sandwiches of the kind that would have fainted at the word 'filling'.

'Great-aunt Dorothy', said his mother, who was not without a certain sadistic humour, 'would like you two to come and stay by yourselves.' Her eyes widened with the tease, knowing they would rather die. 'I've said you would love to explore Edinburgh properly ...' She took pity on her offspring, 'but I think we are rather busy these holidays.'

Jamie had no time to feel relief. A bony hand in the composite mass of great-aunts across the table raised a cup of tea. 'But, Isobel,' said a voice, 'we won't be around much longer, will we?'

One by one, Great-aunts Jean, Ellen and Margery nodded like flowers in a herbaceous border on which the gardener had left the dead heads.

Yes, he remembered it so well, he said to Prue, who was at this point in the long conversation struck by the thought that it was a good thing Jamie was ringing her, else how would she explain the phone bill? The great-aunts, the lace curtains shrouding huge windows, and the silver teapot on the table. Gloom and hush. Annie the maid in black and white, oatcakes and hot scones wrapped in linen napkins. Prints of the Highlands on the wall, soft linen sheets, the old Jacobite wine glass with a spiral trapped in the stem, the agony of repeating 'If' every day after tea and *utter* agony of trying not to laugh when Melly (who had taken up ballet and should not have done) was ordered to do a swan dance to Tchaikovsky on the wind-up gramophone.

Great-aunt Hilda had spotted his giggles and demanded that Jamie apologize to his sister 'Because, little boy, manners maketh man.'

Those were pieces Jamie picked out from the jigsaw of childhood which had gone.

Edward was wailing as Jamie let himself in at the front door. Violet appeared at the top of the stairs, clutching him.

'Thank God,' she said. 'Where have you been?'

Further up, on the second landing, a clearly worried Emmy was hanging over the banisters.

'He hasn't stopped crying for an hour.' Violet sounded frantic. 'I don't think I can take any more.'

'Give him to me.' Jamie flung down his briefcase. 'Have you rung the doctor?' He examined the agonized little face of his son. There was a tinge of blue around the open mouth and flared nostrils.

'He's on his way,' said Emmy.

The doctor took another hour to arrive by which time Violet and Jamie were on the whisky and the baby was limp with exhaustion and pain. The doctor was clearly exhausted, too, but examined Edward carefully.

'I think it's colic, but it's just possible that the gut has twisted.' He fingered the tight little belly. 'I'll give you a letter and if he continues to cry after I've given him some

Calpol, drive him to St Thomas's. They'll have his notes from last time.'

After she had shown the doctor out Violet sank on to the sofa. 'Oh, my God.'

Jamie held Edward close to him. It was warm and comfortable in the drawing room. Violet's carefully chosen paintings were on the walls, her chair covers were tasteful, the grey carpet immaculate. It seemed too insulated a place for this kind of drama.

Love for his son tightening his throat, Jamie breathed into Edward's tiny neck, 'Get better.'

Emmy hovered in the doorway with a tray of tea. She was white and anxious and there were dark circles under her eyes. Jamie warmed to her.

'What about a hot-water bottle on his tummy?' she suggested. 'I think it would help.'

Jamie flashed her a smile of gratitude.

In conjunction with the Calpol, the hot-water bottle wrapped in a couple of tea-towels did appear to help. Jamie sat with Edward on his knee and Emmy held the bottle carefully against the baby's stomach. Gradually, Edward quietened and the stiff little limbs began to relax. Violet sat on the opposite side of the room watching the tableau, and remained silent.

Edward's eyelids fluttered and drooped, then fell over his wet eyes with the suddenness of a steel gate banging shut. Sweating with relief, Jamie looked up at Violet who had turned as white as the lampshade on her expensive marble lamp.

After Emmy had borne the sleeping baby upstairs and retired to a hot bath, Jamie dropped on to his knees by

Violet's chair and put his head in her lap. He could feel damp patching his shirt.

'All right?'

'Yes.' Violet spoke through dry lips. As an afterthought she asked, 'And you?'

'Yes.' In the darkness of Violet's lap, he closed his eyes. 'Thank God, there was nothing very wrong.'

He felt a hand tugging at his hair and raised his head. 'I never want another one,' said Violet, her mouth twisted with emotion. 'Never.'

Jamie sat back on his heels. 'You don't mean it?'

'Yes, I do,' said Violet, avoiding Jamie's eye. 'It's too . . . too distracting. I mean wearing.'

'Don't be silly.' Jamie climbed to his feet and eased his shirt away from his back. 'Of course you do.'

Violet gulped whisky. She looked up and Jamie realized that she was furious.

'Stop patronizing me, Jamie. You have no idea what I think and I'm telling you I don't want another one.'

She put down her glass and got to her feet. Despite her anger, her pallor made her look vulnerable . . . and, he saw with a shock, lonely. Jamie responded by pulling her to him, and kissing the silky hair and the cool, pampered skin of her cheek.

'Don't feel like that, Violet. Every parent must have this sort of experience. Edward's fine now.'

'Yes, you know all about that,' said Violet, harshly. '*And* you keep reminding me.'

He released Violet and took a step back. 'Jenny was five when I moved in with Lara so I don't know everything.'

She gazed down at the carpet with a secret expression. 'Even so, I know you think you've done it all before and this gives you a licence to lecture me. Poor old Violet, she doesn't know nought from ten but I'll teach her a thing or two.'

For a second, Jamie was completely taken aback and then his anger flared. With a little tsk, Violet gathered up the glasses, arranged them tidily on the tray and walked out of the room.

Jamie could hear the clink as she stacked them in the dishwasher.

Along with Scottish great-aunts, Jamie's mother had often indulged in proverbs. He could hear her saying one of them now, in the light, amused, ironic manner she had: 'You've made your bed, darling, and you have to lie on it.'

In her bleached- and limed-wood kitchen, Violet stared down at dirty china in the rack. She was profoundly exhausted and slightly nauseous from fatigue and whisky. Throughout the drama, various thoughts had sifted through a mind that had refused to work with its normal celerity, chief among them that if Edward was ill she would not be able to attend the programme meeting for which she had planned so thoroughly.

The paucity of her reaction to her son's distress appalled even Violet.

Chapter Ten

'Do you have a biography of Charles Dickens?' An anorexic-looking girl dressed in black leggings and Doc Marten's with bright green hair cut into a cockatoo crest, asked Prue the question.

Prue considered the figure. Crested anorexics and Dickens did not figure in her list of obvious combinations. 'We have the Ackroyd in stock.'

'I'll take it,' said the girl. 'And anything you've got on Elizabeth Barrett Browning.'

The bookshop was crowded and Prue was forced to dodge browsers and tables piled with new publications. She stretched up to 'A' on the biography shelf. Where you lined up in the alphabet influenced your success as a writer. Authors whose names began with 'A' or 'B' were read by tall people. 'LMN' got both tall and short.

The girl paid for the books, counting out the money from a leather purse which had almost fallen apart. Prue hoped the books proved to be a fair exchange and did what they were meant to do. Entertain? Teach? Act as a doorstop?

She pressed the till button: the drawer sprang out and hit her in the stomach, as it always did, and the coins clinked into the compartments. Prue recollected that the last time she had seen a pile of coins was at the Ivy when Jamie had emptied his pockets in search of his credit cards. Then, she had remarked on how much loose change he carried.

'Hurry up,' said Gerald who was waiting to ring up a bill.

You see, Prue admonished herself, you're slipping.

She drove home with the delicate scent of flowers for the church filling the car, and the week's shopping rattling and bouncing in plastic bags. At the Dainton turn-off, she remembered that she had forgotten Jane's favourite pizzas and cursed. As part of the strategy worked out between Max and her to help Jane, Prue had arranged that Jane bring a friend back for Friday supper, promising a special meal.

Just because you're busy doesn't mean you let go, she told herself fiercely, meaning, I have a conscience, and spent the remainder of the drive mentally reshifting her timetable in order to propitiate it.

She parked the car in the lane leading up to the church, threw the rug over the bags containing the dairy foods, and extracted the flowers from the back seat. The weather had altered and a warmish wind was blowing, fresh and sweet, along the valley and up towards the airstrip, and the air smelt fresh and soft. The trees' silhouettes were blurring with new growth and the gardens had been given a fresh topcoat of green.

The wind tugged at Prue's clothes, sweeping the moraines of dust and leaves into new patterns and covering a footstep imprinted in mud, a tyre skid-mark – and the evidence of a long winter.

Dazzled and goaded by the onset of summer, Prue trudged up the lane and stopped by a patch of briar which had grown so thick that it impeded progress. No one had got round to cutting it back, which was nothing new. She pulled out the secateurs she always carried and hacked at the worst bits, then decided to send Max up to deal with it properly. She disentangled a blackberry cutting from her sleeve. Someone, Emmy perhaps, had told her there were only ten basic structures in nature which were repeated *ad infinitum.* That prompted her to think: I must call on Emmy's mother and tell her Emmy is doing fine.

Her gaze shifted to the stump of the grand and glorious beech that had been sent crashing to the ground in the Great Storm. The tree lovers in Dainton had mourned it, and Prue was cheered to see that suckers were struggling out of the grass. What did that tell her? Rising from its base, like a glove, were black projections with their characteristic twist. Prue smiled: Dead Men's Fingers made Jane giggle for Carey Scholfield's elder sister had informed the girls they were phallic ('What's "phallic", Mum?').

That was to ignore their strange, almost sinister quality suggesting deformity and ... weirdness. Prue's expression became troubled. The deformity of living a lie when she had been used to truth – or, at least, straightforwardness? Of living on two levels where once one had been sufficient? The fungi's 'third' finger had been broken off near the top, to reveal secret, creamy flesh and rows of spore sacs. What did *those* tell her about herself and the dark fingers that were pushing through her consciousness? Searching for the pattern, Prue touched the fungus with the toe of her shoe.

'Prue, dear, just the person.'

Molly Greer came up behind Prue, and she whirled round. 'Hallo, Molly.'

Molly was carrying a mass of daffodils and catkins from her garden wrapped in the local newspaper. Prue eyed them and knew immediately that her tastefully chosen, expensive offerings from a Winchester florist were destined for relegation behind the pulpit.

'Do you mind?' Molly shoved her hand under Prue's arm. 'The slope is bad on my hip.'

Prue tried not to feel rebellious, to give this gesture of support graciously, and failed. Molly was wearing her sale bargain, a tweed coat designed expressly to keep a dread-nought warm and which exuded a damp smell. Beneath it, she wore socks over thick green tights and sheepskin boots. Molly did not bother with her appearance. Waste of time, she often reiterated, an expert in making a virtue of necessity. My face is my face – which, said Max, who could be moved on occasion to rudeness but not originality, needed to be said otherwise it might be mistaken for a bus.

They deposited the flowers in the church porch, and Molly ordered Prue to fill the vases from the outside tap. Prue bit her lip. Molly Greer might be the keystone of Dainton, fifteen years older and a tireless defender of the village against the threat of motorways, supermarkets and boundary realignments, but unchecked power (particularly if unelected) provokes opposition. Grimly, Prue filled the vases and hefted them one by one into the church, fully aware that any objections to Molly's dictates ranked with present Labour Party jeers – flailings of permanent opposition.

The thought shaped her resolve. 'I'll do the altar,' she said firmly, ashamed of her past pusillanimity and, a little ashamed of her present victory, surged into the church before she could weaken.

When Prue finished she went back down the aisle to judge the effect which, she congratulated herself, was good. Purple freesias and green euphorbia were an interesting combination. To her credit Molly said approvingly, 'Very nice, Prue.'

'Thank you. I thought it was worth splashing out.'

'Oh, really?' Molly gave Prue the benefit of one of her searching looks. 'Prue dear. You're not getting yourself into any kind of trouble, are you?'

'Why do you ask that?' Prue did not turn round to look at her.

'I'm no fool, dear.'

'No, Molly, I never thought you were.'

Prue returned to the altar and made a small adjustment to the euphorbia. I suspect ... she addressed silently the stained-glass window above the altar ... Molly suspects that I am up to something. But she knew as she thought it that the possibility of Molly falling on the right conclusion was not sufficient to arrest what was happening to her.

Molly finished a huge arrangement for a window in the east wall below one of the two wall paintings, or 'Moralities', for which the church was famous. This one depicted St George doing away with the dragon who was about to consume a large-eyed Princess Cleodolinda. Understandably, her parents, on the battlements of the nearby castle, were watching the proceedings with anguish etched into their faces. Parents were bound to their children by a pulsing, tensile rope of feeling and obligation, whether men wore tights and women wimples, or not. Of course. And wept and broke their hearts when their children died, tiny replicas from the mould. Ever since the first caveman dragged a bison back to the cave, the affectionate family had been alive and thriving and parents had torn out their own breasts to feed their young. As Prue would do for Jane. As Max would do for his daughters. Oh, yes. She pictured him, the slumbering giant, provoked to whirling rage, aiming his Purdey at anyone who threatened them.

In this place of belief, as Prue searched the byways of her heart, she forgot that theory and practice were separate issues.

'Can you give me a hand, Prue?' commanded Molly.

Prue resigned herself to several journeys to the wasteheap and to washing out spare vases in the vestry.

'How's that stepdaughter of yours?' Molly asked as they returned to their cars.

141

'Busy. Working. Baby. New house. You can imagine.'

'Flown the coop, that one.' Molly's grip tightened on Prue's arm as she lurched round treacherous mud patches. 'You'd never think she once lived here.'

Violet's gilded, expensive qualities did not belong in Dainton – as perceived by Dainton. This was a little unfair as the village contained a significant number of commuters who were well aware of the world, rather than rural labourers who had never been out of the valley.

Prue steered Molly into the village square which had broken out in a rash of 'For Sale' signs and caught sight of Clive Carter standing motionless in his front garden, which he had taken to doing since he lost his job from his engineering firm. Prue waved at him. Clive did not wave back.

'Time I made the old man's lunch,' Molly said, and added that he was damn well going to have cabbage because she had heard on the radio it was good for heart conditions. Since Keith Greer had made a career out of his bad heart, it did not bode well for Keith. Prue suggested that it was unwise to believe everything you heard. Molly looked her straight in the eyes and said that was true, and one did hear an awful lot of things, didn't one?

While Prue was washing up her lunch, she listened to the radio and Schubert's violin concerto filled the kitchen. Its beauty made her catch her breath and dealt a blow to her heart. She dropped the washing-up brush back into the unecologically acceptable suds. Then she gave up and finished the dishes with tears running down her cheeks into her neck.

Jamie [she wrote]

When Thackeray finally met Charlotte Brontë he expected to meet in the notorious author of *Jane Eyre*

an Amazon. Instead he encountered 'an austere little
Joan of Arc marching in upon us, and rebuking our
easy lives and our easy morals'.

How infuriating the Joans and the Charlottes of
this world are. Except, I think Thackeray's assessment
is wrong. Joan was not so much concerned with the
world as with what she made of herself. She tilted at
the commonly held idea of what a woman should be,
should think, should do, succeeded in doing so and
suffered atrociously.

But she had her moments. I like to think of her
dressed up in breeches, tight boots and the golden
huque that she enjoyed so much (Joan liked clothes),
riding off to battle. That and her communication with
God. Joan was lucky, she lived in an age that allowed a
dialogue with God, you were allowed to speak to Him
and Him to you. Much more than our own, it was an
age that, if it knew it or not, made allowances for the
richness and variety of the human psyche.

Yes?

Nevertheless, I shall take Joan/Charlotte's rebuke
to the easy life to heart, and ask you not to phone me
again. You *do* see, don't you?

Prue knew perfectly well that she was not going to send
this letter, but got as far as addressing the envelope before
she tore it up and threw it in the dustbin.

When Prue opened her eyes the next morning, a fully
dressed Max was standing by the bed looking down at her.

'I thought you were crying,' he said.

He seemed even more impassive than usual – a sign that
he was in the grip of strong feelings.

'No,' she said and forced a smile. 'I've a bit of a snuffle, that's all.'

'You won't forget to pay the gas bill.'

'No,' she said, trying to hide her misery and failing.

Max assessed her expression, then turned and went over to the window and stood gazing out. Outside the wind blew in great racing gulps and exuberant whorls of air. Prue watched his back, so large, so contained, so easy, she knew, to wound. Max always hid his wounds well.

'Good luck for today, Max.'

He swung round from the window. 'You remembered?'

She felt ashamed at the pleasure in his voice and the panic that underlay it. 'Of course, darling. You've got the big brainstorming session on the European set-up. Have you got your notes?'

'Yes.'

Max sat down on the bed and took her hand. 'Are you sure you're all right? I've been a bit worried about you.'

Treachery sat in her heart like soggy mixture in an unsuccessful sponge cake. Prue rubbed his fingers with her own and said, 'Everything's absolutely fine. Don't worry about me.'

Again he watched her and then bent down and gathered Prue in his arms and held her close. 'Is it, my Prue?' he said into her neck, and kissed the hair spilling over her shoulders. 'You must always tell me.'

How lucky, he had said, when Prue had eventually prodded him into proposing. How lucky I am to be given a second chance.

That was twenty-one years ago when Prue had been working as a legal secretary in Stephenson Blackwell's in the City. A bored, underdeveloped, unrealized Prue.

How many women do what Prue did? Mark time. And how many women look up from an uncongenial desk, light on a male figure and listen to the click in their head (*not* their heart) which tells them it is time to take action?

Max was tall – a definite plus for tall Prue – well dressed, Establishment, with the additional advantage of suffering. Two years previously, Helen, his wife, had left him and, in doing so, had rammed her car into an oncoming lorry and taken a further six weeks to die. Max was now struggling to bring up his small daughter by himself, a situation made more difficult by his refusal to move out of Dainton to London.

'It was whisky,' Max said later when Prue had finally willed him into inviting her out to dinner, a process that had taken a great deal of trouble and a fortune in scent and stockings. 'Helen had been drinking for some time and I was drinking it like water too.'

Prue considered. 'It was not your fault that Helen chose to leave. Or your fault that she chose to have half a bottle of the best malt before she did so.' In those days, Prue was armour-plated with youthful righteousness.

Max sat back in the chair. The restaurant was noisy and full, but he was quite still and removed. 'She was so beautiful,' he said at last. 'And my dreams were full of her.'

And Prue had turned away from such feeling and such grief and fled to the ladies'.

Later, she made it her business to find a photograph of Helen and was disappointed for she looked artificial and Prue was forced to conclude that her beauty had been the sort that had to live before it revealed itself. Either that, or the idea of beauty was like Bostik: once it had been applied it stuck.

Still, since competing on that front was out, it left her the task of scoring over Helen on character. Tell me about Helen, she coaxed a reluctant, reticent Max. Tell me.

Clever Prue. For, in the end, Max talked as much as he was capable of, and got Helen out of his system and into proportion. It was not comfortable listening, for Max had inflicted wounds as well as suffering them, but none so deep as the one that Helen made when she told him she was leaving.

'I remember,' said Max, struggling for the precise words, 'the moment she told me. I felt as if a knife had been driven under my ribs. I remember thinking it had reached my backbone and was scraping along it.' He held out the hand marked by Helen's Wound. 'I even drove a knife into my hand to test which hurt most.'

Oh, God, thought Prue, and shut her eyes.

Jack was younger than Helen which, Max said, surprised him. Helen preferred the strong, older types. She had accused Max of growing old before his time, and said it was making her feel old, while Jack was both young and vigorous. Then people grew older younger than they do now, if Prue saw what he meant.

'The irony is,' said Max, putting down his knife and fork at one of their weekly dinners, 'Helen won't be growing old. Unlike me. She will never wrinkle or droop and when I meet her again she will be in her time, and I will be in mine. So, you see, it was a final parting.'

Prue did not think she could bear any more and dropped her head over her wine-glass while she decided on a course of action. When she looked up, it was to corner Max's dark eyes with her own and to ask, 'Will you marry again?'

Max caught on at once. For the first time, he smiled properly. Then he ordered a second bottle of wine. 'It will have to be someone who does not mind growing old.'

'Good God,' said Prue – who by now had fallen thoroughly in love – with all the emphasis of the nineteen-year-old. 'You're only thirty-nine now.'

Their future was set from that conversation. Max would marry Prue, they would grow old together and Prue was determined that the age-gap would make no difference.

For their honeymoon, Max, having been prised from a screaming Violet, bore Prue off to a country hotel tucked away on a Devon estuary. Throughout the short summer night, he told Prue how lucky he was and how he loved and needed her, and this was the beginning of the rest of his life. Then he fell asleep.

Rasping-eyed from fatigue and nerves, Prue lay until pink light slid under the chintz curtains, held her sleeping husband in her arms and wondered why it had not been just a little more, well ... cataclysmic.

Within a month, she felt as if she had been married all her life – falling into a comfortable sofa where she had been expecting a Louis Quinze *fauteuil*. Except for Violet, of course, who set her face against her stepmother with the determination of a seven-year-old.

She had been lucky. But when friends, such as Kate, asked her if she minded about Helen and Violet, she replied, 'No,' and crossed her fingers as she had been taught by her friends when she first went to the convent school.

Knowing the past, its terrible mistakes and the penalties incurred, knowing she had a great obligation to guard Max and Jane, knowing that she endorsed the behaviour that she had perfected over twenty years, knowing she was content in a marriage and in a community, why was it that Prue's flesh felt so firm and expectant this early summer, this growing season, and her eyes hid secrets?

Why not?

Why not?

High Summer

Chapter Eleven

Joan took charge of her own destiny, Prue was fond of telling Max. She made things happen. So did Pandarus, he replied. He had a certain power too. Prue was curious. Didn't Pandarus act as a go-between between Troilus and Cressida? Exactly, Max replied. He arranged the love affair between them.

Prue was not sure she approved. A dirty old man, you mean, she said. At his most inscrutable, Max looked at his wife. There are worse things, he said gently. Far worse things.

What sort of man was Joan's Dauphin, the king-in-embryo, for whom she risked so much? What fusion of lasciviousness, political nous, religious gift and insanity had he inherited from the stockpile of Valois genes?

'The Dauphin's father,' Prue noted, 'had been subject to fits of madness which effectively caused breakdown in the French government.'

The first attack took place in 1392 when the King went berserk and killed four of his attendants. Subsequently, he suffered at least forty-four attacks, 'crying and trembling as if pricked with a thousand points of iron'. The verdict today would, in all probability, point to schizophrenia.

Isabeau of Bavaria, his mother, was not much better.

Despite being embarrassingly short in the leg (a characteristic she passed on to her son), Isabeau had been attractive in her youth but also subject to wobbles in her mental equilibrium. Phobic and agoraphobic, she was terrified by thunder, by the slightest suggestion of disease (not unnaturally given the mortality rate of the period) and could not be persuaded to cross a bridge unless it had railings – a quirk which, again, her son shared.

At first, the quality of Isabeau's mothering was not questioned, but, after 1425, statements wriggled into the records accusing her of neglect. Her extravagance was notorious and so was her intimacy with Louis d'Orléans, her husband's brother. By 1417, jewelled, plumpening disgracefully, Isabeau was the centre of a dissolute court at Vincennes, and scandal reached fever pitch. Rumour was saying that the Dauphin was not the King's son, but his uncle's bastard.

You see, a small but insistent voice spoke to Prue, once a family begins to break down, the effects never end. Think of the stone thrown into the pond. Think of dominoes. Think . . . of what?

The telephone rang in the study where Prue was making these notes.

'Mrs Valour?'

'Yes.'

'It's Emmy speaking.'

'Oh, hallo.' Prue went over various disasters in her mind. 'There's nothing wrong, is there?'

'Everything's fine, but Mr Beckett asked me to call you as he had to leave for the early train. He's coming down to Winchester today for a meeting and wondered if you would like to meet him for lunch at the Coaching House Hotel? He says just turn up any time after 12.45.'

Prue supposed that Jamie supposed that by making the

assignation above board, it became acceptable. If you insist black is white, then so it is.

Sophistry.

Somewhere in the recesses of Prue's chest, a spring released.

'Thanks, Emmy,' she said. 'I might just do that. I'd like to catch up on the news.'

I bet, thought a sharp, less peaky Emmy, as she put down the phone. It sounds all too matey to me.

Prue scanned the reference books on the shelf above her desk where she had been writing up her notes. Vita Sackville-West's *Joan of Arc*, a monograph on jealousy, a critical appreciation of nineteenth-century women writers and *Footsteps: Adventures of a Romantic Biographer*, by Richard Holmes. The wrestlings of biographers, and psychologists, to pin their subject to the page were not as fierce as the battle raging in Prue.

How dare Jamie do this? Put her on the spot. *Force her to make a choice.*

Would you rather, then, that choice was taken away?

What would Emmy make of her role as the pander? Lucky it had been Emmy and not Molly Greer, whose curiosity was as sharp as a predatory bird's beak inserted into his prey. Jab. Jab. Plucking bloody bits of information to wave at the world.

Jamie had counted on her saying yes.

Prue picked up her biro and wrote 'Rouen'. The biro had been part of a job lot bought in Andover market and showed its dicey provenance by its uneven flow of ink. She shook it and a glob landed on the clean page. She stared at her fingers whose secret identification was now whorled and circled into stained relief.

How dare Jamie send messages via a third person? Most of all, how dare he expose her flimsy defences?

She made herself continue.

It can only be imagined how the quicksand of doubt, sown with phobias and madness, hampered the thin, weak, pendulous-nosed Dauphin. Couple that with high intelligence, bouts of drunkenness and physical unattractiveness, and the ground becomes almost impassable. He was capable of attracting great loyalty but, more often than not, only – in the manner of his parents – to betray it.

This was the man Joan sought to ratify as king.

Footnote, wrote Prue: Isabeau became obese, so much so that she was prevented from being regent because it was considered that her size would impede her.

Second footnote. Although she was ostentatiously pious it was doubtful if religion nourished her life. Nevertheless, in one of those curious biographical and historical collusions, Isabeau commissioned an illuminated life of St Margaret of Antioch for her library, a great, jewelled tome. Unlike St Catherine who was associated with virginity, St Margaret was associated with motherhood. Perhaps that was why Isabeau (in hasty retrenchment? fit of conscience?) chose her.

St Margaret was, of course, with St Catherine and St Michael, one of Joan's voices.

Prue looked at her watch and stopped writing but declined to read through her work for, she knew of old, it was at this point that she plunged into a crisis of doubt about her ability to handle the project. Perhaps Rembrandt experienced this blankness half-way through the *Night Watch*? Certainly Tolstoy did not spare Sonya his artistic doubts throughout forty years of writing masterpieces. Why would she be different?

Max was good at urging Prue not to give up when the doubts became an impediment to progress. He was punctilious in encouraging her efforts, talking things over, even doing a spot of research – and it drove her frantic. Joan was hers; her private property. Sometimes Prue dreamed that Max was taking over the project himself.

Quite often he rang in his lunchtime on the days she was at home. 'How's Joan?' he would ask.

Don't, she wanted to say. Don't.

The Platonic ideal decrees that everything has its appropriate nature. Joan came up against that one when she declared her voices had bodies, wore clothes and talked in French. In the medieval Church's view, abstract things should remain so and the Church condemned her for suggesting otherwise. (How Joan, not having had the benefit of Berlitz, was supposed to have understood her voices if they did not speak in French, was not explained by the authorities.)

Upstairs in her bedroom, Prue contemplated the appropriate nature of herself in the mirror. The outer woman, arranged in the scoop-necked Viyella blouse that suited her so well, complete with the unfurled fan of lines at the corners of her grey eyes and the long fingers which were reddened from too much washing up.

The inner, hidden woman? Hesitating over a course that, until recently, had been unthinkable. Unthinkable because it had not existed, said a voice in her head. Prue turned away from the mirror. She began to undress. On went jeans and a white T-shirt. Over those went a navy blazer, which used to belong to Max but, if she rolled up the sleeves, looked stylishly baggy. Prue's role model was the scene from *Pretty Woman* where, thus attired, Julia Roberts signalled that she was now a serious, decent woman united with Prince Charming.

Unfortunately, she did not possess the Roberts haunch but the T-shirt, made of Sea Island cotton, looked expensive and flattering against her skin. Deciding on the jewellery took several minutes. Wedding ring, of course. Pearl studs? Far too small but fake ones did not seem right. Gold chain?

The silver-topped pots on her dressing-table needed cleaning and she rearranged them, thinking what a bother they were. When she opened the drawer containing her scarves, she was as usual confronted by a swirl of materials. Prue fingered the silks and wool, old, of second-rate quality and bought when Max was not earning as much as he did now, drew out an expensive new red one and shut the drawer with a little bang.

The eyes in Max's photograph on her dressing-table followed Prue around the room. She had not noticed them do that before.

Hanging on the handle of the wardrobe Max's ties, mostly striped, established his territory in the bedroom as surely as if he had been there. To Prue, they now seemed thin and worn – like the skin that stretched over his elbows and knees and folded, just a little, over his stomach.

She avoided the photograph and sat down to brush her hair which she tied back with a black velvet ribbon. As she lifted her arm, Prue noted its fullness and the slack which should have been taut. Fear of her age gnawed at her briefly and was routed by a shiver of excited apprehension.

'Don't look at me,' she said to Max's photograph. What she meant was: don't judge me.

She got up, wriggled into a pair of loafers and picked up her shoulder-bag.

Don't go.

Don't.

But she did.

*

The hotel – which Prue knew well – prided itself on chintz, judging by the generosity with which it had been lavished around windows and ruffled on to chairs and stools.

Prue paused in the lounge entrance and Jamie rose from a flower-encrusted armchair.

'Have I kept you waiting?' she asked, brushing back strands of escaped hair.

'Do you like chintz, Prue?'

'Depends.'

'I loathe it and the three minutes forty-five seconds I have been waiting for you surrounded by it have been deeply uncomfortable.'

She laughed and then was serious. 'Why did you ask me to come?'

'Why *did* you come?'

She shifted her handbag strap. 'Because . . .'

'Exactly,' he said gently. 'Because . . .'

He took her hand as he spoke and with the other smoothed back Prue's rogue strands of hair. Registering her quickened heartbeat, she allowed him to do so, and forgave him everything.

He smiled in reassurance. 'I am here on a genuine work project and there's nothing wrong with lunch.'

'That's what Caligula told his victims before eating them.'

Over coffee, Jamie told her about Lara and Jenny, and Prue, listening hungrily, realized with a sense of *déjà vu* that she had heard the story before. It was Max's story, too, and the pain that had been inflicted was as deep as his, although Jamie was not as honest or perhaps as wise in himself to acknowledge it as Max had been. Prue dropped her napkin on to the table. Perhaps there was something about her – face? expression? lack of glamour? – that attracted men who carried these secret histories?

If taxed, Jamie could have explained. Prue was peaceful-looking: so warm and still and intent that she invited men to break their habit of silence.

Later, he suggested Prue show him around the cathedral and they walked down Jewry Street and into the cathedral grounds. The tourist season was well under way and the city was crowded but the precinct escaped the worst excesses. Summer had arrived and the sun had come with it. Hot and vigorous, it shone down on air that pulsed with heat, on flesh slicked with damp, on the rounded curves of women, fattening buds in the gardens, and grass that was still plump and juicy from the spring rain. People sat in groups, or meandered down the paths, and children wheeled, noisy icecream-stained starlings.

Prue and Jamie sauntered towards the entrance to the cathedral.

'Like pilgrims,' said Jamie, who was not usually given to poetry or history.

'Your name *is* Beckett,' Prue pointed out.

Jamie rarely considered the implication of his name. 'A wastrel and a saint.'

'If you're true to it, you'll have a wonderful excessive time and then repent at leisure.'

Prue's hand brushed Jamie's, and flesh whispered together, engendered an impulse to cling and a mutual warmth, and fell apart.

Inside the cathedral, Jamie admired the thirteenth-century floor tiles in the retro-choir and the Great Screen behind the high altar.

'The original statuary was broken up during the Reformation and replaced during the nineteenth century.' Prue pointed at an example. 'That's why Queen Victoria's up there with the Saxons.'

That amused Jamie. Secretly Prue watched him, her gaze

a moth pulled to the flame. He was standing with one hand in his pocket, the other holding a pamphlet they had picked up at the entrance about the cathedral. Absorbed, slightly tense, eyes narrowed, an assembly of flesh tones, of blue veins, of light indrawn breaths, of pulses beating in his neck and at his wrist, of grey suit against the blue-green stripe of his shirt, Jamie, contrasted with the gloom and sanctity of the cathedral, became a voluptuous object.

Assaulted by colour, smell and yet conscious of darkness clutching at the circles of light, Prue inhaled candlewax and incense. Jamie turned to say something to her, something about Queen Victoria not being a Good Thing, something she never could remember and, with a little sigh, Prue yielded and leapt.

Metamorphosed, she soared up into the dark, sweeping spaces in which God dwelt, enriched and at peace before the warfare began. The steps up to this moment had been the tiny steps of the infant. The flailing of a novice. The itch and tease of the tentative. Now, she walked as an initiate.

Shaken and shaking by what had been unleashed, Prue, a forty-one-year-old – with lines, for goodness' sake, at the corners of her eyes – who had not meant this ever to happen, said 'Jamie?' Her tone conveyed that for which, unconsciously, he had been listening and waiting. Very gently, lightly and with care, he touched her fingers with his own.

After a second or two, she moved on down the aisle.

'Why don't you light a candle?' he called after her, producing a coin. Prue looked at it. A simple twenty-pence piece held between lean fingers. He had made a similar gesture at the Ivy, and he was doing it again, only now he was offering it to her as a symbol of whatever lay between them. She hesitated only a second or two, and took it.

'You ought to pray.' She led him towards St Swithun's

memorial where racks of candles were burning and added, to appease God (if he was there) whom she must be grievously offending, 'Not about anything secular.'

'I've lost the habit, Prue.'

A flare from the candles caught Prue's face in profile as she touched the tapers to the wick, and traced her generous features with soft light. Jamie drew in his breath.

The candle joined the others. Flames shifted in the draught, and, mesmerized, Prue gazed at them until the light fused into a dazzling expanse that hurt her eyes.

Outside, the colours were equally dazzling. Prue retied her scarf, which had worked loose. 'Jane Austen died in Winchester,' she said. 'Do you want to see the house?'

She led Jamie through the Close into College Street and he gazed dutifully at the bow-windowed front. 'This is a private house', proclaimed a notice on the door.

'They must be driven crazy.' Jamie ignored the house and looked down at Prue.

'She died from Addison's disease, you know.'

'What's that?' Jamie continued to look into her face, and search her eyes with his own, and she shook her head. It was like having the components of her body taken apart and put together in a different arrangement.

He was due to catch the 4.05 back to London and they turned north and set off for the station. Half-way down one street they passed a shop selling electrical goods and videos. *Dances with Wolves* ... *Thunderbirds* ... *Jean de Florette* ... *Brief Encounter* ... With its distilled forties agony, the expression on Celia Johnson's face accosted passers-by. A camcorder had been placed in the window, trapping pedestrians on the screen. Prue caught sight of them both as they passed, grainy, unreal and turned into fiction, ratified by being imprinted on celluloid – as so much was.

'Look, Jamie.' She stopped. On the screen the space

between them was filled in by a shop front. Jamie moved closer and the image on the screen responded obediently. She felt him draw her closer and his fingers press into her back, exploratory and possessive and she thought that she had waited all her life for that touch. Then she thought: I'm going mad.

'You'll be late,' she said.

At the station, Jamie told her not to wait and Prue obeyed. As she walked down the platform, the down train from London drew into the station. Because she made a point of not looking back, Prue did not see Max alight from the carriage where he always sat.

Max saw Prue. Or rather, he caught sight of the distinctive scarf over the blazer. At first, it did not register in his brain. Then it occurred to him that Prue sometimes wore a red scarf and his navy blazer. Later, as he stood in the taxi queue, having rung home twice for a lift, it dawned on him that it had been Prue.

In the train, Jamie occupied himself by staring out of the window, his neglected briefcase lying beside him on the seat, and analysing Prue.

Little things. Strands of hair that required tying back. A red scarf caught in a knot over her chest. Sharing fried sausages in a kitchen filled with rubble. Her trick of looking at him. Sleepy-eyed but there.

How could unimportant things awake such yearning? Such frantic hunger? And was it not true that the clichés – a pitching stomach, unreliable knees, a wildly beating heart – were part and parcel of falling in love?

Jamie adjusted his position. Violet would never eat two sausages and ask for more. Violet, Jamie now realized with a major shift in loyalties, never listened.

As the train sped through southern England, past back gardens filled with apple trees and a litter of plastic toys, washing and lawns pocked by weather and pollution, past ugly office buildings, strips of wasteland encrusted with abandoned cars, through complicated railway junctions, the life that Jamie had constructed, and which had seemed so solid, began to assume dream-like qualities. As the carriage slid along the tracks so, too, did his sense of direction.

Fear pricked at his neck. Fear that the centre of his existence was not going to hold and that he had been instrumental in its dissolution. On the other hand, Jamie was a male and the testosterone that had driven him to reach and take throughout his adult life was not going to disappear. Like breathing, those reflexes were unconscious.

'Were you at the station today?' Max asked his wife over tea. 'I thought I saw you.'

They were sitting on the patio outside the kitchen. The air was warm and filled with summer scent. Prue poured out her cup of tea and during those seconds made a decision.

'No. Why should I be there? I didn't know you were coming home early.'

'I should have let you know before I left the office and saved the taxi fare.'

'Never mind, darling.'

Prue's teacup rattled in the saucer.

... No, no, Max, where *have* you got that idea from? Of course, Jack and me are nothing more than friends.

Jack and *I*, Helen.

Stop being so pedantic, Max. It's so typical.

Eyes narrowed in anger, hair scraped back over a face

that seemed peeled back to its bone. Scarlet lips mouthing untruths.

Helen later amended her statements to something more approximate to the truth. Yes, Max, actually Jack and I did have a *little* something. Not serious, you must see that. But I get so bored, darling, stuck in Dainton. It wasn't my fault he came sniffing round.

It wasn't your fault that you didn't send him packing?

Helen had got used to a glass of whisky, or four, by this point and had almost stopped eating. Drink and semi-starvation gave her a transparent, insubstantial look, like a leaf skeleton tracked with veins to which flesh had once clung.

And Violet? Max persisted.

Along with the whisky, Helen had taken to shrugging.

And Violet?

Violet's all right, Max. Don't worry about her. Everything's fine if we all calm down. I'll get rid of Jack if that's what you want.

Yes, Max had wanted that but, like everything Helen promised, it did not turn out quite that way. By the finish of the bloody battle of their marriage, it did not matter any longer what Max wanted. It mattered what Jack wanted. And why Jack did not have the grace to get himself killed in the car crash that eventually killed Helen, Max had never worked out, or accepted.

Finding yourself, an ordinary person, at the mercy of a beating, onrushing tide of pain, impotence and ugliness was, at best, bewildering. Max had not anticipated such swirling depths in his ordinary life . . .

Over the teacup, a tempered Max, wise in the art of lying, regarded his second wife. He had known for some time that the twenty-year difference in their ages might surface eventually. No matter, he was prepared. He felt differently now about fidelity than he had at forty. No, the struggle now surely was to yield to the possibility of his wife looking elsewhere with the grace and common sense that he had, in theory, perfected.

Allow her an episode, he had sermonized to himself, falling into the error of imagining that bowing to the inevitable was the only course to take. The past tends to dictate the blueprint for the future – and there was, after all, much to lay at Helen's door. Or, when the thought was too painful, Max amended it: allow that it is probable, that it may happen.

He did not regard his conclusions as presumptuous, which they were. Or that he was traducing Prue by prescribing her infidelity. It seemed right to be sensible, to understand, to take a step back. After all, he had a lot for which to give thanks. He had his home and his daughters, and his feelings for them were so satisfying that they were sufficient.

Then again, he was not getting younger and the pricks (he excused the wordplay) and promptings of his flesh were not what they had once been. To make love these days required a different combination of engorged flesh and triggered hormones. It took the thought and preparation of the voyager embarking on a taxing journey.

In these ruminations, Max forgot another truth: theory is not the same as practice.

Prue refilled their cups, and had an extraordinary feeling that Max was looking at her along the barrel of a gun. She drank the cooling tea and listened to the evening birdsong. Guilt . . . She tried to concentrate on guilt. Guilt creates lies and monsters.

Instead she felt the most complete and utter joy, as wild and beautiful as the swallow's cry from the hot sky.

*

'When?' said Jamie on the telephone the next day. 'When, Prue?'

'I don't know,' she said hopelessly, and tried to be correct and right. 'Never.'

'You don't really mean that.'

'Yes. I do.'

'I'll find a way,' said Jamie. 'Tell me when you can get away.'

She opened her mouth to speak, stopped and tried again.

'Prue. Don't renege. Prue?'

She told him when.

Chapter Twelve

Emmy upended the baby and laid him on the changing mat. The nursery at Austen Road was not as pristine as it had once been. A pile of soiled baby clothes lay on the floor, cotton wool littered the top of the chest of drawers, and baby lotion dripped from a plastic bottle lying on its side.

Edward did not want his nappy changed and squirmed. Clamping one hand on his stomach, Emmy reached for a clean one. After a struggle, she managed to attach it to the baby.

'You horror.'

She bent over him until their noses met. Edward's eyes did a wild dance and he giggled and pulled at her hair.

'No, you don't.' Emmy unlocked his fingers and levered him upright. 'Pull your own.'

The telephone rang as she was negotiating the stairs with a wriggling Edward in her arms. Emmy made herself take the last few treads very carefully before plonking the baby on the floor and launching herself at speed towards it.

'Everything all right, Emmy? I thought I'd give you a quick ring before the meeting.'

She may not have shone at school, but Emmy had quickly learnt that the phrase 'a quick ring' hid many meanings. Because she was charitable and innocent (for it never occurred to Emmy that people might misconstrue her motives) she had, at first, concluded that 'a quick ring' equalled guilt – until she realized she was being checked up on. Violet never deployed subtlety unless she thought it was worth her while. It drove Emmy mad.

Today disappointment made her snippy as well. She pictured Violet at her desk, coffee (real) steaming beside her in the French cup and saucer on which she insisted, perfectly cut and conditioned hair swinging, nails varnished a (perfect) bright red. Perfect because Violet never did the washing-up.

'Fine, Mrs Beckett. I've just changed him.'

At her feet Edward was discharging a pool of dribble into the brand-new carpet. Emmy rolled her eyes at him.

'Make sure he eats his lunch, won't you?'

Safely out of sight, Emmy raised her eyes heavenward and twirled the flex around her finger. 'Steak and chips,' she muttered. 'Rare.'

'What did you say, Emmy?' At her end Violet frowned, suspicious suddenly.

'Nothing, Mrs Beckett.'

'Look, I must go. There's a meeting. Tell him I rang, won't you?'

Emmy replaced the receiver. Either Violet had lost her tea trolley or she was thinking of something else – which would not surprise her. She squatted down beside Edward, grasped each hand and pulled him up until he was half off the floor. The baby's head fell back like a plum on a spindly branch and he made pleasurable noises.

'Your mum rang,' Emmy informed him, blowing softly on his hands. 'Had to dash to a meeting and rule the world so couldn't talk to you. Sent her love.'

Edward had no intelligible comment to make on the subject. Emmy carried him into the kitchen, managing to avoid looking at the telephone gleaming so whitely on the wall.

'Lunch, Teddy-bear.'

Lunch – any meal – required preparations as for battle. Emmy spread a sheet of newspaper on the floor and dragged the high chair on to it. Then she locked Edward into the harness and poked the fastening of a plastic bib that reminded her of a landing-stage on the moon around Edward's neck.

'Steak,' she said, spooning repellent-looking yuck – apparently braised beef and carrots – from a jar (Violet had approved the brand) into his mouth. 'Without the chips. Tough titty.'

Edward sucked at the spoon with the strength of a sumo-octopus and ate the lot. Emmy gave him puréed apple and Edward hurled the spoon on to the floor and bent over to stare, owl-like, at the results. Emmy swore.

The phone rang. Emmy let it ring for precisely five rings and then grabbed it.

'Hi,' said Angus.

Emmy sat down hard. 'Hallo.'

'What are you doing?'

Emmy eyed the horrors on the floor. 'Ducking flying baby food.'

'Fancy a beer?'

She found it hard to articulate and swallowed. 'Now?' she managed.

'Why not? I'm in the area and I've got the van.'

Emmy sighed and proceeded to explain why not. Bring the baby, said Angus. A warm little picture took shape in Emmy's mind of being tucked up with Angus and Edward in a pub with a fire and horse brasses and a beer. A real couple, saying nice, warm things to each other like: 'You make me happy' or, better than that, 'We are so happy together.' (Emmy's experience of real couples was limited mostly to what she had read.)

'Nonsense,' Angus insisted, 'you can bring the baby and his mother won't know if you don't tell her.'

That was how Emmy found herself crouched over a beer-stained wooden bench in a wind made colder because it was supposed to be summer with Edward grizzling beside her in his pushchair. The pub overlooked Wandsworth Common, which was pleasant, but was on a main road and traffic thundered past. Emmy's nose was running and the beer was not marvellous either. A full ashtray lay between her and Angus.

'Aren't you glad you listened to me?' Angus ignored the grizzles.

Emmy had made a discovery. Love – or lust, she was not sure which – did not keep you warm. June had chucked in one of those days designed to keep you on your toes, which conveyed in no uncertain terms that if you had hoped for summer, forget it. Emmy felt guilty about Edward whose little hands had gone almost blue. For the fifth time, she leant over to pull on his mittens.

Edward pulled them off.

'Bugger you,' said Emmy.

Angus was telling her about his latest job, a conversion in Wandsworth.

'Pity the Becketts have just done the bathroom,' he said. 'We've just ripped one out. Practically brand-new. Avocado.'

Pale green, stroked with cream . . . Emmy's fantasies took off. Shimmering, slippery, iridescent temples to cleanliness. Water sliding off skin, flushed pink and white, oozing into folds, between toes, along flat planes. Heat meshed with steam and tuberose scent from the bottles on the shelves.

'Pity,' she agreed, amazed at how quickly imagination could slip the leash.

Angus shoved the ashtray aside. 'What are you doing at the weekend?' he asked.

Emmy shrugged. 'Not much.'

'Fancy coming out with me?'

Emmy wanted to say no. She wanted to get up, seize Edward and run – away from the golden youth who was issuing tantalizing invitations which, she knew, *she knew*, would end in disaster.

Why did she know? Because, it did not make sense that he, beautiful, beautiful Angus, wanted to invite her, plain Emmy from Dainton, out on the best night of the week. Independence, an unscalded heart, caution, were better things by far than the release of saying yes and an aftermath of regret.

'Come on, then,' Angus urged. 'I won't rape you.'

Emmy flushed with distress. 'Of course not.'

'I won't, you know.'

A trio struggled down the street: an old lady in a motorized wheelchair, accompanied by two equally ancient companions in headscarves tied so that they resembled nuns' wimples. The three limped and bumped along, a dance of hovering death.

'Yeah. I'll come,' said Emmy.

Violet dumped her briefcase on the kitchen table. It was an aggressive gesture. Alerted, Emmy looked round from the sink. In his chair, Edward grizzled at the sight of his mother.

'I want a word with you, Emmy.'

Emmy dried her hands. Violet stood with hers on her hips.

'Did you or did you not go to a pub at lunchtime?'

Emmy swallowed. 'Yes, I did.'

'With Edward.' It was a statement not a question.

'Yes.'

'How *dare* you?'

Taken by surprise by the explosion of rage, Emmy backed up against the draining-board.

'How *dare* you, Emmy? I could not believe it when Mary Louder rang to tell me she had seen you with a man outside a pub, drinking. What do you think you were doing?'

'Having a drink, Mrs Beckett.'

'I do not pay you to conduct a social life, Emmy. You are paid to look after my son. It was a thoroughly irresponsible thing to do. Edward might have caught cold. Anyway, I don't allow him near pubs.'

It was only half an hour.

Emmy thought of the countless evenings she had worked late, and the weekends she had babysat ('as a favour to us, Emmy'). Unfamiliar rage – partly at Violet's unreasonableness and partly because she had never truly appreciated until this moment how unfair people could be when their own interests were at stake – which she only just succeeded in controlling pricked underneath her skin.

'I can't trust you.' Violet was speaking in a low, dramatic voice which concealed both a real panic that Emmy was not reliable and the fear that she, the supermanager, had made a crucial misjudgement. 'Looking after a baby is a very serious thing. I *must* be able to trust you.'

How much did trust cost? Eighty pounds, a hundred pounds a week (plus tax and NI, of course)? Cheap at the price, Mrs Beckett. Violet's expression wavered under Emmy's enraged stare and, then, it dawned on Emmy that the boot was probably on the other foot: Mrs Glossy Beckett did not trust herself either.

'Who was this man? Was he a complete stranger?'

'He's . . .' well, what was Angus? Emmy explained that Angus was, at least, known to the family. Thankfully, Violet seized on the let-out (for which she had been searching): at least she would not need to resort to anything drastic and inconvenient like giving Emmy the sack.

'Listen, Emmy. I shall give you one more chance.' You bet, Emmy thought. Procuring nannies takes time. 'But', Violet judged it best to moderate her tone, 'if I ever discover again that you have been doing this sort of thing you will have to leave.'

Perhaps I want to anyway? What do you think about that? Emmy prudently remained silent.

But a curious little pulse beat close to her heart. Hold on, it said. Emmy listened to its thuds. Of what else did it speak? Of stubbornness, a wish to give Violet as good as she gave. Of dawning feelings that would not be controlled.

'I'm sorry,' she said. 'I thought it would be all right to have a drink. I took good care of Edward.' She gave a little shrug which, more than anything, convinced Violet. 'Of course I did, Mrs Beckett.'

Violet opened the briefcase, extracted the latest edition of *Vanity Fair* and tossed it on the table. Her expression had turned remote – the sort of expression that suggested it was unfair she should be so bothered by these domestic matters. From experience, Emmy knew she had lost interest.

'Let's forget it, Emmy. In between drinks did you manage to do the shopping?'

Emmy sighed. Denied attention for so long, Edward opened his mouth and yelled.

On Saturday evening, Angus took Emmy bowling in Streatham with his mates. Violet eyed him when he turned up at the front door in black jeans and boots, said nothing by way of greeting, left him standing on the doorstep and returned to the drawing room. Jamie, however, was more forthcoming and invited Angus into the hall and made conversation until Emmy appeared from the top of the house.

'Have a good time,' said Jamie.

Emmy cast him a look from under her lids and nodded. He was smiling good-naturedly and without the least side.

'Stuck-up bitch,' said Angus, not quite out of earshot of the front garden. 'I wouldn't give her house room.'

Because she was nervous and wanted it to be all right with Angus, Emmy found herself agreeing, although she now realized there were some things about Violet that she quite liked and – almost – admired.

Feminine solidarity can take many forms but perhaps its strongest manifestation is of one woman for another who has been betrayed by a man. Emmy was not at all sure about Jamie and his lunches with Mrs Valour. It was possible that her own newly sensitized feelings were leading her astray, but still she wondered. It was only an instinct, the prod of a half-formed thought, but she sensed a feeling between them, the more surprising for being so unlikely. Unfurling her wings in the world as she was, Emmy had yet to trust her judgement.

She looked back to Number 6 from which sounds of Mozart's *Così Fan Tutte* were issuing. It looked so solid and painted, a cradle for clean shelves, beeswaxed furniture and ironed sheets. The empty home in Dainton hovered in her mind, a boiled, sterilized repository of her childhood, until Angus dropped a gloved hand on to her knee and Emmy forgot everything. Rankled by Violet's attitude, Angus did a lot of accelerator revving, the van rattled noisily and he drew out of the parking space with as much noise as he could muster.

Angus's mates, Ted, Bill and a six-footer introduced as Nails, were distinguished by their earrings, ranks of them, mounting in glittering concordances to the outer reaches of their earlobes. Emmy was fascinated. Serious male plumage had not reached Andover. *One* earring, perhaps . . .

Cherry and Sal, the girls, did not wear jewellery at all, apart from plaited-wool friendship bracelets. Their uniform, however, matched the boys'. Black jeans or leggings, T-shirts, a thicker shirt worn on top, very often tartan, and cropped hair. One of them, Sal, was luscious.

Emmy trembled inside her Doc Martens and cursed the day she had ever heard the word 'perm'. These girls were so sharp, so icily streetwise. So London – and she was so Andover.

They eyed her up and down, these Juliets and Portias of the streets, decided she was a negligible threat and proceeded, in the main, to ignore her. Not surprised, Emmy was gratified, nevertheless, to discover that her bowling skills more than matched theirs.

'Not bad,' said Sal critically at the end of the third round. Underneath her grey T-shirt, her pointed breasts swayed like palms in a tropical breeze and her lips, like plump sofas, glistened.

Emmy permitted herself a mental tick, and then intercepted a look between Angus and Sal, a sultry exchange into which was mixed anticipation. Her satisfaction vanished and a cocktail of terror, jealousy and sick apprehension slipped into her bloodstream. What on earth was she doing here? Here they were, the Sals, Cherrys and Emmys, displayed like buds on the apple tree for the hovering bullfinch, and she reminded herself what happens when the bullfinch has been and gone: no apples.

At the end of the game, Angus came over and slipped his arm round Emmy's shoulders. 'Fancy Indian or Chinese?' His eyes slid from one girl to the other, charm and sex and, yet, a kind of easy tenderness, mixed into his face. He could so easily have been repellent, but he wasn't – he wasn't at all.

Emmy did not like curry, which she tried to hide over the baskets of naan bread and Chicken Vindaloo. The restaurant into which they had piled was cheap, crowded, hot and smoky. The air was like damp cling-film and moisture glistened on the green flock wallpaper. Emmy swallowed a mouthful of chicken and regretted it.

Sal eyed her. 'Not up to your standards?'

Emmy endeavoured to answer, a tricky procedure if the roof of your mouth has been blasted off. Meanwhile, Angus focused on Sal's bosom.

'You eat enough to sink a tanker,' he said.

Sal preened. 'I can take it.'

Yes, well. Emmy shot a covert look at Sal's Titian hair which owed more to Body Shop than to nature.

'If you like it,' said Angus, and leant over towards Emmy. 'Had enough?'

Sal lit up a cigarette and blew smoke in Angus's direction. 'Where to next?'

Next? Emmy had been cherishing fond thoughts of her hot-water bottle and her silent, unshared bed.

'I think it's time I got back,' she said, and reached for her fringed bag. She forced herself to look into Angus's face. 'That was great. See you all around.'

'Don't be stupid,' he said. 'You don't know your way back. Stick with us. I'll see you right.'

They piled into the van and hit the South Circular with a screech of brakes and made for Brixton. The disco there had a couple of fridges mounted above the entrance and the queue to get in was mainly black, funky and noisy. Getting down from the van, Emmy shivered.

Her mental horizons were shifting bewilderingly.

Inside the disco, the noise drilled holes in eardrums. Sal hijacked the opportunity to collar Angus and a dazzling show of body language went into operation. Angus was all male and no male could possibly resist the delights being flaunted – practically unveiled – in front of him.

Keeping a tight clutch on her bag, Emmy watched them dancing amid the shrieks and screams, the coloured lights and smoke-wreathed figures. A dream coalesced, tantalized and splintered, and she was left jolted by shocks of jealousy accompanied by an equally coruscating current of desire.

When Angus disengaged himself from Sal to claim Emmy, he was met by a blank, wooden face.

'I want to go,' Emmy reiterated, her face paled by the light into a ghost's. 'Point me in the right direction. I'll walk.'

'Running away, Emmy?'

There was no point in not being honest. 'Yes.'

The funny thing was, Emmy was sure Angus understood.

'I'll drive you,' said Angus, and flicked her under her chin. 'You are stupid, you know.'

'What about the others?'

Angus glanced briefly over his shoulder at the heaving mass and Sal sent him a smouldering look. 'I'll come back.'

For some while, Emmy had been convinced that a fox was living in the garden of Number 6. A flash of red, a bark in the night, the scatter of refuse around the dustbins, a hint of feralness in the air: these were clues she had quickly picked up. She spent several nights subsequent to the bowling outing watching out of the window in the small hours.

If she was not sure about the fox, there was no doubt about the pair of grey squirrels who had colonized the scrubby bit at the end of the garden. Manky they were, and cheeky chappies, who danced and spun along the garden fences like a chorus line.

During the day, Emmy watched them, and envied their busyness, and the manner in which they cheeked cats who juddered with aggression but who had grown too large and indolent from tinned catfood to do anything about it.

One of the pair had hidden a treasure under the lavender bush, a nut perhaps, and, tail at full mast, he returned again and again to root under the spiky grey branches. Emmy watched him. He knew better than to find what he was seeking.

Angus had bent over her that Saturday night – no, Sunday morning by then – when he delivered her back, and Emmy, suborned by her longings, had raised her face blindly to his. Then she turned abruptly away. She might not have been wise enough to keep her feelings under control, but she knew enough to hide them.

Perhaps it was as well that she was not going to find out what lay behind Angus's golden head and tawny skin for that might spoil the magic, too.

Chapter Thirteen

'When, Prue?' Jamie asked.

When?

Jane's long summer exeat usually coincided with Max's fishing week in Scotland. It was a pity, but there it was. In Max's calendar, the date shared equal rank with his shooting days in autumn, both as immutable as Christmas. Prue had long since accepted these slots in the year and, after the first few occasions when she was inclined to feel abandoned, looked forward to them as a break in the routine and a chance to rearrange her mental furniture.

The departure was generally accompanied by last-minute panics and late-night searches for fishing equipment and the fittings for the special picnic basket Max had inherited from his father. Each year, Prue meant to earmark a place in the attic for them where they could be easily located, and each year failed to do so.

She was up early making egg sandwiches and decanting coffee and tea into the old-fashioned Thermoses from the picnic set. With their echo from another age, she had grown fond of them. They were solid and did not let you down. Prue chopped mint on to the egg, admired the colours, added mayonnaise and spread the mixture on the bread.

Dressed in his favourite corduroys and the jersey that suited him so much better than the city suit, Max seemed pale and preoccupied. Prue put it down to the restless night both of them had spent, which neither had acknowledged to the other. Admitting to insomnia in a marriage was an intimacy only possible when it was going well.

What was unusual was Prue's lack of enthusiasm to sort it out.

Max kissed Jane goodbye and instead of saying, 'Look after your mother,' as he always did, held his daughter tight and said nothing.

'Bring me back some Edinburgh rock,' she muttered into his shoulder. Jane liked its colours better than its taste, and it was a request that she knew would not give her father any bother to carry out.

Max released Jane who, sensing that he was a little troubled, assumed an expression that suggested goodbyes were an awful bore. Max looked as though he had already departed mentally, and he said in a manner that warned Prue not to fuss, 'I'll phone when I reach Edinburgh.'

'Have a good time.' Prue handed Max the fishing bag and the picnic.

Much later, mulling over events, trying to piece together truths from what had happened – truth being as elusive as the scent in a winter garden, a cloud in a wind, or a reputation in politics – Prue remembered that Max had not kissed her goodbye.

'So what shall we do with ourselves before we go up to London, Janey?' she asked, as they sat down to lunch *à deux.*

Jane had spent the morning huddled into the sofa listening to the radio but she perked up at the question and expounded at length on several ideas. These involved an outing to the Romsey Rapids, a definitive update of her wardrobe and an excursion to buy a new pair of roller blades.

'What about taking a picnic tea on the bikes?' suggested

Prue, warming to a mental vision of mother and daughter idling down flower-studded country lanes. 'We could do a day trip somewhere.'

Jane looked at Prue as if her mother had only recently alighted on Planet Earth. 'No way, Mum. It isn't warm enough.'

Prue propped her elbows on the table and cupped her chin in her hands. 'No way,' she conceded.

Jane was quiet for thirty seconds or so. 'I've got some prep to do,' she said, and chewed a tiny mouthful of pork chop. Prue had finished hers and sat waiting. Then she asked, 'Mum, what's adultery?'

Prue fought to control her expression for, quick as any reflex, guilt mastered her stiffened jaw and widened eyes. *Guilt for what she had not yet done.* Unfamiliar with it, untutored in dealing with it, unsure of its properties (did it always stretch, lie, distort?) Prue's panic made her forget that connections did not necessarily exist between things even if they appear to do so. Nevertheless, she *was* familiar with the teaching which held that the distinction between the intention to commit a sin and actually doing so was negligible.

'What *do* you mean, darling?'

'We've been discussing it in RE.' Jane seemed impatient with her mother's slowness. 'You know in the Bible, the story of the woman taken in adultery.'

Prue subsided. 'Oh, her,' she said rapidly. 'I'd forgotten.' Normally, Prue took seriously her parental duty to explain. Today she gave only the briefest of outlines.

Jane considered what Prue had told her. 'Wasn't she stupid, Mum, to get herself into trouble?'

Prue fiddled with her glass of water. 'It's not always straightforward, Jane. You will discover that as you grow older. Think of when you get into trouble at school. You don't mean to but you do.'

As a defence it was not notable. Prue knew that. But at the final count, the matter was simple. You either did something, or you did not.

'But, you see,' said her daughter, pushing away her half-finished plate. 'In a funny way I do want to get into trouble. It's more fun.'

Framed in the window, the beech tree at the end of the garden swayed in counterpoint to the *Prunus autumnalis* which was now fledged in green.

'Bloody hell,' Prue said.

'Mum! You tell me not to swear.'

Prue leant over the table and caught her daughter's hand. Its slightly grubby arrangement of skin and bones lay trustingly in hers and, more than any theory, had the power to make Prue stop in her tracks: to reconsider what can be disgorged from the most ordered and ordinary of linen cupboards or kitchens once they become muddled and out of control.

Prue stroked the hand resting in hers. 'You, my girl, are becoming bossy.'

A trip to *Phantom of the Opera* and roller blades it was, the latter resulting in a crop of bruises to which Jane would not allow Prue to apply arnica because she wanted to display the war wounds back at school.

The plan was to spend two nights at Austen Road, which would allow time for the show and, as Prue explained to Jane, for research in the London Library. Jane enjoyed the show and so, in a masochistic fashion, did Prue, who found herself biting her lip at the spectacle of the Phantom's agonized, racked desire. But such was the decibel level that she emerged from their fabulously expensive seats into the cool night feeling as though she had been hit on the head with a hammer.

'Brilliant,' said Jane happily. 'I love it when it's sad.'

Later, Prue lay in the freshly painted spare room and listened (as Emmy was doing) to the bark of Emmy's urban fox. Max, fortified by several whiskies, would be asleep in his hotel lapped by mountains, shadows and the rainsoaked Highland air. Sleep peacefully, she willed him across the miles, and felt the burn of her treachery work its way down her body.

She endeavoured to concentrate on the things that mattered: the WI meeting, the manure that needed to be dug into the vegetable patch, Jane's half-term report. What had Molly been going on about? Ah, yes. How dreadful it was that the parish magazine had been requisitioned for the debate over fox-hunting, which was rapidly reaching flashpoint. These were the bricks that built a life. Prue's fingers searched for the edge of the pillow case. They mattered and should not be carelessly overlooked. But, faced with a solid, undistinguished municipal building or the breathtaking achievement of Michelangelo's Sistine Chapel, or the grey-tiled fantasies of Joan's jewel-like, turreted cities, it was difficult not to turn away and seek out the beauty of the soaring line.

The unhunted fox in the London garden barked again and Prue dozed on and off. Animals were safer in cities than in the country. No one would dream of setting hounds on the scabby, bone-thin scavenger rooting in the dustbins set out like plastic tombstones along the street.

Along the beige-carpeted landing lay Jamie. She pictured him sprawled under the duvet in the pyjamas that, in a strange anticipation of intimacy, she had washed several times. Prue imagined listening to his breathing and with a curious finger traced the outline of his body.

She hovered. She watched. She breathed kisses over the silent body and tasted cool, silky flesh under her hot mouth, and tried to sleep.

The next morning, she woke early and dressed in an emerald green silk shirt and jeans. She brushed her hair, which she was allowing to grow longer, tied it back and put on a pair of new pearl earrings which were large enough to make a statement about her confidence and finances.

A Woman Taken in Adultery.

The night's dreamings returned as she addressed her reflection. Question: if she had already sinned in her mind, surely it was irrelevant if her body followed suit, all of which argued it was fine to go ahead. The sin had been committed. Had the doctrinalists thought that one out?

Leaving Jane to fuss happily over Edward with Emmy, she assembled her notebooks and said goodbye. Eyes shining, Jane glanced up at her mother. 'Take care, Mum.'

Prue hesitated, and then let herself out of the door.

The foliage in the gardens and on the trees was lit by an emerging sun, and pollution wrapped the road in a thick nap. The tube was hot, slow and littered with discarded morning papers. Someone had been sick and the combination of vomit and sickly sweet disinfectant made Prue gag. She picked up a *Daily Mail* . . . Dan Quayle was criticizing a television soap for depicting a main character giving birth to an illegitimate baby, and was also of the opinion that the Los Angeles riots were due to a 'poverty of values'.

Poverty of values. Prue cast aside the paper.

At the entrance to the London Library, she bumped into Adrian League, one of Max's colleagues who had retired the previous year, a fellow fishing enthusiast. Then he had looked eighty. Now he looked a brisk sixty or so in studiedly casual clothes.

'Goodness,' she said. 'You look twenty—' and realized she was being tactless. 'You look wonderful.'

Adrian had never been one for small talk and got to the point at once. 'What are you doing here, Prue?'

'Research.' She felt she did not sound as convincing as she should. Adrian's eyebrows lifted, the implication being that the last thing he associated with Prue was research. That annoyed her.

'Yes,' she said. 'I'm writing a biography of Joan of Arc. Practically finished, in fact.'

Adrian drew Prue to one side and his expression sharpened. 'Have you got a publisher?'

It was a question that worldly people always asked Prue, and Adrian was very worldly.

'Yes,' she lied, and smiled sweetly. 'In fact a couple of publishers are vying for the rights.' She popped the cherry on the iced bun and completed her perdition. 'I have to make up my mind very soon. Good, isn't it?'

Afterwards in the concealing recesses of the history shelves, Prue's cheeks burned. Not having a track record in lies – hers tended to rebound – she was amazed by the speed and determination with which she had resorted to them. Nevertheless, Adrian's superciliousness had won him a poke in the ribs and she had enjoyed watching him struggle to readjust his expression. How she was going to extricate herself from it she didn't know. Did it matter?

All these lies.

Yes, no, yes? She supposed they did, otherwise she was removing the base on which she had pitched the tent of her life.

Prue bent her head over the books. Every so often she

looked up. The seconds walked slowly past. She smelt dust, assorted scents from the women in the room, a whiff of someone unwashed, felt her own warmth. The books on the shelves seemed so solid, so large, so formed, and their dun, rich colours deep and mysterious.

At twelve thirty, Prue packed up her books into a large, reinforced plastic bag that bit into her fingers and made her way into Oxford Street.

Oxford Street was full of women carrying similar plastic bags and similar secrets, a feminine conspiracy silting down layers to create a petrified forest of lies. The egocentricity of passion and guilt were mixed in Prue's imagination.

At Great Cumberland Street, she turned right, walked north to a hotel set back in a crescent, and halted by the entrance, which was spruced up with a red and white striped awning. A further step forward was required.

Or a turnaround and retreat.

Why hadn't adultery just happened? It was so much easier to be dragged out of turquoise waters on a Caribbean beach and ravished. Or to be thrown down into summer hay. Or to be woken at midnight and told by the equivalent of the man with the box of Milk Tray that you had no option but to yield.

Setting your face north up Great Cumberland Street was harder, an operation edged around with the mundane and small decisions that made it unbearable and took away the joyous, glamorous elements that had made it inviting in the first place.

Then why do it?

The bag was making Prue's arm ache and her back twinged. Strands of hair stuck to her cheek and her tights felt damp around the waistband. She did not feel *fatale*, but shaky and unconvincing. According to novels, and to Kate who listened to tales from other women, other women did this sort of thing with style. Or they should. There was no point in transgressing if you did it meagrely.

I can't do this. The traffic beat on in its uncaring fashion and Prue fled back down the street. She stopped at the first junction and looked back over her shoulder to the red and white stripe.

If you are hungry, why don't you eat? said a voice in her head.

Prue breathed in the traffic fumes, tasted sulphur and carbon monoxide and felt them stream through her blood, alongside the slippery ache for Jamie. Oh, yes, she couldn't deny she *was* hungry.

Jamie.

Max?

Two minutes later she was standing in the hotel entrance, a depressing mixture of cream paint and fake crystal lights.

'Can I help you?'

The clerk at the reception desk was a brown person: eyes and hair of the same colour, and no doubt his thoughts were brown. Prue instantly took against his expression which she imagined combined knowingness and contempt. Because – the voice in her head had switched tack – you are not the first awkward-looking woman to hover in a strange hallway, and certainly not the last.

She declined the offer to be shown upstairs. Number 35, first floor. Prue made for the lift and then changed her mind and trod up the stairs.

Why did this have to be so obvious?

The anchor pattern in the carpet transfixed her, mainly because she kept her eyes fixed on the floor. When she raised them, it was to read the numerals 3 and 5. Her heartbeat jumbled with anchors flashing across her vision.

Jamie was waiting. Two seconds after Prue knocked, he opened the door and she slid in.

'I feel like something out of those made-for-telly American movies,' she said in a tone that did not sound like her.

The door was of a cheap composite wood and it shuddered as Jamie closed it. A DO NOT DISTURB notice swung from a peg on the back with instructions on how to use the fire escape if necessary. Prue found herself reading it.

'Prue,' said Jamie who had not touched her, 'are you here or not?'

Holding tight to the plastic bag, she turned. After a moment, she said, 'I'm here.'

Jamie took the bag from her. 'Are you frightened?'

She nodded. Jamie dropped the bag on the floor and stood quietly waiting. Then Prue knew why she was in this fake hotel. It was lust. Lust to possess the bones, skin and feel of Jamie. To have his flesh bury itself in hers.

He smiled. 'Chintz again.' He indicated the bedspread and she smiled back.

'That's easy.' Prue went over to the bed and rolled up the bedspread and tried to stuff it inside the wardrobe. The material was slippery and refused to go quietly and she found herself laughing.

'Diary of a chambermaid,' she said, and sat down on the denuded bed.

Jamie stood over her and she looked up at him.

'Why, Jamie?' she asked. 'Violet is so new to you.'

He raised his hands and spread the fingers wide in a gesture of non-comprehension. 'It wasn't a process. It just was.'

She looked down at her own clenched, shaking hands.

'You can change your mind, Prue.' Jamie pushed his hair back.

He looked pale and washed out – as if this whole thing was too much. It seemed to Prue that Jamie was looking right through her, and she saw, too, that his hands also were shaking. She concentrated on those tiny indicators, for it meant they were equal. It meant that neither was able to do this lightly.

'But please,' he added.

At one point Prue shrank for she did not want her imperfections to be catalogued. Daylight is not prejudiced, and there was nowhere to hide the slack skin at the top of her thighs or the stretch marks on her breasts. Not that she had minded these stigmata, particularly the stretch marks because they were a result of having Jane and branded her as a mother, but she did not want to spoil things for Jamie. She wanted to save him from the corrosions of her feminin-ity, to save his desire from carrying the burden of varicose veins and compacted fat. She wanted to give him a perfect body.

After that, Prue did not think very much. And after that, as they unfamiliarly entwined, Prue gave up the pretence that it was only lust. Lust had been left behind in the cathedral at Winchester. It was worse, far worse. For what she – used and smarting – knew was love.

Jamie's arm tightened across her body and his hand swept as light as sand running through an egg-timer across her quietened body.

'Prue,' he said with wonder in his voice. 'Prue.'

Violet liked to eat dinner at eight-thirty sharp. Jane, she had informed Prue, was too young to eat with them and Prue had not argued. At half past six she fed Jane pizza and packed her off to bed with *Goodnight Mr Tom*, a favourite book that went everywhere.

In the kitchen, Violet was making a mung bean salad and something unspeakable with tofu. Prue tried not to shudder and rolled a glass of Australian chardonnay between her fingers. The idea of food make her queasy.

'Tell me how you met Jamie,' she asked, needing to say his name.

Violet swivelled and directed an unfriendly look at her stepmother. 'I thought I'd told you.'

'Not properly.'

A piece of tofu quivered at the end of Violet's knife. Prue watched it, fascinated.

'It's funny how you recognize people.' Violet tossed the salad. 'I was having lunch at the Four Seasons in New York.' She paused for Prue to register the right degree of impressedness. 'Jamie was sitting in one of the corner tables. I took one look at him and thought: He will do.' Handfuls of tossed salad rose and fell in a green landslide into the bowl. 'He says he took two looks. The rest was simple. I suppose we're the same kind of people.'

'You've dropped some lettuce,' said Prue and pointed to the floor.

'Blast.' Violet retrieved it. 'Of course, Jamie being in the Four Seasons helped because I knew he was the kind of person I wanted. Seeing him in a Donut Diner drinking through a straw would have been different.'

Violet's honesty was sometimes startling. And, Prue acknowledged to the chardonnay, admirable.

She drank more wine. All of us have a dark side, but it is the fortunate ones who encounter it earlier in life. The reason? If you stumble on your rotten side in, say, your forties, you are unprepared.

Prue went upstairs to check on Jane who was reading in bed.

'Are you having a nice time?' Jane asked pointedly without looking up.

189

Prue sat down. The anti-Violet axis was alive and well. 'Sorry about the early bed, darling. But I wish you'd eaten all the pizza. Violet was put out.' A trace of moisture on Jane's face alerted her. 'Have you been crying?'

Jane shrugged. 'Not really.'

'Sure? You can tell me.'

'It's nothing,' said Jane angrily. Her wet eyes bored into her mother. 'You look odd.'

Prue swept a hand over her face. 'What sort of odd?'

'Odd, that's all.' Jane chucked her book on to the floor where it lay, a broken-backed reproach.

'*Don't* do that.' Prue was extra sharp. 'You know you don't treat books like that.'

Jane pulled the sheet up around her face and said, 'Sorry', in such an offhand manner that Prue wanted to spank her.

'If this is what London does to you,' she told her daughter, 'then we won't be coming back.'

Unexpectedly, Jane struggled to hold back tears. 'You're not so nice yourself.'

Stung, Prue clicked out the light and went downstairs to eat tofu and mung beans. Normally such a careful mother, by the last tread she had forgotten her daughter.

Violet had laid the dining-room table and lit candles. Jamie poured glasses of wine and, outside, the evening dimmed to grey and opal. A white clematis was reflected, pale and thoroughbred, in the dusk from a neighbour's garden and fixed itself in Prue's stimulated imagination – innocence retreating as the dark pulled it further and further away.

The wine played tricks on her body, stretched by nerves and flooded with adrenalin, and sent a rush to her brain. There she sat, suffused by the relief of being defenceless against emotion, and drenched in wet meltingness of desire, opposite the woman she had just betrayed. She drank her wine, watched Jamie and her flesh pricked and burned with love.

Across the table, Jamie ate and drank and occasionally looked directly into Prue's grey eyes and she knew, without question, there was no going back.

As she and Jane waited by the ticket barrier at Waterloo for the Dainton train, Prue constructed a pattern of departure.

First the cluster around the notice-board, followed by an eddy towards the platforms. Then, a whitewater rapid of last-minute passengers who knew the form, succeeded by the desperate dash of those who did not.

Girls in short skirts, opaque tights and high heels, carrying *Bella*s, *Best*s and *Hello!*. Men wearing mackintoshes over Burton suits. City slickers in Gucci loafers or the more solid-looking solicitor types in a three-piece pin-stripe. Women in Barbours carrying Harrods' bags and overlarge brown leather handbags, relics from the seventies. Prue was surprised by how many men were eating sweets.

What transgressions and triumphs lay behind their pallid skins, were housed in slackening bodies?

The carriage filled up within minutes, rustling with paper and snatches of conversation. Flashes of colour, movement and smells: scent, aftershave, sweat and bad breath.

Hands clasped in her lap, Prue looked out on to the emptying platform. A vast, surf-crested tide of feeling roared in her head and swept her away.

'Sorry about last night, Mum.' Jane tucked her hand under her mother's elbow. 'Thanks for taking me to London.'

191

Chapter Fourteen

Rain swept down the glen in sheets and wrapped Max in a dripping blanket. It had that special soft texture of Highland rain associated with skin creams and expensive bottled water, and Max raised his face to the sky and allowed it to stream down his face.

It was not the sort of gesture in which he usually indulged, and he hoped that Peter Broughton, fishing further down the bank, had missed it. He checked the clouds: cumuli nimbi were stacked further to the west with glimpses of blue showing between them. Meanwhile, the rainclouds overhead were thinning, which meant the rain would stop as suddenly as it had started.

Max liked to think of himself as an expert on Highland weather. Years – how many? – of observing it first-hand gave him grounds for this harmless piece of back-patting. All those holidays. All those years lodged in his memory.

As predicted the rain was easing, and the noise of water hitting grass gradually ceased. Apart from the murmur of the river sliding between its banks, silence reclaimed their spot. The silence of solitary sky, earth, rocks and the bleached bones of animals.

Max's silences could be equally terrifying, so much so that, sometimes in their grip, they frightened even him. They were a habit acquired during a childhood of watching adults behave badly and, like all habits, proved half relief, half burden.

Once he had learnt the knack of retreat, it was easy. Silence is a good weapon and, in using it, the wielder conveys all manner of power and self-knowledge. The relief of turning inward, of setting the face against the misery of the dormitory or playing-field, of being bullied and tear-stained (and, later, a man with a spoilt marriage and a successful, but not brilliant, career) and moving to a quiet, sunlit interior landscape, there to crouch and lick wounds.

No panacea remains indefinitely. Bacteria mutate to combat penicillin, ampicillin and trimethoprim. So, the retreat into silence became, as Max's life progressed, less of a life-saver and more of a monster that controlled him. Certainly, to remain silent in the office, where making a noise is essential, was not a wise tactic, and Max's comparative lack of advancement could be ascribed, in part, to this unwillingness to make enough noise. In marriage, silence acts as a vacuum into which evils are sucked.

Helen tumbled to that early on. Coward, she taunted. Why don't you say what you really think? On this, of all points, Helen was justified because she never scrupled to hold back on her own opinions.

Typically, Prue was kinder and sought out the reasons. Please tell me what you're thinking, she had begged him six months into their marriage, after a two-day period of Max barely speaking. (They had disagreed over where to take their holiday.) How can I understand otherwise?

You can't, Max had wished to say. No one can understand anyone else. The secret quarries of the mind are just that. Neither do I wish to be helped.

No?

Prue had helped him, lovingly and carefully. Although Max would not, perhaps, admit it, that was why he had married her. It was not Prue's fault, either, that Max had learnt the art of survival in much tougher hands. In those days, an atheist hungering in his heart for faith, Max found it difficult to accept that trust and partnership could flourish between men and women. Neither, at that stage in their infant marriage, was Prue quite wise enough to point out that if you assume the worst it becomes impossible to accept the best. But they had learnt together.

Max began to pack away his fishing equipment. He was beginning to feel the coarsening effects of being older. It mattered less that his career had not taken him to the top – and for that release he was thankful. Frustration and envy were not good bedfellows. But, from time to time, it concerned him that he no longer minded so much about behaving well. In other words, he had become like his father.

And here, wooed by the air and the drama of the mountains, the impress of his parentage had particular sharpness, the Scottish Highlands, fishing, the annual summer holiday at Northwater House having been one of the gorier battlegrounds of his parents' marriage. The panicked odour of dying fish and fresh blood cracked from their heads on stones, the sting of a midge bite, damp clothes, the acrid tang of peat soil were memories that dripped constantly over the line between the past and the present . . .

'What are you doing, Max?' The voice came out of that past, peremptory and demanding of an answer.

'Nothing, Father.'

'You must be doing something. And if not, why not? Idle blighter. Help pack up.'

Max's thirteen-year-old self had been watching the play of light on the pool formed by a conjunction of rocks and the bridge footings where trout – according to a notice in the guesthouse – lay with the express purpose of impaling themselves on the fisherman's hook. So far this afternoon it appeared that the death-wish had deserted the fish and his father was leaving in disgust.

His father's five-o'clock-shadowed face was darkened by irritation. 'Buggers. I've a good mind to demand my money back.'

In the tundra of post-war austerity, money was not a word to be taken lightly and its value was beaten daily into Max. He thought of the scene that might ensue and closed his eyes. *Please, no.*

This summer the weather on the Ardnamurchan peninsula had been unpredictable: blazing hot one day, sodden the next. Today it was muggy and a storm-cloud of midges rose from the river. Max felt the sweat spring across the ridge in his back and soak into the waistband of his grey flannel shorts. (Don't get them dirty, dear.) Beyond father and son rose the nursery slopes of the mountain, tender green and brown, and, above them, the curlews circled in the breathless hush.

'Get on with it,' bellowed his father.

Max hauled himself to his feet and they stowed away the equipment. A folding army stool (which Max still used), the cumbersome picnic basket, huge mackintoshes stiffened with age, a tin of peppermints, whisky and a battered tin which held the flies. He sighed. Holidays were supposed to be noisy, jolly affairs with campfires, paperchases and fry-ups in the evening.

With a great deal of noise, William Beckett tried to manoeuvre the Rover out of a mud patch in which he had, foolishly, parked it. (He was the kind of person who said, 'Rubbish,' when warned of obstacles.) The Rover stuck and Max piled out of the passenger seat and set his weedy body to shoving. The wheels churned. Mud splattered over the car body – and his shorts.

'Can't *think* what's wrong with the car,' said his father when Max climbed silently back in.

On the way back to their dull guesthouse, they passed a young woman trudging along the road with her shopping. She had a young, Celtic-pale face and hips that swung to the rhythm of her walk.

'I could . . .' said Max's father, slowing down, an expression contorting his features that Max only recognized when he was older as that of lust. 'I'd . . .'

Max turned his head and stared out of the window.

His mother was waiting at the guesthouse in which they stayed each summer. It was a mean-windowed, stone-walled place dedicated to the suppression of high spirits. Not that Max possessed those in abundance, but he was young and, sometimes, the hunger to run and shriek, or merely laugh loudly, tore at him. But he knew better than to indulge it.

On seeing him, his mother attacked him for dirtying his shorts, her air of permanent injury sharpened by having done nothing all day. To compensate herself for marrying Max's father, Antonia took refuge in order. She possessed four pre-war tweed skirts, rotated weekly, and a dozen twin-sets, which were worn according to the season. Today, she sported lime-green – this alerted observers to the fact it was summer – and a string of grey river pearls which reminded Max of teeth.

'It's been a long day,' she said when they assembled in the dining room with the other guests for herring high tea. 'I thought you were never coming back.'

'Bloody waste of time,' said Max's father, camouflaging the first of many whiskies with the water glass. 'We've been bloody had this year. No bloody fish at all.'

Antonia winced visibly and a faint pink tinged her complexion. 'I wish you wouldn't be so coarse, William.'

William's cold eyes raked the dim figure of his wife. It

was not fair, but it so happened that Antonia was sitting in a light that showed her to the worst advantage. She looked more than usually worn and lustreless, not from overwork, for she lived a privileged life, but from disappointment. Deliberately, Max's father raised his glass to his lips and Max shuddered for he knew that gesture.

'And I wish you had breasts like a white dove,' his father articulated, 'instead of the scrag end you have hanging off your chest.' He leant forward, paused and added in a whisper, 'And the wit to fuel a man's needs.'

'Oh, my God.' Antonia looked wildly round the prim dining room. The words fell like stones into the dampish air reminding the occupants of unspeakable things they preferred to ignore. The colonel and his wife at the next table stared like wooden replicas at the window sill on which a dead fly reposed.

'Oh, my God,' whispered Antonia. 'I'll die of shame.'

... After that scene, Max hardly spoke for three days. Along with the silences – which got mixed up with the subject of sex – his hatred of porridge and herrings were acquired at Northwater House.

If porridge and herrings were banished from Max's agenda, it was odd that fishing remained. Each year, he swore he would no longer indulge in the stupendous expense, but back he went to stand for hours in the wind and the rain, or bucket about in a boat and returned with a fresh complexion to tell fisherman's tales. I can't understand the attraction, Prue complained. The point is, Max answered, usually through a cold contracted from a Highland dousing, neither can I.

Throughout our lives we respond, probably without understanding why, to the imprint burnt early on to our memory and spirit.

As Max drove back south with the smell of fish perfuming

the car, damp clothes and muddy boots piled in the back and a selection of fishy parcels wrapped in brown paper, he wrestled with a mental picture that would not go away. It was of soft brown hair blowing in the draught of grimy air created by an incoming train, and a woman wearing a red scarf outlined against a hoarding advertising British Telecom.

He put his foot down and the car speeded past the blue motorway signs, past the rash of ugly buildings in the '*style motorway*' (which favoured clock towers and red paint), through slices of wet, lonely countryside, past villages hanging on the edge of survival and the squat buildings of Britain's industries. Max crouched over the wheel – no car really catered for his height – and aimed to be home by late afternoon.

Jane would be back at school and Prue, he knew, would be working in the library.

Prue's desk was in the drawing room and forbidden to everyone. Her insistence that no one else touched it was the only truly tiresome thing about his wife that Max could think of. He teased her sometimes as to what the desk contained. Now, as he entered the empty house and abandoned his luggage in the hall, Max wished he had not.

The desk was made of rosewood and smelt of the polish that Prue favoured. On the mantelpiece beside it the tortoiseshell clock ticked noisily. An antique blue and white plate they had bought together in Hay-on-Wye hung in its accustomed place on the wall. Dust motes swirled in the afternoon sun which spread a glossy light over a pink and white china ballerina on the desk. It was minus a hand which had been Sellotaped to the tutu. A message in Jane's handwriting was also stuck across the ballerina. 'Don't touch. Very, very precious.' Max grimaced. The ballerina, acquired after seeing a performance of *Swan Lake* in London, was one of Jane's very few girlie manifestations.

Your father is unspeakable.

Your mother is a fucking desert.

My mother.

My father.

My wife.

My daughters.

Myself: a full bag of neuroses, disguised by six decades of living, worn corduroys, tartan handkerchiefs, aftershave, good shoes, a taste for biography (the Richard Ellman was *so* good) and a greed for malt whisky. That is me.

Max stretched out his hand. Like Jamie, his life had been rendered uncomfortable by the effects of the bomb in the City, and the idea of it preyed on his mind. Thus, as he made the gesture, he equated it to the terrorist's action when he or she first pulled a pin or depressed a plunger. His fingers tensed. Once the action was done the result became the only thing that could matter. From then on, normal restraints were in the past, and it was not possible to go back.

One drawer was devoted to bills . . . Sainsbury's, Fenez of Farnham, Marks and Spencer at Marble Arch – Max frowned at that one. There was an invitation to contribute to a pension fund. Max's frown remained in place. He had, he thought, discussed their financial arrangements carefully with Prue, and seen to it that she was provided for when he died. More than anything else, the idea that Prue was thinking independently of him financially suggested that she was evading his control.

No, Max did not mean control – that was just a slip of the mental tongue. Control was not the word he wished to apply to his marriage.

The second drawer contained a mish-mash. A letter from

an old au pair bewailing her new lot and could she come back and work for *dear* Mrs Valour whose good heartiness [*sic*] she so admired and wanted to service [*sic*] again. The postscript to this touching appeal informed the reader that she was only being paid thirty pounds a week as compared to the forty-five Prue had doled out. There was a photograph of Jane dressed as a Merrie Man for the school play. A key with no label. A broken watch. A tiny white hospital bracelet which read: Daughter of Prudence Valour, 24.7.81 at 15.26 hours.

Max's hand shook a little.

Three is a number common to fable and fairy stories. It holds magical properties, the key to structures, the promise of spiritual reward. Three times a prince endeavours to win his lady. The third and youngest son is the one blessed with strength and success. The third daughter is the one marked out by Fate. In 'The Tinder Box' the soldier is asked to choose between copper, silver and gold.

In the third drawer Max discovered the following in Prue's handwriting on a folded sheet of paper. 'I have thought and thought about us and I regret . . .' This had been crossed out and underneath was written, 'One is ready to do anything to find peace once more. I have done everything; I have sought occupations . . . That, indeed, is humiliating – to be unable to control one's thoughts, to be a slave of regret, of a memory, of a fixed and dominant idea which lords over the mind' (Charlotte Brontë to Monsieur Héger).

Underneath that Prue had also written, 'How serious and dangerous it is curiously to examine the things that are beyond one's understanding, and to believe in new things . . . and even to invent new and unusual things, for demons have a way of introducing themselves into suchlike curiosities' (admonition addressed to Joan of Arc).

It took all of Max's self-control not to crush the sheet of paper into a ball. Here, he saw in a flash, his intuition primed by his love for Prue, was the message in the bottle. The tablet of stone. As he replaced the paper where he had found it, he noticed a smear of polish on the rosewood, a curl of dust behind the china ballerina, his big, shambling figure caught in the mirror above the fireplace.

Articles about jealousy had sometimes appeared in Sunday newspapers and, over the years, Max had read them. He knew then from his experiences with Helen, as he knew now, that such journalism usually failed its readers. Nothing could adequately describe the sear of feeling: the isolation, the sensation of being unable to draw breath because it hurt, the shame of being jealous. Second time round was no help either. As with childbirth or injury, the mind constructs its defences and buries the sharper memory.

Max had truly believed that he had found the formula which balanced reason with emotional and physical need. He had believed that at sixty, it was possible to accept what, at twenty-five, was unacceptable and to understand the quirks of sexuality and to place them in a context to a life. To understand that these quirks could be dealt with, and tamed.

On the Sunday following his return from Scotland, Max and Prue were alone. In a further bid to help Jane, Prue had arranged for her to spend the weekend with one of her form-mates who showed signs of extending friendship.

At lunch, Max said he could not finish his roast beef. Surprised, Prue looked up from hers. 'I thought you'd like a roast.'

'It's tough,' said Max, who did not normally comment on the cooking.

'Sorry, darling. Obviously I didn't cook it very well.'

He shrugged and got to his feet. 'I'm not hungry so I won't have any pudding.'

This succeeded in astonishing Prue. 'I've made lemon meringue. Your favourite.'

There was a silence and Prue's stomach contracted. Max looked away. Prue's expression jarred on him: eyebrows slightly raised, a questioning curve to her bottom lip, the mole so marked on her skin. Once, he had imagined that her face was transparent and open. Now, he considered it the opposite.

'I'm off for a walk,' he said, and pushed back his chair with a screech.

'*Max!*'

I sounded like my father. Max paced up the hill towards the airstrip. I talked to Prue as if I was William.

Nature was not in tune with Max's feelings. It was one of those exhilarating summer days with blue sky, warm sun and a tantalizing suggestion of greater heat to come. Washed by winter and spring, colour had spread along neutral hedgerows, through the fields and along the horizon. Mallow and dog rose scattered soft pinks among the green.

As he crested the hill and encountered the breeze which always blew off the crest, Max began to cry. As he was unused to crying, it took him by surprise. He had almost forgotten how the throat ached, or how water could force its way out of the eyes and down the cheeks. He stopped to search for a handkerchief.

'Hallo, Mr Valour.'

Emmy Horton came up behind Max so noiselessly in her rubber soled Doc Marten's that he jumped. Embarrassed, he turned towards her, a big, tear-stained figure and Emmy's heart contracted with pity for she recognized suffering.

Without thinking, she did the only thing possible and touched him on the arm to give comfort. For a moment, they stood frozen, Emmy's hand on the waxed sleeve, and she thought he would protest at her presumption. She removed her hand.

'I thought you were in London, Emmy, with my daughter.' Max blew his nose.

'Down for the weekend,' she replied. 'Wanted to see my mum.'

Fresh air had whipped some colour into her face and her hair – from what Max remembered – had improved.

'Are they well?'

'Yes. Edward has lots of teeth now.'

'I hope my daughter isn't doing too much.'

'Oh, no,' said Emmy and, naturally, Max missed the irony.

A group of birds circled overhead and Emmy's face jerked upwards. 'Bullfinches,' she said, her tone implying that Max would know exactly what she was talking about. 'They must be nesting. They're vegetarian, you know.'

Max did not reply and Emmy felt she should move on. She dug her hands into her jacket pockets. 'Nice to see you, Mr Valour.'

At that moment, Prue came into view over the rise. 'There you are,' she called.

To Emmy's embarrassment, Max swung round 360 degrees and turned his back on his wife. Prue came to a halt.

'Max?'

Emmy looked from husband to wife uncertainly. Aha, she thought and said, 'I must go.'

'Everything all right in London?' Prue asked.

'Yes, I was telling Mr Valour here that the baby has lots of teeth.' She decided to make a run for it. 'Bye.'

Prue waited until Emmy was out of earshot before turning on Max, white with fury. 'What on earth's the matter? Why were you so rude?'

'Don't be melodramatic, Prue.'

She calculated what to say next and modified her tone. 'You've been impossible since you've got back from Scotland. I don't know what's got into you.'

Prue's voice trailed to a close. If she felt her indignation was spurious, why should Max believe it? What if, she thought, he knows? Then she thought: He does. In all her life, she had never felt fear like that which now rose in her like oil from the bore, hot, strong and choking. No, Max can't know ... She struggled to master the fear with common sense. He can't *possibly* know.

'I think I'm owed an apology.'

'Are you, Prue?'

He stared down at his wife and realized that he did not know the woman who stood with her arms folded across her body against the breeze, a typical pose. He had made the mistake of imagining that he did – as he had imagined he had summed up Helen all those years ago.

But what Max really did not know was himself.

Suddenly, he was ashamed. Ashamed of his prying into Prue's desk, of the shaky conclusions that, as a result, had taken up residence in the raw areas of his heart, but on no real evidence – *and ashamed that he could not live up to his own precept that infidelity was merely a spasm of flesh*. And, yes, he was ashamed of the jealousy that raged inside him.

'Max.' Prue, in turn, was beginning to feel sick and shaky. 'Are you ill?'

He wanted to shout that he had had enough of everything. He had no proof, only some words on a scrap of paper – and marriage should not falter on something so flimsy.

'No,' he replied. 'I'm fine.'

'Since we are here,' said Prue after a moment, 'why don't we have a good walk?'

Still struggling with the painful shortfall between theory and its application, Max bit out, 'Oh, do shut up, Prue.'

It was then Prue gave herself away. Normally, if talked to in that manner she stormed off. Now she stood quite still for a second or two, then moved towards her husband.

'Darling, I can't bear to see you angry.' She tucked a treacherous hand into his elbow where it rested against his sleeve. 'Please don't be so cross.'

In silence, they progressed up the road towards Danebury Rings but, since the wind had veered and was blowing sharp and cutting, they turned back before they reached it.

'I'm going to paint the outside of the house,' Max announced the following week.

'Couldn't we get someone to do it for you?' Prue was struggling with WI accounts and not very interested.

'I can manage.'

Prue shrugged. Since the weather had turned wet it was not ideal for painting, but she said nothing. Instead, she was a witness to a great deal of bucket-rattling and virtue up a ladder and could not rid herself of the notion that Max was making a point.

It was a tough, uncomfortable job and Max sometimes felt nauseous from the paint. He also fell off the ladder and bruised his right hip. Watching him limp around with tins of paint was worrying. So were the livid bruises that spread like purple mud under his skin.

He, too, refused Prue's arnica and asked that she please leave him alone.

Chapter Fifteen

Max phoned Violet on Sunday night and asked if he could stay with them for the week. He was sorry to impose, but his club was booked up. The reason he had to be in London, he told her, was Maastricht. Not unreasonably Violet expressed bewilderment until her father explained that the firm's senior partners were holding a brainstorming session on the latest developments in the EC and how it affected corporate law. It was also intended to aid Max to put into place his plan to tie up with other law firms in Europe, and it was vital that he attend day and night.

'Terrific,' said Violet drily when she heard the venue was Claridges. 'You won't starve.'

Glacé nougatine, garnished with praline, cream and white chocolate. A sweet, oozing picture darted and fretted across Violet's unrested mind. Violet replaced it with the steamed fish she planned for supper. She herself had been struggling to master the latest intricacies of the European open market with relation to book publishing and said, 'You can give me some tips, Dad.' Only then did she make a rapid mental review of the fridge and gritted her teeth.

When he arrived on Monday evening, Max seemed tired and to Violet, who was not given to a great deal of observation, older. The more intense for being unfamiliar, a sudden panic made her remember her father's mortality – and, come to that, her own.

THIGH-ABDUCTOR DEATH OF TWENTY-SEVEN-
YEAR-OLD. MACHINE SPLITS RISING PUBLISHING
STAR VIOLET BECKETT IN TWO. HUSBAND SOBS:
'SHE ONLY WANTED TO BE THIN.'

Death bobbed into Violet's mind – a grinning little
mannikin who stuck out his tongue and perched on top of
a toadstool. Violet could not take him seriously.

Apart from his (unhealthy, as Violet pointed out) desire
for meat and two vegetables at his evening meal, Max was
an undemanding guest. He played with his grandson,
entered into the spirit of bathtime and talked to his daughter while she cooked.

'It's good to be here,' he said as they sat in the freshly
painted, sanded, tile-decorated kitchen. 'You've made it
very classy, darling.'

'Thanks, Daddy.' Violet sat down opposite her father and
poured out wine. 'How's the brainstorming?'

Max hunched over his wine. 'Fine,' he said, without
enthusiasm. He roused himself to offer one or two facts but,
clearly, the subject was not uppermost in his mind.

Violet's attention focused on her father's hands. Big
hands, with fingers bruised and slightly swollen from the
DIY, flecked with age-spots. They were gentle hands, and
ones she trusted above all else. Succumbing to a rare
impulse, Violet leant over and held one against her cheek.

'My darling Dad,' she said as those trusted fingers stroked
her hair. Father and daughter stayed thus for a moment or
two and then, as ever incurably restless, she leapt up to
finish the meal. He let her go and drank his wine. Much as
black holes hoover in energy and particles without regard
to other stars, Max's untidy feelings for his daughters were
so huge and volatile and subject to their own laws, that he
could only deal with them in short, concentrated gunbursts.

It was good to have her father in the house, Violet acknowledged, as she turned off the light that night. It made her feel safe.

She turned on to her side. 'Have you had words with Daddy?' she asked Jamie drowsily. 'I noticed you avoided him.'

She felt him edge further away. 'No, why?'

'You've seemed to get on, but you've hardly said a word to him while he's been here.'

'Max understands,' said Jamie, his voice harsh-sounding in the hush. 'He knows about relaxing at the end of a day's work.'

'You selfish toad.' Violet woke up. 'It's not too much to ask for you to be polite. I'm the one that does all the work. All *you* do is dish out the drinks.'

'You've missed my point.' Jamie bunched the pillow around his ears. He tried to woo sleep. The room was too warm and he wished he had opened a second window.

After a bit, Violet resumed the conversation. 'Emmy tells me that Mary Latham has run off with a lover and left the children behind.' Her voice cut like a pair of scissors into the silence. Snip. Snip. Shaping pieces to sew up into gossip – in this case about the family further up the street. 'I've often noticed a strange chap coming out of the door when I get back at night.'

Jamie said nothing.

'Imagine,' said Violet who, to give her credit, did not normally gossip, 'Rod has refused to give her any money or allow her to see the children.'

Engaging in a certain kind of behaviour sensitizes practitioners to fellow travellers. Jamie had been alerted to Mary's activities well before Violet's announcement. He recognized the signals – a strange car outside the house, Mary's lack of sweat when he met her on a so-called early morning jog, her reluctance to mention her husband, her obvious misery and strain. In London, it was easy to run an affair – just like a business, really.

'Poor Mary.' He turned over.

'Poor *Mary*! Poor Rod.'

Jamie did not sleep well and asked himself, over and over, why he was doing what he was doing. He had had no intention of ever risking his marriage, or of disregarding the rules, or losing integrity. But all those things were happening, had happened . . . and he had made the mistake of taking them for granted, of not understanding that they required policing. Why?

The answer was simple. Love.

Love, which involves all-consuming sex, has no regard for social rules, neither does it care about timing (much) and it is unencumbered (unlike the rest of us, whether we like it or not) with morality.

At breakfast, Jamie was horrified to discover that Max was considering remaining with them over the weekend. Fortunately, Violet reckoned that enough was enough.

'You've got the midsummer fête, Dad,' she pointed out.

Max shrugged. 'Somehow I can't work up the energy. It's nice being here and I'm enjoying a break from home.'

The word 'refuge' slid into Violet's mind.

'Don't be silly,' she said, more sharply than she intended. 'Prue would be furious. You've never not done your bit.'

'Grammar,' said Jamie.

Violet whirled round. 'Shut up, Jamie.'

A vision of Dainton bathed in summer goodwill, redolent with a smell of home-baking, decked in bunting, forever sunny, took shape in the minds of the three people around the breakfast table, hand-tinted like an advertisement – and just as reliable.

Before he could stop himself, Jamie asked, 'Does Prue mind being left on her own?'

'No,' said Max curtly. 'I don't think so.' He looked across the litter of jams, butter and plates at his son-in-law and acknowledged the younger version of himself. He registered Jamie's charm, his intelligence (but not brilliance), his habit of smiling with all his face and his knack of focusing his full attention on whoever was speaking to him. The country was not ruled by first-class degrees, it was ruled by charm, and the application of good second-class degrees, like Jamie's.

'Boo,' said Jamie to Edward who was sitting in the high chair. Looking furious, the baby banged his spoon on the rim of his plate. Jamie laughed, reached over and pulled his son into his lap. The baby's expression rearranged itself into contentment. Jamie stroked the top of his head and kissed it.

Then Max perceived youth and confidence and recognized in Jamie a capacity for passion and feeling – elements that, if he had ever possessed them, were slipping away from himself.

Violet made a remark about Prue's homemade cakes and Jamie smiled at her. What that smile contained, Max was not sure, but he knew then he should go home and face whatever was there.

Prue was deep into fête preparations and did not have time to do more than serve Max a scratch meal on Friday evening and leave him to it. It had been a tiring week and she never slept well when left on her own.

'You look exhausted,' Molly greeted her on Saturday morning. 'And you've lost weight.'

'Good,' said Prue.

'Losing weight,' Molly poked Prue in the soft part of her hips, 'usually indicates something.'

'Surely not,' said Prue.

'Waste of money losing weight.' When Prue looked puzzled Molly amplified the statement. 'You have to buy new clothes.'

'That's one way of looking at it.' Prue dumped a load of linen tablecloths on to the nearest bench. 'Shall we get these on?'

'Max back?' Molly shook out the sheet on top of the pile.

'Yes.'

'Been away some time,' said Molly as if it had only just struck her.

Prue turned away to steady a vase stuffed with irises which was threatening to topple. Molly said nothing more.

However well aired, the village hall always retained a lingering, slightly unpleasant smell, a combination of must, used-up air and drains. By eleven o'clock, the stalls were up and overflowing into the courtyard outside. Prue congratulated herself. There had only been one altercation, between the ladies on the cake stall and the ladies on Ideas for Presents, an argument that threatened to take on Joyce Grenfell overtones, as to whom should locate where. After sensitive negotiations, Ideas for Presents was persuaded to retreat to the courtyard where it was deemed to act as a draw. Since Dainton featured in tourist pamphlets and was situated smack on the tourist ley-line between Winchester and Salisbury, and the holiday season was in swing, there would be, Prue concluded, enough potential victims to be seduced with brooches cunningly wrought from dried leaves and paper-clips.

The hall filled up with the as yet imperfectly homogenized mixture of village inhabitants. Elderly couples from the council estate and retired couples of the sherry and Rover variety. The younger generation of tired-looking mothers in leggings ('I really shouldn't but they're so comfortable'), clutching clones of daughters and accompanied by sons wearing T-shirts which bore slogans such as 'Save the Whales'. Their husbands wore olive corduroys and bright-coloured sweaters, and made jokes over oven gloves, lavender bags and tomato plants. The tourists were generally identified by their shell-suits in pear-drop colours.

Whatever, the money spent here today meant that Bosnian refugees, Guide Dogs for the Blind and the Church would be beneficiaries to the tune of a couple of hundred pounds or so. Not much, thought Prue, unaccountably depressed, buying a particularly awful example of macramé and then worrying that she had been patronizing because the macramé would hit the throw-out box by the end of the day. Pity was an uncomfortable emotion and Prue avoided it wherever possible. Instead she concentrated on the broad brushstroke of Russia's leaky civil nuclear industry, the horror of Yugoslavia, the IRA, Somalia and South Africa. Cling to the belief that their hundred pounds would join more and, somehow, something positive would emerge.

Could you apply the same logic, demanded the inner voice that now accompanied Prue to most places, to adultery?

Max only showed up in the last stages of the fête, just before the raffle was drawn by a journalist whose claim to fame was that he once worked for a couple of months on the *Sunday Times* but whose position as 'a Writer' gave him eminence denied him in London.

'Poor sod,' said Nigel Fraster, a self-styled village wit, to Prue. 'Only bit of employment he's had for months.'

Having made a short speech about how flattered he was to be officiating, the journalist picked a ticket out of the metal drum.

'Pink. Number fifty-seven,' he announced.

'Me, me, me.'

Prue heard her daughter shriek from a long way away while a freezing sensation stole over her limbs. The first prize was a ride in a helicopter which could be heard tuning up, untunefully, in the field below the church. The prize had been donated by its owner, a dealer in fertilizers, who had recently bought the manor house and was not, as yet, quite sure of his reception, which veered between acid remarks about the *nouveau riche* and the if-you've-got-it-why-not-flaunt-it? variety.

'It's me. It's me.'

Red-faced with excitement, Jane pushed through the phalanx of disappointed boys who emitted visible hate signals. His moment over, the ex-journalist gave a world-weary smile and turned to Prue. 'The owner insists that children are accompanied by an adult. Just in case.'

'You mean half of the family but not a quarter can be wiped out.'

'Something like that.'

Over the heads of the crowd, Prue sent desperate signals to Max. You go. You go. But Max ignored eye contact and turned away.

Damn him. Max knew that she was terrified of flying and he also knew she would be unwilling to make a scene. He was, in effect, abandoning her.

Damn him.

Someone once told her that you lose consciousness before you hit the earth. Either that or you died of terror.

The rotating blades switched up from a whine to a scream as soon as she and Jane were strapped into the seat of an alarmingly small cockpit and, wishing to disgrace neither her daughter nor herself, Prue prayed for control.

The pilot shouted something that Prue could not hear

and she shook her head. He pointed at the sky, grinned and flicked the switches. Prue watched her hands fasten the seat belt.

The engines crescendoed, and a noise returned to haunt Prue. It was the sound made by the man who had fallen? thrown himself? out of the ninth-storey window in Victoria one ordinary day as she had walked to the station from the Tate Gallery and encountered the cluster of onlookers grouped around the smashed thing on the ground. Fear clawed at her stomach and she prayed that she would not faint.

Jane made an excited face at her mother. The sky loomed large and unwelcoming and, as they rose, the field and church shrank and became toys arranged tidily on a patchwork quilt. The air was as nacreous silk, the type so thin that, allegedly, it can be pulled through a wedding ring. As they rose higher and higher, the rotors tore it apart.

Still placed vertically in the sky, the sun spread blinding light across their vision. The pilot altered course. An ant colony of cars moved along the A13. Beyond that, the curves of the Danebury Rings were peeled back for intimate scrutiny. Further away lay Stockbridge and sweeps of downland country that had settled to the cultivator. An ancient landscape, hugging the past, created by the resonance of past lives.

Poised, free of earth, lit by a wash of light, Prue was rocked into quiescence and, for a moment, she struggled free: of love, anger, fear of the past and fear of the present.

The earth tilted and the sun beat down on her daughter's head. All lives should have such a moment, she thought gratefully.

*

Violet phoned during the week – Prue could hear the hum of office life – and invited herself and the family down for the following weekend. The baby, she said, could do with some fresh air.

'You're not known for your love of the country weekend,' commented Prue.

'Yes, well,' said Violet. 'People change.'

They arrived on Saturday morning with a heap of baby equipment, and the house no longer belonged to the Valours. Once the chaos had subsided, Edward was changed, put into the second-hand cot Prue had bought at Oxfam, and Emmy was dispatched back to her family. Violet cornered Prue in the kitchen.

'Have a drink,' said Prue, who was behind schedule.

Violet ignored the invitation and came straight to the point. 'What's up with Dad?' she said, in the tone that Prue recognized from the days of failing to be a good stepmother.

She chopped at the onions. 'Nothing. Your father is fine.'

'No, he isn't. I know Dad. He's worried about something.'

Prue's knife reduced the onions to pulp. 'He's fine,' she repeated.

Violet regarded the mush on the chopping board and a plucked eyebrow arched upwards. Prue followed the line of her gaze and tipped the onions into the frying pan on the stove. Losing one's moral superiority was harder than Prue had imagined, particularly when dealing with Violet. She gave a final savage chop to a segment of onion and caught her finger. Red trickled over the board. Prue stared at it. 'I can never see French blood,' Joan said, 'without my hair standing on end.' Joan, perhaps, might have understood how it was easy to hate the non-sinner for his reminders of your imperfections, and to love the sinner who shared your darkness.

'I'm not so sure,' said Violet. 'He's not ill, is he?'

'No.' Prue's wooden spoon hovered for a second or two above the frying pan. 'No. But he might be worrying about work, of course.'

At that point, Max came into the kitchen holding a pair of secateurs. Violet swivelled around.

'I was just asking Prue if you were all right.'

And Prue, who knew Max's repertoire of expressions well, was aware that he did not look as surprised as he could have done. Max dropped his free hand on to his daughter's shoulder and let it rest there. Violet smiled up at him.

'I'm fine,' he said, looking directly at his wife.

Prue scrubbed at her wet cheeks with an elbow. 'These onions', she said, 'are very strong.'

Max snapped the secateurs open and shut. Open and shut.

'I've been asked to tackle Mrs Ryder's jasmine,' he said, and did not sound particularly pleased about it. 'It's growing across her window and blocking the light.'

'Don't be late for lunch.' Prue turned back to the stove.

Violet said she had to unpack.

Someone once wrote that to cook divinely required love. Nonsense. Guilt did just as well. Prue fried mince and the onions in virgin olive oil until they were the colour of a sun-tanned thigh. She opened a tin of plum tomatoes and mashed them into the mixture, added orange in the form of grated carrot, and green basil. Then she melted butter in a cast-iron saucepan, spooned in flour and waited until the roux solidified into yellow and back to white before pouring in the milk. A good cheese sauce should be made with Swiss cheese to give it that stringy, tangy flavour, suggesting clean air, hot sun and café life.

A layer of mince, a layer of pasta, a layer of sauce.

A layer of blameless married life. A layer of adultery. A layer of . . . then what?

I don't really want a love affair. I don't want this upheaval, this realignment, this mess.

We have the power to choose, Richard, the vicar, had preached in one of his better sermons. That's what distinguishes us as spiritual beings. Our sense of good and evil sets us apart from the animal kingdom. Rubbish to that. Prue had reacted strongly. We have simply specialized in intelligence, as the lion has specialized in speed and strength, and intelligence feeds on convenient fantasies. Good and evil are myths.

Nevertheless, we *do* possess the power of choice.

She was conscious of Jamie's presence in the kitchen before he said anything. The hairs rippled up her arms and the muscles tightened in her pelvis. Then came a rush of blood flooding into her chest.

'Prue.'

She waited until she had smoothed the final layer of mince and poured the white sauce before she turned round.

'Jamie.'

He was standing just inside the door, cradling a sleepy baby in his arms. Years later, when other details had slipped away, she savoured this epiphany, for that was what it was. She remembered thinking how odd it was to see Jamie in her kitchen and how her kitchen, cluttered with so many familiar things, was the wrong place for him. She remembered thinking: I love him above all else and I *have* no choice.

Jamie looked tired, a little transparent and worn at the edges. She did not know him well enough – yet – but if Max had worn the look that sat on Jamie's face she would have known that he needed her. In return, Prue ached for him, her body suddenly limp, out of control.

She shoved the lasagne into the oven and shut the door with extra emphasis.

'Edward needs some fresh air,' said Jamie. 'Why don't you come with me if you've finished? Violet's doing some phoning.'

As they pushed the baby up the main street, Prue said, 'This feels very odd.'

For a second or two, Jamie looked grim. 'Are you going to say you regret everything?'

She considered. 'That would be another lie.'

His expression relaxed. 'Promise me you won't ever say anything remotely like it.'

'Hush,' she said quickly. 'I see Molly coming our way,' and she asked him about the atmosphere in the City.

'General gloom. Not helped by the muddle over the Maastricht treaty.'

'*Do* you think it should be ratified? The Danes seem pretty adamant that it's dead.'

'If we've elected to go the Europe route, we should get on with it.'

'Nice day,' said Molly, her tone drier than usual as she passed on her way to the vicarage with a bag of spinach.

Mrs Ryder's jasmine did not look pruned and neither, Prue noted, was there evidence of Max. Normally, Prue never gave a moment's thought as to the whereabouts of her husband but now she ran through the places he might be. Now it mattered. Of all the anticipated consequences of an affair, compulsive checking up on the whereabouts of one's spouse had not figured on Prue's list.

'If there is banality in evil,' she said, as Jamie helped her to heave the pushchair up the bank, 'there is, certainly, banality in adultery.'

'Quite,' said Jamie, and held her hand a moment longer than necessary.

The pushchair creaked over bumps and outcrops of dried mud. Prue's skirt was much too thick for summer, and her beaten-up walking shoes had acquired a patina of dust. She took off her jersey and slung it over her shoulders.

Across the pushchair, Jamie looked at Prue.

Memories of what had passed between them surged back – hot, strong, trembling with astonishment and the slap-slither of flesh that had been turned by their wishes into the witchery of high emotion. A rage to possess Jamie, to dig deep under that transparent skin, down into blood and bone, and to seize the sinews of his spirit between her teeth and tear at it, filled Prue.

Embarrassed, she quickened her pace.

'Hang on,' said Jamie.

Prue led them up a track, only just negotiable with a push-chair, towards the footpath leading between Jacob's Farm and the tongue of hazel copse. She gestured towards the latter.

'I wanted you to see it. Old England. Apparently the copse is medieval and the Heritage people are watching it like a hawk.'

At the top of the rise where the path widened, Jamie wedged the pushchair into a root bole and snapped on the brake. Lulled by the bumpy ride, Edward had fallen asleep, his heavy head on one side.

Jamie reached out and pulled Prue towards him. She felt his face join hers, felt the outline of his teeth through his lips, tasted him, smelt him. A fire leapt in her and inciner-ated her disbelief that this should be happening to her, Prue Valour.

Hampered by their clothes, Jamie undertook an awkward passage towards her breast. Prue was still. His hand slid under her blouse and under her bra. His touch was rough – so, too, were his finger-tips on the smoother, warmer skin under her breast. She closed her eyes. Jamie stopped what he was doing.

'Silence, Prue?'

She opened her eyes. 'I don't honestly know what to say. I've not had many lovers. I have not committed adultery before, certainly not in front of a baby. Neither do I understand.'

Jamie's hand now cradled her breast and she added crossly, 'I'm not a cup-cake either.'

He laughed but kept his hand where it was. 'What don't you understand?'

'This is egocentric to the point of eccentricity. But why me, Jamie?'

Not privy to the female psyche, he seemed genuinely puzzled at the question. 'I could ask, why me?'

It was on the tip of her tongue to list his advantages in looks, intelligence, etc., etc., and that she had none of those things, but she stopped herself in time.

Jamie was persistent. 'Well, Prue, why me?'

She turned her head away and presented him with a profile softened by emotion and lust. 'I don't know. I didn't choose you. It just happened.'

Can you retrace the pathways of desire to their source? Pick your way through threads of memory? Select a precise moment when a decision was made?

Oh, yes.

She turned back to Jamie and he brushed the hair back from her eyes.

'I don't know what to do, Jamie.' Prue disengaged herself. 'I can't find it in me to resist.'

'Stop talking,' said Jamie. 'It spoils things.'

'Yes, I suppose it does.'

For the second time, he kissed her, and again, further down the path, against an oak tree.

Edward slept on, a picture of innocence.

*

Because there were so many of them, Prue served the (overdone) lasagne in the dining room. Max opened a couple of bottles of Bulgarian pinot noir. Due for her next assessment at the gym, Violet only sipped hers. Jamie left his almost untouched, whereas Max was into his fourth glass before the cheese.

Outside, the sun shone down on Dainton, revealing smudged windows, curtains in need of cleaning, cracked roads and peeling paint. It shone, too, on FOR SALE notices that had been up for months on end, on the blue rusting Volkswagen, dumped by the village pond, which the owner could not afford to repair, and on the newly heaped grave in the churchyard covered by brown-edged bouquets. Unemployment had finally got to Clive Carter and he had killed himself in the company car before it was impounded by the firm.

The sun warmed, promised, and clarified.

Inside Hallet's Gate, Prue's body was irradiated with lust and what remained of her resolution disappeared as easily as the pinot noir.

I cannot not love Jamie.

Chapter Sixteen

He was nothing if not persistent.

Emmy could not understand why Angus continued to single her out when there was luscious Sal and the rest of the London tribe of hummingbirds for him to, well, ... Emmy did not dwell on the precise nature of what Angus might be doing.

What exercised her was the exhaustion of living with the five senses operating on red alert. She hated her vulnerability, and the way Angus ate up her time.

So much for the independent Emmy Horton.

How about this: when she woke, Angus was there occupying her mind; when she washed up or changed Edward's nappy, vacuumed the hall, listened to the telephone ring, he strutted, preened and made as free with it as only a usurper can. The *Daily Mail, Neighbours* and a novel by Virginia Andrews were no antidote. Neither were her plans to watch for the tawny owl that she hoped would be nesting at Tarrant's barn back home. She had been taken over by an image, a voice and a shape whose powers extended deep into her subconscious. In had slipped cunning Angus, demonstrating to Emmy the limits of her power – and the extent of his.

She learnt that there is no release from the suffocation of a head occupied by the squatter who will not be evicted. As yet Emmy was unaware that time would do the job efficiently.

Come on the hike on the last weekend in June, Angus invited her. The gang's going and there's a good pub to get ratted at the other end. We go in the van.

Thus, one Saturday morning, an Emmy made boneless with nerves laced up her Doc Marten's and ironed her best black T-shirt and jeans and, in the well-rehearsed tradition of Ruth following Boaz, followed Angus to a village near Midhurst on the South Downs.

The group – all right, the Londoners – were displayed incongruously against the green and chalk of the Downs . . . black-clad, flowing-haired townies splattered across the green turf that swept over the ridge and down the fields.

'It looks so green,' said Sal, shading her eyes with her hand.

Feeling superior, Emmy said nothing. Any fool knew that a landscape looked uniform but contained within it variations of colour and texture so minute and myriad that it made the word 'green' meaningless.

On this weekend, the sun chose to beat down and it was hot. Sweat sprouted on Sal's upper lip and her hair hung lank against the tartan lumberjack shirt she wore over her leggings. In desperation, Emmy had bundled her hair into a scarf where it lay on her neck like unaired washing.

Half-way to the pub, Sal and Cherry began to flag. 'Not used to this.' Sal hoicked up one breast with a hand. 'It's tough on the tits.'

Emmy strode over earth crusted into chalky lumps and pitted with flint, felt it crumble under her boots and, framed against the expanse of the world, cautiously admitted to herself that she was happy.

The grass was young, sappy and tough. She bent to pull up a stalk and it bit into her finger. Angus came up behind and poked her bottom.

'Move on.'

Emmy did not appreciate the prize heifer treatment or her mood being broken. 'Naff off.'

They reached the summit of the chalk ridge and the path turned and ran east–west towards a large patch of woodland. Under the tree canopy the sun was filtered of its heat, and the change in temperature made Emmy shiver. The air was still and the light spread in patches over the woodland floor. Violets edged the paths with occasional red and blue splashes of other flowers.

So much texture and so much nourishment on which the senses could feast. Emmy breathed it in, and knew then that her roots ran deeper than she had supposed. She belonged here and her body responded to the changeable light and unmistakable scents of leaf mould and growing things. In a dream she walked on.

'Have some cider,' Angus urged in the pub. It was one of those resolutely fake-beamed and horse-brassed places which served everything in a basket, even the crisps. In a fine example of British inability to handle the weather, a fire had been lit and the place was tropical.

Sal and Cherry were into the vodka, Vince and Nails into the draught bitter. Emmy sipped her cider. The talk was not of jobs for, Emmy and Angus excepted, the group did not have one between them. Neither was it of job prospects, because those had been discounted and the future was something to ignore. No, sensibly the talk was of films, benefits, gigs and *Sun* scandal.

By two-thirty, Cherry, Sal and Vince were drunk and Nails had retired to the gents where he remained. The heat inside the pub had become oppressive: Emmy was sweating and Angus's pony-tail was wet.

'Let's go,' she said.

Sal moaned. 'Why don't the health freaks go back, get the van and pick us up?'

Too late, Sal realized she had ceded an advantage to Emmy. She shrugged – and made an additional mistake of underestimating the enemy.

Emmy could not get out of the pub quickly enough. Angus trod behind her and they walked in silence in single file towards the wood. Once there, the tantalizing, elusive smell of flowers and new leaves again sifted over Emmy and brought her to an abrupt halt. If she could absorb this rioting life perhaps she could steal its confidence and vigour for herself.

Angus's hands slid around her waist. Her thin, whippy, inelegant waist.

'What are you doing, Emmy?'

Drugged by scent and her feelings, Emmy turned and waited the second or two until Angus kissed her. Behind her closed eyelids light splintered across her vision.

'Nice,' said Angus, and released her. 'And you smell nice. I've fancied doing that for a long time.'

Emmy thought about the breasts swinging beneath a black T-shirt. 'What about Sal?'

'What about her? I fancy you both. Have you both. No point in being exclusive.'

'Get off, Angus.'

'Not yet,' he said and turned her face none too gently towards him and kissed her again.

The out-of-body dimension to Emmy's pilgrimage vanished, replaced by a tension that quivered, almost visibly, between the two. Emmy endeavoured to concentrate on the now milky sweep of sky spread between the horizon and the sun, and failed. She thought, instead, of lust, all flesh and tumbled limbs – not that her experience amounted to more than could be written on a full stop. Her good sense also warned her that at this moment her feelings were not reliable.

At the van, Angus fitted the key into the lock and prised back the door.

'Come to my place tonight, Emmy?'

She paused in the act of clambering in, catching a jigsaw piece of her reflection in the passenger mirror. Her lips were uncharacteristically red and her wretched hair had escaped the scarf.

'No, thanks.'

'Why not?'

Emmy shrugged. 'I don't want to.'

'I'll make it worth it.'

She did not doubt it. 'Bad times come after good. I'll pass.'

Dear Marje. What do I do? I am hopelessly, shamingly in love. But he is just after one thing. I'm after several, but I don't know what they are.

Emmy stared out of the window and Angus headed the van towards the pub. There was one advantage of not being a *femme fatale* – a hard head.

Hard head. Soft body.

Angus let his fingers trail up Emmy's leg. 'Quite sure?' His relative indifference stung her until he flicked his pony-tail over his shoulder with a gesture that suggested he knew he was the coolest, hottest lover since Casanova. It was so peacockish, so akin to the male sparrow's mating behaviour ... fluffed-out chest, preened feathers, swagger ... that Emmy smiled.

'Quite sure,' she said.

'Like the bloody Crown Jewels, then? All locked up.'

She turned and looked at him and, after a minute, he slowed the van down and returned the scrutiny. 'I'll get you, Emmy. Don't worry.'

*

Saturday at the Blue Orchid in Croydon was *the* night, Cherry informed Emmy. Angus nosed the van into a parking place only a street away, and the girls immediately headed for the ladies' in the club. It was lit with neon light and smelt of hair lacquer and fags. A row of girls, faces and bodies in various stages of contortion, stood in front of the long mirror.

'Here,' said a big blonde, balancing a lit cigarette on the edge of her Marks and Spencer's travelling cosmetic box. 'Help me lace the bustier up, would you?'

Her auburn friend had a go.

'Not that tight,' yelled the blonde, her breasts rising and spilling over the cleavage.

'What's the point, then?' said her friend. 'You don't want to land up with bee-stings, do you?'

Sal stripped to the skin and pranced around in briefs and long tight boots. Emmy ground her teeth, for Sal's figure was everything that had been promised, and watched as she poured herself into a Lycra mini-dress, with high heels, and Cherry did a paler imitation. Emmy ran a comb through her hair and applied a coat of mascara to her lashes, which gave her a startled look.

'Effing Cleopatra, are we?' said Cherry.

The noise on the dance floor backed up under the roof in a smothering blanket. Glitter balls hung in the ceiling; the room was cut by electric strobes and swivelling light. This was a temple indeed.

Sal raised her glossy arms, wriggled her Lycra rump and her hair flamed around her head – a sleek, confident goddess who ruled over youth, sex and gratification.

'Get on down,' screamed the DJ through the microphone. 'Get on down there.'

The egg-smooth floor was covered first by a trickle, then

a stream, of bodies, oscillating like cornstalks in a stiff breeze.

'Right,' said Sal and sent Emmy a look. She seized Angus, who had emerged with Vince from the shadows that formed the perimeter of the floor. By the look of him, Vince had taken in another skinful and he grabbed at Cherry with a movement that owed more to luck than control.

'Lover boy.' Sal hung on to Angus and moved her hips suggestively.

Oh, yes, Emmy could tell that Angus was not unaffected and she was furious with herself for minding. You told him no, she repeated to herself. No. No. No.

She watched them dance – Vince's lurch, Cherry's spaced-out bop . . . and Angus and Sal – until too many dancers had poured into the space and they were lost to view.

'Fancy one, then?' A dark youth materialized by Emmy, fingering a bottle of beer in a manner that betrayed his nervousness. He was sweating, too: drops sat on his face and blackened his T-shirt.

Emmy stared at him. Somehow, she had got into this and she had to go with it. 'Don't mind if I do.'

A damp hand descended on to her arm, and the youth sent his empty beer bottle spinning into the shadows and pulled her into the centre.

At the edge of the floor, packs of youths hunting females grew bold and ferocious. Their willing prey preened and re-formed in their groups whenever one of their members was snatched away. The music drilled into the brain.

At first, Emmy moved like a wary animal, stiff-legged and eyes flicking. The beat grew louder, the smell of sweat, feet and beer stifled the remaining senses and, suddenly, she heard a click in her head, the distinct, decisive sound of a switch moving from negative to positive, from 0 to 1, and, to the beat of soul, house, rap, whatever it was, to the flash and throb of the strobe, Emmy gave herself up.

Her sweaty youth pressed against her. 'Nice?'

'Nice,' she echoed, lost in the sea of bodies. The youth ran his hand down Emmy's back and between her buttocks.

She let him.

She had no idea how long she shook and strutted with her partner, being conscious only of the sensation of release pouring like liquid through her body. To celebrate her rebirth, she raised her face towards the strobe's fractured glitter.

Angus reappeared and shouted into her ear. 'What are you doing?'

Emmy's face was patched with silver. Angus reached out and pulled her towards him until her body was arched against his.

'Get rid of him,' he ordered.

She was tempted to reply, 'You get rid of Sal,' but the youth had gone. Angus's grip did not slacken and they stood together. Then he began to dance and made Emmy dance with him, and her heart began to beat with a wild rhythm. Angus bent over and Emmy felt his mouth move over her chin and rest briefly on her lips.

'Why not, Emmy?' he said into her ear.

For the second time, Emmy asked, 'What about Sal?'

'She's hotting it up with another guy.' Angus jerked a hand in the direction of the dark, heaving mass where the faces and bodies had been reduced to blanket homogeneity.

'Good for Sal.'

His mouth made another journey across the unmapped continent of Emmy's face and she shuddered.

Later, how much later Emmy was not sure, Angus led her

through discontented prowlers who had failed to make a kill and around couples who did not care or could not wait to find privacy, towards the exit.

He pulled her into the street. They were out in the night where air was cold water and music a dull pulse. Emmy wanted it to stop right there, but Angus had got this far and he meant to go further. He opened the van door and gestured for Emmy to get inside. Felled by panic, she hesitated.

'Come on, Emmy. Get on with it.'

So Emmy climbed inside.

When reflecting on something momentous, memory often takes on the qualities of a dream and brings a sensation of unreality, helplessness, weightlessness. Even of someone else doing the participating.

Between Emmy's pale, slippery body and her mind stretched a gap. Thus, when she dwelt on Angus's naked body and face, sometimes readable, sometimes not, it was with the curiosity of an onlooker viewing a painting. What did those closed eyelids signify? Or the way he rolled over at a certain point? When he whispered, 'That's good'?

She could not remember her own words but she did know that she had wanted to cry out with the love that bound her as tightly as the chrysalis is bound by its carapace. She had wanted to try to convey how she felt, what it all meant. But Emmy lacked the vocabulary, and years of being solitary in the real sense had taken away the habit of many words – or, conversely, nurtured a healthy disrespect for them.

Noises from the street trickled into the hot van. A conversation. A shout, the echo of a can rattling in the gutter. Inside, it was close and lit by ragged filtrations of neon. The blanket Angus had spread on the floor felt scratchy against Emmy's back. Each time she moved her foot, she encountered their clothing or the bulky packages of Angus's work tools.

He lit a cigarette, lay back but made no move to take Emmy into his arms. She coughed and desolation washed her, seeping into the crevasses of her spirit and the hairline cracks of a fantasy that had formed with ill-advised, lightning speed.

She reached for the cigarette packet.

'What's it like having a virgin in the back of a van?' she asked, and could have bitten her tongue.

Angus's hand encountered Emmy's buttock. 'Nice one,' he said.

'Are you sure you're giving Edward enough vegetables?'

'No problem, Mrs Beckett. He likes them.'

Today, Violet was having an acute Working Mother attack, which tended to happen on Mondays, and Emmy was, as usual, the target. She shot Emmy a look which implied that Emmy was guilty of doing all sorts of unmentionable things with the puréed broccoli, including throwing it away. Emmy, who had grown wiser in the ways of her employer, did not drop her gaze. Have you, she was asking silently, ever made love in the back of a van?

Violet prodded a pile of laundry in the basket. 'You will do this today, won't you, Emmy?'

Violet was thinking, It's *so* bloody exhausting having an employee. They never do anything. You have to check, check, check, and you can't ever, *ever*, rely on them.

If Violet had allowed her reading these days to extend beyond the fashionable blockbuster, she would have been reminded that a large proportion of literature has been devoted to the battle between employer and – more power-ful than supposed – employee. Neither side won.

'I'll do the laundry first thing, Mrs Beckett. I was a bit pushed last week.'

Violet's pursed lips apparently suggested that she could not conceive how, compared to the rigours of running an office, looking after one small baby at home could leave you pushed. Emmy was not to know that beneath the Yves St Laurent foundation and Chanel lipstick churned relief, spiced with guilt, that it was not she, Violet, who was having to cope with Edward. In her heart of hearts, Violet suspected she was not up to it.

Emmy of course, was not to know this and she thought, This woman is unbearable.

Violet's heels clicked over the kitchen floorboards. Her shoes were black, very high-heeled and of extra supple leather. Above them, she was wearing a Chanel suit with a long jacket and a short pleated skirt which she had enhanced with an abundance of gold buttons and chains.

Emmy pulled her faded T-shirt down over her bottom and over the leggings which had developed a hole in the crotch.

'How's my boy?' Violet bent over Edward's chair.

Edward regarded his mother solemnly and Violet inserted a finger into the centre of one curled hand. Edward pulled. 'He's getting very strong, isn't he, Emmy?'

At the sound of Emmy's name, Edward loosened his fist and swivelled to look at Emmy. For a moment or two, Violet remained as she was, then she withdrew her hand.

'He's fond of you, Emmy, isn't he?'

Emmy reckoned that if Violet said her name again in that particular tone she would say something shocking. Go away, she willed silently. Go to your work or whatever keeps you so busy.

From upstairs, Jamie gave a shout. 'Are you ready, Violet?'

Violet sighed and picked up her briefcase and an unfamiliar look spread over her features. Emmy knew why: she had heard the Becketts quarrelling the previous evening. The unwilling snooper, the keyhole witness, she had sat in her top-storey sitting room and listened to their voices raised in anger and discord and wondered if they realized how much was revealed. Eventually Violet had retreated to the drawing room and Jamie had gone to bed in the spare room.

'If you could make that vegetable pie, Emmy.'

Emmy looked at Edward. 'Yes.'

Violet lowered her briefcase on to the table. 'Emmy, I think you could call me Violet. After all, we are living under the same roof and I do trust you.'

There, she thought, that will encourage Emmy.

Jamie stood in the doorway. 'Hurry up.' He spoke curtly and without his usual smile.

'Thanks, Emmy,' said Violet.

The front door banged. Immediately Emmy switched from Radio 4 to Capital. Pop music filled the room and Edward banged his spoon as an accompaniment. Emmy picked him up and he settled in her arms with complete familiarity. She nuzzled the top of his head, and smelt his funny little smell composed of nappy cream, talc and a faint echo of regurgitated milk.

'Vegetables, huh?' she said to him.

If the result of making love in a van was a house whose rooms were occupied by separate and angry people, then Emmy knew better than to enter it. She knew she was right to be careful.

Her eye drifted across the piece of garden framed by the window. A clematis had caught blight and hung in a blackened tangle from the trellis. The lawn needed mowing. The frame also caught the bird table on the tree at the bottom of the garden.

Angus's bird table.

Emmy sighed and closed her eyes.

Chapter Seventeen

Prue's love affair was also flourishing. While Emmy's peace of mind was encumbered by caution and anxiety over Angus's motives, Prue's was being fed on a cocktail of intense sexual experience, astonishment, wild joy and terror. Such feeling is greedy and, while it lasts, gobbles up other perhaps more ordinary but no less significant feelings. Thrown into relief by the blaze of novelty, affection and good humour become unsatisfactory and insufficient.

What is *happening* to me? Prue asked herself as she made arrangements, once, twice, three times to meet Jamie at the hotel, and there to sink, shaking and slippery with desire and hunger, through waters of oblivion.

And he as hungry and seeking as she was.

Why is this happening?

But Prue was too happy, too saturated with emotion to do anything other than surrender.

In the early summer of 1429 ('check 7 May correct', Prue wrote in her notes) at approximately 6 a.m. Joan, having spent the night in the besieged city, arrived at the Tourelles (a stone fort held by the English near the head of the damaged bridge across the Loire) outside Orléans and immediately called a council of war. A woman, circumstance and place had come together in one of those significant, delicately timed fusions that make history. Joan's moment had come – *la journée des Tourelles* – and for ever after her name would be associated with Orléans.

Like Prue, Joan was hungry – to put into action what her voices had been instructing her to do. Hungry, and as blazing.

The city had survived the siege for six months so far, partly because the English, under the Duke of Bedford, showed a marked lack of enthusiasm for engaging in action. Instead, from time to time, the English Passevolant tossed its one-hundred-pound stone balls into the city and, from time to time, the French Rifflard returned the compliment. Such was the lack of action that on Christmas Day 1428 the English had borrowed a troupe of musicians from the French ('N.B.' wrote Prue, 'Does that remind you of another war?'). Although Joan was not a soldier, knew nothing of strategy and, above all, was not a man, the citizens were greatly cheered by the news that the famous *pucelle* of Domrémy was to take up their cause.

Joan and the captains discussed tactics, although the course of action was obvious: to storm the earthworks from the south bank of the river before launching an assault on the Tourelles.

It began at seven in the morning and the English fought like animals or rather, as one chronicler phrased it, 'as though they were immortal'. From their advantage on the earthworks, they rained down fire, cannon and lead sling-shot on the French in the great *fosse*, or moat, below and succeeded in repulsing them.

Towards midday, the French retired to eat their lunch. How characteristic, and how trying for Joan, who was famously abstemious in her eating habits and often, after a hard day's battle, had to be coaxed to eat (giving rise in our generation to the conjecture that she was anorexic – another pointer to her extraordinary will-power). Afterwards, they reassembled and launched themselves yet again at the earthworks. Joan helped to raise a scaling ladder. The air was once again ringing with noise and thick with flying objects, and the embattled French and English hacked at each other with axes, lances, guisarmes and bare hands.

It was at this point that Joan was hit by a crossbow bolt which lodged at the junction between her neck and breast, piercing her shoulder. She had predicted this wound. Both St Catherine and St Margaret had warned her. Indeed, a letter exists, written from Lyon a fortnight before the attack, in which Joan states clearly that it would happen.

Predicting a wound is quite separate from experiencing it. Apparently, Joan wept and shuddered with shock and pain. She was pleased that her prophecy had been so exact but a solid wedge of steel-tipped bolt driven at speed into flesh hurts. As she pulled it out of her shoulder to an accompanying gush of blood and splitting of flesh, one of her soldiers offered to put a charm upon the wound.

Joan refused. 'I would rather die,' she said, 'than do what I know to be a sin.'

Such decisions were easier then, were they not? Prue said to Jamie as they lay in bed in the hotel bedroom. You were given a scheme, a set of rules, the notion of direct retribution for veering off-course, all of which left you in no doubt as to how you should behave.

'Sounds terrible,' said Jamie drowsily. 'Who wants rules?'

'People,' said Prue, and nipped his bare shoulder with her teeth.

Potential sinners, of course. The ones born with fleshly lusts and the normal quota of selfishness, greed, cunning and the ability to lie. Natural saints do not require rules for they are never tempted. Their goodness is absolute.

'I don't know about that.' Jamie rolled over and kissed Prue's breast. 'I always thought St Simon the Stylite was a roaring exhibitionist,' he said, and pressed his mouth down into the yielding flesh. 'Anyway, the only way he could manage being good or a saint, or whatever, was up a sodding pole.'

'We're sinning,' said Prue, and sat up in bed.

Jamie pulled her down. 'And very nice it is too,' Prue grimaced. 'If it makes you happy, it could be argued there are rules that apply to us, Prue, and this situation. What's more, we're obeying them.'

'Do you really believe that?'

Jamie shifted on to an elbow so that he could gaze down on the face he had grown to love more than he could say. As a consequence, love, rather than morality or philosophy or even good sense, directed his arguments. 'Things are never as simple as you see them, my Prue,' he said and stroked her cheek.

'That's what I told Jane.' Prue relaxed back on to the sheets.

'But do you believe it?' Jamie's fingers walked light as a feather down Prue's sensitized body. 'We're just us. Nobody else. This is a bit of our lives that is particularly private.'

She had a feeling that she was missing something vital, but Jamie's finger had stopped.

Later she said, 'What shall we do this afternoon?'

It was shaded in the hotel bedroom and Jamie's eyes were dark and unreadable and, therefore, exerted particular fascination on Prue. 'I rather imagined you wished to remain on this bed. Am I wrong?'

Prue bent over him. Her lips were sore and her body felt battered, wonderfully beautifully battered. 'I want to do something with you. Cinema, gallery, anything.'

She wanted the pleasure of walking down the street

holding Jamie's hand. Of being on display as a couple in public. Or sitting at a table in a café. She wanted strangers to look at Jamie and herself and to register the rope of plaited emotion that stretched between them.

The hotel staff knew them by now and the clerk behind the counter nodded neutrally as they walked out of the front entrance.

'He will be used in evidence against us,' Prue remarked.

'Your conscience is guilty today, isn't it?'

'It's always there,' she said. 'How can it not be?'

He took her hand. 'Don't, Prue.'

Wanting to handle it well, she thought carefully before saying, 'It's fine, Jamie. I'm not going to make you carry my burdens.'

She pressed her thumb into Jamie's palm and they walked down to Oxford Street and, via the underpass, into Hyde Park. Here they maintained a space between their two bodies, Prue hugging her shoulder-bag which was full of books. Jamie stuffed his hands into his pockets, looking out of place in his grey city suit among the tourists and children.

'Ice-cream?' he asked. Prue shook her head and Jamie bought himself a vicious-looking thing from a vendor. He had an idea. 'Dinosaurs,' he said. 'Let's go and see them in the Natural History Museum.'

'If you knew,' Prue emphasized each word, 'how many times I've been to see the dinosaurs you would not suggest it. Anyway, you'll be taking Edward later on. Lots and lots of times.'

The thought struck home to Jamie. 'Yes, I suppose I will.'

Instead, they fetched up in the basement of the Science Museum admiring the original Crappers, blue and white china lavatory bowls, old gas fires, early stoves and other domestic developments.

'A bullseye,' concluded Jamie after examining an early

Aga. 'A machine for cooking and a cosy ideal all wrapped up in one parcel. Whoever invented it was quite brilliant.'

'Not as clever as the wheel,' said Prue, who had been very taken by the steam engines upstairs.

Jamie pinched her bottom and she laughed. Together, they gazed into the glassed-in displays of electric lamps.

'When did you first know?' asked Jamie, his breath frosting the glass.

'That time in the cathedral.' Prue knew exactly what Jamie was asking. 'I knew I should be looking for God, but I found you.'

'*Are* you searching for God?'

She pointed at a lamp whose design intrigued her. 'I don't know. Are you?'

'Merchant bankers and God!'

'That's too obvious,' said Prue, 'but I take the point.'

She slipped her hand into his and he drew it up against his chest and held it tight.

Jamie insisted on seeing Prue off at Waterloo. Don't feel too guilty, he said as she got into the train. I'll try not to, Prue replied, but it would be a strange thing if I didn't worry about it. You *are* in it unless you choose to get out, he said, and kissed her quickly on the cheek. He did not mean the train.

No wonder rationalists distrusted love. No wonder Church and moralists have striven to keep it under lock and key and searched for ways to diffuse its power. No wonder love is perceived as a monster that gobbles up whatever lies in its path. Children, spouses, households. Money and good sense.

Yet as the tide rushed towards Prue and caught her in the tow, she bent willingly to receive it as it crashed over her (and pounded over Jamie, too), dragging with it the shingle and debris of her life.

Which was similar to the pounding that took place at the Tourelles on that bright May day where the French fought the English from seven o'clock in the morning until eight o'clock at night, but made no headway.

Her shoulder bandaged with cotton to staunch the blood, Joan took stock and withdrew to an orchard where she prayed. Then she galloped back, seized her standard from the Basque who was carrying it for her and shook it vigorously. 'Whereupon', the chronicler informs us, 'all the Maid's army rushed together and immediately rallied.'

Thus renewed and inspired, the English resistance collapsed and the French seized the day. A triumphant Joan shouted to the English commander to yield to the King of Heaven: 'You have called me whore, but I have great pity on your soul.'

The accusation of sexual impropriety – 'the harlot of the Armagnacs' – was always one that upset and enraged the Maid. She was right to guard her reputation: her virginity, her virtue, was beyond price for it gave her power not so much over women but over men. She knew that to engage in any sexual activity would both corrupt and taint her body, and her power would leach away into tales of lechery and defiled flesh.

It would have been finished for Joan.

Footnote: the English commander who had called her a harlot drowned in the river as the Tourelles was finally taken.

Max observed his second wife as, twenty-five years previously, he had watched his first. He was almost sure that his suspicions were correct. Almost but not absolutely.

She seemed happy, she had lost weight, she was a little abstracted. Nothing significant in itself, and there was danger in deciding, as opposed to knowing, that something was true – because it became so.

Max repeatedly asked himself what was the point of knowing. Of course he would prefer – desperately wanted – his wife to remain faithful, but since, courtesy of the age-gap and the ageing process, it was probably an unrealistic expectation, was he not muddying already dangerous waters? If he conceded the principle then, surely, it did not matter if he was aware of the chapter and verse of his wife's infidelity?

Well, yes. Sufferers from toothache or unhealed wounds will appreciate the desire to touch the spot. Also, curiosity is an electric force.

After tackling the outside paintwork of Hallet's Gate, Max organized a complete programme inside. Dining room. Drawing room. Kitchen. The double bedroom – and began with the latter. When Prue grumbled at the disruption, Max told her to stop complaining, threw a dust sheet over their bed and blotted it out.

'Same again, Prue, I take it?' Max indicated white on the colour chart.

Prue, who had often considered pale pink and grey, but was unsure of what Max was up to, did not dare to suggest otherwise. 'Fine,' she said.

Max prepared the walls. An emptied, echoing room takes on a symbolic dimension. Stripped of colour, it acquires the monastic look and Max was reminded of the reconstruction of a monk's cell in Beaulieu Abbey. How long did it take a blank wall to hone your mind into obedience and equanimity? he wondered. The difference, he assumed, was that the monk considered the blank wall to be a positive statement. Max did not.

Grimly, he washed the walls down, wiped the skirting boards and rubbed them dry. Then he Polyfilla-ed as if it was an art-form, sandpapered until his arm ached, and spent the weekend applying undercoat.

'I'll finish next weekend,' he informed Prue over a dismal Sunday supper of scrambled eggs, and they retired to the single beds in the spare room.

In his dreams, Max returned to childhood. To the discomfort of being born to parents who embarrassed him to the depths of his soul and yet exacted a painful love. How could he not love them? They were all he had.

Max dear, don't put your feet on the settee.

Max, do you have to spread your stamps all over the table?

Max, do . . . Max, don't . . .

When you roger a woman, his father advised him, you must remember that you are in command. It's like driving a car. *You* shift the gears. *You* control the performance. Remember that, otherwise they get the upper hand. Doesn't matter if it's a Morris Oxford or a Rolls-Royce, the mechanism is the same.

Max discovered later that his father could lay fair claim to these statements having taken, as it were, his advanced test and driven a sizeable number of women – in fact, a disgraceful tally. Then, of course, there was the incident with the gun, which drew from Max both pity and horrified amusement. Later, he tried to feel contempt for the big, foul-mouthed philanderer, until he remembered the fishing trips, the cricket, the long companionable car journeys and the pints of beer in the pub, the sense that he was being watched over by a kind of love, and his contempt was replaced by a deep, unhealed loss.

To which Helen had contributed . . .

Sergeant Miles had been one of those textbook soldiers, all 'boogers', handlebar moustaches, a taste for bullying and a righteous mission to knock the scions of England into shape on their National Service.

National Service! National Bloody Misery.

The Sergeant set about his task in a shed, marked out by a double row of beds, smelling of sweat, unwashed blankets and semen expended in loneliness and frustration. Otherwise Sergeant Miles permitted nothing: no pictures, no books. His material was the raw, spotty recruit.

'Now, you boogers. You won't be seeing the outside of these barracks for some time.'

Max willed himself to think of other things. Fishing, pellucid water and undulating mats of underwater weed. A painting he had seen in a Mayfair house. Sex, the non-onanistic variety, a tantalizing taste of which he had been lately introduced to by Betty, his mother's obliging housemaid.

'Are we composing poetry, Corporal?'

'Yessir. I mean, nosir.'

A heavy hand descended on to Max's shoulder. 'It's a funny thing, Corporal, but I have an idea I don't like your attitude. You have a sorta look that tells me that you don't give a tinker's about what I'm saying.'

Clearly, Sergeant Miles's light blue bully's eyes were strangers to finer points of feeling. Max gave in. He knew the type, he knew the score, he wanted to get by and he wanted to get by without being noticed – which was difficult with his height.

'I'll keep your secret, sonny, never fear.'

'What secret, sir?'

Sergeant Miles attacked one of his handlebars. 'That you are a useless, overgrown nancy, if ever I saw one, who thinks he's going to sail through this little episode of slumming with the oiks but who thinks wrong.'

The conversation marked the beginning of a programme of attrition that the Sergeant dished out at every opportunity. During the next eighteen months, Max learnt it was necessary to be tough to survive misery, physical exhaustion and, worst of all, boredom – but it had to be real, bone-deep toughness, not a pretence. Max knew, too, that salvation lay in humour but it was hard to laugh. Fling an intake of youths together, put them in the charge of the Mileses of this world, subject them to every physical coarseness you can think of and what, during those fifties years, did you end up with in the way of English manhood?

Max for one. The aching, trembling thing that was Max Valour at twenty. Somehow, out of the jelly, the fear and longing for death, Max had to shape himself up for life.

Several times he asked himself why it was that, in theory, life contained so much – music, beauty, powerful emotion – when he had been dished out a boil on the neck, sweaty underpants, bloody awful food, hatred of anything militaristic and, at night, the sounds of men snoring.

When he walked into the Boffin nightclub with Dickie Bennett a couple of months before his release back into civilian life, Max spotted Helen immediately. She was talking to a couple of men in grey suits and her beauty struck a blow to Max's starved heart. As a Boffinette, Helen was dressed in a tweeny outfit with a plunging neckline and very high heels which gave her an unbalanced look. Rocking on those heels, she had turned and fixed her eyes on Max and Dickie and the curve of her breasts and intelligent dark eyes (he did not notice the too-thin mouth) and, as yet, an untouched quality in her face almost brought Max to a halt.

He should have deduced from his behaviour on the shooting range (dogged, dogged practice until his aim was dead-eyed and the envy of the squad) that he possessed untapped resources. He had imagined that he had no courage, no terrier qualities, not enough sense of self to endeavour to capture another.

But he did. Endless telephone calls, elaborate arrangements to get out of the barracks, flowers and letters later, Helen agreed to come out to dinner. By then, Max had been past eating and drank instead of the fathomless pools of her eyes and rejoiced that, at last, life was yielding up some riches.

The humour, so painfully acquired, stood him in good stead for Helen was not easy and never concealed boredom. Max's boil refused to heal, and his rawness and over-eagerness bored her mightily. He wanted her body: the white breasts, slightly too full thighs and the tiny pocket of fat that sat on her hips. Above all, he wanted to capture the grubby, selfish, grasping spirit that inhabited the body that so fascinated him.

'Stop it, Max,' she would say through her thin, scarlet-slicked lips. 'I want someone adult.' They were the same age, but Helen imagined she was older.

This was where Max's terrier came in and he held on, with jaws that grew stronger every day.

'All right,' she said at last, worn down by the siege, fixing him with the eyes that promised oblivion and Nirvana, 'we can go to bed. I owe you that. But only once.'

'That's enough,' said ignorant Max, fingers already fumbling at his shirt.

They were at his flat and Dickie had been bribed with beer to stay away. The gas flared in the filaments and gave off its distinctive smell. Outside its ring of warmth, the room was icy and Max's bed occupied a polar region in the corner.

In her electric blue dress (a colour in which Prue also looked good), Helen watched Max. His torso emerged from his shirt and he stopped, unsure how to proceed, failing to take Helen into his arms and to undress her. After a second or two, he continued and took off his trousers and stood, very white-skinned, in socks and underpants.

'My God,' said Helen from the safety of the clothed, 'what have I let myself in for?'

Life may have dealt Max largeness and a boil but he expected such to be his lot. Unlike his fantasies of making love to Helen. Despite Betty the housemaid, he had envisaged that sex just happened. One moment, you are dressed, the next not. He had imagined, too, that romance was a solid thing.

It was not. It fled under the assault of bony knees, Helen's unconcealed contempt, the Arctic temperature, his inability to take charge and his desperate need. Thus, instead of surging like a triumphant fish through tropical waters, Max was brought up against his ignorance.

Helen showed him. He had known she was experienced but it hurt to have it demonstrated quite so brutally. This way, she told him. That way. And Max who had so wanted to lead, followed.

Never, never again, she said afterwards. I want a rich man who wants a wife. Not you. Max argued that he would be reasonably well off as a solicitor. Articles over the next twelve months, then a partnership. Equity partnership within ten to fourteen years. 'Give me ten years,' he begged.

Helen looked at Max as if he was mad, and her dark eyes were contemptuous. 'I'm not sitting in a semi in Guildford wearing gingham while I wait for you to get rich.'

He wanted to slap the jeer from the scarlet lips and take her by the shoulders and shake until her teeth rattled. But he knew he was just as likely to press kisses into the hollows made by her collarbones and suck like a drowning man on that jeering mouth.

'Where will you find him, Helen?'

'There will always be someone,' she said.

After that exchange, Max allowed himself to get drunk and took Helen home. Her flat was in a decaying house off Sloane Avenue in the days before Chelsea became fashionable. At the front door, she said goodbye in a final-sounding voice and turned away. He caught a whiff of jasmine scent and tobacco, and a madness gripped him.

'No you bloody don't,' he said and, grabbing her by the hand, he pulled her upstairs to her room and bundled her inside. Then he pulled off Helen's mackintosh and ripped at her blouse.

'Stop it, Max.'

Helen fought him as best she could but, hardened by two years of army life, he was stronger.

Instinctively, Max knew that Helen enjoyed what followed. As he pushed his way towards what he wanted and ignored her cries, he saw the thin mouth suddenly slacken with desire and felt the white body respond as it had not before. He held her arms tightly and inserted a knee between her legs.

'You will listen to me,' he muttered through clenched teeth.

'You bastard,' she spat back, but the last syllable was teased out, silky and heavy. Triumphant finally, he smiled down at her.

'Got you,' he said.

A month later, Helen knocked at Max's front door and stood, hunched and ill-looking, on the threshold. He had not seen her since that night but his dreams were filled with images of their thrashing bodies that caused him to wake shaking with desire and frustration.

'I've got to speak to you, Max.'

He lit the gas fire and made a pot of tea. She was sullen but accepted a cup and balanced it on the inelegant wing of the armchair.

'What is it, Helen?' Max's cup clattered in the saucer.

'Don't do that,' she said. 'It's irritating.'

'Well?'

'I'm in pig.' She shot him a quick, calculating look. 'And I want you to pay to get rid of it.'

Max went back to the kitchen to replenish the pot, Helen's news knocking around his brain like a loosened atom. Carefully, he directed a stream of boiling water into the china pot. Then he replaced the lid and listened to the pop, pop of the gas fire.

He walked back into the room. 'No,' he said. 'I'm not going to pay for an abortion. You are going to marry me instead.'

With a snarl of dislike, she looked up at him but Max did not mind. He knew he had Helen where he wanted her.

'Got you,' he said to himself.

Thus it was that Max Valour married Helen Beech at Chelsea Town Hall with Dickie Bennett as best man and witness. The bridegroom looked very cheerful in his best, and only, suit. The bride's hair was scraped back into a pony-tail and the waistband of her cheap cotton skirt did not quite meet.

Six months later, Violet was born.

And out of that semi-rape had come adultery and death, and Max had been forced to learn detachment over matters of the flesh.

So you see, my Prue, he told her silently as he mixed paints, rolled walls and inhaled paint stripper on his journey towards his personal Calvary, my armour is heavy and, like your Joan, I risk everything. I have to be vigilant with myself. Coercion does not do. To rout the enemy, I have to give you freedom, that is my gift of . . . love.

I can do no more. Enough. Enough.

Chapter Eighteen

Violet pounded away on the StairMaster. This was the final assault before the holiday. The final push. Clenching her teeth, she switched the programme up to level nine and sweat poured down her face. One, two. Left, right. Gloria Estefan pounded in her ears and her legs followed suit. Up, down. One minute gone. Two minutes gone . . . She visualized the straining muscles, the hasty conversion of her fat into energy, the breakdown into carbon monoxide and the acid left pooling in her flesh, the blood arriving to vacuum it away.

In a gesture that was becoming habitual Violet looked over to the wall, entirely composed of mirror, for a quick check. There she was: body hunched over machine, stick legs working. If the botanist's pin had skewered Violet through the heart, she would resemble nothing so much as a gaudy pinioned insect in the collector's display cabinet.

She paused for breath and, without warning, her mind swarmed with other, forbidden, images, each one as lasciviously detailed and complete as a master pornographer's fantasy. Only this morning, Violet had caught sight of the extra-*extra* forbidden as she had driven past the shop, but the three-second glimpse was sufficient for a starving mind to lick and garnish into luminous temptation. Brushed with whipped cream, glistening with caramelized sugar, light, airy, confident, perfect, it had been a Gâteau St Honoré to outdo all Gâteaux St Honoré.

What a bully the mind was. Violet summoned other images to help purify and rid it of its succulent devils. The Pope. Gerard Depardieu. *Hello!* magazine. She felt her mind bend and strain to her will, as she bent and strained on the machine, but it was useless. Violet was helpless, as hobbled and spreadeagled as Gulliver in Lilliput, when confronted with the powerful chimera of *foie gras*, chips and steak, and chocolate-hazelnut spread smothered on thick white bread. In desperation, she called up the final defence.

Cellulite.

Thick brown circles of fat like potato peelings that snaked and draped and clung to the hips – in pitiful contrast to Violet's Platonic ideal – solarized into her mind. But even the spectre of cellulite failed to force Violet's fantasies to their knees.

Knees . . . Paul Gascoigne's knees. Jamie's knees, rather bony ones. Edward's knees, all pink and plump like sugar mice.

No! Not sugar mice.

Violet scrubbed at her face with the end of the colour co-ordinated towel hanging round her neck, adjusted her position on the machine and stepped up the pressure on her pressurized thighs.

Afterwards, she rested in the changing room and waited for her heart to return to its normal rhythm. It was the lunch-hour and the room was full of women whose flushed bottoms, thighs and shoulders were slicked with sweat and glossy with heat.

The ubiquitous mirrors witnessed, refracted, distorted and told truths, many unwelcome. Violet studied her reflection: sucked-in stomach, sucked-in cheeks, a sweat-splodged Lycra ensemble.

Gâteau St Honoré.

No, you don't. She swivelled to obtain a sideview of her flat stomach and lean thighs.

Mirror, mirror on the wall
Who is the fairest . . .?

Certainly not Prue, and Prue would soon be old.

When Helen, still beautiful, had been dying in hospital from the car crash – and taking some weeks to do it – Violet had saved up and spent her pocket money on a doughnut to give Helen. It was a plain one, dusted with sugar, into which ersatz cream had been piped. This she had presented to her mother in a brown paper bag as she lay propped up by pillows and fed by tubes.

Helen reached out fingers that were by now skeletal, looked into the bag, retched and turned her head away.

Violet now understood why but, at the time, it had seemed that her mother had rejected her gift of love but, then, love offered in a brown paper bag is difficult to accept when you are dying painfully.

Violet had not been sure how to react to Helen's death. Should she cry? Should she be terribly, terribly brave giving onlookers the opportunity to exclaim how extraordinary a child she was? On the other hand, the idea of screaming artistically during the funeral and casting herself down by the coffin in a flurry of smocked dress and Start-Rite sandals, an image taken from a film, rather appealed.

In fact, Violet had been banned from the ceremony because her grandmother declared that children did not go to funerals. Why death was considered only for adults was not explained. Violet beat the ban by sneaking up to the churchyard where she watched Helen's coffin being lowered into the earth with an expression, had she but known it, of avid interest. It is impossible to deny that observing your mother being buried is a unique experience.

Later, she had escaped once again to stand alone and cry, in the pouring rain, by her mother's grave. Just standing, alone, until she was sodden.

Violet got to her feet, peeled off the Lycra and headed for the shower, which she ran until it was ice cold. She clenched her teeth and stepped under it.

I will not think of food, she mouthed the words through numbed lips. I will not think of food.

When she emerged, she felt that her mind had been washed as clean as her body and was now, for the time being, safely under control.

'Hallo, Dad.'

'Hallo, darling.' Max was surprised to be rung up in the office. 'Is everything all right?'

'Fine. How's Jane and Prue?'

Max hesitated a couple of seconds. 'Fine.'

At her end, Violet raised her eyebrows. 'Is Prue still wrapped up in Joan of Arc?'

'To tell the truth,' said Max, 'I wish I'd never heard of the bloody woman. Anyway, why are you ringing me?'

'Darling Daddy. You know you said if I ever wanted anything . . .'

Max's laugh cut across the rest of the sentence. 'What is it?'

'I've run out of money and I need some to buy clothes for the holiday in Italy. I don't have anything to wear.'

'Why don't you ask your husband?'

'I don't want to ask Jamie. It's none of his business. Please, Dad. I love you very much.'

'You are absolutely outrageous.' Max was already reaching for his cheque-book. 'How much do you want.'

'A couple of hundred. Three,' she added quickly.

Max hunched his shoulder around the telephone and wrote one thousand pounds on the cheque. 'I'm giving this to you, my darling, on the condition that you put half of it into the account set up for Edward.'

'How much, Dad?'

He told her, and immensely enjoyed the gasp at the other end of the phone.

'I was thinking about your mother when you rang.' Max stuck the phone under his chin and signed the cheque.

'How funny. I've been thinking about her too.' If Violet was strictly truthful, Helen's memory was like laddered tights in the drawer – there and requiring attention, but only taken out from time to time.

Max's next comment took Violet by surprise. 'Your mother and I did have some good times but, unfortunately, we let each other down. Every marriage makes its accommodations, but perhaps with mine I read the wrong noticeboard. I hope you've read yours correctly.'

'Oh, yes,' said Violet, totally bewildered.

'And we've all survived.'

'Oh, yes.' Violet recollected her dream landscapes and her terror as she ran across them.

'And you, my darling daughter, are more important than anything.' Max's voice dropped and became soft and loving. Sometimes he feared for Violet's bright, glossy beauty and her bright, glossy life. He added, 'And Jane, of course.'

His tenderness reached Violet in a way that she seldom allowed anything to do. 'Thanks, Dad,' she said, with a catch in her voice. 'That's nice to know.'

Because of Jamie's commitments at the bank, the Becketts could not take their holiday until mid-July. Typical, said

Violet. How come we're the only family with a pre-school child mug enough to pay high-season prices?

The destination was a villa in Tuscany and, not to miss a day, they planned to drive there in one all-out marathon down the motorways.

Prue told Jamie they were quite mad. 'How will you cope with the baby?'

Jamie did not often encounter Prue's practical side. Lovers don't, which is part of the seduction for each. Between lovers, there is no need to consider surly teenagers, leaking roofs and the weekly shop. These are reserved for the spouse.

'Edward will sleep in the back of the car,' Jamie said, airily.

'He won't, you know.' Prue poked Jamie with a teasing finger. 'Haven't you learnt yet about babies? They *never* sleep when you want them to.'

'Yes, he will.'

Prue bit her lip. 'I wish, I wish ...' and suddenly the mood shifted back to the one that nourished their passion so satisfyingly, and with which they were now familiar. Yearning, hunger, which was in no danger of being assuaged, spiced with an edge of the illicit, and sadness – the wine and bread of an affair.

I wish I was coming with you, she meant to say.

Jamie understood. 'I know, Prue. So do I.'

'Kiss me goodbye.'

He felt a shiver run through Prue's body, and held her tight. The goal-posts were shifting and, for the first time, Jamie acknowledged that the situation was slipping out of his control.

'I can't bear it, Prue,' he said, spurred by the idea of parting, 'I can't go on like this. When I come back we must talk about it.'

'*Kiss* me, and don't be silly.'

Several times during the nightmare journey Jamie recollected Prue's warning which, of course, he could not repeat to Violet, Violet requiring no encouragement to dislike Prue, particularly as Edward was busy re-creating Dante's voyage into Hell.

The ferry crossing made Edward sick. Violet spent most of the time in the passenger lounge grimly clutching him to her lap with a wad of tissues, surrounded by Rotarians from Yorkshire and schoolchildren giving in to demented urges. Under Edward's assaults, Violet's carefully assembled new outfit of designer shorts and a tartan jacket became stained and smelly.

At Dunkerque, the driver in the car behind them in the queue was distracted by an official mouthing an instruction in French and banged into their rear bumper. Not too much damage was done to the company BMW but, from then on, tempers deteriorated.

'I've forgotten how fast the French drive,' said Jamie, once they were on the motorway.

'Careful.' Violet spoke through gritted teeth.

Jamie put his foot down. 'Just testing the speedometer.'

Violet leant back in the seat. France flashed by. It grew hotter, the tarmac shimmered and in the back, packed into his chair, Edward grizzled without ceasing. The car was not suitable for transporting a baby and the heat accentuated the smell of vomit, which Violet had tried to eradicate with duty-free Chanel No 5. Sweat poured off both of them and Violet's thighs were glued painfully to the seat.

Violet decided she hated both her husband and her son.

'Can't you shut him up?' said Jamie at last, as if it was Violet's fault that Edward was crying.

A couple of small Peugeots shot past and, without thinking, Jamie pushed the accelerator. Violet, who had turned round to see to Edward, was jolted backwards.

'For crying out loud,' she shrieked and, at the sound of his mother so cross, Edward opened his mouth and screamed.

'Stop the car, Jamie. *This minute.*'

'How can I?' Jamie lost his temper. 'We are on the bloody autoroute, remember. I *can't* stop.'

'Well, the next *aire de* whatever it is.' Violet's French had deserted her. Somehow she thrust herself between the two seats and crouched in the back beside Edward. 'Shush, you little beast,' she said, dabbing at Edward's hot, swollen little face. 'You're not making things easier.'

Why didn't I bribe Emmy? she was thinking furiously. Why did I let her go on holiday? The baby's gaze locked on to his mother's. Help me, it said. It's your fault I'm so uncomfortable. Caught between guilt and fury that Edward was not behaving reasonably, Violet hauled him out from the nest of straps and padding and, crouching at a dangerous angle, held him against her swaying shoulder until Jamie swung off the *autoroute* and stopped the car . . .

The villa, which had promised so much in the brochure, fell short. The garden was not the formal sweep interspersed with patches of mysterious, cedary cool that had been suggested, but a dry scrub-pocked patch overlooking the road with no privacy. The rooms were unkempt and the kitchen erred on the side of the primitive. Next door, at least five families appeared to be in occupation, none of whom ever went to bed or turned off the radio.

'What did I tell you?' said Violet bitterly. 'If we couldn't afford a decent villa here we should have gone to Umbria.'

Jamie badly wanted to sit down and drink a glass of wine. He wanted Violet to see the funny side. Suddenly he turned on her. 'Do you ever shut up?'

Violet went quiet.

The baby did not thrive in the heat. 'Why', Violet ground out between white lips, 'are we landed with such a sickly baby?' Edward was hot at night, then cold. Sweat and urine gave him nappy rash which, because Violet did not deal with it quickly enough, suppurated. Then he went off his food, developed a stomach upset and the rash turned from pink to flaming red and his eyes became huge in his shrunken face.

'I think it's time for the doctor. Again.' Violet held Edward's wailing form to her breast. It was their fourth uneasy day and she was shivering from fatigue and frustration. 'God knows how we'll manage the Italian.'

Jamie put down a volume of Larkin's poetry (which Prue had bought him for the holiday) and took his son from his wife. Despite an application of her scarlet lipstick, she had lost her customary gloss, and he was reminded of how dimmed she had been by exhaustion and bewilderment after Edward had been born. Guilt at what had happened since then made his stomach twist painfully.

Experienced in anxious holiday-makers clutching ailing children, the doctor took one look at Edward, issued antibiotics, rehydrating fluids and the equivalent of Calpol. His instructions in broken English were admirably clear. He advised them not to worry, how to proceed and hinted that, in future, it would be better to wait until the baby was a little older before venturing into the heat.

'Point taken, my son,' Jamie told a sleeping Edward in the pushchair, signing away a good proportion of his traveller's cheques for the medicine.

Violet's frustration with motherhood was not diminished by this episode and she weighed it alongside her other resentments. The role of women. The role of men, husbands in particular. Badly equipped villas. Nannies who required holidays. Why, she asked herself as she selected the best tomatoes for their lunch, do babies prevent you doing anything normal, like sleeping? They gobbled you up, babies, and their wailing, smelly forms went suck, suck, suck at what remained of your lifeblood that had not been shed in giving birth.

Chop, chop, went Violet's knife.

Even your head no longer belonged only to you. Everywhere you went . . . Violet chopped on . . . babies came as well. You could not work without thinking about them, lunch without worrying if the baby was getting his, enjoy a drink with a colleague without feeling guilty. A mind split like Morton's Fork spelt muddle, mess and inefficiency, and Violet hated those things with a passion that might have surprised Jamie had it been fully applied to him.

Her friends managed, however. They hefted their snotty beasts under one arm, took them out to diners and restaurants, went on holidays and all seemed fine. Stranger still, these women appeared to enjoy it.

'Better?' Jamie touched Violet on the shoulder and proffered a glass of red wine.

'I suppose so.' She drank the wine and shrugged. 'I keep asking myself why having children is so difficult.'

Once, Jamie would have wrapped his arms around Violet and taken into his keeping whatever anguish was plaguing her. Instead he said, after a moment's reflection, 'We all have to grow up, I suppose.' He inflected the 'suppose' and Violet remained uncomforted.

Still, there was the scent of thyme and hot stone, the sweep of Tuscan hillside replicated in Renaissance paintings, punctuated by the dark green exclamation marks of the cypresses and grey-green blocks of olives. The air felt heavy and scented, and the sun, delicious in the slight chill of the early morning, was a pounding ball of metal by midday. Sometimes in the early morning a chiffon mist was thrown over the valley. Sometimes, a hint of cloud spread like thin paste over the sun moving down the sky. Always, the allure of herb and resin and hot stone filtered through the lazy air, and the seductiveness of the strange.

Now that he was better, Edward slept soundly for an hour or so after lunch, leaving Jamie and Violet free to make their way to their bedroom under the tiles to sleep if they wished, shutters closed against the glare, bars of hot light arranged across the floor, sheets dampening under their bodies. The air in the afternoon felt solid with heat and, more often than not, tension. Or, if both had been honest, disappointment.

Violet's skin had turned light gold, Jamie's an older gold. Both began to look well and rested. Nevertheless, if her hips were satisfyingly slender, Violet's expression was increasingly troubled.

During the Monday afternoon siesta of the second week of the holiday, she turned to Jamie and wrapped her arms around him. He did not repulse her – exactly – but lay on his back, unmoving. She pressed herself against his chest, placed her head on his shoulder and listened to his breath, worrying that her position made her look rather ridiculous.

'Jamie? Do you want to?' Her hand followed a familiar path.

He stirred and responded at last. 'Of course.'

'Of course' was a long way from the approach Violet was used to and had taken for granted. Jamie had always been the one to initiate and had always been gratifyingly persistent. Until recently, that is. Violet thought back over events in the bedroom and the cool nip of reason made her realize that 'recently' had turned into a comparative term. 'Recently' Jamie had not been on form – a state of affairs difficult for Violet to accept, for her mental map of sex was drawn to the specification of herself as the desired object. If the map had been redrawn without her knowledge, it left Violet without a compass.

'Do you think I've lost weight?' she said, stretching so that her tanned and exquisite haunch was displayed to its best advantage.

'Yes,' Jamie confirmed, but without real interest.

He made love to his wife with his eyes firmly shut – as if, she thought indignantly, the sight of her put him off. The episode was not a success. It was too hot, and both she and Jamie were more than a little drunk from lunch. Worse, Violet felt that Jamie had been indulging her.

She lay on her side and stared at the wooden lampstand with its gingham shade. Someone had allowed it to rest on the bulb and it had burnt on one side. A foot or so distant, a motionless Jamie lay with his arm across his eyes. It struck her that things were altering and that it was much easier to control a career than a marriage.

After a while, Violet found herself going over the fine detail of an auction she had set up to take place the day she returned to work. The book was the latest hottest development in diets, and publishers in the States were baying for the rights. Violet totted up figures in her mind. The probable ones first and, as she grew drowsy, fantasies that ran into telephone numbers. Before she fell asleep, she decided to search out a fax machine in the village to ginger up the leading bidder . . .

'Prue?'

'Jamie! Where are you?'

'In a café in Siena. I haven't much time or change. I just wanted to see how you were.'

Prue felt her throat constrict into an aching lump and blinked back tears. 'I miss you terribly.'

'It's bloody hot here. The baby's been ill.'

And Violet? Prue wanted to ask but pride would not let her. 'Hope Edward's better.'

'Yes. Thank God. How are you?'

'Fine. Absolutely fine.' Prue wiped her cheeks with the back of her hand.

'Look, I've got to go. Violet might come at any minute. She's trying to send a fax to the office.'

'Thanks for ringing.'

'Prue. I love you.'

Back in England, Prue sat down with a thump in a chair and wept and wept until her eyes felt like boiled potatoes.

Jamie discovered that the evenings were the worst. Then the light lapped a landscape flushed with pink and gold; a rounded, soft, feminine light. It picked out the dark cypresses and overpainted the gold and brown of the hills over which the early merchant bankers had ridden in search of trade. (It had not escaped his notice that the twentieth-century variety were much in evidence. The biggest villa in the village, which was owned by a merchant bank, boasted security systems, stables, a pool, a personal masseuse and, even, a consecrated chapel.)

'It's so beautiful here,' he confided to Violet, 'that it's almost painful to look at it.'

Violet glanced at the volume of Larkin lying beside him. 'You feeling all right?' she said, and felt his forehead.

He missed Prue, and the light and the ravishing land-scape pressed on a raw spot, which he hoped was not sentimentality. It did not feel like it, for he missed her with an ache and a yearning that he had never before experienced.

To tease and test him, Italy assembled an *enfilade* of ravishing views and buildings, and Jamie's awakened sensibilities continued to suffer for them . . . a hill swelling like a breast, the languor, the aromas, the seduction of the hot nights and good wine. Yes, Jamie suffered because of them.

Quite right?

During the velvet, slumbering nights, he compared the feelings that had once belonged to Lara, then Violet and now, after a frighteningly short time, to Prue, and asked himself what this switchback of loyalty and passion made him. The answer was not that he was facile, because he was not and he knew that. Jamie always tried to do things well, and he tried to think them through. That he had taken an unpredicted deviation forced him to the conclusion that, far from being absolute, love and desire were extremely adaptable.

It did not, however, make them less intense.

He hoped he was not smug, but Jamie prided himself that his life and work were conducted within the limits. He had never cheated on Lara and, in the office, he tried always to take decisions within a context. What did an investment, or the lack of it, mean to local people, the landscape, future generations?

Nevertheless, context had not crossed Jamie's mind when he fell in love with Prue and took her to a London hotel for the afternoon. He had not considered the context of home, wife and child when he ran his hands through her hair and moulded her body this way and that. Or when he had stroked the flare of passion into those grey, beautiful, sleepy eyes.

And what would be the context if he left his wife and son and took another man's?

Took his father-in-law's wife ... and his own wife's stepmother?

Two days before they were due to return home, they were eating dinner, tomato salad, pork chops fried in olive oil with sage, on the balcony when Violet asked abruptly, '*Do* you want another baby, Jamie?' Her manner indicated she had been brooding.

The piece of meat balanced on the end of Jamie's fork dropped to his plate. He must have looked astonished for she leant forward and said, 'It's not *such* a strange question.'

'What's made you decide to consider it?'

Violet leant back in her chair and raised her hands above her head to admire how dark her tan seemed in the candlelight. 'Maybe I was being foolish. And perhaps it is better to get it over and done with.'

'What about the job?'

'That's a bit of a problem as I won't have done my two-year stint before taking maternity leave. But I think I can wangle it.'

Jamie had the sensation of a fish-hook being inserted into the tenderest part of his flesh and yanked. 'But I think you were right when you said no. It would be silly to get pregnant when you've just got your feet under the table at work.'

Violet thought for a moment and then proceeded to astound him. 'I'm willing to take the risk.'

Over the candles, she sent him one of her least aggressive looks. 'What's wrong, Jamie? You were always the keen one.'

'Work, tiredness. Money. The recession is bad. What else do you think?'

'I think ...' Violet got up and walked to the edge of the balcony. Below the house stretched the darkened valley and above the Italian night, laced with stars and a plump, luminous moon. When she spoke again, she sounded unhappy. 'I wish we were back in New York. It seemed easier there. I'm not sure London suits us. If only the recession hadn't meant that you had to come back.'

'We're OK.'

She rounded on him. 'Don't patronize me.' The heat and darkness emphasized her sense of frustration.

Jamie pushed the bottle of wine over the table. 'Calm down and have some more wine.'

He heard her click her tongue impatiently against her cheek. After a silence, he dug in his shirt pocket, produced a packet of cigarettes and lit one.

Her turn to be astonished, Violet looked up in the act of pouring. 'Good God, Jamie. Smoking. What has got into you?'

No decisions were taken. Nothing further discussed. On the penultimate day they made an effort to visit a couple of galleries they had missed. Here, the paintings assembled a colourful, tender theme of maternity: da Siena's *Maesta*, Botticelli's *Madonna and Child Between Two Angels* and Martini's canopied Madonna and standing child.

Jamie had forgotten that strong emotion rubs sandpaper over responses that have become dulled by time and habit, and the radiant Madonnas and Child threatened to overwhelm him. Violet did not say anything much except to roar at Edward when he dropped his teddy for the umpteenth time.

Faced with packing up and driving north, they discovered better teamwork. They had learnt a few things on the journey down and Violet acquitted herself at managing Edward, who was persuaded to sleep at the right times. Keeping to practical topics, she and Jamie talked companionably over the long haul and enjoyed a picnic in the mountains.

While Violet disappeared in search of a convenient bush, Jamie unpeeled a wrapper from a sponge finger and gave it to Edward.

'*Che cosa fare?*' he asked his son.

Chapter Nineteen

Prue waited. In her traditional English village – girdled by custom, sounding the death rattle (which was, nevertheless, taking some time) of *noblesse oblige*, riddled with unemployment and weekend cottages, marked out seasonally by fêtes, Church high days and whether or not its inhabitants wore tweeds underneath their Barbours or sprigged cottons – she waited at Hallet's Gate for her lover to return.

Two weeks. Less than a menstrual cycle, less than a lunar cycle, less than the flowering period of the Fantin-Latour rose. Measured by chronology it was less than any of these things, but measured in *chieros*, the long chilly time of the mind, it seemed to Prue infinity.

Molly Greer caught her as she was backing out of the drive and held up her hand for Prue to stop. Prue applied the brakes and the gravel crunched. Molly motioned that she should wind down the window. Amused by Molly's assumption of command, Prue obeyed. 'Prue. I don't see your name on the flower rota.' Molly's head was framed in the window.

Prue dropped her hands into her lap and smiled. 'I felt like a change and I'm a bit busy at the moment.'

'How can you be too busy for the Church?' Molly was sharp.

'I've been on the rota for a long time. I think a year off would not be unjust.'

Molly's expression hardened but she could not quite

bring herself to say what she thought. She did not have to: Prue knew what Molly was thinking.

'I see,' said the latter, in a freezing tone. 'I do hope this book business isn't going to take you from us.'

Prue was too happy and too absorbed by her happiness to take offence. 'No, I don't think so but I need a little break,' she said and restarted the engine.

'You can't give up on us, Prue, you know.'

Prue shook her head. 'I'll see you soon, Molly.'

She left Molly to stare after the car.

My darling Jamie, I am in the process of retreat, she told him as she drove to Winchester. You won't appreciate what pains I took to dovetail into the rituals of village life because I believed it should be given a chance to survive. Not quite, I know, the bold and dashing manoeuvre of Joan who, after watching the pillage of Domrémy, goes off to save France, but flower rotas and summer fêtes have their place. Don't you think?

Here I am, Jamie, after twenty years of being good at it, and the wadding has been unexpectedly unwrapped from around my heart. I expect it is a commonplace, but to me it seems like a miracle.

What, Prue asked herself again and again, was she going to do with an exposed heart?

'Darling,' said Max after she had collected him from the station and they were driving back to Dainton, 'I know it's a bit late but what about a holiday for us? If I could get the time, how about ten days in Scotland?'

'No,' said Prue, before she could stop herself. 'No. Don't let's this year.'

'What's happened to the I'm-stuck-all-year-in-Dainton argument?'

'I'm just at a vital bit with Joan,' she said, meaning she could not bear to go away just as Jamie returned.

Max hauled the irretrievably crumpled newspaper out of his briefcase and Prue frowned with annoyance. 'Pity,' he said.

Prue concentrated on the traffic and drove back to Hallet's Gate as fast as she could.

What about their marriage, which had nourished and sustained both for so long? Surely with so much change taking place in Prue, Max must sense something. But, apart from his obstinate insistence on redecorating the house, Max appeared to be behaving normally.

True, he was a shade more bad-tempered, more prone to irritation, endlessly pottering with the compost heap, sorting his fishing flies and polishing the guns – the habits accrued from a lifetime.

'How could he *not* know, Bella?' Prue asked the cat who was sitting on the boiler in the kitchen. 'I know I would.'

Bella's green-eyed stare suggested that Prue was fooling herself.

'Yes, perhaps you're right.' Prue stroked Bella's paw.

Blindness to the centre of the other was how a marriage survived. If you knew too much about your spouse, the marriage stood less of a chance when changes occurred.

Prue derived comfort from her conclusions but took to observing Max secretly – from the kitchen window, from under her eyelashes – and to listening for hidden messages in their conversations. At the same time, she was making comparisons and hating herself for doing so: between one pair of eyes and another, between one mouth and another. Not surprisingly, Jamie's face took on the dazzle of the younger and fitter – with the additional allure of the absent – which made Prue want to weep for her unfairness.

'How are we doing with the plan to encourage Jane's friends?' Max asked as they went to bed that evening.

Prue was cleaning her face at the dressing table. 'Lydia is coming over this weekend.'

'We must make more of an effort.'

'You mean *I* don't?' said Prue sharply.

'I didn't say that.'

Prue reached for the tissue box. 'I'm busy at the moment.'

Max flung open a drawer and searched for a clean pair of pyjamas. 'However busy, there are some things on which neither of us should compromise,' he suggested.

'No.'

Prue patted her skin with a tissue while her heart somersaulted and dived. He knows. *He knows.* She folded up the tissue and threw it away. 'No, Max, I suppose not.'

In bed, Max reached for Prue. She submitted, taking a perverse pleasure from her submission, sickeningly aware, so tortuous and labyrinthine is the female psyche, that the frisson she derived from her suspicions added an essential ingredient to the punishment. And Max, suspecting his wife and suspecting that Prue might know that he knew, exacted his dues as he wished, silently and a little desperately, and Prue paid up.

Thus, out of the other's complicity, a strange but mutual dependence was created.

Max rolled away from her. 'Sorry,' he said. 'I'm tired.'

Prue pulled herself upright on the pillows and gazed down at her husband. He seemed more brittle and less substantial than she had realized, and the shadow of her treachery beat its wings over the bed they had shared for so long. There was a tiny scar at the base of Max's neck, a mole on his shoulder and a line had trammelled its way down his cheek. Anguish and the pity she dreaded stirred in her.

'So am I,' she said.

'You've always been good at the soft-soap.' Max swung his legs over the side of the bed and went into the bathroom. She heard the click of the medicine cabinet, the sounds of pills being shaken from a bottle and teeth being cleaned.

Prue threw back the sheets and, clutching her bunched-up nightdress against her, joined Max in the bathroom. He was inspecting his reflection in the mirror and their eyes met. With a sigh, Prue leaned against his back and slid her arms around him, hoping to gather up his tiredness and hurt. Their image merged in the mirror.

'My dearest Prue,' he said and, busy with her own thoughts, she missed the bitter, mocking note.

Perhaps, she thought as she lay later rolling the edge of the sheet under her nails, it was her love for Max that provided the source of her love for Jamie. Perhaps love is like an amoeba; if it existed, it divided and continued to do so. Once you had learnt to love, it multiplied, leaving the original intact.

Darling Prue,

[Jamie's letter had arrived at the bookshop a couple of weeks after the Becketts had come home] I'm sitting in this café and I might as well be on the 88 bus for the place is full of English. We are all in one piece. Just. It's hot. The baby has been ill. Violet is worried about her work. You will sympathize.

Well, no, I don't sympathize, Prue thought, not entirely immune from a little malice.

It is beautiful here and I would love to share it with you. I love the olive trees but I'm not up to describing

on paper what I see. I'll tell you about it instead. It's
also painfully apparent that I've forgotten all my
Italian . . .

Prue was conscious of a tinge of impatience at the
peripheral detail.

I miss you, Prue. More than I can write. Each night
before I fall asleep, I picture you and I imagine
kissing your face. This morning in Siena cathedral
(which looks like a black and white ice-cream) I
found myself lighting a candle and saying your name.
It is not the sort of thing that I normally do but I was
reminded of Winchester. Luckily, Violet was seeing to
Edward. She is doing her best to cope and, I must say,
being very patient, for her . . .

Prue looked up from her letter. The sensation of nails
scraping down the inside of the chest cavity was not an
everyday experience and she was taken aback at how
physical jealousy can be. Violet, the wronged wife, was bad
enough. But Violet, the good and the patient, was unbearable. Violet, who had told Prue repeatedly that she hated
her, that she was only a convenience and boring, boring,
boring . . .

I want to tell you something, Prue, something I find
awkward to say and is easier to show, or to write, but
what I feel for you, Prue, influences everything. It
gives me enormous joy to tell you that, but also
anguish because our lives are arranged as they are
and the situation is as it is.
PS I bought you this card of the Botticelli
Madonna. She reminded me of you.

It is as it is.

The card was one of those small rectangles of thick paper on which was reproduced a religious painting to be sold in Catholic churches and shops. On the back he had written, but not signed, 'I needed you to see Italy properly. I love you.' In the paler English sun, the colours in the figures and landscape beyond glowed with an enigmatic radiance: pink with a green tinge, blue, a hint of gold. Rich, joyous and assured.

Prue destroyed the letter even though she desperately wanted to keep it but decided she could risk keeping the card. There were several caches untouched by the male hand in Hallet's Gate. The plastic box where Prue stored bathroom cleaning equipment, the Hoover and the linen cupboard. But guaranteed absolutely inviolate was the mending bag. Prue hid the card under a torn summer skirt unlikely to be resuscitated and Jane's green polo-neck sweater with a hole in the elbow.

It is as it is.

Prue ran a bath as hot as she could bear it and soaked herself until her skin turned the colour of salmon mousse. She washed her hair in two different shampoos and applied conditioner that had been so expensive she would not dare to confess its purchase even to Kate. The hairwashing was followed by applications of body and face creams and scent.

So had women prepared for men since time immemorial – wives and harlots both – but when Joan, repeatedly harried over this knotty problem, had been asked about her man's clothing, she stated that the matter of dress was a small thing.

Scented and arrayed, Prue dialled Kate's number where Jane was staying for the night.

'Kate? Just checking that Jane's all right.'

'Fine. She and Judy are dressing up at the moment and

arguing as to who should be the tragic Queen of Scots and who the executioner.'

'What are they using for the axe?'

'Good point, sweetie. I'll check.'

Prue listed the possibilities in her head, all of them menacing.

'Prue. That reminds me, let's set a date for the Christmas concert now.' Kate was showing signs of settling down to one of their extended conversations. Prue cut her off.

'Kate,' she said, 'I don't want to do it this year. I think someone else should have a go. I want . . .' she gestured into the air, 'I want time off.'

'Prue! You always do it.'

'Precisely.'

Kate's voice had gone a little cool. 'It's not like you to back off. You were so keen earlier in the year.'

'Sorry. I think fresh blood is called for.'

The silence at the other end indicated that Kate was waiting for the confidences which both women would normally expect from the other after such a revelation. None was forthcoming.

'All right, Prue. You don't *have* to say anything. I suppose Molly did warn me—'

'Molly warned you of what?' Prue gritted her teeth.

'Nothing really. She just mentioned that you had been very preoccupied, which wasn't like you. Apparently, you've signed off the flower rota.' The rising inflection in Kate's voice indicated the friend with proprietorial rights of two decades or so of friendship who suspected something was up and wanted to know. 'Have you and Molly had words?'

Terror that sharp, nosy Molly had worked it out, made Prue reckless. 'Sometimes I wish Molly would jump in the ford.'

'Prue!' Kate was genuinely shocked, but also rather titillated at the spectacle of Prue letting rip.

'I think we'd better finish this conversation,' said Prue and put the phone down. She sat and looked at it, very sand-coloured, very plastic, and came to the conclusion that it was one of the ugliest she had ever seen. Then she dropped her head into her hands and pictured her vengeance on Molly. After a minute or two, she dialled Kate's number.

'Kate? I'm sorry I lost my temper and you're wonderful to look after Jane. I'll reciprocate. Promise.'

'OK.' On occasion, Kate could brood on a slight like a Greek fury but, a true banker's wife, she was reluctant to relinquish capital advantage in the shape of an uncalled-in favour. 'Since you're my friend, I won't tell you what I really think of you.'

Just as well, thought Prue as she sat, tense and excited, in the London-bound train. I'm like an animal, streaking back to its lair. A she-wolf. A jackal, caught on camera lens as it lopes across the horizon. Clever. Feral. On heat.

The train slid into Basingstoke station. Basingstoke apparently had the highest figures for divorce in the south of England. Or was it suicide? Set out in bland, box-like estates – the Home Closes, Hill Rises and Manor Gates – the houses in Prue's line of vision looked too neat and new for divorce and death. Yet behind the net curtains and pots of begonias, messy things were taking place and people were behaving badly.

She considered good behaviour and was forced to conclude that hers – dutiful wife, loving mother and village stalwart – had been easy because it required no special effort, a depressing conclusion for someone who had spent twenty years imagining the opposite.

Unfolding the *Independent*, she tried to concentrate on an

article on whether child benefit should be stopped or not. We should not be selfish, wrote the journalist. Shouldn't we? Selfishness is a sucker which shoots without warning from the main stem and threatens to destroy the whole. Rose manuals counsel that suckers should be snapped off – not cut – at the root base. Prue looked up as the train drew out of Basingstoke. The truth was, she wanted to be selfish. She no longer *wanted* to behave well, but to let go, to step out of her skin and, exposed, pulsating, blood racing, sun-warmed and supple, fly through thin, singing air.

Fleet, Farnborough, Woking, Surbiton ... a litany of southern England rushed past, bathed in a hot yellow light – the kind of places immortalized in black-and-white films starring Kenneth More and Richard Todd when there was forever tea at the Pantiles and everyone played cricket according to the rules.

Discarding the newspaper, Prue picked up the glossy magazine she had bought at the station, which was filled with articles on women's consciousness in African tribes, and the latest in face-lifts and ferocious diets. Inserted among them was one on unfaithful wives, purportedly in-depth. The women recorded their need for fulfilment. Yes, yes, thought Prue. She recognized the power of an affair – the power of a secret – to consume an ordinary life. To make that life seem more significant, precisely because it was secret.

Yes.

The aphrodisiac of terror at being discovered. How to deal with it: run, fight, defend? The need to occupy territory that had nothing to do with your family. A place where you were not viewed as a wife or a mother.

Yes.

None of them spoke of the ravening need, the greed, the hot pulsing rage for another's body. Of lust and tenderness, of darkness and desire, of the sweetness of gorging on another's mind.

Neither did these women speak of the loss of innocence that Prue had found more shattering than relinquishing virginity or giving birth. She *knew* now, for certain, that all of us harbour secret areas of darkness. And those who know this are truly exiles from the Garden of Eden.

Thus, gentle, hitherto contained Prue, hurried along the platform at Waterloo and Jamie, waiting by the barrier, watched her search for him and hoarded anticipation for a few extra seconds before he raised his hand and waved.

They stood looking at each other with famished and desperate eyes. Then, unaccountably, Prue took fright. A summer holiday was a long time and it was possible that things had changed.

'Prue.' Jamie's eyes had settled deep into his tanned face. 'I can't touch you because if I did . . .'

Relieved, she moved towards him. 'You're brown.'

'Boiled to be precise.'

For a second, he was back in the Tuscan hills retasting the vividness of longing, reluctant to yield up the intenseness of the feeling.

'How long have you got?' Prue asked.

'An hour-ish.'

'No time for the hotel.'

'No.'

They walked across Hungerford Bridge to the Embankment Gardens. A hot wind whipped at their clothes and below, slapping at the bridge's moorings, the Thames flowed, dull, poisonous-looking green water in which drifted an assortment of flotsam.

It was less windy in the gardens, and the ground was scabby with dried earth and litter and, because it was mid-morning, they were empty of people, except for a couple of tramps who sat on a bench sharing the contents of a cider bottle. Jamie and Prue sat down on an adjacent one, and only then did Jamie's brown fingers slide up over her hands and catch her by the wrist. 'You've hardly said a word.'

She moved closer and smelt warm body and familiar aftershave. 'Words are not useful at the moment.'

He smiled. 'I wish.'

I wish. She wished. She wished what? That, like a moll in Boswell's London, he would grab her, drag her into the shadows of the bridge and take her against the wall. A knee-trembler, in the hot, airless city, hard and fast enough to assuage the tormenting wen of desire.

She listened to his account of outings, meals, Edward, paintings, the primitive kitchen . . . grateful that he kept his account shorn of Violet.

'And you?' he finished.

Prue supplied an account of house painting, Jane, the disappointing school report, the garden. In her ears, she sounded dull and uninspired but Jamie, observing the movement of her generous mouth and the soft, creamy skin on her cheeks and neck, felt his feelings renew and expand.

'That's all,' Prue finished a little helplessly.

With a sudden movement, Jamie put his arm round her and turned her face up to his.

'Enough,' he said, and kissed her.

Suborned by the mouth on hers, Prue drank of it with the greed of the dehydrated. She murmured his name, her husband, her home, her child pushed into a dark area where she could not see them. Jamie ran his hand across her shoulder, caressing the soft part of her upper arm and gave it a little pinch.

'Fat,' she said.

'Don't you start.' Jamie kissed the area of softness behind Prue's ear which especially fascinated him. 'I love you, Prue, and I missed you.'

Prue stretched and closed her eyes. The sun shone down on the lids and orange and red exploded into her eyeballs. She had never, ever felt so easy in her skin, so absorbed into life. One of the tramps shot them a look and laughed.

'That's right,' he said in a surprisingly cultured voice. 'Go on.'

Jamie released Prue and got to his feet. 'I'll ring you. Soon.'

He's had enough, flashed through Prue and her happiness vanished just like that. She got up from the bench, suddenly weary of her vulnerability and of a situation that absorbed so much of her energy. Jamie took her by the hand, tucking his thumb into the hollow of her palm and they walked up the stone steps in Buckingham Street.

Prue heard herself cry out, 'I don't think this will do, Jamie. It's no good, I can't bear it any more.' She meant the switchback of emotion and despair that she was on, but Jamie misunderstood her.

'I don't think I can either.' Jamie's thumb pressed hard into her cupped hand. 'Let's go to the hotel.'

'That's not what I meant.'

'Let's go to the hotel. I'll make an excuse at work,' he repeated. 'Will you wait? Then we can discuss what we're going to do.'

It was extraordinary how passion diverts pain, uncertainty and commitments. Prue was expected back by Jane, the supper required attention, Kate might be busy. Her absence would look odd.

'Yes,' she replied, shuddering in anticipation, at the mercy of the rolling waves of joy that, after all, he loved her. 'I'll wait.'

She paid no attention to Jane sounding tearful when she rang, to Kate's obvious annoyance, to Max coming home to an empty house – to the sort of considerations that she had poured her energies into over the years and imagined were enough.

Flying through thin, singing air.

No. As she and Jamie tore off their clothes in the hotel, Prue realized that her vision had changed, as once she had made the change from black-and-white television to colour, and could not now remember the former.

'Say you love me.' Jamie was peeling off his socks.

Head inside her T-shirt, Prue told him and pulled it over her head. Then, conscious that Jamie had come from Violet's beauty to her slackening middle age, she folded her arms across her chest. Jamie pulled her to him and she felt the deliciousness of rediscovery, and the burn of his skin against hers.

'I'm so surprised at myself,' he said. 'And I think you are too. This was not part of the life plan.'

She reached up to touch his face. 'Don't say anything. Not now.' She raised her arms towards the ceiling in the ancient gesture – a sun god blessing the earth, or Moloch claiming his victims. 'I'm here, Jamie.'

He ran his hands across her breasts, down her arms and encircled her wrists with his finger and thumb. Then he led her towards the bed.

She thought later, I can't give this up. I can't.

The winged mirror on the cheap dressing table reflected the image on the bed in triplicate and later their separate images as they dressed and said goodbye.

Chapter Twenty

Jane clicked the mouse with her middle finger, once, twice, three times, and the icons on the computer screen arrived and departed at her command.

Click. She conjured up a line that elongated across the screen and which another snap of the mouse turned into a circle. This she wrapped with a ribbon (summoned from the icon treasure box), 'painted' it in with light green and the ribbon a darker green. Underneath she used the mouse to call up HAPPY BIRTHDAY DADDY in green type and centred it under the circle.

Gravely she considered the design, checked it for imperfections and printed it out. The result was just what she had striven for. She folded the paper to make it into a card, and inserted it into an envelope ready to give her father the following morning. Well satisfied, she switched off the computer and tidied the desk.

The swing mirror on her dressing table had tipped over and gave Jane a fine view of her ankles and an empty area of carpet. She got up to adjust it, and her torso and face came into view.

As people are, she was caught by the fascination of the self, and stood for a minute or so absorbing the image. A child's face looked back, on to which she busily superimposed the features she wanted to see. Underneath the fair-skinned face and thick dark eyebrows, there was a body on the cusp of change which she examined with the same absorbed attention, and played the what-will-I-look-like-when-I-grow-up? game.

Tall, blonde, thin? Alice said she looked like a horse without a chin. Implying that it almost was, Lydia had said that wasn't *quite* right, which if it was meant to be loyalty ranked with the rottener variety.

Would Alice and the others like her next term? Apprehension at what might be in store settled on Jane with the weight of a hundred preps undone and a hundred hundred loathed steamed puddings. She hated herself for being weedy and fragile, for minding, but the memory of the previous term's misery made her feel sick.

'You can't run away,' her mum had told Jane (with a catch in her voice) when Jane had cast herself into Prue's lap and begged to be allowed to leave.

'Why not?' asked Jane with the straightforward logic of the child. 'Why can't you run away if it saves you?'

Why not? Prue asked herself, but said, 'We have to stay and stick things out otherwise we would always be running away, because quite a lot of things we find ourselves doing have their bad moments.'

For priggishness that took some beating. Yet if something is priggish it is not, necessarily, untrue.

Prue gathered Jane into her arms and they talked over the problem for a long time.

Jane raised her eyebrows and stuck out her tongue; the image in the mirror responded. She had failed to make her mother understand that *understanding* was not enough: it did not *change* anything. It did not make Alice and the others like her.

'But you will change,' her father pointed out when they took the problem to him for a second opinion. 'Do you remember,' he said, 'when you wouldn't go downstairs because they seemed so large and frightening?'

'Wasn't that Violet?' Jane accused him. 'She was the scaredy one.'

'No, darling,' said Prue, 'Daddy's right. You wouldn't go down those stairs for ages.'

Some comfort was available, for only half the holidays had gone. Seven weeks was a long time, as adults kept informing her infuriatingly. But it depended how you looked at it, and how it seemed to *you*, and Jane was inclined to pessimism. Three and a half weeks would vanish. Just like that. She knew – she just knew. However hard she tried to make the holidays different and special, they would slip from her grasp.

Diverted by the pinkness of her tongue, she waggled it, practised a smile and pulled back her hair to check on the effect. Then she stood sideways to examine the outline of her body and sucked in her stomach which she reckoned stuck out too much. Jane frowned. She was too fat. *Much* too fat. Yet again, she wished that she had a sister with whom to ruminate over these problems. Half-sisters, or rather Violet, were no use.

The inspection over, Jane launched on a hunt for the green corduroy skirt and polo-neck jumper that she planned to wear for her father's birthday supper. The skirt was unearthed from underneath the bed and she smoothed the creases out as best she could. Her next task was to bully her mother into ironing it for her.

Finding the jumper proved a problem, until she hit on where it would be.

Jane winged down the stairs that had once given her so much trouble and launched herself into the drawing room. The chest of drawers in which her mother kept her sewing materials and wools was pushed against the wall under the window and, most weeks, Prue liked to put a vase of fresh flowers on the top. This week, she must have forgotten for the flowers had died. A smell of decay pricked at Jane's nose and she wrinkled it in disgust. Some water had been spilt accidentally on to the wood beside the vase, bleaching a stained whorl of grain into the dark wood. Knowing her mother would be upset, Jane scrubbed at it with the cuff of her cardigan but it was too late.

She opened the drawer.

A couple of hours later, Molly spotted Jane trudging up the main street and hailed her.

'Enjoying the holidays?' Her briskness faltered as Jane turned a blotched and stained face towards her.

It was as if, Molly informed Keith over a supper of mince and cabbage, the child had grown up, almost aged, overnight.

'There was such a funny, bleak look in her eyes,' she said. 'It made me shiver.'

After she had cleared the dishes, Molly got on the phone to Kate.

At the same moment, Max was in a partners' meeting being invited, in addition to his usual duties, to take over administration of the Brussels and Madrid offices. Would he have any objections?

Various thoughts chased through Max's mind, among them pleasure at the recognition. Aware that the purity of a response is often debased by the second thought (in this case, were they offering it to him because no one else would take it?) he concentrated on savouring the sensation before replying that, yes, he would be delighted.

His subsequent thought was that he would be spending less time at home.

Was it worth waiting for? Prue enquired over their after-dinner coffee. Oh, yes, he replied. I'm no saint and, believe it or not, ambition is not necessarily diluted by age. Of course not, said Prue, eyes fixed on his face. Of course not.

At that moment the telephone rang and Max got up to answer it. Prue went out to make more coffee.

'How nice to hear you, Molly,' said Max, at his most impassive.

'It was you I wanted to talk to, Max.' Molly was uncharacteristically hesitant. 'I've just had a word with Kate.'

'Have you?' Max knew at once that the conversation had a subtext, and he marshalled defences to protect his wife. 'But why ring me up to tell me this fascinating fact?'

'We're both worried about Prue. She's sort of gone off.'

'You make her sound like a dairy product. What do you *mean* precisely?'

Although not intimates, Molly and Max knew each other well. At least, Molly reckoned she knew Max well enough to take the bull by the horns. 'Stop being the lawyer, Max. You know what I mean. Do please persuade Prue to do the Christmas concert as normal. Kate is quite upset at having to do it on her own.'

'Why doesn't Kate talk to Prue?'

'She will, she will.' Molly sounded impatient that Max should fasten on peripherals. 'But I thought I would drop a word in your ear first. It's better if you talk to her.'

Is it, my God? Max extracted his tartan handkerchief from his lapel pocket and folded and refolded it. These two women had discussed and weighed and analysed his beautiful, private Prue, and his mood darkened.

'Look, Molly. It was kind of you to ring. But Prue must do as she wishes—'

'There is the *village* to think of and we're not so large that we can afford slackers.'

'Perhaps she's done enough? There are others.'

'Goodness me!' Molly's exclamation contained genuine outrage at the idea that anyone should sign off Dainton – and Max, folding and refolding the tartan material into patterns, had to concede that Molly's brand of – irritating – integrity was the stuff of heroines. Boudicca and Florence Nightingale probably said much the same things. And, of course, the wretched Joan.

'You know as well as I do, Max, it's only a certain type that does things and Prue's one of them.'

'Perhaps she's changed type.'

'Well, she can't.'

'Prue's owed a break, but I'll see what I can do,' he said. 'You'll have to leave it at that, Molly.'

Max terminated the conversation and gave a little smile as he returned the handkerchief to his pocket. Whatever pain she caused him, at least Prue was his, not theirs.

What happened to Joan? asked Jamie on the phone. Many things, said Prue. Abandonment, martyrdom, rediscovery, deification. By the time of her capture, she had become an embarrassment to the Dauphin, whom she had helped to crown, and he made no effort to ransom her. That, she added, in an age when ransoming was as commonplace as presenting a credit card is today.

Poor, wonderful, blazing, sincere Joan who wanted to kick the English out of France, what must she have thought in her miserable cell?

Never trust anyone, said Jamie. She should have known that. Politics always rate higher than religion and morality.

Not always, Prue threw back. They paused at this point to savour the erotic frisson engendered by this tiny disagreement, and became sidetracked.

Whatever happened, said Prue later, this time to Max (these days all her conversations seemed to be conducted three ways, but at different times), it was clear the English were not going to be cheated of their bonfire. 'We like bonfires, don't we?' said Max. 'Guy Fawkes and all that.'

Prue looked at him. 'You don't understand about Joan, do you?' she said. 'Not really.'

'Perhaps not.' Max sighed as he conceded the point.

The Church fell over itself to condemn Joan as a heretic, that most tricky of states to prove and requiring intimate knowledge of the accused.

'How did they do that?' Max asked.

Prue found herself breathing very quickly. The Church's insurance policy was the presumption that the accused is always guilty until proved innocent, this *a priori* conviction being useful in a case like Joan's.

'Ah,' said Max. 'Yes, I see.'

'But,' he queried after a long pause, 'did this not mean that the King of France had been crowned by a heretic?'

'Let us say,' replied Prue, 'that, having ennobled her brothers, the King ordered a certain Guillaume Bouillé in 1450 to prove that the English had rigged Joan's trial. It was the first of many procedures to rehabilitate her – for complicated political reasons, not because she was a saint and a heroine.'

'What else happened to her?' Jamie took up the subject again when he next telephoned.

Her image got used, and by her immediate family too, Prue told him. And the irony is: it was their greed and smallness, admittedly harmless, that ensured, rather like advertising a product, the spread of the story about Joan's extraordinary career. Five years after her death, her brothers pitched up in Orléans leading a woman in armour on horseback. She was, they maintained, Joan risen from the fire. People loved it. They were exposed but, unabashed, the brothers were present in Notre Dame in 1455 to aid the touching tableau of their mother begging a papal commission with cries and groans to rehabilitate her daughter.

In later centuries, when Joan's life and death had faded into a footnote, and she had been almost forgotten, descendants of her brothers used her unimpeachably chaste and chivalrous image to prove that the family was, in essence, noble, and published books to that effect. As a result, Joan was again talked about and the interest in her led, eventually, to her canonization.

'No service to France,' wrote one of these impeccably noble authors, 'can be compared to the Maid's.'

He would, wouldn't he?

'But he was right, wasn't he, Jamie, even if it was for the wrong reasons?'

Ergo. You do not have to ride out to battle with your precious standard streaming behind you and your courage screwed to its limit ... You do not have to be burnt at the stake in front of a howling crowd to be immortal. You do not have to be in almost daily conversation with God and bring off feats of the near miraculous and boot the English out of France. To save you from a second death you merely require a bandy-legged, pendulous-nosed king who can sign and stamp a piece of paper which ennobles your no-good brothers.

The peripherals to the story.

Thus, as a thread of conjecture, half-truth, hasty conclusion and, yes, genuine concern was spun between Max and Prue, Violet and Emmy, Jamie, Molly and Kate, those with peripheral interests played no less a part than those whose lives were primarily affected.

As with Molly's passionate concern for the erosion of Dainton's communal life, with Helen who had not bargained on encountering a car driven by a novice driver coming towards her when she chose to swerve drunkenly into the middle of the road, and again with a torn jumper which lay bundled in a drawer alongside something significant, it is the peripherals that, in the end, matter.

Autumn

Chapter Twenty-One

'Legs apart,' ordered the beauty therapist.

Violet obeyed. She was shivering slightly, having been ordered into the shower to wash off the exfoliant which the therapist had rubbed – a little too enthusiastically – all over her with a loofah. Now, in the tricky part of the operation, Violet was being wrapped in wet bandages, wide flannel ones used in hospitals to conceal gaping wounds but now moulding the contours of Violet's (imaginary) cellulite to her hip.

'You're a lovely colour, Mrs Beckett.'

'Yes,' she said with a degree of satisfaction. 'We were in Italy in June and the tan seems to have stayed.'

'Wider,' said the therapist, whose own face and body glowed electrified and slender, and extracted a roll of plastic wire from the clutter on the shelf. Beginning with the right leg, she coiled it round Violet's bandaged body and a prolonged tussle ensued to anchor it properly. Keeping her legs obediently apart, Violet closed her eyes while hands invaded parts of her body not normally in the public domain and summoned a composite image of Cindy Crawford/Jane Fonda/the Princess of Wales as a compensation for the indignity.

'Hop up on to the table, Mrs Beckett, dear.'

Hop! It was doubtful if Violet was in the running for breathing. Nevertheless, she wriggled herself as best she could into a horizontal position.

'Fine,' she said faintly.

The therapist attached electrodes to what, Violet devoutly hoped, were the correct areas of her body, and wrapped her in a length of plastic sheeting which she anchored with clothes pegs. Thus, like a chicken on a supermarket shelf, Violet lay and gave up her soul – and a lot of her money – in yet another pursuit of the body beautiful.

'Coming up now, dear.' The therapist busied herself with the machine, punching in numbers and flicking switches.

A sensation remarkably like the first stages of labour invaded Violet's torso, which shuddered under the impact. Neither the sensation nor the memory it engendered did she care to dwell on. Reinforcing her unease, an extra strong charge of electricity shafted through her pelvic region and she winced.

'Bear up, Mrs Beckett.' The therapist patted her face. 'Are we all right?'

At least, the injunction was not 'Bear down.' Anything but that . . .

Violet closed her eyes and visualized electric worms – no, centipedes digging with busy legs through her dimpled cellulite and tossing it aside into her drainage system. Gathered up like Nile silt, it surged past pink muscles and vitreous green and red organs the colour of thirties china . . . to where? Not quite sure of the process of excretion, Violet and her Pilgrim's Progress of fat came to a halt. It would be disgorged somehow, in a glistening, creamy flood into the pipes bisecting London.

Bliss.

'We are very quiet at this point, Mrs Beckett, in order to work on our serenity.'

Eyes tight shut, Violet worked on her serenity and counted numbers with a miser's loving, lingering relish: one centimetre, two, three even, off the hips.

The telephone shrilled in the tiny room. The therapist clicked her tongue with annoyance and squeezed past the table on which Violet lay to answer it. Violet tossed one more centimetre into the equation.

'Yes, she is here,' said the therapist with some surprise. 'But my client is undergoing a treatment and cannot be disturbed.'

There was a long pause, interposed by several 'buts' from the therapist. Violet's eyes snapped open. Her first thought was that the auction she was conducting had gone wrong. Her second that Gardener's, the American publishing house who was bidding in the auction, had backed down. If nobody was going to come to the ball she would look pretty damn foolish. Her priorities established, only then was a further thought at liberty to form: Perhaps there's something wrong with Edward?

'Well, if you *must*,' said the therapist in icy tones. 'Just a minute.'

There was a great deal of jerking and pulling of telephone flex and the receiver was inserted under Violet's chin.

'Hallo,' she said in a manner designed to disguise the fact that she resembled a mummy in the British Museum. An evening breeze of electric current played up and down her stomach.

'Violet, it's Lavinia. Gardener's have faxed in with what they say is their best offer of a hundred thousand. I thought you ought to know. They want our answer this afternoon otherwise they're withdrawing it.'

There was no apology from Lavinia for the interruption, neither did Violet expect one. 'They seem dead keen,' continued the voice, which was all breathy and excited. Bound to her sides, Violet's fingers twitched. She nudged the receiver with her head.

'Any more come in?'

'Nope.'

'Right. Tell them I'll get back to them in a couple of hours and could you tell Hayden where it's at, and say I'll be in the office to deal with it in an hour.'

'Yup.'

Almost too late, Violet realized she had made a strategic error. It was not a good idea to let it be known to the managing director that she was out enjoying a long lunch – at least, not these days. She changed tack.

'Scrub that, Lavinia. Just ring Gardener's and say we'll be back to them before close of play, our time.'

The evening breeze switched location and shifted to her bottom where it rippled in and out of the creases.

'OK, Violet.' Lavinia sounded suitably impressed by Violet's decision-making qualities. The phone went dead.

'Sorry,' said Violet, who was anything but at having her status so satisfyingly confirmed, if only to a beauty therapist.

'Well, dear, it seems you can't have much peace.' The therapist returned to dial-twiddling and did not look particularly impressed. She had witnessed this sort of thing many times. 'Not very good for the stress levels.'

'How much longer have I got on?'

'To get the real benefit, I should keep you here for another three-quarters of an hour.'

A brief but violent battle was waged in Violet's head. Three-quarters of an hour on the machine, half an hour to get back – leaving only the minimum to ring round and whip up from other bidders in the ring. If she was going to perform prodigious feats and pull in maximum dollars – and therefore the maximum kudos – she needed to be at the end of the telephone.

On the other hand, there had been an outrageous wait to get on this machine and she wanted to extract every ounce. Correction: she wanted every ounce extracted from her.

'Everything all right, Mrs Beckett?'

Lianas of fat roped Violet to the table. Pound and dollar signs glinted on the ceiling where a fan whirled. What if a decision was taken in her absence? The memory of the disastrous meeting when she had annoyed the managing director had left its scars, and others – notably that prat Sebastian Westland – were keen to gobble up Violet's territory. In addition, the MD was hot on observing good corporate behaviour and had made it clear he thought it would be proper to sell the book to their mother house in the United States. Their mother house was not offering as much as Gardener's but it was just possible that the corporate view would throw a spanner in the works she had so carefully orchestrated.

'Turn the machine off, please,' she said. 'I'm afraid I've got to go.'

'Well . . .' The therapist's expertly tinted skin turned pink with annoyance.

'Don't worry. I'll pay. Do you have another appointment?'

'Except for Monday at seven thirty nothing for two weeks.'

'Fine,' said Violet, and waited to be un-shrinkwrapped. 'Book me in. I'll come on from the office.'

What about Edward? said a voice in her ear as she flagged down a taxi. You're already going out two evenings next week.

Emmy will cope said a second, louder, one. And Edward is far too young to notice whether I'm there or not.

Violet emerged much later that evening from the office, elated. Clever negotiation – a combination of insinuation, nerve and tricksiness – had ensured a deal thirty thousand dollars up on the Gardener's offer, and Violet had been congratulated all round.

'I'll get Julia to run out to the offy and buy a bottle of wine,' said Sebastian, flicking his expensive patterned tie in Violet's direction. 'Or has the little woman to run home?' Sebastian was given to comments like that. He thought they were funny. Violet, who had perfected the art of pretending to scratch her left arm so that she could check her watch without seeming to do so, rubbed at her wrist. Six o'clock. Just OK.

Julia, his secretary, told Sebastian to run his own errands, thank you, which resulted in a sharp little exchange. Eventually, a couple of bottles of chardonnay were opened and the office got stuck in.

Violet did not drink much: alcohol had never appealed to her, and she distrusted its power to make one lose control. She did not mind others losing control, providing they were not too disgusting – it was all grist to her mill. Rather, Violet did not care to let her guard slip but she was happy enough to watch her colleagues make inroads, and concentrated on sparkling. Tonight, however, she felt that her store of energy – which she had come to realize was finite – was being depleted. After a while, she slid off the desk on which she had arranged herself for the others to take advantage of her short skirt.

'Must go, folks.'

Sebastian also disengaged himself from a group. Violet's nostrils flared slightly, a wildebeest having been given a warning signal. 'I'll share a taxi with you, Vi.' He inflected the 'Vi'. 'We go in the same direction,' he said and gazed blandly into her face. It was the look he always assumed before he contradicted someone in a meeting.

Violet opened her mouth to say no, for she wanted some

peace, but remembered the advice she had read in an American magazine – never neglect opportunities to bring enemies round – and thought better of it.

The London streets wore the distinctive air of a wet summer. Moisture oozed from the roads and pavements. Still oily from her session, Violet longed for a bath.

Sebastian indicated the nearest café. 'Like a proper drink?' Thump went the hoof on the savannah floor.

'No, thank you.' Violet was at her most gracious.

He did not press her but hailed a taxi and gave directions. Violet sat with her briefcase across her knees, hoping it suggested the ultimate in female power-broking and debated with herself as to whether it was sensible to bring up the changes she had suggested to the marketing meetings and which were still being discussed. Caution won, and she remained silent. Sebastian moved closer.

'What does your old man do?'

'Merchant banker. Why?'

'Just wondered.' Sebastian's fingers wandered over her thigh and then retracted. 'Sorry.'

Violet opened her mouth to suggest he kept his hands to himself but was forestalled by Sebastian leaning towards her, a mocking little smile stretching his lips. 'You're very beautiful, Vi.'

'Thank you.' Violet suddenly remembered that she had not planned anything for supper and it was seven o'clock.

'Very.' This time Sebastian's hand found its way to the opening of her blouse.

Violet was forced to abandon thoughts of tinned soup and (wholemeal) frozen pizza. She looked at Sebastian. 'Sebastian,' she said. 'Do you mind?'

He squeezed, rather painfully. 'Come on, darling.'

'Sebastian. This sort of thing is very old-fashioned, you know, and politically incorrect.'

He paid no attention and Violet knew she had to make a decision. Bear this ridiculous performance for the sake of her ambitions at work – Sebastian being senior and rising – or not. (Actually, he did smell nice and expensive and obviously had a bit of money.)

Not. She moved her briefcase sharply to the right which blockaded Sebastian's access, wriggled free, tapped on the driver's partition and ordered him to stop. Safely on the pavement, she thanked the driver and said, 'Good night, Sebastian. Thank you for the ride. See you tomorrow.'

Not in the least embarrassed, the smile still in place, he sent a little wave through the window as if to say that this was a scene he had played many times and it was neither here nor there as to how it ended. The implication that she was only a piece of skirt stung just a little. Nevertheless, Violet skimmed rapidly over the implications of the episode in relation to office politics and made the mistake of watching the taxi out of sight. Then, a pleasing thought occurred: she was smarter and tougher than Sebastian Westland and who was to say who would survive if it came to war.

Taxis being plentiful in Waterloo, she decided to walk to the rank at the station, but became confused with the new layout for the Channel Tunnel terminus and found herself in the station concourse.

It was busy with commuters and holiday traffic, including an army of backpackers heading for the night trains. A few businessmen were swallowing beers in the bars, the more prudent, coffee in the coffee bar. Other passengers were bunched by the magazine racks in W. H. Smith and picking over bargain books. Violet sniffed. She liked the smell of a station.

As Violet made for the taxi rank, she saw Jamie.

He was talking to a woman wearing a short-sleeved, stone-

coloured linen suit with her back to Violet. She was familiar
. . . but not, and was looking up at Jamie as she talked. It
took a few seconds for the vignette to register properly with
Violet and she searched for a comparison. Long ago, before
she became ambitious, she had read a novel by Elizabeth
Bowen about a meeting in a station. A residual memory
fought its way up through the depths of her memory. She
then recollected the clever, indulgent, detached French
films she had seen many times in New York because it was
the thing to do in her circle. In those films people were
always meeting in stations. The rendezvous usually constituted or presaged disaster.

The man who looked like Jamie was wearing a grey suit
and paisley tie – she had seen them this morning. Black
shoes, yes. She was sure about those. Pink-striped shirt. Yes,
yes. Grey socks. You see, she acknowledged to herself during
the seconds that had stretched and billowed over her head,
I know my husband down to the last thread on his back.

He would not be here at seven thirty at night because he
comes home on the tube.

In the taxi, Violet stared out of the window into the dusk
and noticed, for the first time, Vauxhall Bridge's disintegrating brickwork and the queue outside the doss-house. One
of the tramps, frail and bearded, was parked in a wheelchair
like an abandoned species. A nuisance who had no use.

Jamie at Waterloo? Why?

Emmy, who was waiting in the kitchen with her fringed
suede bag slung over her shoulder, was uncharacteristically
short with Violet when she arrived home. Violet got the
point.

Emmy hitched the bag over her shoulder and got to her
feet. 'Edward's fine. He ate second helpings of all his food.'

'Thanks, Emmy.' Violet spoke with unusual gratitude and added, 'I'm sorry to have kept you.'

Emmy looked at Violet and Violet found her eyes sliding away from Emmy's direct ones which looked angry. 'Is anything wrong, Emmy?'

Emmy wanted to reply that a few things would benefit from brushing up (wages, hours, consideration) but confined it to one. 'I know you don't want Edward to sleep during the day, but I let him nap this afternoon because he was so tired.'

Violet had issued the instruction on the happy assumption that it would make Edward sleep better during the night.

'You mean *you* wanted a rest.'

The words escaped before Violet could reconsider her management technique. At the end of her tether after a long, fractious day, Emmy found herself shrugging. 'If that's the way you want to look at it, Mrs Beckett.'

Violet did see it that way. Her eyebrows snapped together. 'It means I'll be getting up in the night.'

Emmy's mouth opened to say, 'Tough titty,' but she thought better of it. Violet opened *her* mouth to say something cutting but was forestalled by the mixture of rebellion and genuine anger on Emmy's face. Violet's annoyance shrivelled and, all at once, she felt exhausted, depressed and uncharacteristically apprehensive.

'Well, Emmy.'

'Well, Mrs Beckett.' Emmy resisted the urge to stick her hands on her hips and glare Violet down; she plaited the suede fringe instead. 'I did what I thought best.'

'Yes,' said Violet, 'I suppose you did.'

Emmy was thoroughly taken aback by Violet's capitulation and told Marie-Laure in the wine bar later that her employer was in danger of going soft. Marie-Laure, who came from Brussels, and held dogmatic notions on routine and discipline and who had the misfortune to be working in a liberal family, remarked that Emmy was lucky to know where she was.

'Am I?' said Emmy, struck by the notion, and ordered another beer.

Normally, Violet fell like a stone into sleep from which she was only dragged by Edward's whimpers. Tonight, she read *The Wakeful Toddler: The Problem of Sleep Deprivation and Its Successful Management* until her eyes felt sore. Why she had been vouchsafed a child who considered sleep a form of torture she would never know. Only that she came near murder when other mothers opened their eyes wide and made remarks such as, 'Oh, heavens, mine slept through the night at three weeks.'

Then she lay awake, brain jogged into frantic activity as she analysed the bits of her life: motherhood, marriage, job, melded together into a rock that she was being forced to carry. Worse, at the heart of the rock was the mass – as easily chopped as the tofu she favoured – of her worry and fatigue which she worked so hard to conceal. Of her dislike of her son.

There, she had admitted it. Terrible words. Terrible meaning. But the confession brought no relief, no cooling hand over her hot, burning guilt. No sudden release of the poison draining from a boil.

Violet shifted tack.

No one could accuse her and Jamie of having a *bad* marriage. On the contrary, it was good. Violet thought back over the early days in New York when Jamie could not have enough of her and power came as naturally as breathing.

Jamie would *not* have been at Waterloo, talking to a woman who was so familiar, and yet not.

Under the sheets, Violet slid a hand towards her sleeping husband and touched his hip, as once he had felt for hers. Jamie lay inert and Violet sighed.

She was still awake when Edward gave his first cry, as usual in the wave band between one thirty and three o'clock, and Violet stumbled out of bed. The plan, à la *The Wakeful Toddler*, which had seemed so sensible and constructive during the day, was to give Edward a bottle of water instead of juice or milk, the idea being to bore him into sleeping through the night.

Edward had other, better ideas and fought for them with vigour. The house seemed to ring with the cries of the helpless, dependent – and unreasonable. At one point, Violet raised her face to the dark ceiling and her own face crumpled. She was tired, oh, so deeply tired, of the business of being in a female body, of babies and female curves, and feeding, and monthly rhythms that caged her as surely as the rat in the laboratory.

'Oh, God,' she whispered. 'Is there no rest any more?' Sweating with fatigue and a depth of anger she had never experienced before, Violet held her son's wriggling body and pressed into it with her scarlet-tipped fingers. Edward roared in response, as much from surprise as hurt.

'Just shut up, you little beast,' she hissed at him. '*Just shut up.*'

Edward wailed harder. Beatrix Potter frieze, teddy bears, flickering fires, alphabet wall-paper, and empty space which her mother should have occupied, memory and need whirled like the snowstorm in the paperweight inside Violet's thudding head. Rage, betrayal, bitter grief had been trapped there and almost unfathomable fatigue and Violet, goaded to madness by the whole damn bloody business of what she was, of what had been taken away by motherhood, slammed Edward – her unloved son – back into his cot.

The crying stopped. Just like that. Silence enfolded the room.

'Violet! *What* are you doing?' Jamie stood in the doorway.

Gasping noises came from the cot. Violet pressed her hands to her mouth, 'Oh, Jamie,' and felt the strength trickle away from her knees. 'Oh, Jamie.'

During those seconds, falling like hot coals between husband and wife, anything could have happened – murder, hysteria, welcome unconsciousness.

Jamie pushed Violet out of his way and picked up his son who, red-faced with the effort, was endeavouring to suck in air. Jamie held him up and, for several desperate seconds, Edward struggled. Then he let out a howl, filled with surprise and terror. With an anguished sound, Jamie cradled the little body to his chest and swivelled towards his wife.

'Get out.'

Violet fled to the sanctuary of her bed. Peace. Darkness. Escape?

She was cradled in her conditioner-scented sheets and duck-down duvet from Peter Jones. It was not her fault that she was so tired that she could not think any more. Perhaps not even be responsible for what she did?

An image of her son flailing for the breath she had stolen from him superimposed itself. She turned and buried her face in the pillow where her pulsebeats thudded in both ears.

She thought of death.

When she surfaced, Jamie was standing by the bed. 'I've calmed him down,' he said, 'and given him a bottle of milk.'

'Thanks,' said Violet, looking up at him with an expression that Jamie interpreted as defiance.

'I'm going to sleep in the spare room. I think you need some rest.'

'I'm fine.'

'I also think you should go and see a doctor tomorrow.'

He spoke as if she was some distant, and tiresome, relation.

'There's no need to sound like that.' Violet was aware she should apologize. 'I'm sorry I did what I did.'

'You should be.'

At that point, Violet realized that he was seriously angry – and the enormity of what she had done finally sank in. As she so often did, Violet responded with attack. 'It might help if you were around a bit more. You leave it all to me.'

'I do my bit.'

On safer ground now, Violet reared up from the pillows and her eyes narrowed. 'Oh, do you? Who thinks about the shopping, about what to eat, whether the loo needs cleaning? If we have enough nappies, writing paper, shampoo? Tell me who does all that. And tell me if it's just a question of doing it once or week in, week out?' She wrapped her arms around her slenderized shoulders and hugged herself tight. 'It never ends, Jamie, and it makes me tired. Lunch, tea, supper, ironing, beds, cleaning. Chuck in a difficult baby—'

'Shut up, will you?' Jamie had to make a huge effort to stop himself shaking. Violet watched his fists bunch and his conscious effort to relax them. 'Other women manage, and you have Emmy and Mrs Stone to come and clean.' Only just in time, he prevented himself saying, 'Prue does.'

'Other women don't have full-time jobs.'

Oh, God, she had fallen into that one again. Violet saw her mistake too late. Jamie leaned over her, a hand either side of her body. 'You don't *have* to have one. I earn enough.' His breath jetted on to her cheek.

In a curious way, Violet was beginning to enjoy herself.

'That's right, fall back on the he-man and the bank balance. What if I *want* to work and I'm good at it?' She subsided back into the pillows. 'Anyway, you've missed the point.'

'Being?'

'The buck stops with me. You leave this house every morning confident that when you return you will be given an evening meal, your shirt will be ironed, your bed made. Yes? Who plans all that? Who thinks about it before going to their own work so you can enjoy your meat and two veg?'

There was silence and Violet, sword whirling, drove it home. 'You don't, do you?'

She prepared to continue the fight, to exercise magnanimity in the face of his defeat, to say again she was sorry but, suddenly, Jamie withdrew. Literally. She felt him retreat to a place that did not include her.

And that frightened her most of all – more than the battle, more than her nightmares, more than the selfish, unmaternal side of herself that she did not care to think about too much. More than what she had done to Edward.

'Goodnight.' Jamie sighed, tightened his dressing-gown belt and made for the door, taking this new, puzzling picture of her husband with him.

'Jamie. Wait. Were you . . .' Violet found herself grasping the duvet tight, 'were you at Waterloo station this evening?'

There was an infinitesimal pause. 'No, I wasn't,' he lied. (Prue had met him for a drink before she joined Max at a business dinner, which she was occasionally obliged to do.)

Violet absorbed the information. 'I don't think the bed is made up in the spare room,' she said, with a satisfaction that bordered on the savage. After he had gone she sank down into the bed.

Food, lashings of it, swam across her vision. Muffins dripping with butter. Strawberry shortcake. Beef swimming

307

in thick glossy gravy. Rosy pink shrimps curled into clarified butter, like babies tucked into their cots.

A few hours' sleep were sufficient for Violet to grout the cracks in the carapace – and to convince herself of several things. One: she needed to take a few days off and book into a health farm to recharge her batteries. Two: she had not done anything so very dreadful. Scratch any mother and find a hidden incident, a shaming accident – or four. Three: she had not seen Jamie at Waterloo station with a strange woman. It had been a mistake. A trick of the eye. Thus Violet had no need to worry about her marriage because there was simply no question of failure. Her marriage would survive, come what may.

In the mirror that morning, she drew a line of scarlet around her lips and filled it in.

Chapter Twenty-Two

The summer holiday came and went, and as Prue wished, the Valours did not go away. Max finished the decorating, gardened and watched Prue. Prue grew thinner, took to wearing her hair tied back in a velvet scrunchie and watched Max.

Jane spent a lot of time with Kate's daughter, Judy, hours with her computer, and frequently disappeared on her bicycle. She also avoided her mother, skipping meals and being unusually difficult. Prue, dividing her time between the bookshop and running the house, unable to meet Jamie (apart from that snatched meeting at Waterloo) because of the school holidays, was driven to exasperation and, finally, a burst of temper.

Jane informed her that she was unfair, unloving and furthermore that she, Jane, was too old to be bossed around by someone like *her*, adding that Prue did not care one bit about her daughter.

Not true, not true, Prue wanted to cry out.

But the cry might not have sounded entirely genuine. In her heart, Prue knew she was missing something important about Jane. But that same heart was too full, too greedy exploring new sensations, too preoccupied to look outside itself.

Prue was discovering the fascination of being entirely self-absorbed. She justified it by telling herself that she was allowed to be selfish, that she was permitted a life other than the one devoted to her family, just once.

Eventually Jane was dispatched back to school for the autumn term, with panic, on behalf of Prue, over name-tapes, games equipment and rebellion, on behalf of Jane, over a pair of skin-tight leggings that she had wished to take back and Prue considered inappropriate. Jane went, hugging her software disks, quiet, secretive and distracted, as if, her mother concluded, she was listening in to conversations from another world.

The school always gated the girls for the first two weekends of term and, for the third weekend, Jane was invited to stay with Lydia, a hopeful sign that the friend situation was ameliorating.

Early in the morning on Friday 25 September, the day a twelve-year-old boy in Florida won a 'divorce' from his natural parents, Mrs Harriman, Jane's housemistress, rang Prue. She was brisk but concerned and asked outright if something had occurred during the summer holidays to put Jane off her stroke.

'No,' said Prue. 'I don't think so.'

'She isn't putting any effort into her work, Mrs Valour. In fact, her work is sub-standard for Jane.' Mrs Harriman allowed that information to sink in and then said carefully, 'A little more worrying perhaps is her eating.'

'*Eating!*'

The pause at the end of the phone managed to convey accusation *and* condemnation – and Prue suddenly had a flash of complete understanding of Joan's condition. Even if the Church acquitted her of heresy, it would make sure it handed her over to the English to be tried as a traitor. The defendant was guilty whatever the semantics. 'Yes. I'm afraid Jane is not coping with her food very well.'

'Have you spoken to her?'

'I felt we should speak to you first.'

'I shall come right over after I've finished work.'

There is a world of difference between the detached 'we' of the school and the anxious 'I' of the mother. Prue rang Gerald to warn him she would have to leave early. She also rang Kate and cancelled tea, and Molly to excuse herself from the parish council meeting.

'I see,' said Molly.

No, you don't, Prue wanted to say. You don't see anything. 'I'm so sorry, Molly, but I think I must go.'

'Yes, well . . .' Molly implied that Prue's dereliction of duty ranked on a par with selling her grandmother to pay a Lloyd's debt.

Autumn was beginning to run tongues of brown and gold over the trees and into the folds of landscape and shorn fields, and the light held the season's milky, tender quality. Ready to move off south, birds were gathering on the telephone wires or wheeled in untidy circles.

Hunched at the steering wheel, Prue, for once, took no notice.

Full realization of culpability does not, perhaps, come suddenly. Rather, it seeps into the consciousness, drip by drip, gathering in depth and volume until it is flooded. It is at that point that one fact, apparently unconnected, interweaves with another and the fusion becomes significant. Prue was having an affair. Jane was having problems.

Prue's neglect of Jane came home to roost. She had not strained to listen to the voices in her daughter's head, only to her own. She had not perceived that Jane's quietness was, perhaps, a mask placed over turbulence.

She clenched her fingers around the wheel. The luxury of being able to do something without the rest of your life being dragged in was, it appeared, given only to a few: the very lonely and very determined.

'I've gone wrong.' Prue pulled off the velvet scrunchie that confined her hair the way Jamie liked it and felt a

311

corresponding surge of anger and frustration at the limi-
tations of her existence.

Two minutes later, Prue had convinced herself that she
was being ridiculous, that Mrs Harriman had made a
mistake, and that Jane was only taking her time to settle
down after a long holiday.

Well, no, Mrs Harriman contradicted Prue as they sat in
her austerely appointed room. What they – 'they' again –
had noticed in Jane was not naughtiness. Anyone with
experience of children could recognize the difference
between disobedience and a child who was angry and
withdrawn. *She* knew that and – so went the implication –
Prue should have known. Further, Jane had been caught at
least twice stuffing her food into a paper bag on her lap.

'What do you think it could be?' she asked, directing a
please-don't-trouble-to-pull-the-wool-over-my-eyes look at
Prue. 'Is there a problem at home?'

Her tone suggested that Prue would probably lie. Mrs
Harriman's short tenure as a housemistress had been sufficient to teach her that many parents lied, or at least
fudged the truth, but not long enough to have acquired the
wisdom of not advertising this knowledge.

Unsettled, furious at being judged, guilty, Prue felt a little
sick but forced herself to remember that Jane's welfare
came first and to acknowledge that Mrs Harriman had
experience in this area. Furthermore, losing one's temper
brought only fleeting benefits.

'No, there are no problems, Mrs Harriman,' she said,
and imagined a blush spreading in a great, surging red stain
over her body. She imagined, too, what that blush would
convey to Mrs Harriman. Prue's anger stirred, one of the
new emotions thrown up from the whirlpool that now
swirled inside her.

Why should taking off her clothes in front of a man other

than her husband, an act which had been kept apart from anyone who mattered, not remain private?

Because humans are not rabbits. Pick on any great love story, and an injured party always ends up crying into their pillow. King Mark, Octavia, Mr Karenin, poor simple Charles Bovary. Peter Abelard got it both ways – mental and physical castration (but at least he did not have to hunger and burn for years in a convent like his Heloïse).

Because, said the voice, you don't live in a vacuum.

Oh, Joan, she thought, how clever you were not to have anything to do with the flesh.

Peremptorily, she asked to see Jane.

When she saw her mother, Jane gave a visible start and her bottom lip quivered. Prue held out her arms, but Jane held back and avoided the contact.

'Everything all right with Dad?' she asked anxiously. 'He's not ill?' Her fingers left smudged prints on the highly polished brass door handle.

'Yes. Absolutely fine.' Prue swallowed. 'Can you come here, darling? Mrs Harriman is a little worried about you and I thought we could talk about it.'

Jane ducked her head with a gesture that told Prue nothing – and too much.

'I'm fine, Mum,' she said angrily. 'I wish everyone would stop fussing. I'm just not hungry.'

Prue had not mentioned food.

'Darling—'

'Please don't, Mum.' It was no longer a little girl who spoke, but an uneasy hybrid see-sawing between the baby-skinned, silk-haired image embedded in Prue's mind, and the pale, cross, hungry adolescent into which it had metamorphosed.

Sooner or later innocence is taken away, usually by an adult – that is unavoidable. But if I have been responsible for taking away Jane's innocence too early, I shall never forgive myself. Prue's anger had quite disappeared.

'Darling—'

'Really, Mum,' repeated Jane.

'But—'

'*Don't* fuss,' said the new Jane, tight and unforgiving, and, for the first time in their lives, a door was shut in Prue's face. The blow it dealt, and the grief that flowered like blood after the bullet, shocked Prue into making an audible gasp. Jane's gaze drilled into her mother and Prue imagined that she detected a gleam which was both manipulative – and desperate.

'Darling . . .' She dropped on to one knee. 'Don't be like that.' She captured Jane's hand, the penitent in the painting, and kissed it: the hand off which she had scrubbed dirt and paint, had cradled in her lap after a bath to cut its nails and folded kisses into the damp shell of its palm.

My child.

Jane tugged it away. 'I'll go and get my bag.'

Shorn of her maternal power or, rather, feeling she had forgone it, Prue was left looking stupid on the floor. Children sensed things, did they not? Every act had a consequence, she knew that. Added to which Jane was growing up and quitting the foothills guarded so carefully by her parents.

It was as if, she explained later to her lover and husband (in those separate, three-way conversations), Jane had cut a ribbon and retied it behind her against those who remained. Jamie did not have much to say about it except to tell Prue that she must not put coincidences together – Jane's growing up, their affair – and consider it a case for hanging.

Max said even less.

After saying goodbye to Mrs Harriman, Prue waited for

Jane in the car. A trickle, then a flood of girls emerged through various doorways, the smaller ones still drowned and innocent in their uniforms, the older ones wearing more knowingness on their shiny skins but which was not, as yet, bone deep.

Or so it seemed to Prue.

She waited a long time for Jane. Lydia and Fee, another refugee from the bully Alicia's camp, said, 'Hallo, Mrs Valour,' and disappeared. Still no Jane. Prue fiddled with the knobs of the radio, stuffed rogue sweet papers into the ashtray then changed her mind and put them into her pocket. A draught played on her cheek from the open window and she shut it with unnecessary vigour.

Eventually, Jane emerged from the side door and walked, a little unsteadily, towards the car, her knees smooth bone hub-caps under which ran spoke-like legs, a changeling whose thinness had turned from the acceptable into the frightening. She put out a hand to steady herself before she opened the passenger door. Prue gripped the wheel.

'Thought you were never coming, darling.' Scrambled eggs, she decided, mixed with a little cream. Spinach puréed with cream? No Jane might guess. Pasta? Wholemeal bread?

She started the engine. Jane settled herself.

There was silence. No questions. No 'Thanks for waiting.' No 'What are we doing this weekend?' Just silence. Prue concentrated on driving.

'I've got a nice supper for you,' she said, wrongfooting it by mentioning food. 'And maybe we could go for a walk.'

'I don't want any supper.'

'Don't be silly,' said Prue in a mumsy voice and then wished she had kept quiet. 'Of course you want supper.'

At home Prue made hot buttered toast and tea. Jane took a mouthful and sawed at the contents in her mouth, which irritated Prue. For heaven's sake, she wanted to say, Bosnians are starving. It's good food. Jane piled the toast under her knife. Smudges of exhaustion underlined her eyes.

'How about that walk?' suggested her mother.

The leaves had lost their full-bellied summer note and made a drier, thinner noise, which anticipated their autumn death. Prue listened to the message, and she walked beside Jane down the main street towards the bridlepath that led to the fields. Each day the sun was lodging further down in the sky, sometimes startling red-orange, sometimes diluted by cloud into milky pinks and mauves. A chill threatened.

They passed the village shop and Molly emerged, wearing a navy blue beret and her tweed skirt.

'Any second thoughts about letting us down over the Christmas concert?' she asked abruptly and without preliminaries. She bent over Jane and her chin-wattles shook. 'It's not like your mother to back off.'

Prue shoved her hands into her pockets and grimaced as she encountered layers of fluff as deep as time.

'I didn't feel up to it this year, Molly. Besides, others should be allowed to have a go.'

'Not if they're no good at it. That's doing no favours to anyone. It won't do, Prue.'

It won't do. Some women knew what was what and bullied those who did not. Molly was one and, thus, the world behaved itself. Thank God for them, thought Prue.

Jane loitered behind on the bridlepath and Prue waited for her to catch up.

'All right, my sweetie?'

For a moment, it was like old times for Jane slid her fingers into the crook of Prue's arm, with a touch so bony and insubstantial that no impression was made.

'Fine.'

Prue placed her own hand over Jane's and some of her worst imaginings fragmented. The drag, so slight, at her elbow reminded her that this was where she should be, and had been only a few months back. Connected to her village, to her home, to her family. *There* for her daughter.

But instead of satisfaction and rightness, impatience and frustration beat at the bars confining Prue's existence. Their intense, ruthless quality shocked her.

That evening they lit the fire, the first of the season. Prue had forgotten to have the chimney swept and fretted at the army of birds' nests she was convinced lurked up there waiting to conflagrate. 'It's unlike you to forget,' remarked Max, who was on his knees in front of the fireplace trying to work up the flames.

He hunkered back on his heels with an expression that made her flesh prickle, for Prue recognized it. It was a calculating one. She had seen it sometimes when Max talked of Helen.

'I'll see about the sweep,' he said.

She busied herself clearing up the debris from the grate. The dust brushed obediently into a pile and Prue wished it was as easy to tidy up the untidy rag-and-bone shop of her heart. Max brushed ash from his corduroys.

'Nice to have a fire.'

'Ridiculous, really, so early in the year,' said Prue.

The fire struggled at first and then settled down into a respectable heat. Jane and Max plonked themselves on to the sofa and began to read. Uncertain, Prue hovered, trying to interpret any message conveyed by the back view of her husband and daughter and then told herself she was developing paranoia.

She was making the pasta sauce for the Friday supper-on-the-knees, which had become a tradition, when Max came into the kitchen. He uncorked a bottle of wine and poured some into a glass.

'She *is* too thin,' he said. 'We've got to do something. She must have been losing weight all through the summer and I hadn't noticed.'

'She's growing fast.'

Max swung round and stared out of the window. 'Well, what's the best thing?' His back remained turned.

Prue addressed it. 'I think we should watch her for a little longer before we do anything.'

At this, Max turned and stared at his wife with eyes that had turned hostile. 'Aren't you concerned that it might be something serious?'

'Of course I am,' she snapped.

Max took another mouthful of wine. 'Whatever the situation here,' he said, so softly that Prue was not sure that he said it at all, 'it is not permissible to take risks with Jane.'

'Of course not.'

'Eating disorders are usually a sign of anger,' said Max, 'often reflecting unhappiness in the family.'

Impatiently, Prue cut him off. 'Jane is growing fast. She's had trouble at school and she's never liked the food there. That's all.'

Prue reached for a glass – Max had not offered her one – poured out a generous quantity and drank some in silence. It was almost as if Max was waiting for something, but the trouble with playing games was that you required rules. She offered the olive branch.

'You're right, of course.'

'We'll discuss it later.'

Max quitted the kitchen and left a chill behind. Prue picked up the timer and set it for the pasta. At one of Kate's dinner parties, some years back, she had talked to a doctor.

He had told her that epidemics followed a pattern, a pathology. The irony was intriguing – a disaster that was so far-reaching, possibly final for those at its centre, could be reduced to a predictable curve.

First there was the upward progression on the graph, the passage of a microbe digging into its chosen territory. Then, at the point when the line hesitated, curved and began its downward journey, was a check inserted – the guilt runnelling in dark veins into the love, madness and greed. Then, perhaps, the retreat.

QED: an epidemic shared much in common with adultery. From its discovery – the seeding in the mind and the body's answering counterpoint – to the greedy chaos it engendered. The tug of desire. Senses stretched until they were transparent and aching. Exhaustion that drove the body and did not permit rest. The selfishness.

Then what?

Prue did not know, for she had not climbed far enough up the graph.

'I don't want it,' said Jane, balancing the tin tray painted with pink roses on her knee. 'I'm not hungry.'

'Have a little.'

'Oh, Mum. Stop going on at me.'

Max's large hand descended on to Jane's skinny arm. 'Your mother is right. You should eat.'

Jane flashed a look at her mother, sighed and poked at the pasta with her fork. 'You can't *make* me eat.'

Again she flashed a look at Prue. Help me, it said. Help me express my helplessness.

'Come on,' said Max. 'Not-so-plain Jane.' Using the baby nickname obviously touched Jane for she lifted her face, now infinitely weary and bewildered, towards her father. He slid his arm along the sofa and pulled her gently towards him. With the other hand, he picked up the fork with a mouthful of pasta.

'Open up,' he said. 'Storm troopers.'

Jane grinned at the reference to her latest computer game. 'Stupid, Dad.'

All the same, she opened her mouth.

'Chew,' he ordered gently. 'Go on. Bandits nine o'clock.'

Above her full mouth, Jane's eyes locked on to Max's and filled with tears. Prue found herself holding her breath in an agonizing lungful. Jane's jaw began to move. Prue's breath released in a sigh. She watched as Max, murmuring to his daughter, gently smudged away the moisture on her cheeks with his thumb, held her to his large body and fed her, forkful by forkful, until the plate was empty.

Then, cradled by her father, Jane went to sleep in front of the fire.

Max spent most Saturdays in the garden. In fact, he spent more and more time there, and the garden was beginning to acquire an obsessively manicured look.

Currently, his obsession was relocating the compost heap.

That morning, he stood under the plum tree at the end of the garden, which was delineated by a stone wall between it and the road. It was going to be a warm day, but the warmth had not got going yet and the early mist was still in the process of being shredded by the sun. Plums in various stages of decay lay in the grass, jewels exuding a sweet slime above which hummed cones of flies. Amid the richness and plenty of autumn, he seemed a curiously lonely figure.

Or that was how he struck Emmy as she walked up the road.

'Hallo, Mr Valour.'

Down from London for the weekend, she had been walking up by the airfield and could not resist returning via Hallet's Gate, for the family's doings were, she informed Anna, beginning to really intrigue her. (Anna demanded a full-scale report and she wasn't to spare the dirt, and wasn't Emmy getting a bit toffee-nosed herself as she hadn't been in contact for ages?)

Sharp Anna. It was true, Emmy was changing, which was akin to being dragged into a room she had not planned on entering or being given glasses that widened the vision. Still, it was unlikely she would wake up as Cindy Crawford.

Max looked up. 'Hallo, Emmy. I was deciding where to put my compost heap. The old one isn't doing so well.'

This was a red rag to Emmy. She leant over the wall and squinted in the direction of his pointed finger. 'Are you planning to build one or two?'

'Build?' Max's shadow looked huge on the grass. 'I was just going to reposition the heap.'

Emmy got into her stride. 'It would be much better if you built a wooden one. That way the air won't get in and you can keep two on the go.'

'Why don't you come and advise me?'

Emmy didn't require asking twice. At once Max pinpointed the change in Emmy, who was looking much, much better – the jeans and Guernsey sweater moving her from one category to another, as did the short hair, liberated finally from its perm by Mr Twist of Clapham.

'Look . . .' Emmy hauled a piece of paper and a biro out of her pocket, 'you can build one like this. You need four three-by-one corner posts. Four one-by-one, thirty-inch and twenty-seven inch floorboards. They're cheaper from a demolition contractor.'

'How do you know all this?' Max squinted at the paper.

Emmy shrugged and swiped at the flies. 'I like this sort of thing.'

She appraised the garden and Max suspected that she did not approve of the precise herbaceous border and circular bed in the lawn. It also amused him that he minded.

'I've been trying to get my mum to buy a wormery.' Emmy's face shone with inner conviction. 'But she won't have it.'

'Have you? Tell me.'

Max was fascinated. Emmy obliged and they settled to a conversation in which figured liquid manure, worm casts, air circulation, bacteria and slime.

Max borrowed Emmy's paper and was noting various things on it. 'You dig it twice?' He stooped over the paper and the sun struck his face, opening it to Emmy's inspection. He's upset, she thought in a rush of compassion and decided that she liked him far better than the more obviously attractive Jamie. Particularly if what she suspected – only suspected, mind – was true.

'How long will this take me to do?'

Before she could stop herself, Emmy offered to help. He smiled his sweet, tired smile. 'That would be very nice. Are you by any chance free now to help me buy the materials?'

. A motorbike roared down the road and applied its brakes. Like a puppet jerked by its master, Emmy whipped round.

'*There* you are.'

A leather-encased giant leant over the wall and Max was fascinated to see a pony-tail straggling from under the helmet.

'Angus.' Emmy looked from Max to the Adonis, every line of her thin face alight with longing, and Max shuddered for her. 'Sorry, Mr Valour. I can help you another time.'

Naturally, Max could not compete with the testosterone-charged Angus – never would have been able to.

'Tomorrow?' Emmy was being pulled out of the garden by an invisible force.

'Of course.'

Extraordinarily, they were back the next day. Both Emmy and Angus.

Building compost bins is a cohesive activity. Nails, planks, posts and fingers – more often than not wrapped in Elastoplast – are the constituents. Those, and the smell of wood: dry, resiny, strong enough to tickle the hairs in the nostrils. That, too, and the smell of earth, which blends the sourness of impacted soil and freshly turned sods, dampened by September rain. Fixing together four simple wooden sides and a lid to ensure that weed seeds and pathogens are destroyed establishes a bond, between material and maker, between bacteria and rubbish, between the cold outer layer which shields and conserves the heat at the core.

Max and Prue should have built a compost bin.

Chapter Twenty-Three

Jamie suggested to Violet that it would be a gesture if they took the Valours to the theatre. 'Since when have you been a theatre goer?' Violet replied. 'But yes, fine. Get your secretary to organize it and it better be Shakespeare.' Perceiving he was puzzled, she added, 'Don't be witless, Jamie. Shakespeare is educational for Jane.'

They met in the foyer of the National Theatre. Neither Max nor Prue had been to the theatre for some time and Jane was excited. The theatre was brightly lit and humming with noise. As she pushed through the glass doors, Prue felt a stir of anticipation, a pleasing sense that she was out in the world, and it was an interesting place to be.

Violet, who looked in especially thin and confident mode, but felt uneasy and strangely rudderless, gave Prue a peck on the cheek.

'You look pale, Prue. Stewing too much over Joan of Arc?' She made it sound as if it ranked with unmentionable practices.

'Not over much.' Prue's fingers made their customary excavation of the fluff in her coat pocket.

'Perhaps it's the grey then. I never thought it was your colour.' Violet ran her eyes over Prue's crêpe suit.

Prue had not looked at Jamie, but now she did. 'This is very good of you both. I used to go to the theatre a lot before I married your father.'

'Ah, yes, the fifties,' said Violet, quick as a flash.

'I'm not *quite* that old,' said Prue.

'I know,' said Violet. 'Some days you really don't look your age.'

'Hi,' said Jane to Jamie.

Jamie bent and kissed her, and said, 'I've been looking forward to seeing you. I need some advice on a computer I want to buy.'

Jane lit up like an evening star.

Violet kissed her father. 'Get us some drinks, will you, darling Father. Mineral water for me. With ice and lemon.'

Max obeyed.

The foyer filled up and Prue felt the noise and colour stir her senses into action.

'By the way,' said Violet, placing herself adroitly in Prue's line of vision. 'I've booked in at a health farm.' There was a pause and Prue adjusted her expression into polite interest. 'I've been a bit exhausted lately and I thought it would do me good.'

Jamie appeared surprised. '*Have* you?'

Violet shot her husband a look. Jamie was back in her bed, but, these days, that was about all. 'I told you the other day.'

Jamie slipped a hand into his trouser pocket. 'I must have forgotten.'

A signal tactic of spouses existing in an uneasy silence at home is their rudeness to one another in public. It was a tactic that Violet was indulging in. 'Jamie, you're so stupid these days. Don't you ever listen?' She underlined the role of the-one-who-kept-things-on-course (which she played to the hilt) by casting her eyes to the ceiling.

'You're going somewhere nice, I hope,' said Max, the only one of the party who appeared to approve the idea.

'Yes, very.' Violet's attention was temporarily diverted by the sight of a woman eating a large smoked-salmon roll.

'I'm thirsty,' said Jane.

'Why didn't you say so earlier?' said her father.

Violet ignored them. 'It's near Newbury,' she said. 'I chose the one closest to Dainton . . .' Prue knew then what was coming. '. . . and I wondered if you could look after Edward for me. Just for the Saturday and Sunday. Jamie or Emmy could bring him down.'

'No,' said Prue, her sense of well-being vanishing. 'I can't.'

'*Can't* I have something to drink?' asked Jane crossly.

'I haven't told you the dates, Prue. How can you say no?'

'Very easily.'

'Mum, you are impossible to get through to these days.'

Prue glanced at Jane, and perceived, instead of her loved daughter, a lanky, avenging angel with a sulky mouth. Outside, the river shone with light, illuminating a thousand, thousand other lives.

Jane tossed back her hair in remarkable imitation of Emma Hughes, a sixth-former with whom, judging from the number of casual references slipped into the conversation, Jane had fallen in love. 'Mum pays no attention to anyone but herself and she's slipping. We had *packet* custard the other day.'

'Jane . . .' Max spoke softly but with a warning. Going in to play against a cross-grained adolescent probably resulted in the same queasy mixture of rage and laughter as embarking on a tennis match against John McEnroe. Prue flashed a smile at Max, the referee.

Violet ploughed on. 'About Edward, Prue. He wouldn't be any trouble. And Jamie can help out. And Emmy's only down the road.'

The bell sounded for the performance and Jamie ushered the party through the doors to their seats. Prue's determination not to give in hardened. She thought of heavy, immovable objects: the Stone of Scone, the pyramids, the Giant's Causeway.

'Violet,' she said as they made their way down the aisle, 'I don't think you understand. I don't want to look after Edward. I have other things to do.'

'Do change your mind, Prue.' Settled in the middle of a row in the stalls, Violet leant across her father and prodded Prue on the thigh. She had no intention of giving up, and dropped her voice a note or two to add urgency, skilfully conveying surprise that such a reasonable request was being refused. 'Don't worry about the packet custard.'

Acid welled to the surface. The acid distilled from years of distrust, dislike and of knowing that whatever she did, wherever she turned, Prue had failed with her stepdaughter, both failure and guilt sharpening dislike. Prue struggled not to be small, struggled with the obligation, as she saw it, to treat the world with care, struggled to forgive if she could not forget. Against that she had to lay the wounds of an ego which knows it has failed in its bid to be liked.

She turned in her seat and said, loud and clear enough for the audience in the seats around to take an interest, 'Will you shut up, Violet?'

'Violet,' said Jamie, obviously uncomfortable – almost, Prue observed, aghast at Prue's response, as if he had been betrayed – 'why don't we leave the subject?'

Violet gave her husband one of her wide-eyed looks. 'I was trying to tell Prue not to worry too much about everything.'

She looked so earnest, believable and beautiful. Clever, clever Violet, hiding her secrets so well. Jamie touched his wife on the shoulder. 'Careful, darling,' he said and, metamorphosed by jealousy's mischievous alchemy, Prue's determination melted into a hot tide and she wanted to cry out, 'Don't, don't touch her. Touch me.'

Jamie registered Violet's sharp shoulder blade under his hand. He had never seen Prue in a temper (neither, of course, she him) and the experience would alter, subtly, the image he carried. Jamie was learning about flux: the mutation from one state to another of the people he loved. Or, perhaps, he was learning to see what was there in the first place.

Violet leant forward. 'Prue,' she hissed, 'are you by any chance menopausal?'

'My God, Violet. You're the limit.'

Rage streamed through Prue, plus the urge to behave badly and she gave in to it. She leapt to her feet and squeezed her way along the row, provoking disgruntled murmurs and a great deal of rearranging.

'Mum.' Jane's uncertain, muted whisper followed Prue's progress. 'Mum?'

Prue ignored her daughter. Another black mark. Another cold stone for Jane to lay on the wall building between them.

At the door to the foyer she turned and looked back. Jamie seemed stunned, Max impassive, Jane frightened and Violet, well, Violet looked like Violet when she had won an encounter. Otherwise, they were a perfectly ordinary group on an outing to the theatre.

No doubt her rage was perfectly ordinary too, but, like the frog whose brain cannot process all that it sees, Prue felt she had not managed to develop sufficient neural pathways to deal with the changes in her life.

Outside the theatre on the river embankment she drew in London air, feeling the weight of her emotion choking the oxygen out of her lungs: pain, jealousy – and a passion that was in danger of going sour from too much weight upon it.

She was missing the first act of a play that she had wanted to see.

A wind blew off the Thames, a dank, sour wind, smelling of people and lives lived too close together. She wanted Jamie. How she wanted him. She also wanted her daughter, as perfect and unblotted by the world as the day she entered it. She wanted the second baby she had never managed. She wanted Max not to mind. She wanted to be in charge of herself again.

'Before you get caught in a great passion,' ran the letter of a seventeenth-century Portuguese nun, which Prue had come across during her research, 'think well of the excesses of grief, of the uncertainties, of the diversities of impulse, of despairs, doubts and jealousies . . .'

Prue had not considered well at all. So unlike her. She had let herself slip into a rushing stream and had not cared about the rocks. The nun, she should have remembered, had been abandoned by her aristocratic French lover.

Prue breathed in the alien river smell, traffic fumes, and a sense that she had lost her way.

In the interval, she sought them out to apologize, the old Prue on whom they relied. Of course she would look after Edward, it would be no trouble. Jamie was welcome to stay, too, and she was sure Emmy would not be needed. After all, Violet was a busy working mother and needed all the back-up she could muster. (Prue trusted she sounded convincing.)

Max and Jamie heard out this orgy of repentance in silence. Violet was repairing her make-up in the ladies.

'That's very good of you, Prue,' said Jamie at last. 'We appreciate it and realize it's a big favour.'

'Fine, I'll tell Violet.'

'Don't worry,' said Jamie, 'she said you'd come round.'

Prue stared at him. That was possibly the most tactless thing her lover had ever said to her and her faith in him was shaken. To stop herself from saying something irretrievable, she drank a slug of gin and tonic. Max slipped his arm round her shoulders.

'Well done, darling,' he said softly into her ear.

His tone conveyed complicity and understanding of her bad behaviour, and Prue was filled with gratitude for Max's goodness. She turned in the circle of his arm and kissed first Max's cheek and, then, his mouth.

Violet could be seen making her way towards them through the crowd in the foyer. She stopped to speak to an acquaintance.

You and I, thought Prue, are both prisoners of our gender. Lipsticked, scented and moistly compliant receptacles. Joan understood the predicament and tried to hack through the casing. But even she failed.

Jamie gathered up their glasses and, as he passed Prue, touched her haunch in a secret gesture. Prue's flesh burned and the blood drummed in her ears.

She was helpless.

As they parted after the play, it was agreed that the Becketts would come down to Dainton for the following Sunday.

Since the Sunday morning looked promising, Prue revised the catering schedule and suggested a walk to Danebury Rings and a late lunch.

'Fine,' said Jamie.

'Not fine,' said Violet who, to do her justice, looked tired.

'I don't want to lug the baby up there. Besides, I've been there hundreds of times. I'll drive the car and meet you.'

Prue retrieved a stew from the larder and asked if Violet could put it in the oven.

'Oh, don't bother with lunch,' said Violet, repressing a vision of roast chicken, rubbed with tarragon, and roast potatoes. 'Cottage cheese and apple will do.'

Prue looked Violet straight in the eye. 'The rest of us would like lunch. You can eat apple and cottage cheese if you wish but I would be grateful if you did not make too much of a song and dance about it in front of Jane.'

Violet's expression darkened – and Prue turned away.

You betrayed me, Prue. No, worse. You did not supply what I needed.

I hate you, I hate you. Daddy only married you because you were convenient.

What nonsense. Helen had betrayed her daughter long before Prue replaced her, or failed to, but, if replacement equals betrayal, then so be it.

But what of Prue's betrayal of a stepdaughter – for, surely, Prue stood, and must be judged as such, *in loco parentis*? But perhaps all families are busy practising the point-counterpoint of deceit and revenge on each other. Prue was at it; the next-door neighbour was at it. The nation was at it.

Reluctantly, Prue faced the question, as a patient is forced to look at a swelling tumour. Was revenge the fuel of her love affair?

The weather threw up one of those warm golden days in which autumn specializes, and the morning heated up. The party filed along the lane, crumbling dry, crusted mud underfoot and watching air shimmer above the hedges. Naturally, the fields had been harvested and, patchworked with brown and gold, they rolled up the contours of the land, framed by a scattering of late poppies, hogweed and cascades of blackberries. In the verges, pimpernels made their tiny orange statements and periwinkle crawled up the stems in the hedgerows. A smell of hot fruit and vaporizing dew, of cool earth and ripeness was in the air. Notwithstanding the assaults made on it by chemicals and humans, the earth appeared in good working order.

Jamie stopped to shift the rucksack containing water and rations.

'Apple, anyone?' said Prue.

Jamie moved closer and his hand made contact. For a second, she closed her eyes. Jamie's thumb rubbed briefly on her flesh and then was gone. That's your lot, she thought.

They moved onwards down the path, lumpy with outcrops of chalk and summer drought. For some reason, an avenue of pine trees which led nowhere had been planted to their left. Rabbits played in the grassy ride between the pines where the shadows were cast, uneven and dark.

That grass: green and thick. To brush through it with bare feet, moisture squeezing up between the toes . . . She imagined sinking to her knees, waiting for Jamie. Lying back, allowing the damp to lap her body in a blanket, the nettle to lash her skin and the outcrop of dry earth to lacerate the tender places on her body as she drew up her legs, and the sun striking them.

Jamie would blot it out and then, boneless and shaking with desire, she would give herself up to hot, juddering strokes of sex and love. She imagined, too, what she would look like afterwards: nettle-lashed, reddening, imprinted by grass, invaded and sated.

Prue chewed an apple. Jane needed new jeans. The freezer needed defrosting and Molly, apparently anxious to restore their *entente* back to the *cordiale*, had donated a quantity of tomatoes from the Greer greenhouse. They begged to be turned into sauce. The harvest supper committee required ten apple pies.

The vision of her naked, sated body fled down the pine trees, turned transparent, floating. And vanished.

The party halted by the edge of the biggest field lapping the perimeter of Danebury.

'Let's cut across.' Jamie squinted up at the slope beyond.

Max tested the soil with his boot. 'Too soft going. You'd end up with a sackload in your shoes.'

'Nonsense,' said Jamie, and struck out over the field confidently, stuck it out for approximately fifty yards and beat a retreat. The sun picked out his fair hair and the sheen of sweat on his forehead. He looked young and untroubled, and Prue drank him in greedily.

'You were right,' he said to Max and sat down to empty his shoes.

Once again, he brushed against Prue and her naked, desire-tormented body ran over the stubble and too-soft earth and sank to the ground.

They squeezed over a professional-looking fence at the foot of the ring and found themselves facing a clump of dense woodland which circled the lower slopes.

'Up, then.' Max beat a path through the undergrowth.

Jane disappeared through an interlaced hazel and beech after her father. Prue tied her sweater around her waist and drew in her breath.

'Damn and blast.' Max could be heard swearing. He slithered back down towards them. 'Someone's put a sodding great barbed-wire fence up. We'll have to walk round the ring and come up the other side.'

Jamie peered through the trees. 'We can get over that. Fences are for getting over.'

Max sent him a look. 'I don't think Prue can manage.'

'Yes, she will.'

Max shrugged. 'She won't.'

'Yes, I will.' Prue surged forward. 'You lot can have the privilege of helping me over.'

In the event, Max held the wire down and Jamie draped his sweater over the barbed wire and Prue stepped across. The wire bit her hands, gave under her weight and every movement had an edge of danger.

Then they were up and over and into the open, treading ground impacted with history and myth.

Hundreds of years ago – 1000 BC? – an Iron Age people had singled out this outcrop in a valley basin. Actually, Prue explained in her best local-historian manner, it may be as old as 2000 BC, the height of the outcrop allowing the settlers to dominate the valley – unlike the village situated in the dip – and giving security from enemies.

The fort itself revealed considerable administrative, engineering and military sophistication. For instance – by now Prue had warmed thoroughly to her theme – the east entrance is cleverly placed at the intersection of several trackways.

'Rather like Sainsbury's,' said Jamie. 'Bagging the intersections outside towns.'

'It was well organized.' Max indicated the central area where sheep were grazing. 'That bit contains hundreds of storage pits, one for each family, which were jealously guarded. You could probably steal your neighbour's wife but woe betide you if you pinched their grain.'

There was an awkward silence.

Max slid down the slope and landed, neatly for such a large man, in the ditch below.

'Catch me, Dad,' Jane yelled, and windmilled down the bank, which was knotted with treacherous roots.

'Catch her, Max.' Prue's heart was in her mouth.

Jane teetered and wobbled, failed to grasp at a branch, gathered speed and shot down like a bullet.

'My God!' Without a moment's hesitation, Prue launched herself after Jane.

But it was all right. Max assessed the angle of Jane's descent, moved into position and when his daughter tumbled towards him, caught her. He did not wait for Prue who was having difficulty making the descent but assisted Jane to climb up the inner earthworks. Thus, Prue finished in a heap at the bottom and, as she went over, she felt her ankle wrench, not badly, but it made her gasp all the same.

'Are you OK?' Jamie shouted from the outer earthwork.

She got to her feet and tested her ankle. 'Fine.'

Jane and Max had reached the top and were walking in a clockwise direction. Prue took a few experimental paces. Apart from a twinge, the ankle was fine. She looked up at Jamie, silhouetted against the sky.

'I'm going to find an easier way up,' she told him.

None of the party looked back at Prue, and she was left alone. She began to fight her way along the ditch, slashing through the undergrowth and densely packed grass. Once she glanced up, and there were Max and Jane walking in single file to her left, Max with his characteristic lope, Jane pattering behind him. Jamie had vanished.

Prue was alone with the muttering trees and a chorus of sheep cries. Above her was a sky with whipped-cream clouds and hot sun, around her, the slippery, treacherous sides of the fortified camp.

Wait for me, she wanted to call out to her husband and daughter, but felt, where once she had unquestionably possessed it, she no longer had the right. Solitude is supposed to give strength – if it is chosen. Think of the mystics. If it is imposed, then it makes bitter bread for the eating. A bramble whipped at Prue's ankle, which sprouted a spray of needle pricks, and she cursed herself for not wearing trousers. She stooped to rub at the scratches. Suddenly she understood why God was in demand as a companion, and why Joan had needed him above all else – more than the homage of a king, quickly transferred, as we know, more than the embroidered *huques*, the pure-bred stallions and personalized banners sewn with fleurs-de-lis. More, even, than the badge of blood, the martyrdom, that, unconsciously, she had sought and found at Rouen.

Searching for the way upwards, Prue pursued a path towards knowledge.

'Still there?' Jamie stood above her.

She gazed up at her lover, so close and yet so removed, and never loved him so well.

'The others are coming.'

She turned to watch Max and Jane as they approached.

'This is cool fun,' Jane called out.

Across the divide separating Prue from the others, Max and Jane regarded each other and Prue, who could not bear to watch, bent her head and turned away. Max muttered something under his breath, slipped his arm around Jane and held her tight.

'Aren't you coming up?'

Prue swivelled towards her husband. He was looking down at her, eyes wrinkled in the sun, mouth compressed with his knowing, complicitous look.

What *do* I want? she cried silently.

'It's much easier to walk up here,' said Jamie.

Irresolute, confused, she looked from one to the other. She knew that this moment was significant, that the old Prue was gone, replaced by a woman who acknowledged both duality and the seeds of decay in herself, and accepted that these things were true of others.

It had been a difficult process, but there it was. Darkness creeps into most souls, leaving them lost, suffering and frightened. It had crept into Prue's life.

Gradually, her fists uncurled in her jacket pockets. Superimposed over the sun, the chain on a gate flapped in the autumn wind, and a flurry of sharp air blew over the stubble which made it rustle. Black on gold, crows rose in an aimless cloud. Prue stood motionless. For the first time, she understood what she had done by annexing her stepdaughter's husband, the measure of the transgression she had dealt Max in violating his family.

'I'll stay down here,' she said.

But a hundred or so yards further on, Jamie called down, 'I'm coming to get you,' which he did, pulling Prue up by the hand to the outer path where they walked in silence, in the opposite direction to her husband and daughter.

Chapter Twenty-Four

From the first-floor landing window in Austen Road, Emmy watched a couple of redwings and a fieldfare feast on the red traffic-light berries of the *Viburnum opulus* in the next-door garden. Not natural democrats, the birds made a great deal of fuss although there were plenty to go round.

Emmy moved one of Violet's statements-in-bronze out of her way and propped her chin on her hands.

'Did you know that birds are attracted to red?'

'Nope,' said Angus, slipping his hand under Emmy's red jumper.

'Yes.' Emmy's flesh crawled with pleasure. 'If there's a choice between red and white berries, they always choose red.'

'Yes,' said Angus, and continued.

Emmy bit her lip. 'They prefer that end of the colour spectrum.'

'So do I.'

She turned her head over her shoulder. 'What about Sal, then? She wears black.'

'So she does.' Angus edged closer. 'Can we go upstairs and explore other spectrums?'

Emmy's mouth twitched. 'No, you devil. I've got the baby to look after.'

Angus cocked his head to one side and listened. 'Sounds as if he's asleep. I can tell.'

Downstairs in the kitchen, the washing machine and the

dishwasher were banging out a cacophony. The drawing room had been cleaned, Edward's things ironed and Emmy had been on the point of tackling her own room. She had not been expecting the doorbell to ring, or Angus to step into the hall, kick off his boots as he always did and say: 'I was passing.'

Somehow, despite the faithful teachings of *Cosmopolitan*, sex at ten o'clock on Monday morning did not seem right. Emmy swivelled her body towards Angus so that her meagre breasts were pressed against his chest.

'Why were you passing?' she asked, curious to know.

'Just was.' He grinned. 'I hadn't seen you since last week.'

Four days, actually.

'Been with Sal, then?' Emmy kept her gaze fixed on the birds. 'Over the weekend, I mean?'

'Always knew you could read my lips. How did you know?' Angus shifted so that he could trace interesting pathways over her breasts.

'I can smell her.'

Indeed, traces of that ghastly musky perfume Sal poured over herself lingered on him. Emmy turned her head. Angus made a dive for her trousers and she squeezed her legs shut.

'Go away.'

'No.'

'Go away, Angus. Go back to Sal.'

His fingers arrested at the junction of her thighs. 'Do you really want me to? Shall I?' He was tracing small circles of desire which fanned out through Emmy's concupiscent body. 'I don't know why I bother with you, Em, but I do.'

'Don't bother, then. I can get along fine.'

'Do you believe that?' Angus went further. 'Aha.'

'Will you stop it?'

Angus feinted, grabbed for and captured Emmy's arm,

and pulled her into the nearest doorway, which happened to be the main bedroom – Jamie and Violet's bedroom. She struggled and protested but by this time his hand had found the target it sought.

Sex at ten o'clock on a Monday morning was fine, she thought afterwards. Absolutely fine. But after such abandon, how did you face the rest of the day? The rest of the week?

Angus rolled over on Violet's lace-edged (and staggeringly expensive) pillow-cases from Macy's in New York and kissed Emmy's naked shoulder. She closed her eyes, the better to savour the gesture. Then she stiffened, and shot upright.

'What if they find out?'

Angus pulled her down and made himself more comfortable. 'Stop fussing.'

She tugged at the hair trailing over his shoulder. 'Stop being a nag.'

'Nag, nag.'

An hour later, Emmy's eyes flapped open like a submarine hatch. Oh, my God, she thought, sleep vanishing. The baby. She raised her head and listened, but the house was quiet – even the machines were silent. Breathing quietly, Angus lay beside her, muscles and skin slackened by sleep.

For a few precious seconds, Emmy bent over him and allowed herself the luxury of a private view.

There was the slope of his haunch, and the line between the tanned chest and the loins which were paper white. The sinew running down his forearm, the angle made by ankle meeting foot . . . He was a map on to which she routed her desire but not her hope.

'Nice, aren't I?' Angus sounded slow and sleepy. 'An oil painting.'

'Yes, oh yes,' she found herself murmuring in that unguarded, private moment.

Slowly, he reached up and touched the slight mound of her breast. 'So are you.'

Emmy jumped out of bed and pulled on her under-clothes. 'I must check on the baby.'

'Sure.'

In the doorway, she turned to look at him sprawled shamelessly over the bed. He returned her look and said something that took him as much by surprise as it drove the breath from Emmy's body.

'I want us to get hitched,' he said. 'How about it?'

Over a mug of Violet's decaffeinated coffee and with Edward on her lap, Emmy explained the reasons why she had no intention of getting married at the moment.

She was too young.

'Twenty,' said Angus. 'Hardly a chicken.'

She wanted a career and to travel.

'You could have fooled me,' said Angus. 'Have a career looking after me.'

She was not sure if she agreed with marriage.

'Shack up with me, then,' said Angus.

He leant forward over the table and sent his pony-tail up and over his shoulder, and asked her why she was making excuses. Did she not love him? He asked so sweetly and with such tenderness that Emmy felt faint, and promptly succumbed to a tidal wash of fear that Angus was playing the worst of tricks, and could not, for the life of her, understand why.

Neither did it escape Emmy that he had not mentioned loving her, a prerequisite she rather thought was necessary in a marriage proposal.

Did she not love him?

'I'm not sure I do. Love you, I mean,' she lied, and had

the doubtful satisfaction of watching his expression darken. She shifted Edward, who was playing dangerous games with the empty mug at the edge of the table.

'Yes, you do. I know you do.'

He leant back in the chair and folded his hands behind his head. It took a lot to crack Angus's confidence.

'Not enough to marry you.' Emmy's lips shook as she forced out the words. 'I want someone I can trust.'

Angus listened in silence and then got to his feet. 'You're out of date, Em.' He picked up his jacket. 'I'll be off, then.'

'Angus . . .'

He padded out of the kitchen into the hall and reappeared, boots in hand. 'What?'

'Sorry.'

He stuffed his feet into the boots and bent down to lace them. 'Don't bother to see me out.'

Too late, she realized she had hurt him, and badly.

The front door clicked shut and Emmy was left holding a wriggling baby and contemplating the empty coffee cups on the table. Edward made noises that indicated he wanted a drink and Emmy put him into his chair while she fetched one. He drank thirstily and Emmy interpreted the squall that followed as a demand for a refill. After he had finished, she carried him upstairs and peeled off his sopping nappy. Delighted with the attention, Edward kicked his bare legs into the air and made cooing sounds. Emmy cleaned him up and smothered his bottom with cream. At that, he laughed.

A clean bottom, a dry nappy, a drink . . . if only life was that simple.

Downstairs the kitchen seemed so quiet and empty that Emmy switched on the radio and cradled in her hands the mug that Angus had drunk from which still retained a residual warmth. The vision she had once nurtured of the house, with cork matting and potted plants, seemed dim and inappropriate.

The mug was empty, Angus was gone, and Edward was due his morning walk.

Jamie first noticed the change in Emmy.

'She's gone very quiet,' he said to Violet.

Nowadays his and Violet's conversations tended to domestic topics – a tacit acknowledgement, perhaps, that for the moment it was best to keep to safe ground. Violet searched in her briefcase for the minutes of a meeting she meant to go over.

'She looks fine to me.'

'She seems different.'

'Rubbish. There's no difference at all. There's still a layer of dust in the spare room which I've told her to clean several times.'

'Her heart doesn't seem to be in the job.' On several occasions, Jamie had caught Emmy staring out of the window in what struck him as a despairing fashion. Her misery sounded an echo with him, an empathy rooted in his own confusion – and who was to say if that empathy was less acceptable because it had been born out of deceit rather than honesty?

Whatever. Jamie now perceived how little he had understood, how life had flowed around him and how he had not taken the trouble to take note. This shamed him. (Don't be ashamed, said Prue, when he confided this. How can we understand everything all at once?)

'Her heart not in the job?' Struck by the implications of Jamie's statement, Violet slumped back on to the sofa. 'Jamie, are you serious? Do you think Emmy wants to leave? Had I better talk to her?'

'It might be an idea.'

Violet ran through her schedule. 'I've got Frankfurt in a couple of days, then the States in November. She *can't* leave.' She seized on a solution, the easy one. 'Maybe we should give her a pay rise.'

Jamie shrugged. 'We can't make her stay if she isn't happy.'

'Yes, we can. I'll make her stay.' Violet stuffed the minutes back into her briefcase. 'She owes it to me.'

Jamie's expression was not kind. 'You have funny ideas sometimes, Violet. Emmy doesn't owe you a thing.'

Violet began totting up figures on a smart black leather notepad. 'I'm sure it's the money. They always want more.'

Jamie sighed. Alerted at last, Violet's head jerked around. 'Don't go all snooty because I mention money. You work with it all day, so don't pretend you're above such vulgar preoccupations.'

Until this moment, Emmy had not registered the exact honey colour of the kitchen floor: yellow, dashed with transparent wax, its mirror brightness now washed with the slight cloudiness of cream cleanser. As Violet talked, she stared at it. These days, most things had an unpredictable quality. Her feelings. The workings of her body. The patches of wakefulness during the night when she woke and stared into black and nothingness. The sudden pitchfork into exhausted sleep. Surprise at what she herself said and did.

Above all, Emmy was conscious of astonishment as to how hidden her feelings were, had been, from herself, the person who obligingly provided the receptacle in which they sloshed. Question: what were the chances of comprehending others if the chances of understanding yourself were pretty low?

'I mean, is there anything that's worrying you, Emmy?' Violet was saying. 'You seem so quiet. So unhappy. Do you need anything?' Far too shrewd to mention money in the opening moves of a negotiation, Violet was banking on the I'm-terribly-concerned-about-your-welfare approach, which worked a treat on the staff at work.

Emmy swallowed. 'I'm fine, thank you.'

The kettle boiled and Violet poured water over mint teabags and fished them out with a spoon. Then she placed a mug in front of Emmy and sat down opposite with hers.

'You would tell me,' she said, opening her eyes wide – yet another tactic that conveyed the appearance of absolute sincerity – 'if you needed help.'

Oh, yes, I do, I do, thought Emmy desperately.

'I mean, Jamie ...' Violet still hesitated a little over the Christian names, 'Jamie and I would hate to lose you. We feel you're almost family.'

This gave Emmy the opportunity to reflect on the number of times she had been requested to take her supper upstairs on a tray, to fetch and carry shopping, forbidden to socialize during her work hours and had her movements scrutinized. The funny-peculiar aspect of it was: compared to the silence and isolation of her own home, it *had* been more like belonging to a family.

Across the table, Violet's lips moved and her glossy hair undulated and flicked obediently into its expensive cut. From a distance, Emmy watched her. Then Violet turned, glanced out of the kitchen window, and Emmy was hit by a clap of recognition. For Violet's expression revealed a fleeting uncertainty and, even more unexpected, loss.

She, too, thought Emmy. How extraordinary that, after all, she and Violet shared the same skin.

The moment passed as quickly as it arrived. Violet sipped the mint tea, argued the toss with herself and plunged in.

'You're not thinking of leaving us, Emmy, I hope? We would be very sad.'

Emmy grimaced and stared into her mug.

'Would you prefer camomile?' Violet asked.

'I'm fine,' said Emmy and, to her horror, tears welled in her eyes. 'Absolutely fine.' She struggled with herself. 'Would you like me to take Edward to the clinic today? He's due his twelve-month injection.'

It was Monday morning and Violet was not up to dealing with tears before work. She followed on the lead thoughtfully provided by Emmy. Waiting with a hot, restless baby in a hot, noisy clinic had not been written into her blueprint of motherhood when she devised it in those pre-conception days of sunlight and balm. Neither was it now. She looked at her watch.

'Yes, do.'

She dickered with the idea of trying once again to get to the bottom of whatever was worrying Emmy, then decided that ignorance on the behalf of the employer was the better part of valour.

Alone, Emmy resisted the impulse to ring Anna. What's up, then, you old cow? Anna would say, heavy with the weekend's excess. Keeping your legs tight together? Tell us the gen on Madam. How many pairs of knickers has she got through this week? Have I got news for you . . .

No, Emmy would say. Have *I* got news for *you*.

Instead, she plodded up the stairs to the first floor. The door to the main bedroom (Emmy could not bring herself to look through it) was open, revealing abandoned clothes and an unmade bed. The cistern in the bathroom gurgled quietly.

She held on to the newel post and hauled herself up the next flight to her flatlet. Here the doors were kept tight shut, for Emmy's standards had dropped lately and she was pretty sure that Violet checked up regularly on the rooms. Well, Madam could get her eyeful of piled clothes and overflowing wastepaper baskets.

Her sitting room smelt . . . of what? Despair? It should. Disuse? Certainly, the room *looked* despairing and out of sorts. Emmy stabbed her finger down on the table (a cast-off from the garage and Hallet's Gate with a split top) and wrote 'Fool' in the dust.

It was no use ignoring any longer what she had to do.

The bathroom door made its familiar popping noise and the displaced air raised the edge of the carpet, which had not been fixed. Emmy registered the wet flannel lying in the bath, the shell-shaped soap dish floating its burden of jelly and soap, five bottles of shampoo, each with a different set of promises, and one of Edward's rubber ducks.

A moth to the flame, her gaze was riveted on the test-tube she had left on the shelf above the basin.

Hundreds, no millions of women had crossed this bridge. No, no, nothing so comforting as a bridge, more a thin, rotting plank balanced over a big question mark, with the scatter from spoilt lives clotted into heaps underneath – like the discarded cars, bits of pushchair, kitchen waste and old clothes of the council tip.

It was Emmy's luck that she had had no practice at plank walking and was the sort of person who developed vertigo on a deep-pile carpet.

Imagine inching forward and hearing the rotten fibres give under her weight with the sodden, sullen sound! Imagine the shake of her body and the freezing blood forcing its way through her arteries and, down below, the gap into which she was falling.

Twenty, thirty years ago – Emmy did not know enough to

estimate precisely – she would have had no choice. Stuffed, finished, probably banged up in some home and saddled with the stigma for the rest of her life. Now Emmy had three options, which made it worse because she did not know what to do – either what she wanted, or what was right.

Emmy surprised herself, for she was not in the habit of considering ethics and it did not come easily.

Jamie stepped neatly out of the way as Emmy jumped down the last six stairs into the hall. It was odd activity for an adult, and Jamie was transported back to the time when he did just that for a dare with his friends, the era of long shorts and scratched knees. He did not associate Emmy with those moments of shivering abandonment and free fall.

'Are you practising for the next Olympics?'

Emmy flushed and muttered something unintelligible, but there was something in the manner in which her eyes glittered that told Jamie that she had been crying.

'I thought it was only Eddie the Eagle who did that sort of thing.'

Emmy regained her balance. 'I don't know what came over me,' she said, with perfect truth.

Jamie looked at her thoughtfully. Guilt had unpredictable and physical results, and Jamie had been suffering from a diminished appetite and fretful sleep. But it also led you to another door. Jamie wanted to find out about other people, was ravenous to do so, because it gave him a sense of being earthed. By contemplating the mistakes and suffering of others, Jamie gave himself licence not to think too badly of himself.

Quite forgetting that it was loose, Jamie leant back on the radiator and sprang forward again when it cracked and shifted in its moorings. He collided with Emmy.

'Oh, Lord, sorry, Emmy.'

He flashed her a wry grin. 'If there's anything we can do, Emmy, you only have to ask.'

Peaky, thin, shivering in the recently intensified autumn chill, Emmy was the incarnation of misery. A spot of red crept into her cheeks and Jamie mistook it for anger. Later, he realized it was a badge of courage, for Emmy shook as she said: 'I'm going to have a baby.'

Then Jamie made the reply that was to haunt him for many months: 'Is that all?'

Violet's reaction was not much better.

'I hope she doesn't want it,' she said, but had the grace to stop there. A flush suffused her cheeks and her red mouth twisted. 'I mean, I don't want to make it sound as if a baby is a disposable asset.' She paused, thinking of the offer she had made Jamie and which had never been spoken of since. 'They're not.'

'Well, we agree on one thing.' This time, Jamie's smile was a formality.

Well ... in a way, a baby was. Helen, darling mother Helen, had thought so. Bye, bye, little daughter. I'm off and I don't want you hanging on my arm like a weekend bag (the sort that Violet had bought from exclusive shops: elegant but hell to carry). It doesn't suit me to have you along with Jack.

Violet often wondered if it would have been better if Helen had popped into the local pregnancy advice bureau and, hey presto, Violet would have been disposed of down the municipal drain. (Presumably, she would have been in good company down there. Consider all those film stars, politicians, aristocrats who found themselves lumbered with the prospect of an awkward weekend bag, let alone the career girls, potential unmarried mothers, mistresses and one-night stands.)

The strange thing was: Violet did not think the worse of them for it. Life had to be got through. Far worse to be born and then not loved. Correction: not to be loved enough.

Violet's analysis terminated at this point. She did not make the connection between Helen's treatment of her and her attitude to Edward.

'Do you want it?' she asked Emmy, who was retching over Edward's meal of puréed soya beans and tomato. 'Here let me.' She wrested the spoon away. 'Go and sit down. I'll feed him.'

Endeavouring to be practical was no defence against bone-deep confusion and anxiety. 'I don't know.' Emmy's hand fluttered in the region of her stomach.

'Well, you must decide quickly, otherwise it becomes worse.'

Violet remembered her surprise when she woke up one morning, twenty-four weeks pregnant, to encounter the definite, writhing bulge under her ribs and thought: Legally, I could still get rid of it. And also, Not now. It is *alive*.

Emmy sat down in the kitchen chair. Even now, Violet was no expert in the business of shovelling food down her son and, the bout of nausea having subsided, Emmy was able to watch with scientific interest the false moves and baffled impatience on Violet's beautiful face.

'If you wait between mouthfuls,' she said at last. 'He likes to eat slowly.'

Clearly, this was news to Violet but she took the advice and harmony was achieved between mother and son for the remaining mouthfuls. At the finish, Edward threw himself back in his chair and flashed his mother one of the smiles that came from nowhere. Violet found herself smiling back.

'Cheeky monster,' she said, softer than Emmy had ever seen her, and dabbed Edward's face with a wet flannel.

Emmy breathed out slowly, and tried to imagine that her stomach did not belong to her. Violet captured one of Edward's flying hands and held it at an exaggerated distance while she tackled the grunge clinging to the fingers.

'Is it tactless to ask who the father is?'

Emmy swallowed and waited for the word Angus to form on her lips. It did not. If she expected something sharp and stinging from Violet she was mistaken, for Violet returned Edward's hand to him – rather as if it was a bag full of rubbish – and said: 'Don't worry. It's none of my business.'

Emmy revised her ideas on Violet.

Two days later, the postman delivered a parcel for Emmy elaborately tied up in string.

'You don't see that often,' Jamie commented as he passed it over to Emmy, who knew at once who had sent it. She held it between her cold hands, knowing that it contained the books she had lent him and her CD of Shakespear's Sister. The string, so carefully and determinedly knotted, undid Emmy – it was so like Angus to wrap things up well. To her surprise, she dropped her head in her hands and wailed from sorrow and nausea.

Within seconds, Jamie was on his feet. 'Violet, I'll leave you to sort this one out.'

Violet shot him a look which said, 'Typical', but the next thing Emmy knew was an arm circling her shoulder.

'Look,' said Violet in her ear, 'you've got to wise up, Emmy. You can't go on like this. I suggest you get along to the clinic this morning and get some advice.'

She glanced at her watch – Piaget and new – saw that she was running late, but made an effort. 'I'll ring up and make an appointment for you if you like.'

Emmy promised to do something, blew her nose and

unpicked the string surrounding the parcel. Inside was the novel by Virginia Andrews that Angus had kidnapped before she had finished it. It was a novel about children in danger. Inside it, he had inserted a note: 'It was nice knowing you, Em. Don't worry about anything. Me and Sal have gone off to live in the country for the winter.'

It was so like him, too, to return everything.

Autumn had settled heavily over the city. Ringed by the ceaseless traffic, Wandsworth Common was damp underfoot and mud-clogged. Here and there a light shone out of a building, or the bright red of a bus cut through air layered by damp and pollution. Trees, roofs, gates dripped. Emmy's feet left dark footprints on the grass and the buggy bucked and snagged.

What do I do? She watched a couple of mothy Canada geese by the edge of the pond, panic routing her resolution to be sensible. A jumble – abortion, welfare payments, coping alone, labour, a council flat – clogged her mind, which had lost its ability to concentrate.

She strove to pin down a rational thought, to settle on a concrete plan that would help, and failed. Her thoughts slid, despairing, muddled and without much hope, to the only thing she wanted to think about: Angus.

She had sent him away, and she did not know if she had the language to call him back.

Chapter Twenty-Five

Prue noticed that the photograph of Helen in Max's study had been returned to its prominent position on the table.

'I hate you,' she told it, then admitted, 'but I think I understand you a bit better now.' Helen's face glistened mistily with non-comprehension.

She attacked the pile of papers on Max's desk and emptied an ashtray, releasing a whiff of stale tobacco and dust. It was then she noticed the box of gun cartridges on the right-hand side of the desk. Frowning a little, she checked the contents and refastened the lid. It was almost full, and should not have been left lying around. It was a strict house rule that the guns and the cartridges remained in the gun-safe.

Upstairs, Prue retrieved the key from its hiding place under the bathroom basin and unlocked the safe. There was plenty of room so she pushed the cartridges inside and relocked it.

Later, when she was ironing Max's tartan handkerchiefs into the precise rectangles he preferred, Prue remembered something. The iron, which was on its last legs, hissed and an overabundance of rusty-looking water spilt on to the linen. Prue cursed and propped it on its side. Why, she asked herself, had there been so much space in the gunsafe?

In her mind she ran over the contents. Max possessed two guns: the one he had inherited from his father, and the other from an uncle. Max preferred the latter and it was his father's that was missing.

She tackled a shirt. Perhaps it was being overhauled.

The shirt-sleeve panned out under the iron, crisp and smooth. The smell of clean, hot clothes filled her nose. Strange that the cartridge box had been practically full. But not absolutely. Was Max becoming careless? The iron hissed in protest as she jerked it upright. Where was that gun? Prue snatched up the iron and ironed until there was a pile as high as her shoulder.

She was in the kitchen when the phone rang.

The phone call had been Jamie.

'Will you come, Prue?'

She had glanced at the kitchen clock and the clutter of cooking ingredients and utensils. This was as good a moment as any to say, No. It's over. Enough. Finish.

'Please, Prue. We haven't been together since the summer, and I can't wait any longer. It's been difficult.' Jamie meant Violet, work, a creeping restlessness, some money worries for, healthy as Jamie's salary was, its chief characteristic was a tendency to melt.

No, Jamie, she could choose to say. I no longer wish to be overwhelmed. By guilt. By deceit. By love. It has to stop. Sometime. It will stop. Why not now?

But her body said something different, and Prue was already opening the drawer and putting away the kitchen knives and frowning as she tried to remember what time Max was coming home and whether or not there was a stew in the freezer.

There was, and she left it to defrost on the sideboard and moved quickly around the kitchen wiping surfaces and stowing saucepans in cupboards. Since her affair, Prue's kitchen had changed. The more she entangled with Jamie, the more snowy and starched her tea-towels, the more polished the furniture. All of these achievements (snowy tea-towels, for goodness' sake!) would offer clues to the observant, for Prue had never been a fussy housewife. Now, providing the sink was rid of its coffee stains and supper was on the table, Prue felt a balance had been struck, and part of a bargain held.

She draped the dishcloth over the tap. In other words, adultery is an activity grouted in between cooking, washing and dusting, after birth and in the short space between marriage and death.

From her position on the boiler, Bella stared at her mistress and folded her paw carefully underneath her plump body. 'Not quite as simple as that, Bella, is it?' she informed the large, unblinking eyes.

Prue drove a third of the way to Winchester and, at the last minute, turned the car back. She had been using her country handbag, a terrible old plastic number, which accommodated her notebooks, and had neglected to transfer her cheque book and credit cards into the smarter London leather version. Ergo, no train fare.

She swore and headed back at top speed.

'How do you manage to get away from the office?' Prue asked Jamie when they eventually caught up with each other in room number 35. Prue was late and Jamie a little irritable as a result. 'Surely someone must be putting two and two together?'

It was, perhaps, significant that they did not fall on each other but sat down to talk.

'Office life is a monastery requiring poverty and obedience, until you have learnt the rules . . .' Jamie sat down on the bed, '... which are to do precisely as you wish and explain later.'

'How is the office, and is anything happening?' Prue tossed the leather handbag on to the chair as if it had not cost her extra petrol, panic and most of the things she required in a handbag for it was much too small.

'Work? Busy. And Dyson is still very difficult in meetings.'

'Tell.'

Jamie's eyebrows twitched together. 'There's nothing *to* tell, really. His views and mine are poles apart and we clash. Meanwhile, the Serbs are cutting a swathe through Bosnia, the phylloxera bug is ravaging Californian vineyards and Clinton is going to be US president, after all. The infuriating thing is, the problems with Dyson take up far more of my energies and attention than anything else.'

Prue touched Jamie's knee. 'We're not so far apart, then. I've realized that I spend my life tiptoeing between alliances and hostilities. But it's not such a terrible thing.' She was silent for a minute while she considered what she wished to say. Her hand fell back into her lap. 'I have a feeling Max knows something,' she admitted at last.

Jamie went quite still. 'You're sure?'

'No, I'm not sure. It's a feeling. A feeling that he's watching me all the time.'

When you have wronged someone, it is helpful if they behave badly, too, however slight the transgression. The idea that Max was watching Prue provided Jamie, who tried not to think of his father-in-law, with a small opportunity to think less well of him.

Prue read her lover's thoughts and her protective instincts towards her husband were roused. 'Don't,' she said almost sharply. 'Don't think badly of him. Didn't you do the same with Lara?'

Lara? Golden, lying Lara. Ah ... as golden as a young

man's carelessness chose to make her and as lying ... ?
Be honest, Jamie Beckett. As lying as he himself had turned
out.

Jamie caught Prue's hand and pulled her roughly down
beside him. She gave a little laugh, and pretended to
protest. He brushed his mouth along the line of her jaw
until it rested on the soft point pulsing beneath her ear.
'Yes,' he said. 'I watched her long before she knew I knew.'

She drew in his subtle smell, and turned her head so that
their lips were almost touching. 'How did you find out?'

Jamie's mouth lingered on Prue's and she nipped his
bottom lip luxuriously. 'Jenny was the one to tell me about
Lara. She didn't realize she was doing it, of course. She just
said that Mummy was spending the afternoon with Uncle
Robert.'

'Poor Jenny.'

'Poor Max.'

Prue was still amazed by herself. How was she capable of
talking about Max while she slid her hand under Jamie's
shirt? Perhaps, perhaps, the things she had chosen to dictate
the shape of her life had merely been props.

'Max may well suspect something,' she said. 'I'm distracted and forget things. I keep dashing up to London and
I lose my temper. Relations between me and Violet took an
all-time plunge at the theatre. Then there is Jane – and her
problems.' She paused. 'And there I do blame myself.'

Jamie covered her hand and pressed it against his well-
exercised stomach. 'Shut up, Prue.'

She pictured what lay beneath the still faintly tanned skin
– a pulsing, coiled and looped landscape that existed to
service Jamie's taut, fresh-skinned body.

'Max once said, Jamie, that there are worse things than
being a pander. I couldn't think what he meant at the time.'

With the sharpened hunger of the condemned man, for

Jamie sensed that he and Prue had moved to another stage, he again plundered the closed eyelids with his mouth and the line between the clean silk of her hair and her temples. 'I do need you, Prue.'

She put her arms around his chest and held him. Their intimacy, a compound of sex, gratification, danger, shared guilt and indecision, intensified.

'What do you want to do, Prue? For I think you do want to do something.'

She hesitated. 'No one knows where a wave comes from but it rocks the ship all the same. But – but I don't wish to be responsible for a shipwreck.'

'I see.' Jamie disengaged himself and got up from the bed. 'So we don't go on till we're old and past it?' From his height, he bent over Prue and twined his fingers into the hair at the nape of her neck and pulled her head back. 'Plenty of people live double lives, you know.'

'I understand that now,' she replied, feeling the tug at her neck like the tug of sexual desire. 'I just hadn't been looking before.'

Jamie tried to imagine what it would be like to be normal again, to conduct a normal Monday-to-Sunday life minus Prue. 'Have your feelings changed?'

'No.' Prue stretched out her hand, fingers quivering. 'Look, Jamie, it shakes for you. My mouth aches. My legs are weak . . . and all the rest of it. Can I prove it any other way?'

Jamie had a sudden, disconcerting vision of the future – Violet (where had all his feelings gone?), Edward, the office, bills, office cars, a little gardening, negotiations, last-minute holidays in Italy – and yearning and loss flooded him.

'Leave Max.'

He had spoken on the spur of the moment, but the sensation of an oiled, purposeful spring uncoiling inside him suggested that he had been thinking about it for some time. Buried in the wrinkles of the human psyche are fantasies and, once they are aired, they can be dressed up in any costume to look plausible.

'What did you say?' Prue's face twisted with a mixture of joy, fear, but not surprise.

'Leave Max.'

Against all advice, Joan had been desperate to take the impossible, the city of Paris. The largest city in Christendom, with its hundred thousand citizens, moats, guns on the ramparts. Ranged against it, Joan's army and a wavering king who was conducting secret negotiations with the enemy and pursuing his own agenda. Joan had also broken her sword – the one she claimed had been given to her by God – by striking a camp prostitute with the flat of its blade. It was a bad omen and was seen as such. The offensive against Paris was a doomed enterprise, too, and Joan lost badly. Paris refused to be taken and she was borne away on the tide of a retreating, surly army.

Thereafter, Joan's luck, her vision, her whatever-you-choose-to-call-it ran out.

Leave Max? It seemed as impossible and as wrong as taking Paris. Prue's thoughts traced circles like the skylark's, high on a cocktail of thin air.

'I could get a job abroad. It would be exciting, Prue. You'd like it. You need a change.'

Do I? Leave Dainton? Leave jam-making, gardening and flower-arranging and the balancing of the WI's accounts with which she did battle each year. Abandon a home, a husband and a child. Abandon the idea that a marriage should be made to work. Shut the door behind her, shake the dust from her feet – it had been done before, often. Helen had done it. Statistically speaking, women do it more frequently than men. The ideal soured by years of wielding

359

Brillo pads and baby lotion, they leave their husbands, not the other way round.

'What about the children?' she asked him.

'Yes, what about them?' He sounded bleak.

Silence fell between them. Jamie looked down at his hands. 'Let's go out,' he said abruptly.

She glanced around the room which, over the months, had been scaled of its glamour, rather as the scales were flaking away, in little pearly scabs, from Prue's eyes. Once, its shoddiness had been exciting, now it appeared unjoyful and makeshift. They left the bed as smooth and unoccupied as they had found it.

A November afternoon in London exudes a lost quality of threatening fog, congealing cold and orange neon. Oxford Street was dense with shoppers and fractured by coloured slabs of Christmas decorations. There was a hum of noise, the grind of traffic and the restless beat of shoppers pressing in and out of the stores. The pavement was too crowded to walk two abreast, which made their progress uneven. Jamie's irritation returned.

'Where to?' Prue slipped her hand through his elbow.

'I don't know,' he said, wishing it was late enough for a drink. 'Coffee?'

They made for the coffee shop in Selfridges and commandeered a table. Cappuccino arrived, foamed and flecked with chocolate. To give herself time before she tackled the issues, Prue stuck her spoon into the foam and scooped it up, struck by the childishness of the gesture.

As powerful as the released genie, a picture of Max in his city suit forced its way into her mind, followed by a thin white Jane. She watched them walk into the distance, knowing that for a long time she had ignored her connection to them. Or theirs to her. She looked up at Jamie and her mind cleared. What was left? A drained coffee cup, shame and regret mixed with intense happiness, the knowledge that she had grown, and a half memory of the old Prue.

She tinkered with cup and spoon, aware that Jamie's scrutiny was accompanied by a certain acerbity, which she was also aware indicated he was determined on something.

'I had no idea that kicking over the traces . . . sinning . . . would be so exhausting.'

'What do you mean?'

'It intrudes into your mind and acts like the magnetic pole. Everything is pulled towards it. And you can't stop thinking about it.' Prue pushed her empty cup into the centre of the table. 'Instead of being automatic, everything becomes self-conscious. I didn't think it would be so difficult. I imagined it was just a question of taking off your clothes and that was that.'

Jamie was conscious of a tinge of impatience. He gave one of his half-smiles which clients had learnt meant he was thinking strategy. 'Whoever sent you to a convent, Prue, did you a disservice. Sin does not come into it.' Jamie had the benefit of a more or less secular education, which allowed him to be more direct. He leant towards her. 'You haven't answered my question, Prue. Will you leave Max?'

'I don't want to answer it because I can't.' Prue took a deep breath, terrified suddenly at the thought of losing Jamie. 'I don't know what to think, or what to do.'

'Perhaps,' said Jamie wryly, 'you need a head-on collision with God to test he's there.'

She appreciated the joke. '*Touché.* I'll shut up.'

Jamie looked at his watch. 'I've got to go.'

For the first time ever, their meeting had proved unsatisfactory. Prue watched him pay the bill and leave. She knew she would never fully understand how or what she had got herself into, only that she was overflowing with a feeling to which she had become addicted, so strong, so consuming was it and she wondered what on earth she had done with her life before Jamie.

Prue emerged into the street and, skilled now in managing London's crowds, threaded her way through the crush along Oxford Street towards Marble Arch. She had no fixed idea as to where she was going, neither did she care very much. At the junction, she paused and then descended the stairs to the subway.

Underneath stretched the tunnels of no-man's land, spiked with sudden turns, blind alleys and hidden entrances, urine-impregnated, splashed with dirt and pulverized food, lit by a dirty light from yellow lamps.

Half-way along, Prue became aware of footsteps. They were gaining on her – fast. Various thoughts jostled for precedence, but she set herself to walk purposefully: there was no reason to panic. She debated turning round to look, decided against it and hoisted her bag further up her shoulder. Despite these precautions, her heart tattooed against her chest with stabs of panic.

The subway lights blinked, and time elongated into seconds of intolerable tension, long enough for Prue queasily to construct a case that she deserved this: a squalid mugging, the stinging corrective of assault. Should she turn to receive the lash and the bruise, much as she had her lover's caress?

'Prue!'

She came to a dead halt, swivelled and, relief and ruefulness making her furious, cried, 'Jamie. *Why* did you do that?'

He gripped the lapels of her coat and dragged her towards him. 'I wanted to frighten you. And I did.'

'Not very nice,' she whispered, as her head fell back and her knees trembled with both fear and desire.

'No.'

When he kissed her, she tasted grime and exhaust fumes and supposed that he tasted it on her. Breathing rapidly, she buried her head in his shoulder.

A woman passed them, glancing at their locked figures with an expression of distaste. Prue recollected the times when she had been confronted by couples eating each other, and did not care.

'Jamie, we can't stay here.'

They moved off down the subway, up the stairs, and into the park, which was still open. Welded into a mass by the dark, the trees were tipped by neon and hugging blackness at their centres. A solitary man walked towards Speaker's Corner, his shoes clicking on the path. Otherwise, it was deserted.

'Why did you want to frighten me, Jamie? Why? *Why?*'

His hand forced its way inside the fastenings of her coat. 'If I was able to explain the things I feel about you, and as a result of you, then I would be a rich man.'

Prue shook her hair loose from her coat collar and arched her head back so that Jamie could cover the exposed skin with his mouth. Then he pulled her, smiling, towards the blackness and concealment, their feet leaving matching depressions in the damp ground.

'Here,' said Jamie and pressed against the furthest tree. 'And don't say no, otherwise I'll make you.'

'Yes,' said Prue, as his hands travelled roughly up her skirt, experiencing the triumphant thrill of yielding, of being at her most female and feminine. She moved a little to accommodate him. Jamie pressed closer.

'Wait,' she said, and altered her clothing, shivering as tongues of cold air licked the inside of her thighs. Then she said triumphantly: 'Now.'

Afterwards, Jamie leant slack and heavy on her and pinioned her to the tree. He was panting and laughing.

'I never, ever imagined . . .'

Prue let her head rest against the bark and smiled at the lights of an aircraft moving in an arc through the sky. Where in the world had it come from? From plague, starvation, political uncertainty? She did not care. The episode had taken only a couple of minutes but she, Prue Valour, had travelled to the outer limits of lust.

She turned his face towards her. 'I love you,' she said, searching for his face in the dark.

He appropriated her hand in his and ran his thumb over her palm in the intimate and tender gesture that made Prue catch her breath.

'I love you,' she repeated, imprisoning his thumb by curling up her hand. 'And I must go home.'

Gently, he buttoned her blouse and straightened her skirt and she brushed at her hair with her fingers. The temperature had dropped and their combined breath streamed into the night.

'When do I see you again?'

She took a deep breath. 'I don't know, Jamie.'

On the train at Waterloo, Prue searched in her too-small handbag for a piece of paper, and began to make a list of Christmas presents. Then she divided the page into 'food' and 'things to organize'. Gradually, the wild, primitive feelings rocking her body dispelled along with the longing, and the urge to touch the stars. The train swayed from side to side, and the smell, peculiar to electric trains, seeped up from the floor. The dark outside the window was as thick as a blanket. Prue let the list drop into her lap and closed her eyes.

*

'Is that ZBD Software?'

'Yup,' replied a terminally bored voice.

Prue squinted at Jane's list of Christmas requirements, which made no concessions to legibility. 'Look, I don't know what I'm talking about but I want to order some things for my daughter.'

'Name on credit card, please.'

'Before I order I want to check it will arrive before Christmas.'

'Sorry, can't do anything without credit-card details.'

After a tussle over the spelling of Dainton, Prue asked for a Universal Printer Sharer, Standard 2-1 Parallel for an Acorn Archimedes.

'We don't have that one but could supply a similar model.'

'Could I send it back if it's not right?'

'We charge an administration cost.'

The telephone emitted a dead silence. Prue took the plunge. 'OK, I'll order.'

'That will be five pounds postage and packing.'

'But it only costs *nine* pounds.'

'Do you want to order?' The voice had turned impatient.

'I'd better have something else to make it worth it.' Prue held up the ZBD advert. 'Could I have Saloon Cars Deluxe.'

A keyboard tapped away. 'That will be an extra six pounds postage.'

'But you've just charged me for the Universal Printer Sharer.'

'Each item has a postage charge I'm afraid.'

Prue slammed down the receiver and dropped her head into her hands. If I sit very quietly, she thought to herself, then perhaps everything will go away. If I am extra, extra still and quiet perhaps it will turn out to be a dream.

Christmas presents, school runs, hotel rooms, making

wild, outrageous love in a public park, a hurting, bleeding husband, a lover who had hacked his way through the hedge of thorns to the modest house (and modest life) where she had lain sleeping. A stepdaughter. A daughter whose accusing face and bewildered eyes were locked on her mother's.

Life had to go on.

Chapter Twenty-Six

It was lunchtime, and, against all expectation, an early Christmas rush in Forsight's bookshop had gathered momentum. The shop was unusually full and stuffy. The more swingeing the recession, it seemed, the more the book as a present grew in political correctness. 'Indisputably cheaper than caviar,' said Gerald, propping up a sagging dumpbin. Either that or the free warmth and an undemanding dose of piped classical music kept the customers coming.

For the umpteenth time the telephone rang and Gerald held it out to Prue, who balanced the pile of paperbacks she was sorting against the counter and took the call pressed up against the wall to avoid the crush. It was Mrs Harriman.

'We would like either you or Mr Valour to come and collect Jane today,' she said. 'We think she needs a few days at home.'

Fear took Prue in its jaws and shook her. She could barely articulate. 'Why?'

'Jane has been very under par this week. So has her work.' Fatigue and real concern toned down Mrs Harriman's disapproval but she managed to suggest – yet again – that the situation was Prue's fault. Buried in the part of Prue that did not want to listen, a voice said: She may be right.

Over the years complacency had provided a stout shield for Prue against the buffets, and feeling squarely in the wrong was something else with which she was coming to terms.

Time to plant the standard on the ditch? Time to admit that life was tougher and more draining than she had allowed? At forty-one Prue observed her fingers curled round the receiver, and concluded that, for most of her adult life, she had been in retreat.

'Yes, Mrs Harriman,' she said.

'The headmistress had a word with her this morning and it seems to have upset Jane a great deal, in fact she grew quite hysterical, so we judge it best that she goes home to calm down,' said Mrs Harriman. 'We have been keeping an eye, as you asked us, on her eating.'

'So have we,' said Prue, ironing any suggestion of defensiveness out of her tone. 'Her weight is stable at the moment, yes?'

On this occasion, Gerald was not so accommodating when Prue asked if she could go early. He took off his glasses and slammed them into their case.

'If the job is becoming too much,' he said, 'you must tell me.'

'I'm sorry to let you down.' Prue looked Gerald squarely in the eyes but he merely extracted his glasses from the case and turned away.

Prue's gaze roved along the bookshelves and stopped at Fict.: W. Wasn't it in Evelyn Waugh's *A Handful of Dust* where Brenda Last, having been informed that John is dead, lets out a sigh of relief when she discovers that the dead John is not her lover, but her son?

Prue understood now – for she *knew* there had been times during her battle when she would not have given up Jamie. Never would, perhaps. Recognizing a truth can result in an extreme reaction, and Prue had to remember that if she shared a complicity with Brenda it did not mean that they were the same person. But yes, she and Kate had agreed during one of their no-holds-barred talks (that were not honest enough, it seemed) that they would never put their children in jeopardy. Both had spoken from innocence but, then, the so dedicated, so home-centred Prue had not learnt that you cannot make general rules, least of all for yourself.

Feeling guilty about Gerald, Prue sorted the paperbacks into the shelves and went to fetch her coat. 'Letting down' people had become a regular debit on her account. Who else could she let down? She had already let down her employer, her husband, her daughter, her friends. The cat?

Jane was waiting in the front hall of the school and plainly in no state to be lectured. The junior mistress who was guarding her, handed her over with the jolliness that hides extreme embarrassment and Prue bundled her into the car.

'Home,' she said.

'Home?' Jane made the word sound as if it was recently acquired foreign vocabulary.

In Hallet's Gate, Prue stood her silent daughter in the kitchen and unwound her scarf, removed her woollen gloves and eased the school coat off bony, unresponsive shoulders. Then she rubbed Jane's hands between her own. They felt cold and unlived-in.

'Jane.' Where once Prue would have been confident, she was now uncertain. 'Can you tell me what's the matter?'

Jane shook her head. 'Leave me alone, Mum.'

'But something's wrong.'

Prue did not require verbal confirmation, and nor could Jane give it. She allowed her mother to fuss over her and, while Prue did so, she observed her with a grown-up pair of eyes. This was not the parent who had guarded Jane and taught her the shape of the world. This was no longer the mother who was on her side but, apparently, a stranger with a secret. Jane knew, she just *knew* that the secret was harmful. Above everything else, Jane hated Prue for changing.

Back at school, Victoria (she of the divorced parents) had said that people always stopped loving each other. Jane was disinclined to believe her, but Victoria insisted. 'It always happens. Wait and see. Then you get someone else.'

Of course, Victoria had no option but to say that, and Jane did not know about the theory of relativity. Imperfect as her knowledge was of what took place between men and women, however, Jane grasped enough to know that the card with its glowing painting and hasty inscription that had rested against her jumper had the power to hurt her father.

Her *mother* could hurt her father.

Jane thought of the loneliness of being teased, the bewilderment of realizing that the world was ranged against you, and not knowing why, of hearing girls snigger as you passed, of finding unwelcome objects in your desk, of lying awake at night, alone, cold and afraid. She could not bear the idea that her father might feel the same. Jane spent so much time thinking about the card, puzzling out what it meant and what to do, that she could not sleep and her appetite, which had picked up a little, dwindled.

'I want you to have a cup of tea, darling.'

'I don't want one.'

'*Please.* I'll have one, too, and then we'll talk.'

The regulation shoes looked frighteningly too large for Jane's feet and her tights were baggy around the ankle.

'How about hot buttered toast?' Prue reached for the bread board.

Wanting to throw herself on her mother and bury her head in her shoulder and, in the same breath, wishing to inflict hurt as she was hurting, Jane glared at her. 'I don't want to talk to you. I don't want anything to eat. I want to watch *Neighbours*.' She added under her breath because she liked the effect it would have on her mother, 'And I'm going to make you watch me starve.'

Prue went white, then red. Then she sat down and put her head in her hands. Trying to forget I'm here, I suppose, thought Jane angrily.

She left Prue to contemplate the corpse-like shape of Jane's outdoor things on the floor. Bending down, she picked up the coat and smoothed out the sleeves. Then she folded the scarf and restored the gloves to their proper shape. Such everyday, mundane things whose wool was soft and worn to the touch, and she held them as tenderly as if they contained a breathing imprint of her daughter. She looked up and her gaze locked on to the garden. In the winter dusk, the *Prunus autumnalis* looked stark and unyielding.

'Joan's life', wrote one of her biographers, 'had been led on the high planes of feeling and it was fitting that death should meet her in the same high key.' In other words, it would never have done if, after the Paris débâcle, Joan had meekly returned to Domrémy to tend her sheep or sat down and hemmed handkerchiefs for her bride chest. It was required by everyone that she died dramatically – the ones who loved her, or rather her image, the ones who hated her and wished for the tongues of fire to sear her bones. Courageous, heroic, the woman who, voices ringing in her head, had done much to change the idea of what a woman could be, Joan required it of herself.

Imagine. If you have stood beside your sovereign in Reims Cathedral as he was anointed by the holy oil and crowned at your instigation, the oriflamme grasped in your hand. (All other standards were excluded but Joan's. As she said: 'It has borne the burden and it was right that it should have the honour.') If you have ridden with the wind in your ears and the sun at your back, smelt the sweat and horse and blood, wept with anguish and pain at your own wounds, experienced the noise and exhilaration of the charge, fought with your comrades over the white dust and through black mud, listened to their oaths, the sound of the trumpet signalling victory, and the quiet commands of God, how could you give it up? How could you return to the spinning and dusting?

It is strange, the same biographer comments, how an individual's life 'adjusts to the key imposed on it from the first'.

That does not give the postman or the fishmonger much of a chance to adjust to a higher key, or the average woman who spends a significant part of her life chopping onions and hoovering. Or Prue, whose existence had not been very special. A marriage. A birth. An affair. Then what?

Imagine, too, standing on the ramparts of the city of Mélun and listening to the voices of St Catherine and St Margaret telling you that you would be captured shortly, that you must not be surprised, that you must take every-thing as it came, however difficult.

That God would look after you.

Then what?

'I want to talk to you, Prue,' said Max that evening, and rose from his armchair, his face set and drained of all humour. He walked to the window and looked out, one hand shoved into his pocket. 'We've got to do something.'

She did not dare to ask what he meant and sought refuge in evasion. 'Oh.'

'We have to face some things, Prue.' Max swivelled round to look at his wife. 'I . . . We . . . are failing to do so.'

She heaved up from the chair with the sagging seat which she had always meant to replace and went over to stand beside him. 'Are you talking about Jane?'

'Partly.'

She noticed that his hand was trembling and she put out her own to touch him. Quick as a dart, he moved back out of reach and she was left, hand suspended, with a sensation that he had kicked her.

'I see.'

'No, you don't.'

Prue said quietly, 'You're angry with me, Max, aren't you?'

He turned back to contemplating the dark garden that reminded him of the one through which in his childhood dark monsters had slid. The frog monster. The bad fox. The fanged weasel. Clever, hungry killers. 'I'm angry with myself.'

Impatient that, at the crucial moment, she should feel so weak, Prue wanted to say, So am I.

Nevertheless, if confronting the worst about yourself when you had hoped not necessarily for the best but for the average is to be done, it should be expected that it hurts. Prue swallowed. For the maximum damage limitation, she needed to be canny and wise, much wiser than before.

'Prue. Go and sit down. I can talk to you better from a distance.'

The past *was* a different country. How many times over the years had she and Max talked, sitting close to one another, often with his arm draped over her shoulders? How many times had he played with a strand of her hair, or wrapped his big fingers around her longer, finer ones while they debated this or that? Which car to buy. Which school for Jane. Which holiday to take. Countless.

And how many times had Prue cast herself on Max's

shoulder and wept over Violet, then the baby who came, and then the baby who never did, with fatigue, with frustration? And how many times had he comforted her, and she him? Many, many.

Life was made up of a series of losses – loss of confidence, faith, love, money, health, taut muscles, eyesight . . . Max had imagined that he had that knowledge safely under his control, and understood how to use it. From the opposite side of the room, he regarded his wife and knew that he had lost the will to remain silent.

Added to which, Max was aware that to anticipate is to control. 'That's your trouble,' Helen had bitten out during one of their disagreements. 'You won't let me breathe.'

'Stay there, Prue,' he said to reinforce the point.

Back in the sagging seat, she flinched at what was to come. Courage, she muttered to herself. Courage, courage.

Max cleared his throat. 'We *must* sort Jane out, Prue. The situation can no longer be ignored.'

'I agree.'

'Do you know why she is like this?'

'No.'

The silence that followed her denial was broken by the clink of keys of the gun-safe which Max tossed from one hand to the other.

'I think I know, Prue.'

Stop, she wanted to cry cravenly. Turn the clock back. I don't want anything to be said. Let's leave it at that point when the balance goes neither one way nor the other.

Clink went the keys.

'Are you . . . are you unhappy, Prue?'

Perhaps Max had meant to ask other questions outright but at the last minute, pulled back by caution or an understandable shrinking from pain, failed to do so. His expression was quite calm and no one, not even Prue, could have gauged what it hid.

As the one who had built and consolidated for as long as she could remember, Prue found herself cast as an agent of destruction: on a par with the vandal and the Stanley knife – or with Joan's men, who plundered the city of Orléans after her first great victory.

'To go back to Jane,' she said desperately. 'Puberty. And she's being teased.'

The keys disappeared inside Max's fist. 'I thought you would answer a direct question,' he said. 'You disappoint me.'

She sighed. 'Of course I'm happy.'

'You forget I have experience and I know the signs.'

'Yes,' said Prue bitterly. 'You do have experience and I'm sorry for it. I know I lag behind you in that. But, Max, I paid the dues. Helen and Violet were hung round my neck until I thought they would stifle me, and I could never get away from them. They've always been there in our marriage.'

As she spoke, a memory nagged at Prue of someone else saying the same thing.

'You never said.'

'I suppose there's a lot I've never said.' She moved slightly and the light played on her thinner face and accentuated the strain visible on it.

Of course. Jamie had told her once that Violet had accused him of hanging Lara round *her* neck.

'But you would not lie to me, Prue?' He knocked his fist gently against the wall. 'I wouldn't like to think that.'

'No, I wouldn't, Max. There's no reason.'

'So, there is no need for me to worry?' Max had got himself under control.

Her grey eyes met his blue ones. I understand perfectly

that the price is silence, was the message in hers, provided I do nothing to rock the family boat. So why are you asking me now?

Darling girl, take what I offer in the spirit it is meant. I understand better, far better, than you can imagine. But have pity, for it's tougher than I had imagined.

On such collusions do marriages draw their nourishment, grow and even bear fruit.

'No need is there, Prue?'

Prue took a deep breath . . .

At the beginning of May 1430 it was clear to anyone with strategic nous that the town of Compiègne would be besieged by the Burgundians, with backing from the English. Compiègne had remained loyal to France but its bridges were vital to any army wishing to dominate that area of the country known as the Île de France.

Joan, who had spent an uncomfortable nine months after the coronation hanging about the French court champing to get back into the field, rode out anxious to act as its saviour.

She was in Crépy-en-Valois where news reached her that Compiègne was finally under attack. Under the cover of night, Joan and a chosen few rode through the thick forest, harnesses jingling in the sleeping hush, their chargers' feet sinking into the soft forest floor and, without alerting the besiegers, entered the town during the hour of the false dawn.

'I'll ask you again,' said Max. 'There's no need for me to worry?'

Prue stared at him.

These were Joan's last moments of freedom and, Prue hoped, she spent them as she would have wished. The last time Joan felt the steady roll of her horse between her thighs, smelt leather, sweat, listened to the rapid exchanges between her men, looked up at a peaceful sky.

By five that afternoon, Joan was ready to attack. Mounted on a demi-charger, the lilies on her standard undulating in the wind, she rode out through the tender May evening with its long shadows, its scent of growing things and promise of heat to come, and charged the Burgundian camp.

The going was hard and, in the end, Joan's retreat back to Compiègne was cut off by a detachment of Burgundians and English. Pushed off the causeway into the boggy land by the river, Joan was seized by the floating panels of her scarlet and gold *huque* and dragged from her demi-charger.

She was taken . . .

Prue did what she thought best. 'No,' she said. 'There's no need to worry.'

Max stuffed trembling hands into his pockets.

The sight of those shaking hands brought a lump into Prue's throat. Joan had to suffer, had to yield her physical freedom, and so, without question, did Prue. Only in her case, Prue was lying and would carry the weight of her lie on her back, up hill and down dale, until her skin was bruised and torn and beaten – as a result of her daughter starving herself because she suspected something was wrong, and because her husband's hands were shaking with grief at the effort of sustaining a marriage.

'We must concentrate on Jane.'

'I am thinking of Jane.' Prue felt her heartbeat return to normal. Relief made her terse. 'I think of her most of the time.' She continued, 'I think we should keep her at home for the rest of the week and then send her back. Otherwise she will fret at missing what her friends are up to. In the holidays, I will help her make up some of the work.'

'The eating?'

'Worrying. But I've checked out her weight with Matron and she tells me she has not lost any till this last week. So I think she was eating more or less OK. Plus, she's growing fast ... Mrs Harriman did say that the girls had been talking about anorexia among themselves and one or two of them had been trying it on.'

'Dad?'

The door was pushed open to reveal the figure of their daughter in an old pink nightdress that she insisted on wearing even though Prue had bought her new ones. She was hugging her copy of *Goodnight Mr Tom*.

Max looked up with the softened expression he reserved for his women. 'Why aren't you in bed?'

Pale and huge-eyed, Jane advanced into the room. 'I was listening at the door,' she said, her mouth stretched in a smile that neither of them recognized on the face of their eleven-year-old daughter. It was a smile which belonged on an older face and with an older spirit.

'You naughty girl,' said Prue. 'Straight back to bed.'

She put her hand on Jane's shoulder. Jane fixed her with a look which combined hatred and yet love – betrayed love, Prue supposed – and shrugged herself out of Prue's grasp. The book fell open in her hands and a piece of thin cardboard fluttered to the floor. It fell with the painting face up.

Max picked it up. He looked at it, then turned it over. Prue felt the rushing and beating of her pulses build to a crescendo and, for a second or two, was in danger of fainting. Max looked up. Jane hovered by her father's chair, one leg bent behind the other in the attitude of innocence. A smile remarkable for its bitterness pulled at Max's mouth, but his eyes were damp.

It is true, said those eyes as he handed it over to Prue.

'Is that yours?'

The pulses shrieked in Prue's ears and wrists. You knew, said her eyes in return. She took the card and examined the serene, sinless Madonna. 'Oh,' she said. 'That's Kate's. I liked the picture, so she gave it to me.'

'What does it mean, Mum? What does it all *mean*? Why was Dad so sad?'

Prue was putting Jane to bed, removing the pile of computer magazines from the bed, brushing the fair hair and proffering a toothbrush in front of her daughter's nose. 'Funnily enough, grown-ups do get sad. One day,' she said, 'I will explain but not now.'

'Why not?' Jane mumbled through a mouth full of toothpaste.

'Because you are too young and you must accept that.'

'But who was the card from?'

'From an old boyfriend of Kate's, I think.' Prue watched Jane in the mirror. Jane rinsed her mouth and spat out quantities of toothpaste.

'Oh,' she said, and Prue relaxed a little.

When Jane was in bed and tucked in, Prue bent to kiss her. Her lips made contact with the sweet, fresh skin and lingered.

'But you see, Mum, it's frightening when I don't know about things,' Jane said out of the blue.

Prue sat down on the bed. 'I agree. But in good time. Till then, you must trust Dad and me.' She ran the edge of the sheet under her fingernails. 'Why did you take the card? It wasn't yours.'

Jane's eyelids masked her expression. 'I don't know,' she said. 'I just did.' She was silent. 'Why was it there, Mum?'

Downstairs in the drawing room, Max was sitting quietly

in his chair, his hands on either arm. A glass of whisky stood untouched on the floor by the armchair.

As she came back into the room, the twilight had been finally routed by the dark, and his figure was shrouded. She bent to turn on the table-lamp and went over to draw the curtains.

'Is she settled?'

Prue nodded.

'I love you, Prue.'

Unlike his wife, Max was used to solitude and suspected that, as in the past, it might be his portion in the future. He was well acquainted with it; it was his companion in life. Its prospect emptied the mind and cleansed the spirit and allowed the emotion and feeling to wash within the bone shell that housed his brain.

Life had to go on, and tranquillity was a luxury. Wars may lay waste, tornadoes lay waste, recession was laying waste, but, surely adultery lays waste far more lives than any of these.

'Have a glass of whisky,' he said, 'and we could watch the news.'

Prue thought her heart was in danger of breaking.

Chapter Twenty-Seven

Half-way back from Winchester on Saturday morning, Max remembered the gun.

It was due for collection from the gunsmith's where he had taken it for repairs. The repair had not really been necessary and guns were best left in their safes. Nevertheless, Max had taken it to the gunsmith.

With an exclamation of impatience, he guided the car into the centre of the road, checked that it was empty and made a U-turn.

The detour would make him late for lunch. Not that that mattered too much, except to Max who was hungry, for the house was in chaos on account of the Valours' annual pre-Christmas drinks party due to take place the next day.

The Becketts were also staying for the weekend.

'Do you want to go ahead with it?' Prue had broached the curious – and ominous – calm that suggested everything, but also nothing, which had settled over their home life. 'Shall we drop it for this year?'

'Why?' he had replied.

Because, Prue had begun to say, feeling much as Joan must have done as she kicked her heels at the French court, requiring the catharsis of some sort of battle, some point of engagement, some reference as to where one was. But Max cut her off.

'Then if you want the party,' she conceded, 'that's fine.'

If, thought Max, one reflected hard enough on events it

was possible to predict what was going to happen. How the same things, betrayal, disappointment, lack of love, greed, foolishness, repeat themselves in each generation, in each family, in each relationship. People grew used to their patterns, or they were born with a predisposition to them.

Max drove on. He needed time to rebuild the dignity he now perceived as more important at his stage of life than he had bargained on. *If* he was to survive, Max had to think of himself, and Prue must make allowances, as he had done for her.

With difficulty he located a parking place, for Winchester was crowded with shoppers (and garish with Christmas lights), and retrieved the gun.

'It's a beauty,' said the assistant, running his hand over the butt. 'Capable of doing big business. I see you take great care of it.'

'Yes, I do,' said Max. 'I do.'

It lay beside him in the car and, from time to time, he glanced down at the age-cracked leather case. He never used this gun on his shooting days. It had belonged to his father.

When people asked Max about the incident – and there were not many around to remember it now – he shrugged the question aside. At the time it had been newspaper fodder, and caused his family acute embarrassment.

What it was exactly that tipped his father over the edge Max had never been sure. Drink? The drip, drip of disappointment and frustration? A wish to make the day different from all the others stacked up on each other like old newspapers, and clumped into years.

Anyway, one morning in late spring, William had got up, eaten a hearty breakfast and then turned a gun on Max's mother whom he threatened to kill.

Of course, he did not. Instead, he had blown a small hole in Antonia's foot and a large one in the kitchen floor.

So much for the grand Wagnerian finale crescendoing to a terrible howling end with wind and storm that William craved. Instead it had been a muddled, not terribly bloody, incident in a suburban kitchen, the Tristram with a whisky-mottled face and the Iseult in flowered print overall. Between them the spoilt promise of the years.

Extraordinarily, prison life contented William and, on visiting days, he enquired with more interest after Max's affairs – exams, games – than he had ever shown previously. When he emerged, considerably less ruddy and stout than when he went in, he went to live in a remote cottage on the Ardnamurchan peninsula where he chopped wood and planted trees (having become something of a tree expert in prison) until he dropped dead of a heart attack. Max stayed with him often and they spent companionable evenings in the pub drinking the local malt and walking the hills above the glen.

Once the initial shock (and discomfort) had diminished, Antonia also flourished and spent the remainder of her life happily in Croydon with a spinster cousin. Accommodations, however bizarre, having been made with the general messiness of life, everyone, it appeared, was a great deal more content.

But Max never liked the gun.

'It's the Christmas season, all right,' said Max, forty-five years later, edging through the kitchen door at Hallet's Gate. 'The men are all demanding whisky. Either that, or the party is awful.'

The kitchen at Hallet's Gate was unrecognizable under a

sea of glasses, bottles and remains of the not-very-imaginative snacks, which Prue, in an uncharacteristic spirit of grudge and groan, had put together early that morning.

'Tough,' she said, wrestling with a tray of ice-cubes. 'I only bought one bottle. Make them drink the sherry. It's a good one and they should think themselves lucky.'

'Hallo,' said Kate brightly from the doorway. 'I haven't really talked to you yet.'

In honour of the occasion, Kate had progressed from Lycra leggings into a pleated wool skirt. She looked wholesome, straightforward and keen-eyed. The ice-cubes ejected out of the tray and shot over the sink. Prue made a grab for them.

'Take these, will you, Kate? I'm just coming.'

Kate was not in any hurry and lingered by the sink.

'Molly is having a go at Richard over the church cleaning rota,' she reported. 'Richard ain't too pleased.'

Prue had a distinct impression that Kate had levelled her radar at both her and Max with the aim of gathering as much information as possible.

'Will you see to the refills?' Prue turned to Max, and stopped herself adding her habitual 'darling'. She whipped open the oven and extracted prawn vol-au-vents. They looked overdone.

'Earn your keep,' she said to Kate. 'Open those packets of Kettle Chips, and dismantle the radar.'

Kate's eyebrows suggested outrage and innocence, and that she had no idea what Prue meant.

Prue flipped the oven gloves over her shoulder. 'If you must know, Max and I are going through a bit of a bad patch, in fact a bloody one, and I don't know how it's going to end. Somehow, the Valour party went ahead and I've got to get through it.' She smiled in a way that was new to Kate. 'Is that a good enough update for you?'

Kate looked like the woman who, having determined to

learn the worst, decides to stick to the Noddy version of life from now on. 'Oh, Prue,' she said with distress and some distaste. 'I'm sorry.'

Too late, Prue realized that Kate would rather not have known about her marital problems, and felt some sympathy with this ostrich position. Oh, well, she thought. What did I expect?

The drawing room had been denuded the day before of most of its furniture, and echoed slightly. The party had reached the half-way point between the stiff beginning and the we-must-go-home-the-joint-is-overcooking stage and the atmosphere had worked up into a fug of cigarette smoke and bodies meeting central heating. Prue's arrangement of red ribbon and fir cones (not her best) sat below a water-colour of a Highland scene. As she came into the room, Violet was pointing out the painting to a guest, a woman dressed in an outfit that shrieked Emporio Armani.

Molly pounced on Prue. Molly was not dressed in Emporio Armani. As a concession to the Valour party, she had unearthed a shirtwaister dress of the type Doris Day favoured in the fifties, plus sensible lace-up shoes.

'Where's Jane?' Molly cast a beady eye around the room.

She made Prue feel uncomfortable. 'She's over with Judy. The two of them decided the party was boring news,' she said.

She was glad when Richard, the vicar, bore down on them both, cherishing his empty glass rather obviously. Prue grabbed a bottle and filled it for him. God knew, Richard had little enough luxury in his life.

'Now you two are together,' he said gratefully, 'we can discuss the cleaning rota.'

Every sense aware that Jamie was standing only a couple of feet away, Prue refilled Molly's glass. Molly launched into a tirade and Prue knew that if she had any shreds of grace left, if her love for Jamie was to mean anything, she must concentrate.

You could not drop in and drop out of your life, however tempting, however badly the frenzy of sexual desire itches and frets, however secret your inner life, however far you had travelled.

'. . . dusting,' said Richard.

If the pew-polishing rota was the vehicle by which the collective life in Dainton was conducted, so be it.

'. . . dusting,' she said, watching Jamie out of the corner of her eye.

Over by the window, Emmy held out a cross, crumpled-looking Edward to his mother.

'Why on earth didn't you change him? He's smelly.'

'Sorry, Violet.'

Edward was suffering from a slight stomach upset (he would, thought his mother grimly). Violet's glossy head ducked in annoyance. She had taken to wearing lipstick of an even brighter scarlet, which suited her and which acted as a beacon, although that was not necessarily her intention, for if Violet craved attention, she did not wish to take it further than that. (She was merely copying the look of a very OK author interviewed in depth in *Vanity Fair*.) A couple of the older men at the party had brightened at Violet's entrance, and hovered hopefully.

'It's better to journey than to arrive.' Prue nudged Kate and indicated the hopefuls.

'I particularly wanted to show Edward off,' Violet whispered to Emmy at a level calculated not to be heard while her red lips smiled and glistened with – false – invitation. Bet you did, thought Emmy. 'I can't if he smells.'

Unaware of the exchange, Edward gazed out of the window at a couple walking their retriever who, as non-invitees, were pointedly not looking towards the window of

Hallet's Gate. At the sight of the dog, his face creased in a sudden, devastating smile and he bounced up and down on Emmy's shoulder.

'I'll change him,' said Jamie, materializing out of the group which contained Mrs Patterson, known as the Praying Mantis because she had presided over the deathbeds of three husbands, who had followed each other with staggering rapidity.

Edward was handed over and his father bore him off. Violet frowned in the direction of her hopeful cavaliers who backed off hastily, picked up a handful of dirty glasses and made for the kitchen. Emmy was left with a damp stain on her T-shirt, clutching a muslin nappy. Uneasy in the company, yet fascinated and just a tinge envious at the affluence in the room, she twisted the nappy between her fingers, knew she could never belong and wondered if she could make a bolt for home.

'Hallo,' said Max, waving the sherry bottle in her face. 'Would you like some?'

'No, thank you, Mr Valour.'

'Max,' he said.

He smiled his gentle smile which made Emmy, whose life for the last two months had been a compound of fear and a churning stomach, feel almost witty and beautiful and normal.

'Actually, I've been wanting to talk to you.' He placed the bottle carefully on the window sill and paused. 'I gather you're going to have a baby.'

Emmy felt a blush the colour of peonies mount her face, but there was no point in denying it.

'Have you decided what you will do?'

'Yes,' she said. 'No. I mean, yes.' She bit her lip and her peaky features were accentuated by her obvious agitation. 'I'm going to have the baby.' She paused. '*That*'s final.' Her fingers clutched the nappy. 'Mum can have me for a bit, I think. I can live off the social and then when the baby is older try and get a live-in nanny job with the baby. Some nannies get flats, you see.'

She made Max feel infinitely old. In his day, the social was somewhere you went for a good night out. He winced, too, for the trust that underlay Emmy's sad little plan.

'Don't fret,' he said suddenly, and his kindness made her want to cry. She looked up at him, and a strand of her hopeless hair lay against a cheek now so white that Max could swear no blood ever pulsed in it. As ever in situations like this (and Max had experience in dealing with pregnant women), his chivalry was stirred.

Acid was burning in Emmy's stomach and she longed for something starchy to mop it up. 'Mum's got to talk to Dad first. She's waiting for the right moment.'

'I've had an idea.' Max took Emmy completely by surprise. 'And I'd like to make a suggestion.'

It took a couple of seconds for Emmy to absorb what he said. Then her eyes widened and hardened with suspicion. You dirty old man, she thought, deeply disappointed. I thought *you* were straight.

Max understood. He took a step back until a space was between them. 'Don't worry, Emmy. This is perfectly above board. No question about that. I'll be in touch.'

Thoroughly bewildered, Emmy reckoned she could make a dash for it. Without a muted goodbye, she slid past Max and disappeared.

In the hall, she struggled into her inadequate jacket.

What will you do?

The answer was: I don't know, so stop asking me, everyone. Alongside the nag of *that* question was the ache and mystery of her love for Angus which she tried so hard to pretend did not exist – unlike his baby inside her.

Lady Truscott polished off her third glass and swayed, just a little, as she accepted a fourth. Smiling, Prue circulated and did her best to draw in a shy bachelor who appeared inextricably welded to the wall and debated introducing him to the Praying Mantis.

His nappy-changing duty completed, Jamie was back in the room and talking to Major Hutton. His attention remained fixed on the Major – except for once when he raised his eyes and met Prue's.

Prue moved in measured fashion around her guests offering vol-au-vents as if her heart was not beating to a wildly sexual rhythm, her conscience was as light as the flaky pastry and her home was not crumbling around her.

After Joan was taken by the Burgundians, her former friends and allies abandoned her. The King, her King, in particular did nothing, he for whom Joan had risked so much. (Jean Jouvenal des Ursins, a contemporary observer, was brave enough to reproach the sovereign for his unwillingness to help, unaware that detachment, especially in the face of danger, is considered a characteristic of the children of schizophrenics.)

Poor Joan. After capture, she grew so desperate and exhausted from constant questioning and prying that she threw herself from the tower at Beaurevoir, a leap of sixty to seventy feet. Astonishingly, she survived almost unscathed. She must have been very, very desperate, and she must have believed very hard.

Prue gazed out from the tower of Hallet's Gate on to the unyielding terrain below.

The last guest having been steered out of the door, the Becketts and the Valours sat down to eat bread, cheese and salami.

Max put down his knife with an expression, the careful, impassive, lawyer's expression that Prue knew well.

'I have some things I wish to discuss,' he said, 'and I might as well do it here.'

A hand grasped Prue's heart and closed, and she was not sure if it indicated fear, or a curious exultation that the worst could be about to happen. Oh, Mum, Jane had said, hadn't the Woman Taken in Adultery *wanted* to get into trouble?

Once upon a time, Max would never have broached a subject publicly without first consulting Prue. If her life equalled the reading of a book, Prue sensed she had reached the crisis or drama in the story where events cried out to be tied up. How perverse are the contradictions in human psychology which beg to be free and, yet, beg to be sorted into the correct pigeon-hole. Like the mail, Prue thought a little hysterically.

She had wanted and taken Jamie: she had wanted him badly and allowed the flames of that desire to lick and burn her body, as Joan's had been seared on the pyre. But, at the bottom of her only half-explored female soul, Prue expected to pay a price.

Prue, of course, was not alone in distrusting joy.

'This may surprise you . . .' Max did not seem agitated, 'but I will be living in London for the next six months or so in the company flat.'

Prue helped herself from a bowl of fruit salad. 'Max!'

'I'm going to be heading up the Brussels and Madrid offices, plus working to set up the additional European offices, and I feel the commuting is too tiring. Prue's staying here.'

Prue's spoon assumed a life of its own, and clattered back into the bowl. Apparently, she had misunderstood the bargain that had been struck.

She thought of Joan's Dauphin bowing out.

'I'll come home for some weekends, of course, if it's possible.'

Imperceptibly Jamie relaxed but Violet's mouth opened.

'What on earth are you going on about, Dad? Leave Prue for six months?' She gave Prue one of her examining-an-animal-behind-zoo-bars looks. 'Do you mind, Prue?'

'If that's what your father wishes to do.'

Prue's tone, and the rigidity of her body, alerted Violet that there was more to this announcement than lay on the surface. Violet's eyelids closed over eyes that were suddenly suspicious, and hid the calculations she was making. Then she looked up and the obstinate look had settled into place. 'Jamie,' she ordered her husband, 'tell Daddy this is a bad idea. Not only bad but unnecessary.' Jamie hesitated, and she tutted impatiently. 'For goodness' sake, Daddy, you've been commuting all your life. What's different?'

Max smiled at his daughter. 'There's no need to get upset, my darling.'

'You can't,' said Violet, and Prue could have sworn Violet was close to tears. 'It isn't good, and it isn't done. If we all went galloping off into the sunset every time we fancied a change, which is what I suspect this is, everything would collapse.'

Violet had no idea that she had hit the target.

Full marks, Violet. For common sense and for a certain courage. Reluctantly, then with a rush of admiration, Prue thus conceded to her old adversary.

'Darling,' said her father, 'you can't organize everything, much as you'd like to.'

'Think of Jane,' responded his daughter, who, over the years, had not made a practice of it herself.

Taken aback by Violet's late discovery of sisterly responsibilities, Prue picked up her spoon and chased a cherry-stone around her bowl. 'I don't think it's as dramatic as all that.' She assessed her husband. 'Is it, darling? You do have a lot of work with the commission.'

'The reason I'm discussing this with you,' Max continued, 'is that I will suggest to Emmy that after she leaves you she comes to me in the flat in London until she can sort herself out.'

With a noise that sounded suspiciously like a wail, Violet dropped her face into her hands. 'You've gone *mad*, Daddy. What will people think? You'll be accused of child molesting or something. Or they'll think the baby's yours.'

'She needs a helping hand and I will need a housekeeper.'

'For God's sake . . .' Violet raised her head and bunched up her napkin on which lipstick was imprinted in bloody rings. 'You have a wife.'

Lipstick, thought Prue, searching through the house-wifery manual kept in her head. How do you get it out? Paraffin? Petrol?

'Pregnant women are no trouble,' said Max, as if he had not heard. 'They're easy to look after. It's what comes afterwards that's the problem.'

For a couple of seconds, Prue was bewildered and thrown off the scent, and then she understood. Helen. In many ways, what had happened to Max, and to her, was the result of Helen and that story.

She, too, wanted to drop her head into her hands and wail. Instead, with a curious disappointment, she looked at her watch and said, 'It's time to pick Jane up from Kate's otherwise we'll be late for the carol service.'

*

St Mary's held its carol service earlier than most parishes. Otherwise, said the admirable and wise Richard, Christmas was an indigestible lump.

Once again, St Mary's had been decorated – over-decorated in the opinion of some – by Dainton's army of flower-arrangers (which this year did not include Prue). Swags of ivy hung from the pillars, snaked over the pulpit and lectern and wreathed anything that possessed a circumference and did not move.

The much-argued-about candles had been lit in their dozens and the effect *was* magical, both familiar and yet mysterious. The church smelt of hot wax and was spiced with evergreens. Every last seat was taken, and parishioners who could not face the trials of Series B and tub-thumping, hugging and kissing matins, which Richard insisted on for younger members of the parish, were there in force to store up their annual tally of grace.

Once-in-Royal-David's-Citying, the choir progressed up the aisle with Richard in tow, his expression serene. We must live and let live, it said. (Anyway, only a moment's reflection brought a forward-looking vicar to the conclusion that the majority of those who clung to the old ways would be dead quite soon.)

Violet had stayed behind at Hallet's Gate, declaring she needed a bit of peace or she would go mad, but Jamie had come. Most people live on the assumption that, however badly they have behaved, there remains a residue of forgiveness waiting to be granted them. Standing in the pew beside Jane, Jamie on the other side of her husband, Prue felt sick and shaky and, perhaps for the first time in her life, completely alone.

'What about Jane?' she had whispered to Max in the hall as they collected their coats. 'What about her?'

'I think about her more than anyone,' he had replied.

'Why didn't you talk to me first? In fact, we *must* talk, Max . . .'

It was then that Prue saw Max was crying. She wanted to tear her heart out of her chest in expiation and give it to him to do with as he wished.

'Max . . .' She tried to touch him, but Max put up his hand to shield his face and turned away.

The Angel Gabriel saluted the Virgin Mary and, via St Luke, gave her the news of her impending pregnancy, which Molly read out at gunfire pace. Clearly, she did not feel easy with the subject.

'Il est né, le divin enfant' intervened in Prue's thoughts. It was sung in a jolly fashion by the choir, and then St Luke took up the story again, read beautifully this time by Mrs Paulton who owned the village stores.

In the pause, as choir and congregation gathered for the assault on 'Adam lay y-bounden', Prue felt the candlelight lap her like a second skin, and its tongues of flame run through her body. She turned her head and looked at Jamie.

A hunger has woken in me, she thought, and it will be impossible to quiet it yet, for I am not yet old and dried up.

The high, clear voice of Jane beside her singing 'O Little Town of Bethlehem' made Prue screw up her eyes in pain. Where had her hunger led her?

'Do you believe you are in a state of grace?' was the trick question posed to Joan by Cauchon, her inquisitor at her trial. The question was so unfair that one of the other judges (who were there, after all, to condemn her) protested. But canny, passionate Joan knew that there are many answers to a question. Always.

'If I am not,' she said, 'may God put me in it, and if I am may God keep me in it.'

How did they take the reply, these men of God? Actually, not so much men of God as men of the Church, a distinction that should be noted. Further, they were men of the Church caught up in a civil war and those trying Joan in Rouen had chosen to work with the English and the Burgundians. To be fair, the Duke of Bedford and Philip the Good of Burgundy represented a decency and order that neither Joan's schizophrenically inclined Charles nor his cohorts could match.

Middle-aged, celibate, learned, these men were faced by a young, obstinate, extraordinary female who went to a great deal of trouble to hide her sex. They were men of peace. She was a woman of war. Her message was political – unheard-of for a woman. Boot the enemy out of France was Joan's cry. Further, she declared, she did not have to pay attention to those who sat in judgement on her unless God (through her voices) told her she must. In other words, Joan was not going to pay lip-service to the theological or ecclesiastical orthodoxy of the day.

You can imagine their horror, their bafflement, their fury that their authority and stature – the existing structures of Church and state – should be, thus, so undermined.

But when she was brought to face the court and the crowd at the cemetery of Saint-Ouen at Rouen at a stage in her trial when it was deemed it should be made public (remember, she had been in prison for over nine months and was weary from ceaseless questioning), Joan was placed at all times so that she could see a waiting cart and executioner. Unlike many martyrs, she did not seek out pain and had a healthy wariness of suffering. Perhaps the sight of that silent bringer of death was too much.

Joan recanted. She disavowed her voices, she renounced her male clothes, she submitted fully to the Church.

What agony she suffered as a result can only be conjectured, especially when she discovered she would not be set free. Her voices angrily informed Joan that she had committed a crime in confessing, and the rough English soldiers made her cell almost unbearable with their daily petty assaults. Joan was probably at the end of her tether when the more imaginative among them took away her woman's clothing so that she was forced to resume doublet and hose.

Once Joan had done this, the die was cast. Her determination returned with them and she was again ready for battle. Anyway, she would rather die, she told Cauchon, 'than endure longer my pain in prison'.

Then she informed him that it had been solely her fear of dying by fire which had made her sign the confession.

Nothing could have been more satisfactory to Cauchon, who desired only her death and, with those words, Joan had delivered up to him the disposition of her physical body.

She had also made a choice: to die. In the wrong done to her and the wrong she had done to herself by confessing, there had also been a rightness.

I was wrong, thought Prue of her own actions, but also right. In the bleakness there is also to be found healing, because there are many answers, because nothing is black and white and people need the grey as much as they need absolutes. I did not know that before.

At the end of the service – Prue swore she would never willingly sing 'Hark the Herald Angels' again – the congregation filed past the collection tray by the door into the cold, dark world. Prue put in five pounds, Jamie twenty.

'Buying your way into good grace,' she muttered at him.

'Correct,' he said. 'It's traditional at Christmas.'

After exchanging greetings, the congregation dispersed and groups, breath streaming into the cold air, walked briskly back to their homes. Max had gone ahead with Jane and Molly, and Prue tugged at Jamie's arm. 'Wait.'

He half turned, and she sensed at once how tense he was. 'Max has won, hasn't he?'

Their faces were barely discernible in the dark. Prue permitted her hand to linger on the smooth cashmere nap of his overcoat. 'No,' she said. 'Not Max entirely. But the whole thing. It is too much to ask of us all.'

'Hasn't Max decided to make the break? That's what I assumed.'

She stopped by the recent grave of Molly's sister and stared down at it. 'I don't know because I haven't talked to him about it.'

Jamie did not reply.

They walked past the other graves with their uneven headstones, their carvings obliterated by lichen, and plodded up the slope from the church to the lane above. The grass was slippery and treacherous. Prue tripped, and landed on her knee. Jamie waited until she had brushed herself down. Then he said, 'You mean it is over?'

Further down the lane, a large, shambling figure beside Molly came to a halt.

Chapter Twenty-Eight

Was television like life? Or life like television? Compare and contrast. The articles of the examination drill that Prue had learnt so well at the convent hammered in her brain.

Conditioned reflexes never die. They may lie down and sleep a little, but it takes only the lightest touch and they spring up again. Prue looked up at Jamie, felt the dust clogged under her fingernails, and compared and contrasted. No glossy television drama, no scriptwriter, no director could convey the impression that she was being cut into pieces, the rawness and anguish of her feelings, or the answering pain and desire on her lover's face. Neither would a director choose a backdrop of a sloping piece of grass slicked with dried mud.

The dialogue would not have passed muster. Neither Prue nor Jamie was capable of saying much, certainly not capable of articulating what this moment *felt* like or how they perceived the future without each other.

He licked his finger and scrubbed at her cheek. 'You've got a smudge.'

Prue submitted to his finger. 'Do you think Violet has any idea? It seems impossible that all this feeling is being expended and she hasn't sensed it.'

'No, I don't think she does.' Jamie considered Violet. 'That is her strength.'

'Don't ever tell her, will you, Jamie? Not even when you're old and grey.'

'That's my business,' he replied savagely.

'We don't all have to fall down.'

'*What?*'

'Ring-a-roses. Atishoo, and we all fall down.'

'I thought that was about the plague.'

'Exactly.'

Negotiating his way in the dark, Jamie sighed, full of regret, and aware that he was thoroughly netted. Not so much by his wife, but by being his age, a parent, and by who and what he was. Depression lowered a blanket over him.

'Won't you reconsider, Prue?' he asked abruptly.

She swallowed, and Jamie waited. Two or three seconds stretched out, and slipped into the past.

'No,' said Prue. She scrambled up the slope and into the lane, and contemplated a life once again simple and conducted on one level. 'I can't explain, but I know you know.'

At this point, Jamie probably understood less than Prue imagined, but it is one of love's delusions that each has exclusive access to the other's mind. This deceit, however, does nothing to lessen the pain.

'I didn't know how much it would hurt. That's all,' Jamie told Prue, frowning with the effort of talking sense.

Nothing he had said before had ever hurt Prue so much. Nevertheless, she managed a half-smile while she battled to put her life back on straight lines, to return it to the mundane where preoccupation with sausages, clean sheets, cat fleas and Hoover bags would help to blot out the radiant, shining, scented, achingly happy landscape that she had walked with Jamie.

'The others will be back by now and wanting supper,' she said.

Without warning, Jamie pulled Prue towards him. For a

couple of seconds, she allowed herself to lean against his shoulder and closed her eyes.

Swaying circles of light in the lane indicated the torches shone by returning parishioners. They dipped and swayed, an *aurora borealis* sweeping back to base for gin and sherry, comfortable in the knowledge that church had been done, some even having found nourishment in the service.

'I say,' said Molly to Max, 'shouldn't you go back and see what Prue's up to?' It was too dark for Max to see Molly's expression.

It was at that instant that Max stopped walking. 'I'll see you on Sunday, Molly.'

'Right,' she said and, shrugging her dreadful tweed coat more tightly around her, set off home where Keith was waiting for her to serve him yet another supper with cabbage.

Max's large shadow moved back along the patched and rutted surface of the lane, dipping in and out of the light directed by the wind ripping over from the ridge, which was sending clouds scudding across the moon.

Max was about to say, Are you coming Prue? when the words were stillborn.

In the freeze-frame, looping and spooling in slow motion, he watched his wife, who was outlined in the light from the church porch, climb the bank and lean towards his son-in-law. He saw, too, Jamie's hand touch his wife's cheek, and pull her to him. Then he understood.

Prue looked up from Jamie's shoulder, the rough fibres of the material rubbing her cheek and saw a large figure back away, then turn and run.

'Oh, my God, Max has seen us,' she said.

And with that, Prue pushed Jamie away and also ran, like

an animal, its hunting finished, streaks home like a bullet from a gun.

At the entrance to the drive, she skidded to a halt, her feet sending a spume of gravel across the grass verge. Something moved and the security light flooded the area. Then she froze. 'No, Max,' she said, her hand across her mouth. 'No, not that.'

For Max had materialized out of the darker patch of shadow where the car was parked. The gloom made him appear even bigger, his face more set and white than she had ever seen it. In his hands gleamed the polished barrel of his father's gun.

'Where did you get it?' asked Prue in a stupefied fashion.

'It was in the car,' said Max.

'But you *always* put the guns away.'

'I didn't this time, did I?'

'Get back, Prue,' said Jamie urgently from behind her. 'Get out of the way.'

But Prue was not listening. She took a step forward but Jamie's arm swept out and pushed her aside. The shock made her gasp and she stumbled.

'What are you doing, Max?' Her voice rang thinly in the night. The gun shone into her face.

Max loomed over his wife. 'I want to kill you,' he said calmly. 'Painfully and slowly.'

She scrabbled at the fluff in her coat pockets. 'Max, where's Jane? Tell me where Jane is.'

'I don't know. Inside I imagine.'

Husband and wife stared at each other. The guns. Those guns had been there all their married life, waiting to be used.

'Max,' Prue inflected her voice into that of a supplicant, 'please don't do anything silly.'

A second later, she thought, How funny that I never

realized the gun barrel was the colour of beech leaves in autumn. Another second elapsed, and she reflected: Max is going to kill someone. How will Jane cope with a murderer for a father?

'Put the gun away, Max.' Jamie sounded in control. 'It doesn't solve anything.'

'I know the truth now.' Max moved the barrel up to the level of Jamie's chest. 'The truth . . .'

'Yes,' said Jamie. 'And I'm sorry.'

'*That* makes it worse. At least, if you're going to fuck my wife you should be wholehearted about it. If you were going to betray my daughter—'

Max could not finish the sentence and took a gasping breath. Jamie was silent, and edged an inch or two across the gravel so that part of his body came between Max and Prue. 'I am. I was wholehearted. And this', he gestured at the gun, 'is not a resolution.'

'Shut up,' said Max.

Every movement the trio made appeared magnified, and so was the silence, broken by the shuffle of their feet, and their urgent whispered conversation.

How strange, and yet how not strange, thought Prue, grasping at straws. I thought we were so civilized. Then she remembered the wild hot lust and tumbled bodies, the urgings, pantings and satiations, the greed for more, the ruthlessness that went out and took it, and knew that, ultimately, no one was civilized. Why should Max and a gun be any different?

Max felt a darkness fogging his brain, the rage he had been hiding from himself for so long. For a lifetime. Slowly and patiently, he lifted the gun and pointed it at his wife.

'What's the pattern, Jamie? A quick foray and then off? Do you hang around to estimate the damage? Is that the form?'

'Believe me,' said Jamie, breath streaming into the night, 'I do not make a habit of it.'

'Max.' Suddenly Prue was furiously angry. 'You know that's not what you think. You know what's been happening and you sat on the sidelines. You *cannot* take issue now.'

He looked steadily at his wife. 'I never thought you were stupid before. Adulterous . . . maybe. A liar . . . of necessity. There are worse things. But *stupid*.'

'Oh, my God!' Prue understood. 'It's because of Violet, isn't it? Not me.'

She stretched out her arm. 'Max, my darling. Listen, listen to me—'

With a gasp of rage and pain, Max tightened his grip on his father's gun. 'Was it not enough that you had your freedom, Prue? I could take that. I could manage it, and understand. And cope. Just. But I can't forgive that you have transgressed against my daughter.'

'Max!'

'Was it some sort of revenge for having to take on Violet when you married me?'

He only married you for convenience.

I hate you, Prue.

'Max. Shooting me or Jamie is only a gesture. It won't erase what's happened. What happened, whatever the suffering, is worth more than just a gesture.'

Prue's teeth chattered uncontrollably and inwardly she wept with pity and grief. She was frightened, my God, she was frightened. Demons take up residence in the wronged, even in gentle, wounded giants like Max.

'Max,' she said, knowing now that it was she that Max wished to kill, not Jamie and, strangely, accepting it, 'would you like me to get down on my knees?'

Down she went on to the gravel, the sharp stones biting

her flesh like toothed animals. A St Joan of the shires. Penitent, but hungry. Awoken but grieving.

Sensing that this exchange between a husband and wife excluded him, Jamie remained motionless where he was. He found he could not bear the sight of the figure kneeling in the drive and he turned his head away.

'You threatened Violet's happiness, Prue. That is your greatest sin against me.'

'Is it? Are you sure?'

Prue would never understand fully the complicities of her marriage, and terror blunted her responses.

'To harm my daughters is to harm me,' said Max heavily. 'How could you think so little of it?'

The wind was rising. A dead, cold smell of winter blew in with it, and the silence of suspended life settled around the group in the drive. Prue's knees ached and stung and the shapes under them indented her flesh, but no less punishingly than Max's words stung and wounded.

Somehow, in the dark woods and ravines of blindness and folly, reason, humour and wisdom *had* to be found. Prue got to her feet.

'You must understand, Max, it did not seem like that,' she said, savouring (for the last time?) the beat of passion for Jamie deep in her body. 'When you're in prison, it's difficult to care about the jailer. No, I don't mean it like that. But you must appreciate that I saw it from a different angle.' Prue took a deep breath. 'If you kill me, Jane will suffer.'

Jamie's eyes suddenly narrowed as he saw that Max's aim had slackened.

Prue raised her arms in a gesture asking for forgiveness. 'The awful thing is, Max . . . that it doesn't have anything to do with you, or with Jane. It was to do with me, that's all.' She pointed towards the gun. 'Max, please let me have it.'

With a cry of pain, rage and release, Max raised the barrel, aimed and squeezed the trigger – and shot the sky.

The report ripped apart the silence and travelled through the village. Prue imagined she felt the air part above her fingertips and the passage of hot metal. Her hands dropped to her sides.

Edward began to cry inside the house and the curtains at Jane's bedroom window were ripped apart. The back door was wrenched open and Violet peered out.

'What on earth . . . ?'

Then the telephone rang.

Behind Prue, Jamie tensed, leapt forward, and took the gun from Max. The muscles in both men's jawlines were rigid – the still-young versus the ageing. Sweat sprang out on Jamie's forehead.

'Don't worry, Violet,' he called out. 'The gun went off by mistake as Max was bringing it in from the car. Tell Jane not to worry.'

'How stupid of you, Dad.' Violet disappeared to answer the phone.

'I'm sorry, Max,' Jamie said. 'For all the reasons in the world.'

With a little cry, Prue snatched the gun from Jamie and cradled it awkwardly to her chest. 'Sorry, I'm so sorry,' she whispered to it.

A minute dragged by as the three remained, frozen and unmoving. Then, together, they entered the house.

'That was Molly,' Violet said as they entered the kitchen. 'For some reason she wanted to know if you were all all right. Since you could have blown us all to pieces, I said it was lucky that she was keeping an eye on us. Then the vicar rang to enquire what the shot was.'

'Hot chocolate, anyone?' asked Prue. 'I'm going to make some for Jane.'

'Yes, please,' said Jamie, and caught Prue's eye. Hot milk, passion and a threat of death, was the message it conveyed. How does that strike you?

It struck her as absurd, comic and profoundly truthful. 'I'll take Jane's up,' she said.

She shrugged off her coat and went into the study to put away the gun. The patina on the barrel gleamed at her, expensive and cared-for. She touched it with her fingertip and then locked it away.

When she returned, Violet and the two men were sitting at the table discussing the stock-market. She joined them, cradling her mug loosely between her hands.

It was in the sum of existence that stock-markets and clean socks could not be denied their place, and that love, sex and passion had to be given theirs. But if that was true, which the tableau around the kitchen table appeared to confirm, neither was it deniable that in between the interstices of life's little infrastructures (shopping, cooking, getting pensions) flourished deep-rooted and tenacious emotions that sometimes erupted into violence and bloodshed. Then they disappeared.

Sometimes an irony lurked at the heart of these flaring eruptions. For Violet, who had done so much to cause trouble, was the reason – the reason, at any rate, to which they clung in the carnage – that the three remained sitting round the table and kept silent, and would continue to do so.

Jamie drained his mug, a freebie from a petrol station that Jane had insisted on collecting, and got to his feet. He gestured towards the empty mug. 'Thank you . . .' he said, and for one farcical moment, Prue thought he was going to thank Max for not killing him. Violet stretched and pushed her mug towards Prue, which the latter took to mean she should wash it up.

'I'm going to have a bath,' she said.

How unprivate Prue's love affair had been. How impossible it was for it to exist as an island. Falling in love with a man other than your husband was a public exercise, and she had lacked the perception, or experience, to realize this.

'I won't be staying.' Jamie tapped the mug, which gave off an echo. 'I'll square it with Violet. Fabricate a work crisis.'

Max did not look at Jamie. 'I want you gone,' he said, and now he did not sound at all civilized.

Jamie appeared to approve Max's attitude. 'I'll go back by train in the morning. Violet can drive herself up later in the evening.'

'Right,' said Max.

And that was that.

Violet insisted that, even if her stupid husband was insisting on working through their well-earned, statutory weekend, she was not. She wished to be with her family.

In fact, Violet did not relish the idea of a Sunday on her own with Edward in London.

'Look, Daddy,' she said, bending over Max who was sitting by the drawing-room fire after breakfast. 'This is our pre-Christmas get-together. If Jamie wants to abandon his family, so be it. I'm staying put.'

Prue, who was writing yet more lists at the desk, fingered the silver paper knife and stared into the omnipresent photograph of Helen. Helen who had run away from her daughter. You launched more than a thousand ships, you witch, she informed the image, with a shiver of knowledge that left her cold, but at least you were honest. Yet if Helen had introduced the dogs of war into the family, it was Prue who had let them loose.

For the ten-thousandth time, Helen's glistening beauty accosted Prue but, for the first time, Prue acknowledged complicity.

The patter of pine needles falling from the Christmas tree interrupted the silence. The movement caused one of the silver balls to rotate, catching the light.

Max reached up and grasped Violet's hand. 'Whatever you wish, my darling.'

'Right,' said Violet. 'We'll dispatch Jamie to his London vastness and we'll make ourselves comfortable. In some ways, it's easier without him.' She thought for a moment. 'You know what, Dad, I just might stay until Monday morning.'

She slipped her arm around Max's neck and rested her cheek on the top of his head.

Thus it was that Prue found herself delivering Jamie to Winchester because Violet wanted to watch the cookery programme *Gourmet Dieting*.

'You can drop Jamie off anywhere, actually, providing there's a station.' Violet made him sound like dry-cleaning. Max said nothing, but Prue suspected he was allowing her to say goodbye in private. Max had always been generous.

It was a cold, raw morning and the wind whistled up the line, bringing the sting of salt, smut and sewage from the coast. The tiny waiting room on the platform was stuffy and smelt of gas fire. A couple of women in sensible shoes were discussing their planned assault on Christmas shopping. They glanced at the intruders and their conversation broke off. By mutual consent, Prue and Jamie retreated outside. Here, the damp and rawness stung their exposed skin.

'*Annus horribilis.*' Jamie addressed the foot passenger bridge. 'Is that what it's been, Prue?'

Prue managed a joke. 'At least we haven't been photographed sucking toes.'

They were silent. She dug her hands into her pocket. 'Where next, Jamie?'

'I thought it was goodbye. In one sense, anyway.'

'For you, I mean.'

'Abroad,' he said, with a little shrug of his shoulders. 'I think I can arrange the old job back in New York.'

'Violet?'

'She'll be pleased.'

The future stretched out, for the moment flat and dispiriting, a jigsaw puzzle into which the pieces still had to be fitted. Jamie paced away up the platform, then he stopped and returned to where she stood and put both hands on her shoulders.

'Prue. Darling Prue. I'll ask once more. Come with me.'

She stared into the face she loved so desperately, alarmed and unnerved by her desire to say yes. The price of her love for him had been her sense of wholeness, of belonging to the garden of Eden. But whatever the discord of the lost harmonies and innocence, it had been worth it. It had to be, otherwise all the mess and pain caused to others would have been for nothing.

The train came into sight, a steadily enlarging dot on its front plate registering like a borehole on Prue's vision. With a hiss of wheels on the rails, it drew into the station. Doors clicked open and shut with a hollow sound. A couple of voices rose above the noise, shouting instructions to one another. Passengers went in an untidy stream towards the ticket barrier.

Prue rubbed her fingers together, feeling the roughened texture from too much washing-up without rubber gloves.

'Prue?' Jamie questioned, his hands heavy on her shoulders.

'It's impossible.'

'It's perfectly possible.'

In the end, I would not have wanted not to have been buffeted, she thought – the sheet fluttering on the washing line, bouncing and whipping in the wind. Even though the end of this is going to half kill me. I have been fortunate in journeying beyond Monday to Friday.

Faith? Prue possessed only the form, not the substance. Belief in marriage? Yes ... and no. A sceptic's view of passion? Never.

'The real reason,' Jamie prompted.

'Jane is the reason.' She smiled into the face of her lover. 'And Edward.'

'Are they the only reason?'

'They are quite good enough,' she replied, 'but no.'

She had been searching through sleepless nights and the fret of sexual frustration, and longing for the formulation which had, so far, eluded her.

Weeping copiously, Joan went out to her death wearing a black shirt, and a kerchief on her head. Nailed to the stake was a board which said:

Joan, who had herself called the Maid, a liar, pernicious deceiver of the people, sorceress, superstitious, blasphemer of God, defamer of the faith of Jesus Christ, boastful, idolatrous, cruel, dissolute, invoker of demons, apostate, schismatic and heretic.

Such a small sign to carry so much invective – and wasted on nine out of ten of the waiting crowd who could not read.

And as if this panoply was not enough, the sermon directed at a frightened, weeping girl waiting for the fire to strip the flesh from her bones took as its text a quotation from the First Epistle to the Corinthians: 'Whether one member suffer, all the members suffer with it.'

Joan was then formally cast out by the Church and handed over to the secular authorities to finish off. Then she was crowned with a mitre. 'Heretic, relapsed, apostate, idolater.'

They must have been very frightened of Joan, all those men, and of her power to change things.

Perhaps the key lay among the puzzle of Joan's death. Because the scaffold had been built so high, she had taken a long time to die, longer than necessary, because the executioner had been unable to climb up and strangle her, as was the custom. She would not have been aware of that little detail when she threw back her recantation in Cauchon's face and, thus, gave her enemies everything they needed to structure the careful wall of faggots and wood.

Nevertheless, Joan had made her death her own decision.

Prue's decision was also her own. She spoke slowly, fighting to find the correct words. 'If I give up the marriage, it will have been for no good reason,' she said. 'There is no reason not to see it through. It's the same for you, Jamie. There is no reason to abandon Edward and Violet, and every reason to stay.'

To his credit, and this was one of the many things for which she loved him so passionately, Jamie saw the point.

'My darling Prue.' His hands dropped from her shoulders and he bent to pick up his bag. He stood upright. 'I did try.'

'Yes, you did,' she agreed.

When the train had become a dot on the horizon, Prue finally quitted the platform. She walked over the passenger bridge, through the ticket barrier and out into the station car park. She sat there, surrounded by cars belonging to day-trippers. A man also sat on one of the benches, holding his poodle as carefully and tenderly as if it was a child. Every so often, he bent and whispered into the dog's ear and the dog raised his face and butted his master's cheek. Prue tried squeezing her eyes to see if it hurt less. Then she dug her nails into her palms so hard that they left red crescents. The corresponding pain made absolutely no impression on what she felt inside. The homeopathic approach did not work.

She started up the engine of the car and drove home.

It came as something of a shock to Jamie staring at the newspaper in the train that he was probably suffering more than Prue. It is, of course, always easier to take decisions than to have them imposed; that is why men insist on being the decision-makers.

The landscape was transmogrifying into suburbia, and the variety and colours of heaped and abandoned plastic toys in the back gardens stretching down to the line struck Jamie, and he wondered if his mind was similar – cluttered with soiled, greyish detritus that had once given the illusion of being inviting.

Had he really meant to leave Violet and his son? *What if this happens again?* also flashed across his mind.

Is this the pattern?

The train drew into Clapham Junction. Jamie looked without interest at the station sign, picked up his bag and stepped down on to the platform. The station had recently been tarted up with British Rail paraphernalia. Even so, it exuded a lost feeling and the litter rattled in the December wind.

He ducked down into the underpass.

As he made his way home, Jamie planned tactics and the

strategy for the job in New York that he had already discussed with his boss. His bag grew heavy and he shifted it from one hand to the other and lengthened his stride.

The morning wore out over London.

In Hallet's Gate, Violet fastened Edward into his travelling high chair and surveyed the lunch laid out on the table.

'I'm glad Jamie's out of the way,' she said, 'because I want to talk to you about this London business.'

Max helped himself to ham, salad and a baked potato and sent a wintry smile in the direction of his daughter. Prue sat down beside him. Not now Violet, she thought wearily. It was one thing to make life-turning decisions and to choose what was right, or at least best; it was quite another to be lectured.

Violet returned to a favoured theme. 'Daddy, there is such a thing as the *male* menopause.'

Red stained Max's face and his fork stopped half-way to his mouth.

'It happens all the time. Middle-aged men get restless and do all sorts of funny things. But it's hormones, nothing more. They'll soon settle down.' Violet turned in her chair to pinion Prue. 'Aren't I right? When you get older you mourn your lost youth.'

In all the battles and uneasy peaces that had attended their relationship, Prue had never once imagined that Violet would end up defending her position.

'So they say,' she managed to get out.

Violet pressed on. 'It's worse for women because they lose their looks, isn't it, Prue?'

Prue felt unable to comment.

'There,' said Violet with some satisfaction. 'She does understand.'

'Darling,' said Max. 'I do think you have to be careful with your advice. You can't always be sure what you're talking about.'

Violet dropped back against her chair. 'But I am, darling Pa. I've read about it in a lot of places. You really mustn't go shacking up with young girls, however innocently. It gives one a bad name. You can't have Emmy living with you.' Having grasped a line of attack, Violet was, as ever, reluctant to relinquish it. She added as the *coup de grâce*, 'Think of Jane.'

Max and Prue found themselves looking at each other, their shared thought passing silently between them, as the warp and the weft shares the thread in the cloth. Indeed, there was a price for ensuring the well-being of children.

Chapter Twenty-Nine

Emmy had been brooding all weekend over the letter she had been sent the previous week.

> You might think it odd that I am writing to you, but I ask you to read this letter before making up your mind whether to ignore it or not.

A lawyer to the last, Max's formality was accentuated in his correspondence.

> As I mentioned last time I saw you, I have been thinking about your position. I am writing this on the assumption that you will be bringing the baby up on your own. (Please forgive me if I have got this wrong.)
>
> I will be living in London during the next few months, possibly longer. I know that Violet feels that it is difficult for you to continue with your job with them, especially when you have the baby. This, I imagine, leaves you with a problem and I would like to suggest a solution. I am offering you the post of housekeeper. Duties would be minimal – to cook and clean and shop. *Nothing* else is required. I am suggesting this because I think it might be of use to you, and I would like to think that you and your baby would have a roof over your heads.

Emmy reread the letter – written on Max's high white laid paper – and looked out of the kitchen window of Number 5 Hallet's Lane. It was very much the same view that could be seen out of the kitchen of Hallet's Gate, but the eyes and mind processing the visual information thus received assessed things differently. However, after a year of living with the Becketts, Emmy had seen enough to know that the general messiness of life applies at all levels.

Her father was in the pub, well on the way, no doubt, to oblivion, and her mother had caught the Ride'n'Shop Christmas Saturday Special bus into Salisbury. A faint smell of disinfectant overlaid by the sicklier one of ceramic hob cleaner assaulted her queasy stomach. Powered by a crystal battery, the clock stared down at her from a wall that glistened with endless applications of cream cleanser. It did nothing so old-fashioned as to tick.

Tick, tock, Emmy.

Whatever she did, whatever happened, Emmy decided that the first thing she would do was to buy a clock with a proper tick.

In the midst of the muddle in which she found herself, someone had bothered to stretch out a hand to help. To help her, witless, ugly Emmy, who had fallen into the oldest trap of them all. Max's gesture touched a healing finger to the abraded areas of her spirit.

The view outside failed to provide any definitive answers, and she dropped her head into her hands, pressing them against her eyelids. Angus threaded his way through the dancing circles and blobs of light. He did not look happy and Emmy, no saint, felt better.

*

Mrs Horton shrugged her shoulders. It was not a gesture designed to give reassurance and Emmy took none. 'Your dad's livid,' she said. 'And doesn't want you here.'

Emmy was not surprised. 'Don't worry. I won't bother you.' Inside, her guts heaved with dread and panic.

'Why on earth did you have to go and fall?' Mrs Horton attacked the microwave with a specially impregnated cloth and rubbed vigorously. Emmy pictured the war between loyalty to her daughter and loyalty to her husband being waged behind the frosted perm, and was rendered speechless when her mother announced that Emmy was a chip off the old block because she had married her dad for the same reason.

Emmy reached for a chair and sat down. 'You *never* said, Mum.'

It was only when, later that evening, she lay sleepless on nylon sheets so clean that they emitted sparks every time she moved that Emmy asked, Why don't you bloody help me, then?

Consequently, the idea of a roof over her head, a place for the baby, help and support, grew rosier. She pictured putting the baby to sleep in a freshly painted room in which hung a dancing mobile of grey and red elephants like the ones she had seen in Mothercare. She pictured, too, sitting at a kitchen table eating soup and fresh bread, with the radio playing.

These were stubborn, hard-to-ignore images, and they featured Emmy alone.

Emmy had no feminist axe to grind, or any views on the absolute necessity of looking after yourself which allowed her a degree of flexibility and willingness to contemplate surprising courses of action. Lucky Emmy.

I could make myself live with Mr Valour, she informed

the darkness. It's easy, really. Just for a little while. Until I'm on my feet. Then me and the baby will bugger off.

She regretted the element of self-serving in her plans, but it could not be helped for she understood intuitively that being on your own did not guarantee liberty – rather the opposite. It took away the freedom to be soft and generous.

The bedroom was chilly and Emmy's lips felt dry. She heard a scuffle outside in the garden. A fox? A rat up from the river? She pictured the latter trotting, head down, from its damp moss-licked mud-hole to the frost-scented, hollow pile of leaves under the beech, its feet leaving the imprints of curtain hooks on the lawn.

Did she have to be alone?

Towards dawn, Emmy got up and stood, shivering, by the window, still fogged with night vision. Soon, the missel-thrushes would be waking, shaking out their white under-wings and pale wingtips. Soon, they would signal the new day in harsh, rattling chatter and set about the business of finding a slug, a snail, a berry. After the breeding season, missel-thrushes often fed together in family groups.

Dix points the missel-thrush. *Nul points* humans.

It would not be so bad living at close quarters with someone you did not care for. After all, Emmy claimed experience in non-affectionate co-habitation. Her parents had done it for years.

She washed, brushed her obstinate hair into some kind of shape and put on her black leggings. Black and white were magpie colours. Apt for someone who was about to occupy someone else's husband's nest.

She trod stealthily down the stairs to the kitchen – anything to avoid her father and his temper this morning. Two spoonfuls into the Frosties and her stomach rebelled. Her knees went odd, too. She bet she'd been right about what was up with that nice Mrs Valour and Mr Valour. She just knew something was wrong. Mind you, Madam and her husband were not exactly a pattern for the young and in-love. At least, she still had the energy and interest to be curious. That was something.

All day Emmy hovered by the telephone, notting. That is, not picking it up, and wasting considerable time and energy in not doing so. Yes, please, she *could* say to Max. I'll come and be housekeeper. I'll have the baby in Winchester, stay with me mum for a bit and then I'll come. That would be very nice, he would say, and puts my mind at rest.

Emmy recollected the thick carpet, the dry-cleaned curtains and pretty china of Hallet's Gate. She smelt the drift of pot-pourri and the expensive beeswax polish Mrs Valour favoured. Was she selling her baby for a brand of furniture polish? Her soul for a bowl of rose petals and a cushion with tassels?

For in her heart, Emmy did not *quite* believe that the housekeeping bit would remain so.

And what of Angus, wherever he was? Did he ever think of her as he stripped the knickers from the Sals and Cherrys and buried his body in theirs? Did he remember their secrets, the jokes, the whisper of breath over their passion, the drift of hair on a pillow and a shared thought?

Emmy did, but also hugged the knowledge that memory was a mist: it distorted the shapes of objects, and concealed hazards.

Just before he had left the house in Austen Road that last time, Angus had turned back, boots dangling from his scarred, tough-skinned hand.

'I never thought you'd be frightened, Em,' he said. 'I thought you were made of strong stuff.'

'I'm not,' she had told him. 'I don't want risks.'

What was she doing now if she wasn't taking a risk? And

how much more, silly cow that she was, would she prefer to be taking the risk with Angus?

Seventy pounds a week *in hand* from Mr Valour. Tax and insurance paid (unlike his daughter who had not got round to it). It meant she would not be able to go on the social once she had started, but the deal was a good one.

Emmy did what she always did when she felt trapped and went out. Christmas trees shone red and green pinpoints, mixed with dazzling white, from windows on to a day that was not going to bother over much about getting light. Emmy looked up. The huge beeches that dominated this end of the village were still, frozen into dormancy.

The village and its occupants appeared to Emmy's fevered, bothered mind to be waiting. For what? Christmas? For the recession to end? For more optimistic times?

She trudged on, her life wedged awkwardly in the lap of others. Someone else's house, someone else's husband to look after.

The light at the top of the rise was dull and flat, the land dripped brackish water and the puddles were frozen around their edges. Was she still capable of discerning the beating life in the woods and under the hedgerows from which she derived so much pleasure, which she needed to exist as she needed the glass of pure, cold water? Was that also suspended, and driven underground so that she could not find it? Suddenly, Emmy found herself clinging to the gatepost into Oven's field and sobbing.

Emmy dialled Cherry's phone number and a woman answered. Her voice was familiar.

'Is that Sal?' Emmy asked, surprised.

'Yeah.' She did not sound friendly.

'This is Emmy. Remember? Do you know where Angus is?' And why aren't you in the country? she wanted to add.

The voice hardened further. 'Since you ask, I haven't seen the bugger for weeks, which is typical.'

Emmy swallowed, paused and made the hardest request of her life. 'Do you know where I can get hold of him?'

'What's it to you?'

Emmy licked her lips. 'Plenty.'

Boredom, disenchantment or perhaps a spirit of mischief overcame Sal's reluctance. She gave Emmy the number and, in a rare moment of feminine solidarity, offered the following advice. 'He'll always have his hand up a skirt, you silly idiot. Do you want that?'

No, Emmy did not. Neither, judging from her tone, did Sal, after all. Well, well. On balance, there were worse things. Lack of understanding. An ultra-clean kitchen and a bare heart. The mess and suffering of Angus and his women terrified her, but she had learnt that terror was portable and life was composed of a series of loads ... the basket of shopping into which purchases were chucked, heavy breasts – not that she had any idea of those, not yet anyway – the overdraft weighed down by failure to deal with it.

Thirty seconds later, she dialled the number.

'Can I speak to Angus, please?'

'Who is it?' asked a bruising sort of voice.

'Tell him Emmy.'

She heard the echo as Angus's name was shouted through the house. It took some time before anyone came to the phone, and her mother's colourful china plate beamed down on a shaking Emmy.

'Who is it?'

'Emmy.'

'Hell. Are you all right?'

Emmy found that her throat was blocked and her eyes were streaming. 'Of course.'

There was a silence. Clearly Angus was not going to be cracked easily and Emmy realized she had been stupid. She could not ring Angus up, coolly inform him that she had changed her mind, and then reveal her little bundle of news. You cannot declare the war over and then drop nuclear tonnage when signing the peace treaty.

'Are you going to say anything, then?' Angus sounded frighteningly cold and distant.

'No. Yes. No.' Emmy's voice did not sound right either.

Angus softened. 'You *are* OK?'

'Yes. It's nothing. Forget this.'

'Where are you?'

'At Mum's. I'm staying till Monday morning. Look, Angus, it's all right. I'm fine. Bye.'

The receiver was back in its cradle and she was left to stare at it and the pad beside it which, for some reason, was disguised as a liquorice allsort. Emmy pressed a hand to her stomach. It's you and me, she thought. You and me. Us.

After their tea, Mrs Horton sallied out to an underwear-selling party. Her father was sleeping off the day in his bedroom. In desperation, Emmy turned on the television. The script-writer on *Casualty* had decided that a stomach haemorrhage was highly entertaining. Shackled to the sofa by repulsion, Emmy watched for a few minutes and then turned it off, just as the luckless doctor and the wall were being artistically splattered by an actor who, to his credit, looked as though he could wring the script-writer's neck. If that was entertainment, then Emmy was beautiful.

She went to bed and slept.

Up at seven o'clock, she went through the routine. Teeth.

Hair. Leggings. T-shirt. Since she was feeling masochistic, Emmy stared at herself in the diamond-bright bathroom mirror. The sight was not reassuring. On impulse, she reached for a relegated bottle of Charlie and dabbed some behind her ears and on her wrists. Too late, she forgot that scent made her feel sick.

A noise like a wounded aircraft coming in to land advanced up the lane and, bottle in hand, she froze. It brought back the days when Angus flew down the lane on his gleaming machine and swept her away, a knight on a bike, smelling of sump oil.

Her sadness and loss made her throat swell and she watched in the mirror as tears dammed in her eyes and slid on to her cheeks.

Look at me, jeered the image. That's all you've got, Emmy.

So absorbed was Emmy by this touching vision of tragedy that she did not, at first, take on board that the noise had stopped. By the house, in fact. The gate banged shut, and someone squelched up the path.

Only one person did that.

Emmy screwed the top back on to the scent bottle and put it with extreme care in its place on the shelf. Pregnant women were known to have funny ideas – think of the stories of them eating coal, or longing for exotic foods.

Someone thumped on the door and her father bawled, 'Go to hell.'

Emmy went down the stairs and opened the front door. There, looking cross and tired, stood Angus. Emmy's hand flew to her mouth.

'What . . . ?'

Angus yanked her outside on to the concrete doorstep. 'I've come to find out what's going on.'

Emmy began to shiver from cold and excitement, the

smell from the scent making her nausea rise in retch-making waves.

'Well?'

There are times when defences drop and, an inadequate garden fence in the wind, Emmy's fell with a crash.

'Oh, Angus, help me.'

He watched her for a moment or two, long enough for Emmy to grow really frightened. Then he said, 'What do you think I'm here for, you silly cow? So. What is it?'

She lifted her pale, tear-stained face to him and her lips formed the words, but nothing emerged. Instead, she laid her hands on her stomach. Angus's eyes travelled down Emmy's body and came to rest on the bunched fists.

'Oh, Emmy,' he said, enlightenment percolating slowly into his brain. 'You would.'

'Shut the door,' Mr Horton roared from the top of the stairs.

Angus cocked his head. '*Are you coming with me this time?*'

This time, Emmy did not hesitate. She pulled the front door shut and said, 'I'm here.'

'*Good* girl.'

She followed him down the path and through the squeaking gate. Angus rummaged in his carrier and chucked her a pair of leathers and the spare helmet. Emmy caught them with both hands.

She imagined the comments – the sort she had learned while living with the Valours – being uttered behind the doors of Dainton's houses and cottages as they passed with an ear-splitting noise emitting from the bike's engines. Yobs. Selfish. Should be shot.

Hallet's Gate and its damp, heating compost heap peeled away to their left.

It was a nice idea, Mr Valour. I'm sorry. I would have done my best. I *would* have done my best.

A few cars were straggling out of the drives, driven by men in shirt-sleeves, the white bloom of their aftershave still overlaying their complexions. As usual, the traffic on to the main road had clogged to a standstill, apart from pin-striped cyclists in trouser-clips, who sailed past. A bus drew up at the stop by the junction and a couple of girls in short Lycra skirts, Doc Marten's and permed hair shining with moisture got on.

Emmy was shivering uncontrollably. She tugged at Angus's back. 'I'm going to die of cold.'

'We'll stop at the services.'

Andover now lay behind them and Emmy sang a farewell to the town she knew best. In the market place, stalls – pink polythene mushrooms – would be springing up, and those in trouble and on the dole would begin their creeping progress in search of bargains.

Good oxtail there, and cheese, Emmy told them silently. Rabbits are cheap, too.

The doors to the precinct would be reset for their daily open/shut performance, and synthetic aromas would waft from the shops specializing in potions and knick-knackery. How do they make a living?

An assistant would paste up another 'Special Pre-Christmas Sale' sign on the china and electric store, and the butcher would assemble shrink-wrapped chicken thighs, ham, and mince the colour of terracotta. Barclays Bank would continue to shine its hideous turquoise signs into the arena, a reminder that shopping and money were as linked as peaches and cream, love and marriage.

She and Angus?

Goodbye, said Emmy, heart thumping, teeth chattering, baby fluttering.

Angus rode up to the Fleet services as if Hell's Angels were on his tail. He stopped the bike and helped Emmy, frozen into a state resembling *rigor mortis*, on to the ground. Her knees buckled and he grabbed her.

'Tea,' he said. 'Egg and chips.'

'Can't wait,' said Emmy.

The Muzak was hard at work in the restaurant, which was already fugged with steam and cigarette smoke. Angus steered Emmy past the smokers and settled her by the window.

'I'll get you the best breakfast of your life. Trust me, Em.'

That was it. Emmy must wait and trust. Trust, even though it was a risk. *Precisely* because it was a risk.

Half dreaming, she closed her eyes. Then she opened them to watch as Angus balanced a loaded tray in one hand and two bottles of milk in another. He slid the tray down on to the table. Both plates were lapped in fried eggs, baked beans, overdone bacon and grilled tomatoes. Once again, Emmy's eyes closed.

If you make me sick, she told her baby silently but fiercely, I'll never forgive you.

'OK?' Angus flicked at Emmy's chin with a finger that stung her skin.

The nausea that threatened at the sight and smell of grease and food rose alarmingly.

Don't you dare.

It subsided.

'OK,' said Emmy and picked up her knife and fork.

Chapter Thirty

Prue took the phone call later that morning.

'Yes, Emmy,' she said eventually, after a prolonged interval. 'If I told you how delighted I am at your news would you believe me?'

She went to find Max. He was in the study, polishing the butt of the gun that Prue had last seen illuminated by the moonlight. Weak at the knees, she stopped abruptly in the doorway, reliving the sensation of stones biting into them, and smelling the cold night air scented with smoke and leaf-mould.

'Shouldn't you put it away?' she asked after a while.

If twenty years did not qualify you for superior knowledge or wisdom when it came to dealing with yourself, they certainly did not qualify you when it came to dealing with a spouse. The only thing of which Prue was now sure was that she knew less than at the beginning, and that life was a state of flux, but cunningly hidden.

Max shrugged. 'Don't worry, I won't use it again.' He did not look up.

Prue bit back the temptation to reply: That's what they always say. Instead she slid her hands into the pockets of her cardigan and wrapped them over her middle, aware that the gesture revealed her nervousness.

'Emmy's just phoned to say she's sorry but she can't take the job, after all.'

Plainly disappointed, Max looked up at last.

'She's going to live with her boyfriend, the father. That's very good, though goodness knows how they will manage.'

Max contemplated the perfect gloss and smooth grain of the butt. 'I should think they'll manage perfectly well,' he said, and his tone suggested that Prue had been guilty of patronage.

So she had been. She advanced into the room, which felt cold and, because no one had cleaned it lately, sported a thin veneer of dust on the furniture.

'Can we talk, Max?'

Asking for forgiveness was akin to the executioner asking the victim to absolve him. (Joan's executioner never was absolved. He pitched up at the Frères Pécheurs shaking with terror. God would damn him, he wailed, for burning a saint. He is also said, traditionally, to have insisted that, despite the quantity of oil, sulphur and fuel he had thrown on to the pyre, he could not get Joan's heart or entrails to burn. They, and anything else left of her, had been thrown into the Seine.)

Still hugging her cardigan around her middle, the old, soft, sleepy-eyed Prue stood by her husband – except that she was not. 'Max, please put that thing down, the gun, I mean, and talk to me.'

Her closeness stirred his senses, honed after twenty years into the conditioned reflex. He knew now that the image he held of his wife was deceptive – and why should it not be? So was his own. Funnily enough, the one person who had not bothered to hide anything had been Helen, and how thin a person she had proved. Max sighed, and placed the gun in its case, shifting his bulk out of the daylight coming through the window into the shadowed area of the room.

'Do you want a divorce?'

The locks on the case snapped shut and Prue breathed a

sigh of relief. Max inhaled her scent and the freshness of recently ironed clothes, lifted the case off the table and opened the gun-safe.

'It's curious, isn't it . . . ?' Prue held her breath and Max continued. 'You imagine your life has a certain foundation . . .' Prue winced. 'In answer to your question, Prue. I'm not sure what I want, or what is going to happen.' He stowed his father's gun in its place and took out the Purdey.

Prue thought of the clichés in which she could take refuge. She and Jamie were separate from her and Max's marriage. The itch of her flesh made no difference. Max and Jane were too important to throw away. Although cracks will be apparent from the inside, possibly from the outside, a smashed vase can be put back together with time and skill . . . None of these words would do because Prue had loved Jamie and it had mattered, and had altered things at home.

'Do you have to do that?' She gestured towards the Purdey.

He squinted over the bifocals at his wife. 'Yes, I do. They need attention.'

A sigh escaped her. 'I am sorry I hurt you, Max. I wish I hadn't.'

'You showed admirable judgement in finding precisely the point where I would hurt most.' Max took off his glasses and rubbed his eyes. 'Why weren't you cleverer, Prue? You could have been, you know.'

'Forgive me, Max. Forgive me.'

Yes, Prue *could* have been a great deal more clever. More principled, tougher, she could have stayed at home. But she (as are others) was locked in an unconscious drama, propelled by ancient, primitive forces.

Prue looked at Max and raised her shoulders. Oddly enough, Max understood the gesture. It embodied the spirit in which he had married Helen, against reason and sense.

You did something because it was unavoidable. He decided to talk and laid the Purdey on the table.

'As I said before, I knew about it for some time,' he said, 'but I did not know whom.'

'I was so careful.'

'You forget that I know you very well. I may not know what you think, but I know your mental geography. It changed, Prue, and I couldn't find my way any more.'

This was true.

'Anyway, you bought a new set of underwear and there was dust on your St Joan notes. But, you see, I had prepared for all that.'

'Was I that *obvious*?' Prue looked at the carpet, so in need of the Hoover. 'It's a cliché, I know, but it was nothing to do with you.'

'That's one of your sillier statements.' Max went over to the drinks tray.

'Isn't it a bit early?' Prue watched him pour a whisky.

'Shut up.' Max measured out some water.

She thought of Jamie bending over her in the bed at the hotel, tense with passion, kissing her naked shoulder and thought she would die from the pain.

Loss does not arrive all at once: it comes as an injection that drives under the skin and floods the system. Then it disperses until the next time when, summoned by smell, a word, a memory, the needle jabs into the flesh.

'I imagined you together,' said Max. 'I thought of what you did when we made love and I wondered if he took that bit of you which was mine as well. Or were you different with him?'

She felt a tidal blush flood her face. 'I never compared notes.'

Max leant against the mantelpiece and toyed with the glass. 'I know I'm getting older, Prue. We all know what happens to potency and I realized that by marrying some-one so much younger I had to make allowances. In a way, I felt you were owed an affair. My mistake was to think I knew it all. You see, I thought Helen had taught me that the flesh was everything, but also nothing. I did not see what it would cost. I did not foresee it would involve my daughter. My daughters. And that cannot be.'

She turned away her head, and fought her tears.

'Anyway,' Max continued, 'it taught me a thing or two about sex. The degrees of complicity. Imagining, you see, which is what one does a lot of at this stage of life, instead of doing.'

The tears slid down Prue's cheeks. 'So the gun and that stupid scene *was* for me as well as for Violet . . .'

Max's fingers tightened on the glass. 'I found it unforgiv-able,' he searched for the words, 'unbearable, wicked, that you had taken my daughter's husband, and I had to do something for her.'

Prue knew then that she would never be free of Violet. Ever. Ever. That was her punishment. 'The dustman or the mayor would have been fine, or any old Tom, Dick or Harry, but not Violet's husband,' she said.

'You must see that, Prue.'

She accepted it in silence. 'The tiger principle,' she said eventually and wiped her tears with the back of her wrist. 'You've made the point. Will you have me back?'

Max's whisky made a glugging sound and displaced dust pricked at Prue's nose. She waited.

'For Jane's sake, probably,' said Max.

'No. *You*'ve missed the point. Not for Jane's sake, for mine. Because I've asked you. Because I decided to ask you to help rebuild our marriage.'

'And Jane?'

'It has to be between the two of us.'

Max turned away from Prue, and jiggled the contents of his glass from side to side.

Prue held out her hands, fingers stretched and quivering. 'Max, please.'

He did nothing. She gestured again. 'Give me your hand, Max.'

Still he waited.

'Give, Max.'

Slowly he put out his hand and laid it in hers, his cool, manicured lawyer's hand, so familiar against her hot, unsteady flesh. Their fingers held, moved and twined together.

'Oh, Max,' she said, her gaze fixed on the white slash of Helen's wound.

'There's a brick coming loose in the wall by the gate,' he remarked. Then he said, 'What's for lunch?'

After a while, he picked up the Purdey and replaced it in the gun-safe, which he locked with a click of metal on metal.

The Reverend Richard Williams looked a happy man. Although Easter was, of course, hugely important, Midnight Mass was the colourful highspot of the year. Lit by candles, the church looked so beautiful, so swathed in mystery and light. Unlike the world.

Regardless of his parishioners' sleep quota, Richard had decided to give a sermon. He felt something was needed to mark a bad year, financially, politically and spiritually. Was there anyone left untouched by cynicism and who trusted a politician? He thought not, although the Church could be said to have benefited from the misery brought on by recession even if the unemployed *arriviste* churchgoer was only there because it marked out a day in the week.

Keith, her husband, relegated to the seat behind the

pillar, Molly sang 'It Came Upon the Midnight Clear' loudly enough for two, and Richard suspected she had had a couple of nips. The Valours were in the pew behind. Mrs Valour looked strained and he wondered if she was sickening for something. Mind you, the daughter was very pale and, now he looked properly, far too thin.

His sermon was one over which he had brooded long and hard, in the belief that, in the end, you must stand and be counted. Vicars were there as sacrificial lambs or, worse, Aunt Sallies, but also examples to their flocks. He knew he was going to cause offence and viewed it with trepidation, but with a sense of martyrdom searched for and found, he mounted the pulpit.

'The family,' he announced, 'is under assault and I want to talk to you about it.'

Prue stole a glance at Max out of the corner of her eye, but he was staring ahead.

'Easy options ...' Richard was warming nicely to this theme, 'It's easy to conclude that your spouse is dull, or doesn't satisfy you, and to decide to seek out someone else. It is far harder to stand by the vow of marriage and to make a go of it. I accuse those who are listening of giving in to these temptations at one point or another.'

Several stifled yawns issued from the Paulton family and Keith Greer had taken advantage of his cover to slip quietly into a doze. Quite a few in the pews adjusted their expressions into blankness and wished that the vicar would shut up. Jeremy North thought of several little episodes with some pleasure, Fred Stokes with less. Old windbag, the latter thought, keeping his eyes fixed on the vicar and attempting to look stern.

Prue thought of the tides beating inside her body that would take years to subdue and subside. Of extremes of feeling, of the scars still unhealed, of the moments when she soared above ordinary levels, of her daughter's misery, and thought, savagely and stubbornly. Even so, I *can't* regret it.

'What do we want?' Richard Williams's question was rhetorical for he did not wish to run the risk of being given the wrong answer. 'Security, real security, for our children to grow up in. We want families, real families, to make our communities and to set an example to future generations. We want standards.'

Newly married, newly arrived in the parish, exuding a fresh-minted quality, Carole and Peter Danby shifted closer together and tried to disguise that they were holding hands. Max turned his head and indicated the Danbys with a nod.

What's in store for them? he asked Prue silently.

She returned his gaze, and took on board its new speculative quality and concluded that, in a strange way, the events of the last year had revitalized Max. In some indefinable manner, repossessing had turned out to be an aphrodisiac.

Against that, Prue had to remember that he would not forget what she had done, and that she must accept his anger. Recession had changed the face of the village, of the country, and shone a dim but, perhaps, honest light on them all, rather as an unwise love affair had exposed the wrinkles in her marriage. Prue could never again regard her husband in the same light, neither would Max her, but her vision was wider.

She turned her attention back to the vicar.

Yet that was not quite how Max viewed the situation. He was thinking: There is no fool like an old one. Nevertheless, when he looked at his wife his eyes suggested that he accepted the perversities of the spirit – the oxymoron on which deep-seated, long-term relationships often thrived. Particularly his own.

'We should consider divorce the last resort and ...' Richard paused to milk the drama '... deviant sexuality should be helped and pitied but should never be regarded as anything but *outside* the norm.'

There was an audible rustle as Joe Tatchett got up and walked out, throwing his prayer book on to the table by the door with a thump.

The candles burned lower and the yawns got louder.

Jane moved restlessly beside Prue and Prue bent over her.

'Not much longer,' she whispered.

'So boring,' Jane whispered back, and leant briefly against her mother.

'The promises we make to ourselves and to others,' Richard wound up with a flourish, 'should be made on the absolute assumption that we try to keep them. Not on the I'll-give-it-a-go basis.'

I suppose, thought Prue, concentrating on her love for Max and Jane, the Church has to say that and it *is* useful. But it is not the whole story. Not at all.

Twelve days later, the tree needed to be dismantled and the decorations replaced in their box. Max would put them back in their place in the attic beside the fishing rods – at which point he usually retrieved the latter to look them over.

Prue and Jane were wrapping silver balls in tissue paper when, true to form, Max entered the room and dumped canvas-shrouded rods and a cobwebbed fishing bag on the sofa.

Prue got in quick before he became sidetracked. 'Can you help with the tree? I think we'll have to cut it up before we take it out.'

'Plain Janey,' Max used the old nickname, 'can you get the clippers from the shed and a black plastic rubbish bag?'

Prue held up a ball to the light. It was made of delicate, transparent glass and the light slid over it like coloured oil. 'Pretty,' she said.

Both Max and Jane were reflected in its curve, distorted, distant reflections. I've been away, Prue told herself, suppressing her grief. I went and looked at another land, and wandered beside a river flowing with honey. But I had to come back, and I had to find the way home.

The image blurred under the warmth of her fingers and, after wrapping the ball carefully in the tissue, Prue put it in its place in the box.

Many women turn back from strange lands to light the fire and tend the hearth. It was not a bad decision – quite the contrary – but not every woman's. But to arrive at it, it was necessary to beat it out in blood and pain, otherwise the fire would not burn with heat and light.

Prue had an idea that the roar and buffets of the battles ahead would strengthen her power. Love, after all, was an act of will. Passion was not.

Jane returned with the clippers and handed them to her father.

'Hold the tree steady,' he said. 'And hold the bag open, Prue.'

Cursing gently when the needles punctured his skin, Max pruned the tree of its branches and stuffed them into the bag. It rained needles on to the carpet, which disappeared under a green sea, and the tree shrank and became bald.

After the last branch had been disposed of, Max straightened up. 'That's Christmas over,' he said. 'Let's get this thing outside and I'll chop it up.'

Prue bent over and fastened the plastic bag because she did not want Max or Jane to see that she was crying.

Jane watched her mother. Her expression suggested that she had learnt something about the precariousness of the adult world. It also contained a provocative element – how can I use this knowledge? – but mainly relief. 'Hurry up, Mum,' she said. 'I'm hungry. What's for supper?'

Joan did not disappear with the casting of her mortal remains into the Seine and with the scattering of the pyre's ashes to the wind. Neither did Prue's love for Jamie. Nor his for her. But as Joan was reborn as a myth, a legend, a heroine and, finally, a saint . . . as she had danced, as another of her biographers phrased it, down the centuries, first one shape, then another, Prue learnt to accommodate her experience.

The past tangles with our lives, deny it as you might, and the peripheral characters in the drama sometimes play as big a part as the hero – what *had* Molly been doing when she made Max turn back? But Prue knew, oh, she knew, that forgiveness is, perhaps, the greatest virtue, and she was fortunate to have experienced its healing.

You might consider that for a young ignorant girl with androgynous leanings, a taste for battle (but not for killing) and a highly developed notion of her country in an age when the boundaries were confused, it might have been better to stay at home. But we would have been denied the spectacle of passion, sincerity, courage, extraordinary vision and burning – the term is not ironic – faith. We would have been denied a heroine for all times.

You might consider it would have been far better for Prue to have remained inside her comfortable existence and never ventured out. In fact, she should never have jeopardized her family, hurt her husband and daughter, and embarked on the dangers and disequilibrium of passion.

Yet, that was how it was.